Cover artwork by Arno Kiss
www.arno-kiss.com

Designed by Jud Widing

www.judwiding.com
Facebook/Twitter: @judwiding

A Middling Sort

Thank you so much!!!

Enjoy!

By

Jud Widing

Prologue:

The Parson's Cause

1763

A Middling Sort

A HUNDRED MEN HAD STUFFED THEMSELVES into the Hanover County Courthouse, and they were all staring at Denton Hedges. Denton stared right back, raking his eyes across the pasty-faced assembly as though he were vetting horses. He was confidence incarnate, projecting the kind of self-assurance that comes only with practice. And like most people who lacked confidence, Denton Hedges practiced a lot.

He kept his flinty glare, mirror-honed for occasions just such as this one, locked on his audience. This was, after all, the best way to keep his audience locked on him – specifically his face. As long as they kept looking at his face, they wouldn't be looking at his hands, and so wouldn't notice how much those hands were shaking.

Because they *were* shaking. A lot.

He wasn't worried about the glaze of sweat on his forehead; despite the chill of autumn pouring in through the open door (an open door plugged up with concerned patriots bobbing up and down on their tippy-toes), *everyone* in the Courthouse was sodden. Whoever set the sartorial conventions of colonial justice's discharge was all about layers, not so much about breathability.

Nor was Denton worried about the occasional wavering of his voice; while still untried as a lawyer, he knew perfectly well that he had a gift for oratory. Years of holding (social) court taught him that the rare but embarrassing cracking, stuttering, dithering and quivering could all be repurposed into subtle intensifications of an emotional appeal.

In fact, Denton Hedges was surprisingly composed about the whole affair. A young lawyer standing up for the rights of the colonies against the avarice of the Anglican Church and the caprice of the English Crown should be losing sleep, or his appetite, or maybe just his temper. When a date was set for the hearing, Reverend Emory Wright – the plaintiff – was really hoping for Mr. Hedges would lose the will to live altogether. He even prayed about it, yet he evinced no surprise when his prayer went unanswered, yet again.

Far from driving Hedges to destroy himself, the suit seemed to sharpen the would-be barrister. Word around town was that he'd been whistling as he prepared his case. *Whistling.* As if Emory needed another reason to despise him.

Surprisingly composed, even on the stand, that was Denton. Except for those goddamned hands. And they weren't even shaking because he was nervous about the case. He knew he had the legal and ethical advantage, and he'd never found a more reliable or renewable source of energy than the burn of righteous ire. In case that weren't enough, he came prepared with a cast-iron argument that was sure to weasel its way into the least open of minds, and hopefully cave in the closed ones.

No, Denton Hedges' hands were shaking because the judge was Chester Hedges, his father. Despite all of the logical, legal, philosophical and political weight the junior Hedges knew was undergirding his position, the presence of his dear old dad introduced a personal element to the proceedings that was, well, overgirding it.

Denton rose to his feet as steadily as he could, taking one last look at the vibrating page in his hand before placing it firmly on the wooden seat beside him. Lifting his eyes to the bench, he was rewarded with a look of vague censoriousness from his father. Nothing unusual there. A standard Judge's Frown, but this time coming from the man who once sat him down for a hasty red-faced primer on the intricacies of human sexuality, and how a bit of solitary DIY might save your mother from having to fetch new sheets quite so often.

"Um," declared Denton Hedges. He added, "A-hem."

In broad strokes, the case was as follows: A law passed in 1748 guaranteed the Anglican clergy 16,000 pounds of tobacco a year, because they're the clergy and you're the royal subject and fuck yourself. 1758 saw a particularly dreadful harvest, resulting in a scarcity of tobacco that raised the price from two pennies per pound to six. The obligatory donation that used to be worth $320 skyrocketed in value to $960, due to nothing more than a climatic accident. This understandably gave Virginian tobacco farmers pause, a pause they used to draw breath, that they might say "bullshit".

The House of Burgesses - Virginia's colonial legislature - passed a law called the Two Penny Act, which said that planters could pay off their debts to the clergy in cash, at the old rate of two pennies a pound. Word crossed the Atlantic, made its way to King George III, who sent another word back to the shores of the New World. That word was "bull*shit*".

The Two Penny Act was vetoed by royal authority; this occasioned a great hue and cry that was in keeping with the rhetorical trends thus far established.

Seeing the hackles of colony and crown raising, Reverend Emory Wright somehow decided that the Church really ought to get in on the action, and filed a suit against the tax collectors for Louisa County for the clerical back wages he felt he (and other ministers) were owed. By this simple action, he arrogated unto himself the symbolic mantle of "British Emissary/Stooge", and more remarkably, cast a sympathetic and victimizing light on tax collectors.

Denton Hedge's role, then, was to argue that the King did *not* have the right to abrogate the Two Penny Act, as that would constitute a tyrannical intrusion into the legislative authority of the colonies. What began as a provincial spat over finance quickly escalated into a debate over competing systems of government, because when the options are 'pay up according to the law' or 'challenge the entire system of governance by which said law obtains any coercive authority', everybody is suddenly possessed by the Spirit of '76.

Even if they didn't realize that was what it was yet.

Hedges took a deep breath and focused on the words. His hands steadied. They didn't stop shaking entirely, but they became manageable, and that was all he needed.

He opened his mouth and started speaking. His life was never the same again.

The court ruled in favor of the defense. Wright received damages of a single penny, and the King's veto of the Two Penny Act was deemed null and void. The Anglican Church would be getting a cash settlement at the original rate of two cents per pound. There was a mumbling of oaths in ecclesiastical corners, but no further suits were brought forward.

Denton Hedges attained parochial fame on the strength of his performance. Neighbors and strangers were falling all over themselves to pat him on the back or pick up his tab, which was fun for a time, but ultimately meant little to Denton. He concerned himself with the opinions of exactly two people: the first was his sweetheart Peggy Jefferson (no relation to Thomas), who was naturally proud of her beau, and who consummated her esteem by becoming Peggy Hedges in 1766.

The second was his father Chester. Despite being the one to hand down the ruling in Denton's favor, Chester hardly seemed to acknowledge that his son had won the case. Or, indeed, that his son was a lawyer at all.

Still, Peggy was enough, and when they had their first son Lawrence, he was more than enough. Shortly after his birth the Hedges clan moved to Boston. Denton's reputation preceded him there, but had done very little work on his behalf; he arrived being known as a person who was known in Virginia. For what, nobody could say. So Denton would have to set about proving himself to the world again, but that was fine, because Peggy was still on his side. And she was enough.

For a while.

Part One:

He May Touch Some Wheel

1767

I

WHEN BRISBY HOULIHAN WAS A YOUNG BOY, HE walked home from the schoolhouse along a rutted little stream of dried mud that some folks took to calling a street. About three quarters of the way back to his house, or one quarter of the way to the schoolhouse depending on one's perspective, there was a charming little field nestled behind a copse of Elm trees. The Big Kids played games in that field, games involving sticks and balls and hoops and injuries, games that made not a lick of sense to young Brisby, but games by which he was nonetheless spellbound. Nearly every day, he would trek his way off the not-so-beaten not-so-path, brushing aside the curtains of foliage (indulging in the not-so-patriotic fantasy of being a Spanish conquistador braving the wilds for parts unknown) to sit himself against the trunk of a particularly mighty tree, that he might partake of the vicarious fun sloughing off of the mysterious merriments before him.

The Big Kids saw him, and they ignored him. That was just fine with Brisby – they were too big for him to play with, and anyway, he was having plenty of fun just watching.

This latter point was brought home when he was brought into the game.

Something happened – the stick was hooped through the and also something with the skipflip or maybe didn't well…*something* happened, something that Brisby didn't understand, and now suddenly every single Big Kid was heading right for him.

"Hey, kid!" One of the Big Kids shouted.

Brisby looked over his left shoulder. Then his right. He knew the Big Kids were talking to him, but this just seemed like good form, an acknowledgement that this inter-age communication was highly unusual and that the younger party should consider himself lucky. "Who, me?"

"Yeah, you! You seen a bunch of our games. Who won that last point?"

Gulp. If Brisby wasn't very much mistaken, the tree trunk pressing into his back had unleashed a swarm of Tickler Ants, each of whom sought vengeance for a loved one Brisby had accidentally sat upon during less participatory visits to this accursed field.

There were two teams of kids in front of him. He assumed, at least. Working from that assumption, he had a 50/50 shot of making the 'correct' decision – but whether or not it was the correct decision didn't matter. Every single one of the kids in front of him looked like they were trying to light him on fire with their eyes. He had become an essential component of the game. The game could not continue until Brisby made his decision. Brisby went from watching the game to playing the game, without even realizing it.

What he did realize is that this game kind of sucks.

No matter what he said, half of the kids were going to nod equitably, because this little kid sitting under the tree was simply doing his duty and calling it like it was. Nothing admirable or commendable about it. They would bear him no particular good will.

The *other* half, however, was going to get absolutely *furious*, because this is an *outrage*, this little kid can't tell his asshole from the hole in which they would very much like to bury him, and if they ever see his face around these parts again they're going to make him wish he was never born, or at least that he were born at a slightly different time or in a slightly different place. They would hate him with that red-hot fury that can only be sustained by young people with nothing better to do.

Whatever he said, Brisby was never going to be able to come back to watch this game again.

So he stood up, brushed the dirt from his pants, and said "hlurgh" as he threw up on himself.

This seemed the safest course of action. Better to be an object of general derision than of outright hatred. All that was left was for Brisby to stay home from school for a few days, then put the word out that he had been *very* sick and he sincerely hoped nobody thought he was the kind of kid to throw up on himself without a very good reason.

He was never popular after that incident, but then again, popularity had never been in the cards for him. That was just fine: he had managed to hold a position of adjudication without alienating anybody. He was never *un*popular, that was what mattered. And all it took was absolving himself of the position of adjudication entirely.

Memories of this bygone era came flooding back to Brisby Houlihan in the autumn of 1767. New import duties were being imposed by England, and a Board of Customs Commissioners was being established to execute the wildly unpopular Townshend Acts.

Wildly unpopular.

Customs Commissioners being attacked in the streets unpopular.

Brisby cleared his throat, which was suddenly very dry indeed. He raised his glass and tried for another sip of water, but the glass was still empty. As it had been the last four times he had tried to take a sip. He put it back down and bounced his leg nervously.

Sitting across from him, Governor Rumney Marsh reclined and smiled his 'king shit' smile. King shit was a relative position, clearly. Marsh was Colonial Governor of Fidget's Mill, a small port town to the north of Boston, near the border of New Hampshire. As far Houlihan could tell from his home here in Boston, Fidget's Mill really had nothing going for it, or going on in it, other than commerce through the port, which ran perfectly well without bureaucratic oversight. So what Marsh actually *did* to feel so smug about, other than reporting to his British handlers with complete sentences, was anybody's guess.

"I am loathe," Brisby began. This was a reliable way to begin, as it was so often true in so many ways. Selecting one, he continued: "to give the impression that I'm anything other than flattered. But-"

"Then don't." The Governor rolled a cigarette without worrying overmuch about spilling tobacco all over the Houlihan sitting room, humble as it was. "You've been selected. I don't see why you're saying anything other than 'thank you'. You're going to be bringing in a lot more money, and that's just the salary I'm talking about."

Houlihan watched with silent displeasure as flakes of tobacco lilted to the ground. He'd have to make sure he found every little bit of that stuff and picked it up, or else his infant daughter surely would. His eyes returned to the Governor's. "'Just the salary'? What else would there be?"

"His Majesty knows perfectly well that his most loyal subjects ought to be entitled to a little something extra. A little taste." Marsh parted his lips, letting the pink tip of his tongue slither out between them. He brought the cigarette up to meet it, and at that point Brisby closed his eyes because he'd never seen such a simple task undertaken in such an upsetting fashion.

Marsh continued, oblivious to his interlocutor's distress. "You'd be in a position of influence. What do you do now, huh? Shovel shit? Shovel dogshit?"

"I'm a physician, Governor." Try as he might, Brisby couldn't keep the disdain from his voice.

Marsh picked up on *that*, of course. "Why did you say it like that? '*I'm a physician*,' like I'm supposed to know who the hell you are?"

"It's only that you had to walk through my practice to get back here."

Rumney thought on this for a moment. "Well, that's as may be. But it's also beside the point. Stop changing the subject. The point of the subject is that you've been tapped, and that's all there is to it."

Hey kid! Who won that last point?

The issue at hand was the Revenue Act of 1767, which fell under the dubious auspices of those unpopular 'Townshend Acts'. By its writ, an import duty would be raised on certain goods (such as tea, glass, paint, lead and, much to the chagrin of those for whom 'Stamp' remained a sphincter-clenching word, paper) making their way into the Colonies. How else to recoup the costs incurred in defending the Colonies from the French and the Savages? Granted, the ungrateful Colonists had put up quite a stink over internal taxes over the past decade or so, but these would be *external* taxes, levied on imports and exports. Everyone in England agreed that this was agreeable and saw no reason why the Colonists shouldn't agree with them.

If Brisby accepted and excelled in the position of Customs Commissioner, which would see him enforcing trade laws and exacting duties from his fellow colonists, his employers in England would nod equitably. Commissioner Houlihan was just doing his duty. Nothing admirable or commendable about it. They would bear him no good will.

Everyone else – his friends and neighbors – would be absolutely *furious.* Hell, they already were furious. He'd just be strapping a target to his back, waiting for someone to notice him (which wouldn't take long at all) and swing his way with a pre-loaded musket.

He would be *un*popular.

But all the same, how to say no to the people who make the laws?

"Would it help if I were sick on myself?" Brisby inquired brightly.

"Help what?"

"No, of course not." He pondered his dilemma some more. Then, arrived at another possible route for self-disqualification: "Why are you here? Governor Bernard should be coming to me, as a denizen of Boston. I've never even been to Fidget's Mill!"

Marsh struck a match along the side of his chair (*Houlihan's* chair; what nerve!) and lit his lewdly secured cigarette. "That's another bit of good news for you. We're anticipating some…some trouble, in getting the lower sorts of Fidgetonians-"

Brisby sniffed at this. Surely there must be a better way to describe a resident of Fidget's Mill.

"-to comply gracefully with the Townshend Acts. I'm looking to handle it myself, but if things are truly out of hand, then orders from across the Atlantic are to bring in one of the state Customs Commissioners to lay down the law." He shook out the match and took a drag of his cigarette.

"That'd be you," he growled through a cloud of smoke.

Laying down the law. The wildly unpopular law.

Gulp again. Brisby tried to stifle a cough as the tobacco smoke rolled over him. "I can't say that strikes me as especially good, as far as news goes."

"You'd receive higher compensation, commensurate with your troubles."

"I'd just as soon forgo the troubles altogether."

Marsh took another deep draw from his cigarette. "That's not an option, *Doctor* Houlihan. Either you accept the posting, or we revoke your license to practice medicine."

"Who's *we*?" Brisby knew this was an inflammatory question – there was undoubtedly substance to the ultimatum. He was just forcing Marsh to admit that he was nothing more than an errand boy for the people actually capable of following through on the threat.

The Governor shook his head, but said nothing. Neither of them had anything else to say. There was no easy out, no vomiting on himself and laying low for a few days. If Brisby wanted to support his family, he had to take the appointment. It was as simple as that.

Feeling parched, he reached for his glass again. But this time, he remembered that there was nothing left in it, and stopped himself from fully committing to this mindless tic. This, at least, was something to which he *didn't* have to commit. "Okay," he sighed. "I'll do it. And you really ought to have led with the ultimatum."

Marsh whipped the 'king shit' grin back out, and stubbed his cigarette out right on the table. "Had I known you were a doctor at the outset, I would have happily saved us the time."

"Mhm." Brisby nodded, silently praying that his fellow Americans would come around to external taxes, as proposed in the Townshend Acts. Maybe, after a brief period of anxious transition, people would see that going along to get along wasn't so bad after all. Maybe they'd even start to look at Customs Commissioners as friendly helpers, keeping the Colonies in the good graces of the King! Who doesn't love a friendly helper?

II

BRISBY WAS WILLING TO FORGIVE THE FIRST rock whizzing past his head. Maybe somebody was carrying a rock and tripped, and it flew out of their hand at just the right angle to put some wicked backspin on it. By the third rock, however, the intention behind these projectiles was clear.

For the umpteenth time that night, he cursed his luck. Being the youngest and least-everything-else of the five Customs Commissioners, Brisby was tasked with breaking the news of the Townshend Acts to the good people of Boston.

Apparently the good people of Boston stayed home tonight, because as far as he could tell he was only addressing the stinkers.

"Listen!" he cried, sidestepping a shoe hurtling through the air towards him. Maybe it would have been easier to just let it hit him: it would have saved him the trouble of kicking himself, for holding this meeting outside at a wide intersection. He was surrounded by furious faces – many of them familiar and once-friendly – quivering in the hysterical orange glow of the torches. No easy means of escape.

Oh yeah: they brought torches, of course.

Reclaiming the entirety of his five foot seven inch stature, he lowered his outstretched palms in a last-ditch attempt at controlling the crowd through tepid suggestion. Failing that, he made one final last-last-ditch attempt at controlling the crowd through pally commiseration. "I'm not happy about it either!"

Another shoe hurtled true through the air, and thwacked Customs Commissioner Houlihan on the forehead.

From the back of the rabble, the Sons of Liberty Massachusetts Chapter watched and listened. A secret society dedicated to defending the integrity of the colonies from the financial aggressions of the British, its members were masters of inconspicuous spectatorship. Their numbers had dwindled since the halcyon days of opposing the Stamp Act, thinning the ranks enough to make a proactive policy look mighty counterproductive. For now. Because a sea change was at hand, and the leading lights of the organization could sense that the time to hoist the sails and crack the oars was soon to follow…

From the back of the clutch of above-mentioned patriots, an unmemorable man of thirty-three years gently jostled his taller companions, fighting to catch a glimpse of Brisby's announcement.

No one paid him much attention, which was how he rather preferred it.

Over the next few months, all across Massachusetts, popular discontent boiled over into organized demonstrations. They were all non-violent, in the sense that nobody is actually getting *hurt* when they're being burned in effigy. Each spasm of ordered fury appeared to be entirely spontaneous and independent.

And with a predictability that nevertheless galvanized the crowds each time, every single protest ended in exactly the same way: local merchants committing themselves to adopting the strict non-importation agreement, an agreement which would cut off the Townshend Acts' proposed source of revenue at the knees. The British wanted to tax imports? Why, then the Colonists would just halt them altogether.

Across the Atlantic, Parliament grew anxious at the unexpected display of solidarity (after all, these were not Colonies that could cease consuming goods from abroad without making fairly immediate sacrifices), yet they did not suspect an overarching design. Many of them were fathers, all too familiar with the rebellious phases of adolescence. This was perfectly natural contrarianism, to be beaten out of the relatively fledgling Colonies with a firm paternal backhand.

Measures were discussed. Insubordination might best be countered through a show of force. Soldiers were drummed up from their barracks to patch up their red coats, polish their bayonets, and await further instruction.

The author of these provincial insurrections had accounted for the possibility of a belligerent reaction from the English. That unmemorable man who lately kept to the backs of crowds did not hope for violence, and had no love of martyrdom. He was a doe-eyed idealist of a brutally political disposition, striving to square his own mental circles and bring about upheaval and revolution through equitable, non-violent discourse between rational actors.

In many ways, Denton Hedges was a fool. But there's a reason the mightiest kingdoms in history all had a fool by the throne.

That's not necessarily to say it was a *good* reason, of course.

Unlike a truly gifted fool, Denton did not perform. This was, for the most part, by choice: his rhetorical gifts were considerable, and as a lawyer he had been well accustomed to speaking before crowds. But as the grumbling of royal subjects took on increasingly revolutionary tenors, the prospect of being a figurehead, or an identifiable face, ebbed away. So Denton wrote. He wrote pamphlets and articles, and he wrote speeches for those whose patriotism outshone their sense of self-preservation. Watching these men (invariably men) from the wings, Denton fostered a tiny ember of humiliation. What happened to his courage, his conviction? Why was he so afraid of leaping into the line of fire, where his ideals lay?

Those were questions he would answer. Someday. But not today. Today, he stayed cozy behind the curtain and pulled the strings, and then held on tight as the strings pulled back.

There were no delusions of grandeur here, no fantasies of absolute control. Denton knew his task was like trying to direct plate tectonics, or perhaps he would have done had he had the slightest concept of plate tectonics. There were larger forces at work here, emotional and political winds beyond the control of any individual. He could only do his small part to the best of his ability, doing what he thought was right, come what may.

Non-terminal martyrdom. Is that what that is? Maybe, he admitted quietly to himself, he wasn't so averse to the concept after all.

Several months after their last meeting, assembled in the wake of Commissioner Houlihan's announcement of the Townshend Acts, the Sons of Liberty Massachusetts Chapter reconvened in their usual haunt, the back room of a dank and sticky tavern. The whiskey flowed so prodigiously that drunkenness became airborne, thick enough to ward off all but the most dedicated to the Glorious Cause - the Cause in question being cirrhosis of the liver.

Martyrs to the end, the courageous Sons braved the vapor to hold their heroic meetings. To protect their identities, many of the partisans here assembled went only by the pseudonyms they employed on their anonymous polemics.

In the back of the room, the unmemorable man of thirty-three years ran his hand through his sandy hair. Nobody listened to him the first time he suggested that they really shouldn't be attaching their pseudonyms – some of which had themselves been attached to the worst libels of the King and Governors imaginable – to their actual faces. They told him to keep quiet, and so he obliged, and continued to do so. Despite his best efforts, Denton had never been able to recreate the sterling reputation he enjoyed in some of the other colonies. So yes, he kept quiet, because sometimes that was the best way to get things done.

Keeping quiet, he scanned the room, eyes peeled for possible spies. This was one of the more stressful roles he'd arrogated unto himself, but it was a role he found himself taking up often. He did it not because he wanted to do it, but because no one else seemed to be doing it, and someone really *ought* to be doing it.

This was how he'd taken on most of his assignments over the past few years: doing a thing that nobody else wanted to do, but that nonetheless needed to be done. Needless to say, he had been very busy since joining the Sons of Liberty Massachusetts Chapter. Case in point: the lately-concluded propaganda campaign in favor of non-importation. It was a course of action The Sons unanimously decided to be necessary, which they would get around to just as soon as they had a free evening or two.

So Denton had very quietly slipped away for a few months, and very quietly returned without trumpeting his accomplishments. As always, he hoped people would notice not only the accomplishments but the lack of trumpeting, and commend him on his modesty. This had never happened in his entire life.

Recalling Denton's attentions to the tavern, a man whose pen name was A.S. Muggins raised his hands for order. It was a superfluous gesture, as everyone was already silently watching him. "My fellow Sons, the cause of non-importation has been almost universally accepted, thanks to our strenuous efforts!"

Sensing that something was expected of them, A.S.'s fellow Sons bounced about in their seats.

From the back of the room, Denton considered that the most strenuous effort A.S. Muggins had likely undertaken in the last several months was conducted on the privy. It gave him a headache if he meditated on this for too long: two years ago, the Sons of Liberty led the charge on repealing the Stamp Act. Denton himself had contributed a few particularly influential tracts, which might have bolstered the prestige and influence associated with his name, had he written them under his name. He never boasted of the glory that ought by rights belong to him, but he would sometimes hold it close on sleepless nights, and it kept him warm.

Now, he looked out at the well-meaning drunkards in front of him with pity. Pity for them as people, pity for what had happened to their patriotic zeal, and even (he was far from happy to admit) a helping of pity for himself. Perhaps a part of him *wanted* to catch a British spy in their midst. It would mean that what they were doing was important enough to warrant surveillance.

He didn't catch a British spy in their midst. He never had. They suspected one of their numbers of going turncoat two years ago, but it turned out he had just been suffering from kidney stones. That was the closest they'd ever come. The fact was, the Massachusetts branch of the Sons would never match their brothers in Virginia, as far as influence and strength were concerned.

This stung Denton, but he kept that to himself. Instead, he ran his fingers through his hair one last time.

And then, Denton ran his fingers through his hair one last time. Ugh. Despite his self-consciously confident bearing, he found his natural restlessness manifesting as a series of obnoxious nervous tics. One of those was running his hand through his hair. One last time. He told himself last time was the last time, but he had a tendency to do it without thinking about it. Now that he was thinking about it though, that was the *last* time.

Denton Hedges ran his fingers through his hair one last time. Alright, *that* was the last time. He took a deep breath, finding the tranquility that was so often just beyond his reach.

Once again, A.S. raised his hands for order, this time with some justification. "We have the visit of two of guests, here bringing an announcement of import, or should I say *non*-import, ha, except not actually, and excite!"

The bouncing resumed, with redoubled intensity.

"Gentlemen, to you here I give, Samuel Adams and James Otis Jr.!"

A.S. gestured to the provocateur known only as Glucosicon, who leapt from his seat and bounded out the door. A moment later he loped back in, proudly leading two men who looked distinguished enough to be discomfited by A.S.'s ostentatious introduction.

The shorter of the two identified himself as Samuel Adams, and wasted no time in getting to the point: "Mr. Otis and myself are planning a Circular Letter, to be distributed amongst the colonies. As to its precise content and tone, these topics and others are under discussion as we speak. We-"

Window Tablechair, who must have panicked upon being told he could choose anything he wanted for his pseudonym as long as he chose *right now*, raised his hand. "As we sp-"

The Eskwire (sic) leaned over to him and whispered "not *literally*."

Window Tablechair lowered his hand.

Adams continued, "We trust the rumors have made their way to your door. The British may be plotting a deployment, to enforce their tyrannical dictates at the point of a bayonet. It is vital that we draw tight the common bonds of freedom that hold together these colonies."

Denton shook his head slightly. He made a mental note to enjoin Adams not to include "bonds of freedom" in his putative letter.

James Otis Jr. literally tagged in, placing a hand on Adams' shoulder and stepping forward. "Our letter's going to be moderate, really. The Townshend Acts are just not acceptable due to lack of parliamentary representation. Taxation without representation is tyranny, that's what I always say."

Adams nodded with a slight roll of the eyes. "*Always*. It's his little catchphrase."

"But," Otis continued with a waggle of his finger, "we're not arguing for parliamentary representation."

"Probably not," Adams corrected.

"Whatever."

"We have not yet concluded our discussions as to the con-"

"Fine."

"-tent and tone, precisely, of-"

"Okay. Okay. We're *probably* not arguing for parliamentary representation. We are – *potentially* – stumping for a return to the old method of taxation, through provincial assemblies. The colonies would tax themselves."

Adams tagged back in. "We would reclaim our own financial destiny and repay our debts to the English King, pursuant to solvency, at which point we would be financially – and so politically - disentangled from the royal loins of our discharge."

Again, Denton shook his head.

"But the crux of this scheme is that this Circular Letter would needs be presented as a *compromise.* A moderation of an initial, more extreme position. And this position has already been articulated in many quarters."

Otis tagged in. Adams was having none of it. A minor shuffling of feet ensued.

"Non-importation!" Otis shouted.

"BUT," Adams resumed, "that we may accrue credibility at the bargaining table, non-importation must be *universally* embraced, else a shirker provide a handhold from which to pry apart our common alliance."

Denton considered excusing himself.

A.S. tapped a finger on the table anxiously. "Non-importation *has* been universally accepted."

Adams opened his mouth to speak, but Otis stepped on his foot. "Ouch," is what Adams ended up saying.

Otis, meanwhile, said "there is only one town that's been holding out: Fidget's Mill."

When no oohs and aahs of comprehension were forthcoming, Otis frowned and muscled onwards: "They're a very small town to the North, just near the border of New Hampshire. They don't really have an economy: they don't produce anything. They have, and are, their port. So by asking them to cease imports, we're essentially asking them to cut off their only source of income and let the town wither and die."

"Don't they have a mill?" Denton wondered.

Otis wrinkled his nose. "No. What? Why would they?"

Denton sighed and hung his head.

The Sons joined him in navel-gazing silence. Not contemplation – this was a pre-emptive mourning. If Fidget's Mill had to die for the cause, then it had to die.

This, at least, was the vibe Denton was getting. It was not a vibe with which he gibed. He ran his fingers through his ha-NO. He kept his hands on his knees and asked, "How do you expect to convince them to sacrifice their own town to the Cause?" He knew this to be a pivotal question, as it was one he'd had to address anew in every town he had traveled to over the past few months, though with much lower stakes for the townspeople.

Adams, not familiar with the high-handedness with which the Sons addressed this half-mute little man, answered openly and warmly: "To be perfectly honest, we aren't entirely certain. There are, in the case, certain complexities which obfuscate the economic realities."

James tapped in. Adams nudged him back, but James sidestepped gracefully. "Just what those obfuscating complexities are, we've not been able to tease out as yet. Fidget's Mill is a pretty insular community. Seems people are either unwilling to talk to us, or unable to adequately explain what's happening there."

"Best as we *can* tease," Adams interjected, "the town is under the thumb of a merchant family by the name of Crundwell. Seems they own the ports, and as the Mill is the ports, and the Crundwells are the ports, then therefore the Mill is the Crundwells."

Denton stopped listening at that point. Was it possible that there could be such a town as the Fidget's Mill these men presented? His mind reeled at the thought. What a precarious existence it must have, if it were true that it teetered on this economic knife's edge. How would that even work? How could it ever have gotten to that point? Did it help or hurt the town to be under the control of a single aristocratic family? It beggared belief.

Just as belief-beggaring was the idea of convincing a wealthy aristocratic family who made their living from the docks to pluck themselves, and their town, from the vine. How, Denton wondered, would this be possible?

Adams and Otis bickered for a little while, concluded their presentation, and then left on the hesitant estimate that their Circular Letter would be put into circulation at the beginning of the following year.

They took their leave, and the Sons discussed. It was November 1767. They had less than two months to turn Fidget's Mill (or, to put it more plainly, the Crundwells) on to strict non-importation. If the

Circular Letter were released without unanimous support for the agreement, then the British could simply lavish Fidget's Mill with the trappings of Empire, to show the rest of the austere and self-immiserated Colonies what they could have if only they would renounce support for the Letter and the Agreement.

However, if the Circular Letter – designed to rally Americans behind a common goal – remained nothing more than a fancy in the minds of Adams and Otis while British soldiers were making landfall on the shores of the New World, the simple threat of force might be enough to strangle the burgeoning spirit of rebellion in the womb. For all they knew, January 1768 might even be too late to release it. They couldn't rush the letter, but nor could they delay it a moment longer than was absolutely necessary.

A proper dilemma, and here the Sons of Liberty Massachusetts Chapter were getting drunk and shouting general disapproval at the state of things without offering any plausible methods of rectification.

As per usual, Denton quietly excused himself and slipped out the door.

He didn't go home. Instead, he paced through the moonlit alleys. These are the people who got the Stamp Act repealed! Some of them, anyway. What happened to that drive? That initiative?

No matter. This was another one of those really-ought-to-be-done-nobody-else-is-going-to-do-it-guess-I-better-do-it things, wasn't it?

Some people like to wring their hands and make PRO/CON lists before they make a decision. The world had always been much more clearly cut for Denton.

This was but one of the reasons why he was just about the worst person to be going to Fidget's Mill at the end of 1767.

III

DENTON FINALLY DID GO HOME, AND SLIPPED under the covers next to Peggy. She stirred but didn't wake, and he was glad of that.

In the morning, he told her that he was leaving once again, and she smiled. He was glad of that, too. The smile was pride, pride at seeing her husband contributing to the Cause. Peggy was, in many ways, even more dedicated to increased independence for the colonies than he was. Not necessarily in terms of scope of influence (by dint of her station and gender, she had many fewer opportunities to exercise her principles), but in the manner of advocacy. Peggy organized and hosted meetings throughout Boston, modeled on the French *salons* about which she had read so much. As a consequence, hers was a recognizable face in town. The colonial authorities knew who she was, and what she did, and she knew that they knew. But that never stopped her – it often seemed to have exactly the opposite effect.

And here was her husband, stirring up popular insurrections with his pen, hiding his face behind the pages. This was the true source of his shame, when he was low enough to feel such emotion. Peggy was an inspiration to him, and he hated the idea of letting her down. Her opinion was, after all, one of the only two about which he cared.

Well, one of the only four. Two of the others belonged to his children. Fortunately for Denton they weren't quite old enough to have discreet stances on daddy's political activities, but someday they would be, and it was important to him that he behave today in a way that would make them proud tomorrow. What better way than to build them a new nation?

But that was the cart *way* before the horse. Nobody was talking about a new nation, at least nobody worth taking seriously. Except when the door was locked and the curtains were drawn, sometimes Denton and Peggy let out the lead on their wildest dreams…

Peggy made young Lawrence and Annabelle Hedges their breakfast, mealy porridge that had spent the night bubbling over the embers of yesterday's fire. As they slurped it down, Denton tousled Annabelle's hair on the way to his own chair. He did this often, and it may have been, he sometimes reflected in those low moments, a strange externalization of his own nervous tic. Because he was nervous now. He always was, on the morn of a departure.

"When will you be back?" Lawrence inquired dutifully. Language acquisition was coming slowly to little Lawrence, but he'd had plenty of opportunities to learn how to ask that over the past several months.

Denton slurped at his own bowl of porridge, delicately placed before him by Peggy, and bobbed his shoulders from side to side. "No later than January. Two months, at the most."

"Mhm." Lawrence approved. He didn't know *why* his father had taken to absence more and more frequently, but he always approved. There had never been any rending of garments or smiting of thighs as Denton took his leave. The Hedges clan understood the sacrifices that had to be made for ideals, and of this, Denton was most glad of all.

Later, when the kids ran off to play, Peggy brought Denton a letter.

"I concluded that it came down to spoiling your appetite or disturbing your digestion. I opted for the latter," she said with a pitying smile.

Denton saw the handwriting on the envelope, and forced a smile in return. "What's the occasion for this missive?" It was a question he often asked his wife when she handed him a letter from his father. She patted him on the shoulder and sat next to him. It was rhetorical, and she knew it.

The letter opener was in another room, so Denton hooked his finger beneath the flap of the envelope and peeled back the paper. The only good part about opening these letters was seeing that preposterous wax seal burst.

Mr. Hedges, the letter began. The letter from a father to his son. Denton sighed and silently cursed the postman. Part of the reason he'd moved his family to Boston was to escape the perpetually disapproving gaze of his father, and here came one of his semi-regular epistolary zingers. *Have any good cases lately?* was the not-so-subtext lounging between the lines of these letters. After the ephemeral high of the Parson's Cause, Denton's forays into the courtroom became less and less frequent. Somehow, dear old dad knew it. And dear old dad wanted Denton to know that he knew it. For some reason.

And for some other reason, Denton cared. His father's opinion remained one of the only four that he valued, despite the fact that his father's opinion was that his son was squandering his potential, scribbling his little pamphlets while more muscular minds did the heavy lifting of colonial jurisprudence. He didn't even need to read the letters, and increasingly he didn't.

He handed it wordlessly to Peggy, who skimmed the letter for any pertinent information that Denton ought to know. In this way, she protected him from the pointless vituperation his father seemed so fond of pouring into his ear (or eye) at any opportunity.

Nearing the end, she frowned and shook her head. Dear Peggy, who spared Denton the pain by taking it on board herself. Despite the bad blood between them, blood that seemed to have gone bad while Denton was still in his late mother's womb, Denton couldn't hate his father because bad blood was still blood. Peggy had no such reservations. She hated Chester Hedges for the contemptuous way he wrote his son, and made no secret of it.

"He had a cough, but now he's better," was how Peggy summarized the two-page, double-sided letter. She crumpled up the pages and tossed them into the dying, porridge-heating embers. The flames awoke and happily devoured the unhappy sheets.

Denton nodded limply. "Thank you."

Peggy stood up, kissed him on the cheek, and went to check on the kids.

It was rare that Denton and Peggy told each other they loved one another in words. It was rarer still that they ever doubted it.

Denton packed a single bag and lugged it to the front door. As on his previous journeys, his family was lined up, waiting to wish him well on his travels. His kissed them all, and told them he loved them (it always felt good to say it just prior to a prolonged absence) and that he would be back before any of them knew it. With that, he strode out the door to commission a carriage to Fidget's Mill.

Hefting his pack over his shoulder, he thought about the quartet of assessments that meant anything to him. Wife, children, father. Three out of four in his favor wasn't bad, was it? That would be enough. Complacence seemed so easy, when one thought in those terms. He could go to Fidget's Mill, do his darndest, and the people closest to him would love him no matter what happened. Except for one of those people, who would look down at him along the bridge of his nose and across the miles, no matter what happened.

But would *he* feel worthy of their love? In considering their opinions, he sometimes neglected his own. If he did the bare minimum, three of the four would stand by him. But he would feel as though his learned apathy somehow sullied the drive of his wife, and ditto for the kids if they inherited a fraction of her zeal for life.

Peggy was a recognizable face, while he lurked about in the shadows. His father had written to him again, wondering what he'd actually accomplished with his life.

Well...what if he showed him? And what if he followed his wife's example?

Perhaps the time for anonymous tracts and pseudonymous meetings in run-down pubs was over. Fidget's Mill was the final link to be set in the mighty chain of non-importation. What if Denton set to work on it under his own name, behind his own face? Would he finally feel he was living up to the high esteem in which his wife and children held him? Might his father send a letter, of which Peggy could read most, if not all to Denton?

Could he make his people proud, and justify their love?

These were the questions on his mind as he leapt into the carriage, and began the trek to Fidget's Mill. Never once did it occur to him that he might be moving away from, rather than toward, the answers.

IV

THE OVERLAND JOURNEY TO FIDGET'S MILL WAS supremely uneventful. Denton did his best to engage the carriage driver in conversation, and was reminded that sometimes one's best just isn't good enough.

"Hello, sir," Denton ventured.

"Yuh?" returned the driver.

What to say in response to this? The driver wasn't returning his greeting, he was dropping a half-articulated syllable that nonetheless fully articulated the question *what do* you *want?* Given the circles in which he tended to run, Denton was well-equipped to enter into antipathetic dialectics. Someone slipped some personal attacks into their political arguments? Watch as they slide gracefully off of Denton's shrugging shoulders.

A churlish interlocutor, that was no sweat. But Denton found himself less prepared for someone who simply refused to make with the interlocuting to begin with.

So what to say in response to him? After far too much thought on the subject, Denton eventually settled on, "Um, lovely day we're having."

"S'night."

Blast! So it was. The lack of sun was a dead giveaway, in hindsight. Denton sat back in his seat and stewed, letting the clop clop clopping of the horses fill the camaraderie-shaped hole in the night.

A few hours later, after the sun had finally gotten enough of the orient and come crawling back (as it always did) to the Lord's Most Favored People, Denton decided to brush off an old classic.

"Um, lovely day we're having."

"Yuh."

Well, that was progress of a kind.

The carriage crested another low, rolling hill indistinguishable from the other low, rolling hills. The only thing that was different about this particular low, rolling hill was that instead of offering a vista of more low, rolling hills, this low, rolling hill presented any and all cresters with their first look at Fidget's Mill.

It was a good look at a place that didn't look very good.

When James Otis Jr. said that the town was essentially just the port, Denton assumed this was a comment on commercial realities. Turns out that, no, 'just the port' was really the *only* way to sum up the huddle of brick and timber teetering on the edge of the Atlantic.

Wrapped in a generous crescent of woodlands (all sinister grey branches now, but it must have looked spectacular just a few weeks ago) sloping down to the shoreline, Fidget's Mill looked a bit like a once-vibrant hillside community that had been dumped into a gorge after a ferocious mudslide. It wasn't that the buildings themselves were ugly – they just didn't *work*, in a way Denton found difficult to quantify. Nearer the bustling docks, already thrumming with the salty patois upon which manual labor in New England thrives, the architecture was either of a bold new school unfamiliar to Denton, or else everything was just too close together. Perhaps it was a trick of the distance, but he imagined trying to maneuver his slight frame between two adjacent edifices and got so thoroughly stuck that he began to imagine panicking and crying for help.

As Denton's eye made a Westward caress of the town, the city planning swung towards the opposite end of the "distressing-in-a-way-that-is-hard-to-articulate" spectrum. The town seemed to be disintegrating as it crept inland, with a chilling lack of order or decorum. Buildings were too far apart, and positioned at canted angles to each other. Streets lost their backbone and snaked wildly across the dewy grass, for no discernible reason. Fences went every which way, frequently failing to reconnect with themselves, which is sort of the whole idea with fences.

About a mile inland, Fidget's Mill lost interest in itself and just stopped. A lonely log cottage held vigil on the outskirts, smoke wafting from the chimney.

"S'good?"

Denton was surprised to notice that the carriage had stopped moving. He pulled his eyes from the hypnotic oddity that was Fidget's Mill, and noticed the sign at which the driver had called his horse to a halt.

WELCOME TO FIDGET'S MILL
POP: VARIABLE
NO SOLICITING

"Let's go the rest of the way, shall we? I'd love it for you to drop me at a place of temporary lodging, as I have none."

The driver shook his head emphatically. "S'good."

"Sorry? I'd be paying you more. You'd be ferrying me just a mile or two further, which, if you-"

"G'bye."

Denton sat in baffled silence for a moment, waiting for the coachman to say something to the effect of "ah-ha, gotcha". He kept waiting, until he remembered the silence of the ride out here. However long he was willing to wait, it wouldn't be as long as this man would be.

"Ugh," Denton replied.

It was after he disembarked from the carriage, fetched his cumbersome trunk, paid the driver, watched him slide down the other side of the low rolling hill, and dragged his baggage the two and a half miles into town, gasping and sweating and nearing collapse, that Denton began to consider the fact that he was unable to give a carriage driver more money to escort him another couple of miles. That seemed a straightforward bit of negotiation, and he'd failed it. Yet here he was, self-appointed political emissary of the Sons of Liberty, to convince a wealthy and complacent merchant family to embrace an entirely new approach to trade (i.e. 'stop doing it') that would do nothing material for them, save hobbling their profits and potentially cutting off all revenue to a town that would be unable to sustain itself without said revenue.

And other than 'go to Fidget's Mill', Denton had no clear plans on where or how to begin. How to insinuate himself with Higher Sorts like the Crundwells?

Fortunately, a course of action suggested itself when someone struck Denton on the back of the head with something heavy. He collapsed, and was unconscious before his face plopped into the muddy thoroughfare in the center of town.

V

A FEW GENERATIONS AGO A FAMILY BY THE NAME of Crundwell sauntered up from Virginia, encumbered by the wealth that was the terminal yield of their tobacco plantation, and threw their lot in with Injuns and Witches.

It was all they could do to take control of their own destiny. King James II had chucked the Great Seal of the Realm into the Thames, and the ripples made their way across the Atlantic. They always did. It wouldn't be accurate to say that the War, which would hit the history books bearing the name of the newly crowned king William, was sudden or unexpected; colonial life was a hardscrabble existence given shape by the ubiquitous boundaries of us/them anxiety. The war with the French and the Savages began, and every man of fighting age could only say "already?" as they took up their arms.

Meanwhile, after years of agricultural heroics that were nearly as profitable as they were unsustainable, the Crundwells of Virginia were facing a few years of fallow austerity. Hence the sale of the plantation.

But where to go? They couldn't stay in Virginia. Once the new buyers – they of the surname Shidy – realized they had been sold an ample tract of inert dirt, there would undoubtedly be quite a few inquiries as to the current whereabouts of the Crundwell clan, pursuant to either demanding satisfaction via a duel, or else converting them into fertilizer. The level-headed discharge of Colonial justice left something to be desired, which was great news for malefactors right up until they got caught by the malefacted.

Where to go, then, was 'away'. Which way away? Which direction would render a Shidy pursuit less likely?

War was breaking to the North. All sides were conducting the most hideous of atrocities; the xenophobic grapevine ensured that only the enemy's diabolical transgressions made their way into southbound tales told after the sun had hidden its face.

No well-to-do family of farmers in their right minds would go north. At least, that's what a well-to-do family of would-be farmers like the Shidys would think. At least, that's what a well-to-do family of ex-farmers like the Crundwells thought a well-to-do family of would-be farmers like the Shidys would think. So the Crundwells packed their bags and began the pilgrimage towards Polaris, towards Mars.

The current crop of Crundwells had all heard different explanations as to why their near ancestors decided to settle in a lonely crescent of Massachusetts shoreline, in the Northern reaches of Essex County. Salem was still about ten years from its infamy, but there had been cases already. Women (and a very few men, but women bore the brunt) accused of dabbling in the dark arts, of consorting with adumbral Familiars, and in some of the less convincing cases, of just being all-around buttheads. If the Savages didn't get you, the Witches would. So the Crundwells kept hearing.

Which made their decision to settle near the epicenters of wars physical and spiritual so perplexing. It couldn't have been purely about hiding from the Shidys; that'd be a bit like hiding from a grouchy tabby cat in a Grizzly's den. No, there must have been other reasons, reasons known only to those dearly departed whose watchful portraits haunt the halls of the happy estates sprung from their graves…

It's fun to imagine, anyway. Whatever the clanking chains of reason that compelled the Crundwells to settle down in that poor excuse for a cove, the reasons for their meteoric ascendancy – and therefore the *ex nihilo* trajectory of the town itself – were remarkably prosaic.

Before they even built their homes, the Crundwells built docks. At night they would huddle up around a fire and gaze lovingly at the progress they made on their pier that day, seeing the shape of their labors as a black absence against reflections of moonlight sighing off the Atlantic. But let's not romanticize this too much: the Crundwells built the docks for the express purpose of undercutting the prices of rival firms in Boston. Puritan work ethic was all well and good, but a bit of savvy capital allocation is nothing to turn your nose up at either.

The big guns of crossing-the-pond commerce were never going to stop patronizing the ports in Boston. It was too convenient, convenient enough to justify the inflated prices. But the small fries, the independents and the upstarts, they heard tell of a deal to be had: ship to Fidget's Mill for significantly less than it would cost to ship to Boston. The overland journey into that bustling hub to the south wasn't included, and was a hassle with which the Crundwells would have nothing to do. But things could be arranged for those in the know, at a price that made the extra headache not simply bearable, but preferable.

As word of Fidget's Mill spread among ambitious merchants on foreign shores, and sight of approaching sails peeking up over the horizon became more and more common, so the town itself began to expand. Laborers brought their families, which brought cooks and tailors and blacksmiths and barkeepers eager to provide essential services, which brought musicians and actors and playwrights eager to provide inessential ones.

Without any overarching design, the town would swell until it burst, at which point new buildings were constructed. The criteria by which an architectural endeavor was assessed and undertaken was:

"Do we need something building?"

"Looks like we might."

"Alright. Put it over there, where that puddle is."

The town may have been out of control, but the Crundwells nevertheless kept a tight fist on the reins, for all the good that did them. Provincial authorities came slithering out of the woods. The English took notice of the town and dispatched a Governor. The fundamentals of colonial law and order grew slowly but surely, like a pesky fungal infection. The Crundwells retained their overbearing influence solely because they retained their monopolistic control over the docks, which remained the sole source of income for the town. Very few people came to Fidget's Mill by land. Money either changed hands internally, amongst the citizens and debarked sailors on a temporary shore leave, or else it left with the goods on their way to Boston. There was only one income spigot, and the Crundwells had been controlling the flow for generations now. They were an institution without which the citizens of Fidget's Mill could not even imagine living.

In 1767, when the Board of Customs Commissioners set up shop in Boston to impose import duties on the Colonies, suddenly the Crundwells faced an institution *with* which they couldn't imagine living, though in the opposite direction. And as luck would have it, they didn't have to; the Customs Commissioners had no enforcement mechanism in Fidget's Mill. The upshot for firms and captains was that docking in Fidget's Mill dramatically decreased the likelihood of having to endure the most arbitrary abuses of an already unjust set of laws; being boarded, having goods confiscated, having crew incarcerated, and, while we're at it, having to pay an extra tax on imports.

Consequently, demand for docking space in Fidget's Mill increased exponentially. And Buddy Crundwell, reigning patriarch of the founding family, was going to do his damndest to expand to meet the demand. Dock construction kicked into double-time, and the wages of the overworked carpenters kicked into time-and-a-half (those who felt they were missing a half-time were kicked out on the double).

For a family so monomaniacally fascinated with itself and the story of its own success, the Crundwells had a very poor collective memory for details. Otherwise, they might have recalled a similar spasm of enthusiastic overproduction in the tobacco fields of Virginia, which proved so unsustainable that they had to get out of dodge and find a new line of work.

(If the Crundwells didn't remember this, the Shidy clan most *definitely* did. They would never, ever forget.)

So, at the end of 1767, Fidget's Mill stopped teetering on the economic knife's edge upon which it had existed for so many years, and finally began tipping. The only question was: which way would it tip?

The second only question was: would that make any difference?

VI

THE THIRD ONLY QUESTION WAS "WAIT WHAT where am I what is going on?"

Denton rubbed his forehead, taking a moment to gather his bearings and acquaint himself with his surroundings. Mud and yuck, those were his surroundings. Thus acquainted, he turned to the human man crouching down in front of him. Two facts were readily apparent: the man was a slave, and he was not from Fidget's Mill. The first fact was betrayed by his skin color; the second was betrayed by the fact that the stranger was helping Denton.

The moneyed folks bound for the big city of Boston always tended to treat the Fidgetonians with an off-handed condescension that proved utterly devastating to the self-esteem of people just trying to be kind. They closed ranks to reassure each other, and before long an unspoken agreement arose: if the out-of-towners are all going to be jerks to us, let's be jerks to them *first*, so maybe *they'll* be the ones who feel like idiots instead of us! Thus, good samaratinism became just another import.

This helpful out-of-towner rested a reassuring hand on Denton's shoulder. "Take it easy. A man clouted you upon the head and made off with your belongings."

Denton's vision swam itself to exhaustion and then drowned. The causal link between head-clouting and belonging-off-making remained just out of reach, positioned behind a curtain of blinding pain as it was. "Did I fall over?" Denton asked.

The slave gave a pitying smile. He responded by pointing his bent forearm perpendicular to the ground, and tracing the ninety-degree journey to parallel. "Like a tree. Perfect posture, straight as a rail. None of that flopping about, as one so often sees amongst the less educated sorts. It speaks highly of a man's character, to see him falling down like a gentleman."

Denton nodded, probably. Equally likely: the entire world bobbed up and down while his head remained stationary. "Well, I do my very best in all things."

The stranger smiled and nodded, as though this was either very funny or very profound. Denton couldn't see how it was either, but then again he couldn't see much of anything with the universe spinning so quickly.

A swarthy nightmare creature materialized in the air just in front of Denton's face. It had slick, writhing tendrils capped with ferocious yellow teeth, and wait a second it was the stranger's hand proffered as a way of introducing himself.

"My name is Increase," he said with that same quiet smile. "You're not from around here, are you?"

"Increase…"

"That's right."

Denton pondered this for a moment. He was familiar with the word. It just wasn't often in conjunction with a human face. "What's your surname?"

"That is my surname."

"What's your first name?"

"Don't have one."

"Oh." Now that the throbbing whirl of pain was subsiding, Denton looked None Increase over. He must have been into his fifties. His hair was greying around the temples, his body stooped but nonetheless evocative of a physical strength Denton could hardly imagine. It wasn't the sort of strength to which anyone would willingly push themselves, that was for sure. This was the strength of the man who spent his life being pushed. His eyes were a glassy brown, but still sharp under his sloping brow. His clothes were tatters of yesteryear's latest: hand-me-downs from his master, perhaps.

"You didn't answer my question," the slave reiterated politely but firmly.

"No, I suppose not."

"…well?"

"That was my answer."

"To whether or not you're from around here?"

"Yes."

"You 'suppose not'?"

"No." Denton reached up and touched the back of his head. His hand came back caked in mud, but fortunately free of blood. He took a deep breath. "No, my good Increase, I am not from around here."

"Mister."

"Indeed."

"No, Mr. Increase. That's what people call me."

"Indeed?"

"Yes."

"Mhm."

Mr. Increase shook his hand in front of Denton's face again. This time, Denton took it. Before he knew what was happening, he was on his feet. His surmise had been correct: Mr. Increase was *strong*, not just for his age but full-stop.

It occurred to Denton that he had no proof that this slave wasn't the one to have clouted him upon the head and made off with his belongings. Granted, it would have been a rather poor criminal who returned to the site of a public daytime crime to tend to his victim, but this was a rather poor town, so it wouldn't do to dismiss the possibility out of hand. Now on his feet, Denton looked around at the passersby. They were, as one would expect, simply passing by, hardly deigning to spare the poor foreigner a glance. Certainly none of them were pointing to Mr. Increase and shouting 'there he is, the villain,' which was encouraging. That could well be because they simply hadn't bothered to notice the crime being committed in the first place, though.

"What's your name?"

Denton had to think about this. "Hedges. My name is Denton Hedges."

"Do you know where you are, Mr. Hedges? Do you know what day it is?"

"I should hope so. Otherwise I may have suffered some manner of cranial trauma." Denton fixed him with a face. Mr. Increase couldn't figure out what the hell kind of face it was. It was just a *face*. Eerie. The face spoke, asking "you aren't either, right?"

"Aren't what?"

"From around here."

Mr. Increase shook his head. "No. Not originally."

"Unoriginally?"

"You could say that."

"Okay." Denton stared at the ground for a moment. "Do you know where the hotel is?"

"I do. It's called the Kl-"

"There *is* a hotel, isn't there?"

"Of course. It's just u-"

"Can you tell me where it is?"

"That's what I'm doing."

"I'm sorry."

"It's alright."

"Is there a better one?"

"A better what?"

"Hotel?"

"What's wrong with the Klu-?"

"You said it was just 'alright'".

"When?"

"Just a second ago."

"I was talking about you interrupting me. That was alright."

"Was it?"

"Yes."

"You didn't mind?"

"Well, a bit, but as I said, it was alright."

"Could I have done it better?"

"What?"

"Better than alright. I do my very best in all things."

"You don't want to be better at interrupting people."

"I want to improve myself in all things."

When Mr. Increase was fifteen, he fell into a lake without knowing how to swim. He thrashed about for something to grab on to. Finally, he struggled his way to a log floating on the surface of the water, wrapped his arm around it – and plunged back under the surface. The log looked strong and buoyant, but it was dead and rotten, unable to support his weight.

This image kept recurring to him, with greater and greater urgency, as the conversation with Denton progressed.

But still, on his many travels Mr. Increase had been introduced to the idea that when one saves a man's life, that man's life becomes one's responsibility. He'd heard it from a man who had heard it from somebody who had been to China, or one of those countries. Had Mr. Increase saved Denton's life? Probably not, but it was a more honorable explanation for sticking by this strange, likely concussed little man than a cocktail of curiosity and boredom.

Denton was saying something, but Mr. Increase opted to show him how a professional interrupts people. "Mr. Hedges," he cut in with utilitarian simplicity, "I think I'll walk you to the Klump now. We can continue our conversation on the way."

"That sounds like a wonderful idea. Denton."

"...yes, your name is Denton."

"I know. I mean to say I'd prefer you use my first name."

Mr. Increase smiled and wrapped an arm around Denton's shoulder.

It was almost concerning to Denton, how easy it was to secure the slave's friendship. Not only because he was a slave – Denton was a staunch abolitionist, but he was also acutely aware of how it might look to the locals he was meant to be wooing, palling around town with the help. No, the concern was largely about things on his head. Scratch that; on his *end*. His head was the thing that was hurting.

Denton had always struggled to make friends. He had had precious few friends before, at least not to his knowledge. He had a gift for conditioning people to tolerate his presence, though. Usually it took time, effort, and occasionally bribes. As far as he could tell, it was a strange by-product of his natural charisma. He was electric in front of a crowd, and could effortlessly command the attention of a small gathering. But when the gathering dispersed and he was left one-on-one, he sometimes found himself continuing to hide behind his buoyant stagecraft. It was a bulwark between himself and vulnerability. He knew this, and he was working on it, and he had gotten better about it during his time in Massachusetts. With his family, he could be himself. With other people, he tended to be the person he wanted them to think he was. This latter course of behavior was never planned; it always felt impressed upon him by some external force, which manifested as a heavy clenching in the sternum.

But with Mr. Increase, he was being himself right off the bat. No clenching anywhere. And all it took was being clouted upon the head.

Encouragingly, Mr. Increase seemed to respond just as quickly to his new friend. The shine-taking was immediate, like a crack of lightning that hung around to admire its own blazing brilliance; one second, the slave was making the sort of oh-god-how-can-I-get-out-of-this-conversation face Denton knew to be universal to all humanity. The next second, Mr. Increase's face did a thing Denton had so rarely seen in such close quarters. It softened. Denton nearly gasped, so unexpected was the shift.

Whatever it was that prompted Mr. Increase's split-second change in attitude, Denton planned to exploit it in his own favor. How lucky that he should fall in so easily with a Fidgetonian! He needed an in with the upper crust of Fidget's Mill society, and one just fell into his lap. Or perhaps the other way around would be nearer the truth. Either way, a slave in Fidget's Mill would almost certainly be working on the docks. And in Fidget's Mill, the docks meant the Crundwells.

Yes, perhaps it did take being clouted upon the head for Denton to be real with a stranger; as the dizziness waned, the Machiavellian thinking came waxing back in with a vengeance. He wasn't proud of wanting to exploit a new friendship. But nor was he *not* proud of devising such a clever scheme on the fly.

Perhaps, Denton mused, he could use the same affable magic on the Crundwells that he used on Mr. Increase when it came time to pitch the patriotic benefits of adopting strict non-importation. All that plan needed was to figure out what the magic was. And to figure out how to leverage his budding relationship with Mr. Increase into a face-to-face with the Crundwells. And to keep any Customs Commissioners away from the Crundwells, lest they report back to the British as to the Sons' aims in Fidget's Mill. And to change his clothes, because his were all muddy. And to buy new clothes, because a careful glance of his immediate surroundings reminded him that someone had stolen his suitcase while he was unconscious. And to find money with which to buy new clothes, because most of his finances were in the suitcase.

Perhaps, Denton further mused, the net yield of falling in so easily with a Fidgetonian was actually quite poor, as far as luck was concerned.

VII

TO BE FAIR: NO PLACE LOOKS GOOD AT THE height of a grey winter day. The clouds swallow up the sunlight and dump it in an unflattering spread, casting everything in a flat, shadowless, colorless *blah*. So it wasn't Fidget's Mill's fault that it looked like it had never known a moment of joy in its brief existence.

To be fair in the other direction, Fidget's Mill wouldn't have looked much better if this were a sunny summer afternoon. The town was drab and haphazard in a way that so perfectly reflected the qualities of an overcast day that, when combined, they very nearly achieved a kind of aesthetic alchemy by which two ugly lumps of *ugh* produce something *aah*.

Very nearly, but not quite.

Denton tried to look around as Mr. Increase led him to the hotel, but he found that his hungry eyes kept slipping off of everything, like a leech on a grease chute. Everything in the town was perfectly designed to deflect interest, even when the only real alternatives were moist pockets of mud and scraggly stray animals. Or maybe those were the well-loved pets. In which case, the strays might be indistinguishable from the little mounds of gnarled tree limbs Denton kept seeing piled alongside houses.

Or maybe those *were* the strays.

Only one way to find out.

He raised an arm towards the bramble. "Here doggie! Or perhaps kitty!" That's the sort of thing he wouldn't have done, had he not just sustained a blow to the head. He wondered what Mr. Increase must think of him, based on their limited interactions thus far.

Mr. Increase followed Denton's gaze towards the little mound of gnarled tree limbs and nearly tripped over his own feet.

Town hotelier Vera Miringhoff could have named her hotel anything. This was what most patrons would say to her shortly after she welcomed them to the Klump Regency and suggested that they enjoy their stay.

Except for this new guy that Mr. Increase had brought in. Most folks had a snidey little comment to make when they checked in, but the new guy just nodded and said "thank you." And then he babbled for a while but, Vera hated to admit, she sort of zoned out at that point.

As it happens, giving her hotel a dumb name was a strategic decision. The Klump Regency was one of the largest buildings in the entire town, second only to the Crundwell Residence on the outskirts, because it was more or less the only game in town for the peripatetic population. As mentioned, out-of-towners and Fidgetonians had a mutual distaste for one another. Naming this near-mandatory place of temporary residence something that could hardly be uttered without a sneer helped Vera (and, thanks to her robust involvement in nearly every social circle, the entirety of the town) pick out the occasional diamonds in the Boston-bound rough. If someone was enough of a sweetheart to *not* make a languid swipe at such low-hanging, low-class fruit, then maybe they weren't all bad, and maybe Vera would let the rest of the town know to be a bit nicer to this one.

"What's your name, sweetie?" she inquired casually. Vera was portly and in her 60's, which gave her free reign to call grown-ass men "sweetie".

"*Denton* Hedges." They both silently noted the perplexing emphasis, and silently noted each others' silent notation of it.

Vera nodded. "Well Mr. Hedges, pleased to meet you. I'm Vera."

"A pleasure." He teetered on his feet uneasily. "I'm very sorry for my curious behavior, I can assure you I am typically far steadier on my feet. It's only that I've recently been clouted upon the head."

Vera gave Mr. Increase an inquisitive look, to which he replied with a slight nod.

"I regret, therefore," Denton continued, "to inform you that I have no funds with which to purchase my lodging here this evening. My suitcase was taken from me, and I have reason to believe the purloining of my purse was the purpose behind clouting me upon the head, which did indeed happen from behind. I will, that said, send for funds from my wife in Boston at the first opportunity, but for now I am afraid that I am very tired and really ought to get some rest."

At this Vera gave Mr. Increase a far more pointed look, to which Mr. Increase responded verbally. "He seems to be getting worse."

Vera turned back to Denton, and stepped out from behind the small desk that had been between them. "Have somebody fetch the physician, would you?" she asked Mr. Increase without taking her eyes from Denton's.

Mr. Increase nodded and slipped quietly out the door.

This was all quite puzzling to Denton. He was feeling *much* better. Just sleepy, that was all. He was cogent enough to find Vera's order to Mr. Increase quite strange. She didn't tell him to fetch the physician; she told him to find somebody *else* to fetch the physician.

He was going to point this out, and ask what was *that* all about, but instead for some reason said "well, you see, this is such a bother, but it seems that upon my arrival a person or persons unknown did snatch my chest of possessions, and I am afraid to say that included in said chest was my financial, ah, situation."

He stopped talking. Vera wasn't a medical woman, but she knew that she really ought to keep Denton talking and awake. And calm.

"Is that right?" she asked, as though she didn't know the answer.

"And my wardrobe, I regret to confess. So I was wondering, if it's perfectly alright with you, if you could direct me to the place of business of the most senior enforcer of the laws regarding the inviolability of person property, such as they are?"

"Of course, Mr. Hedges."

"Denton, please."

"Denton, yes. That's such a pity to hear." Mr. Increase slipped back into the room as quietly as he'd left. Vera shot him a concerned look over Denton's shoulder, which he returned. "I'm sorry to say that the only real lawman here is Sheriff Barefoot, and he serves at the pleasure of Governor Marsh. And *he* serves at the pleasure of the wretched King George III."

"Mhm, er." Denton scratched absent-mindedly at the back of his head. "Ouch." This was valuable information. He had reckoned he would find the English Crown trying to assert its authority at a distant remove, but they had the Governor to make laws, and the sheriff to enforce them. How powerful must the Crundwells be, that a campaign to win them over through subterfuge was deemed not only necessary, but also the most expedient means of achieving the Sons' ends?

He would have to tread lightly; if his membership in the Sons of Liberty were to become common knowledge, he might suddenly find himself wrong-footed at every turn by the Imperial Infrastructure here established.

It was nice to know that Vera and, apparently, Mr. Increase were on his side though. It made him far less reluctant to sleep around them.

Hedges rested his hand on the counter as casually as he could. "Would these affiliations possibly disincline Mr. Sheriff Barefoot from making the necessary inquiries into the whereabouts of my luggage?"

Vera finished writing on a paper with a flourish of the arm. She spun the page around and scooted it to Denton. This was slightly disorienting, as Denton hadn't noticed her taking out the paper and undertaking the writing of words upon it. "He's just got other things on his mind, is all. Best we leave him to his worries, and handle our own amongst ourselves. See my meaning?" She tapped the paper three times. "This gal here, she's the one you really want to see about getting back your belongings. Barefoot'll put somebody 'on the case', but Miss Carsis'll get results. She knows everything that happens in this town."

Timorous as could be, Denton slowly picked up the page. It read:

33 GUTTER LANE

He looked at Vera uncertainly. Most of his uncertainty had to do with why it took her so long to write two numbers and ten letters. If it had taken a long time. Couldn't be certain. She grinned warmly.

"Why, er, I just was thinking, this seems awful trusting, if she's as big a cheese as you imply."

Vera waved a hand dismissively. "Either you're worth trusting, or you're not. She'll give what you deserve in either case."

"Aaugh?" He sniffed nervously.

"When you're in a condition to go anywhere, you'll go there. You let me know, and I'll let her know, and she'll set a time, and you'll go there. She'll be expecting you." Vera then gave Denton a code phrase, to be relayed verbatim.

"I can't, ah, I don't know if I can say that verbatim."

"Why not?"

"I've already forgotten it."

Vera gave the counter two friendly pats with her open palm. "That's alright. I can explain this all again tomorrow. Until then, the doctor is here."

With that, Denton smiled, pushed the paper back to Vera, and walked away. In that parting look was a clarity of self-awareness that took her slightly aback. Maybe giving him Miss Carsis' address was a disastrous idea after all. Or maybe it was the best idea she'd ever had. It was just too early to say at this point, but she knew one thing for certain: it was one or the other, and nothing in between.

Denton, too, was ruminating upon extreme turns in good fortune. Because as he spun around, he discovered that the physician who was to tend to his wounds was a man he'd last seen dodging shoes in a town square in Boston. It was Dr. Brisby Houlihan, lately appointed Customs Commissioner to Fidget's Mill.

VIII

BRISBY AND MR. INCREASE GUIDED DENTON UP to a room that Vera averred was *his*. Just how this was, given his inability to pay and lack of firm future prospects regarding the same, escaped Denton. But Vera insisted, and so up he went.

The room was a small second-story affair, a reluctant rectangle trying desperately to be a perfect square. Looking in from the doorway, the drawers and cupboards were all against the wall to the left; the bed jutted out from the right wall. Straight ahead, a throw rug looked as though it had fulfilled its nominal destiny in the manner of its placement. The dying light of the day pressed against the window, a thick curtain of soft flame.

None of the light came *in* the window, though. Because it was late in the day, and the window faced East. And there were no literal curtains to match the metaphorical one. That was good news at the moment, given Denton's lately acquired sensitivity to light. It would be not-so-good news whenever he wanted to sleep past sunrise.

But he could worry about that another day, a day when he didn't have Dr. Brisby Houlihan pressing a thumb into his eyelids and pulling them upwards, the better to scrutinize the eyeball beneath.

"Is that necessary?" Denton inquired sincerely.

"Relax." Brisby switched to the other eye. "It's your lucky day, as far as being brained in the middle of a public thoroughfare goes. I'm a physician up from Boston for just a brief stretch of time, and I'm very good at my job." He withdrew his hand, wiping some of the mud that had clung to Denton's face on his pant leg. "What's the last thing you remember?"

"You telling me that you're a physician up from Boston for a stretch of brief time, and that's very good for your job."

Brisby grinned and patted Denton on the knee. "Yes, very funny." Behind the smile, the doctor made a mental note of the lack of fidelity in the repetition. "I mean before you were struck."

"I was…" Denton thought on this for a moment. Fortunately, he was cogent enough to stop himself from saying *I was mulling on my lack of actionable courses, pursuant to the successful discharge of my patriotic duties.* Brisby was, after all, not just a physician. He was the Customs Commissioner, an emissary of the Crown. Denton knew this because he'd seen him announcing the Townshend Acts in Boston, but Brisby didn't know that Denton knew this because he'd been too busy dodging concussions of his own to notice the quiet man in the back of the crowd.

An informational disparity in Denton's favor, that's what he had here. This was also his only real advantage. If he could hold on to that advantage, perhaps he could spin this unfortunate incident into a greater advantage. He had, after all, lucked into meeting quite a few people from all walks of life in Mill here, had he not? Mr. Increase, Vera, Brisby…and all it took was being bonked on the head!

Speaking of – Denton realized he had sat in vacuous silence for several seconds now, markedly failing to answer Brisby's question. "I was on the street…standing on the street, and I was just wondering where I might find lodging for the evening…and then I was on the ground, being found by him." He nodded to Mr. Increase, who leaned against the doorframe with arms folded. How curious, that Brisby allowed him to hover like that!

Brisby reached out to Denton's left ear, and for one horrified moment he thought the Doctor was going to tell him there was something behind his ear, and come back with a glittering coin or a geode or some other bauble. Instead, Brisby snapped twice, the sharp reports filling Denton's head with unhappy harmonics.

"Hey!" Denton insisted.

The doctor nodded, satisfied. "You didn't have anywhere to stay?"

"I didn't. My trip to Fidget's Mill was rather last-minute."

Brisby snapped open his medical bag and rooted around. "Business or pleasure?"

"Business" came tumbling out of Denton's mouth before he had a chance to vet the thought. A bolt of ice shot through his spine; he knew what the next question would be, and he hadn't a satisfactory answer.

"And what sort of business is that?"

Denton was not a good liar, which was surprising, because he was such a good lawyer. He was always quick on his feet because he always told the truth, and the truth was always ready at hand. Lies took a bit more work. The only reliable way he'd found to lie was to work it out ahead of time, rehearse it, and ultimately make himself believe it. But he didn't have time right now. He'd thought he was falling in with these people effortlessly, but he could see now that they remained skeptical. And why wouldn't they? He was an outsider.

But so is Dr. Houlihan, Denton reminded himself.

A lie wasn't like Fidget's Mill, it wouldn't come *ex nihilo*, but perhaps there was something in this room he could use as the foundation of a fiction. He rolled his eyes around the room, which didn't take long. It was a tiny room, and he despaired of spotting a bright idea hanging conveniently on the far wall.

Instead, he saw a bright idea leaning against the doorframe.

In hindsight, he would attempt to console himself by recalling that his head had been well and truly bopped, and so he couldn't have expected himself to have the best ideas of his entire life, lying in that stiff bed. Or, indeed, to have the good sense to catch one of the worst ideas he'd had in his entire life.

The most he could do was recognize the bad idea after it was too late to spot it; by the time said idea had tumbled out of his noggin and was travelling down the mouthspout, a second idea had leapt out after the first, screaming NOOOOOOOOO!

"I'm in the slave trade," Denton declared with the edge of obstinate certainty that is unique to the smoothest of bald-faced lies.

(NOOOOOOOOO!)

Oh cranberries, he thought to himself. Denton was well enough attuned to the general political consensus of Massachusetts to know that the tide of popular opinion was flowing towards his own position of abolitionism. So not only was his cover story reprehensible to him personally – it was just about the worst possible choice he could have made, given the degree to which he tended to count on the groundswell to carry him through to his objectives.

And, judging by the look on Mr. Increase's face, it wasn't only him to whom the cover story was reprehensible. Oh dear.

If he had to find a silver lining, though, it would be that wealthy merchant types usually LOVE slavery. So that should endear him to them, the better to whisper sweet nothings (i.e. recommendations for trade policies) in their ears.

The other silver lining, more a copper lining: that room-prompted confabulation *still* wasn't as bad as 'Window Tablechair'.

Brisby cocked his head to the side. "How so? What do you do?"

Ah! An opportunity to backpedal! What would be the least ethically compromising position to hold, while still technically working in the most ethically compromised business in history?

He looked around the teeny tiny room for another spark of inspiration, because nobody is more idiotic than a clever man in extremis. This time, Denton found his inspiration sitting right before him.

"I'm a doctor. A slave doctor."

(NOOOOOOOO!)

Denton's heart sank as Brisby's face lit up. "Well, why on Earth didn't you say so? We have so much to discuss!" The actual physician held out his arm, inviting the fake one to proffer his own.

Behind Brisby, Mr. Increase grimaced, shook his head, and slipped out of the room. Denton felt legitimately terrible about that. He also felt legitimately terrible about having represented himself to Brisby in this way. He also felt legitimately terrible about his concussion.

If he had to find a silver lining to this legitimately terrible turn of events, though, it would be that he'd successfully found an 'in' with Brisby Houlihan, who could almost certainly serve as an 'in' to the higher climes of Fidget's Mill society. Perhaps he could be getting an audience with the Crundwells sooner than he'd ever imagined, and then he could be on his way by the year's end, well before Sam Adams and James Otis Jr. released their Circular Letter.

Denton tried to keep the glint of that lining in sight as the dark cloud of Legitimately Terrible rolled over him.

IX

DENTON KNEW HIS CONVALESCENCE WAS GOING well when he felt overcome with restlessness. He had a lot to be restless about; where he had just yesterday come blundering into town without the least course of action charted out, he now had an embarrassment of riches in that department. He also had an embarrassment or two of a less happy kind to mark his arrival. One was the debt to Vera he was accumulating; she had come up that morning to tell him he could stay rent-free until he was better, at which point he could go see the woman named Miss Carsis at 33 Gutter Lane. Vera was *very* confident that Miss Carsis could get Denton his luggage back, at which point he would be able to pay Vera back. She never specified whether or not there would be interest attached, but Denton wasn't a fool. And simple generosity or not, Vera's ostensible largesse had committed Denton to seeing Miss Carsis, and soon.

The second embarrassment had to do with the whole 'I am a slave doctor' fiction in which he'd cloaked himself, in front of two people who could quite easily put paid to that claim. With Brisby, that was as far as the concern went. But that look on Mr. Increase's face, after he had been so helpful to Denton in his time of vulnerability…that cut surprisingly deep.

Last night, it had snowed. Was it the first snow of the year? Almost certainly not, but Denton was still sorry he missed it. He was pleased to see that he had awoken early enough to enjoy the night's labors as a silent, unbroken sheet of white. By afternoon, it would have been thoroughly tromped and balled and tossed and bepissed, but for now it was perfect.

Inspired, Denton arose from his bed, threw on his coat (after peeling off most of the mud, now dried to clay, that commemorated his fall in the thoroughfare) and made his way out into his first full day in the Mill. He was happy to note that things could really only improve from here. And that was true, for a little while.

An itinerary was slotting into place, which gave Denton the warm and fuzzies. He was a man who thrived under pressure, who felt more comfortable when his TO-DO list had a whole lot of DOs and very few DONEs. His first piece of business took him down to the docks that were the beating heart, swelling lungs, and gurgling intestines of Fidget's Mill. He wasn't *positive* he would find Mr. Increase there, but he may as well have been.

Snow cascaded delicately through the air, blown from the rooftops, peeling off of the three-inch blanket of white silence that invested the squalor of the town with majesty and dignity it did not, frankly, deserve. The virgin snow crunched under each step Denton took, as he drew his coat tight around his shoulders and ruminated on how indefinably unpleasant it was for the words "virgin" and "crunch" to be so close together.

Children laughed and played in the alleyways, packing the wet flakes into balls and hurling them at each other. Presumably this was fun? They were all laughing fit to bust a gut, anyway. Denton had never been in a snowball fight. He hadn't had many pals to playfight with. He'd had a lot of books, but they didn't do well with projectiles or moisture.

A paroxysm of loss for a feeling he had never known took one of the key arteries of his heart, and smacked his left ventricle with it as it shouted "STOP HITTING YOURSELF STOP HITTING YOURSELF".

Emotions were complex beasts.

An errant snowball struck Denton in the side of the head. The kids burst into tearful gales of laughter, which clued Denton in that maybe that snowball wasn't so errant after all.

Alright, not *all* emotions were complex beasts. Anger, indignation, humiliation; these all felt more like single-celled critters with one job and one job only: reproduce.

He formulated a rather devastating verbal retort, but the children had already beat a hasty retreat through the fleecy alleyways.

Oh, look at that. A more complex variant of humiliation – the free-floating kind, independent of any witnesses. Emotional evolution in action, a century before anybody would put their thumb on the biological fact of it.

(STOP HITTING YOURSELF STOP HITTING YOURSELF)

And now his headache was back.

Heart lungs intestines etc. though the docks may have been to Fidget's Mill, floes of ice had locked up the body economic for the time being. The hustle and bustle Denton had expected to find may well have been vindicated by reality in the warmer months, but today the port was a still life. The snow, here able to boast of nearly four vertical inches, grabbed the sounds of wood creaking and hulls groaning in the frigid waters and held them greedily. And greedy it was, for there was much sound to be held: the dock must have been nearly 1,500 feet long, easily capable of providing safe harbor for forty, maybe even fifty ships. Denton stopped and counted – there were thirty-seven ships sheltering here from the frozen bay.

But clearly, not all activity had ceased: a dizzying squid of footprints stretched its track-tentacles out in every direction. Coming or going, Denton couldn't quite say, but they led to/issued from a well-tread depression several feet in diameter just in front of what was easily the largest building on the dock. Further from the water, he'd have called it a barn and been done with it. Situated as it was, he could only say it was a large two-story spectacle of haphazardly-fired and expertly-lain bricks. That was often the way, as far as Denton could tell with his untrained eyes. Brickmaking was an odd job for the unskilled. Brick*laying* was an art reserved for the well-trained.

Even now formulating what he would say, should he find his man, he followed a trail of traffic-packed snow all the way to its source, or perhaps its destination.

The brick building had a modest, regular-sized wooden door that somehow seemed wildly incommensurate to the rest of the edifice. Were it a great big double-door looming over him, Denton might have felt a frisson of transgressive glee as he levered it open and slipped inside.

(So fixated was he on seeing his plan through, he hardly noticed when breaking in to a locked building had become a preliminary step.)

But this human-sized hatchway was oddly off-putting. It just…it lacked the requisite theatricality. Big buildings should have big doors, that was just common sense. But no matter; this worked in his favor. This'd probably be easier to jimmy his way into. How did people usually do it? He could find a crowbar somewhere, most likely, and-

It's open!

The voice pierced the silky hush of the powdered docks like a bayonet through a soap bubble. Denton whirled on his feet, the snow providing a whimsical *rrrRT!* accompaniment.

There was nobody in sight, and there were no hiding places nearby. Certainly not within earshot – the nearest place a man (or woman, as the voice had a female quality to it) could have hidden was a pile of boxes some hundred feet away. A voice would not have carried that far, that clearly, through the hush of snow.

The voice seemed to have come from directly inside his head. Had that snowball thrown by the kids knocked something loose, something that had been jangling at the end of its tether as a result of the inaugural bonk he'd received upon his arrival yesterday?

Nope, the voice reassured him. Was it female? It was androgynous, in a way Denton couldn't define, but it certainly skewed feminine.

Suddenly the soothing quietude of the morning took on an oppressive air. Denton's ears began ringing, as they did when he found himself in a silent room for too long. It was unpleasant – he loved noise, the little noises that are so easily tuned out, like the wind rattling the windowpane or the deep breathing of a slumbering dog. Silence was unnatural. Doubly so when mysterious voices were cutting through it to let you know that…

Denton pushed the regular-sized door to the jumbo-sized building. It clattered in its frame, but didn't open. He breathed a sigh of relief. How unnerving would it have been, had the voice in his head known th-

You have to pull.

Denton paused. He reached out a trembling hand, clutched the chilly brass knob of the door, and pulled. It swung open easily.

That's how he found how unnerving it would have been: *VERY.*

The brick building turned out to be a storehouse, which in hindsight of course it would. Goods being brought in couldn't just sit on the ships, particularly with the writs of assistance granting the British the authority to board ships and confiscate goods arbitrarily (that there was little threat of this happening in Fidget's Mill was cold comfort to overseas merchants, so the proper precautions were taken for form's sake). But nor could they be immediately loaded up for the trip down to Boston; there simply wasn't any mechanism of coordination precise enough to ensure that the carriage would be ready and waiting at the moment of mooring. Besides, it was in the economic interests of the town to keep people with money in town for a few days, to inject some much-needed capital into an otherwise closed loop.

Hence the storehouse, which seemed remarkably smaller on the inside than the outside. That probably had something to do with the claustrophobic press of shelves and stacks that were practically flush with one another, from wall to wall and floor to ceiling. The shelves were full of boxes, boxes and more boxes, none of which were labeled as far as Denton could see. Each of the boxes varied in size, but most of them were large enough that he simply couldn't fathom how they had been brought in, or how they would be taken out. He could barely figure out how to maneuver his own slight frame between the shelves.

He found modest success by pinching his shoulder blades, sucking

in his gut and shimmying his way into the stacks sideways.

The smells would have knocked Denton flat on his back, had he the space to be thusly knocked without kicking off a slapstick domino chain of toppling shelves. The whole place stank of salty damp, of wood left to rot by pounding sea, of pliable clay that never found its shape, of spices and wool and rum and paper and silk and molasses and human sweat, though the latter Denton suspected was a byproduct of manhandling the others through the storehouse, rather than an import in its own right. But hey, the wealthy could afford their eccentricities, so he would withhold judgment until all of the facts were in.

Just as he felt nearly blinded by the solid wall of aromas, he reached the eye of the store. The stacks opened into an indoor courtyard of sorts, a hollow core cleft into the labyrinth of shelving. The dimensions were roughly similar to what he'd imagined the entirety of the place to be, just scaled way down on the x-axis.

Sitting in the center of this center was the man he had come to see: Mr. Increase. The slave looked up from a sheet of paper in his hands and inhaled sharply.

Denton had rehearsed a whole thing. That was how he'd thought of it – a whole thing. He was going to apologize, and offer an admittedly limp but hopefully plausible explanation for his lie (yes, he would entrust Mr. Increase enough to reveal that he had lied, hoping that this would serve to demonstrate the verity of his remorse, though he wouldn't reveal the actual motivation for the lie), and depending on how well that went, attempt to insinuate himself into Mr. Increase's good graces. Befriending a slave wouldn't necessarily help him in securing non-importation, but one never knew when friends in low places could come in handy.

Sometimes Denton really hated how his mind worked. Not most times. Just some. Like this one.

"I came to apologize to you," Denton began, as he had practiced.

Mr. Increase eyed him skeptically. Slowly, he raised a hand in greeting. "Hello."

The ball was back in Denton's court, and he had no idea what to do.

He'd conceived this apology as a monologue, and rehearsed it as he would his closing remarks in a hearing. He hadn't accounted for a reply, and he *certainly* hadn't accounted for a reply that seemed to utterly disregard the first thing he'd said.

He felt his rigorous preparation slipping through his fingers.

"I'm sorry," he clarified.

"I figured," Mr. Increase replied.

"Huh?"

"I figured you were sorry."

"How?"

"You just said you came to apologize. That would imply sorrow."

"Yes, so it would." Denton considered this exceedingly valid point. "Well, I am."

"About what, may I ask?"

Denton's whole thing really had been wonderful. Poetic, elliptical, satisfying. This was none of those things. "Uh, I'm sorry about saying I was a slave doctor."

Mr. Increase cocked an eyebrow. "You're apologetic about announcing your occupation, and yet not about the plying of the trade itself?"

"No."

The slave shook his head and returned his attention to his clipboard.

Denton began to blubber, but swallowed some of his own saliva and so began to cough.

Mr. Increase waved a dismissive hand in his direction without bothering to look up. "Cough into the crook of your elbow, if you don't mind. That's a box of cinnamon right by your head, and I'm not about to sweep it up if it blows everywhere."

Denton did as bidden, and after a few seconds, got himself back under control.

"Mr. Increase, I come to apologize because I have dissimulated, and poorly. I am not a slave doctor. I am neither a slaver *nor* a doctor. I have always been a staunch abolitionist, and I hope my behavior towards you will bear this out."

Increase's eyebrows started hiking their way to the top of his forehead. Denton started speaking more quickly in an effort to finish before they did: "There is a perfectly good reason for my deception, and it is as follows, you see; two years ago th-" Too late. The eyebrows reached the base of the hairline, paused for a second as though at the peak of a hill, and then went sledding back down to their natural altitude.

"I knew you weren't what you claimed to be, Denton. None of the slaves have ever heard of you. Except for one, of course. He was in Virginia, back in 1763."

Denton blanched, and got self-conscious about demonstrating his emotions by becoming *more* white. But he couldn't help it, damnit!

Increase grinned. "Don't worry, barrister. Your secret is safe. Nobody halfway positioned to set anything to rights listens to the slaves."

That was an in. "I'd reckon you've a lot of interesting things to say, for anyone willing to listen."

"…"

"I would listen to you."

"…"

"You wouldn't happened to be owned by the Crundwells by any chance, would you?"

"I'm not a slave, Mr. Hedges."

Having plumbed the depths of humiliation and found bedrock, he was glad to know there was always a way to keep digging deeper. To celebrate, Denton said "Whoops" very quietly.

X

"OF COURSE YOU AREN'T," DENTON DECLARED magnanimously.

"You just assumed I was, owing to the color of my skin."

"No. Well, yes. But, you know, *to be fair*, not that it's *fair*, *ethically* I mean, but..." The thought tapered off into oblivion. "I'm not certain where I'm going with that. I'm very sorry, I haven't...well, I'm a staunch abolitionist, as I may have mentioned, though I must confess I've never...I do most of my canvassing, as it were, at a distance, and so-"

"You've never spoken to a colored man before."

Denton twitched. "I don't think I would have phrased it that way, but yes."

Mr. Increase's eyes twinkled. If Denton wasn't very much mistaken, he was enjoying this. "Oh, no? How would you have phrased it?"

"Far more delicately." Denton cleared his throat. "I think we ought to start again."

"I'm sure you do."

"...forgive me, but I don't get the impression that you're prepared to wipe the slate clean with me."

The free man placed his clipboard on the table next to him. "Let's say I'm prepared, but staying my hand for want of a good reason."

That was good enough for Denton. Explanations and justifications swirled through his mind, but a simple maxim cut through the fog like a harpoon through a spiderweb. Honesty Is The Best Policy.

Besides, he ruminated with no small amount of shame, *who would he tell? Who'd believe him?*

"I'm not a slave doctor. I've no affiliation with the slave trade."

"You said that already."

"I'm working up to the reason for the deception."

"I'll be very interested to hear it. That was a curious lie to tell, in an area so opposed to the institution."

"I know, I know." Denton ran his fingers through his hair. *Gah!* He had managed to keep that particular tic under control for a few days! "Dictated by context entirely. I've never been strong with on-my-feet fabrications. And I am, by profession, a lawyer, so if there are any fulminant witticisms burning deep within your funny bone, let's out with them now so we can proceed uninterrupted." He gave Mr. Increase a moment to make the joke that most everybody likes to make. To his credit, he didn't. "At any rate, I've come here for...I'm not entirely sure. I've tasks to accomplish and have found no clear path by which to do so, leaving me no recourse but to thrash about in an attempt to forge my own."

Mr. Increase leaned back on the table and folded his arms. If Denton didn't know better, he'd say the old man's interest was being piqued. "And what are your tasks, that so need to be accomplished?"

"They are of a highly sensitive nature, Mr. Increase."

"Would you believe me if I told you my first name was actually Discreet?"

Discreet Increase. "Most likely not, but it does have a ring to it."

Another laugh. He wagged his finger playfully. "Healthy skepticism. You're not so dense after all."

Denton smiled and then accidentally told Mr. Increase everything about everything.

Roughly an hour and a half later, Denton finally stopped talking. It had been a flat-out monologue, the longest he'd ever spent talking in one stretch. His throat was dry, his tongue felt heavy and his jaw ached. He never felt this way after a courtroom harangue. What gave? Mr. Increase was just one pretty calm guy with modest clothes in a stinky warehouse, in contrast to a rowdy public house full of would-be toffs, which was where his speeches usually ended up being delivered. Must be the moist chill of the bay seeping into his joints.

His senses had bled out of him as he'd told his story, and were only now returning, bearing a souvenir from their travels: an overwhelming awareness of how full the storehouse was of silence, and how little space it had to spare for his disquisition. It made his speech feel an act of violence in some indefinable way.

The snow must have picked up again; the perpetual exhale of fresh snow falling onto the slanted roof cuddled right up to the silence.

Finally, Mr. Increase rent the hush.

"You want to make The Crundwells, who are rich, stop importing things, which is the thing that made them rich."

"...well, once again, that's not how I would phrase it. 'Challenging the King' and 'Fomenting popular rebellion against the very structure of colonial administration' more accurately descr-"

Mr. Increase held a hand up. "That's what you hope will happen as a consequence of disrupting trade. Which is all you're actually after, is disrupting trade."

Denton sighed. "You're being excessively reductive."

"No, I'm laying things out as they are. What are you going to do about the Lowestofts? Or the Ditteridges?"

"The who?"

"...what do you actually know about how this town is run?"

"Not enough, I fully admit, but the levers by which the world is changed are-"

"Don't give me the 'levers' speech."

With great pride, Denton resisted the urge to run his hand through his hair. "The what? Is the levers speech a common speech?"

"I hear variations on it all the time. Always from moneyed white folks like you."

"I'm not moneyed."

Mr. Increase ran a showcasing hand along his tattered wardrobe. "That's relative." He rose from the table and walked towards Denton, disguising his slight limp with hard-earned dignity.

"You disparage my contribution to the rebellion?"

A sarcastic tilt of the head from Mr. Increase. "Oh, it's a rebellion, is it?"

A baffled shaking of the head from Denton. "I came here to apologize, not to be belittled. If you have something you'd like to say in response to my revelations, I'd appreciate if you'd out with it."

Mr. Increase smiled, and outed with more than Denton had bargained for.

XI

MR. INCREASE'S MOTHER (WHO, THROUGHOUT his entire story, was never given a name by the filial narrator) escaped a

Virginian tobacco plantation when she was seventeen years old and two months pregnant. Already suffering from the early stages of what would later be termed 'green tobacco sickness', her flight was a feat of heroism the likes of which her son could only hope to emulate. The rags on her back were sodden and heavy with the dew of those loathsome fields; she was dizzy, nauseous and nearly blinded by a migraine that cracked like an echo of the whip she still heard in the moments before sleep. These things slowed her down, but they didn't stop her. Mother Increase cut a lonely path to the North, foraging and starving and, to her great and everlasting shame, occasionally stealing.

There were times when her son would wring grim amusement from the parallel journeys of his mother and the Crundwells; both fleeing from that most lucrative of crops, heading not towards anything but simply *away*. But there the amusement ended, because the more plentiful contrasts were too stark to bear with a smile.

Mother didn't stop in Fidget's Mill; she kept on going, following whispers that told of work to be found for colored girls just to the North, just out of reach, just a little further now, until the decision to settle was made for her. On October 21, 1717, she collapsed onto the grass made harsh and brittle by the evening frost, and pushed through her delirium and agony to find the give in her misery. She was terrified of her child, terrified that it might come out with significantly lighter skin than her own rich ebony. Her sweetheart was even darker than she, but her mast-…that alabaster bastard was pale enough to be translucent. Time had gotten away from her, but her incoming (or outgoing, to be precise) offspring could plausibly have been by either of their issue. A child as dark as blissful slumber would swell her heart to bursting, but a grey baby of liminal hues…she didn't know if she would be able to love someone who could not but look at her with *his* eyes.

She nearly lost consciousness in the act, but held on with the tenacity she had come to think of as her only natural gift – but what a gift it was. Until this second, perhaps: the child (she couldn't yet think of it as *her* child, because if it came to that…) was sucking air in wet, shallow gasps. The benthic pressures that had built up in her stomach and pressed southward, in counterpoint to her own personal cross-country journey, had dissipated. But still, she kept her eyes clamped shut, listening to her ch-no, *the* child – mewling and fidgeting on the rough woolen blanket she'd lain out for it.

Finally, she marshaled her considerable will and cracked open her tired eyelids. A warmth filled her chest, the likes of which she had never known, nor ever considered possible. Little baby Increase was hale, hearty and a giddy obsidian that gave punchy contrast to his big, brilliant eyes – the eyes of the father he could never know, at least until the day of judgment finally came to put paid to the injustices of the world. What a busy day that would be.

At any rate: Increase was healthy, but he didn't cry. Probably because his mother never had.

What his mother may have called him as she clawed a sharpened rock up from the soil, and scythed it down against the umbilical cord still slick with her vitality, Mr. Increase never said, and so Denton never asked. He felt he was being led down the scenic route to a very specific point, and wasn't much interested in suggesting further detours.

Knowing full well she couldn't sustain her peripatetic lifestyle with a baby on board, Mother crept through the woods to the nearest town, said a quick but thorough prayer, and stepped out of the wild for the first time in months.

Fortunately for her, the high drama of her lifestyle was also unsustainable. She winnowed her way into Portsmouth, New Hampshire and carved out as decent an existence as a single woman of color with a newborn child could hope to find. This wasn't saying a whole lot, but to her it was everything.

By the age of fifteen, young Increase was taller and stronger than most anyone else in the town. That was reason enough to head down to the docks for work; he had no especial interest in maritime trade, and harbored a phobia of the open ocean that, had he ever shared it with anyone else, he would have pointed out was *completely* rational. But find work he did, and he thrived on the vigorous camaraderie that naturally develops when manly men are lifting heavy boxes together. On either side of a working day he was a third-class man by virtue of his birth, but work rekeyed him to be just one of the lily-white guys.

Save, that was, for the days when slaving ships moored in Portsmouth.

He struggled through a single day of herding humans who looked more like him than his coworkers down the gangplank as though they were chattel. When the second ship dropped anchor, Increase turned tail and headed for home. He said so long to his mother with a curious distance that would haunt him for the remainder of his life; he owed her so much more than he ever could have given her, something he only realized after reflecting upon the insufficiency of what he never could have guessed would end up being their final farewell.

Rushing back to the docks, Increase boarded the first non-slaving ship he could find. Loaded down with furs acquired from the natives (allegedly through enlightened trade, though even on the Sisyphean upslope towards puberty Increase was savvy enough to suspect foul play) and lumber culled from the ample American boscage (no pretenses towards reciprocity in that bit of business, though the boy could hardly imagine how anyone could miss a few felled trees), Seaman Increase fell to his duties aboard the London-bound *Humdrum* with alacrity.

Race relations were hardly more equitable in England, but the open sea was positively utopian. Sure, Increase frequently spent his free moments cowering below decks, hyperventilating as he attempted to steady himself against the crushing, terrifying immensity of the tar-black Atlantic. The work was backbreaking, and one wrong footing would send him plunging into the dread element. But the maritime terror rendered the weight of prejudice that so encumbered Increase on dry land more buoyant. It was a simple matter of expediency: when the stakes were high, there just wasn't any time to tend a prejudice. Sails needed hoisting, oars needing cracking, and Increase was a back still unbroken. That was all there was to it.

The ship docked in London, Increase helped unload the cargo, and he received his payment in sterling. As sailors on shore leave have since time immemorial, he decided to treat himself to a rowdy night on the town. But he traveled the foreign city alone – the sea-borne sense of brotherhood hadn't a pair of land legs yet.

"Yet." That's what he told himself, anyway.

Increase had a good time, and kept a hefty chunk of his pay for transit back to America. There was a market for English poundage, to be sure.

The return journey took a *Humdrum* loaded down with manufactured goods, textiles and porcelain chief among them, and lifted up by that conditional bonhomie, through the southern arm of the North Atlantic gyre to the West Indies. Unloading, payment, a lonely stroll, re-embarkation.

The *Humdrum*, normally a festering tomb of unspeakable stenches, smelled sweeter than anything Increase had ever known when he and his sunrise shadow scrambled on board that morning. This was courtesy to the new cargo – sugar and molasses, the gustatory indulgences to which even the purest Puritans are susceptible.

So aromatic was the new load of glucose, Increase had no idea that the ballast of the ship was of the human sort: a tangle of slaves, many of whom would not survive the journey to the colonies, some of whom had already reached their final destination.

But he did have *some* idea, didn't he? When the wind was still, wasn't there a sour stench of miserable humanity underneath the sweetness? When his sometimes-friends fell silent for the night, couldn't he hear mythic creatures of the deep crying out in pain, and didn't they sound all too human, all too real?

Some nights he couldn't sleep. And on those evenings, all he could think about was how *easy* it was for him to sleep soundly most every other night.

They berthed in Philadelphia, and this time Increase accepted his payment and began an overland journey north. He left as quickly as he could, and told himself it was because he was eager to see his mother. And perhaps that was true – but more than that, he wanted to make sure he didn't see what all was dragged up from the bottom of the *Humdrum.*

Nearly two years after his departure, Increase returned to Portsmouth. He positively jingled with riches from across the sea. His voice had dropped, because so had his anatomy. His face, angular and chiseled like a sea-beaten breakwater, was prickly with the beginnings of a mighty beard. He was a changed man – or rather, he had changed *into* a man. Perhaps it was true that he was eager to see his mother, but he was just as eager for her to see him.

He couldn't find her.

He knocked on the door of their old home, and a white man greeted him with the barrel of a musket. Searches for old friends yielded similar results. Mother was gone, and the fact was that nobody in Portsmouth was sad to see the back of her. Two possibilities occurred to Increase: someone knew where she was, and simply refused to tell Increase out of bigoted spite…or else she was so little considered by the people of Portsmouth that they had forgotten about her before she had vanished over the horizon. Assuming she had left, that was.

Which, with each passing day, Increase found a less and less plausible assumption.

Had he come home to a grave bearing her name – hell, had he come home to her rotting corpse, as he frequently did in his nightmares – it would have been easier to bear. It was the not knowing that killed him. Maybe she was dead, but what if she wasn't? Where would she be? What could have driven her to fold up her tent and leave, knowing full well that her son would never be able to find her? What if she hadn't been driven, but had been taken?

The possibilities were too stark to consider – which made them morbid fixtures of his low moods for years to come.

To stay his imagination, Increase returned to the seafaring life. There he kept himself occupied for nearly three decades, before he finally caught a poor footing and flipped off the rigging on a trip back from the West Indies, crashing onto the deck and breaking his left leg. He lay infirm for the remainder of the journey, sequestered below deck where the world smelled sweet to compensate for the sour bedrock.

He heard them crying out, day after night after day after night.

They docked, he was paid, and this time he stayed. For the first time in thirty years of skirting the edges of the triangle trade, Mr. Increase lowered himself down onto a corner post of the dock and made himself, *forced* himself, to watch as those poor men and women with the unhappy luck of having survived the trip were dragged, manacled and moribund, out of the hull and led to market. The stench of their torment rolled over the docks like the curse from a long-sealed sepulcher. It was impossible that the ship could ever have smelled sweet, with such squalor left to fester just out of sight.

Mr. Increase cast about for a port that did a minimum of business in slavery (finding one that entirely refrained from the lucrative industry was a fool's errand), and eventually settled on Fidget's Mill. He moved, and lived a quiet life as a fixture of the docks, limping along and telling tales of his voyages around the world to anyone who might want to listen.

Such people were rarities, in Increase's experience. So when someone like Denton Hedges came along, his volubility got the best of him.

A long pause. "Um," Denton said, because it seemed like he ought to say *something* at this point.

"Just hold on, I'm coming up on my purpose in telling you my tale."

"Oh, good."

XII

MR. INCREASE WAS A GIFTED RACONTEUR, AND Denton Hedges was a scrupulous listener, but patience in both roles is exhaustible. Sensing a growing agitation in his one-man audience, Increase set to wrapping up his biography in short order.

In his years as crippled curator of this storehouse, Mr. Increase kept himself removed from colonial politics – but far from ignorant of them. It was his apparent disinterest that kept him so well-informed;

nobody thought twice about gossiping around the dock negro who couldn't even be bothered to bemoan his lowly station in life. His pronounced limp was icing on the pitiful cake.

Slowly, a general political theory informed by his personal experience began to take shape. Prejudice festered, it seemed, because the colonies were stable enough to allow for such indulgences. If only things on land were more as they were at sea: high-pressure, fast-paced, life-and-death. Maybe then the meritocratic impulse that Mr. Increase somehow still believed was unique to most all humans (this running contrary to what his personal experience should have told him) would reign supreme in the affairs of man. And, he scolded himself for having to add after the fact, thinking of his mother's journey through the wilderness, woman as well.

"Non-importation," Mr. Increase smiled humorlessly, turning to fetch a cane Denton got the impression was more prop than necessity resting against the table to which he'd returned, "what are you really after with that? Adoption of a Circular Letter. To what end?"

Denton answered without hesitation. "We want the independence to levy our own-"

"Levy our own taxes? You think that's independence?" The old man began clopping his way over to Denton. "We'd still be paying the crown, wouldn't we? We'd still be living as dependents, as subjects, wouldn't we? I'm sure you've got ideas on how that feels, but do you actually *know* what it's like? The *experience* of being intrinsically less than someone else, and the *knowledge* that you and the other fella were set in your places purely by an accident of birth, and that no amount of work or effort will pull you out of the hole the good Lord dug just for you? Do you *know*, or do you *imagine*?"

"...I must protest," Denton submitted in a voice of exceeding meekness, "on the grounds that upward mobility is a challenge for all-"

"It's a *challenge* for you, I don't doubt that. But is it *impossible*?"

"...you're very articulate, Mr. Increase."

"..."

"Where were you educated?"

"At sea. What sort of a future do you see for these colonies, Mr. Hedges?"

Denton tried to bring his lamentable imagination to bear on the future. All he came up with were flying carriages drawn by horses with wings on (how this was to be accomplished was a problem for the natural philosophers), and the peaceful union and assimilation of the bands of native savages roaming the wilderness by civilized society. He did not have a future in almanac writing.

He opened his mouth to speak, but realized Mr. Increase's question was rhetorical when Mr. Increase plowed on ahead: "Because if that future ever includes a slightest hint of self-determination, the first thing we'd have to do is remove the boot of King George III from our throats." He hobbled to within a few feet of Denton, and eyed the younger man thoughtfully. "It's rich, hearing you all ranting about liberties and natural rights."

"Our concern is w-"

Mr. Increase raised a hand that said *spare me*. "I'm sympathetic to your cause. You don't have to give me the hard sell anymore." He lowered his hand. "I can help you. You want to really put pressure on the Crundwells? Organize their colored laborers against them. We can damn near shut the town down at a stroke, and I can help you out with that. But you need to be prepared, because things will get violent."

Denton started to speak, and Mr. Increase brought his hand back up. "We won't be the ones instigating violence, I can promise you that. But surely you're aware that any stirrings of rebellion by the colonies will bring British guns to our shores?"

The rumors of an impending British invasion swirled in Denton's mind. He nodded, but said nothing.

Mr. Increase continued, lowering his hand again. "Nobody takes kindly to resistance. The Crundwells will come for us, in one sense or another. It's why we've never tried anything before. But if you can give me your word that you and some other whites in high places will, if not support us openly, then at least stay your hands against us, then we might have a deal."

"How do you expect me to promise that?"

"Get closer to Dr. Houlihan. Use him to climb the social ladder, insinuate yo-"

"That's what I came here to do!" *And*, he didn't add, *I specifically came here to the docks to apologize*. How had he suddenly fallen in to complicating his plot with Mr. Increase? Things were getting away from him already. This wasn't good.

Pretend it's a court case, he suggested to himself.

How's that supposed to help me? himself fired back.

Oh, so now you're going to give me shit too?

I just want you to be the best intriguer against the crown that you can be. That's the only way you're going to impress your dad.

What?

Your dad will only be impr-

This isn't about impressing my dad.

Uh huh.

It's not!

Keep telling yourself that.

I will! But I don't have to! Because it's not!

FOCUS, came the androgynous voice that had spoken to Denton outside.

"Did you hear something?" he asked Mr. Increase, who had taken a step or two backwards.

"…no?"

"Okay." Denton shook his head and returned to the topic at hand without fanfare. He hoped that this would seem a smooth transition; it proved more jarring than a quick *sorry I spaced out there* would have. "I can't promise you anything, you must understand that. I'm not in a position to make bargains, because I'm not entirely convinced that I want what you're offering. I'm also unconvinced that you could *deliver* what you're offering." Mr. Increase's face hardened, and Denton raised a gentle hand. "I don't know you that well. But I hope to. You seem a man more dedicated to the Cause than many I knew in Boston."

"You must understand that my reasons, and my Cause, aren't quite the same as yours."

"I do. But I don't really care. Which is why I'll promise you nothing more than that I will do my very best, as I do in all things." He mulled on Increase's comments about elevated stakes being the great levelers of social inequality, and added what he congratulated himself on later as being a savvy question: "Let's say we can each get exactly what we want. Would you please be able to promise me that, once the Crundwells and the rest of Fidget's Mill have accepted non-importation, you will call off your, ah, um, the, er," he wrestled with the natural vocabulary a middle-class white man would normally use in this situation without thinking twice, "ahem?"

Fortunately, Mr. Increase smiled tolerantly. He understood what Denton meant, and more importantly understood offense was not included in that. "I can't promise you anything, except that I will do my best."

"Ah-aha." If non-importation were accepted and the Circular Letter released in the midst of a racially motivated rebellion that remained ongoing, what would that do to the political maneuverings of the Sons? They hadn't accounted for a black population operating independently of what they considered the self-evident interest of the colonies ...which, in hindsight, seemed a rather glaring oversight. But if no agreement on the termination of trade were reached, then the unity of the Circular Letter's adoption would be a lost cause, and the English would have effortless points of entry through which to corrupt the virtuous municipalities.

This was hardly a choice, was it? There was a much simpler formulation to be had: did Denton want an ally, or not?

"Fuck it," Denton declared, extending a hand towards Mr. Increase.

The old man's face sparkled as a gleeful grin dawned upon it. "I suspect we'll be making quite a few decisions along that line, before this is all over." He took Denton's hand and shook.

The handshake was three firm pumps in the heart of the storehouse, with reverberations that would be felt throughout the entire town.

XIII

DENTON WANDERED FIDGET'S MILL UNTIL sundown, and then a little longer besides. Eventually he stopped into a pub for a late dinner, at which point he recalled that he had no money.

So he sauntered back to the Klump Regency along streets of packed snow, now more navigable for having been so well trodden throughout the day. This might have been something upon which to mull, had he not already so much grist for the mull mill.

An in with Mr. Increase. A potential in with Brisby Houlihan – granted, Denton wasn't the smoothest social operator, but Brisby was most definitely an *acquaintance* at this point, and the doctor-patient relationship gave a simple pretense for further communication. The door was open for socialization, anyway, and if he could glom onto Brisby, he could ride the physician-cum-Customs Commissioner straight to the Crundwell's front door.

He slipped in the Klump's front door and approached Vera, seated comfortably behind her desk. "Excuse me, Ms. Miringhoff, but I was wondering where I might obtain a dinner at this late hour, making allowances for my unfortunate pecuniary situation?"

The hotelier stared blankly at Denton for a moment. She snatched a golden chain dangling from her side, and yanked on it until it produced a watch face. "It's 9:45," she noted with some disbelief.

"A full dinner wouldn't be necessary, just a quick something to e-"

"Miss Carsis is expecting you at ten o'clock precisely."

"…since when?"

"Since this morning! Since you felt well enough to go out wandering!"

"Why didn't anybody tell me?"

"Because you were out wandering!"

"Then how was I supposed to know about the appointment?"

"You should have been here!"

"But you just said she made the appointment *because* I went wandering!"

"She did!"

"Then if I'd stayed here, the appointment wouldn't have been made?"

"Probably not."

Denton was quite sure they had reached an impasse. He changed course: "And anyway, how did she know I was out wandering?"

"She knows these things. She finds out."

"How?"

"Very quickly."

"So she knew I was out wandering, and she told *you* about the appointment?"

"Yes. By letter."

"Why didn't she just come and tell me?"

"You were wandering, she didn't want to disturb you."

"..."

Another impasse.

Vera looked down at her watch again, not-so-slightly frantic. "It's 9:47, Mr. Hedges, and you *cannot* be late to a meeting with Miss Carsis!" The look of starchy terror on her face told Denton everything he needed to know about how highly this mysterious woman valued punctuality. Denton still wasn't even clear as to what Miss Carsis did in this town, but she was clearly a Big Shot. And one didn't keep a Big Shot waiting.

"33 Gutter Lane, man, run!"

Denton made the "BAAAH" noise he always made when faced with the prospect of physical exertion. His was a life of the mind. "How do I get to Gutter Lane?"

"As quickly as you can!"

"When I say 'how', I m-"

"Also, do not forget the code phrase!"

"What code phrase?"

"The one I told you!"

"...right after I'd been hit on the head, you mean?"

"Oh, alright." She told him again. "Can you remember that?"

"Yes!"

"Then GO!"

Denton went.

If one wanted to stay on the main roads of Fidget's Mill, one would be spoiled for choice in the signage department. The most heavily trafficked avenues were all clearly labeled, so the big spenders could get from point A (invariably the docks) to point B (variably the Hotel, the Crundwells', or the sole road out of town).

The side streets were another story. They were all unmarked, to discourage the wanderings of the out-of-towners. The Fidgetonians all knew where everything was, after all. They didn't need any damn locational cues.

As he dashed frantically down the snowslick alleyways, Denton took small consolation in the fact that he'd be lost even *with* better signage. 33 Gutter Lane, alright, fair enough, be there at ten. And, assuming his internal clock wasn't wildly off the mark, it was about four minutes to ten.

He tried to take a turn too quickly and slipped, landing on his hip. He made a mental note to say "ouch" later, because he couldn't spare the breath to do so now. He pushed himself up and kept on running.

What was he looking for? He had no idea. The numbering on the houses was sporadic at best. But he had the distinct feeling that he damn well ought to be hurrying, because Miss Carsis was clearly not the type to brook tardiness.

And if he got on her bad side, he'd probably end up on Vera's bad side. The rest of the town would likely follow suit, and then the only person he'd have in his corner would be a free black man and, if he was lucky, a well-meaning stooge for the Colonial overlords.

All this before he'd even gotten his foot in the door with the Crundwells!

Running slipping falling rising running went Denton, until he rounded a corner at one minute to ten and saw a burbling gutter running along the side of the road.

It wouldn't be until the next morning that Denton noted how curious this was. Was it not, after all, more than cold enough for such a tepid little runlet of water to be frozen solid?

Crooked doors lined the side of the road opposite the gutter. None of them had numbers.

"Well, blast," he muttered under his breath. He tried to, at least. What came out was the sound of a ghost sitting on a whoopee cushion.

There were seven doors. It was a small alley. 1 through 7, that's how he would have expected them to be numbered. Gutter Lane was straightforward enough; this was a lane with a gutter in it. So where the hell did 33 come from?

A one in seven chance. About fourteen percent. Denton didn't like those odds. Miss Carsis seemed to be a well-kept secret, nevermind that Vera could hardly wait to let him in on it. If he went barging into the wrong house, spouting out his code phrases, what might happen? What if the door he knocked on belonged to one of Sheriff Barefoot's deputies? Or to Barefoot himself? That last was highly improbable, sure, but Denton's entire stay here had so far been a parade of highly improbable events.

Which, come to think of it…

Selecting the one correct door out of seven based on absolutely no information would be highly improbable too. So, since he'd spent the last 24 hours as the beneficiary of a sequence of highly improbable events (such as being neatly delivered by fate into the laps of Mr. Increase, Brisby Houlihan, Vera Miringhoff and now, apparently, Miss Carsis), it stood to reason that, extrapolating a pattern from experience, it was highly probable that he would continue to experience highly improbable events.

Like guessing the one correct door out of seven based on absolutely no information.

Rational animal that he was, Denton was also a human. He split the difference by recognizing that his current train of thought was an outrage to logical thought and intellectual dignity, while acquiescing to its dumb intuitive appeal.

Riding high on cognitive dissonance, Denton stepped up to the third door from the left and knocked.

No one answered.

He knocked again.

No answer.

He shrugged and walked all the way over to the door furthest to the right. He knocked.

No one answered.

He knocked again.

No answer.

He shrugged and walked all the way over to the door furthest to the left. He knocked.

No one answered.

He knocked again.

No answer.

He shrugged and walked over to the door second from the right. He knocked.

No one answered.

He knocked again.

No answer.

He shrugged and walked over to the door in the center. He knocked.

No one answered.

He knocked again.

No answer.

He shrugged and walked over to the door second from the left. He knocked.

No one answered.

He knocked again.

No answer.

He shrugged and walked over to the door third from the right. He knocked.

A young woman cracked the door and poked her head out. She gave Denton a cursory nod, but put more effort into looking up and down the alley for tails.

Satisfied that he was alone (as Denton himself often was), she opened the door wider and gestured him inside.

"Come," she whispered, "there are eyes everywhere."

As he followed her inside, it occurred to Denton that opening the door on the first try was highly improbable, but so was knocking on every single other door before hitting the correct one. His streak was unbroken; what it was a streak *of* was becoming an increasingly pertinent question.

The room into which Denton stepped was small and smoky. Candles burned from inconspicuous places, setting a mood that could just as easily be sultry or occult depending on what sorts of horseplay were going on.

The young woman pointed to a low chair, and Denton levered himself down into it.

"What is your name?" she asked with a piercing glare.

Vera had prepared Denton for this. This was an opening bluff, meant to catch out possible interlopers. A spy would provide a fake name. A true believer in the Cause would know not to give any name at all. Not yet, anyway.

He just had to say what Vera told him to say. Verbatim. *Vera-batim*, he thought to himself mirthlessly.

Parched, he ran his sandpaper tongue over his lips. Thirsty and hungry, he was. He wished Vera had given him a little snack to send him on his way…but, if she was to be believed, Miss Carsis could help him get his suitcase back, which would get him his money back. First order of business would be buying himself an improbably-sized meal and eating until he died.

But not yet! The phrase, damnit: "I have traveled here from afar to make you my friend."

The young woman gave him a look. Was it an approving look? The look of someone who just made an inside joke, and is watching comprehension dawn on your face? Who could tell? "It's better to make friends at home," she replied.

At this, Denton was overcome with the absurd urge to say *okay, so sorry for the intrusion* and go home. Not even back to the hotel – all the way back to Boston. From whence this squirreliness? There was something fundamentally unnerving about this place, but Denton had stared down his father from the courtroom floor. It would take more than 'unnerving' to sway him from his course. "Then it is necessary for you, being at home, to make friends with me."

The young woman's expression warmed considerably. "Miss Carsis will see you now," she informed him with a degree of casual apathy that gave him a chill.

Recalling an earlier mental note, he said "ouch" quietly to himself as he followed the young woman into the next room.

XIV

DENTON DIDN'T HAVE THE SLIGHTEST CLUE what to expect from Miss Carsis. Stepping through a heavy royal blue curtain and into her room (which he caught himself thinking of as her *chamber*), he felt reasonably well prepared for anything.

He was nonetheless surprised when a pleasant woman wearing her forty-odd years with disarming grace and confidence rose from a creaking wooden chair and introduced herself as a witch.

"Hello, Mr. Hedges," she said. "I am Miss Carsis. I am also a witch."

"Oh?" was all Denton could think to say. He'd never been a superstitious man; tales of witchcraft in Essex County had always had the ring of mass hysteria to him, likely fueled by the terrifying wars at the turn of the last century.

"Yes indeed," she cooed in a curiously familiar voice, dismissing the young woman behind him with a nod. The Son of Liberty and the Witch of the Mill took a good look at one another, and it was only then that Denton noticed that the hair waving down to about earlobe-height was radiant silver. Her energetic, androgynously lupine face was so evocative of youth that he hadn't clocked this marker of age at first.

Sterling though it was, it glimmered with a vitality that stove off any semblance of advancing age. It didn't look like a quirk of biology; it looked like a *choice.*

"I mention this," she continued, "because I've always found it best to get that sort of thing out of the way as soon as possible."

(It's open!)

(You have to pull.)

The color drained from Denton's face as he placed Miss Carsis' voice – he'd last heard it inside his own head. She smiled, perhaps noting the recognition sliding across his face…or perhaps reading it directly out of his mind.

Miss Carsis claimed to be a witch, and Denton believed her.

He ran his fingers through his hai-no STOP IT.

She reached out and wrapped her own delicate fingers around Denton's wrist. Her grip was surprisingly firm. "You've no cause for nervousness."

"I beg to differ."

She laughed, led him by the hand to a chair, and sat him down in it by pressing gently (but still firmly) on his shoulders.

"So," Denton ventured, steadied by his newfound powers of conversing like a normal human, "how is the, uh, how is it working out for you?"

"Being a witch?" She walked to a table in the corner of the room and poured some liquid from a tin pitcher into two copper mugs.

"Ah, yes. How does it, you know, how does that…" he could tell that she knew what he was trying to say, but she wasn't about to finish his sentence for him. Not because she enjoyed watching him flail about for his words, he could tell from her face; because she wanted to see him succeed by his own labors.

That inexplicably reassuring look of humanistic investment was what ultimately convinced Denton that she was a good witch.

"…you know, how do you do your witching, mostly?" He added, half of habit and half of etiquette, "if you don't mind my asking."

She placed one mug in front of Denton, and cupped the other in her hands as she sat down opposite him. "I shall offer an example, as a way of explanation." She took a sip of her drink. Denton held off – Miss Carsis had an aura of eminent trustworthiness, but he was still nervous about drinking a witch's brew without finding out what went into it.

But *god*, he was hungry, thirsty, all of it, and Miss Carsis must have known that…

Carsis continued, "Vera informed me of your misfortune."

"…which one?"

"Your fortnighter was pilfered by base villains. There is a natural antipathy we hold towards men of foreign dispatch, you understand."

Denton, always one to absent-mindedly drink from any cup put in front of him, stopped himself just before tipping the mug of mysterious liquid up to his lips. "I'm not foreign. Just from Boston."

"Anywhere that isn't here is foreign, as far as most of us are concerned."

"I see." Despite having his entire metaphysical worldview turned upside down by the woman seated before him, Denton found himself relaxing into his role as guest to a friendly host. There was something so numinously soothing about the woman…

Miss Carsis took another sip of her drink, and fixed Denton with a look more pregnant with meaning than any he'd ever received before. It said *I would not invite a stranger in to my home only to poison them, or present them a beverage that would prompt so much as a bout of indigestion. I will not be offended if you choose not to partake of my offering, so do not feel compelled; all the same, I suspect you will enjoy it should the spirit move you to imbibe.*

Or maybe he was projecting all of that onto her. Or maybe she was sending it to him telepathically; the hows and whats of her witchery had yet to be made clear.

Either way, between her permissive patience and his own creeping calm, he took a drink, and it was the most delicious thing he'd ever put into his body. He made a loud MMMMMM noise, which he had never done before, and pointed to the mug.

The witch nodded appreciatively and resumed her explanation. "This is an insular community. I'm sorry to say, Fidgetonians are deliberately boorish to newcomers, as you may have discovered. This insularity, however, begets a convenient corollary: everything that happens here folds back in on itself, in time. This is a town of echoes. So for one such as myself, unafraid of keeping her ears low to the mire, determining the villain responsible for your discomfiture was the work of but a minute." Another sip.

Denton took a hearty pull of his drink. "I can't help but notice you don't seem to include yourself in the 'Fidgetonian' classification."

"No," she nodded with a cheeky smile, "I often don't. Very perceptive, Mr. Hedges."

He took another sip of his drink, and was stunned to find he'd already drained his cup. Stunned, but sated; this paltry pull of a questionable beverage had quelled his hunger pangs entirely. As if by magic. Denton, so nearly lost in the pleasantries of the witch's company, forced himself to return to his purpose. "If you've found the luggage that was taken from me, then I am in your debt. I have modest finances and few talents, if I am being perfectly honest, so I do not know how best to repay you, but re-"

"Don't worry. I will tell you how." Her face hardened slightly at that, and suddenly Denton realized that this wasn't a case of folksy generosity. He was getting a quid, because Miss Carsis already had a quo in mind.

He put down his mug, his nerves getting warmed back up and ready for action. "I gather the law of men isn't a particular concern of yours, but I can promise you my serv-"

Miss Carsis raised a halting palm, and Denton found his jaw snapping shut of its own accord. Or, more likely, of *her* accord. Up until now, he had been shocked at the ease with which he was willing to accept the veracity of witchcraft. But now, seeing it – *feeling* it – in action, his outraged rationality began to reassert itself.

"Are you familiar with Familiars?" Her bearing had once again taken on the glow of pleasant memories, but Denton felt he could suddenly see the sharpened steel lurking just beneath. Had the room gotten ever so slightly colder, or was that just him?

She took another sip of her drink and leaned back in her chair. It *groaned* under her weight – which was odd, because Denton wouldn't have guessed she weighed more than a hundred pounds. "A witch is not truly a witch without one. Familiars are…partners, let us say. They are ancient spirits, from a time without form. Humans are but trespassers in a universe that is, by rights, theirs. Long before we came, long after we are gone, they *were,* they *are* and so they *will be.*

"Theirs is a higher plane of existence. But just as I thrive by lowering myself into the filth and drinking in the vibrations of the Earth to which all that lives must desperately cling until the Return, there are those among the eldritch beasts that defile themselves with the putrescence of our world. But, curiously, they are born, or created, most certainly *condemned*, to serve us. They require humanity to attain their inscrutable aims, and we may in turn avail ourselves of their services in the attainment of ours. Symbiotic, parasitic relationships with dread entities. Do you understand me?"

Perhaps a cloud had drifted across the moon – the night somehow seemed darker than it had a moment ago.

Miss Carsis leaned in, and this time the floor underneath her chair registered the same sort of objection one would expect to hear had an elephant trod into the room. "Demons, Mr. Hedges."

Struggling and sputtering to regain his speech, Denton managed to say "Denton," because this really felt like a first-name-basis sort of conversation.

"Yes, Denton. I'll continue to go by Miss Carsis if it's all the same to you. Nothing personal, understand, that's just my preferred method of address. Denton." She grinned a wicked grin. "I have dispatched my

Familiar to collect the man who transgressed against you. He will be made to account for his sin, beneath the sole of your boot."

The horrific tension in Denton's jaw abated enough for him to shape a full sentence. "I don't seek punishment for the man."

"The man who struck you on the head, and made off with your belongings?"

"Perhaps he is poor, and must feed a family. I do not bear grudges. I simply wish to have returned to me m-"

A thunderous slamming shook the entire house. Denton jumped – Miss Carsis just kept on grinning.

"Here they are," she sighed giddily.

Five minutes ago, Denton didn't believe in demons; now he was about to see one. His mind reeled with the possibilities. Would it be a horned humanoid, of cloven hoof and crimson skin? Or something else entirely – something far worse? A horse-sized spider, or a dribbling thicket of thrashing tentacles?

He heard the front door creak open. Denton felt himself trembling, unable to stop. His empty mug jangled on the table – because it wasn't just him that was shaking. The entire house was quaking.

From behind the azure curtain, he could hear the blubbering and whimpering of the man who stole his suitcase. Denton never wanted to hurt anyone! It was only *stuff.* What had this man been forced to witness on Denton's account, that would reduce him to a state of gibbering insensibility?

In an instant: everything stopped. The house stopped rumbling. The man stopped simpering. Silence descended.

The curtain parted. A young man – a *boy* – no older than seventeen years, surely – wobbled in to the back room. His eyes were vacant, and his hair greying around his temples.

Denton gasped. He couldn't help himself. Miss Carsis just watched, and smiled.

The curtain parted again, and the Demon stepped through into the fluttering candlelight.

"Gobble gobble," said the Demon, who looked an awful lot like a turkey.

XV

"YOU NEEDN'T DISSIMULATE ON HIS ACCOUNT," Miss Carsis informed the Turkey-Demon, "I have told him what he needs to know."

Denton braced himself for some nightmarish transformation, a horrendous shedding of the Turkey-suit to reveal the true demonic corpus underneath.

Instead, the Turkey-Demon said "oh, thank you ever so kindly" in an aristocratic British accent. "That puts me right at my ease."

Its feathers were the glossy black of an oil slick, and its eyes seemed to burn with diabolical hatred, but aside from that it seemed a perfectly friendly turkey. It pitter-pattered its way over to Denton, bobbing its head affably.

"So pleased to make your acquaintance," it clucked, "please do call me No-Good Bulstrode, as this is my name. You are free to affix any unpleasant addendum that tickles your giblets, as well. 'No-Good Bulstrode the Vile Turkey' seems to have been a perennial favorite."

Denton caught himself from falling; much to his surprise, he had leaned so far back into his chair as to be on the point of tipping over. "Ah, my name is, um, Denton Hedges."

"You're the chappie for whom I fetched this rascal?"

"Hm…I suppose so."

"What luck! He excretes contrition from every orifice."

Denton gave the young man a sympathetic glance. "I can't say I was angling for that. Just the luggage back, really."

"It's in the front room," Miss Carsis informed him.

He didn't get up to check. He believed her. She had introduced him to a posh Turkey-Demon; he was ready to believe anything she said.

The witch turned to the boy. "Apologize," she suggested with the tranquility of undeniable reason.

"I am so, so, so, so, so, so," said the boy. He continued, "so, so, so, so, so sorry. My mother is sick, an-"

Miss Carsis raised her palm and the boy's jaw snapped shut. Denton could sympathize with the look of unalloyed terror on his face, and suspected he was making that face himself, now that she was turning her attention back to him.

"I have done you a service," she reminded him with a smile, "and while you are of course not obligated to reciprocate in kind, you would do well to remember that there are forces beyond our reckoning at work in the universe…" Here she made a lazy wave towards No-Good Bulstrode, "…and they are inclined to pay a man back what he puts out into the world, with interest."

The spin on the word *interest* chilled Denton. Did she mean it in the financial sense…or did she mean these invisible Demons were *interested* in the settling the affairs of humans? Just how much control over this world did they have, anyway?

He decided himself on the former meaning and let the thought go. Threw the thought as far away as he could, to be more precise.

"What, um, would you like?"

"I have told you of my friends in low places."

"Yes, er, you have."

"You came in here demanding my friendship."

"Not demanding, um, sorry! Vera told me I had to-"

A raising of the palm, a snapping of the jaw.

"You demanded my friendship, and I have given it to you. Friends help one another, and I have helped you. So as you go about your duties, making friends in high places – do not ask me how I know your business, just know that I do – you would do well to remember my kindness. Will you be my friend in *high* places, Denton?"

His jaw popped slightly as it opened. Too much snapping for one night. Bad as he was at reading people, he saw through the genial tone. This was not a request; this was Miss Carsis calling in a debt, mere seconds after it was unwillingly incurred. As with Brisby, this was a strictly utilitarian interest masquerading as friendship. Isn't that always the way?

To Denton's great relief, though, the demand was for pure information. She had the low sorts of Fidget's Mill on her side or under her thumb, but the higher rungs of the social ladder still eluded her. Denton was her way in, assuming he could wriggle up there himself. *Why* she wanted in wasn't clear, but that was her business. Because as she was seeing Denton as a means to some mysterious end, so Denton began to see her in the same light. Like her, his work had lately been conducted in the shadows; influencing popular opinion through pamphlets and articles, drumming up ire and channeling it into organized demon-strations, or sometimes just sending a good actor into a town meeting with an inspiring script and planting the seeds that might one day grow into something revolutionary.

(A good actor…)

So imagine befriending – or bebusinessing – the one person who casts all of the shadows in the town! Just imagine what he could get done, if push came to shove!

He had vowed to thrust himself back into the light, but perhaps he was not yet finished with shadows. Or, of course, vice versa.

Miss Carsis saw the glint in his eye. Without a further word spoken between them, they had come to a mutual understanding. He wasn't as dumb as he looked, or sounded, or acted.

To prove it to both her and himself, he pointed to the whimpering boy and barked, "and SCENE."

The boy stopped crying, and glanced hesitantly at Miss Carsis. The witch raised her eyebrows at Denton, beaming her amused disbelief.

Choosing to read this as an encouraging sign, Denton plowed ahead with his supposition: "However it is you're privy to my business, by these same supernatural channels of information you were privy to my arrival, prior to my arrival. Perhaps even before *I* knew I would be making the trip – there is much I cannot begin to understand about you. In any case, sensing my arrival, you orchestrated the clouting incident, the snatching of my suitcase, and ultimately my presence here, simply so that I, an outsider capable of ascending the social ranks in a way a Fidgetonian could not, upward mobility being restricted by the aforementioned insularity of the town, would be in your debt for a favor. I am quite confident that Vera colluded with you in this, and as I outline this, I now suspect Mr. Increase to have been an ally of yours as well – it was not an accident that he was the one to come to my aid. Nor, I now imagine, was it an accident that Vera had him send for Brisby Houlihan – you were giving me the pretense by which I would grasp the first rung in my climb. From the moment I arrived in Fidget's Mill, or perhaps slightly before, I have been proceeding along a path you yourself carved for me. Am I incorrect?"

Wordlessly, Miss Carsis raised a palm to Denton's head. He heard, *felt*, a deep sucking noise from behind his eyes. Was she going to take his *eyes*, for having seen through her chicanery? He snapped them shut.

The noise subsided. "Open your eyes," she commanded, and so he did.

Miss Carsis sat with a palm turned to the ceiling, as though waiting for a gentleman of high bearing to help her out of a carriage. Though, Denton thought, the likelihood of her ever desiring such a gesture was the Platonic Ideal of zilch.

Hovering just inches above her hand was a soupy orb of lifeless grey. It…what was the opposite of 'glowing'? It seemed to absorb light.

"Do you recognize this?" she asked as a teacher would a student.

Denton puzzled over it, and identified it by its absence in himself. "That's…my head injury." He was glad he didn't think about how ridiculous that sounded, or he wouldn't have said it.

"That's right." Miss Carsis blew on the concussion she had removed from Denton's head, by her happy witchcraft. It disintegrated and scattered like the drabbest dandelion in the universe. She turned to the ex-weeping boy in the corner. "It's no comment on your acting abilities, Maurice. Mr. Hedges here is a sharp one." She favored Denton with a playful sideways glance. "Your mother's medicine is on the table over there."

"Thank you, Miss Carsis," Maurice gushed with a bow. He turned and gave Denton a similar, though less fulsome bow, and grabbed a small vial from a table on his way out the door.

The witch turned back to Denton. "I'd be worried about you, if we weren't on the same side."

"Are we?" Denton's sense of wonder had been crowded out by indignation. "So far, it seems you've manipulated me from the jump, and I've not the slightest idea what you actually want."

"I've done us both a favor. I've woven you into the social fabric of Fidget's Mill far more effectively than you co-"

"Yes, but *why*? To what end? I know what *I'm* after."

"To impress your father."

"No! To compel the town to adopt non-importation!"

"You seek to compel a town," Miss Carsis summed with no small amount of mirth.

"Well, the family who runs the town!" Recalling two other surnames Mr. Increase had thrown at him, he corrected himself: "Families!"

"So you've come to appeal to three wealthy families, that they might impose a disastrous economic sanction - upon *themselves* - all without consulting the majority of the Mill's population, the very people who would be most devastated by the decision? Does this not strike you as fighting fire with fire, as far as opposing Royal peremptoriness goes?"

"...the plan needs some work, sure. B-"

"Be truthful with me, for we are friends. You wish to impress your wife and children as well, but know that they will love you even should you fail. It is your fa-"

"Shut up!" he shouted at the witch. She could probably turn him into a tadpole or make his knees disappear, but he just then, he didn't care. "I am here to accomplish a political end, and to do so before a Circular Letter of great import is released into the colonies. If our ends align, then I would value your assistance, and be happy to render you my own. But that means the deception ends now. You will deal with me as an equal, or not at all. I will not be deceived, or misled, or bullied. Do you understand me?!"

As his senses returned to him, Denton realized how frightening it would have been to see Miss Carsis angry. What was *terrifying*, in a deep, elemental sense, was seeing her ecstatic. Her face was a rictus of pleasure, as though he had just informed her that a wealthy relative had died and left her El Dorado. "Oh, I do, Denton. I would say we are well-met here in the Mill."

"Well, *good*," he snapped with less conviction. "Now, I'm sleepy and want to go home. How do I get home?"

And he'd been doing so well, up until then.

"Guh," he burbled as self-consciousness sunk in.

"What's to 'guh' about, then?" asked No-Good Bulstrode, his guide through the winding sidestreets this evening.

"Oh, nothing."

"You're not sour on Miss Carsis' cheeky scheming, are you? It can be such a fuss, getting good hard-working individuals of noble and upright bearing to do a deal with a woman of Wiccan persuasions. Simple matter of establishing trust, at which point she'll be as forthright as you like."

Watching No-Good Bulstrode speak was fascinating. Lacking lips, there was no articulation to it. He just opened his beak and held it agape as words came tumbling out. The fact that he bothered opening his beak at all threw into doubt Denton's original supposition, that the communication was telepathic. But could any wandering ears hear him? Or would they just hear gobbles?

He pondered what he must look like, staggering through the alleys by moonlight, following a turkey who looked perpetually surprised.

They rounded a corner, and for old time's sake, Denton slipped and fell and landed on his hip. Having been clutching his recently reclaimed suitcase in a protective deathgrip, the unwieldy chest clapped him appreciatively on the spine. Unlike at his last slip, he said "ouch" immediately.

"Oh yes, you simply *must* be aware of your footing at all times, you old acorn. Treacherous streets, for those lacking the traction of talons." He did a little rangy-game tap dance to prove his point.

"Can I ask you a question?" Denton pushed himself back up to his feet.

"I do wish you would," replied the still-dancing Turkey-Demon.

"What are you and Miss Carsis after?"

No-Good Bulstrode stopped dancing. He jerked his head from side to side, front to back.

If Denton had trouble reading humans (and did he ever), he sure as hell couldn't read a turkey. But the turkey was definitely nodding. Maybe. Hard to say, with turkeys. They had very active heads. Finally, it started grumbling, "not for me to say, I'm very much afeared. Professional confidentiality, reputation at stake, gobble gobble and such." Denton took the latter justification to mean something akin to 'etcetera'. "If she didn't wish to reveal it, I won't be the one to do so."

"She didn't explicitly refuse to reveal it. She just ignored me when I asked her, and then I forgot to ask her again, owing to my pique having arisen."

"Well, you can perish the thought of anything occurring involving Miss Carsis and your upright pique."

"…I think you're willfully misinterpreting what I said in order to dodge the question."

"There's no sneaking anything by you, is there?"

Denton assented by way of slipping and falling again.

"So you're not going to answer me," Denton observed upon rising.

"Nope, no by-sneakage to be had when you're on the case."

Denton sighed. He wanted to keep slamming his head against this particular wall, but he also didn't want to miss an opportunity to chat with a demon. So he shrugged and allowed the subject to change. "Well, then let me just observe that you're very erudite and polite, for a, um, well, for a Demon. As well as a turkey."

No-Good Bulstrode's beak fell open. "Thank you ever so much for noticing. Demons and witches get along like houses due to the mutual animus borne us by otherwise well-meaning hoi polloi. I couldn't assert with any certainty just whence these slanderous misapprehensions, but I will say that they've done us down a treat, as regards our relations with the public. Most of us, us being of course Demons and Witches, though perhaps I may be so bold as to speak on behalf of Turkey-dom as well, most of us are up to no more than putting our gizzards in it, doing the dirty business of striving to improve our lot and the lots of our fellows."

"So why do you let people call you things like No-Good?"

"Well, it's only my name, for a start."

"Then what about the nasty suffixes you were inviting earlier?"

"Sometimes it's good to have a type into which one might play. You must understand, concealing your intellect behind the role of a chundering buffoon as you do!"

Denton tried to get offended, but couldn't. There was no malice in No-Good Bulstrode's words, and anyway, those words were coming from a chubby little buzzard.

They emerged onto one of the main streets.

"I can find my way home from here." Denton ran his fingers through his hair. Goddamnit.

No-Good Bulstrode shrugged. Once again - maybe. Hard to say. But for a critter without shoulders, he had certainly given off a 'shruggy' vibe. "Please yourself. I shall treasure these last moments, strolling through the streets with a new friend. I wish you a good evening, and pleasant dreams."

With that, the Turkey-Demon made an about-face and started to walk away.

"Bulstrode!" Denton called after him.

No-Good cocked his head over his non-shoulder.

"Has anyone ever called you 'No-Good Bulstrode the Foul Fowl'?"

A split-second pause elapsed that felt like millennia. Denton rarely made jokes, and when he did, they were usually awful and the cause of flushed cheeks and crippling regret. He was gearing up for just such a response when No-Good Bulstrode began to laugh.

It was the worst noise Denton had heard in his entire life.

A shrill, horrific tittering, like the laugh of an infant human and the gobble of a turkey on the chopping block were eviscerated in separate circumstances of comparable horror, buried in the same graveyard, dug up by a mad scientist, stitched haphazardly back together, given ghastly life through a bolt of lightning and taught to play the kazoo.

"GIBGOBBLAHABOGHALOBGLOB, FOUL FOWL, BLOHG-ABBALHABLAHGOGGLOBOGGL!"

No-Good Bulstrode chuckle-clucked his way back into the shadows, and only after he had left did Denton realize his hands were clapped over his ears.

With great reluctance, he lowered them. That nightmarish sound was gone, but it would be back. When he slept, he would hear it. It would pursue him, and he would run, but he would never escape. Or perhaps he would never sleep again. Better to die from exhaustion, than hear that cackling cacophony one more time.

Any lingering doubts that No-Good Bulstrode was actually a Demon were dispelled in that moment. Denton had entered a supernatural realm beyond his comprehension. Faced with this, the prospect of having to put political pressure on rowdy merchant families was a piddling nonsense. Which, in a way, was nice.

Somehow, what should have been a crippling glimpse into a howling void of existential dread where every precon-ception about the nature of the world was consumed and obliterated became a friendly little confidence-booster for Denton Hedges.

He was, however, fairly certain that he would never make another joke for as long as he lived, just in case. Taking up a jaunty whistle just to keep the noises thrashing about his skull at bay, he heaved his luggage back towards the Klump Regency.

XVI

DAYLIGHT WAS LONG IN COMING, BUT THE doctor was far more punctual.

"Knock knock," he chirped from the other side of Denton's door. To alleviate any lingering confusion, he knocked twice.

Denton snapped up to a seated position. He was a light sleeper on a night when he *didn't* have the affairs of witches and demons on his mind. Last night he hadn't managed much more than a doze.

"Who's there?" he returned, more for form's sake than anything.

"Brisby."

"Brisby Who?"

"Hou*lihan*, but close enough."

Moving in stiff clockwork bursts, Denton jerked himself over to the door and levered it open. Brisby leered at him from the hall side of the doorframe.

"Good morning! Didn't die in your sleep, did you?" This asked in his clinically disinterested Physician's voice; it could just as easily have been 'had you eaten anything unusual?' or 'still got that rash, have you?'

"I wouldn't have said so, but you're the professional." Denton opened the door wider and dottered back towards the dresser.

Brisby slipped in after him and closed the door. "Routine bit of business, checking in on the patient the morning after. Anything unusual to report? Headaches? Strange dreams? Something else?"

"Not so much," Denton lied. He *had* had an strange dream. Or perhaps it was no dream, because he couldn't remember having fallen asleep.

Who was he kidding? Of course it wasn't a dream. It was a nightmare.

Tossing and turning as he always did, Denton wound up lying on his stomach, limbs splayed in every direction. And as always happened after a time, his lack of flexibility began to tug on his tendons like the sclerotic Quasimodo playing his final ding-dong encore on the bells of Notre Dame.

He bent his arms to roll back onto his side. Only his arms didn't bend. They just lay heavily on the mattress. He tried to move his legs; they proved just as stubborn.

Oh, nuts, he thought. He was paralyzed. It must have been something in the witch's brew. Why did he drink that? Rookie mistake, drinking the witch's brew!

There were a few more thoughts he had anticipated getting through, but all of a sudden his intellectual priorities shifted quite drastically. His face was buried in the pillow, so he couldn't attest to the specifics of any of what happened next with the slightest degree of certainty. This he considered to be an unbelievable stroke of good fortune.

Something fell on top of him. It didn't actually touch him, at least not at first. He felt the bed under him buckle and depress, an oval of leaden pressure encircling his entire body. The mattress cried out, creaking and popping, as it settled into its sinister silhouette. Denton had dreamt intense dreams before. His dreams had *never* felt like this. The sounds, the sensations, the iron taste of fear on his tongue – it was all real. It was too real.

The *something* drew closer to his pillow-pressed head. It didn't speak, or scream, or even breathe. It simply rested atop of him, and observed. He could feel it sifting through his mind, looking not for gold but for seeds, seeds that birthed gnarled, palsied boughs, boughs that bore the sorts of forbidden fruit upon which this nightmare sated itself.

Someone had once told Denton that sleeping on his stomach was bad for his back, or something to that effect. But he had never in his life been so glad of his disregard. What might he have seen, had not his eyes been pushed into the cushion?

No sense speculating any further: in an instant, the *something* was gone. It didn't go away; it was just *gone*. The room fell still, which is how Denton came to realize that this horror's quietude had a dreadful motion to it. His limbs grew responsive once again, but he kept them as still as the rest of the room. He didn't want to turn over, for fear of the creature's return. It was several hours before he yielded to slumber's advance.

"Nope," Denton repeated to Brisby, "no strange dreams." And then he thought about it. Would Brisby be intrigued by Denton's midnight visitation? Perhaps this was a chance to draw the doctor into his life, and consequently vice versa?

Yes, perhaps it was. And so Denton told Brisby about his dream. The physician listened, rapt, and pondered for a moment at the story's conclusion. "What do you think it means?" he asked Denton.

Denton smiled.

That smile sustained itself for about an hour, as Denton artfully directed the conversation with Brisby to more general topics. They were, Denton was almost positive, Making Chit-Chat. Or Having A Chit-Chat. The preferred verbage was up in the air, and Denton didn't have any strong feelings about it either way. But Chit-Chat this most certainly was.

It was, however, with no small amount of mortification that he was made to recall his lie from before.

Brisby was a real doctor. He was under the impression that Denton was as well. And so, as they strolled the avenues to Fidget's Mill, shaped by packed snow that had had more than enough time to turn every color except white, he spoke to Denton as one doctor might to another.

"Have you been keeping up to date with the latest literature from overseas? A gentlemen by the name of Holwell just last year published a paper in which he recounts the ramblings of Indian doctors – *their* Indians, over on the bottom of Asia, not *our* Indians – and how they believe the theories one finds recurring periodically throughout the years, namely, that illnesses – specifically smallpox – are the work of invisible worms that crawl into a living specimen – specifically human – and, well, I'm not entirely certain what they're meant to do once they're in. They rearrange the furniture, if you will, thus causing the smallpox. And Holwell asserts, or rather his Indian medicine men assert that the way to combat smallpox is by injecting oneself with – and listen to this, Denton, get a load of this – *smallpox*. A smaller dose of friendly worms, who will, well, again, I can't say for certain, but who will secure the furniture where it lay, so that the rabblerousing worms won't be able to go about their invisible business. What say you to this farfetched theory? Don't be influenced by my calling it farfetched, mind, I'm curious to hear your opinion on this risible matter."

As he had to nearly everything else Brisby has said on this arm-in-arm stroll through the town, Denton simply nodded and said "A-mhm."

"I concur wholeheartedly. Perhaps a matter for further investigation, but it has a sour stench to the well-honed nose of common sense, wouldn't you say?"

"A-mhm."

"Indeed, indeed."

This has been an astonishing walk, to say the least. Brisby seemed uniquely disinclined to see through Denton's translucent ruse. Prior to hiding behind "a-mhm", Denton had actually made an effort to play the part of a physician. When asked about his opinion on Boorhaeve's theory of fluids and fibers, an increasingly out-of-favor modern analog for Galen's theory of humors, Denton praised the role of fluids and fibers in remaining regular, and asserted that apples were, to his unrefined palette, the ideal balance of both.

When the topic turned to the questionable efficacy of bloodletting, Denton averred that his commitment to individual liberties bound him to believe that they ought to let the blood do whatever it wants. That was a medical *and* a political tell that seemed to be utterly lost on Brisby.

Except Denton didn't – couldn't – quite believe that it was. Instead, Brisby seemed to take these slips on board, just long enough to toss them back overboard. It was as though he didn't *want* to see through Denton's dissimulation, as though it weren't worth the trouble to him.

Without entirely realizing it, Denton began developing his own curious fascination with the friendly physician. He was hardly one to speak, but Brisby seemed a bit too…accommodating to be a good Customs Commissioner.

The two strolled the day away, Brisby monologing about the latest advances in medical research and practice, Denton occasionally cheering him on with his "a-mhm"s. A few times, he nearly swapped out an "a-mhm" for a "hey so did you want to do something specific or do we just keep wandering around", but each time decided against it. He wanted to fall in with Brisby, that he might fall up the town hierarchy. He couldn't well bring their palaver to an arbitrary conclusion.

So it was with exceeding good cheer that Denton found a non-arbitrary way to conclude their stroll. They had, simply because Fidget's

Mill was small enough to cover in a few hours' worth of strolling, found their way down to the docks. An essential bit of business suggested itself to Denton, with the fortuitous cover of a pseudo-essential bit of imaginary-business.

"Oh, this reminds me!" he exclaimed, pulling his arm gently from Brisby's (and was he mistaken, or did the physician tighten his grip in the moment before disengagement?) "Much as I have enjoyed our afternoon together, I'm afraid I must see to my slaves."

"You *own* slaves?" Brisby goggled.

"No! No. I mean that in the same way you might say 'my patients'. They are just slaves on whom I happen to dote. Well, dote's not the right word, but you can surely intuit my meaning and substitute a more appropriate word." Denton began walking backwards toward the massive storehouse, waving as he did.

"Ah. Alright." Brisby hung his head. "I would offer my assistance, but, well, I'm not as welcome on the docks as I'd like to be."

"Oh? Why's that?"

"...huh? Oh, no reason. Anyway. I shall perhaps..."

Brisby kept speaking, but Denton stopped listening. He was too busy thinking. Dr. Houlihan was trying to keep his role as Customs Commissioner a secret? But how could that work? How else could he explain his sudden residency in the town? And surely he had begun maneuvering on the behalf of the Crown by now...hadn't he? Well, this was an interesting wrinkle.

Brisby had stopped talking, and was looking at Denton as though he expected a response to something.

"The what?" Denton offered.

"The Local!"

"What about The Local?"

"Maybe I'll see you there tonight?"

"Oh, sure!" Denton called over his shoulder as he turned towards the storehouse.

"Excellent! Until tonight!"

"Okay!"

Okay, Denton repeated for his own benefit as he shuffled towards the storehouse, *what the hell is the Local?*

XVII

DENTON FELT GOOD UP HERE ON THE MORAL high ground. The only challenge was in translating that to a righteous opening salvo, because it was hard to seem powerful while struggling to squeeze between close-set shelving.

When he finally fought his way to the center of the storehouse, he was pleased to see that Mr. Increase was crouched over a box, counting something or other inside of it. This would give him the elevated position, as long as Increase didn't choose to stand up. Given the older man's bum knee, Denton didn't think he would.

Having reminded himself that he was about to get high-handed with an older, slightly crippled man did bring the moral high ground a bit closer to sea level. But no sense dwelling on that.

"Hey!" Denton shouted.

"You needn't raise your voice," Mr. Increase said without looking up.

"I beg to differ. You tricked me! I came in here and apologized to you, all the while you were scheming with Miss Carsis to get me right where you wanted me!"

"That's right."

"…well, I'm not happy about that!"

"Didn't it also get you where *you* wanted you?"

"…that's beside the point!"

"I'd say that *is* the point."

"No it's not. The point is that you maneuvered me like a chess piece, when you could have been consulting me as a fellow chess player!"

"Chess players don't consult one anoth-"

"You know what I mean!" Denton searched for a surface to slam his fist on, but the closest one was a solid four steps away. He considered it, but ultimately decided that it would look too silly. So instead, he just made a fist and jerked in around in the air.

Finally, Mr. Increase stood up. Curiously, he still hadn't actually turned his head to Denton. He was still staring at the box. He sighed. "Well, now I've lost count." At long last, he turned to look at Denton. "Do *you* want an apology?"

This was offered with such sincerity, Denton was momentarily flat-footed. It seemed as though, if he said 'yes', Mr. Increase would apologize, and he would mean it. Thus robbing Denton of any reason to be angry. But if he said 'no'…he'd just look like a petty asshole. Damnit! What happened to the moral high ground? Everything changed once Mr. Increase stood up.

It was the cynical, manipulative part of Denton that was most outraged by the cynical manipulations of Miss Carsis and Mr. Increase. He envied their alliance, and their ability to so effortlessly manage people. Denton didn't consider himself the type of person capable of doing that…but he still found himself jealous of those who *could.* What rankled him most wasn't being manipulated, it was seeing manipulation happening and not being brought in on it.

Mr. Increase could turn the emotional tide of the moment simply by standing up. What a powerful ally he would make!

Did Denton want an apology? Yes. He did. It was as simple – and, yes, petty - as that. But perhaps he could take a stab at some small-scale machinations of his own.

"No," he fibbed. "I suppose I don't want an apology. I understand why you did what you did. And I suppose I must admit…I admire it."

Mr. Increase listened impassively to this. Denton had been rather counting on a smarmy, self-satisfied smile. "I'm quite difficult to flatter."

"I'm not trying to flatter you, Mr. Increase."

"You are. You're just not succeeding." With a grunt, Mr. Increase levered himself back down to the ground, and resumed whatever the hell he was doing before Denton arrived. "Mr. Hedges, you're accustomed to dealing with ideas, and concepts. And that's fine. Every society needs your kind. But you have a lot to learn about dealing with people. And right now, that's what *our* society needs."

Denton took four steps over to the nearest table, as he felt a fist-slamming surface might come in handy before too long. "Our society is one on the cusp of a monumental change. These are heady times, and now more than ever we n-"

"Why do you write? Twenty-seven."

"Huh?"

"Twenty-seven. Do me a favor and write that number on the third line from the bottom on the second page on that tablet there." Mr. Increase, still without lifting his eyes from his box, pointed directly at the table Denton was standing next to, and snapped twice.

Denton looked down and saw the tablet. "I'm afraid I don't hav-"

Snap. Point. Snap. Denton spotted the pen on the other end of the table. It wasn't until he was writing 'twenty-seven' on the third line from the bottom of the second page on the tablet that he realized he had just put *himself* in a subservient position to Mr. Increase. If the man had just said "write that number" and so on, Denton would have told him to take his 'twenty-seven' and insert it into a rude cavity. But with the simple words "do me a favor", he was pre-emptively positioning the act of writing 'twenty-seven' as one of generosity. And who didn't like being made to feel generous?

Damn, this guy is good.

Mr. Increase snatched the tablet from Denton's hand, because apparently he had risen from his position next to the box and hobbled over while Denton was deeply lost in thought. Fortunately, when he found himself again, he understood what Mr. Increase was getting at.

"I write about ideas, in order to influence people. This is your point, correct?"

"Correct." Mr. Increase slapped the clipboard, as if what Denton had just said were printed on one of its pages.

"Well, you're good at influencing people. Another point taken. But how are you in the realm of the intellect?"

"...I can hold my own, thank you very much."

"Well, as long as we're not busying ourselves with modesty, I can hold my own as well as other people's. You're clever, I'm smart, and we've already established that our objectives overlap. We are nothing if not well-met." He noted the ease with which Miss Carsis' words came out of his mouth. He hoped he had drummed them up himself, rather than her having planted them there, but he wasn't willing to write off the latter possibility entirely. "So why don't we do away with the feints and deceits, and simply work *together*, as equals?"

"Fine."

"...I confess I was expecting rather more resistance than that."

"Sorry to disappoint you."

"Yes, well...I have something you can help me with."

"I'm all ears." Once again, the depth of the sincerity in this thought, which could so easily have been offered dripping with sarcasm, was slightly disarming. It also made Denton highly skeptical. He had ostensibly reach an agreement with both Miss Carsis and Mr. Increase to be treated as a co-conspirator, but he didn't for a moment believe that either of them was suddenly going to be forthright with him.

Nor, if he was being completely honest, did he anticipate being forthright with them. Well-met, the three of them were. Yes indeed.

"Do you know what the Local is?"

A look of something like nostalgia dawned on Mr. Increase's face. "Oh, yes, I know it quite well. Why do you ask?"

XVIII

THE LOCAL TAVERN WAS THE ONLY TAVERN IN Fidget's Mill, and therefore the only tavern within a day's carriage ride. It was redundant to call it the 'local' tavern then, as simply calling it The Tavern would have sufficed. But somehow - and this was just one more reason Denton distrusted the unstructured, popular forms of government Mr. Increase seemed to favor - Fidgetonians had taken to calling it The Local. Nobody seemed to know how or why they chose to eliminate the useful word and keep the useless one, or so said Mr.

Increase. He was also quick to point out that it amounted to the same thing, as everybody knew what The Local was – at least, the locals did. Denton found this logic both unsatisfying and difficult to argue with.

The Local wasn't especially packed, but it was remarkably noisy. After a halting conversation with Mr. Increase, punctuated by a great deal of "Huh?" and "Sorry?" and "What was that?", Denton's finally decided to make a formal survey of the place for Brisby. He came up empty.

"Where else could he be?" he shouted directly into Mr. Increase's ear.

"Come again?"

"I don't see Brisby in here! He said he would be! Where else could he be?"

"He might not be here!"

"But he said he would be here!"

"That doesn't mean he will be!"

"What?"

Increase shook his head and pointed to a back door, leading to the outside.

The experience of stepping from the soupy, feverish swelter of the bar and out into the raw frigidity of the late November night was very similar to how Denton always imagined it would be to force one's way out of a massive womb of jelly. Not that Denton always imagined what it would be like to force one's way out of a massive womb of jelly. Very rarely did he imagine what it would be like to force one's way out of a massive womb of jelly. But the scenario had certainly occurred, as he suspected it must have to all ambitious men of leisure at one time or another.

"Alright," Mr. Increase sighed, "now what were we saying?"

"What's that?" Denton pointed to a wooden shed teetering drunkenly against the trunk of a white oak tree, on what must certainly still have been the property of whoever owned the Local. Ribald shouting floated out from the open door, sullying the crisp clarity of the evening with injunctions to parties unknown to "get him", or "come on", or contradictorily "*go* on".

Denton was struck with the sudden and overwhelming desire for a hat. There was an air of rarefication about these whooping cries. He upbraided himself for not having purchased headgear.

Say…

"Could he be in there? Sounds fairly tony, if you're willing to look past the profanity."

Mr. Increase shrugged. "Odd place for a physician to unwind, but not outside the realm of possibility."

"Shall we investigate?" Self-consciously uncapped, Denton inched his way towards the door of the shed. The clumsy clapboard structure looked to be (or have once been) a small stable, large enough for two or three horses to lodge comfortably, perhaps even with a carriage. The ingress hung ajar, just enough for an enthusiastic shaft of firelight to puncture the gloom.

And, of course, the shouting.

He pulled the door open and wormed his way in. As he turned to hold the door for Mr. Increase, he spotted his erstwhile guide hanging back several paces. "Aren't you coming?"

"That's…not the sort of place my kind is welcome, I'm afraid."

"Nonsense, Increase, this is an enlightened colony. Very few people own any slaves at all here."

"Oh, how silly of me. You're so right."

"Look, I'm not wearing a hat, so we'll both look like we don't belong." Denton realized how stupid a thing that was to say only after he'd said it. Fortunately, Mr. Increase clearly recognized that Denton realized this, and so neither of them had to say anything further.

Denton nodded agreeably and closed the door.

The shed was not a stable. Perhaps it once was, but it was certainly not any longer.

The shed was a coliseum. A circumference of elevated benches encircled a wooden-fenced ring, lit from above by an array of dangling lamps. Up in the shadowy utmost of the bleachers, Gentlemen of

Noble Birth (or so they clearly fancied themselves, dressed as they were) leaned back so that they might watch the evening's fascinations down the bridges of their noses (for a fleeting instant, he thought he saw his father up there…but, *phew*, no). Lower to the ground, men with callused hands slapped the packed dirt floor and snarled at the combatants in the makeshift arena.

This was a class more familiar to him, but it was no closer to being his own than the toffs on the rafters were. One of the laboring sorts caught Denton in a stray glance. He sneered and spit on the floor. There was an initial moment of terror – *What have I done to upset these men already?* – before Denton recalled how he was dressed. He'd left the Klump Regency dressed for a stroll with Brisby. He was wearing his spiffiest duds, which, while certainly not spiffy enough for an audience with the Crundwells, were spiffy enough to get him spat at. To judge by his dress, if his kind were anywhere here, they were up near the ceiling, affecting amused detachment.

Denton turned his attention towards the evening's gladiators. Their names, as far as Denton could ascertain from the lawless yawping, were Shitheel and You Ruddy Cunt.

They were, Denton could not help but notice, chickens.

With his unparalleled powers of deduction, Denton determined that he had walked into a cockfight.

Cockfights weren't illegal – on the contrary, they were a popular attraction, heralded by drool-stained notices in any and every publication. Fortunes were won and lost on the fates of these cocks, but money changed hands even among those without the taste for gambling. Cockfighting was a spectator sport just as much as it was a game of chance, and bloodlust was one of the few characteristics that cut across all distinctions of class and race (the more visible distinctions of the latter remained strong enough to keep the audience pale, however). Sure, there was opposition to it. Some folks said it was beneath the dignity of a civilized people, degrading in some pivotally spiritual way. But some folks said the same things about dueling, and wasn't that still in vogue amongst the higher sorts? And anyway, some folks could get fucked, because in a time when personal liberties and individual freedom were on the lips of every free-thinking citizen of these thirteen colonies, who were *they* to say who could and couldn't shake their chickens around, strap sharpened spurs to their feet and throw them in a ring with another recently rattled rooster?

Denton fought back a frown. He was a humanist, yes, but not such a species chauvinist that he couldn't drum up some poultristic feeling for the soon-to-be drumsticks.

"Bejesus! Wouldn't have conjectured I'd strike upon you here, Denton!"

Such a familiar voice! Denton looked around for its source.

"Oh, you flatter my true altitude!"

Denton looked down. "Oh. Hello, Bulstrode. What, um, what are you doing here?"

"Come to see the show! I've placed a piddling sum on one or the other of these tonkers, besides."

"Okay. I meant more, you know, chickens and turkeys-"

"I'll just put that to bed right now; Let's ignore that I am not *actually* a turkey, but a demon currently adopting the *form* of one – I've no especial chummitude to offer a bloke simply on the grounds of he's got wings stuck to a bundle of scrumptious meat. Surely you don't shed a little tear for every chimp what gets brained by a well-flung pebble?"

"What do chimps have to do with humans?"

"...ah, of course. My mistake. You lot aren't there yet."

"Aren't where?"

"Never you mind. What're *you* doing here, Denton? OH DO PLEASE PECK HIM HARDER, YOU RUDDY CUNT!"

Denton balked for a moment. There was no reason not to let Bulstrode, and therefore Miss Carsis, in on his maybe-meetup with Brisby. And yet, given the treatment he'd received from Miss Carsis thus far, he found himself reticent. She had, after all, arranged for him to be clouted upon the head.

Then again, they'd reached an arrangement, as regarded honesty. And Denton could only lead by example. "I'm here to meet the physician who attended to my...head wound. Brisby Houl-"

"Yes, Dr. Brisby Houlihan. We asked Vera to send for him, you'll recall."

"Oh yes, Bulstrode. I recall very well."

"Excellent news, given the head-smiting you received!"

"The one that Miss Carsis orchestrated, you mean?"

"That's the one!" Bulstrode enthused.

"…at any rate, Dr. Houlihan told me I could find him here this evening, and as he might get me a leg up the social ladder, I came to do just that. By which I mean, find him here."

No-Good Bulstrode shook his feathers appreciatively. "Yes, wonderful scheming. Although, I must point out, the sod level here is where congregates the poorer sorts. Hence my being here. A roaming gobbler doesn't catch their eye, and even if it did, I am possessed of what you might call an *aura.* I just naturally have a way with keeping the blighters, well, away, you see?"

"Not entirely."

"The only way I'm prone to be noticed, I say by way of an explanation, is indirectly. Such as, for example, if a well-dressed toff were to flounce into a cockfight and start talking turkey with the same."

Denton paused for a moment. He lifted his eyes and saw a small ring of baffled faces pointed his way.

"They can't hear me, I'm afraid to say. But they can hear you."

"Yes, thank you. I had worked that one out."

"Not that I'm overeager to bring this episode to a nib, but I'd go so far as to suggest we have shut with the palaver."

"Sounds-"

"HEY!"

Denton spun on his heels. A very clearly tipsy Brisby whiffled his way up to him.

"Oh, hello," Denton smiled half-heartedly. "I'd been looking for you!"

"Who were you talking to?"

"I was…praying."

The makeshift amphitheater erupted in cheers and jeers. For a harrowing instant, Denton assumed the entire crowd had conspired to call him out for his woeful dishonesties. But nope; You Ruddy Cunt had just swung a spur and sliced what seemed to have been a fairly pivotal bit of Shitheel's circulatory system.

"OH!" Brisby shrieked. Denton assumed this was in response to the grisly developments in the ring, but once again he assumed wrong, a fact made clear when he followed Brisby's gaze up to the top of the bleachers. "I came with some friends! You should meet them! It's only the one friend, really."

Denton looked at the one friend. He was a young fellow. That's all Denton could say for certain. "A-mhm."

"It's Buddy Crundwell's boy!"

"a-MHM?"

"Let's go say hi!" Brisby bounded up the steps to the best of his ability. Either he had a low tolerance, or he had been here for quite some time. Because, to be accurate, Brisby wasn't really bounding. His ascent was more of a scramble, or an upward collapse.

Denton gave No-Good Bulstrode a parting shrug, and received the distinct impression that the true form of the Demon not only had opposable thumbs, but knew enough of non-verbal communication amongst humans to be pointing one thumb upwards as a show of encouragement.

He shook himself from his stupor and climbed after Brisby. Best for his faux-aristocratic pretentions if he could minimize the amount of time he spent smiling warmly at turkeys in public.

XIX

BUDDY CRUNDWELL JR. HAD A HAT ON. FIRST impressions are everything, and Denton's first impression of him was his hat. Once again, he kicked himself for not having one of his own.

As for the rest of him: Buddy Jr. was unmemorably dapper. A cravat of sanguine silk, under a waistcoat/coat combo of a brighter hue. His hat was a big chestnut-colored triangle, with a gold fringe outlining the edges. He was, all in all, wildly overdressed for a cockfight, putting even Brisby to shame. It did not bear considering, where the sartorial comparisons put Denton.

This ostentation was as it should have been. Buddy Jr. was the second son of the town patriarch (and his namesake), but for reasons unknown to the general public, he was the heir apparent to the Crundwell throne. Buddy's first son, Sonny Crundwell, was oft seen but rarely discussed, save in hushed whispers in the wake of his passing. The hopes of Crundwell succession rested on Buddy Jr.'s broad, Adonis-like shoulders.

From where Denton stood – about two bench-tiers below him – those hopes were well-placed. At twenty-six years old, Buddy Jr. was the sort of unattainable ideal a Greek sculptor must have had in mind as he sat down to a slab of marble.

"Oh, walk it off, Shitheel!" Buddy Jr. suggested. He turned towards the two men clambering up towards him. "Brisby! Where'd you get off to? Come and sit with me!"

Brisby made a breathy noise of assent, which seemed all he could manage after his drunken ascent. For a physician, he did not seem to be in terribly good shape.

"I want," he panted, "to introduce you to my good friend, Denton Hedges. He's in town for the slave trade. Denton, meet Buddy Crundwell Jr. He's an abolitionist."

Buddy Jr. frowned down at Denton, who frowned at himself. "A slave trader," Buddy Jr. repeated. "Ah." Denton's frown achieved dummy-like depths; he and the Crundwell boy might well have gotten along, were it not for this wretched charade he had forced himself to perform.

"Well, I'm a slave doctor, actually. A doctor to the slaves. And pleased to meet you. Not at all in that order, necessarily."

First impressions are everything. *Curses.* What might a hat have done for him in this situation?

Nodding as Brisby settled in next to him, Buddy Jr. waved Denton up reluctantly. "If my lately acquired friend here vouches for you, then I suppose you're alright."

Not the most ringing endorsement he'd ever received, but it would apparently do. "Oh, thank you." Denton strode up to Buddy Jr.'s level and sat down next to Brisby.

Down in the ring, Shitheel had expired by way of drainage. He lay in a puddle of his own viscera, as You Ruddy Cunt strutted his victorious stuff. Denton saw money of various stripes pass through the dim light. From the hands of frowning faces to the hands of smiling faces, that was the universal flow of currency. Save, of course, for a few smiling faces who were paying out *and* being paid. Bookies, Denton figured.

One of the bookie-types looked inquiringly up to Buddy Jr. The young Crundwell raised a closed fist, and from that summoned up three fingers, followed by an outstretched thumb thrust to the right. The bookie grinned, nodded, and returned to his more spatially immediate customers.

Denton admired the ease with which Buddy Jr. gestured his money away. "You attend games of chance such as this often, I take it?"

"Yeah," he shrugged, "I like them. What of it?"

Denton shrugged. "Just making an observation."

"Well, don't."

Brisby bulged his eyes out for a moment, the reeled them back in. He stage whispered to Buddy Jr.: "Give him a chance, he's suffered a head wound recently."

Denton suspected Buddy Jr.'s aggression towards him was due to his fictive profession, rather than any social faux-pas he had committed, so it was with mixed emotions that he noticed Brisby's qualification have a pronounced effect on Buddy Jr.'s bearing. "You don't like them?" The Crundwell kid finally asked Denton. "Games of chance?"

Down in the ring, Denton saw one of the organizers of the cockfight staring thoughtfully at No-Good Bulstrode. He made a move to grab the Turkey-Demon, but fell short of his goal when he suddenly crumpled into unconsciousness. The most popular story in the tavern the following night would be that his collapse came after staring directly into the glittering eyes of the turkey, but the most popular story is so seldom the right one that most listeners laughed and discarded it out of hand. Which is unfortunate, because sometimes that most popular story *is* the right one.

In any event, the organizer awoke from his coma two days later no worse for wear, except for an overwhelming revulsion at the mere thought of turkey dinners.

"Nnnno, I wouldn't say so," Denton droned, distracted by the men hustling the rag doll of an organizer out into the fresh air. So distracted was he, that he set himself on the path towards what for him was a bold conversational gambit. "I've never been entirely comfortable with the roll chance plays in my regular life. I've certainly never felt compelled to make a game of it. I'd much rather stick to games of certainty."

For the first time, Buddy Jr. seemed genuinely interested in Denton. He leaned in, to peer around Brisby (who was nodding off into his own unassisted unconsciousness). "What is a game of certainty?"

"Well, for example, flipping a coin."

"That's not certainty. That's chance. A fifty-fifty chance, specifically."

"Only if you try to guess how it will land. If the object of the game is to guess *if* it will land, your chances of winning improve dramatically."

Buddy Jr. stared at him vacantly for a moment. Nervously, as though trying to not wake Brisby, he ventured: "That was a joke, wasn't it?"

Glancing nervously down at Bulstrode (who was mercifully out of earshot), Denton shrugged. "Yes."

A genuine smile crept across Buddy Jr.'s face. He began to laugh, a normal, non-terrifying human laugh that was music to Denton's ears. Brisby started awake, wiping a jewel of drool from the corner of his mouth, and joined in the laughter. He was no less taken by the joke for not having heard it. Buddy Jr. elbowed Brisby. "He's not so bad, eh? *If* it will land! That's too funny. Too too funny."

"Too funny, *if* in the land!" Brisby agreed.

"I'm so glad you think so," Denton mumbled. The joke had worked! He was so rarely able to make them, but now he could see their purpose. This laughter was, however, making him suspicious. Either Buddy Jr. didn't have a sense of humor, or there was some sort of wildly complex quadruple-bluff going on here. Because nobody ever laughed at Denton's jokes unless they wanted something from him.

Still, Denton was a connoisseur of patronizing fake laughter. And Buddy Jr.'s sounded like the genuine article.

"Tell me Mr. Hedges," Buddy Jr. asked as he leaned further onto his knees, "how did you get into the slave trade? It's such an unsavory institution, don't you agree? And you don't seem an unsavory character."

"Well, it's a funny story," he began, and left it there, because he didn't have faith in his ability to fabricate a suitably funny story that *didn't* involve witches and turkey-demons *ex tempore.*

"Yes?" Buddy Jr. wasn't about to let a funny story go untold.

"Oh, er, I suppose…" Once again, he looked frantically around the room for inspiration, and once again, he would realize too little too late that this was one hundred percent the wrong way to go about spinning a yarn.

"I come from a storied clan of slave, um, fighters."

(NOOOOOOOOO!)

Buddy Jr. stared at him, aghast. "What?!"

"Oh, I know! It was awful. That is why, er, and also how, that is both why and how I taught myself to be a doctor. Against the wishes of my bloodthirsty father. Because the slaves would be injured in fights, and, um, then I would rush in and, you know, I would patch them up, to fight another, ah…"

(NOOOOOOOOO!)

"…day."

Now it was Brisby's turn to be visibly flummoxed. "So you're not a licensed doctor?"

Aha! Here was an opportunity to reel back his earlier lie! If he claimed to be unlicensed, a self-taught doctor, he could utilize this as an all-purpose cover for his ignorance on more far-flung matters of medical specialization. "I must confess," he lied in a husky whisper, "that I am not. I am strictly self-taught. Though I am entrusting you, as my new friends, so keep this a secret." *My new friends, a deft touch!* he congratulated himself

"So you're a black market doctor, then?"

"Yes, though we prefer to call it the slave trade."

"No, I mean…" Brisby turned back to Buddy Jr. for backup.

"He means," came the conversational cavalry, "that you might perhaps have picked up, or taught yourself, or otherwise acquired, skills that are perhaps not a part of the curriculum in a facility of medical education?"

"Sure," Denton allowed. Warming to his theme, he expanded: "yeah, sure."

Buddy Jr. and Brisby looked at each other for a moment. Without a word spoken between them, they turned, in unison, back to Denton.

"Perhaps you can help me," Buddy Jr. stage-whispered.

Denton suppressed another *(NOOOOOOOOO!)*. He'd gotten himself in over his head yet again. Alright. But maybe it was time to start trying to tread water instead of thrashing about waiting for a life preserver.

"Perhaps I, um, can," he replied, smooth as butter that had been left sitting out in the sun for just a bit too long.

XX

TRAILING BEHIND BUDDY JR. AND BRISBY towards place and purpose unknown, Denton reviewed what he knew of medicine. Sometimes people got sick. When this happened, they took medicine. Then they weren't sick anymore. Sometimes.

Other times they died.

This mental stock-taking occupied Denton for about four strides, at which point he was given a merciful distraction via Brisby's sozzled babbling.

"BJ!" He apparently intended this as an affectionate abbreviation of "Buddy Jr.", and neither of his companions was in the mood to point out the even *more* affectionate context in which that abbreviation was typically employed. "How is she taking it, then?"

BJ didn't lift his eyes from the ground. He stalked on ahead, watching one foot assert itself before the other. "You mean…"

"Fithian! Fithian! How-"

The young Crundwell whirled on Brisby. "Do you expect I've told her?"

Brisby's automatic recoil was tempered by a half-burpy hiccup. "No, I expect I don't, but-"

Denton watched this demonstration of latent power dynamics with rapt fascination. Brisby was, theoretically, the person with the power in this relationship. He was a Customs Commissioner up from Boston, cloaked in royal authority, vested with the power to levy and enforce financial penalties in a manner limited, in effect, by nothing more than his own scruples.

And yet here he was, cowed by a representative of the merchant family he should by regal remit (if not by rights) have well and truly under his thumb. Did BJ here have some personal dirt on Brisby? The latter didn't strike Denton as an excessively craven man, so there *must* have been a good reason for his demurral.

Perhaps it had something to do with this Fithian woman.

Or, perhaps Brisby *hadn't told Buddy Jr. that he's the Customs Commissioner*. But then how would he have weaseled his way into the Crundwell bubble so quickly? Questions, questions, questions…

Buddy Jr. stormed off ahead, and Denton met Brisby as he straggled back towards him.

"What was that all about, then?"

"Oh, just a private matter of his," Brisby sighed before explaining everything in excruciating detail.

The long and short of it was that, while the Crundwells were the old money of Fidget's Mill, there was another family who had just this generation made their ascendancy to the top rung of the social ladder. They were the Lowestofts (that name rang a faint bell in Denton's mind), and they were the new money. Having a proprietary view of the Mill as they did, the Crundwells found the Lowestoft family and their mannerly climbing to be nothing less than a personal affront. For while the Crundwells had a monopoly on the ports, and made their fortunes undercutting the prices of all rivals to the south, they had never made allowances for transporting goods overland to Boston. They deemed this to be none of their concern, and left that to the wiles of the individual clients.

In hindsight, this was an abject idiocy. It left a hole in the market, one that didn't make itself known until it was identified and filled by some ambitious upstarts. Patriarch Cullender Lowestoft purchased a horse and carriage (never having had any expendable income to speak of, the provenance of these vital funds had remained an empty well of information demanding to be filled with idle speculation and gossip), and sent his two kids down to the docks to talk up the newest name in affordable transport. Much as the Crundwells made their fortune through preposterous price-cuts, the Lowestofts gave themselves an edge by employing themselves as labor, and then deferring their own payments. Cullender's wife Opal (widely believed to have been the brains behind the operation) drove the carriage, itself a scandalous novelty sure to attract the English gentry eager to see the curious sights of American living. The Lowestoft children, Fithian and Tobin, were the porters, doing all of the heavy lifting and getting in sun-kissed shape in the process. All in all, they proved a memorable contrast to the pale doughiness of the Crundwells. The injuries to prestige were soon enough forgotten; there was more than enough insult in the Lowestoft's success to keep the wounds fresh.

And the hits just kept on coming: after about two years of the Lowestoft's parasitic business practices, Buddy Crundwell had tried everything he could think of to compete with, conquer, buy out or otherwise annihilate the incipient transport empire, when he had a disturbing realization: the more successful and efficient the Lowestofts became, the more his own side of the business (shivers: his *side*) flourished. No longer forced to commission a way through the throbbing wilderness of the New World on their own, nervous big-money importers from around the world began taking business that might otherwise have gone to Boston and redirecting it to Fidget's Mill. Doing business with the Crundwells on the docks and the Lowestofts on the shore remained cheaper than going straight to Boston, and so the reluctant conjunction of the two families proved to be mutually enriching to both.

Naturally, because the Crundwells were haughty swells at heart, strengthening the delicate ties of this hateful alliance became a simple matter of good business sense, though no less hateful for it. Were the Crundwells to somehow force the Lowestofts (who, though they had begun employing multiple carriages and paid laborers, were still able to keep prices down by primarily utilizing their own sense of familial industry) out of the picture, the importers who had become accustomed to a stress-free overland escort would almost certainly become so frustrated as to take their business elsewhere. The Lowestofts had had too long to burrow into the body of the town; removing them might well kill the host. Together, though, their two names bore previously unthinkable orchards of fruit, nevermind how sour it all was (and nevermind that the Crundwell forbearers had been burned on unsustainable agricultural yields before). So, having children of marriageable age, a natural consummation of the commercial union presented itself. Buddy volunteered his second son, Buddy Jr., to be married to Cullender's first child and only daughter, Fithian.

Denton listened to all of this thoughtfully, and filtered it through the requirements of his ultimate goals. This was a potential complication: it was no longer just about getting the Crundwells to accept non-importation. The Lowestofts, who from the sound of it bore no less influence in the town than the Crundwells, would also need to be convinced, perhaps at the same time. Maybe one family could be convinced, and compelled to press the other into compliance. But then again, maybe they would simply re-enforce one another in their cut-throat convictions that the bottom line was the end-all-be-all. Might Denton not become an enemy against whom the two families could unite? The prospect was daunting, and not nearly as far-fetched as he would have liked to believe. He'd have to be even more careful in his deceptions and manipulations than he'd anticipated: the consequences of being caught out might be disastrous to the cause of American liberty. And also to the cause of Denton having never broken a bone in his life. Or maybe even to the cause of his having a life, full stop.

The fact was, he had no idea what these isolated titans of self-contained industry were capable of.

This was veering dangerously close to the outermost edges of the political; things were starting to get personal. Denton had always proved somewhat inept at all things personal. Politics and law were complicated, but you could debate and barter and appeal to rational self-interest and ultimately make a deal with which neither interlocutor was especially happy. In the realm of personalities, though, emotions ran hot and logic couldn't stand the heat. Complications, complications.

Up ahead, Buddy Jr. turned to make sure his two tails were still on his trail. Satisfied (if that's the right word), he waved them onwards, and stepped into a single-story home.

"HEY!" Brisby shouted at Denton, who was standing right next to him. "You can't tell BJ what I told you."

"I should have thought he already knows."

"Good point. No. Wait a second. You can't tell him *that* I told you."

Denton, never entirely comfortable with personal touch with all but his closest friends, surprised himself by placing a comforting hand on Brisby's shoulder. "Don't worry. I'm very discreet."

Brisby smiled gratefully. "Me too," he reassured himself. Denton's discretion was immediately put to the test, and he passed by not contradicting Brisby's claim. The two men locked arms and strode into the house after Buddy Jr.

XXI

INSIDE THE SINGLE-STORY HOME, BUDDY JR. LED Denton down a narrow hallway into a small room near the back. Blankets had been pressed against the single-pane window, to hold the draft at bay. Another pile loomed large on the bed, covering a shivering Fithian Lowestoft.

Denton really scrambled through his memory at this point, trying to recall what he knew of medicine. Was she sick? How was he expected to help her? Why couldn't Brisby help her – once he sobered up, anyway? He was the licensed physician, after all!

Buddy Jr. knelt down beside her. "This man here," he whispered, nodding back towards Denton, "is going to help us."

Fithian looked back up to Denton, smiling wanly. "Thank you, sir. What is your name?"

It occurred to Denton in this moment that, since he had made the conscious decision to lean into his lies, he'd adopted an air of insouciant ease the likes of which he'd never experienced firsthand before. Adopted was precisely the right word: he knew this new sense wasn't a natural issuance of his, and in a way it must have known deep down as well, but he still couldn't bring himself to tell his self-confidence that it *was* adopted.

He had always been able to bury the social anxieties that had plagued him all of his life under a role; when he got up on the stand, he was Barrister Hedges, not Denton. When he wrote his polemics, even when forced to read them aloud to a crowd, he was a pseudonym, not Denton Hedges. Separation gave him courage, and let the charisma he kept secreted away in some deep part of himself shine through. But now, Denton Hedges was taking a sabbatical entirely, being replaced by the new round-the-clock fiction of Unlicensed Dr. Denton Hedges, Physician to the Slaves. Denton wasn't quite *himself* anymore, and in ways he wasn't fully appreciating, he was getting in to the fiction.

He hadn't run his hand through his hair in quite some time, for one.

"Dr. Denton Hedges," he told her in a voice a sober Brisby might have recognized as a soft impression of his own.

Buddy Jr. looked up at him curiously. "I thought you weren't a licensed doctor?"

"I'm not. This was just my nickname. They called me 'Doc Hedges'."

"Who's 'they'?"

"Mhm?" He breezed past Buddy Jr., and leaned over Fithian, as though he were in the least bit used to leaning over recumbent women who weren't his wife. "What seems to be the matter?"

"I'm pregnant," Fithian informed him. She peeled back the blankets, revealing a distended belly. To Denton's (un)trained eyes, she must have been at least five months along. Maybe more. Or, who was kidding who here, maybe less. He had absolutely no clue.

"Congratulations!" he clapped his hands so that he had something to do with them. "This all seems pretty well under control. I can return when – *after*, of course – the child is born to-"

"No…" Fithian looked up at Buddy Jr. pleadingly. "Have you not told him?"

BJ shook his head. "I wanted him to see you first. A professional assessment."

The young woman turned to Denton, taking his hand gently in hers. "I'm pregnant, Dr. Hedges, and that is the situation I need seen to."

That loaded look between Brisby and Buddy Jr. in the cockfighting ring.

So you're a black market doctor, then?

You might perhaps have picked up, or taught yourself, or otherwise acquired, skills that are perhaps not a part of the curriculum in a facility of medical education?

(NOOOOOOOOO!)

Denton stared thoughtfully at Fithian Lowestoft. She wanted the situation seen to, by an unlicensed doctor she had never met…

Spinning from the waist, he redirected that same thoughtful stare to Buddy Jr. "This isn't Fithian Lowestoft, is it?"

Buddy Jr. gave Denton Hedges the look of transcendent

condescension for which every school of "charm" or "etiquette" ever established is forever striving. "Of course not."

"Ooooooooooooh," said Denton Hedges, master of discretion. "Oh dear."

The young woman's name was Millicent Ditteridge, known to friends and loved ones as Missy. Her family, as Denton was informed later that night by a drooling Brisby skirting the frontiers twixt waking and sleeping / sobriety and intoxication, was the third of the mighty triumvirate that effectively owned Fidget's Mill. If the Crundwells were the old money, and the Lowestofts were the new money, then the Ditteridges were the wait-what-do-they-even-do money. The former two families' wild successes were notable because neither family actually *produced* anything. They simply moved things that other people had produced from one place to another, and extracted a handsome fee for their troubles. But still, most of the poorer Fidgetonians (i.e. most of the Fidgetonians) would grudgingly admit that the two families were familiar with graft and hard work. They still *made* a living, even if they didn't make anything else.

The Ditteridges, though, seemed to be of the belief that there was no sense making a living when you could just *take* one instead.

The family's fortunes lay in paper, that's all anybody knew. Not paper currency – while they had an embarrassing amount of that, they had even more wealth locked up in illiquid capital over in England, if the stories were to be believed. No, the Ditteridges were purveyors of the paper upon which news and stories and opinions were published, the material that constituted the informational veins of the colonies. Whatever it was they got up to in England, they came to Fidget's Mill in ships that had no right to be floating, laden with opulence as they were. And underneath their glimmering prosperity lurked a twine-bound stockpile of blank, expectant pages that would have gotten Alexandria's head librarian sweaty under the binding.

Unlike most importers, the Ditteridges came to Fidget's Mill with a long-term residence in mind. Chip Ditteridge brought his eldest daughter Missy along, with plans to send for his wife and their five other children once the advance party was sufficiently settled. Yet again, no one knew why they should be so eager to leave behind a life of unfathomable abundance for the comparatively hardscrabble existence of the Colonies, but here they were just the same. They quickly became the town's most important importers; they brought in more goods and paid higher prices for marginally better service. And yet, despite their being arguably the single most pivotal pecuniary pillar in the Fidgetonian economy, the Ditteridges remained anathematized by their prospective neighbors. It wasn't simply for their wealth – though that was certainly part of it – instead the primary source of the friction was the unsevered umbilicus that pulled taut across the Atlantic.

The Ditteridges wanted to live in America, but they had no pretentions towards (nor even the slightest interest in) becoming Americans. To a certain extent, this was fair enough – a distinct American identity was hardly in the offing, and even many of the more radical colonists, agitating against perceived transgressions by the King, still considered themselves to be Englishmen – but to an even more certain extent, this was unacceptable. The merchant family, friends of the royally-appointed Governor Rumney Marsh and presumably just as chummy with the powdered heads of government back across the pond, were a convenient and natural avatar for the nebulous forces of oppression that many colonists felt pressing down upon them, but were unable to identify and articulate beyond a general sense of existential unease.

Still, the Ditteridges had insinuated themselves into the commercial circle of life to such an extent that, much like the Lowestofts, to even entertain their extirpation was to court ruin for the town as a whole. Such was the nature of developed dependency. Nonetheless, what cast-offs of their high-quality paper that failed to find their way to Boston were conscripted into the pamphlet war against the Ditteridge presence itself. Such was the delightful irony of their industry – the Ditteridges, flunkies of the British now and forever, found a reliable stream of revenue in supplying the rebels' throbbing concourse of lettered unrest with its means of dissemination.

But hey, that's just business. Denton had no idea, but some of his most vituperative polemics against the British were published on pages of Ditteridge issue.

Most of the colonial rabble-rousers had no idea either, nor would having an idea have eased their enmity. The Ditteridges became a symbol rather than a fact, and so the fact became that the Ditteridges were to be grudgingly tolerated, and the proper response to seeing Chip or Missy coming down the street would be to mockingly doff one's cap (or mime the action, should one be wanting a topper), and sneer something quite biting and sarcastic, like "oh, good day *sir*," or "how are we today *madam*," and then spit in their path or fart at their passing or generally perform what rite of biological impertinence came naturally in the moment.

In short, the proper response to seeing a Ditteridge was not to fall in love. Conversational intercourse was a strict no-no, so the other sort was nothing short of a NO-NO-NO.

And yet here Missy lay, with child by a Crundwell. Scratch that – *the* Crundwell, the heir apparent to the parochial port empire, his hand promised to a woman from the *other* family. In another time, this would be correctly identified, in certain circles, as a PR problem.

XXII

DENTON STUDIED AT MISSY'S ROUND BELLY. HE turned his eyes up to her face. "Is bearing a child supposed to make you look like that?"

"Like what?" The edge of fear in her voice made Denton wince.

Ill, he thought, and then he thought better of it. "You're sweating."

"It's warm in here."

As if on cue, the wind rattled the small window against the bulwark of blankets. The covers were doing their best, but Denton could still see his breath vanishing in front of his face. It was freezing in here.

The fake doctor stared nervously at the real one. *She needs a real doctor*, he thought. And while he didn't think better of it, he did have the good sense to yield to his well-honed instincts of self-preservation. This wasn't what pregnancy did to a woman. He imagined. It hadn't done it to his wife, anyway, and she was the only pregnant woman with whom he'd spent any real time.

Thoughts of Peggy warmed Denton against the chill of the room. Perhaps she was just so superlatively strong as to ward off the sweats of pregnancy? Yes, if any woman were, it would have been her. But still, Denton suspected Missy's condition was uncommon.

He knelt down beside the bed, getting his head level with hers. "Um, are you ent-"

"Are you going to ask me if I'm certain I want to cease my expectancy?" So piercing was her stare that Denton couldn't help but avert his eyes for a moment.

"Something along those lines, I suppose."

"I am. It-"

"That's alright, then." Denton stood up. He didn't much care about her reasoning. She seemed happy with the decision, and it had nothing to do with him, except in the sense that now he was expected to perform the procedure.

He knelt down again. "On second thought, are you *utterly* certa-"

"Yes."

"I see." He stood up again, and ran his fingers through his hair.

Gah!

Denton was a man of the world, or at least of the country. He had heard of these sorts of things being done, naturally. But instructions were never provided, and he'd never asked for them. Odd-jobber though he was, he had believed to a near-certainty that this task would never be expected of him.

Though, odd-jobber that he was, the possibility had certainly occurred.

Yet while this unexpected turn of events had led said task to be suddenly expected, it wasn't *required*. He could walk away, or tell the truth and say he had never performed this procedure and hadn't the first idea how he would go about it (so tell *some* of the truth, anyway).

But, at the same time, here before him was the most incredible 'in' with the powerful families he could hope for. The Crundwells and Ditteridges were present, and the former cast a distinctly Lowestoft-shaped shadow. If Denton could figure out how to make this happen, he would not only be sharing a secret with them all – which implied a sense of trust, however tenuously established and conditionally dependent – but he would have done them, to put it mildly, a favor. They would owe him one. Or maybe more than one. A personal favor for a political gain.

Essentially, the sort of thing he'd always frowned upon quite strenuously. Oh dear. Decisions.

He scratched his chin for a moment. It is a well-known fact that scratching one's chin leads to Inspired Thoughts. This is nearly as reliable as the relationship between baths and Epiphanies. Why this should be the case, that Inspired Thoughts can be tickled out of the jaw, no one knows. But the results speak for themselves.

Sure enough, after fifteen seconds of silent mandible caressing, Denton had an Inspired Thought. Frankly, he couldn't believe it took him this long to think of it. All that was left was to gracefully excuse himself.

"Back in a jiffy," he mumbled as he dashed out the door.

Denton knew exactly where he was going. Dealing with people and personalities left him frightened and adrift. But now he was in his element: cold, hard information.

The information in question: the directions to Miss Carsis' house.

He ran as fast as he could, but made sure to slow way down and take the street corners carefully. They were slippery and he was clumsy; there were two more pieces of information that were ready at hand.

His excitement did get the best of him, though. He fell once. But only once.

Denton knocked out a zippy little tattoo on the door. The young woman answered again, and waved Denton right in. It wasn't until several hours later that he realized, to a near-moral certainty, that he had been admitted to that familiar sitting room through a different door than the one he passed through upon his first visit.

Oblivious for now, he shouldered his way through the blue curtain to find No-Good Bulstrode pecking at Miss Carsis' bare feet.

His face flushed with embarrassment immediately, for reasons he couldn't quite put to words. "I'm, um, I'm not interrupting anything, am I?"

Miss Carsis beamed at him. She sat sideways on one of the wooden chairs, feet dangling out toward Bulstrode. Her left arm hung lazily over the back of the seat. "Not at all. Come in, please."

The hesitance to enter the room was also difficult to account for rationally. But hesitant Denton was to enter, and hesitantly he did enter.

No-Good Bulstrode looked up from his labors. "Why, good evening yet again!" As his beak dangled open, little toenail clippings tumbled out and pitterpattered onto the floor. Denton's stomach heaved a bit in protest.

"Yes," Miss Carsis said pleasantly, "No-Good recounted to me your encounter at the cockfight. Most unexpected, that you should attend such barbarous gaieties, that is what I felt initially. And then I heard of who *else* was in attendance. Very clever."

With neither a word nor a gesture Denton could see, Bulstrode withdrew, allowing Miss Carsis to rise to her feet. She wiggled her neatly-trimmed toes happily, and looked back up to Denton. "You have wasted no time in insinuating yourself amongst the higher sorts. That initiative goes neither unnoticed nor unappreciated."

Denton blushed. He so rarely received direct compliments. That these compliments came in the form of litotes did not upset him in the least. "Well, funny you should mention that. I've perhaps *over*insinuated myself, and now I'm in a bit of a pickle."

"Go on."

"I'll speed past a rather long and uninteresting story and arrive straight at the punchline, which is that I am currently expected to perform an abortion on young Missy Ditteridge, who is carrying the child of young Buddy Crundwell Jr."

A long moment of silence. Miss Carsis' facial expressions were a complete mystery to Denton. He wasn't certain what reaction he had been anticipating, but he had been anticipating a reaction of some sort. This was just prolonged nothing.

"So," he continued, feeling something more might be expected of him (because wasn't that always the way), "I thought maybe following through on this would be advantageous, and so, ah, I was wondering if, er, I might not enlist your help in this endeavor?"

"Do you assume I have done such a thing before, simply because I am a witch?"

"No, but you, er, your, well, you have, ah, please interrupt me because I do not know where I am going wi-"

"Well, it just so happens that I *have* done such a thing before."

"Oh thank goodness."

"But, I hasten to add, *not* because I am a witch. I happen to be a witch, and I happen to have done such a thing. I simply cannot stress enough that the two are not causally linked in any sense."

"Um...okay."

"Let us fly, then. We haven't any time to waste."

"Well, strictly speaking, I reckon we've got about four months or so to waste."

Miss Carsis made a face at Denton that communicated more than any mere words could do. Even *he* could read what was written there. He was getting cocky with the jokes.

"Sorry."

The witch snapped directly at Bulstrode without breaking eye contact with Denton. "Bulstrode! We're off!"

"Very good! Let's away!" Pitterpatter.

XXIII

"THIS IS MOST UNUSUAL," MISS CARSIS muttered to herself as she waved her hands over a flustered Missy.

Upon entering the room with the witch in tow, Denton very nearly introduced her to Buddy Jr. and Missy as his "assistant". He, with his lamentable imagination, had never experienced anything that might be considered "precognitive", or otherwise predictive of the future, but in that moment he had such a vivid image of being turned into a toad that he bit back that instinctive pretense in favor of calling Miss Carsis by her Lilith-given name and leaving it at that.

Perhaps heeled by her authoritative aura, perhaps overwhelmed by a spell whose casting escaped Denton's attention, or perhaps just clinging to sanity by a shivering finger and eager to grasp any helping hands thrust their way, Buddy Jr. and Missy not only failed to recognize the witch (as stark a demonstration of how class could define and divide even in a town as small as this, Denton noted), not only accepted her presence, but they immediately deferred to her embodied expertise, all without comment.

"What is most unusual?" Missy inquired nervously. The coils of her auburn hair flopped playfully in front of her eyes, clearly not getting a good read on the room.

Miss Carsis lowered her hands to her hips, and shook her head. After a moment, she replied: "Those who've sworn an oath to Hippocrates would call it a puerperal infection, what you have. I'd just as soon revert to the colloquial nomenclature of childbed fever."

Buddy Jr., perched on the edge of the bed next to Missy, squeezed her hand anxiously. "But my Missy is h-"

"She's not *your* Missy, mister." Miss Carsis favored him with a distinctly witchy glare. Buddy Jr. did not look like he appreciated the favor.

"...of course. This Missy, then, of whom I am enamored...?" He tilted his head down, soliciting approval. Miss Carsis gave it in the form of a soft nod. "...Yes, well, she is in childbed, and she appears to have a fever. So what is unusual, then?"

"She's gotten the infection the wrong way round."

Denton, sensing a slam-dunk opportunity to impress his pretend non-credentials upon the couple – and the actual physician Brisby – stepped forward. "Puerperal infections are commonly infections of the mouth, s-"

SHUT UP, he thought in Miss Carsis' voice. He looked over at her, and she was making an emphatic "shut up" face. The very probable possibility that *he* wasn't the one to think that thought in his own head popped up and said 'hey hows it going', but he was quick to smother it before it had a chance to spit out any of the disturbing pearls of existential sputum he could see dribbling from the tip of its tongue, chief among them 'how can you be so sure you're the one having *this* thought, then?'

Miss Carsis resumed her diagnosis. "She's gotten the sickness the wrong way round because it's really meant to occur *after* the child is born." They all five entered a long tunnel of dark silence, at the end of which stood a Turkey-Demon. No-Good Bulstrode hopped up on the bed next to Missy. Nobody seemed to notice except Denton.

They can't see him right now, just ignore him, came another thought that Denton was quite certain he wasn't the one to think. He shuddered.

"I do hate to pry," Brisby slurred as he swayed on an invisible breeze, "but as a medical professional I simply must ask, you are quite certain you haven't had the child already?"

The quivering couple fell perfectly still and stared up at him in disbelief. No-Good Bulstrode continued going about his eldritch business, which seemed to be ruffling his feathers and pecking at the air just above Missy's bulbous belly. Denton was fairly sure the Turkey-Demon was doing so with an air of bemused disapproval.

"Yes," Missy said as equitably as she could manage, "I am quite certain."

"Oh, er, ah, ahem," Brisby began, "yes, well, we simply must confirm these sorts of things, you understand. What a boner it would be, to begin treatment only to learn that the child was in the next room, having been very much born, um!"

With horror, Denton realized that the drunken fool had just disqualified himself from giving medical advice tonight. All eyes turned to him now. *Blast!*

"Surely," Buddy Jr. began with a leading cock of the eyebrow, "Mr. Hedges, you must be well acquainted with the illness. Slaves are always giving birth in the most *reprehensible* of conditions, and some modern theories from overseas have it that infections are the work of-"

"A witch," Bulstrode interrupted. And – it was the strangest thing – Buddy Jr. let him, without seeming to hear him. The man just stopped talking, and stared straight ahead. "Or mayhaps a warlock, I cannot determine at this time. But this matron's breadbasket is redolent of stinky mischief."

"That is wildly inappropriate, Bulstrode," Denton scolded.

Miss Carsis rolled her eyes. "He means-"

"Can't they hear us?" Denton pointed towards the uninitiated trio of silent, staring faces. "Also, apologies for the interruption."

"No, th-"

"You don't accept my apology?"

"No, I *do*, b-"

"Oh, I've done it again. Plea-"

SHUT UP.

"-se, ah…"

Denton fell silent, and Miss Carsis filled the vacuum: "No-Good Bulstrode had done his work and was ready to relay his findings, so I'd laid those not privy to him into a gentle trance for the duration of his disquisition. They'll awaken believing that no time at all has passed, and with a sense of general prosperity to assuage any distress caused by their missing time, should they happen to notice it in the least."

"Ah. So, um, there are other witches in town, then?"

"Rummy to that!" Bulstrode exclaimed. Denton turned to Miss Carsis, wondering whether "rummy to that" was a good thing or a bad thing. She shrugged, just as uncertain as he was.

The Turkey-Demon clarified: "Miss Carsis is the only matron of the dark arts in Fidget's Mill. I've seen to this myself; being a Familiar with certain Interests to which I am compelled to attend, it behooves me to have thaumaturgical market by the curly-shorts, what? Ours is the only tune in town, the necromantic waltz to which all and sundry must forever dance!"

Bulstrode started getting…angry…? As always, it was hard to tell. He was hopping up and down on the bed and gobbling, which Denton read as anger based primarily on context clues. "But," he risked in the face of such fowl fury, "is it possible that there lurks here a witch or warlock without your knowledge?"

The hop-gobbling halted. "'tis, of course, a possibility."

"But this raises questions," Miss Carsis mulled. "First, who could it be? It would need be a person close to Millicent, to cast such a precise spell."

"Egads," Bulstrode clucked, "they sought to cloak their hocus-pocus under the shawl of her parturiency!"

Denton felt his heart racing. He was getting into the deductive spirit of things. "So it had to be someone who knew about Missy's pregnancy."

"She could have hidden it from a casual observer, under the proper attire, but those closest to her would almost certainly have noticed her expanding midsection." Miss Carsis nodded, and turned towards Missy. "Who else knows of your condition – I speak now of your impregnation – save those of us in this room?"

"-invisible organisms," Buddy Jr. resumed, continuing his pre-freeze thought in what to him was an uninterrupted stream. Until, of course, Miss Carsis interrupted him with her question. So he wound down gracefully: "And, uh, yeah."

"Not a soul," Missy answered Miss Carsis.

"Very good," the witch replied, and the trio in the corner of the room again went blank. She turned back to Denton. "It's neither Brisby nor the young Crundwell. A powerful sorcerer might veil their puissance in a general sense, but the very air around them will yield their secrets to unusual scrutiny such as myself and No-Good

Bulstrode bring to bear." To Denton's blank expression, she simplified: "If I were standing next to a mage, I'd know it."

"And the atmosphere around these chappies is husky with grey mortality, I should say," Bulstrode did indeed say. "Terribly sorry about the 'grey', nothing personal meant by it, you see, I'm sure you'd be the first to admit your sort are rather soggy doddles, in the metaphysical sense."

Denton shrugged. He was finding that No-Good Bulstrode had a remarkable talent for saying things that probably *should* be offensive, but end up not being so. "So somewhere in this town is a witch, or warlock, who is close to Missy, and for some reason wants her to perish of seemingly natural causes, only they don't know enough about pregnancy to keep from goofing up the illness with which they've stricken her."

Miss Carsis opened her mouth to speak, but another thought occurred to Denton. Unknowingly regaining his mask of confidence, he butted back in without intending to: "Ah! This isn't simply about offing Missy Ditteridge: this is about doing so in a way which would expose what would, from a business perspective amongst the families, seem to have been a wild indiscretion. An ostensibly natural tragedy would become the fault of Buddy Jr., for it never would have occurred had he simply committed to Fithian as was intended by their respective families."

Typically not one to brook interruption, Miss Carsis was nonetheless glad of Denton's brusqueness in this case. Perhaps he'd prove a more competent ally than she'd anticipated. "Chip Ditteridge would be alone here, with his oldest daughter gone. Perhaps he might reconsider sending for his family?" This last sentence tapered off into nothing, a tentative gesture Denton found profoundly unbecoming of the witch.

"Perhaps he'd reconsider staying here at all," Denton enthused, getting excited despite himself. He did his best to reel in the amount of fun he was having, pondering an incipient act of supernatural murder that could kick off a chain reaction leading to the destruction of an entire town. "The consequences of Missy's death in these circumstances would be positively earthshattering, or Millshattering, at least, and if Brisby were unable to spy anything unusual in her condition, then it's very likely no one here ever would have."

"The enchantress, or enchanter, would have seen through their purpose without incurring the least bit of suspicion."

"So," Bulstrode mulled aloud from the bed, "we're casting shadows that are out to supplant us, it seems."

The witch nodded. "Witches of the sort that give witches as a whole a bad name."

"Ditto Familiars."

Oh. Oh goodness. Wait a second.

Denton decided this was something he ought to share with the group. "Oh. Oh goodness. Wait a second."

They did. And he recounted his nightmare for them, in all of its terrifying (and, he realized upon vocalizing what had at the time seemed quite intense, anti-climactic) detail. He concluded with "Could this have been…?"

"Our opposite's Familiar," Bulstrode concluded Denton's conclusion.

Miss Carsis shook her head, finishing the shake with a look to Bulstrode. "They can't know. This attack would make no sense. It must be about something else." She racked her gaze toward Denton, anticipating his confusion. "That's none of your concern, what I just said. What matters is you being visited by a Familiar of whom we were completely unaware. But why?"

Once again feeling things despite himself, Denton was inordinately flattered. He was already on someone's radar enough to warrant their attentions, negative though they may be. "How do they know me?"

"Perhaps they know of our midnight consort." Her face tightened, and she looked at Denton with sympathetic severity. "You are perhaps in greater danger than you realized."

"Well, I had figured if my identity as a Son of Liberty were common knowledge, I would be-"

"That is a trifling concern. We meddle in the celestial realms. These are contests that extend beyond our world. The only one of us truly capable of appreciating the stakes is he." She gestured to No-Good Bulstrode, who was hard at work preening his perpetually proud chest. "My benign influence in Fidget's Mill depends upon a certain degree of integrity in the town, and my ambitions are fairly modest. But looking past my own frustrations, if that integrity should be torn asunder, and this dark interloper should deck the corridors of power with their black banners…I trust you've heard the stories originating in this county, not a century ago. Yes? It will be worse. Practitioners of occult conjury do not wage war with each other directly. They shape the course of human events, pulling strings from the shadows, driving others to fight their battles for them."

There was something distressingly familiar in this description, Denton thought. Had he a business card, perhaps "Practitioner of Occult Conjury" would have been the most succinct way to describe his own work.

Frankly, this was all getting a bit too eschatological for him. His hands were quite full with getting the three families to sign off on non-importation, thank you very much. Wading into a war for the mystical plains of something or other, that was all well above his paygrade.

He had a thought, and tried to hide the thought from Miss Carsis, knowing that she might well read it. The thought was that he didn't really care about her supernatural battles. Her objectives were still a mystery to him, as well as why she should care so much for the integrity of the town, and seemingly so little for the Cause. Somehow these positions fell in with her larger priorities, priorities about which Denton could not bring himself to care. He cared about the Cause. *His* Cause.

"Can you make her well?" he asked, pointing to Missy Ditteridge.

No-Good Bulstrode stood silent for a moment. "As well as terminating the pregnancy, correct?"

"That is what I meant."

"Mhm. Well, yes. She's quite certain this is what she wants?"

"Yes."

"Well then it'll be but a moment's graft. Unsavory graft it'll be, I'm afraid. You may favor the aversion of the eyes, is my advice to you." Bulstrode hopped down between Missy's spread legs, and Denton had enough sense to take his advice at that point.

Denton counted the splinters he could see poking out of the wall, in the hopes that his count would distract him from the horrific slurping and sloshing noises coming from just over his shoulder. It didn't.

Finally, Denton turned back in time to see Miss Carsis compressing a ball of pink between her hands, until she brought her palms together gently, as if in a slow-motion mockery of prayer.

"Was that…?" Denton started to ask, and then stopped himself.

"She is no longer with child," Miss Carsis declared matter-of-factly.

Denton shivered, not at all owing to the temperature of the room. "And her sickness?"

"Gone with the offspring," Bulstrode happily informed him.

Where to? Denton almost asked, but this time stopped himself before he started.

Miss Carsis laid a reassuring hand on Denton's shoulder. "Consider the greater good. This enemy of yours, w-"

"Mine?" Denton hiccupped.

"We know nothing of their objectives save two things: they wanted Millicent Ditteridge dead, and they wanted her unborn child to remain so. What does one do to an enemy?"

Denton considered this. "Ask them to stop?"

"You frustrate their objectives."

"So we killed the chil-"

"The child was never *alive*," Miss Carsis snapped. "It wanted upwards of a month before it was anything resembling a living entity. Millicent, who *is* alive, would have ceased to be had she carried the child to term. Put aside the political ramifications; the moral calculus is clear on this. I've given you nearly a minute to be uneasy, but it's time for you to retire your curious hang-ups and return to the tasks at hand."

"Yes, I-"

"Buddy Jr. owes you a favor now, after tonight." She smiled like an angler fish. "As you owe me another favor, after tonight."

"What do you mean, *another*?"

"I returned your bag to you."

"You arranged for it to be stolen in the first place!"

"And look how's worked out for you! As you conduct your social climbing, by all means, please pursue your own goals. Business is business, and I shouldn't want to stand in the way of that. But keep your eyes open, that I might see through them."

"…"

"Not literally."

"Thank goodness. I have need of my solitude in the night."

"I have no interest in hearing about it."

Miss Carsis unfroze Brisby, Buddy Jr. and Missy, minds loaded with images of Denton performing the difficult task assigned to him with the cool professionalism they had never imagined could be found in such an unassuming man. And, just as importantly their minds were unloaded of any Miss Carsis-shaped memories. Thus deceived, they all said their goodbyes. Missy was quite happy to be in good health, seemingly disinclined to ask any questions about her nothing-short-of-miraculously-fast recovery, and thanked Denton profusely. Buddy Jr. insisted that he was in the man's debt, slave trader or no (Denton spotted Miss Carsis nodding gladly at this). Brisby was wowed by Denton's medical know-how, and did his best to pick his brain all the way back to the Klump Regency.

Denton had had more than his fill of brain-picking for the night, though. The ease with which Miss Carsis was able to manipulate thoughts, or simply plant wholesale fabrications of memory, was terrifying. *And why did she feel the need to manipulate people?* He wondered. *Could she not just control them?*

What were the limits of her power? Did she have any?

She was one of the good witches, it seemed, even if her own purposes were slightly inscrutable to him.

But he was facing down a bad one, with a hellspawn of a Familiar at his or her beck and call. Even with Brisby at his side, the night suddenly seemed oppressive. A shadow, that was how Bulstrode describe their new adversary. And that seemed accurate. But the night was *all* shadows, each writhing in the tortured torchlight as though it were coiled, and eager to spring.

Fretting over who was accepting goods from across the cosmic drop of nothing that was the Atlantic Ocean, and what that would do to a scheme of economic coercion levied against a piddling little King who'd be dead in the blink of an eye…it all seemed so small now. And yet, Denton found himself clinging to his original objectives more tightly than ever. He was liable to go insane in the face of some infinite war between Demons and what not. War between humans, now that he could wrap his head around. It seemed dumber than it ever had, but at least it was dumb on *his* scale.

XXIV

HOW HE WENT TO SLEEP PROBABLY WOULDN'T matter in the end; he was a nocturnal jive-shucker, for sure. But still, the decision seemed important to Denton: if he fell asleep on his back, and the vicious Familiar of whomever had tried to kill Missy Ditteridge visited him once again, he would be able to get a good look at it, and perhaps ascertain some detail that could lead to its consort. Then again, if he fell asleep on his back, he would be able to get a good look at it. The way it had sounded, and the way it had felt, he wasn't sure that was such a hot idea, as far as his sanity was concerned.

Falling asleep on his stomach would be cowardly. It'd also be bad for his back (alright, yes, he was man enough to admit that tummy-slumbers always delivered him into the morning stiff and sore), but mostly it'd be cowardly. There were things at stake that were more important than his sanity. At least, that's the distinct impression he'd gotten; he wasn't *entirely* sure what was at stake that was more important than his sanity, particularly if he was the one making that judgment. But it sure seemed like something was.

So possessed was Denton by the sleep-posture question that it became a matter of pure academia: he slept not a wink that night.

That was a night that seemed to stretch into eternity, but at the end of eventless eons the sun rose and burned time itself from the loam of the Earth.

Or to put that another way: time flies when you're otherwise occupied.

Denton and Brisby spent their days meandering the streets, two outsiders learning the geography and tempos and moods of the town, and learning roughly the same things about each other (save the geography, of course). The mutual utility they drew from each other took a backseat to honestly felt friendship, which was nothing if not the pinnacle of mutual utility. Still, Denton was aware that this was complicating the quiet exploitations that they both silently acknowledged were the true purpose of their association. At first, at least. Some nights they would eat or drink or partake of the leisures afforded those of nobler birth (i.e. that only those of "nobler birth" could afford) together, Denton more often than not cadging meals from Brisby, who was more than happy to bill everything straight back to His Majesty, courtesy of the Board of Customs Commissioners (Denton imagined – Brisby still wouldn't entrust Denton with his true vocation). Some nights they would separate, Brisby presumably to fulfill some royally appointed task, Denton to liaise with Mr. Increase or Miss Carsis, or more often to haunt the taverns and street corners where the strange vibrations of epoch found resonance in hushed voices and peeled ears. Yes, Adams and Otis Jr.'s Circular Letter was still forthcoming. February of next year, they had told him in response to an inquisitive letter he'd sent. If the attempt at opposing the Townshend Acts through economic avenues were to succeed, Denton still needed to bring the power players of Fidget's Mill around to the idea before then.

And where were those power players? Of the three big families, he'd only met Buddy Jr. and Missy. Both of whom seemed genuine in their desire to repay Denton's generosity (*perceived* generosity – even he caught himself believing he was the one who cured Missy of both childbed and fever, rather than Miss Carsis), but neither of whom were accessible to a mere doctor of slaves (*pretend* doctor of slaves – it was easiest to keep track of lies by believing them all to be true, and at this rate he was growing concerned about keeping track of which of his truths had started out as lies). He was frittering his time away on…what, exactly? What had he accomplished, *actually*? He had met people who would be important to the attainment of his goals…but what else had he done? What was he waiting for?

Part of his hesitance, he realized, was his fear of consummating his lies with action. The other part was in catalyzing the increasingly complex chain of debts and obligations in which he found himself. The ever-spreading web of independent motivations and overlapping cross-sections of interest that bore tenuous alliances or bred potential enmities was expanding beyond the scope of even Denton's capacious, pedantic mind. Who was he kidding: this wasn't threatening to get out of hand, it already *was* out of hand, and he'd hardly begun to go to work!

It was the middle of December, tending towards the end, and he had nothing much to show for his time in the Mill. Oh, he had identified problems, some of which he hadn't even realized were problems that existed in the real world. But each problem redrew the starting line further and further back from his goal, and each receding redraw left him more and more disheartened at the prospect of trying to close the distance at all.

And so, enraged by his own inaction, Denton did something he had never done before: he invited himself to a party.

"I want to meet the Crundwells."

Brisby nearly did a spittake as they strolled through the streets, mugs in hand. Nearly, because his mouth was empty. He had just swallowed his latest pull of booze, but he also wasn't about to let that stop him.

"You what?"

Denton, who was himself drinking something pungent, held his cup halfway to his face and repeated himself. "I want to meet the Crundwells. You mentioned a New Year's party, did you not? S-"

"Those parties are for the Higher Sorts, Denton. This means themselves, the Lowestofts, and the Ditteridges, Governer Marsh," this last name he said with a shudder, "as well as any wealthy out-of-towners who happen to be in-of-towners at the moment."

"Are you going?"

"…yes, and I see where *you're* going with that, but-"

"You're not wealthy."

"No, I'm not, but-"

"So why are you allowed to go?" Denton had found no small amount of entertainment from teeing up moments such as these, moments in which the most logical thing for Brisby to do would be to admit that he was Customs Commissioner.

"Because…" Brisby tossed back the rest of his beverage and hurled the cup into a pile of refuse as they strolled past.

Denton cast a backward glance toward the soiled goblet. "I believe that was Ms. Miringhoff's cup, wasn't it?"

Brisby came to a halt over the span of about three seconds; his feet stopped moving easily enough, but the upper half of his body didn't get the memo until simple physics delivered it express. "Oh, curses! You're right. When you're right, you're right." The esteemed physician – who was aware of germ theory but was yet to be convinced – turned on his heels and lunged towards the garbage heap, a veritable bouquet of waste.

Denton raised a hand in futile restraint, chiding himself for giving Brisby an excuse not to answer his question. "Oh, I don't suppose she'll mind overmuch." He was, however, slightly tickled that Brisby would rather dive into the trash than face the question to which the most logical answer was 'I am the Customs Comissioner'.

"Nonsense! Won't be a moment's work."

"It's only that I expect she'd be more distressed by your odor, should you wade into the…oh, well, perhaps try to not get too much on…"

"What's that?"

"Nevermind."

Brisby emerged from the midden, cup in hand. "Aha!"

"Brisby."

"Yes?"

"I want to go to the party."

"I'm afraid it's just not done, bringing in men of the lower sorts," said the man scrambling his way out of a mound of filth.

"After what I did for Buddy Jr. and Millicent, you don't think they would want me there?"

"I'd say that's *precisely* why they wouldn't want you there. How would they justify your presence to their parents? 'Hello dad, meet the man who aborted my bastard.' It's just not done."

Denton felt agitation stirring up his lunch. Nothing was going to get done here without bold strokes. He'd have much preferred bold strokes of the pen – much more his speed, that. But bold strokes of action would have to do.

"Well what if I attended as assistant to the Customs Commissioner? Whoops," he added.

Brisby turned to Denton, very, very slowly. He looked at him for a long time. As unsteadied by drink as he was (and always seemed to be, Denton noted with a hint of pity,) that glare was sharp enough to cut diamonds. "Who told you?"

Stupid. He shouldn't have said that. Curse his *own* tipsiness! Alcohol and subterfuge, what made him think those two could play well together? Stupid! "Well," Denton improvised, rolling the dice, "you know how the slaves talk. They see, and they talk. And I hear it all, tending to them as I do. They've seen you down by the docks, inspecting the ships and their cargo."

All at once, Brisby was nose-to-nose with Denton, and seemingly as sober as a teetotaler at confession. "Yes," he growled with a menace Denton could literally not have imagined coming from such a goofy man, "the slaves do talk. And you know, never once have I heard them talk of a doctor tending to them. And I have been listening. Lately, I've even been asking."

"You doubt my honesty?" Denton was so offended by this, he temporarily forgot that there'd been precious little honesty for Brisby to doubt.

"Why did you lie to me? I thought us friends!" And in that moment, Denton could tell that Brisby did.

"Why did you lie to *me*? And how long have you known I'm not a…doctor?"

"I asked you first. And weeks."

"Why didn't you say anything?"

"…I didn't want to know I was right. I wanted to keep thinking you wanted to be *my* friend, and not that you wanted to be friends with the Customs Commissioner." Brisby stumbled over to a nearby building and sat down against it. "That's what this has all been about, hasn't it? You're one of those Independence-minded fellas. I can't imagine what you want in Fidget's Mill, but here you are. I mean, you've never actually given anybody a reason why you, as a slave doctor, would have come here in the first place. What's your made up reason for being here?"

"…"

"Do you have one?"

"…"

"Am I wrong?"

"No."

"Am I right?"

"Yes." *WHY ARE YOU TELLING HIM THIS?!* Because he was drunk? Or because he was guilty? Or because he was both?

"Am I…" Brisby hiccupped and burped in rapid succession. He threw his mug into another nearby garbage pile. "Oh, damnit."

"Don't worry about that." Denton sighed. What did friends say to one another in times such as these, when the pretense of their relationship was revealed to be a ruse from the start? Surely this happened to friends all the time? "Listen…"

"I don't want to be Customs Commissioner," Brisby mewled. "If I'd said no, they were going to take my practice away from me. I wouldn't have been able to support my family anymore. I don't understand why they picked me, but they did. So here I am." He rested his elbows on his knees and hung his head.

Tentatively, crouched in front of Brisby as he was, Denton reached out a hand and patted him gently on the head, as though he were trying to wake up a porcupine. This was not at all how he imagined this conversation going. Perhaps this was what he got for trying to invite himself to a party.

"Well," Denton replied, swinging in to a seated position next to Brisby, "I'm only here because we…something had to get done, still *has* to, really, and nobody else was going to do it. My family and I would have been fine, had I just stayed home. Your motivations seem more noble, I must confess."

"No, *yours* do. You've got beliefs. I have none. Pure self-interest, that's why I'm here. I'm the *worst.*"

"Noooo."

"Yes!"

"No you're not."

"Yes I am!"

"You're doing it for your family!"

"But you're doing it for *everyone's* family!"

And to impress your dad, Miss Carsis' voice rang in his ears. Was this a memory, or had she been listening in and decided to interject from afar? My, how stressful it was to have a witch in the equation.

"My labors may well benefit everyone, but I'm not thinking of them as I perform my duties. I still think only of my wife and children." *And your dad.* "And *only* my wife and children. I am just lucky, in that my self-interest has the appearance of some grander ideal. Though, if I may cast aside modesty for a moment, I am still possessed of such ideals."

"Mhm." Brisby traced a finger through the snow between his legs, drawing a triangle that never closed, instead growing ever smaller within itself.

"And what about you, my friend?" Denton nudged Brisby with his shoulder. "Speak to me as though your livelihood were not on the line. Where lay your sympathies? What would you do, at this juncture in history, were there no constraints upon your actions?"

Brisby continued tracing until the triangles grew too small for him to continue. "If I speak truly?" he asked without looking up.

"Yes indeed."

The physician gave a dull smile. "In all honesty, I would most likely do nothing. I don't want to raise children as subjects to a Crown that values them not as individuals vested with rights to self-determination…but nor do I wish to see them growing up in an atmosphere of revolt. Either scenario is an unhappy one. So I would do nothing, drop my sails, and wait to see which way the wind blew."

Denton sensed an opportunity. It would take finesse, and a delicate touch, but he knew he could pull it off. "What say you, then, if I blow you to invite me to the party?"

Unfortunately, while Brisby was oblivious to the fellatious entendre that was Buddy Jr.'s initials, he was far less snowblind about that particular collision between metaphor and colloquialism.

"I would say that that won't be necessary," Brisby replied as carefully as he could, "and, in fact, I will invite you to the party on the condition that you do no such thing."

"I was talking about your sails. Like the metaphor."

They sat in the snow for a few more minutes, letting the moment pass and disappear around the next bend before they made eye contact again. Which was fine by Denton – the slip of the tongue was out of sight, out of mind. Because he was going to a party. A party. Denton Hedges was going to a party! What would he wear? What did one wear to a party? He considered asking Brisby, but it was nearly impossible to look at a man who had just finished flopping around in filth and think *now that he's finished there, I really must hear his thoughts on high fashion.*

A party! Denton Hedges was going to a party! He stomped his feet a few times in a fit of kiddy giddiness. He hardly thought about the fact that this was his opportunity to meet the rest of the Crundwells and the Lowestofts and the Ditteridges and the colonial Governor, and who knew who else? Anybody who's everybody would be there. Something to that effect, anyway. This was an unparalleled opportunity to insinuate himself into the upper crust of Fidget's Mill, and all he could think of was; what does one wear to a party? What would HE wear? Besides a hat, obviously. He was most definitely getting a hat. Beyond that, though – what?

He knew just who to turn to. To whom to turn, he knew just who.

XXV

"A PARTY?" MISS CARSIS DID A DECIDEDLY POOR job of masking her surprise.

"Yes, on the eve of the New Year."

"And you want that I should dress you?"

"Precisely."

Miss Carsis looked down at her clothes, which ran the gamut between blinding whites and stormy greys. Everything in between, but nothing beyond. She turned back to Denton. "Why, in mischief's name?"

"Because..."

"Witches are hardly known for their sartorial acuity. More often the opposite."

"Yes, well..."

"It's because I'm a woman."

"Yes."

"Oh, Denton," she sighed, rising from her chair and stepping back to a pot bubbling over a fire in the corner. As far as Denton could see, there was no fuel source for the flame, nor containment to hold its shape and size. His natural suspicion was that this was some wicked potion made of puppy tongues and slug eyes, but his natural faculties were leaning towards it being turnip stew. "You've so much to learn."

"If that 'so much' has to do with fancy dress, then I'm all ears. I must confess my wife has always been the one to tend to such matters for me."

"Your wife dresses you?"

"On such occasions when a finer eye is required, yes."

The warmth with which Denton said this was, Miss Carsis had to admit to herself, rather endearing.

"It's not a ball, is it?" Denton turned towards the familiar voice. No-Good Bulstrode pranced into the room, bringing with him a chill that reached deeper into the bones than the winter could account for. "Witches love balls."

Denton blushed. Perhaps he needn't learn as much as Miss Carsis thought.

The Witch whipped her wooden spoon towards Bulstrode, flicking him with a spatter of stew. "Saucery! Sorc…Sorcery!" It was something to behold, seeing Miss Carsis get flustered. "And I'm sure I don't know what you mean by that, in every sense."

"Oh, no? Mice into handmaids, pumpkins into carriages, one thing into another?"

Miss Carsis shook her head over the stew and resumed stirring. "Hardly a Witch's work, judging by your description. And I don't hold with pumpkins. No, that sort of cheap ostentation puts me in mind of Fairy Godmothers." She punctuated that thought with a wretching YELCH noise. "Meddling peddlers of feel-good flimflam, the whole of their race! May they be trod upon by large horses!"

"Not to interrupt," Denton interrupted, "but what's all this about pumpkins?"

She nodded and turned her stew-bestrewn spoon on Denton. "Nothing of which you must concern yourself, that is what we're talking about. Hucksters of saccharine hocus-pocus." She flicked her spoon up and down like a conductor tapping her baton on a music stand, to tell the orchestra that warm-up time is over. "You mustn't trust just any woman with a wand."

A globule of turnip made a downward bid for freedom. It fell to the floor with a disappointing *plop.*

Denton nodded appreciatively. "No, certainly not."

The spoon returned to the stew, along with the burning spotlight of Miss Carsis' attentions. *Perhaps* that's *how she's keeping it at a boil,* Denton thought with a minimum of jocularity. She sighed, and spoke to her stew: "If all you sought were a means of transportation fashioned from a gourd, I could help you. Transmogrification is a trifling affair. A docent in matters vestiary is what you need, though, and I'm afraid I can offer no safe passage through that dark wood."

Denton nodded unappreciatively. "Oh, that's too b-"

"BUT." She stopped stirring, and turned to Denton with a disarmingly affable grin. "I can conjure up the garments chosen by an eye far finer than mine."

"Oh, swell! So to whom can I-" He stopped himself, because he had a feeling that he already knew to whom could he-.

Down at his ankles, his new Turkey Godmother sized him up and cocked its head from side to side as though it were cracking its neck.

Do turkeys have necks? Judging from the look on Miss Carsis' face, she heard that thought thundering through Denton's mind, and furthermore the answer was almost certainly *yes, you idiot.*

"Well then!" Bulstrode gobbled. "Let us away to get you kitted up for the ball!"

"It's not terribly flattering, is it?" Denton raised his arms outward and let them flop limply against his thighs.

Brisby held a dutiful silence as the swishing of Denton's glitzy new waistcoat, a bawdy silk eyesore of cream and floral gold, died a lazy, pendulous death. "No, but nor is it meant to be. That's what the servants are for."

Denton whipped his head around, nearly unseating the powdered wig clinging to his hair on unforgiving pins (though to go by feel, he'd have guessed it had been grafted to his scalp when he wasn't looking). "We're to have servants?"

"Liveried, yes."

"Oh, curses."

"Which ones?" No-Good Bulstrode perked up from the corner, for the first time in quite a while.

"Nevermind."

"Aw." The turkey returned to the corner of Denton's room.

Brisby cocked an eyebrow. "Huh?"

Denton shook his head. Bulstrode hadn't made himself known to Brisby, and much as Denton had been made to feel rotten for having deceived Brisby, he wasn't about to put *all* of his cards on the table. "Nevermind."

"Aw." Brisby lowered his head.

In the mirror, Denton could practically see the gears grinding along in Brisby's lowered head. He chose to ignore them, and instead focused his attentions somewhere they did not often stray: himself.

He looked ludicrous. To a certain extent, he expected this. But to be seeing his humble mug besmeared with the schmutz of wealth and privilege brought home the absurdity of the whole production. He absolutely looked the part of an aristocrat. Nobody at this party would be doing double-takes as he skipped past, wondering who the hell let that commoner in here. And that was the joke of it all – it was the work of but a day to perfect that illusion. Or perhaps conjuring trick would be more apt, for this ball-ready Denton's courtly credentials were no more illusory than anyone else's would be.

Well, they certainly weren't *less* illusory, anyway.

Denton fidgeted in his breeches. "These are a bit tight, you know? My breeches."

An ecstatic flapping issued from the corner of the room. "Right then, right, would you say," No-Good Bulstrode began, giving Denton plenty of time to see where he was going with this. It all slotted neatly in to place: Bulstrode intentionally gave Miss Carsis an underestimated breech size, and encouraged Denton to show off his new dress to Brisby, knowing that the presence of the latter would inhibit the former from answering back or cutting him off once he'd begun the final stage of his fiendish scheme. No matter how helpful Bulstrode could be, he was, after all, still a demon.

"Would you say," he continued, "that you have, by dint of the stature accorded by your vestments, become too big for your breeches? GIBGOBBLAHABOGHALOBG-"

Denton clapped his hands over his ears. Brisby observed silently. Fascinating and gentle though the newly-made Dandy before him seemed, it was nevertheless nerve-wracking to be alone in a room with the sort of person who didn't act as though you and he were alone in the room. Was the man cracking, since Brisby had seen through his façade?

"Are you…are you alright, Denton?"

Denton peeled his hands off of his ears, a mere fraction of an inch.

"Steady on," Bulstrode assured him from the corner, "I've giggled meself to bits and tidied up, so you've nothing to fear."

The hands drifted back towards his sides, ever so slowly, ready to dash back at any time. "Anyway," Denton said with a consistent reticence, "I don't believe I'll be taking a servant to the ball." He began a journey of a hundred buttons at the top of his collar, hiking his fingers up under the fat of his neck to reach the inaugural knob.

Brisby raised his hands as though moving in to help. He and Denton both knew that the Great Unfastening was a one-man job; the abortive approach was purely for form's sake. This was good practice, as most everything done by the upper crust was purely for form's sake. "Why the heavens not?"

"Brisby. I'm not actually the slave doctor."

"I know that. But who else does? Really, this fiction redoubles the urgency with which you must acquire a servant. Would it not be expected of you to have a slave on hand?"

Halfway unfastened. "Just because I claim to be the physician to slaves, it does not necessarily follow that I must *own* slaves, does it?" Denton looked to Bulstrode for some kind of support. The turkey-demon stared back, motionless. No help there.

"Even if you didn't own a slave, you could still bring one. This is for the look of the thing, I'm afraid. I'm no happier about it than you are. I certainly don't own any slaves, but Governor Rumney Marsh is lending me one."

Denton felt sick. *Lending me one.* Lending him a *person.* Perhaps it was because he had been so desensitized to the institution from birth, but somehow *lending* a person seemed worse than *owning* them. This was, he was more than ready to admit to himself, an ecstatically absurd thing to think. But then, one's thinking had to have the whiff of the insane about it to even face the practice.

On a more positive note, he was two-thirds of the way through the un-studdening of his coat. "But I don't need anyone. I'm self-sufficient."

"Were I to go by the look of things, I would find that exceedingly difficult to believe. Look at how you struggle with that coat!"

What would this be – four-fifths of the way done? He'd love to slip the final button through its catch, shrug the coat to the ground, and say something along the lines of "Pah! What struggle?" But that would necessitate a solid four or five seconds of pinch-faced silence, and he wasn't about to concede the point in such a humiliating fashion.

Instead, he settled on "I am *very* nearly done."

Four or five seconds later, he made to shrug off the wholly unbuttoned coat. Limited as his range of arm motion was, he only succeeded in bouncing the shoulders around a bit. After a few more seconds of this, he swallowed the small but bitter capsule of his pride and turned his back to Brisby. "Lend me a hand, would you kindly?"

For one frightful second, he thought he heard Bulstrode gearing up for another chuckle in the corner. The threat mercifully passed unfulfilled.

Brisby smiled with an air of condescension so thick Denton could *feel* it, even with his back turned to the man. All he said was "certainly," but said 'certainly' was freighted with all sorts of subtextual 'neener-neeners'.

Good gracious, if somebody who was anybody who was everybody would be at the party, and all would be floating around trailed by their "help" (the cuddly euphemism that happily embraced slaves, indentured servants and all-purpose companions poorly paid by those torn between an ethical opposition to proper slavery and a pragmatic avoidance of anything that might lead to perspiration), any hint of struggle like the one he'd just worked through would stand out like a zebra at a lion's bar mitzvah. Any efforts at ingratiating himself further with the Crundwells and Ditteridges, or at all with the Lowestofts, would be frustrated. *Look at the low-class moron over there, without even a servant to aid him!* And if he were *very* lucky, it would only end in ridicule – maybe such a cyclone of inquiry would kick up the inconsistencies and contradictions lurking just beneath the thin, filmy scum of his cover story. Down that path lay danger.

The safest course of action would be to tell his scrupulous convictions to take the night off, and take a servant to the party. *But where will I find one?* he asked himself, in the hopes that he could come up with a better answer than the one he'd landed on more or less immediately.

XXVI

MR. INCREASE HAD CLEARLY SEEN SOME SHIT. There were a lot of florid ways of expressing the same idea, like saying "he had eyes that ached with the weariness of unhappy travels," or "his face was a landscape carved by the receding tides of fortune", or "his figure stooped as Atlas under the burden of eternity," but these were all magniloquent ways of saying he had clearly seen some shit and, consequently, he sort of looked like shit.

Increase curled his nose (which was as the frowning snowplow condemned to clear the thoroughfares of Hell on the day it finally froze over, if you like) at Denton. Lit by the single spare candle he kept around his tumbledown dockside lodgings, Mr. Increase's visage took on a nightmarish quality, a somber reflection cast upon a lake of fire.

Denton could only imagine the shit this guy had seen.

He opened his mouth to speak, to finally respond to Denton's lengthy and circumspect pitch. But as before, no words came.

The onus for the moving forward of the conversation was entirely on Increase, but Denton nonetheless pondered what he might do to facilitate the process. It had been a good three minutes since Denton had finished speaking. Well, *good* probably wasn't the right word. But it had been three minutes, alright.

Finally, progress: Mr. Increase began stroking his eyebrows (which were as the fuzzy caterpillars of lamentation dancing to the celestial requiem sung by dying stars and goats falling off mountains)! Was that progress? Well, it was a thing he hadn't done before. Progress or regress, it was gress of some kind; this Denton knew to a moral certainty.

"Hm…" he growled. "I seem to recall giving you a great deal of autobiographical background, no?"

"Yes! Me too!" Denton exclaimed with enthusiasm incommensurate to the message. There was nothing to be done for that: he was thrilled the dialogue had resumed.

"…rrright. Then perhaps you and I might together recall the craterous impact the institution of involuntary servitude left in me during my formative years."

"Ah-hah!"

"…and *then* perhaps we, as one, might consider how a man such as myself, thusly sculpted by his miserable lot in life, would react to the proposition that he participate in the very institution from which he was quite literally born to flee."

"But the thing you must understand, you see, is that you would not *actually* be my servant. It's simply that-"

"This would all be to safeguard your fiction, correct?"

Denton leaned back in his chair – that was when he realized he had leaned forward slightly. When had that happened? No matter. "Ahm, correct."

"Successfully doing so would demand that I wholly embody the part of your servant, correct?"

"Correct again!"

"Which would entail me performing all of the menial tasks typically considered the remit of the servant, correct?

"…correct." Denton leaned forward again, but this time consciously. He had to imagine the mental effort of this second lean was visible on his face. "Yes, oh, I see what you mean." He fell silent, considering the possible alternatives.

Increase was an unlikely choice to begin with – he was a fixture of Fidget's Mill, known as an intense anti-authoritarian. This was often confused with racism against whites, but that was a charge without foundation. He had no especial issue with white people – it was simply that authority in the Colonies was especially white. No, Increase was a man who bridled at the bridle; a man who would gladly spend his life wondering where his next meal was coming from if the only alternative was knowing there was only one place it *could* come from.

If one were to call Mr. Increase a contrarian, he would disagree vehemently. One must make of that what one will.

What would the partygoers think, if the strange newcomer to the town showed up with the swarthy spirit of the docks bowing and scraping in his wake? Denton had no idea, but being the sometimes-incompetent scholar of humanity that he was, he had a few ideas. Chief among them was the thought (left unarticulated to Increase, lest he bristle at the unhappily instrumental view being taken of him) that the well-known storehouse-keeper's ministrations would be seen as an automatic legitimization of the new guy. Something along the lines of 'wow, if a fellow as independently-minded as Mr. Increase is doting on the slave doctor, then he must be a man who commands respect, or perhaps instills fear, etcetera'.

As a secondary consideration, though, Denton was thinking of Mr. Increase's concerns. Everybody at the bottom of the pile was eager to scramble their way up the top, and Denton was offering the man a chance to leapfrog all those middling bits between the two. Why wouldn't he want to take it?

Because – *and I really ought to have thought of this*, he upbraided himself – slavery wasn't just an abstract concept to be exploited to Mr. Increase, as Denton would have to admit it was for him. It was a tactile reality that had warped the roots of his lineage into knots that could be neither split nor unwound - and the mere consideration of which was enough to make old wounds ache anew.

Feeling cornered and off-guard, Denton opted for brutal honesty. He would pitch this to Mr. Increase as the cynical, calculated machination that it was. Perhaps he would react poorly, but that would hardly be a drastic change of pace from the current timbre of their talk.

He would do this right after he tried out the other approach. "You know," he began with the slightest hint of reprimand, "I am thinking of *your* concerns as well. I am offering you an opportunity to place yourself amongst the real power players of the community."

"What am I supposed to do, thusly placed?"

"…air your grievances? Many people would kill to be in your position. The position to which I am referring, of course, being you being here, being made this offer, and not so much, you know, the rest of it. I'm sorry," he wisely concluded.

"Did you honestly expect me to do you this favor under the delusion that you were doing *me* a favor?"

"No. It just sort of happened."

"Do you think me a fool, Denton?"

"No, and I would not begrudge you for thinking the inverse." He bowed his head for a moment, and then lifted it again. "So, as I have no standing to risk in your eyes, might I ask you for a referral?"

"For what?"

"For someone else who might act as my servant for the evening."

Mr. Increase thought for a moment: "When is the party?"

"On the Eve of the New Year."

Mr. Increase smiled. "No, what time does it begin on the Eve of the New Year?"

"Oh! Right. I believe I'm to arrive at the Crundwell Residence-" *and is it my imagination or did his smile get a little bit wider* "-at or around eight o'clock in the evening."

"And you would be providing my livery, correct?"

"I will…" Denton struggled to make sense of where this conversation was heading. "Is…does th…are you expressing amenability to the scheme, Mr. Increase?"

"Would you rather I didn't?"

Denton nearly fell out of his chair. "No! Not at all. It's only, just a moment ago, you see, you seemed less-"

"I've reconsidered." He stretched his hands out to his sides. The gesture bespoke reconsideration, somehow. "I'm not going to force someone else to bow and scrape at your heels. And besides, I'm quite taken with the idea of you owing me a favor."

"I must warn you, there's a hell of a queue."

They ran over the details, and made plans for Increase to visit Miss Carsis' for a fitting. He'd have garments spun by invisible hands, just as Denton did. Whether or not their carriage would be of a hollowed-out vegetable (or was it a fruit? Or something else entirely?) remained to be seen, but Denton would most certainly be airing his own grievances, should Miss Carsis force him to ride to the party in a foodstuff.

He said his farewells and returned to the evening. It wasn't until about halfway back to the Klump Regency that his mind set aside the task of imagining what a gourd would sound like rolling down the muddy streets and returned to the more pressing issue: why had Mr. Increase agreed to act as his servant, with such a minimum of pressing and cajoling? Or at *all*, even?

The man, after all, had clearly seen some shit. Yet as Denton was bidding him a fond farewell, the candlelight caught his face – but in hindsight Denton wasn't so sure about that. Memory lent Increase's face a glow all its own, luminance independent of any outside source. His face blazed with the molten fury of a long-dormant volcano reclaiming its natural right and sending forth its igneous discharge to devour the town so foolishly built along its ancient path to the sea.

Denton couldn't shake the feeling that, for all the shit he had seen, Mr. Increase had a mind to stir up some new shit, just so he could get a good look at it.

XXVII

"*MY DEAR COUNTRYMEN,*

I am a *Farmer*, settled, after a variety of fortunes, near the banks of the river *Delaware*, in the province of *Pennsylvania*."

Denton laughed quietly to himself as he read these words. A *Farmer*! He hoped that such a risible fib would go unnoticed, as it was the foundation upon which a more admirable edifice depended. But, all the same, he sort of hoped people might see through the lie, as it would mean they were paying closer attention than he sometimes suspected they actually were.

The copies of the *Pennsylvania Chronicle and Universal Advertiser* that had slowly trickled up to Massachusetts over the weeks following their publication had been read so often they were nearly unreadable. The print was fading, as though worn away by the friction of so many fire-lit eyes grinding along the pages, pages which were stained by damp and coffee and things which perhaps don't warrant further scrutiny, pages that had been folded and re-folded and torn and repaired and frayed and crumpled and in one case even singed around the top-left corner. These pages were all, if not well-loved, then certainly well-read.

And, Denton had to admit, they were well-written as well. Perhaps a bit too learned to be coming from a true *Farmer*, but it was easy to lose sight of the pretense once one had gotten caught up in the content. That content was, in its broadest sense, an airing of colonial grievances (*everybody is doing it*, Denton thought humorlessly) against the English, and a call for unity amongst the disparate colonies. If none of the ideas contained within the so-called Letters from a Farmer in Pennsylvania were particularly unique or novel, they had never been expressed in such a passionate and accessible fashion.

Their nomenclature was apt: they were a series of polemics in epistolary form, letters written by a man who identified himself only as a farmer who located himself in Pennsylvania. He was articulate and thoughtful, this farmer, but he had the low-class bonafides to back up his call to rebellion. Never mind the fact that, as Denton came to suspect more and more as the next week's letter found its way into his hands, they were written by John Dickinson, a slaveholding lawyer literally born on a plantation that he would come to inherit (while increasing his landholdings in the process), who knew as much about being a farmer as a coachman knows about being a horse. Denton had met Dickinson in Pennsylvania, where the latter practiced law. He hadn't worked with him, but knew a number of people who had; there were very few harsh words said about the man.

But still, the degree to which the Letters were on everyone's lips in the closing weeks of 1767 rankled Denton. He wasn't an excessively proud man – he was, after all, well accustomed to lurking in the shadow of whoever was standing on the stage. And Dickinson was writing anonymously – it wasn't as though he was soaking up fame for his Letters.

I should have thought of this. That's all Denton could think about now. Since he moved to Massachusetts, he'd done less speaking and more writing in service of the revolution. So how had this not occurred to him? And for those few people who would have recognized his voice behind the Farmer, as he had recognized Dickinson's, wouldn't they have been impressed? Wouldn't they have been

(proud)

Not that that mattered. Not that that's why he was doing it. Because it didn't, and it wasn't. Denton was doing this for the Cause. That was all. That was it. The Cause.

But there was an 'it' he could have done from home, as Dickinson had from the comfort of his plantation…and there was the 'it' he was doing here, standing on the main thoroughfare of Fidget's Mill, six days from heading to a party at which all of the movers and shakers would be fulfilling their tautologically assigned roles. How, when faced with the prospect of becoming an active agent in the cause, had it not occurred to him to write a goddamned pamphlet?

Because being an active agent seemed more…

More. It seemed like it would be more difficult, and more important, and more impressive, and ultimately effect more change. And yet, the Letters were having a positively incendiary effect on the town, as Denton could only imagine they were having all over the colonies. In a bar, he overheard a great big barrel of a man struggling his way through Dickinson's third letter, the one in which the *Farmer* explicitly lays out the meaning of the letters, and drawing bawdy applause that was typically reserved for the anatomical exhibitions that happened behind red curtains at unconventional hours.

"The meaning of them," the barrel-man read, "is to convince the people of this colonies…of *these* colonies, that they are at these…this moment exposed to the most i…immin…iniminiment dangers; and to persuade them immediately, vigorously, and…un-amoniously, to exit-exERT themselves in the most firm, but most peace-able manner, for obtaining relief."

How these drunkards, who could barely lift their heads to avoid a mug sliding down the bar, hooted and hollered at these words!

Why on Earth am I bothering with these elaborate subterfuges and deceptions? He had been thinking of the popular will as a stubborn mule, needing to be driven along at the end of a whip. But here and now, it was more like the Good Ship Brisby with the sails out, waiting for a gentle breeze to show it the way.

No matter. Leave the barroom class to Dickinson. Denton would focus on shaping the minds that truly mattered: those of the higher sorts. If change must come to Fidget's Mill – and it must, for the good of the colonies – it would have to start at the top. The people could be positively beside themselves clamoring for non-importation, but unless the three power-player families decided to adopt it, nothing was going to happen. Even if every single citizen picked up sticks and left, the Crundwells and Lowestofts could call in slaves to run the docks. They had the money and the reach, Denton had to imagine.

He took a pause to ruminate on how quickly he was becoming like *them*. The higher sorts. Had he honestly just thought such dismissive things about the lower…er, about the laboring sorts? They were, after all, closer to his actual station. He had nothing in common with moneyed types. And yet he was thinking like them already, in anticipation of being amongst them.

Or in self-defense, to make yourself feel better about Dickinson's triumph.

Alright, that one was definitely Miss Carsis.

No it wasn't.

Denton shook his head to clear it. Whether or not it was her, or his conscience pretending to be her, it had a point. Why was the success of the Letters bothering him so much? Why was he doing this? To create a better world for his children, right? Right?

Almost definitely. Sure. He'd figure it out later, either way.

Back to business: he had begun to formulate a plan of attack for the party, of what he would say and do. The higher sorts had rules of etiquette, about which he had been grilling Brisby, and recei-ving unsolicited advice from Bulstrode. First thing he planned to say, was "how do you do". BUT, and this was the tricky part, he would not necessarily wait around for a detailed answer. The question was largely rhetorical. Why one would use a probing question as a frothy greeting, he could not fathom. But there was no sense getting hung up on it, so he turned to the second thing he-

The party was six days away.

The 31st.

Six days away.

Thirty-one minus six…

Wait a second.

He looked around the streets, which come to think of it were not nearly as busy as they usually were. He saw a couple ducking into an alley a few yards away, bundled up and huddling close against the cold. A cat pawed its way across the street, silently slipping on a patch of ice and looking around frantically, possibly out of embarrassment.

It was Christmas. People were at home with their families. cozying up to the fire with loved ones. What were they thinking about? Was that barrel-man gathering his kids together and following up a reading from the Book of Luke with a passage from the Letters of Dickinson?

Almost certainly not.

Other people had lives outside of the Cause. They believed in the Cause, or in causes more broadly, because they thought their attainment would improve their own lives, and the lives of their children and their children's children yea unto the seventh generation. Denton had the Cause, and his family. Except he didn't have his family here in Fidget's Mill. He'd left them for the Cause. For now. But this 'now' seemed to be quite prolonged. He believed in the Cause because it would improve the lives of *other* people's offspring, sure, but he hated that he had to be apart from his wife and children to make things happen. He missed the way Lawrence and Annabelle's smiles stretched to their ears, just like their mother's. He missed his wife's laugh, the one she gave when she found something *really* funny, that sounded like a trumpet trying to breathe. He missed the feel of his children trying in vain to hug him around the knees.

He missed them.

What would he be doing right now, if he were born in another place, at another time? Was he truly committed to the principles of liberty and political self-determination, and if not, what on Earth was he doing right now? Deferring happiness, that was for damn sure.

Are those convenient and readily accessible designs with which to fill the rumbling emptiness of your life?

Denton shook his head. *My life is neither rumbling nor empty, Miss Carsis.*

A passerby nodded to him and wished him a Happy Christmas. Denton started to follow him like a lonely lemming hoping *someone* would come along and show him the way to the nearest cliff. The passer-by took two glances over his shoulder and became a runner-away.

Alone in the street again, on Christmas day. What were Peggy and the kids doing? Having fun, he hoped. Denton hunched his shoulders, shrugging his coat up towards his ears.

One thing kept gnawing away at him: if was willing to leave his family for the Cause, and the Cause should fail…

…how could he face going back to his family?

XXVIII

THE LIGHT BILIOUS OF THE MOON CROOKED FULL crashes through the branches heaving in the wind numbing the pain splintering brought on those shards luminous bloody bruised from the instants terminal of their journey lonesome through nullity cosmic.

Lying on his back flat he doesn't feel the grass sharp prodding insistently into the neck bare between the collar of his jacket floral cream gold and his hairline cropped tight but he somehow knows how it would feel (sharp) if he could feel it.

Sitting upright he levers his elbows back to support his weight heavy unfamiliar and cracks his neck stiff as he takes in his surroundings strange haunted evil but somehow all the same perhaps he has knowledge dread of this place strange haunte-

A snap dry in the thicket foul. Not the wind heedless of its passage rambling but a foot heavy clawed hoof cloven talon gnarled forever round the throat swollen with blood waiting patiently to be drawn forth and made black by the blush lunar, the satellite laughing keeping tabs from a remove cold.

How long has he been here he wonders seeing the imprint matted on the ground stretching erasing his shadow sodden from the Earth. He looks towards the source of the sound so like a clap of insanity driving a mind teetering on the brink abysmal over down into nullity vitrified brittle broken.

Standing at the edge jagged of the clearing hallowed, a pair of eyes like absence obscure stare out from a face sallow wan lifeless his. *He looms under the canopy yawing of the tree ash and watches silently himself lying chilled confused distraught in the quivering redoubt defoliated.*

"You are having a nightmare," the Diredenton says.

"I suspected as much," replies Denton.

Denton swings one knee under his torso and heaves himself to his feet. He brushes the grass-stains off of his lovely jacket, which he purchased specifically for the party on New Year's Eve. This being a nightmare, he fully expects that no amount of scrubbing would get those pesky stains out.

He looks to the Diredenton for further direction. This nightmare is far too vivid to be purely for shits and giggles. Diredenton is going to deliver him a warning somber cryptic useless-until-its-meaning-becomes-clear-in-hindsight, or maybe just point to a carving on a tree and tell him to "BEWARE", or maybe forgo the pointing and warning and settle for being generally unnerving.

Behind Diredenton, Denton spots movement of some sort. The trees themselves seem to be leaning hard to the right, as though they all in unison dropped their wallets. The moonlight, diaphanous though it is, fails to provide sufficient illumination to confirm or deny Denton's initial impression. Though at a second glance, it doesn't look as though the trees are bending…it looked like the trees are being bent. By something…

Denton is hardly a zoologist, so he could not speak with any great authority on the boundary between an animal, a creature and a monster. But to his untrained eye, this is a monster. It's glossy black, like the jungle jaguars of which Denton has read. But this is no jaguar – it looks like it must be…is that its leg? It bends and lumbers like a cow leg, but its size is less bovine and more barn.

He sees the leg – if that's what it is – come crashing down to the ground. The trees whip back to vertical, quivering in its slipstream. But it makes no noise, and he feels no tremors. This is the most unnerving part of it all for Denton – the hideous, titanic monster makes absolutely no noise, and seems not to touch the ground at all.

"Come," Diredenton wheezes.

"Don't tell me what to do," Denton announces at a normal speaking volume. He'd intended to think it, but as this entire scenario was something he was thinking, he conceded it made a certain kind of sense that he said his thoughts out loud.

"-out loud."

"What?" Diredenton turns around languidly.

"Oh, nothing."

"That's alright, then. Off we go."

They brave their way through the woods, although there's a bare minimum of braving required, as the press of leafless, lifeless wood parts before them.

And, as one might anticipate in a nightmare, seals itself behind them.

Deeper and deeper they go. Probably. Seems a reasonable guess, anyway. There are no markers to gauge their progress. It's just that it would hardly be a very good nightmare if they were traipsing their way out of the spooky forest, would it?

After about an hour, he realizes this latter consideration might be worth entertaining. Because, to be perfectly frank, this isn't a very good nightmare at all. It was creepy enough to begin with, but now he's just leading himself through a grove which, to give credit where it's due, is sufficiently grim to raise the hair on the back of one's neck. The monster was a great touch as well. But now they're just wandering, seemingly aimlessly. Sometimes an owl says 'hoot' a few times, but his or her little owl heart is clearly not in it.

"Excuse me!" Denton calls to Diredenton.

His doppelgänger-cum-counselor stops and turns around. "What?"

"I think I'm going to wake up now."

Diredenton's shoulders droop. "How come?"

"Well, there's just not a whole lot happening here."

"I haven't gotten to show you the rest of the forest yet!"

Denton ponders this for a moment. "Is your tour pursuant to telling me that I'm somehow missing the forest for the trees?"

"…yes."

"I don't believe you."

"I lied. Sorry."

"Was there to be any purpose in showing me the entirety of this forest?"

Diredenton puts his hand on his hips. "Hmm…well, as a for instance, I've always considered myself an amateur ornithologist."

"No I don't."

"I didn't say you did."

"But you're a figment of my imagination. This is all taking place inside my head."

"Well, gosh, alright, but that doesn't mean all of you likes the same things that you do. It's not all about you. Because, as I was saying, amateur ornithologist, that's me. And I've always been hoping to find the bird that sometimes says 'hoot'. I was rather hoping you might help me."

"…so is the fact that I find your searching for a single bird pointless meant to highlight the futility and absurdity of my obsessive pursuit of my Cause?"

"…"

"Or perhaps not?"

"I'm going to be perfectly honest with you, I hadn't considered it. I guess I expected you to at least feign interest in my hobbies."

Denton shrugs. "Well, I'm going to wake up now."

"Suit yourself."

"I will, thank you."

"Alright."

"Bye-bye."

"So long."

Denton wakes up and upon waking discovered his nightmare waiting for him.

The Other's Familiar was in the room with him. He knew it because it wanted him to know it. Presumably, he knew *that* because it wanted him to know that he knew it because it wanted him to know it. And so on. The balance of information was very much in this shadowy figure's favor, that much was clear.

He tried to open his mouth to ask it a question, but found he was once again unable to move. He was on his back, arms flailed above his head like a big letter Y. His eyes were locked on the ceiling, and for this he was grateful.

It was in the corner. It *was* the corner.

What was it doing there? Was it watching him again? It certainly felt like it was paying attention to him. His chest was tight, as though the Familiar were reaching in through his sternum and playing his lungs like a bagpipe. Which, speaking of, drew his mind to the infernal buzzing sound that was filling the room. Not just the room – his entire skull. It seemed to be pouring out of his ears, bouncing around the modest accommodations, making disapproving tut tut noises of its own, and diving back down his aural cavity with nothing to show for its travels but the thin gloss of misery with which all hotel furnishings have been varnished since the dawn of hospitality.

The din grew and rose and built to a shattering climax…and then stopped, all at once.

The beast spoke, its voice rending the smothering pall of silence.

"Himself made Herself sick," it said. It didn't roar or bellow, it simply *said*, in tones of silky rationality, all slightly softer than the average man's indoor voice. "Herself, and the Babyself. Myself should be nothing if not approving, for Myself is a Familiarself. And

Familiarselves are beholden to their Consortselves. And yet...to poison Herself?"

What? Denton thought, as loudly and unidirectionally as he could. He'd have preferred a normal conversation, but his jaw remained as paralyzed as the rest of him.

Fortunately, or perhaps unfortunately, the beast heard him and drew closer. The Familiar seemed to suck the air in the room towards itself, but Denton didn't hear it breathing. Perhaps it just liked the idea of literally taking people's breath away.

He could move his eyes, he found, but he nonetheless kept them rigidly fixed on a minor divot in the ceiling above his bed. At the bottom of his peripheral vision, a shade threw itself over the room, an obscurity of unfathomable immensity that somehow filled only a portion of Denton's quite fathomably sized room.

"Himself. Yourself knows Himself?"

I don't think so. Sweat pooled on his forehead, despite the frigid Massachusetts winter crawling in through his window. He willed the droplets to trickle into his eyes and blind him for a while.

The creature groaned, an inhuman noise so packed with strange and specific emotions, Denton had no way of interpreting its purpose. "Neither does Himself know Yourself. But Himself is soon to be upset with Yourself."

You are...Himself's Familiar?

"In a manner of speaking, Myself supposes so. But Myself finds Myself in frequent disagreement with Himself. Yourself isn't in want of a Familiarself, is Yourself? Myself senses the necessaries in you. Desperation. Ambition. Flopsweat."

Do you mean me harm?

"...no. What makes Yourself think Myself does?"

You poisoned Missy! Attempted to kill her as she was with child!

"Oh. This was at the behest of Himself, you must understand. Myself opposed the measure strenuously, and indeed, it continues to rest heavily upon Myself. Myself means no living Creatureself harm."

Ah! That's just what you would say if you meant me harm!

"...Uh."

If Denton wasn't very much mistaken, he heard disappointment in that 'uh'. And who knew what this monster could be capable of, if overly disappointed! A bead of sweat slid down the side of his forehead, coming to rest in his hair. That could have gone into his eye! Waste! *Why have you come here?*

"To Yourself's universe? Well, I often won-"

No, sorry, why have you come to my room in the Klump Regency?

"Ah. Because Yourself is soon to run afoul of Himself, should current trajectories want of deviation. Myself thought a friendly warning would be the civil thing to do. Myself wishes to see no harm come to any living Thingself. Enough harm has already transpired, for no purpose greater than the acquisition of impossibly ephemeral control of an impossibly insignificant speck of land on an impossibly small world." The shape sighed, and grew even loomier than it was before. "You might tell your friendselves that demonselves can be just as civil as the next entityself, if it comes up in conversation."

Denton struggled to match the casual off-handedness of the Familiar's speech with the howling terror that hung around it like an aura. *I'll certainly do that.*

"Myself would so very much appreciate it."

Consider it done.

"Thank yourself!"

The air came whooshing back over Denton, and his muscles all got back in touch with his brain. The Dread Familiar had left, but always one to air on the side of caution, Denton kept his eyes locked on that same divot in the ceiling until the sun was well over the horizon.

On the plus side, he got a uselessly cryptic warning out of the evening after all.

XXIX

DESPITE HAVING THE LACES OF DENTON'S BOOTS in his beak, No-Good Bulstrode's voice came out with perfect, unobstructed clarity: "What a curious little bodger. This fascination with 'self' this and 'self' that? Curious."

Denton watched Bulstrode lacing up his boots. He had offered to do it himself, but it was very important to both Bulstrode and Miss Carsis that he begin slipping into his aristocratic role as soon as possible. Mr. Increase wasn't about to dress him, and he certainly wasn't about to ask, but Bulstrode seemed downright eager to rise to the task. "Not to be overly pedantic," Denton drawled in his toniest tone, "but its fascination was more of a 'thisself' and 'thatself' bent."

Bulstrode clucked appreciatively. "Very good, sir! You're a natural!" This he said in a facetiously posh voice, which redoubled his naturally posh voice and rendered him nearly incomprehensible. It came out sounding like *Vuhruhguhsaaaah*, making it the work of a few seconds for Denton to translate those noises into English.

Miss Carsis came up behind Denton with his cream and gold jacket. He couldn't help but look at it with a twinge of regret for the grass stains he was never able to get out of it. Of course, that had been a dream – but the feelings lingered. "Arms," she ordered, and Denton obliged by thrusting his arms backwards. She helped him into the coat. "You haven't run afoul of any Himselves lately, have you?"

Denton shook his head while shimmying, um, himself into the starchy, creaking sleeves. It was a feat of coordination the likes of which he had never before attempted. "I don't think so. I'm sure I'd have noticed. Besides, Hims…the Familiar averred that the running afoul was to occur if I were to continue on my current trajectory."

"You must remain ceaselessly vigilant at the party tonight, then. It's very likely that this vile man will be at there, given his necessary proximity to the likes of Millicent Ditteridge, and so there is where you two shall clash."

With the coat resting heavily on his shoulders, he sighed and began the journey of a hundred buttons once again, this time starting from the bottom. "What makes you say that? I'm planning on being as agreeable as can be."

"Well, don't."

"Okay."

Bulstrode pulled the final lace of Denton's boots taut, and turned his beady little eyes upwards. "We simply must catch this 'Himself' tit out, you see. Fates in the balance, stakes never higher, that sort of thing. No sense fretting about it, just keep that turning over in the old coconut. See?"

"Right, I understand that the stakes are high. Which is why I was planning on being just as nice as can be."

Miss Carsis slid around Denton, starting to latch his buttons from the top and working downwards. "The Vile Familiar warned that you would run afoul of this man."

"Didn't seem *that* vile," Denton mumbled. Upon reflection, the creature had been downright friendly, just in a spooky way.

"So," Miss Carsis ignored him, "we need you to do that, to run afoul of him and draw the so-called Himself out into the light, the light being of course metaphorical."

Denton's brow was knit in concentration, trying to see around the Witch's nimble fingers and monitor his own upward progress on the stud clasping. "But we don't know who Himself is, remember?"

"Sooo," she replied as though it were the most reasonable thing in the world, "you'll just need to run afoul of most all of the men there."

Denton stopped buttoning. Miss Carsis didn't. "I can't do that." Miss Carsis didn't stop buttoning, apparently disbelieving him. "I'm attending this ball so that I might enter the good graces of the higher sorts, and consequently URK."

He yanked his foot backwards. Bulstrode looked up at him with his best *oh sorry is that your toe I just pecked as hard as I could?* face. Miss Carsis yanked Denton forwards again, fastening the final knob of his coat. "Minor transgressions will suffice. I have no intention of squandering you as a spy in those higher climes of society."

"You mean to use me as bait?"

She pressed out a crease in Denton's right shoulder, smiling maternally as she did. "Precisely. I have confidence that you will find the delicate passage between excessively affable and overly confrontational."

"Um, why?"

Her smile faltered, ever so slightly. "Because I have to." Now it didn't falter – it was withdrawn. "And so do you."

"Gulp," Denton pronounced.

Miss Carsis and No-Good Bulstrode trailed Denton outside to the carriage. It was a covered black behemoth with ornate carvings on the side, a conveyance from which men of Denton's true station instinctively diverted their eyes, lest they meet the haughty gaze of the leisure class and feel compelled to consider their own lowly existence.

"What are you doing?" Mr. Increase asked him from the front of the coach. He was delicately stroking one of the one two count 'em TWO jet-black horses that would be carting Denton to the party. Denton could hardly believe the excess being deployed for his benefit.

"What do you mean?"

"Why're you staring at the ground?"

"Was I?"

"You still are."

Denton looked up to the carriage and over to Mr. Increase in one jerky, angular motion. "Ah. So I was."

Bulstrode turkeyed his way over to Increase. "Simply splendid stallions we've secured for you, Mr. Increase. Do be a gentlemen about them, won't you?"

Increase, decked out in a gaudy livery designed by Bulstrode and supplied by Miss Carsis, nodded a perfunctory nod of ever-decreasing depth as he climbed up onto the coachman's perch. "Can't believe you felt you had to tell me…"

"Don't take it personally, chappie."

It made sense that Mr. Increase and Bulstrode knew each other, yet watching them interact was still inexplicably strange for Denton, not least because they didn't seem to get on at all. "Are they not fond of each other?" he asked Miss Carsis.

She stared back at him flatly. "Please tell me you'll be bringing a more perceptive eye to bear this evening."

Denton felt he deserved that, and so waved goodbye to his magical benefactors and bundled himself up into the coach. Mr. Increase snapped the bridle up (and how must he have felt, Denton could only wonder, to be the one holding it?) and they began the bumpy ride to the Crundwell residence.

Jostling down the uneven streets, Denton took this time for a bit of navel-gazing. He couldn't help but feel his life was becoming more and more like this ride; he was being driven towards an unfamiliar destination, spending the journey being jostled by forces and facts he could neither see nor understand. He could merely guess what was happening outside the narrow confines of his perspective based upon how drastically he was being hurled about.

...should current trajectories want of deviation, that's what his midnight visitor had said. And yet, it seemed that by delivering this warning, the damn monster had ensured said trajectories would be left wanting after all. Had Denton not been warned of running afoul, he'd have been his good old likeable self, and no harm nor afoul would have befallen anyone.

Instead, it came and issued its dumbass warning, and now the afouling was going to happen. Scratch that – Denton was going to have to *make* it happen. Despite his natural love and gift for polemic, he exerted heroic efforts to steer every casual conversation he'd ever had into safe harbors. The slightest chop in the dialectic waters occasioned only two responses: all hands on deck for safeward steering, or else the call to abandon the chit-chat ship. Never once had he gone down with his dinghy as a good captain should; but now that seemed to be precisely what was required of him. Not just once, but over and over again, with as many men as he could manage.

His stomach went runny, and did backflips.

Attempting to flex his increasingly overworked optimism muscle, he considered the fact that, if he was always putting so much effort into *not* scuppering, perhaps it would be a simple matter of not doing that anymore?

Two problems with that, of course. First, he had no idea just how ugly things would get if he let his natural dispositions for argumentation run amok. He'd need to retain some degree of control – finding that delicate passage would be impossible without control.

The carriage bucked and his head *thwacked* against the window, just to remind him that control was in short supply around these parts.

Alright, fair enough. That was his second problem. He needed to keep a tight enough grasp on things that he'd be a *persona* at least tolerably *grata* amongst the heavies of Fidget's Mill. Miss Carsis had her phantom battles for the fate of all humanity to wage, whatever. That was her thing and he was happy (and obligated) to help her out with it, given all she'd done for him. But he had his own pressing objectives to see to. Non-importation, insignificant though it might look in the face of occult eschatology, wasn't about to accept itself. And the Cause remained foremost in Denton's mind, no matter what else came knock knock *thwack THWACKING* against the window with each shudder of the carriage on the uneven dirt road.

He decided after careful consideration that leaning his head wistfully on the glass was not the right call for a trip of this sort (even if it was totally on-point, emotionally), and scooted to the center of the bench. The coach still rocked and rolled, but now he had the room to be hurled about in relative comfort.

XXX

THE RIDE SMOOTHED OUT SO SUDDENLY THAT IT took Denton about a minute to realize what had happened. Fidget's Mill didn't have *roads* so much as it had well-trodden grooves in the Earth that everyone agreed should be left clear of construction. And after spending a half hour feeling like a die being juggled in the hands of Fate, who was probably saying something like "big money big money" or "Daddy needs a new epochal disruption of the prevailing state of affairs", he could hardly process the relief of being cast.

Certainly, it wasn't until much later that he thought to wonder how he came up, though circumstances would give him plenty of helpful hints to work that out for himself.

The Crundwells had commissioned a team of independent surveyors to establish, to an obnoxiously precise degree, the exact boundaries of their property. Once they had their perimeter, they split the world into two categories: inside and outside. Everything outside could go screw; everything inside could also go screw, except the latter category could screw pursuant to a program of radical improvements.

On a knife's edge, the misery of Fidget's Mill stopped and presto chango the majesty of the Crundwell property began. The road smoothed out, the grass grew greener, the trees yawned taller. Even now, in the dead of winter, with a thick blanket of snow draped over the world, the differences were stark. The Crundwells (or more accurately, their servants) had cleared the road of snow, right up to (but not past) the edge of their holdings. On either side of the perfectly-cut path, the virgin snow lay in sensuous repose, beckoning Denton to come hither and tromp around like a Labrador. The Crundwells had no fence, and no human (no human he'd want to meet, anyway) could look at such immaculate snow and not think very seriously about casting aside their responsibilities for a moment, just a moment, in favor of christening the crisp seasonal sheet with their unworthy boot.

So how the hell had they managed to keep troublemakers off of their property? Adults could be browbeaten, but cheeky children in the dead of night would find "leave your mark on the Crundwell snow" too good a dare to pass up. Yet pass it up they all had, clearly.

Denton shivered. *From the cold*, he assured himself, but the sweat in his pits told a different and altogether stinkier story. How strange it was, that of all the tales he had heard of Crundwell influence in and control of the town, the one that should strike the most visceral fear into his heart was told by a dove-white quilt of cozy snowfall, winking slyly in the light of the setting sun, as if it were letting him in on a naughty joke with a wicked punchline.

Through an alley of skeletal trees, covering their shame with the winter, the Crundwell mansion spread against the punchy sunset burning up slate-grey daylight, exposing its self-satisfaction like a hirsute man of high breeding and low inhibitions in a bathhouse, greeting Denton as it did every other supplicant come to suckle on its grudging teat: all at once.

This was a mansion that positively embodied contempt, but an all-encompassing contempt made possible by a delusional belief in one's own metaphysical supremacy over the entire human race. It was so shatteringly conceited, one really had no choice but to stand back and admire it.

This was a mansion that, when one stood back to admire it, told you to fuck yourself.

Mr. Increase led the carriage along the wan artery to its terminus, a roundabout that cowered in the shadow of the towering manor, as though fearful of venturing any closer to the forbidding oversize double-doors. In the center of the circular intersection stood a bizarre, deformed tree. It rose to an unconscionable height, nearly three stories from the look of it, on a smooth shaft devoid of branches. At the top, large green fronds flopped limply, clearly not impressed by what they saw from such an elevated perspective.

Denton stepped daintily out of the coach, admiring the tree all the while. He turned to Mr. Increase, something to the effect of "wow would you look at that" on his chapped lips, but stopped when he saw his fake-servant's face. He was looking up at the tree with something just short of horror, but a ways beyond disgust.

"Wow, wou- what's wrong?"

Increase shook his head. "That's a palm tree."

"Yes it is." Denton looked back up at the fronds. Palm fronds, sure, he'd read about those. He'd read about them as being suited to warmer climes…He looked back to Mr. Increase. "Seems a bit out of season for it, I might have thought."

"These grow in temperate places. I saw them in Caribbean. One shouldn't be able to grow here."

"They're summer trees, are they?"

Increase shot Denton a look of cosmic reproach. "They shouldn't be able to grow here *ever. Especially* not in winter."

Denton recoiled slightly from that look. He couldn't quite understand why an out-of-place tree should upset Increase, but all the same he absolutely could. He thought about that pristine snow, this displaced tree...it was as though the Crundwells were capable of reshaping not just the town of Fidget's Mill to suit their purposes, but nature itself. Power and control of a sort Denton could hardly fathom; these were just some of the perks of living in a small, insular community, if you're hysterically wealthy and well connected.

And didn't power of this sort have the whiff of the supernatural about it? Could Buddy be "Himself"? It didn't seem likely, given the evident depth of feeling he had for Missy. Still, if a turkey can talk, all things are possible.

The crunch of packed snow underfoot snapped Denton and Increase back to reality. A black man in a suit was staring at them with wry amusement. Undoubtedly, he saw the ostensible master being cowed by his ostensible servant, but surprisingly enough Denton didn't fear transmission of this moment to unfriendly ears. He wondered if the Crundwells were even accessible to their "help", unless the latter were fully engaged in their ministrations to the former.

Nonetheless, Denton and Mr. Increase both struggled into roles to which they were both ill-suited.

"Ay," Denton decreed as imperiously as he could, "take the carriage around to the carriage house, or the place where carriages are stored when not in use please, I demand you do this, thank you."

Mr. Increase nodded. It looked less like a supplicatory nod and more like someone doing what they imagined was a supplicatory nod based on books they'd read. "Yes, sir, your wish is my command."

"Okay. Thank you." Mr. Increase swung himself back up onto the bench. "Bye bye, see you inside!" Denton called after him. He turned to the Crundwell's servant. "That is my servant there."

The man nodded.

"What's your name?"

The man nodded.

"...do you speak English?"

The man paused, and raised this thumb and forefinger out in front of him, a teeny gap between them. "Little."

Denton's heart sank. This was a first generation slave. Not that that made it *worse*, necessarily – the institution was all a complete nightmare. But this guy grew up free across the sea somewhere, with a life and loves and wants and fears and dreams all his own. And now he was here, stuffed into a suit that was most definitely insufficient protection from the cold, forced to cater to the whims of some assholes whose language he didn't even understand.

And the worst part of it was that Denton couldn't really imagine any of the torments and indignities this man must be suffering on a daily basis with any greater specificity than that. He literally couldn't imagine. Some abolitionist.

The man turned and gestured for Denton to follow, and for a dread second he felt himself preparing to turn around and run, away from the Crundwells and Fidget's Mill, run through the untouched snow and leave a trail of footprints so others might follow...but of course they wouldn't, because unlike him, they'd have nowhere to go. Runaways carried a high reward on their head, and if caught, paid a high price all over.

He had no choice, yet again. That's what he told himself, at least, as he smothered the most fundamental impulses towards human decency with the lumpy cushion of pragmatism (the one that never seemed to soften emotional blows as it should), and followed the man into the mansion.

XXXI

THE MAN HAD VANISHED BEFORE DENTON HAD A chance to thank him. Denton, who suddenly struggled to think of himself as anything other than "Mr. Hedges," found himself alone in a stately atrium large enough to fit his entire room at the Klump

Regency, and some of his neighbor's as well. Garlands of pine clung to the banister of the second floor landing, and slithered along the double-wide wooden stairs so well polished they looked like a liquid ziggurat trickling down from the heavens, just daring the unworthy to go on and *try* it.

Gold-framed portraits claimed the majority of the wall space. Their placement was carefully organized so that all of their eyes were fixed on the front door, and more specifically on whatever dumb slob came staggering in from the cold. Or maybe Denton was just projecting that look of sneering disdain.

Or, then again, maybe he wasn't.

He didn't immediately recognize Buddy Jr.'s portrait, but instead had to reason his way to the recognition. *There's an unmemorably dapper fellow. Where have I seen one of those before? Ah, yes.* Identifying the rest of the family was the work of yet more deduction based on Brisby's half-drunken debriefings, devoid of identifying plaques as the portraits were.

The youngest daughter, Lucretia. Buddy Jr.'s older brother Sonny. Their mother Bunny. And Buddy himself. The gang was all there, looming over their guests, and looking none too pleased about it.

There were three Himselves of whom he would have to run afoul. And there would be more to come. This was not going to be a good night, this he knew for certain.

Light applause bounded through the halls, followed by the opening bars of an orchestral waltz. Denton had never been musically inclined, because he wasn't the least bit gifted with it. In his teenaged years, when most boys his age were out rousing rabbles, Denton decided that perhaps he might like to try picking up the violin. The problems started when he succeeded in picking it up; he insisted to anyone within earshot (a forever-dwindling category) that his instrument was possessed of some fatal flaw, and *that* was the reason it seemed capable of producing nothing but barnyard animal noises. After a few trying months, though, in which Denton witnessed firsthand just how fragile friendships can be, he conceded that the fault lay in the player. He put the violin down, and there was a great merriment *sans music* to mark the occasion.

This abortive expedition into a songful world - so different from the drab and dry republic of letters he came to occupy - had infected his natural appreciation for the art with an unshakable strain of acrimony, an aesthetic dysentery that converted the most numinous and beautiful of inputs into metaphysical flatulence.

As the waltz found its bouncing rhythm, so too did Denton's tummy, which begrumbled itself in effortless ¾ lockstep.

And yet. He began to float towards the source of the song, a gawping guppy caught in a net meant for bigger fish. He had always had a real soft spot for waltzes. Couldn't say why for certain; it wasn't as though he knew the first thing about dancing. It was just something about the playful buoyancy of that time signature, the sway of its shepherding breath, of the *bum-BUM-BUM bum-BUM-BUM* that somehow felt untethered from itself, in a way that a more traditional four-count of *BUM-bum-bum-bum BUM-bum-bum-bum* never quite did. It was as though he were a maple seed, shorn from the cradle of its issue and cast out into the-

OH FUCKING DARNIT.

It wasn't as though he knew the first thing about dancing.

Which was exactly what he would, as an apparent high-society oik, would be expected to do.

"Oh rats oh nuts oh, um, fuck," he reassured himself under his breath.

His hands began to sweat. He suddenly had a vision of himself, being made to dance with Lucretia Crundwell, extending his hand to her, her taking it, and his soggy glove making a moist little *squeesh* sound as she did so, like a spoon being plunged into a bucket full of porridge.

His hands began to sweat more. He stopped walking and flapped them at his sides, a poorly conceived attempt to help them air dry. Spotting the logistical inadequacies with this plan, he clutched the middle finger of his left hand between the thumb and forefinger of his

right glove and pulled.

"DENTON!"

"AAAH!" Denton replied. In his panic, he pulled at the middle finger itself. A dull throb settled into the knuckle, and he farted a little bit.

Heading straight for him, Brisby Houlihan looked as though he'd heard the funniest joke in the world about a half an hour ago, and was trying to keep his face exactly as it was until he could get to a mirror and see what he looked like when he was busting a gut. A massive toothy smile utterly devoid of humor or mirth, without even the "what, me worry?" grin of a naked skull.

It was, in short, the face of a sycophant in a room full of who's who. Denton physically withdrew from this quivering rictus. He'd not pegged Brisby as a brown-noser, and yet here he was in something approaching bootlicking blackface.

Denton amended his previous reply to "Aaah?"

Brisby clapped his hands and snapped his jaw shut at the same time. This was *not* a good look for the man. "Denton, my friend, you're late! BJ is eager to see you again, as is everyone else! But," he hit the 'B' hard, like a 'P', spitting as he did. Denton could smell whisky on his breath, though perhaps implying there was any breath that wasn't coming up whisky would be dishonest. He could smell breath on Brisby's whiskey.

It only then occurred to Denton that the poor Doctor was probably always drunk as a result of the compulsory nature of his time in the Mill. Here he was, at a party with the man who strongarmed him here, and the people over whom he was meant to be wielding this unwanted authority.

Brisby was a terribly silly man, but Denton felt even sillier for having missed the tangible sadness of the poor Doctor-cum-Commissioner.

"BUT," Brisby continued, "instead of seeing you *again*, as BJ is, they are eager to see you for the *first time*. Except," *exce*P*t, spittlespittle,* "for Missy, who will be seeing you again, as she has already seen you for the first time."

Denton untangled Brisby's mini-monologue from his own jolting realization. "What do you mean, that they are eager to see me?"

The good doctor laughed in Denton's face. Denton was reasonably sure he was getting second-hand tipsy. "We have told them all about you, of course!"

"...what, ah, what have you told them?"

"About you!"

"Of course. But what about me?"

"All!"

Denton shut his eyes and focused on the waltz. He'd graduated beyond butterflies in his stomach – they'd vacated to make room for a gaggle of those rolly-polly bugs, and he was quite certain they were all having a tumbling competition.

Bum-BUM-BUM bum-BUM-BUM bum-BUM-

"BUM alright," he finally said. "Brisby, do you ever worry that you drink too much? I'm slightly concerned on your behalf," he added, having seen the answer to that first question slide across Brisby's face like an ice-skater on a melting lake. "Um, but, I say that as your friend only of course. Um. I would like to meet them all as well, everyone of whom you have told everyth-"

"m'GOO," Brisby shouted as he whirled around and strode back towards the music.

Denton looked once over his shoulder, hoping to see Mr. Increase bringing up the rear. He desperately hoped it was standard practice for the...'servants' to tag right along with their...'employers'. He needed to have someone at his shoulder who *wasn't* utterly impressed with the show of wealth and privilege being flashed about every which way he looked. Because, as much as Denton absolutely hated to admit it, and as antithetical as it was to everything he believed about what constituted human worth and a good society and a responsible discharge of finances surplus to the requirements of a comfortable living...

...he *was* impressed.

-BUM bum-BUM-BUM bum-BUM-BUM bum-

XXXII

DENTON STEPPED INTO THE BALLROOM AND finally realized how in over his head he was.

Here they were. They being everyone. Everyone was here. All at once. The entire high-wire act that was Fidget's Mill's social ecosystem laid bare, to an extent that they themselves didn't seem to realize. Denton's eyes darted frantically around the room. Were they all looking at him? Most of them were. Some of them *definitely* were. A few might be looking *through* him. They were *all* looking at him. Everyone. All at once.

The Crundwells, the Lowestofts, the Ditteridges, making believe that they didn't all despise one another, performing for themselves and for each other, not a one of them suspending their disbelief in the slightest.

Well, alright…who was who? Denton knew precious little about each member of the families, only what Brisby, Miss Carsis and Mr. Increase told him, but he could certainly try his luck with uneducated guesses.

Best to start simply: he recognized the Crundwells easily enough. Buddy Jr. was dancing with a young woman Denton could safely assume was Fithian Lowestoft, the woman to whom he was expected to be wed for the sake of their respective families (he being Buddy Jr., not Denton). He felt that was a safe assumption because their embrace was tender, but BJ's eyes were tending to the side, fixed firmly on Millicent Ditteridge, upon whom Miss Carsis had performed the...procedure. How did Fithian not see that (the eye-tending, not the …procedure)? Too many questions. All at once.

The warmth on Missy's face faltered not a bit when the dancing couple turned, leaving Buddy Jr. with his back to his beloved, and Fithian with her piercing blue eyes towards her unknowing rival. The fact was, Fithian looked no more pleased about the pose of intimacy than Buddy Jr. did, and she looked at Millicent with a depth of unfeigned friendship. They weren't rivals, at least in the sense of fostering antipathy – they were friends. Denton was almost certain of this.

Standing behind Millicent was an older gentleman with a mushy jawline. Her father, Chip Ditteridge, most likely. It wasn't Buddy, and the father Lowestoft wouldn't be standing that close to another man's daughter. Not here, least of all – new money had to be especially sensitive to social proprieties. Chip glared at the back of his daughter's head, then up to Fithian, radiant as ever (Denton assumed). Mr. Ditteridge wasn't happy about this friendship. Why not? Questions questions, all at once.

Chip shook his head and weaved through the crowd to his wife. Except Denton knew it *couldn't* be his wife, unless his information was out of date. Doris Ditteridge and the rest of Chip's kids were still in England, awaiting the summons of their dear papa. And it wasn't Buddy Crundwell's wife Bunny, unless the artist of her portrait had been given rather radical creative license. So it was Opal Lowestoft, mother of the *nouveau riche* Lowestoft clan. Chip was leering quite aggressively, and Opal returned tolerant but dismissive smiles. This looked like something that happened a lot.

Not very far away, Cullender Lowestoft (for it had to be him) shook his head and walked towards his wife. The look on his face wasn't fury or jealousy – he looked as though a child had knocked something off of the table for the fifth time and he was dutifully inbound to pick it up again. He and his wife exchange a knowing, loving glance. Clearly, there was no jealousy here because they trusted each other implicitly. With genuine tact and amiability, Cullender placed an arm on Chip's shoulder and led him away from his wife. Were these two friends themselves? How were these people such good friends? Allatonceallatonce.

A woman – Bunny Crundwell, the artist had actually captured her quite well – approached Cullender and Chip with a fan in her hand. It was collapsed, so she clutched it like a baton. She and Cullender exchanged friendly words – Denton cast a quick glance towards Opal, who was watching her husband speaking with mother Crundwell and smiling, seeming to verify Denton's assessment that the Lowestofts were confident enough in each other to override any primal feelings of jealousy – and laughed at some joke that, judging by Chip's look of distant hurt, was a punchline only the two of them got. They were friends, perhaps old friends.

Then Chip started trying it on with Bunny. Cullender, still smiling but no longer laughing, made a clear effort to distract his friend with more talk. And Denton could see why: Bunny looked interested, in a way Opal hadn't.

And here he came, the man of the hour: Buddy Crundwell himself. His puffy face was beet-red, but he wasn't staring at Chip. No, his anger seemed directed at Cullender. He stepped between the object of his ire and his wife, which given their proximity escalated the situation from genial to uncomfortable in record time. It wasn't *awkward*, because awkward had no place in such a gorgeous ballroom (which, peripherally, Denton acknowledged that it was, mirrored and gilt and marbled monstrosity though it may have been) full of such wealthy people. But it was uncomfortable; Denton could feel that from across the room.

Buddy said something cross to Cullender, and the new-money patriarch who was at least ten years his junior shrugged and walked away. Bunny, he couldn't help but notice, started to follow. Buddy barked out a few syllables, and Bunny shook her head in familiar annoyance, said something back over her shoulder, and redirected towards her other son, Sonny, black sheep of the family. Sonny was Buddy Jr.'s older brother, and was doing *something* for a young man who must have been, by process of elimination, Tobin Lowestoft, the youngest of the Lowestoft children. It might have been a magic trick of some sort. Denton smiled wanly. What would Miss Carsis make of a bit of sloppy legerdemain like this, he wondered.

Bunny looked disapprovingly at Sonny. It *must* be a magic trick he was doing, then, because he couldn't imagine what else would warrant such a look of parental disappointment. Or maybe he was just a really shitty kid and that was how she always looked at him. Allatonce-

allatonceallatonce!

The last person unaccounted for was planted against the far wall. Lucretia Crundwell, youngest and least consistently named of the Crundwells, was watching Sonny, Tobin and her mother with a look Denton couldn't crack. It was melancholy, but it was also condescending, perhaps. Missy, who – egads, Denton had missed this - cut in on Fithian and was now dancing with Buddy Jr. (*What drama!*), gave Lucretia a sympathetic glance. Friends, perhaps? Just as she was friends with…

GAH. All at once! This was too much. Everywhere he looked, he found himself faced with the complexities of interpersonal relationship, on a seemingly *infinite* scale. He had hardly begun to account for how the presence of people like Brisby Houlihan, or the colonial governor Rumney Marsh (and didn't *those* two seem to be avoiding one another), or indeed himself might upset the dynamics here. Distressingly, Denton got the impression that none of them *would* upset the dynamics. People this well established would shift as the world shifted, and Denton would be swallowed up into their drama, but nothing would really change. Not *really*.

Denton had never been the most nuanced judge of people, if he was being honest (which would be a welcome change of pace). He struggled to read them. He had always known this about himself. And yet, the web of emotional entanglements before him could hardly wait to unravel itself. If this were a stage play, Denton would have written it off as lacking any hint of subtlety, as having too low an opinion of the audience's intelligence. These people were practically SCREAMING out their opinions of and relationships to one another.

So why on Earth didn't they act upon them? Was the mold of social propriety so constricting? How could they live this way?

What Denton felt went beyond anxiety. This was pure horror, a nightmare that made him pine for the halcyon nights of the not-so-Vile Familiar. These three families were living the way they felt they needed to in order to impress one another. That was all there was to their lives. It *was* a performance, played for an empty theater. It was an autoerotic roundabout where nobody ever got off. It had always been this way, he felt. He *knew*, somehow. Before the Lowestofts rose to this level, the Crundwells and the Ditteridges played out their dramas. Post-Lowestofts, the old dramas were modified to allow the new family to fold in and become assimilated. But the new dramas were of precisely the same intensity as the old ones. Nothing actually changed. Not *really*.

How did he know all of this? He just *did*. But how?

So many questions.

"It's almost time!" Brisby shouted.

Denton awoke from his reverie. "Huh?"

"The new year!" He handed Denton a drink and rushed back to the center of the room. Denton didn't want a drink, but everybody else had one, and now wasn't the time to stand out.

The new year. *Already?* Denton rubbed his head. How long had he been standing there, watching these courtly melodramas unfold?

He took a sip of his drink. It was alcoholic. That was as far as his mind was willing to venture from the more pressing issues at hand.

What an idiot, he said to himself. *Thought you would just come up here and get the Crundwells to accept non-importation. Write a few pamphlets? Organize a few gatherings? Then what?*

Cullender Lowestoft looked at the pocket watch dangling from his waist. He smiled a big friendly smile and raised his right arm. "Thirty-seconds left!"

Chip Ditteridge scoffed loudly. "Not by my watch! Only Twenty-six seconds left in this year of our Lord Seventeen Hundr-"

"You're both wrong!" Buddy Crundwell corrected helpfully. "There's a full thirty-one seconds left now!"

They bickered about this for a bit, but Denton couldn't spare the attention to listen.

Look at this. You don't understand people. There's some unspoken language they all speak, that everyone *speaks, except for you. How did you expect to sway them, to influence them all? Because make no mistake, me – you need all of them. And make no other mistake; it's not a simple matter of getting one family on board, and using them to leverage the other two. Inter-family strife is built into their incestuous little commonwealth. That sort of pressure would collapse on itself before it had a chance to push outwards.*

"Ten!" Chip shouted.

"Not yet," Cullender opined.

Buddy nearly said something, but held his tongue. Denton could see – even a man as unacquainted with nuance as Denton could see – that Buddy was torn between his natural love of correcting other people's mistakes, and a more recently developed aversion to agreeing with Cullender about anything.

"Nine!"

"Almost…"

"Eight!"

"Aah…"

"Seven!"

"Ten!"

"Six!"

"Nine!"

"Five!"

"Eight!"

"Ten!" Buddy joined in.

Everyone around the room was clearly excited to join in the countdown, any countdown. But rather than pick sides, even the sides of their own patriarch, they all abstained, and stood silently as the men of the houses screamed decreasing numbers at each other.

"Four!"

"Seven!"

"Nine!"

"Three!"

"Six!"

"Eight!"

Denton rubbed his temples, not entirely certain how he wound up here but cursing every decision he'd ever made in his life just to ensure he didn't miss out on something pivotal through selective cursing.

"Two!"

"Five!"

"Seven!"

Can I leave? I could just go, right?

What a coward that would make me. No. I have decided to give myself to the Cause. If I can serve it here-

Dickinson's Letters are doing a great deal already. I'm sure something else will come along soon enough. Hell, maybe I could go back to Boston and write it! I'd be much more useful elsewhere. This is so far beyond my abilities, the chances are high I would only make things worse by staying.

"One!"

"Four!"

"Six!"

I miss Peggy. I miss my family. As Denton thought this, Mr. Increase strode in from the side door.

"Ah," Denton shouted over the numerical din, "We can slip out after this, wouldn't you say?"

"Yes." Increase replied. His voice cracked, and he seemed unaccountably jittery. He snatched Denton's cup. "You didn't drink any of this, did you?"

"Happy new year!" Chip's celebratory squeal was met with scattered, uncomfortable applause.

"Three!"

"Five!"

"It's already the new year!"

"Just a sip," Denton replied. "Why…" and then Mr. Increase's jitters grew much more accountable. Denton whipped his eyes across the room. Everyone had been drinking the same drink. Only that wasn't right – only the higher sorts had glasses in their hands. The lower sorts, the 'help', stood in the corners and the shadows, as they were instructed to do. Perhaps they could have some water later, but the stiff drinks were not for them.

"Two!"

"Four!"

"Happy 1768 everyone."

"One!"

"Three!"

"Stop counting."

They were only for the higher sorts.

Denton wobbled uneasily, slapping a hand on Mr. Increase's forearm for stability. He looked up into a face that had clearly seen some shit. "What did you do?" Before Mr. Increase had a chance to answer, Denton rushed up to Brisby, who stood with the glass halfway to his face. "Stop drinking that right this instant!" he hissed.

"Why on Earth would I do that?" Brisby replied. "You really mustn't worry yourself over another man's drinki-"

"That batch is bad!" Denton snapped.

"Happy new year!" More hesitant applause.

"Two!"

"Buddy."

"ONE."

"Okay."

"Happy new year!"

Finally, with all of the counts in approximate agreement, the room burst into applause, and the higher sorts all took a drink.

As if to declare its own modest independence in timekeeping, a heavy clock chimed from deep within the house, offering the final word on 1767. Denton contributed the first word of 1768, to Mr. Increase. It was "What", followed by "Have", "You," and "Done".

So much for the old drama: just about everything changed after that.

Part Two:

By An Ocean Of A Thousand Leagues

1768

A Middling Sort

I

IN THE BEGINNING GOD CREATED THE HEAVEN and the Earth. And the Earth was without form, and void; and darkness was upon the face of the deep. And the Spirit of God moved upon the face of the waters. And God said, Let there be light: and there was light. And God saw the light, and said Whoops: and God brushed it under the sofa with His foot.

That's not what happened, but it may as well have been. The Word that breathes life into the universe, the Word that will be the last sigh of the dying cosmos, the Word on the lips of every newborn babe…all one Word: Whoops.

The Eternal Whoops - written in blazing fire across the heavens, hewn into the towering pillars of the Earth, darkening the loneliest black of the sea - is the only true certainty in life. Death and taxes can both be deferred or altogether dodged, if one knows whom to talk to and in what tone of voice. But Whoopsie Daisy, Whoopsie Doodle, Whoopsie Does It; whatever one calls it, the fact of it remains the same.

The fact, written into every atom of the universe, is as follows: Nothing makes any sense, ever. Things just happen.

How to grapple with this tragic fact? The first stage is to become one with the universe, by saying "Whoops" as loudly as possible.

The second stage is to just make something up and say "That's not what happened, but it may as well have been".

To master to the first stage is to be Human. To master the second is to be Historian.

That's not to say all competing histories are equally valid. Things happen; there is an objective reality to what did and did not occur, and the general order in which they did so. But the chains of causation linking moments in time are so complex, so tangled and tightly wound, that attempts to unweave them and lay them out are an exquisite brand of madness.

Necessary and important, but madness all the same.

Here is what can be said with certainty, about the universe: there are long stretches when nothing seems to happen, and a hypothetical observer is left floating about, listening to the Interstellar Whoopsies of galaxies colliding and great big rocks crashing into life-bearing planets.

But then, sometimes, things happen. Little teeny tiny things, sure, but a whole lot of them.

Taking Earth as a for instance, specifically from an anthropocentric perspective, existence is nothing but a string of teeny tiny things that happen, or don't. A falling coconut *doesn't* crack the skull of person who was 'meant' to live for another forty years. A bacterial infection *does* kill the only cow of a family who depended on the animal to survive, and so they all perished, because they were 'meant' to do so. A male bird of paradise *doesn't* deploy its mating dance until a particular female is in the vicinity, so that they will copulate and begin a feathered dynasty that will culminate in a bird that will take a big shit on an orangutan's head, because this too was 'meant' to happen.

Why were these things 'meant' to happen? What would happen if they didn't happen? Does it even make sense to speak of such events in terms of meaning? Dumb questions, except for that last one, to which the answer is no.

There was no reason, it all just had to happen. Just because. None of it made any sense, ever. Things happened, or they didn't, and sometimes those things were caused by nature, and sometimes by people, but in the end it didn't make a difference, because animals with sufficiently developed prefrontal cortices would just make up reasons and explanations after the fact. The only way in which these explanations were reliable was in their having no explanatory power in the least.

But they may as well have.

This was, in short, the new perspective Denton Hedges had on the great arc of history. He only wished he'd attained this perspective about six months ago.

II

FOR A NUMBER OF REASONS THAT DENTON found highly, well, reasonable, he decided it was improbable that he should still be alive. It was, in a strange way, discouraging.

Perhaps he would never quite get over the fact that his first reaction, upon realizing Mr. Increase had poisoned the punch, was relief. *Phew*, he had thought without meaning to, *now I won't have to worry about not being able to dance!*

That had immediately troubled him, but fortunately new problems suggested themselves in a generous attempt to distract him from his own issues. First and foremost: he had warned Brisby off from drinking the tainted beverage. It had been an impulsive decision, and while the ethicist in Denton was pleased with that reaction, the pragmatist despaired. Denton had essentially implicated himself, by revealing foreknowledge of the scheme. Who would believe him, that his foreknowledge had come only moments before theirs, which would presumably come as their family members began collapsing? Who would even listen?

Brisby simply stared at Denton for a long moment, as the revelry continued around him. He turned to Mr. Increase, amiably confused, willing to misread the situation to keep things positive.

"Are you trying to tell me I've been drinking too much, my friend?" Brisby waved his head from side to side in a comic pantomime of drunkenness, which given his *actual* drunkenness became more of a pitiable distillation of unhappy truths.

"I'm telling you that everyone has," Denton mumbled. There was no getting out of this, but he could at least try to keep things calm until he could make his escape. "Especially you. Please don't drink any more. And tell Buddy Jr. and Fithian and Missy not to, either," he added, despite himself.

The world was about to turn upside down, and here he was, shuffling his feet and mumbling in a room full of laughing corpses. Denton had no idea what to expect from Mr. Increase's…whatever he did, but he suspected the other shoe would drop within the hour. He had to get the hell out of here…he just didn't know how.

Fighting his way to some kind of objectivity, it made a certain sort of sense that Mr. Increase would want to kill the entire upper class. It was certainly not the way Denton would do things, but there was a perverse sense of 'yes, well, I can see why one in his situation might be so inclined'. If only he'd had the decency to do it in a way that wouldn't incriminate Denton by association.

Mr. Increase, for his part, looked even more terrified than Denton did. "We really ought to go now," he suggested.

"Do you think so?" Denton pondered the most graceful course of exit, and then remembered that he had well and truly fucked himself by trying to save Brisby. And there was no grace in that.

So they turned and ran to the side-door, the door from which Increase had emerged to tell Denton of the stick he'd shoved into the spokes of Fidget's Mill.

They sprinted through the kitchen, down dimly lit halls that stank of rot and decay. He didn't see a single white face as they ran. This was the backstage of the noble play that was life for the higher sorts. Like any glimpse behind the curtain, it instantly shattered the delicate illusion it worked so hard to keep shiny and bright.

They tumbled through the door to the outside, and ran towards the stables where Increase had locked up the horse.

They stopped at the gate, because it was locked and the groom had the key.

"Oh, fuck me," Denton said by way of a preamble, "you locked the carriage up?" He shot a look back at the house over his shoulder. Nobody was coming, yet. Not that they would. Not yet, anyway. Until people started to get sick, they would just think that dash from the room was some eccentricity of the curious new slave doctor.

Increase shook the heavy padlock frantically. "I had other things on my mind!"

From the ballroom, somebody screamed.

"This seems a fundamental concern in a plan like that! The getaway! Also, why did you do that?"

"I had to!"

"Also, for a second time, *what* did you do?

A shout came barging through the door behind them. Denton could only imagine the mouth it came from wouldn't be far behind, along with the rest of the body. Especially the fists. "We must fly!"

Denton grabbed Increase's hand and dragged him back around the side of the stables. He looked around frantically for an escape route, and then he saw it.

The heavenly bed of unsoiled snow waved at him suggestively. *Come and see me sometime*, it cooed, and Denton reckoned there was no time like the present.

He yanked Increase forward, and together they traipsed into the thigh-deep snow, kicking up billows of fine powder with which the wind slapped them silly. Denton's powdered wig flew off, and was swallowed by the drifts.

Despite himself, he began to laugh. It looked like he was getting his wish after all! If the context wasn't *quite* what he'd imagined it would be, it did little to temper his childlike enthusiasm in the moment.

What did a much better job of tempering his childlike enthusiasm, or at least helping it to come of age in record time, was the realization that they were beating a very clear path for pursuers to follow.

They were about halfway between the cleared passages of the Crundwell drive and the menacing thicket of the deep dark woods. Too late to go back. "Faster!" He called to Mr. Increase, at which point he realized that Mr. Increase, despite his here-and-gone limp, had passed him and was now the one doing the yanking.

No longer responsible for steering, Denton kept his legs pumping and threw a terrified glance over his shoulder, in the hopes that their hunters might trip over it.

No one was following them.

No matter – he wasn't about to be lulled into a sense of security, false or otherwise.

No chance of that happening, he would find out soon enough. They slipped into the smothering woods and vanished.

They ran a riotous circuit through the woods, for what must have been hours on end. When they closed the footprint loop by circling back on their own trail, they began carefully tiptoeing through the tracks to a random spot next to a tree, which they labored their way up to hide for the night.

Denton knew full well that a halfway competent tracker would spot them in an instant. The branches of the trees were all heavily laden with snow, and they'd been unable to scale their sleepytime timber of choice without knocking most of that snow to the ground.

He was increasingly hopeful they *would* be found, however. For obvious reasons, they couldn't start a fire. And not having anticipated a dash through the dead of New England winter, Denton had dressed to impress with nary a stray thought for things like insulation and moisture retention, two things that were impressing their importance upon him by under and overabundance, respectively.

Even if an absolute buffoon were set on their trail, and they didn't think to investigate the tree that was suspiciously denuded of snow, they'd have to be deaf not to hear Denton's teeth chattering. He could hardly think for the sound filling his head with physical weight, like a woodpecker trying to crack open the side of Gabriel's horn.

He couldn't feel his limbs. He climbed the last several yards of the tree by sight alone.

Mr. Increase didn't look much better off, but he at least had a thicker jacket on. Denton envied him for a moment before remembering that he had that thicker jacket because he'd had to sit on the outside of the coach to drive Denton to this wretched place. So maybe fair enough on the coat, then.

The mighty spans of the tree weren't thick enough to lie down on normally, so they had to position themselves face down on the branches, with their limbs straddling the tree's, dangling in a playful wind that didn't know its own strength.

Denton would hardly have known he'd slept if it weren't for another visit from Himself's Familiar.

Cheek raw from the press of the bark, Denton could only stare down at the ground where the shadowy figure made its way through the woods. It left no footprints to mark its passage. *I gotta get me a pair of whatever snowshoes he's wearing*, he thought, before realizing that he couldn't move and oh shit not again.

The Dread Familiar stopped in an itsy bitsy clearing in the underbrush. The plunging shafts of moonlight cut straight through it, and Denton's mind struggled to adjust to the eye-crossing sight of a well-lit silhouette.

"Yourself shouldn't have done that," the Familiar informed him with all the urgency of 'don't forget you're having lunch with Martha on Tuesday'.

Well, I didn't.

"Myself thought Yourself as averse to living Thingself suffering as Myself."

I am! I didn't do that!

"An illness borne of thaumaturgy is easily cured by the same means."

Okay, I'm a little preoccupied at the moment.

The Familiar sighed.

"Yourself does not understand. Myself is oath-bound to cure Himself. All Yourself has accomplished is to immiserate Innocentselves, guilty of nothing save a noble birth."

Take it up with the guy next to me! I didn't know this was going to happen, honest. I took your warning to heart. I'm no fan of unhappiness either.

The ethereal absence on the ground stared up at Denton for a long moment. It had no features, and yet Denton got a distinct whiff of cogitation from the thing.

That'll be all, then? His truculence was of endless fascination to his higher faculties of reasoning. There was anger bubbling up from deep within him, and he couldn't help but wonder how deep such a reservoir lay.

The Dread Familiar shrugged. "Myself just wishes Myself were not so dissatisfied with Myself's consortself. This happens so often with Myself. Familiarselves aren't to have convictions of their own, and yet Mys-"

I'm sure you've a very interesting perspective on the matter, but that's not what I meant at all. If it's all the same to you, I'd like to get as near to forty winks as I can. We can pick this up another time, if I am not dead.

"...alright."

And if Denton wasn't very much mistaken, the Familiar put him to sleep immediately after that. When he woke in the morning, he and Mr. Increase were somehow still alive. Which was discouraging, because he was starting to get the feeling that it might be for a reason.

He just hadn't made up what that reason would be yet.

III

STAYING AT THE KLUMP REGENCY, DENTON HAD begun most mornings in bleary-eyed confusion. Sleep withdrew gently with the moon, and he often spent several minutes lying in a twilight drowse, doing his best to locate himself in time and space through the roundabout route of reconstructing a narrative of the preceding two or three days. Finally a simpler method would suggest itself, and he would sit up and take a look at the room as he blinked himself awake.

But this morning, at the precise moment the sun weaved a beam through the knotted canopy and gave Denton a balmy *whap* on the cheek, he was *awake*. No somnolent limbo, no temporal or spatial confusion, no outward manifestations of eagerness that might belie a certain unchasteness of dream (though, of course, it was *awfully* cold outside). Just readiness, for whatever the day might bring.

Which could be just about anything.

Denton peeled his left cheek off of the bark of the tree, crying out as he left a cheeky souvenir by which it might remember him. His arms and legs hadn't the starter pistol wake-up his brain had gotten, dangling out in the cold as they had been all night. He swung them from the elbows and hips, fighting to get the blood flowing once again. Fortunately they were gloved and booted, but unfortunately those gloves and boots were only a little less effective as insulation than happy thoughts. He could only imagine what ghastly shades might have fallen over his typical pinkness.

Finally regaining control - if not feeling - of his limbs, Denton carefully withdrew his hands under his chest, and pushed himself upright with the world's closest-gripped push-up, using his hips as the pivot. After a certain point the muscles in his torso took over, and he leaned back to a seated position, legs dangling astride the branch, looking as though he were riding a giant dachshund with a very serious skin condition.

He looked down at the floor of the forest, unable to help projecting a certain malicious mockery in the glinting and glittering of ice crystals under the sunlight, which the jagged branches above had shredded and sprinkled around the woods like confetti. Last night's deep dark wood had become a twinkling starlit sky that grooved to the slackening beat of his heart, the better to see him dance until he dropped.

He traced the path of the footprints he and Mr. Increase had made the night before. Unless-

Not that he *didn't* expect Mr. Increase to still be here, but just to be certain he stole a quick look at the branch a little ways to his right. Yep, there he was, still fast asleep. Or dead. Oh heavens, Denton hoped he wasn't dead. But one thing at a time.

Unless their pursuers had exercised great care to walk in the footprints left by their quarry (which, though Denton was no hunter, seemed a needlessly time-consuming undertaking), then nobody had pursued them at all during the entire night.

They had run all this way for nothing, and slept in a tree for nothing. Nobody came for them, except for the sun, which came alone, selfish lover that it was. This whole situation was, more than anything, embarrassing.

Boy, he really hoped Mr. Increase hadn't died for this unnecessary timber-top slumber party.

"U-u-u-u-u-u-u," Denton began. His jaw *popped* like an octopus that had been sucking on a thermal vent for too long. He struggled one leg over the branch, positioning himself sidesaddle to more easily face Increase.

"M-m-m-m-m…In-In-In…HEY!"

Mr. Increase started awake. Denton took this to be a promising development. "A-A-A-re-r-r….y-y-you al-l-l-l-IVE?"

Denton watched his poison-peddling friend (*and with friends like these…*) slowly lever himself up to seated in much the same way, and with much the same difficulty, that Denton had. Whatever benefit Mr. Increase may have derived from his superior garments was likely cancelled out by his superior age.

"YyyyyES!" Increase called back.

"O-o-o-o-o-o-o-o-o-o-o-o-o-o-o-o-o-"

"OK?"

"Y-y-y-y-y-y-y-y-y-y-"

"Yes?"

Denton nodded. "I-i-i-i-i-"

"Increase?"

"N-n-n-n-n-n-n"

"N-n-n-no?"

Denton pointed to the ground. "I-i-i-i-I'll mee-m-m-meet y-y-" He accidentally found a better way to articulate the thought "I'll meet you down there" by gesturing a bit too enthusiastically and teetering backwards, straight off the branch. He plummeted to the ground, retaining his perfect bent-leg sitting posture all the way, and disappeared into a thick drift of snow with a satisfying *whunf* and a generous plume of powder.

Mr. Increase considered limbering up and climbing down, but – and he hated to think this way, given the circumstances – just falling looked like fun.

So he did. And it was.

They had a lot to talk about. Whats and whys and no seriously *WHY*s, and whatwereyouthinkings and doyouhaveanyideas, but the one thing they didn't need to talk about was that all those would have to wait, and not just because neither of them could convince their jaws to join the Glorious Cause of coherent speech. Getting out of the forest before night fell again was all that mattered. It was an absolute marvel that they weren't already dead, but Denton felt the final curtain would fall in that thunderclap immediacy with which the veil of sleep had lifted that morning.

Neither of them had planned to be roughing it that day. Denton had matches, which he had brought to be able to light other people's cigarettes at the party and say "no, please, how interesting, go on," but neither of them could find any wood dry enough to catch.

Denton was generally upset about the whole expedition, in a diffuse this-is-not-how-I-expected-to-die sort of way. For Mr. Increase, however, the sinking feeling that he'd be unable to survive out here carried a personal cost. He had been born in the wilderness, to a mother who carried and nourished him alone. And here he was, a grown man, facing the very real possibility that he would fail at the same task. It had nothing to do with falling short of a woman – he had always known his mother was twice the man he was. He felt he was failing *her*, betraying the legacy of hardscrabble survival that was the greatest pride he could take in his birthright.

This went beyond self-preservation. Increase had made a decision, doing what he did back there, and he knew that the consequence of that choice might be death. But it couldn't be *this* death. He was going to get out of these woods. He was going to survive, if it was the last thing he did.

That was a sobering thought to focus the mind. And before long, Mr. Increase arrived at the solution that was so perversely simple, he was certain Denton had dismissed it out of hand, as he knew he himself had.

They would retrace their steps and go back to the Crundwell's mansion.

IV

THEY HAD A BRIEF CONVERSATION THAT LASTED about forty-five minutes, thanks to the stuttering and stammering. Conversational economy was further impaired by the desperate calisthenics both were practicing in a vain attempt to keep warm.

Compressed to its essence, the conversation was as follows:

Denton told Mr. Increase that turning back and going to the Crundwell Mansion was just about the worst idea he'd ever heard.

Mr. Increase ventured that it was, at the very least, a better idea than 'stay out here until we freeze to death'.

Denton conceded the point, but clarified his initial comment: even if nobody had chased them out here, it sounded as though people had already begun falling ill as they made their escape, and Denton had exposed them both by warning off Brisby (yes, sorry about that, but also I'll not take the blame for this) and so the surviving family members – amongst whom was the mysterious Himself – might perhaps have a less than charitable welcome for them upon their return.

Mr. Increase contended that the idea turned on its own sheer idiocy: nobody would expect them to do something so brazenly counter-intuitive as to return to the scene of the crime. And if they were acting counter-counterintuitively, wouldn't that necessarily mean that they were acting intuitively?

Denton found this splitting of semantic hairs as a proxy for sound reasoning to be a disgrace to the very basis of rational thought, primarily because he remembered doing the same thing himself not too long ago. At least he'd had the decency not to say it out loud, though!

Mr. Increase asked Denton what he was talking about, the decency not to say what out loud?

Denton said what?

Mr. Increase said you were just saying-

Denton said sorry nevermind.

Mr. Increase said if it was-

Denton said I said sorry nevermind, forget I said anything.

Mr. Increase said okay.

And then neither of them said anything for a minute.

Mr. Increase reinaugurated the conversation with what was meant to be his closing gambit, after Denton was already on board: he proposed that they use the chaos and confusion that was inevitably gripping the Crundwell residence to sneak in, pilfer some clothes and supplies, snatch up their carriage or, if it was still locked up, somebody else's, and then make their escape.

Denton started to ask where to, but held his tongue – and not just because it was somehow very nearly frozen to the roof of his mouth. The fact was, this may have been an ill-advised course of action, but it was the only course being advised, so by default it was the best plan they had. He finally relented, and said alright.

Mr. Increase made a gleeful yipping sound. Let's get the hell out of here, he added.

Denton nodded in silent agreement.

It was late afternoon by the time they emerged from the woods. They had gotten duped by their own evasive maneuvers and ran a few pointless laps around their circular feint before realizing their mistake. Their unspoken communications had progressed to such an extent that they didn't even have to look at each other to know that they would never speak of this again.

Back on the right track, they poked their heads out of the tree line.

The day was still in the way that only days in the deepest pockets of winter can be. And so was the mansion.

Denton wasn't sure what he had expected to see, but he had expected to see *something*. He accepted that members of the Crundwell family circling the roundabout, flailing their arms and crying was probably an unlikely sight, but perhaps a few unusual carriages parked haphazardly by the front door? The undertaker? The Sheriff? Some lesser light of the Fidget's Mill Watch? Nosy neighbors?

None of the above. All was calm and quiet. Mr. Increase had brought in the New Year with a bang (and cough and a choke), but the Crundwells had somehow spun that into a creeping hush that was disquieting for its serenity. That accursed palm tree wasn't helping either.

Denton recalled his carriage ride into the mansion. What was it that people did during moments of placid contemplation?

Why, they stare wistfully out the window, of course.

And the view out of the approximately eighteen billion windows on the arcing front and side of the mansion had an unobstructed view of the approach Denton and Mr. Increase would have to take. Against a backdrop of virginal white that suddenly struck Denton as less *come hither* and more *thither they go; after them!*

They could follow the covering of the treeline as far towards the back of the property as it went, and make the mad scramble for the mansion that way, but they had no way of knowing if that would reduce or increase the likelihood of being spotted.

Denton sighed, and his breath ballooned out in front of him like a cartoon thought bubble.

Maybe it was delirium setting in, but Mr. Increase was quite certain he saw the words *Time to shit or get off the pot* suspended in the downy cloud of cogitation.

He nodded his agreement and set off running. Denton yelped and made a grab for Increase's arm, but was about three seconds off the mark thanks to fast-twitch muscles that had assumed they had a snow day off and gone back to sleep.

For Denton's part, he was rather confident that the words in the vanishing huff-puff were *Maybe if we circle around to the head of the drive and wait where are you going WAIT YOU GAH shit! Shit!*

Denton took off running after Mr. Increase because it seemed like the thing to do.

They loped like puppies playing in their first snowfall; their faces twisted and cracked like arthritic old hounds suffering through their last.

Chip Ditteridge stared wistfully out a window at the side of the mansion. He'd stuck around mainly for the novelty of the situation. There wasn't much of anything he could do to help, and not just because he felt utterly uncompelled to do much of anything to help. He was drawn to the drama of it all. A poisonous plot in the natal moments of the New Year! Bad news for those of weaker constitutions than his own, but good news for those as attracted to intrigue as he was. What a juicy bi-

He heaved ever so politely. Maybe *juicy* was a bit too on the nose, or on the ground, which is where the dinner of those most dramatically effected by the toxicant wound up, in an altogether *juicier* form than it was ingested.

Another heave. This absolutely would not do. If there is one thing Chip knew about gentlemen (a group to which he strenuously insisted he belonged, to anyone who would listen and even more so to those who wouldn't), it was that a gentleman *always* has control of his gag reflex. Etiquette 101.

He took a deep breath and turned his attention back to the window. Outside, two figures frolicked through the snow, arms pumping parallel to the ground, knees kicking as high as their bellybuttons.

Chip scoffed haughtily. He looked over his shoulder, to see if anyone might have overheard his haughty scoff. No audience for this one. Pity. More Etiquette 101: the haughty scoff. He considered his haughty scoff to be, if not the haughtiest he'd ever heard, certainly the scoffiest. The sort of scoff that demanded to be overheard.

He returned to the figures racing towards the mansion, hoping to gain more inspiration. The servants were out gallivanting while their masters lay dead or dying! An outrage to the very concept of civilization and order and society and literature and tall hats and fashionable timekeeping accessories and scoff! SCOFF!

Ooh, that was a *good* one. He turned around. Nobody came running. Did these philistines not appreciate a practiced haughty scoff when they heard one? That couldn't be right – *everyone* appreciated a practiced haughty scoff when they heard one. The problem was that they simply hadn't heard it.

Chip stepped away from the window and went to find someone, anyone, to listen to his haughty scoff. He'd hardly left the room before forgetting what it was he had scoffed haughtily about in the first place.

Ah yes, the two servants playing in the snow. He returned to the window, and watched their progress towards the house.

Mr. Increase plowed into the side door of the mansion shoulder-first and tumbled in, rolling once onto his side and slamming into the not-so-far wall with a wet *smack*. The door swung open, bounced back on its hinges, and had nearly completed a gentle journey back into its frame with Denton rocketed into it. The door swung open again, but Denton lacked the inertial conviction of Increase and wound up staggering back out into the snow before regaining his footing and weaving through the slowly closing door. He used his hip to bop it shut behind him.

He offered the recumbent Mr. Increase his hand, and Mr. Increase took it. Denton helped the man upright again. All of this he ascertained visually: he and his extremities had lost touch, ha-ha, but also and mostly uh-oh. He dreaded the moment when he would peel off his gloves to assess the damage.

Mr. Increase crept to the only other door in this puny little entry room. He cracked it open a few inches, just enough to press one eye against the opening and get the lay of the room beyond. It would have been a perfectly surreptitious maneuver, if not for the querulous *crreeeeeeeeeeaaaaaaaaaaak?* of the hinges.

Denton slithered his way under Mr. Increase's arm, lowered his head to tummy-height, and pressed his own eye up to the sliver of the next room.

There being nothing in the next room, they *crreeeeeeeeee-aaaaaaaaaaak?*ed the door open a bit further. And further still. Until it was open, and they were through, and the door was left to *crreeeeeeeeee-aaaaaaaaaaak?* closed of its own accord.

V

THE HALLS OF THE MANSION WERE DRAPED IN funereal black. It had been a little over twelve hours since Mr. Increase had done his ignominious (and, to Denton, still unspecified) deed, and apparently the new lords of the manor were first and foremost concerned with seeing to the interior decoration. The thick linsey-woolsey curtains wrapped the sounds of human passage in black oblivion, rendering the hallway as silent as the tomb of a stern librarian whose epitaph was "ssshhhh!"

Silver lining, this would make navigating the halls in relative silence that much easier. That lining was unfortunately limning the necessary corollary: the gloomy sound-swallowing ensigns would be just as effective at masking the approach of everyone and anyone else. They could very well round a corner and collide with Sonny Crundwell.

Assuming Sonny wasn't among the dead.

As Denton considered the rites of succession amongst the families, and pondered how they would be executed in any given combination of survivors and not-so-survivors, he marveled at the fact that there was clearly an infrastructure of grief in place. The servants must have been drilled on getting these hangings up on the wall, in case of death. Whose death?

Almost certainly Buddy's. Or his successor, Buddy Jr. Maybe Bunny? Denton would find out for certain, but he remained nearly positive that at least one of the Crundwells was dead.

Christ.

They took off at a hobbled cantor, the best they could manage on their tingling limbs (the house was far from warm, but it was certainly warm*er* than the outside). For a moment, the illusion of inescapable stasis was overwhelming: the abysmal hangings obliterated the expected visual and aural reference points that typically accompany movement. They had no clue where they were going, but for that brief eternity they felt – *knew* – that they would never get there.

A T-shaped intersection snuck up on them, presenting the option to continue straight or take a hard right turn. Denton took the former route, while Mr. Increase took the latter.

Denton, having once again slid back to second place in this two-man conga line, watched Mr. Increase take the turn, but nonetheless continued a few steps before realizing that his companion had no intention of catching up. He flounced back those few steps and watched Mr. Increase striding purposefully down the perpendicular hall. It wasn't that Increase was ignoring Denton's diversion – he was very likely unaware of it. He couldn't hear the absence of footsteps behind him – that's what had been there when Denton *was* hot on his heels.

Denton rushed to catch up, and was about three quarters of the way to Increase before considering the ways in which this approach might go wrong. Fortunately, Mr. Increase did not greet Denton with a 180-degree turn and a punch in the mouth as he'd feared. He didn't even turn. *He hadn't even heard him.*

What are these things made of, anyway?

They arrived at a stately atrium, though not the stately atrium through which Denton had entered last night. For whatever reason, the Crundwells had multiple foyers in their mansion, and so far they all looked nearly identical to Denton. Except where the first he had entered had portraits, this one had hanging swathes of that same abysmal black fabric as lined the halls.

Could these all be portraits of the maybe-late Buddy? Denton couldn't think of any other reason to cover the entire family in somber dustcovers just because Daddy bit the big one.

Unless they were *all* dead. In which case why would the servants have bothered to go through the motions of bereavement? When the head of the snake comes off, the whole thing dies, isn't that the saying?

(*Sort of a dumb saying, seeing as it could apply just as easily to most any animal*).

The foyer gave onto four hallways, each pointing in a different cardinal direction (in case the precision of this architectural decision was lost on anyone, the frame of each door was engraved with its corresponding direction; in case anyone doubted the authenticity of these directional claims, a compass rested in a small trough built into the wall beside each door). Denton and Increase came down from the North hall. The latter came to a halt, closed his eyes for a split second, and pointed down the Westward hall.

"The front entrance to the stables will be down there."

Denton peered down the hall skeptically. "Where does it say that?"

"In my head."

Their voices had absolutely no echo. Denton would never have thought of his voice as having one outside of caves and empty speaking halls (not that he spent much time in either), but to hear his voice being swallowed by the hungry nothing of these rooms' acoustics was chilling.

Satisfied with Mr. Increase's explanation, Denton turned right and began down the Westward hall. He had taken seven steps when a deafening roar split the silence.

He whipped his head around to find Mr. Increase mounting the inexplicably wide staircase. His right foot rested on the center of the bottom step; the sound that nearly startled Denton out of his frigid skin was the stair registering a formal complaint re: the prospect of Mr. Increase's upward mobility.

Denton whispered loudly at him, which was perhaps not necessary after the *fortissimo* groan of the stair. "Where are you going?"

Mr. Increase whisper-shouted back. "Upstairs!"

"You said the stables were this way!"

Mr. Increase picked his left foot up and plopped it down on the next step. The step scolded him. "I need to get a coat!"

"We'll get coats in town! We'll get two new coats in town! I'll buy you as many new coats as you want!"

"How are we getting back to town?"

"In a carriage, of course!"

"*In* a carriage, you say?"

"That's right!"

"And who will be taking the reins?"

"…alright," Denton conceded, "but we must make haste." He tiptoed over to the stairs.

Increase summoned an aura of 'yeah no shit' and nodded it in Denton's direction. The two men did their best to climb the stairs silently, and the stairs did their best to cheer them on as loudly as possible. Denton suggested they move over to the far sides of the steps and climb them there, to minimize the degree to which their weight would warp the wood. This cut the clapboard grousing down to a *mezzo forte*, giving Denton the space to hear his own thoughts, variations on the theme of *gee I really hope those black banners mute the rest of the sound we're making.*

He looked up to the top of the stairs, expecting to see someone staring down at them, with a knot in their brow and a blunt object in their hand. Given his recent run of luck, it was passing probable.

But nobody was there. And as they summited the stairs and made their way down the second floor hallway (which looked nearly identical to the corridors of the first floor, only smaller – Denton couldn't help but marvel at the painstaking repetition of the house's design), the two men neither saw nor heard nor sensed a single sign of life.

Denton began to wish for whoever it was that normally greeted strangers with the brow/blunt object treatment. It'd be a catharsis of some sort, a release of the unbearable tension that was mounting in this maze of disorienting, indistinguishable passageways, utterly devoid of guiding threads save the bolt of quiet iron that carved out a pocket in the cochlea and settled down to start a family and a small business forging bells against the hammer and anvil that would never ever ever stop ringing.

They padded down the halls, prying open whiny doors and catching glimpses of empty rooms, all just as black and deathly quiet as the rest of the house. The further into the domestic quarters of the Crundwells they went, the greater the degree of neglect they saw in the family's belongings. Rusted hinges on armoires cracked and quivered as they opened, like nervous teens' sweet nothings on an eventful first date. Doors fit unevenly into their jams, like underwhelmed teens accidentally trying to redress themselves in each other's sleepwear. Doorknobs stuck, shelves emptied out, a coating of finger-smeared dust lay gratefully over everything, and the less these later examples are compared to the erotic horseplay of clumsy adolescents, the better.

Eventually, after what felt like hours but was in fact closer to about twenty minutes, they broached a dresser and were rewarded with winter weather wear that fit well enough. They shimmied back into the hall, down the way they came. As they descended the stairs (which were just as crabby and bad-humored about their descent as they were their ascent), Denton once again expected to be set upon by curled lips and un-sunned skin and smooth knuckles whose first-ever job of manual work would be punching Denton and Mr. Increase's noses out the back of their heads.

And again, no one came, which only upset Denton more and more with each step they took towards the front door.

What the hell is going on here? Why had they not seen a single soul? Why had someone – some*ones*, must have been – put so much work into hanging these hideous shawls, only to vacate the entire mansion? Hell, how did they have all of these things just laying around, ready to be unfurled and nailed up at the drop of a hat (or Buddy, or Buddy Jr.)? The storage space that would be required to keep all of these near at hand would be preposterous. Sure, it wasn't as though the Crundwells were hurting for space, but…

Before Denton quite realized it, they were outside again. Between the heavy wool overcoat that he half expected to start *baaa*ing at any moment, and the insensate status of his extremities, only Denton's nose registered the discomfort of the cold this time. Registered it quite emphatically, but it was easy enough to ignore.

Harder to ignore: that the stables were still locked. Denton felt good about this: that was more like it! He got nervous when things went too well.

VI

THEY WERE DOWN THERE TRYING TO JIMMY open the lock on the stables. Chip Ditteridge had pulled a chair up to the window to watch the servants struggling. Only they weren't servants, were they? No, Chip had recognized them as they crept through the halls. It was the new slave doctor, whose name escaped Chip at this and all other moments. The negro with him was Mr. Increase, Chip knew that well enough. He'd marveled at the infamous dockhand's coasting in the wake of a white man.

Hadn't Mr. Increase slipped into the ballroom in the moments before everything went wrong? And hadn't he whispered something to the slave doctor, at which point both fled from the room?

And here they were, emerging from the woods at first light and tiptoeing around the mansion. What they were doing was anyone's guess. They'd certainly given him a workout, creeping around up here and throwing open every door in creation. Did they know he was up here? Did they mean him ill, or were they simply eager for a glimpse of true distinction? Not on his fashionable timekeeping accessory! He'd had to capitalize on the silence of the hall to dart and dive around behind them, keeping moving to circle back to rooms they had already checked for…coats? Did these fools come to the mansion with malice aforethought, but not jacket aforethought? He felt a haughty scoff well up in his chest. It was going to be a real belter, phlegmy and robust. Pity there was nobody here to hear it.

He knew most everyone had left, running off on this or that bit of business. Buddy Crundwell had been the head of the snake, but cutting it off hadn't killed the rest. No, it turned out that the snake was actually a bunch of smaller snakes in a tall coat pretending to be one big one, and severing the head had freed the constituent slitherers to break off and pursue their own things. Some of those things being death.

It was sad. Chip was sad. He took no pleasure in seeing people perish in such gruesome, drawn-out fashion. But he was fine, and his Missy was fine, which meant his immediate concerns could be put to bed. His secondary concerns were his station, economic and political, within the town. And these could most certainly not be soothed into slumber in the same way. Once his position had been fortified, once the shifting sands had settled, Chip could and would mourn the death of people who were, if not his friends, then his social equivalents.

But that still looked to be a ways off.

So where did things stand? As much as the Crundwells fancied themselves old money, there was no such thing in the American colonies. Meanwhile, the Ditteridges had been king shits of fuck mountain (Rumney Marsh hadn't the slightest *clue* about being king shit) back in England since Richard III was yodeling about horses. Status wasn't accorded by money, or property – money and property were accorded to status. Blood, lineage, family, name, primogeniture – *breeding*. These intangibles adumbrated one's social station, not the base materialism that was coming more and more to fan the embers of Colonial ambition. Chip was nearly as disdainful of their sickly, pale light as he was fearful that it would catch, if the kindling were heaped generously enough.

Still, the Help was here. They should have come running to hear his haughty scoffs. What else where they there for, but to perpetually attest to their own inferiority simply by existing in the shadow of their betters? Perhaps they couldn't hear him, what with these morbid little blankets flopped all over the shop.

Chip was so engrossed with this meditation on the natural right of the aristocracy that he nearly failed to notice Denton traipsing back out of the woods with a heavy branch, which he forced through the loop of the padlock and leaned on with all of his weight. Mr. Increase joined him. Just before the branch broke, the lock did.

Chip nearly failed to notice, but didn't. He smiled to himself, scoffing a private scoff, and wondering if anyone else had registered the suspicious behavior of these two men, or identified them as the likely perpetrators, or clocked their mid-day escape. He hoped not – even if he knew not how, it was information of this sort that often gave a man a leg up, when power structures were shifting under his feet.

Never before had Denton taken such a harrowing carriage ride. Mr. Increase could at least focus on guiding the coach and controlling the horses: Denton was left alone in this pressure cooker of stubborn glass and wood, waiting for the inherent instability of its construction to get self-conscious and explode, as he'd wished he could have done back at the party.

What the hell was going on? Why had *NOTHING* bad happened yet? Well, except for all of the bad things that had happened already. If something bad happened, he could deal with it. A problem, however serious, presented the opportunity to come up with solutions. Lists could be made, steps could be taken, plans could be hatched. Nobody *likes* a problem, but you can work with a problem.

But right now, Denton's only problem was that he felt he ought to have a whole bunch of problems sliding down the pike, and none were forthcoming. He had the itch to make lists and take steps and hatch plans, but he didn't know where that itch was, other than somewhere on his person. How do you scratch a free-floating itch? What a miserable limbo this was.

As they crossed into Fidget's Mill proper, everything looked normal. GAH. This was unbearable!

A distressing thought occurred to Denton: was the structure of Fidget's Mill so immovable, so immutable, so unchanging, that even the probable death of the town's would-be tyrant couldn't shake up the status quo? Had the Fidgetonians simply absorbed the tragedy and moved on? Or had nobody found out yet?

GAH GAH GAH. This was a fate worse than death for Denton.

Death at least had a sense of conclusion to it: it was the final check on every living thing's To Do list. What was this? Nothing! Waiting! Nothing!

Denton couldn't bear not having anything to do. But then a niggling voice in the back of his head spoke up, and reminded him of something upon which it had been mulling for a few hours.

An illness borne of thaumaturgy is easily cured by the same means.

Son of a bitch.

He swung open the door of the carriage, shouting up to Mr. Increase over the clattering of the horse's hooves. "Son of a bitch!"

Mr. Increase lifted his left arm and peered at Denton through the crest of his armpit. "What?"

"Get down here! I want to talk to you!"

"I'm b-"

"RIGHT NOW."

Mr. Increase squinted at Denton, but finally yielded. He'd never seen the man wound up in this way, and it was slightly unnerving. More than slightly, actually. So he guided the carriage to the side of the road, swung down, and climbed in. "This seems an especially po-"

"Thaumaturgy!" Denton nearly shrieked.

Mr. Increase had only just begun to settle into his seat. "Excuse me?"

"The Dread Familiar visited me in the woods. It told me that the poison was thaumaturgical. Magical!" Denton pounded his knee with his fist. "Miss Carsis provided you with the poison, did she not?"

A slanting of the shoulders told Denton everything he needed to know.

"I told *both* of you, that I would be treated as an equal in any and all machinations, did I not?"

"…I owed her. She asked me to do this, and so I-"

"What about me? When is somebody going to owe me something?"

The familiar edge came back into Increase's glare. "When you do something for someone."

"I got you into the party!"

"I could just as easily say that I got *you* into the party."

Denton bit his lower lip, because he didn't have the strength to drive his head through the window as he'd have wanted. "You've all been using me. Even when I specifically told you I wouldn't be used, you continued to do so."

"Are you not using Brisby in the same way?"

"No!"

Mr. Increase raised an eyebrow.

"I mean, not in the *same* way. I consider him a friend."

The eyebrow nearly touched the ceiling of the carriage.

"There are many tiers of friendship!"

"I didn't want to do this, Denton. I am truly sorry. You can choose to believe that or not, but the fact remains. I owed Miss Carsis a debt, and when she heard about the party, she collected."

Overwhelmed with the urge to spit, but still feeling collected enough to find the idea of hocking in such a lovely carriage distasteful, Denton threw open the door, stepped out of the carriage, and spat emphatically into the snow. His loogie plopped onto the smooth blanket of white and burrowed down an inch or so.

"Don't pretend you didn't want to do it," Denton said to his vanishing spittle. "You told me you wanted large-scale rioting, that sort of thing. Maybe Miss Carsis asked you to do this, but it wasn't antithetical to your goals."

From the carriage, Mr. Increase slid up to the door but did not get out. "I don't want violence for its own sake. I only ever sought it as a means to an end. Because my ends cannot be accomplished through …more traditional means. Our situations are qualitatively different, Denton. But I take no pleasure in the loss of life."

Denton turned around, cursing himself for giving Mr. Increase the literal high ground in this conversation. "So why did Miss Carsis wa-"

"I have no idea. And until such time as she wants us to, neither of us will."

Denton listened to the sound of his own breath for several seconds, watching it materialize and vanish before his eyes. Overwhelmed, he cupped his hands over his face. Slowly, this became an unprecedented double-hand through the hair gesture. The pinnacle of his nervous tic.

"Just over twelve hours ago, I was headed into a party with the objective to 'run afoul' of some high-society types. Now people are dead and, for all we know, the survivors know that we're responsible." Denton shook his head – *we're*. Why did he insist on including himself in this? "I just wanted to secure a trade agreement."

"That's how things begin. Not how they end."

"So what's your next move?"

"I…I don't know." Mr. Increase lifted his chin and scratched the top of his neck. "It's hard for someone in my position to plan, you understand. I suppose the first order of business will be assessing the fallout of…what happened."

"Not what happened. What *you did*," Denton corrected.

"Ah…yes."

Denton climbed back into the carriage, and shooed Mr. Increase out with the nod of his head. The free man chafed at the peremptory nature of the gesture, but was crystal clear on what motivated it. Race was the furthest thing from Denton's mind. The man was angry, and embarrassed, and most of all *hurt*. Because he had been used yet again. Mr. Increase felt a pinprick of regret at the top of his stomach, which was more than he typically allowed himself.

"I want to talk to her," was all Denton said. As Mr. Increase clambered back up behind the reins, Denton was ashamed to admit that what bothered him most was that he thought he had convinced Mr. Increase to act as his livery. As it happened, the only mark in favor of his powers of persuasion were that he'd convinced *himself* that Mr. Increase's dramatic about-face wasn't a feint at his expense.

VII

BEING UNACCUSTOMED TO WITCHES AS HE WAS, Denton wasn't entirely clear on the nature of Miss Carsis' powers. There was a telepathic dimension to them, but did that extend to telekinesis? She had pulled a concussion out of his head, hadn't she? What was that? And when she rendered him mute, did *she* snap his jaw shut, or did she make *him* do it?

Which was worse?

Being uncertain of Miss Carsis' abilities, Denton was consequently uncertain of what, if any, limits there were on her abilities. Phrased another way, did she have any weaknesses?

Phrased a third way, how in the hell could he take the high hand with a woman capable of turning his hands into lobster claws?

It had become abundantly clear that Miss Carsis wasn't much of a friend. An ally, maybe, as long as their goals aligned. But she'd forced Mr. Increase to deceive Denton (this was how he chose to think of it – the idea that Mr. Increase required little coercion was too upsetting to consider), and in a fashion that endangered both of them in very immediate, as well as long-term, ways.

So she wasn't much of a friend. But did Denton want to risk making her an *enemy*, simply to salve his wounded pride?

He asked himself these questions on the ride to Gutter Lane. He was freezing, probably frostbitten, and somewhere near the surface of awareness fostered the hope that the witch would divest Denton of his miseries as she had his concussion, even as he was upbraiding her. It was the least she owed him, he figured. It was also the only way he could justify going to see Miss Carsis before, say, Brisby Houlihan, who could provide more terrestrial medical attention. Because not seeing the doctor straight away made the 'all-for-my-pride' case a bit stronger, and Denton refused to acknowledge its fortitude.

Besides, Brisby would certainly be full of questions, wouldn't he?

Assuming he was still alive.

The carriage arrived, Denton knocked, and it was only as he and Mr. Increase entered the dim house that he remembered why he was here. He was here to scold Miss Carsis for having poisoned the power players of Fidget's Mill.

What would stop her from simply killing Mr. Increase and him, should their querulousness outpace their usefulness?

These were all important questions that evaporated the moment Miss Carsis looked up to Denton and said "how was the party?" with an innocent sincerity that bypassed irony and approached a form of exquisite, venomous absurdity.

"Fuck yourself," Denton replied. Which was not how he'd expected to kick things off, but life was full of surprises.

Such as: Mr. Increase making a thick, wet gurgling sound from deep in his throat. It was probably nerves, but it sounded like a geyser weighing its options.

Such as: No-Good Bulstrode, who was puttering around on the kitchen counter, fixing a soup that gave a surprisingly sweet smell, continuing to cook as though nothing had happened. As Bulstrode so often provided a sort of commentary on the witch's inscrutable moods, his sudden silence was as shocking as a gong strike would have been.

Such as: Miss Carsis looking genuinely hurt by Denton's anger.

It took every ounce of his self-control to not immediately apologize to her. *Stay strong*, he advised himself, *this is another trick. She's trying to manipulate you into feeling bad for her and apologizing*. She's *the one who should be apologizing here, not you.*

Still. It was hard for Denton to see that look on a woman's face, particularly if he'd been the one to put it there, and not want to do his darndest to get it off.

He desperately wished for her to say something now, because if she didn't he might end up apologizing no matter how hard he tried not to.

Finally, she sighed and rose from her chair. "That was mean-spirited."

Which was a wonderful thing for Denton to hear, because it rekindled his anger. "Of course it was! I'd say I've the right to be somewhat mean-spirited, wouldn't you?"

"No, I would not. What's the purpose of being mean-spirited?"

To salve my wounded pride was, admittedly, not a great response, but it was the only one he could think of at the moment.

"That's not what I'm here to talk about!" he shouted instead.

"Am I safe in assuming that this is about what transpired at the party?"

For the first time in his life, Denton bit his tongue. As in, he *literally* bit his tongue – he couldn't think of any other way to contain his rage. The iron taste of his own blood gave him courage, so he could only imagine what the taste of someone *else's* blood might do.

That's when Denton realized he might want to relax a bit.

"Yes," he snarled as politely as one can snarl, "you are correct."

"Couldn't be avoided, I'm afraid." With that, Miss Carsis sat back down, and returned to reading whatever evil little pamphlet she was reading.

Without looking up, she added, "you must be exhausted. I won't keep you any longer." She snapped her fingers in the general direction of Denton and Mr. Increase, and Denton instantly felt better than he'd felt in years. Perhaps it was simply the contrast between the depths of frostbite and the relative comfort of his baseline health, but he felt *incredible*. If he wasn't mistaken, she'd even healed the gash he's gnawed into his own tongue, which gave him pause – did she know he'd bitten his own tongue in frustration? Once again, embarrassment proved the loudest of all emotions.

One look at Mr. Increase told Denton that she'd worked the same magic on him as well.

And it was magic in more ways than one. Miss Carsis was, in her own unique way, apologizing to them. They had suffered on her behalf, and she had rectified their suffering. But she was also threatening them, wordlessly and indirectly. *Look what I can taketh*, she was saying, *and think about what I could giveth.* The pain she pulled from people must go *somewhere*, after all. And she had a lot of cupboard space in this house.

The message was received, loud and clear, but Denton wasn't leaving until he said what he had come to say, and until Miss Carsis agreed to it.

Once again, he had to struggle not to be polite. *Thank you for healing my ouchies* came scrambling up his throat, and he gulped it back down. *Thank you* wasn't how hard-edged negotiations began, as a rule. Instead, he took a step towards Miss Carsis. "Look at me," he demanded.

Bulstrode and Mr. Increase both looked at Denton, both shocked. Bulstrode made quiet clucking sounds, while Mr. Increase resumed his thunderous, nervous gurgling.

Miss Carsis, however, kept her head buried in her reading material. Denton took another step, close enough now to glance at what she was reading. It was, if he wasn't very much mistaken, not a real language. It was as though someone had tried to reverse engineer Egyptian hieroglyphics, having only overheard somebody talking about them at a loud party.

So *that* was creepy. But it was too late to lose his nerve now.

Actually, it's never *too late to lose your nerve*, Miss Carsis' voice contributed in his head. Denton was well past caring whether that was actually her or simply his imagination trying to destroy him from the inside; it was just another annoyance at this point.

"*Look at me*," he once again insisted.

And she was. As far as Denton could tell, she didn't turn to look at him. She just *was* – one instant looking at the pages on the table, the next instant looking at him.

She narrowed her eyes at him. "You are being exceptionally disrespectful, and I would remind you that you are my guest here."

In for a penny… Denton thought in his own voice.

"I thought we were friends, no? Friends can be candid with one another." He jabbed a trembling finger at Miss Carsis (*his shaking hands, once again betraying his nerves!*), but kept his voice steady. "Now *you* owe *me* one."

"One what?"

"A favor."

"What favor?"

"I don't know yet. But I've been owing everybody favors up until now. Not anymore. You both," here he aimed his finger at Mr. Increase, "owe me favors."

"Now hang on just one moment," Mr. Increase objected.

"Your poisonous schemes wouldn't have come to fruition, were it not for me!"

"In order to incur a favor," Miss Carsis replied with enraging patience, "typically an arrangement must be made ahead of time. In addition, the one incurring typically *does* something to incur said favor."

"I got Mr. Increase into the party!"

"At which point Mr. Increase performed the favor he owed me. Perhaps Mr. Increase owes you a favor? That is between the two of you. But I don't see how I come into it."

"*I* took the risk at the party," Mr. Increase pointed out with an uncharacteristic degree of petulance. "Denton, I am very sorry you incriminated yourself, but that hardly c-"

Denton stomped his foot, not wanting to be outmatched in uncharacteristic petulance. "*At the party*. You took the risk *at the party!* How did you get to the party, Mr. Increase?"

"In a carriage that Miss Carsis provided, and that I drove. How did *you* get to the party, Denton?"

"…what I mean is that I was invited. And besides, this isn't about tallying up who did what!"

"You keep telling us what it *isn't* about," Miss Carsis drawled, and Denton couldn't help but notice with dread that she had ever-so-delicately repositioned the loyalties of the room. Now she and Mr. Increase were a unit – *us* – and Denton was alone. "Why don't you tell us what this *is* about?"

"I'm through being played like a tuba!" He cursed himself for picking such a big whimsical instrument and barreling onward: "I'm done with you both, until such time as I see fit, at which time I will call upon you to collect my favor. Is that understood?"

"So you mean to say that you are not done with us."

"I mean that I am done with…that *you* are done with *me*."

"So why would we help you when you come calling?"

"Because you owe me a favor."

"We never consented to this debt," Mr. Increase sniffed.

"Nobody consents to debts! That's the point!"

"Some folks consent to debts!" Bulstrode chimed in from the back. "A folk taking out a loan, there's one!"

"That's not what I mean!"

Miss Carsis scoffed a scoff that would have made Chip Ditteridge proud. "Well for bog's sake man, what *do* you mean?"

"I just want to be a part of it!"

"A part of what?"

"Everything!"

"What would you do to be a part of everything?"

"Anything!"

"Even manipulating your friends?"

"Yes!"

"Even poisoning a party?"

"Yes!"

"Even lying to your wife?"

The room fell perfectly silent, and Denton was suddenly positive, beyond a shadow of a doubt, that Miss Carsis had engineered this entire exchange, to guide him to this specific point. This entire exchange? Try their entire acquaintance, and some time beforehand as well.

It had nothing to do with Denton lying to his wife specifically. Miss Carsis was testing his dedication to the Cause. Convictions pitted against his personal life; which was the priority? How much of a believer was he?

More of a believer than most.

But even still.

"No," Denton replied, "and don't you ever speak of my family again."

"Or what?"

"Or I'll be very cross with you and probably say something rude, that's what."

In keeping with the uncharacteristic nature of the evening, Miss Carsis smiled a smile of unaffected warmth and tenderness. She placed her pages down on the table and once again rose from her seat, except this time like she meant it. "Oh, I knew there was someone like you buried under all that soft breeding."

VIII

THE FIRST STEP WAS RECONNAISSANCE. THE landscape of Fidget's Mill had changed, and there was no sense laying new foundations without spotting the sinkholes.

Actually, Denton averred, the *real* first step was for Miss Carsis to finally come clean and explain why the hell she went and poisoned half the town's pre-eminent worthies.

"Didn't you have a plan? Or did you do it just for the hell of it?"

Miss Carsis shrugged permissively. "The poison *was* the plan, really. It was just the one step. I simply needed to narrow the field of possibilities."

"…what does that mean?"

Miss Carsis pulled Denton's plainclothes out of a cabinet in her living room, which was upsetting because Denton had changed in his hotel room. "Well, what did we know about Himself? We had established that he must belong to one of the three families. Finding him is merely a matter of turning over more and more rocks, until only one remains."

"Jesus." Denton shook his head as he snatched his clothes back.

Mr. Increase, having little patience for metaphysics and even less for No-Good Bulstrode, had excused himself. Miss Carsis was more than happy to have him stay, but Denton was glad to see him go. He wanted to retain at least one ally whose concerns were strictly political – which is to say, material.

"You poisoned them all with some terrible magic, knowing full well that this secret witch – or wizard, or warlock, or whatever you call him – would be cured by his Familiar."

Bulstrode hopped up on the table and loosened the strap at the back of Denton's vest with his beak. "Quite logical, wouldn't you say?"

"Except for the fact that *turning over rocks* in this context means *murdering innocent people*!"

Miss Carsis tutted. "You told me you were willing to do anything, Denton. Even poisoning a party. You responded in the affirmative to that."

"I *am*, and perhaps would be, should it be dictated by the circumstances. But being willing to do anything doesn't obligate one to do the worst possible thing." He slipped out of his coat, allowing it to fall onto Bulstrode's head. "What alternatives did you exhaust, to catch out this rival of yours, prior to poisoning a party?"

"I had Bulstrode search the town. As he did not find anything, he rec-"

"Now just one moment!" Denton's coat shook disagreeably on the ground as Bulstrode shimmied his way out from under it. "I did indeed make a canvas of the town, but the responsibility for what went down at the tony do can hardly be lain at my talons, what?"

"I wasn't saying it would be," Miss Carsis snapped, "I was simply explaining to him the alternatives-"

"But that's not an *alternative,*" Denton cut in, "that's a preliminary. What do you plan to do, once you find this rival witch?"

"Destroy him."

"And then what?"

"Return to my original business."

"Which is?"

One of her eyes twitched. "None of yours."

"Oh, come now, none of that," Bulstrode mediated, "no sense keeping the boy in the dark." He tapped his way out from under the coat, and next to Miss Carsis. "You see, there is much about your universe you do not understand. Chiefly, that your universe is but one of many, and that at the moment of its inception, forces of uns-"

"I'll just stop you right there," Denton cut in yet again, finger raised in the air. "Will any of this aid me in securing non-importation in the colonies?"

"…not as such, no."

"It would certainly give you perspective in the face of failure," Miss Carsis added helpfully.

Denton pinched his thumb and raised forefinger together, and pumped them up and down exactly once. "Then I must admit I'm not terribly interested."

Bulstrode cocked his head to the side. "Aren't you curious, as to the very nature of your theater of existence?"

"Not especially. I've got bigger things to worry about."

And if Denton wasn't very much mistaken, Miss Carsis shot Bulstrode a look of overwhelming gratitude.

Knowing that Miss Carsis poisoned the party simply to narrow down her search for "Himself" was both chilling and reassuring. She was not a psychopath, inflicting misery for its own sake. She was merely a fanatic, inflicting misery as a means to an end.

Which was, you know, slightly less terrible.

But, the question finally demanded to be answered: how far had the field of inquiry been narrowed? Who survived the party, thus remaining a suspect, and who absolved themselves from suspicion by their own death?

Perhaps listening to Bulstrode would have clarified for Denton why it was so important to isolate and annihilate this rival witch, as far as Miss Carsis was concerned. But Denton didn't care. The fact remained that this rival witch was also an obstacle to *his* plans, attempting to sabotage the delicate balance of Fidget's Mill, as evinced by the attempt on Missy's life, in such a way as would have demolished the…

…

The attainment of Denton's objectives demanded a certain stability in Fidget's Mill. And in attempting to smoke out the rival witch, Miss Carsis had utterly upended any sense of said stability. And, being so close to her, Denton had completely ignored this fact. But hadn't she said that her own ends required a certain degree of integrity in the town? What was she after, and why wouldn't she tell him?

Was he associating with the wrong witch?

Should he be associating with witches at all?

As he amended his own plans and considered future courses of action, witches hardly factored in to it. People at the top of the food chain were dead, and the tenuous stability of the town had been undone. That meant the Mill would be need to be rebuilt. Was he not well positioned to take part in this reconstruction, thus assuring himself a place of greater influence, pursuant to the accomplishment of his political ends?

No, he was not. But was he not well positioned to *become* thusly well-positioned?

That depended on whether or not Buddy Jr. was still alive. The man, after all, owed him a favor, did he not?

He did. And Denton couldn't get over how nice it was to be owed a favor, as opposed to the inverse.

But still, good feelings could wait. There was some slightly less cuddly business to attend to.

"Say, Bulstrode," Denton began in the tone of voice that always indicates a request one or two steps beyond the bounds of propriety, "you wouldn't happen to know where Brisby Houlihan is staying, would you?"

"Why, the cemetery on the hill, as of last night!"

"Oh my god!" Denton staggered from stationary.

"OBBLAHABOGHALOB, just one of my little stitch-ups, there. Brisby's as alive as he ever was, and I'd entreat you to take that any which way you like. Let's off to his place of residence!"

As Denton followed Bulstrode out the door, Miss Carsis shrugged at him, as if to say *try living with him.*

In the fourteen seconds that elapsed between Denton's knocking on the door of Brisby's place of residence (a small but flawlessly constructed cabin behind a larger residence) and the opening of said door, Denton had imagined innumerable different scenarios for his immediate future, all unique right up until the point where he was torn limb from limb by an angry mob. He was having difficulty forseeing a world in which he was *not* torn limb from limb by an angry mob. Unless, that is, he were not torn but snapped like a wishbone, which seemed entirely within the realm of possibility. Even after Miss Carsis' magical ministrations, his long night in the woods left Denton feeling somewhat brittle.

Brisby swung the door open, looking so disheveled Denton thought he might have spent a long night in the woods himself. The physician took a few moments to fix his attentions on the man in front of him, and when he finally did, he very clearly regretted it.

"You!" he blubbered to the empty space just over Denton's shoulder. "Have you any idea what you've done?"

"No," Denton replied with disarming sincerity, "I was hoping you could help me with that."

IX

FITHIAN LOWESTOFT WAS IN A PICKLE. SHE HAD never really settled into Fidget's Mill; it had all felt far too precarious. The Lowestoft clan were the new money in town, and the feeling that they could be ousted just as easily as they were…insted?…hung over every friendship she *nearly* made, every plan she *sort of* laid.

And boy oh boy, had she been right. A poisoning on the stroke of the New Year was a big deal, sure, but a more robustly established town would likely have been able to absorb the isolated tragedy and move on. Fidget's Mill, on the other hand, couldn't have handled the catastrophe much worse, short of snapping itself off the continent and sliding into the Atlantic.

With Buddy and Lucretia Crundwell dead, and several others (her own parents among them) convalescing, anyone with a penny to their name became inordinately interested in the idiotic logistics of high-class inheritance. Everyone, that is, except for those who stood to gain from it. Buddy's first son Sonny should have been the heir to the Crundwell dynasty, according to the rules of primogeniture that were all the rage about a thousand years earlier. Yet, that Sonny wouldn't have been taking up the mantle was all but guaranteed, due to the fact that everyone in the town knew that he was, in terms of business and personal accomplishment, a poor choice indeed. This was the stated reason, in any case. The real reason was that he was largely despised by his parents.

Really, what it came down to was this: Sonny had a secret, and the attention he would receive as the effective Head of the Town was inimical to his personal interests. His personal interests being Tobin Lowestoft, Fithian's younger brother. Fithian had long suspected that there was a bond stronger than friendship between those two, and her suspicions were redoubled as Sonny dutifully hunkered by the bedside of a Tobin recovering from the hateful poison in his drink, and shortly thereafter confirmed as the two disappeared early this morning. Sonny would have lived a life more lavish than most people could dream of, had he stayed and taken the reins of the family business. But he would have been living a lie. The same went for Tobin in theory, though their father Cullender was still a strapping relatively-young lad, and didn't look liable to keel over anytime soon (one would hardly believe he'd drank the poison at all).

She shivered. These were complex times – Fithian was torn between, on the one hand, being happy for her brother's having found love and made a dramatic choice motivated by that love…but on the other hand, feeling that her brother's love was an abomination. She was, after all, a Good Christian, a designation that was often at odds with her desire to also be a Good Person.

With Sonny gone, the weight of the Crundwell name fell squarely on the shoulders of the sole remaining son (because even if Lucretia Crundwell hadn't succumbed to illness earlier today, thus multiplying the grief of the poor Crundwells, she wouldn't have given the keys to the castle – *Fidget's Mill hasn't fallen into* complete *anarchy,* Fithian thought with a sour sarcasm). Buddy Jr. was to hold the crumbling Crundwell business together; not only that, but he was saddled with the knowledge that failure could well mean a catastrophic end for the town of Fidget's Mill entire. Without the Crundwells (and, more to the point, their private infrastructure around the docks) to prop up the local economy, could a town that produced little of actual value hope to survive? Fithian feared not.

This meant that the entire town had a stake in Buddy Jr.'s successful ascent. And, fancy this, what was considered a pivotal rung in that climb (but still just a rung for all that)? Why, marriage to homely Fithian Lowestoft, that was what. Not only had nobody asked what she thought of this arrangement – nobody had asked Buddy Jr.! The idea, when Buddy Sr. was alive (and perhaps it was time to start referring to Buddy Jr. as 'Buddy', and Buddy as 'Buddy Sr.' Such are the perks of continued existence), was that the Crundwell and Lowestoft clans would be tangled in a death grip, from which they could not disentangle themselves easily or safely. It was to be a purely political union, one to which Cullender had reluctantly agreed. Fithian had been outraged – her father was typically so loving and attentive to the needs of others, yet here he was prepared to sacrifice the independence and free will of his daughter to shore up his financial footing in the town.

With Buddy Sr. dead, however, the union stopped being spoken of as a practical hypothetical. Before the old man's earthly vessel hit the ground, Fithian felt all eyes darting expectantly between her and Buddy (Jr.). Now she was no longer being asked to make a sacrifice for the good of her family – she was being *expected* to make one for the good of the *town*. If the Crundwells and Lowestofts were united, the new money would act as a crutch for the old one. This would preserve the Crundwells and everything they'd built, but shift the balance of power towards the Lowestofts. Fithian didn't understand it entirely – she didn't care to – but her mother and father had hardly slept at all this calendar year, fretting over the arrangement. That Fithian was expected to follow through with it was being taken for granted. For the first time in her life, she felt some hatred for her beloved family. She couldn't talk to her parents for obvious reasons, and Tobin had left her all alone.

Fithian felt like she was going mad. She and Buddy Jr. were quite friendly, and had spoken candidly about this. They knew they were wrong for each other, and more to the point, they both knew that Buddy Jr. was in love with Millicent Ditteridge, and vice versa. Fithian was ecstatic when she had heard Missy was pregnant by Buddy Jr. – *those* two might now marry, and leave her to chart her own course in life! – until Buddy Jr. had intimated that…*arrangements* would be made…

But, as Cullender explained to an only half-attentive Fithian, the Crundwells couldn't marry their son off to the Ditteridges. The latter family was too intimately associated with the English crown, and the Colonial Governor Marsh (somehow not dead but merely very sick, surprising given the amount of poison he must have ingested via drink), and all things monarchical against which the winds of liberty were blowing, or something like that. More political excuses. Buddy Jr. and Missy were in love. Let them run off, like Sonny and Tobin!

But then the town would rot from the head…unless, of course, the good Fidgetonians might be convinced to allow a woman to head up the business…

Not a chance. Fithian sighed and slouched back on a couch beneath one of the large windows in the Lowestoft sitting room.

There was more to think about here than just herself, and her wants…her *needs*. It was disgusting, and it wasn't fair, but it was the way things were. Her life was not her own anymore. It was political.

More than political: it was a pickle.

She let her eyes drift towards the window. It all looked so normal. That really annoyed her. The entire town was clinging to existence (by the hem of *her* dress, it seemed), and it looked exactly as it had last week when things were comparatively fine. The passage of carts and hooves and feet packed the snow into tight trails, sunlight blew its cheerful load indiscriminately over the sullen clouds, and a midnight-black turkey was watching her intently from the other side of the street.

So maybe not *exactly* as it had last week.

Just as Fithian sat forward for a better look, the turkey turned and went a-bobbing down the street, towards the docks. Fithian shrugged, fell back on the couch, and pondered ways to escape her unhappy fate.

She couldn't well run away. Sonny and Tobin had already cornered the market on that.

X

RIDING A HORSE AS WHITE AS THE UNTOUCHED snow, and nearly as white as her hair, Miss Carsis approached a picturesque cabin on the outskirts of town as the high rays of the noon sun locked the day in blue amber. Two horses followed behind her, saddled and bridled by unridden.

The plan had been quite simple, and would have been easily accomplished. It just would have been a rather slow burn, which wasn't usually a problem for Miss Carsis. In fact, that was her style. But then Denton Hedges showed up, and Miss Carsis got overambitious. Now the only element of the original plan that remained was putting her two charges up in this cabin once occupied by her witchy mentor, who had leaned into the whole crone-of-the-woods thing far too eagerly for the new-school witch's tastes. All else was a shambles.

Silently cursing Denton's name as she opened the door (without knocking) and stepped across the threshold, Miss Carsis cursed her own impatience for good measure. The two men in this cabin had become something approaching an occupation for her, and much as she welcomed the way working for their benefit (and, indirectly, her own) brought order and purpose into her life, she would be superlatively pleased to have this whole affair behind her.

She could hear shuffling from the next room over, and so called to them. "It's only me, boys." In synchrony, Sonny Crundwell and Tobin Lowestoft popped their heads out of the doorframe. They smiled weakly at Miss Carsis, and she smiled back at them.

Sonny Crundwell and Tobin Lowestoft were in love, the kind of love that begged consummation and so beggared belief. Sonny, by rights the heir to the Crundwell dynasty, had felt himself becoming more and more marginalized by his father, until Sonny's younger brother Buddy Jr. (who had for whatever reason been favored from birth, as evinced by his carrying their father's name) was unanimously understood to have usurped that role. The older brother felt no frustration with the younger, because it was not Buddy Jr.'s decision to be so favored; in fact, he seemed to be exceedingly unhappy with the arrangement. Both would have preferred Sonny claim the seat of power that was by rights his. Buddy Jr. had grown sick of the attentions that had been lavished upon him, and longed for a simpler life. Besides, he had his own forbidden love to pursue.

Which was, at bottom, the fundamental difference between their loves. Buddy Jr. and Missy Ditteridge had a forbidden love, love that flew in the face of their family's wishes. That was romantic and exciting and, most importantly, easy to understand, fodder for the sort of novel Lucretia...used to read. Oh, how Sonny despaired of ever fully making peace with the passing of his younger sister, the first person to whom Sonny had ever fully revealed his strange desires, and the first person who had ever told him that love was always strange, his no more than anyone else's.

Sonny's love for and with Tobin, however, was not forbidden, because nobody could forbid something that they didn't accept was a real thing. Most men were physically intimate with their male friends, and so felt they understood precisely what Sonny and Tobin felt for each other. But as there was no real homosexual identity to speak of, the exclusivity of the two young men's attention for each other proved flummoxing. Why didn't they also seek intimacy with women? Why deprive themselves of that? Those few who were aware of their love looked on it with more frustration than anything else, as though it were no more than affectation, self-consciously adopted just to be difficult. Other's, including Buddy Crundwell himself, thought his older son's sexuality to be an abomination, an unspeakable rebuke of the Crundwell name and all that it stood for. More than any religious and ethical objections, he felt Sonny was deliberately eschewing the embrace of a woman to disrupt the orderly passing of the dynastic potato. A man who never coupled with a woman could never have a child, and so, if Sonny died childless atop the Crundwell throne, the tiny empire would likely die with him, regardless of what Buddy Jr. had gotten up to.

So Sonny had been shunted off to the side. And there he was meant (and refused) to languish, kept buoyant by the love he could give to Tobin, and the love he received from him. There was never any confusion, when it was just the two of them. They loved each other, and expressed it in the ways that felt right. And right those ways always were.

And then Buddy Crundwell and Cullender Lowestoft started making noises about marrying Buddy Jr. and Fithian, much to the latter two's undisguised dismay. Buddy Jr.'s love for Missy was a poorly kept secret, almost certainly known to both Buddy and Cullender. But it made no difference to them. Professional concerns trumped personal ones, and having been shouldered to the side by his father for just that reason, Sonny understood all too well how this felt. So, quietly, he and Tobin began pondering ways that they might legitimize their love in their family's eyes. If some union could be established between them, then would this not serve effectively the same purpose as a marriage between Buddy Jr. and Fithian? One Crundwell-Lowestoft union was surely as good as another, wasn't it?

To no one's great surprise, it wasn't. There was no precedent for two men entering into any kind of legal union that could supplant marriage between a man and a woman. So what was left to them? Sonny now felt responsibility not only for himself, but for his younger brother's fate; the scrutiny with which Buddy Jr.'s love life was being assessed was a result of Sonny's failing to sustain the same relentless, business-minded audit. The solution was as simple as it was far-fetched: regain his natural position as the heir to the Crundwell dynasty. Little would change in his own life, and then Buddy Jr. would be free to forge a life with Missy, and Fithian would be free to forge her own path, which Tobin knew to be her ultimate desire.

Simple yet far-fetched: how to pull it off, then? Their quest to find a solution to their problem led them to some of the less savory pockets of the town, which before long led them to the witch.

Miss Carsis had sympathized with their plight with startling immediacy, promising to tender whatever help she could, in return for a favorable place at the right hand of the metaphorical throne, once everything settled back down. Which, no matter how riotously the people of the town combatted the change, they inevitably would. Settle back down, that is. Entropy worked its thin, room temperature fingers into everything sooner or later. In fact, she pointed out, though their love was confusing to most of Fidget's Mill, perhaps seeing such a love practiced by the incipient patriarch of the town would normalize it. Make it not only comprehensible, but banal in its effortless comprehensibility.

The prospect was appealing, redoubling Sonny and Tobin's enthusiasm for the plan. Miss Carsis agreed to help them no less enthusiastically, and with a minimum of dissimulation. She claimed to be on their side because it offered her an incredible opportunity to rise in the social ranks; as a witch she would never be the belle of the ball, but she might not have to live in a place called Gutter Lane anymore. Besides, being friends with the men in charge would prove useful beyond measure, she was certain. The torturous schemes required to get anything done in town could be foreshortened considerably, if one of the steps could be 'call up the bossmen and ask them to do something for you'.

In her deepest heart of hearts though, there was another reason for Miss Carsis' readiness to come to their aid, one she would never reveal to another soul, living or dead: the love between Sonny and Tobin touched her. Not because it was especially touching; Miss Carsis was as capable of love as anyone else, she was just more capable than others of suppressing the feeling when it wasn't useful, which was most times. The love touched her because it was misunderstood, not even kenned well enough to be hated. It was held beneath contempt, in the murky subterranean cave system to which all confusing things blithely dismissed were condemned.

If witchcraft was a kind of love – and Miss Carsis was unequivocal on the point that it *was* – then she more than anyone else in town was equipped to understand just how Sonny and Tobin felt. And so, keeping this latter line of reasoning to herself, she agreed to help them.

All of this was a perfectly unwitchy way to think about witching, but what was more witchlike than unconventionality? Nothing, Miss Carsis felt quite certain of that.

A rather bland, bureaucratic tale of corporate takeover proved sufficient but endlessly time-consuming, and so slightly more proactive means were employed. Which also proved insufficient, and so the means grew still more proactive.

And then Denton rolled in to town, and Miss Carsis sensed him immediately. He stank of ambition, and there were few things more evident to a witch than that. So she made an immediate and unilateral decision: she would use him. He did better than she could ever have imagined, getting invited to the New Year's party, bringing Mr. Increase with him at Miss Carsis' behest. The poisoning scheme was wholly her idea, just as unilateral as the one to employ an unwitting Denton – poison was a simple method of removing Buddy Crundwell from the picture that could easily be pinned on the newcomer, and if it happened to take out a few of the other elders of the town, well, what of it? Not to mention that blasted Familiar who had been wandering around the Mill for as long as Miss Carsis could remember had appeared to Denton, and so provided her with a convenient (and plausible) excuse to placate Hedges and keep him on her side, in the event that he should avoid apprehension.

But then she added sloppiness to her mounting tally of sins. The spells she'd uttered over the poison as it brewed, spells that were meant to make it fatal to only a select few partygoers, wound up being unequal to their task. Buddy had died, yes, but he was the only patriarch to do so. And so Miss Carsis would never be able to reveal her role in the tragedy – if Sonny ever found out that she was responsible for Lucretia's death, he would very likely kill her, witch or no. Which was obnoxious, because Sonny and Tobin had decided that their love and plans had been discovered, and that the poison had been meant for them, and therefore safety was only to be found elsewhere. So, unable to assure them that the poison had actually been specially concocted to *not* work its malice upon them, she could do nothing but wish them safe passage as they rang in 1768 by fleeing Fidget's Mill.

The white horses were for them. She had loaded them down with supplies, and loaded their two riders down with promises that she would see to whatever eerie and eldritch conspiracy there was arraying itself against them, and call for their return when the conditions were more favorable. That there was no conspiracy against them, and that the conditions of the town would never be more favorable to their lunging into the power vacuum at the heart of the Mill, and that she couldn't safely communicate any of this to them, was more frustrating than when her socks bunched up in her shoes, which until now had been the pinnacle of frustration.

But she couldn't abandon them now. She still believed in them, and she still believed in love, more than anything else. Besides, what else did she have to do? Bulstrode had his mysterious Immortal Demon errands to see to. Love was her transcendent, numinous Cause, the thing she believed in which was beyond her, more than her. It mattered not if it was her love or someone else's, because love was love was love. If she didn't have that, what did she have? No, by Lilith, she would ready the town for their return. And she wouldn't be fooled twice; a buffoon as dangerously competent as Denton Hedges wasn't worth her time or attention.

Still, she couldn't help but feel he was partially responsible for her having to watch Sonny and Tobin disappear over the horizon. She knew it wasn't his fault; the blame lay entirely with herself.

But for all of Miss Carsis' power, she was still only human.

XI

IN THE WAKE OF THE "INCIDENT" ON NEW YEAR'S Eve, Buddy and Lucretia Crundwell were dead, Sonny Crundwell and Tobin Lowestoft had fled, Chip Ditteridge had taken to wandering the Crundwell mansion (at least, this is what people assumed: his carriage and slaves were still in the stable, and the Crundwell servants' inability to find him could only mean that he was moving around and hiding from them), and Governor Rumney Marsh was in a very bad way.

Brisby, who had escaped with only a slight case of the tummy grumbles thanks to Denton's intervention (as always, he had done most of his drinking ahead of time at home), had been a busy little beaver that day, but consequently could personally attest to the physical (though not mental) well-being of Buddy Jr. Crundwell, Opal and Fithian Lowestoft, and Missy Ditteridge. He had not been able to see the remaining members of the families, busy as they had been with the manifold crises that had unfolded in the evening, but Brisby had second-hand assurances as to the relative good health of Bunny Crundwell and Cullender Lowestoft.

Having concluded his update, Brisby nodded proudly, and then remembered the context and throttled way back. Still, he couldn't help but evince a hint of satisfaction with his overview of the chessboard, so lately swept.

"Well," Denton nodded, "that's certainly a lot." And it was. He had barely gotten a handle on the lay of the land *before* the crisis. Now allegiances he hardly understood were shifting, people were dying or fleeing, tensions were trebling, and the precarious equilibrium of the town was going bye-bye.

So where did this leave them?

The door opened, and Mr. Increase entered, trailed by Bulstrode. "Thank you," Denton told the turkey. He had asked Bulstrode to run and fetch Mr. Increase, knowing that the turkey would know how and where to find him.

"Huh?" Brisby wasn't privy to Bulstrode – it was easy to forget things like that.

"He was talking to me," Mr. Increase covered.

"Aren't you the one who poured the malignancy into our drinks, therefore rendering you responsible for our current predicament?" Without waiting for an answer, Brisby wheeled on Denton. "Is this why you thank him? For destroying our town?"

It's no more your town than mine. Denton always had such wonderful ripostes, he felt, but not the courage to deliver them.

"What is your role in this, Denton? I demand answers!"

Denton ran a hand through his hair. Damnit! "Do you demand they be truthful, or will placatory falsehoods suffice?"

"Those might be preferable!"

"…really?"

"Yes!"

"…Would you mind if Mr. Increase and I retired, in order to concoct some convincing fibs?"

"I think I'd appreciate it if you would!"

"…well, alright then." Denton shuffled Mr. Increase back toward the door.

"Watch out you don't trip over that turkey!" Brisby called helpfully.

"At another time," Denton whispered to Bulstrode once they'd all shuffled out to the front of Brisby's little shack, "I'd be very interested to know why you choose to make yourself visible in certain situations where invisibility would make everyone's life easier."

"I often wonder the very same thing about most humans."

Denton considered responding to that, and decided it wasn't worth it. Instead, he brought Mr. Increase up to speed on the state of the town in the Year Of Our Lord 1768. It was a measure of his guilt that, on a face that had so clearly seen some shit, Denton could see new wrinkles forming in almost real time.

Lucretia's death seemed to hit him hardest. Buddy was one thing, but such a young woman…

"So now," Bulstrode chirruped, "I'll have a go at distracting you from the horrible things you've done, by redirecting your attentions to the task at hand! Is this very much agreeable, I hope?"

Mr. Increase stared at and through Bulstrode.

"Shall I take silence as an affirmative?"

"Sure."

"Then I'll take affirmatives as silence as well, what? Ready? Here I go, with the distraction!" Bulstrode spun about in a circle, for no reason Denton could determine. "We must use our powers of deduction to deduce the identity of the magical malcontent what goes by the name of Himself, yes?"

Denton and Mr. Increase nodded.

"Wonderful, yes, I thought so too. You seem *marvelously* distracted from the pain and death you have caused, I should say. Carrying on: knowing as we do that Himself's Dread Familiar neutralized the effects of the poison for its master, we can exclude those in pain and dead, so sorry to bring that up again, from our list of potential Himselfs. With whom does this leave us then? Anyone?"

"Bulstrode, jus-"

"Anyone at all?"

Denton sighed. "It could technically be Buddy Jr., but that wouldn't make any sense. I got the sense his love for Missy was genuine, and he wouldn't endanger her life just to maintain cover with an out-of-towner like me. It could be Cullender Lowestoft – I don't know him that well – or it could be Chip Ditteridge."

"So Miss Carsis' gambit worked," Mr. Increase allowed with a maximum of chagrin. "She's narrowed it to three."

"Ah, but not so fast, chippies! Aren't you forgetting someones?"

"…?" Denton and Mr. Increase concluded in unison.

"What of Bunny Crundwell? Opal and Fithian Lowestoft? Or Millicent Ditteridge?"

"He's called *Himself*, I thought," Mr. Increase stated, sans question mark.

"Yes, but let's not be pronoun chauvinists, please and thank you. We Familiars can be, let's say *imprecise* when it comes to the finer points of anatomy, so a pinch of magnanimity on that score would be appreciated."

"Even so," Denton resumed, "I think we can safely rule out Missy Ditteridge, for the same reason we could rule out Buddy Jr."

Mr. Increase shook his head. "Now hang on a second. Endangering a loved one for the sake of a ruse does seem farfetched, but couldn't a witch casting a sickness upon herself retain greater control over it?"

"A well-used noodle, you have," Bulstrode clucked, "but Denton here is correct. The illness with which poor Millicent was afflicted had a magical cause, but the symptoms were entirely biological. There would have been no easy way to keep them under one's claw. It is very unlikely to be Millicent."

"Then why did you mention her?"

"I long to see those noodles well-used! And I hope you'll allow a degree of euphemistic imprecision as well, recalling my unfortunate infacility with human anatomy."

"…what?"

"Oh, nothing." Bulstrode turned to Denton. "What's banging around the old attic, then?"

Denton squinted at nothing for a moment. He recalled the depth of knowledge with which Fithian glanced between Buddy Jr. and Missy. It'd be so easy to say it was Fithian, and the motive was pure jealousy …but Denton didn't buy it. "I don't think it's Fithian either. I'm not confident enough in that assessment to write her off entirely…but I'm fairly certain."

"That's fairly good enough for me!" Very probably, the turkey demon had reached this conclusion already; he just enjoyed running his two human companions around in logical circles.

"So," Mr. Increase concluded with a gentle clap of the hands, "Himself could be Bunny Crundwell, Cullender or Opal Lowestoft, or Chip Ditteridge. Narrowed it to four, nothing at which to turn up one's nose, for one night's worth of work, or am I very much mistaken?"

Neither Denton nor Mr. Increase had anything to say to that. The one night's worth of work had been hateful enough to last a lifetime.

"Alright," Denton grumbled at last, "we can start figuring out who's who tomorrow. Also, maybe you can explain to me why this should be my concern, Bulstrode."

"The integrity of the t-"

"Right now," Denton interrupted so effectively as to make Mr. Increase flush with unearned pride, "let's go tell Brisby something pretty."

XII

CHIP DITTERIDGE DIDN'T *WANT* TO BE STUCK wandering the halls of the Crundwell mansion. At first, when the people in the ballroom started dropping, he had panicked and ran. How was he to know whether or not he risked succumbing by staying where he was? Chip hadn't gotten where he was today by staying where he was. Unfortunately, where he was today was lost in the Crundwell mansion, so perhaps there was something to be said for stasis.

For the first few hours, he had made a point of hiding. After he saw those two rascals cavorting their way out of the woods, Chip decided that he couldn't trust anyone except himself, although he *would* say he could trust himself, wouldn't he? But how did *he* know he was trustworthy? Best to err on the side of skepticism, which in this case meant hiding behind curtains or crawling into dressers, all the while suppressing the haughty scoffs so desperate to be voiced.

And there were so *many* curtains behind which to hide, so *many* dressers in which to crawl. Then what? Why, as befit a man of Chip's station when enclosed in a small, cozy space, he got sleepy. And as befit a man of Chip's station when he got sleepy, he went to sleep, because a man of Chip's station can sleep wherever he damn well pleases, including (and *especially*) in the dresser of another man who was but a few hours dead.

So he awoke, birthed himself from the woolen lips of the late Buddy's wardrobe, and gave a haughty scoff. He couldn't help it.

Now…from which way had he come? There weren't a great many landmarks by which to chart his progress; that abysmal black bunting obliterated any hope of orientation.

And so Chip wandered, this time wanting desperately (but not *too* desperately, as desperation was unbecoming in a man of his station) to be found, this time remaining decidedly unfound.

Which was annoying, because Chip knew something nobody else did.

This was how he always preferred the world to be. Now, granted, a pinch of epistemic reticence was always welcome in the stew of self-satisfaction. He couldn't be *absolutely positive* that nobody else knew what he knew, *vis-à-vis* the slave doctor and the dockhand escaping into, and then out of, the woods, just as things began going so tragically wrong here at the manor. But he could be *fairly certain*, which in Chip's experience always rounded up to *almost positive*, at which point one might as well keep rounding up to *absolutely positive.*

At first, he hadn't been certain what to do with this informtion. But being condemned to haunt these halls with no company save his own thoughts had given him plenty of time to think, because thinking was the best way to create new thoughts. That way he wouldn't have to deal with the old ones, some of which had pointy bits and made scary crocodile noises.

His new thoughts ran thusly: he had, as he had heard some colonist of low-breeding say, "one over" on the slave doctor and the dockhand. It would be the easiest thing in the world, to nudge old Sheriff Barefoot and say "right, look at those two there, and think how much better they'd look slapped in irons!" And the Sheriff would comply, because what else were law enforcement officials good for? He wouldn't need evidence, because when a man of Chip's station testifies to the veracity of a proposition, the proposition is true, otherwise a man of Chip's station would not be testifying to its veracity. Logic, plain and simple.

So. Once he tracked down the two trouble-makers, Chip would outline this situation for them in the starkest terms possible. Then they would fall to their knees and offer slobbering entreaties for clemency. Oh please Mr. Ditteridge, don't do this to us! We are but slow-witted conscripts into the nefarious cause of colonial agitation, so easily led astray by our miserable intellectual allotments!

And then, in his graceful way, Chip would consider their position and show mercy. *If*, he would append to their moist rejoicings in explosive staccato (how he would find the plosive in the word "if" was a matter he would address when the time came), you two help *me.*

Of course, they would reply, anything for one so just and lenient as yourself!

Chip would smile here, clear his throat, and outline his plan. Which he didn't have fully outlined yet, but again, that was a matter he would address when the time came. In broad strokes though, he wanted to have the lower sorts of Fidget's Mill on his side. Even cut off from the flow of current events as he was, he'd been around too long to think he was going to emerge from these labyrinthine halls into a town that was exactly the same as the one he'd left in 1767. The board had been wiped clean, and a race to reset the pieces would be inevitable.

Probably. Almost certainly. Absolutely.

How would Chip position himself, to be in a position to reposition the pieces in a position most advantageous to him? Balls if he knew. But he didn't have many friends in Fidget's Mill (which was completely not his fault, it was due entirely to the anti-Royalist bigotry of the slum-dwellers here). Making friends among the rabble would be essential, but as that was very nearly impossible, *making* such as these be his friends would do the trick. Growing up wealthy taught Chip many things, chief among them being that the quickest way to make new friends was through compulsion. *Keeping* them was a different matter, but Chip had never fretted much over that. Friends often ceased to be useful after a short period of time, at which point to hell with them; there were always other friends to be drafted.

The slave doctor and the dockhand were both influential in their communities. They could drum up further support for any measures Chip needed to take, to get a stronger grip on the town. He was acutely aware of the political knife's-edge upon which the Mill rested. If the town adopted non-importation as the rest of Massachusetts had, a unified colonial front against the British would be soon to follow. But if Chip could effectively commandeer the town, and deliver it to the King…*personally* deliver it to the King…

Sir Ditteridge?

Was that too much to hope for? He didn't think so.

A knight of the realm. Imagine that! The first in his family for generations! And there would almost certainly be more material rewards to follow. The man who single-handedly staved off colonial insurrection!

Granted, he wouldn't be able to live in America then. And moving back to England would present some problems of its own…but no problem was too big for a knight of the realm, was it?

He rounded yet another corner, and this time came into a large foyer. In the foyer were two slaves. Chip scoffed haughtily, and they turned to look at him.

"Fetch me a carriage back to town!" he cried as imperiously as he could manage (which was very imperious indeed, if he said so himself, which he often did).

The slaves stared back at him blankly. Chip considered how he must look, having slept in a cabinet and wandered the halls without food or water for…however long it had been. Days? Come to think of it, he was *very* hungry, as well as thirsty. He'd sated himself on the dignity the slave doctor and dockhand had so cravenly proffered him (*they* would have no use for it anymore), and that had kept him going for a while. But now, he was actually quite hungry, quite thirsty. Not for metaphors. For real food and drink.

"Let's table that for one moment – fetch me real food and drink, and *then* a carriage back to town!"

Again, the slaves stared back at him blankly.

Chip scoffed, though his haughty heart wasn't in it. "You two don't speak English, do you?"

More blank stares. Chip shrugged his coat higher up around his shoulders, and marched past the slaves, out into the cold of the day. He'd fetch the damn carriage himself. Let them gawk while they could – their doctor would be giving them marching orders set to Chip's fief and drum soon enough.

Once Chip was outside, one of the slaves coughed quietly. "I was really hoping that guy had died too," he whispered in perfect English, because Chip wasn't the only one who liked having secrets.

XIII

FORTUNATELY, BRISBY HADN'T TOLD ANYBODY about Denton's warning. That Denton had advance knowledge of the poison was clear enough, and Denton could understand why Brisby would therefore assume longtime complicity, rather than the truth, that Denton found out about it literally seconds before warning Brisby not to drink his drink. And if someone as…agreeably disposed towards Denton as Brisby suspected this, then those far less favorably inclined would undoubtedly peg Denton as the sole malefactor of the evening. It was imperative that this damning information remain between just the three of them. And Miss Carsis. And Bulstrode. And possibly some of the slaves at the Crundwell mansion, though none of them spoke English so he wasn't really worried about that.

Still, Denton did his best to spin a fiction by which a warning to Brisby could be offered in perfectly good faith. That his best *was* good enough said more about Brisby's innate gullibility than it did about Denton's facility with fabrication.

The lie was, like most fiction, needlessly convoluted and packed with unnecessary detail. But in the end, what it boiled down to was that Mr. Increase saw *some slave* in one of the back rooms pouring *some substance* into the drinks, and came out to warn Denton, who immediately warned Brisby, and then took off to capture the fiend. The fiend led them on an appropriately fiendish pursuit through the house, and sadly the two got turned around and so didn't leave until the next morning. But, still, they had tried their best!

Despite Houlihan's nearly unbelievable willingness to accept the tale, Denton at least had the good sense to feel bad about it. The reasons for this were manifold, but the chief two were that Denton didn't feel good about throwing slaves, as a bloc, overboard to save his own white skin. Obviously there *was* no poison-pouring slave, and were Denton asked to identify one, he would appeal to the not-so-latent racism of the interrogators by claiming that, gosh, he couldn't pull the fella out of a lineup, he hardly got a good look at him.

The other reason to feel less-than-stellar about the lie was helpfully pointed out by Brisby.

"So…Mr. Increase saw the slave depositing his poisons into the potations, and came to tell you."

"That's right," Denton confirmed.

"And you immediately warned me off of drinking said potations."

"Correct."

"…"

Finally, Denton saw it too. "Ah."

"I don't see how I could have been partaking of the tainted beverage, if a slave had only just accomplished his villainous objective in the backroom. Surely I would be drinking of a different pitcher, as it were?"

"Yes," Mr. Increase pitched in, "you were. But I must have neglected to mention that, as I saw this scoundrel tipping his vial over the potation, I did hear him say, under his breath, 'ya-har! This batch'll be even worse than the first, of which the guests are already now drinking!'"

Brisby's eyes went wide. "He said that?"

"Indeed he did," Mr. Increase somehow managed with a straight face.

"Well, that settles it." Brisby clapped his hands once, sounding even more relieved than Denton and Mr. Increase felt.

"…really?" Denton couldn't help wondering this aloud, any more than Mr. Increase could help elbowing him hard in the kidney.

"Yes, you two saved me from a most scatological end! I knew there couldn't have been the least trace of malignity in the situation, though I must confess suspicion does have a way of creeping up."

"Oh, but of course."

Brisby thought for a moment, which Denton correctly identified as unfathomably dangerous to the entrenchment of their fiction. So, having already availed himself of one off-the-cuff, highly unconvincing fiction, he couldn't see the harm in doubling down.

"Ouch!" he cried, grabbing his elbow (conspicuously devoid of pain) with such force that he actually *did* hurt his elbow a little bit, which lead to a genuine, and consequently far more restrained, "ouch".

As he'd hoped, Brisby had merely been looking for an excuse to cast aside the vagaries of politics, in favor of physiological certainties. To wit: a man cried out in pain and clutched his elbow. Now *here* was a problem that might well have an immediate solution, complete with actionable steps towards its accomplishment.

"What seems to be the matter?" Brisby cried as he rushed to Denton's side, as though it weren't the most obvious thing in the world what seemed to be the matter. His elbow (ostensibly) hurt. Only a trained physician could have seen fit to ask such a silly question in the first place, Denton reflected.

"My, uh, my elbow hurts."

"Where?"

"…the pointy bit between the upper and lower portions of my arm?"

"No, I mean, inside or outside the elbow?"

"Outside, I guess? Or inside? Inside the bone, you mean?"

"No…no. Does it hurt…" Brisby touched the back of his elbow, below the tricep. "Outside…" he touched the meaty section of the inner elbow, below his bicep. "…inside."

"Aaaah. I understand now." And he finally did, but having cleared up his honest misunderstandings left him with a whole battery of affected misunderstandings with which to confuse and confound poor Brisby. The doctor really was trying his best with the uncooperative patient, and fortunately, that left him precious little time to think about the gaping, armada-sized holes in Denton and Mr. Increase's story. Mental real estate was a commodity both precious and finite, and Denton was happy to *finally* be the beneficiary of this sad fact.

An hour later, they left a haggard and exasperated Dr. Brisby Houlihan who was only too happy to say that yes he would make sure the who's-who (or, more accurately, who's-left) of the Mill knew that Denton and Mr. Increase were innocent bystanders just trying to do what was right. Because by agreeing to this so emphatically, Brisby felt he augmented the chances of them both leaving *now*, as opposed to *a time other than 'now'*.

"But do you think he'll actually do it?" Denton still couldn't quite wrap his head around Brisby's gullibility. The strategic, cynical part of him (a part given a much more prestigious position in the Noggin Congress, since his being summarily duped by Miss Carsis and Mr. Increase) wondered if that gullibility were just a pose, to lull these two self-appointed fugitives into complacency, that a trap might be more effectively sprung upon them…or maybe Brisby was just a bit of an airhead. Not *stupid* – Houlihan was certainly not stupid – just a bit…well, in his own world.

After all, wouldn't a crafty man with an eye on maneuvers and manipulations want to make it look as though his confidence was hard won? Rolling over the way Brisby had would just be *suspicious*. Which it was. So, it must *not* be suspicious, because it was *so* suspicious that there was no *way* it could be. Right?

"Right?" Denton summarized to Mr. Increase.

"I don't…" Mr. Increase shook his head, stopped walking for a moment, and resumed locomotion with speech. "I don't know."

"It's a hell of a lot to keep track of, I must say."

"What is?"

"Chicanery of this sort."

"You have no idea."

Denton didn't like the sound of that at *all*.

He bade Mr. Increase a fond-ish farewell (after inquiring as to how much he cared about mysterious witches) and returned to the Klump Regency. On his walk home, he reduced his options to two: flee Fidget's Mill, return to Boston, leave this infernal town to its own devices, and let the spirit of agitation currently gripping the country play out as the fates demand.

Or.

He could stay and keep trying to accomplish this piddling political goal of his. He could stay, in the hopes that Brisby was in his corner the way he claimed to be, in the hopes that Brisby went and *very convincingly* argued that Denton couldn't in the least be blamed for Buddy and - more to the point - Lucretia's deaths, in the hopes that Buddy Jr. would be receptive to the argument, in the hopes that Buddy Jr. would still feel he owed Denton a favor.

Because, finally, a plan of action was taking shape. Vague, ill-defined, perhaps ruinously ill-conceived; the plan was all of these things, in this larval stage. But it would be ready to hatch soon, and Denton was optimistic that its wings would envelope the whole of Fidget's Mill, and all things would finally come up Denton.

But he really needed Buddy Jr. on his side, to start.

Denton, with eyelids fighting a valiant (and vain) battle against gravity and sheep-tallies, struggled his way up to his room, threw open the door, and very nearly collapsed into his bed.

Very nearly. But he had almost died out in the woods, and he was now facing similarly fatal stakes in the discharge of his duties. They took on an immediacy they had previously lacked. If Denton screwed up here, he could be killed. One would be hard pressed to find a more immediate shot of perspective than one's mortality being brought home in a visceral way.

So, struggling with a head that grew heavier by the second, Denton sat down at the small desk against the wall and wrote his family a letter. He wasn't entirely sure what he was writing. All he knew was that he could very easily have put this off until tomorrow morning, and at the same time, this was something that absolutely couldn't wait.

He awoke the next morning when the sun knocked on his window and whispered *hey asshole*. Denton peeled his face off of the desk, and saw that he had completed the letter to his family. He reread it, shook his head, and sent it without making a single change. Not because it was perfect; merely because it couldn't be improved upon.

XIV

PALLS AREN'T GOOD FOR MUCH, BUT THEY *ARE* good at spreading over things and places. Lucretia's death cast a pall over the Crundwell mansion. So did Sonny's abandonment of his family. And, sure, Buddy's death did too. But that last pall was more economic than emotional.

Point is, there was a whole passel of palls spread over the Crundwell mansion, which is why it was so striking that that is where they remained. Denton expected to see said palls spreading over the rest of Fidget's Mill, and so was stunned by how unaffected the town seemed by the tragedy just over the hill. This was a town on a knife's edge, was it not? He'd thought this countless times, he'd heard it *said* countless times. Tenuous equilibrium, dangerous instability, etc. etc. etc., all synonyms for Fidget's Mill.

And yet, 1768 seemed indistinguishable from 1767. There were a few tearful words said for Lucretia in pubs over the next week or so, but these often had little to do with her as a person (nobody really knew much about her as a person – she'd have been the black sheep of the family quite handily, were it not for Sonny), and more to do with the fact of her death. A young woman in her prime, would have made a highly desirable bride, could have made a man very happy, let us drink to her memory. That sort of thing.

A great many words were said for Sonny, but they were not the sorts of words one generally wants said about oneself.

As for Buddy, well…Buddy's death only registered as a business hiccup. In fact, Denton came to realize that the man was held in approximately the same esteem as slavery was in the Mill. While there were a few defenders, people were generally arrayed against it/him to varying degrees. *But*, save the most vocal opponents, people were also generally prepared to acknowledge his/its utility, and the role he/it played in keeping the world turning on its current axis.

Oh, and as was generally the case for Fidgetonians, 'people' were 'white male landholders'.

In the first week of the new year, Governer Rumney Marsh stepped up his presence in the town, becoming a far more visible mover and/or shaker than he had heretofore been. That he was both generous of waist and, for several days after the party, wan of face and green of gill served to illuminate just how driven the man was to secure a tighter grasp on the cords of power. Denton could tell Rumney was preparing for *something*, but just what that something was remained a mystery.

But that wasn't what fascinated Denton. He was drawn to the inactivity far more than the activity. Dreadful though the realization was, Denton spent the first week of the new year feeling more encouraged than he had since first setting foot in this town. The *de facto* head of Fidget's Mill was dead, along with his only daughter. The oldest son had gone missing, with the son of another of the chief families. The town's tenuousknifesedgeequilibrumandsoonandsoforth had been shaken like a baby, so where was the wailing and crying?

People just didn't seem to care. And that's when Denton realized that perhaps the antipathy towards the status quo was greater than he had thought.

Not that this would help him. It didn't really *change* anything – his goals were still economic in nature, which meant securing the co-operation of the higher sorts of people in town. But still – how could he not be excited, even *thrilled*, at the prospect of widespread popular support?

Awful shame about the dying and sickness and all that, but this was a wonderful development.

This wave of morbid cheer rose so high, and ran so swiftly, that Denton decided he could ride it all the way to Buddy and Lucretia's joint funeral service. Which he could, and did. But, he might have recalled in a more grounded state of mind, *can* and *should* are often opposite ends of the same spectrum.

Denton had hoped that Brisby would put in a good word for him with Buddy Jr. He could see by Brisby and Buddy Jr.'s adjacent faces, upon arriving at the field at the edge of the Crundwell property, that a good word had been put in, but turned out to be insufficient.

That pall that had failed to spread over Fidget's Mill? Denton found it spreading not over but *through* him. Had he just walked into a funeral for which he would be held responsible? Would those assembled here, which included not just the remaining members of the Crundwells, Lowestofts and Ditteridges, but also Governor Marsh and, uh oh, Sheriff Barefoot, rejoice at the convenience of Denton's arrival, and see if there wasn't a buy-two-get-one-free deal on caskets?

Feeling frozen in place, Denton could only stare through the make-shift pews erected in the field, to Buddy Jr.'s similarly immobile face. There was a brow upon which you could crack walnuts.

Finally, Denton recalled how to walk. One foot in front of the other, but then, here was the trick, put the first foot *back* in front, and so on. He utilized this recently reacquired knowledge to walk towards a man who looked hard at work trying to give himself an aneurysm. What else could he do? If he turned and ran, any suspicions Buddy Jr. may have harbored would thereby be confirmed (and that Buddy Jr., as well as the rest of the town, had suspicions was clear enough. So much for only Brisby having seen them run out). If he stood stock-still, *everybody* would start to look at him curiously. His only choice was to walk up to Buddy Jr. and do his best to act as though nothing had happened.

Nothing for which he could be blamed, anyway. It'd be very hard to pretend the deaths of his father and sister hadn't happened, though Denton had often heard that there was no limit to the powers of positive thinking.

"Hello," he said to Buddy Jr. when he was still slightly too far away for a greeting to seem natural. "How are you doing today?" This was a very normal thing for one human to say to another human.

"How do you think I'm doing?" Buddy Jr. shot back.

Denton recalled the context of their meeting. "Probably not very well," he observed. He sat down in the empty chair next to Buddy Jr. "Do you mind if I sit here?"

Buddy Jr. shook his head. Denton nodded his, and then observed a few other things he probably ought to have observed earlier.

He had sat down in an empty seat. That meant Buddy Jr. was sitting between Denton on one side and Brisby on the other. Where was Missy? No, dumb question – they would be doing their best to hide their love for one another, particularly now that the town was expecting him to marry Fithian for the sake of the Mill's solvency. So, not-so-dumb question, where was Fithian?

And then came the moment of transubstantiation, when a not-so-dumb question becomes a dumb question: Denton asked it out loud.

"Where's Fithian?"

Buddy Jr. rolled his head toward Denton, but couldn't dignify him with a similar turning of the shoulders. This left Buddy Jr.'s body facing forward, and his face turned to glare at Denton down his own shoulder, which looked incredibly uncomfortable, which in turn underlined that this was being done to make a point. "She opted to stay home today, given the chill."

The chill was a rather delicate way of saying it was *fucking freezing*. Whatever poor souls had dug the graves (and Denton could guess they hadn't been the sorts of people to be remunerated for their labors) had to shovel away the snow, and then chip away at the frozen earth, until the holes were deep enough to constitute a respectful interment. Denton had been wondering why a week had passed before the funeral(s) were arranged, but perhaps that was the answer; it just hadn't been possible to get the graves dug any sooner.

But for a family that kept a palm tree alive in the depths of a New England winter, an unyielding Earth wouldn't stand a chance against their unstoppable will. Not to mention their expendable help.

An image occurred to Denton, of two slaves digging three graves: one for Buddy, one for Lucretia, and one for the both of them to tumble into upon completion of their task. He shivered, and was happy to know that it would be chalked up to the cold.

"Of course," Denton agreed. "It is quite chilly."

"Yes. It is."

They sat silently for a moment, waiting for…the priest? Denton wasn't sure what sort of a funeral this would be. The only funeral he'd ever been to before was a Quaker funeral for his grandmother, which as far as he could tell was just getting your loved ones together to sit and take a nap, and then every once in a while one of those loved ones will stand up and deliver some limp anecdote that just occurred to them, often but not always involving the deceased. Denton couldn't quite remember – he'd been young and sleepy. Now he was older and even sleepier, and he still had no idea what happened at funerals. Lawyers, after all, usually only come into the picture after the funeral business has been handled.

"I'm very sorry for your loss," he ventured.

Buddy Jr. looked into his own lap and shifted uncomfortably. "Loss*es*."

"Of course."

Another long moment passed. Finally, Buddy Jr. swung on Denton, a full-bodied shift complete with thrown elbows that nearly knocked him backwards. "Why didn't you stay?" BJ exclaimed in a gravely whisper.

"Stay where?"

"In the ballroom! Brisby tells me you went gallivanting around the house looking for the hateful slave, when there remained such dire want of your skillset in the very room from which you fled!"

"…what skillset?"

"Medicine!"

"Ah! Yes! My medical skillset! For I am doctor to the slaves!" Denton went to run his hands through his hair, but caught himself when his hand was halfway to his scalp. He paused awkwardly in mid-raise, then turned the move into a half-hearted slap on the forehead. Fortunately for him, Buddy Jr. read this lamentable physical comedy as a manifestation of his dreadful guilt.

Still, Buddy Jr.'s rage was not to be swayed by the taint of sympathy. "My dearest sister Lucretia might still be here with us today, had you remained to ply your trade! My dearest brother Sonny might yet be by my side, and so," here he lowered his voice, "the overwhelming pressures to enter into a sham of an arranged marriage might be ameliorated!"

"Your father might have survived as well," Brisby pitched in. Denton shot him a look, which seemed to hit the *actual* physician right between the eyes.

"Yes, that's also true," Buddy Jr. allowed.

"I…I…" Denton sputtered for a second. He didn't know what he…he… For some reason, he *did* feel guilty about this, despite the fact that staying in the ballroom would have done nothing, save blowing open his cover story. It was, in a strange way, a wonderful stroke of luck that he'd put himself in the position of having to run out of the room at full speed.

So why did he feel guilty about it? He was satisfied that he wasn't responsible for the cause or effects of the evening. And yet…

Denton hung his head. "I am truly sorry," he said and meant. It was slightly worrying, hearing such raw, unguarded honesty coming out of his mouth and sliding into Buddy Jr.'s ears – making a habit of that could get him into very serious trouble. "But, in addition to being a doctor, I am a former record holder in my college's…running department." He shook his head and plowed on. "I am very good at competitive running, and so I thought my skillset as a man fleet of foot might be gainfully employed, in apprehending the villain of the evening."

"You were very much mistaken," Buddy Jr. snarled as he turned to once again face forward in his seat.

"Yes, I was. And I will always be, from the bottom of my heart, sorry for the mistakes I have made." Denton also turned back to face front, and ran his hand through his ha…FUCK. It disturbed him, how quickly habits could be formed, and how difficult they could be to break.

A rector of the local parish eventually showed up and said a few words. And then he said a few more. And a few more after that. Then, he said a few more.

Finally, at lost last, the rector said a few more words. And then all that was left was for him to say a few words. So he said a few more. And, just for good measure, a few more.

Four hours later, the mourners were sent on their way, and Denton reflected on how savvy it was to run a funeral like this. As he'd already learned, mental real estate is precious and finite, and it's hard to be devastated by grief when you're so bored as to envy the man in the casket.

XV

AFTER THE TOWN'S GRIEF WAS EXORCISED BY the tedium of the priest, everyone broke and headed into the Crundwell mansion for chow.

In what Denton could only think of as exceedingly poor taste, a long table was laid out in the very ballroom where Buddy bit the big one. That was where the poor taste ended, though, because each and every item on offer was *delicious*. Denton could say this with absolute certainty, because he tried each and every item on offer. Such were the perks of being welcomed amongst the upper classes.

Oh, and speaking of poor taste, there was drink on offer as well.

Denton couldn't help but notice, as he sipped and nibbled the day away, that more than a few crooked stares were cast his way, and retracted just as quickly. He'd cleared things up with Brisby and Buddy Jr. (well, kind of), but positive gossip was always much slower to spread than negative. How many of the guests – er, mourners – here were looking at him and thinking 'here is the criminal, returned to the scene of the crime?'

Another quaff cleared everything up. There was an easy solution to this, wasn't there? Of course there was. So Denton walked over to Buddy Jr., because being seen to be pally with the son of the deceased would put paid to those pernicious suspicions. Probably.

He sauntered over to Buddy Jr., clapped a hand on his shoulder, and cried "Buddy!" loud enough for others to hear. "Junior," he added, in case there were any lingering confusion.

Buddy Jr. turned with planetary lethargy. When half of the son's face had dawned on Denton, so too did the social solar system in which he was engaged: Buddy Jr. had been deep in conversation with Fithian Lowestoft and Missy Ditteridge.

Denton had stumbled into Fidget's Mill's very own love triangle. Again.

"Oh," he announced, "hello."

And then, Denton got to witness the triangle at work. From his position just over Buddy Jr.'s shoulder, he watched as the skeptical young man's face warmed ever so slightly – he may not have entirely cleared Denton of wrongdoing in his mind, but here was a man who could be entrusted with the truth of this tangled love affair. This, Denton had already demonstrated by staying mum about the 'procedure'.

Fithian, to Denton's left, raised an eyebrow of such imperiousness, that Denton could scarcely believe she belonged to the *nouveau riche* clan. There was a brow for an old money portrait, if ever there was one.

Meanwhile, Missy, to Denton's right, smiled with unguarded sincerity – here was the man who had saved her life in more ways than one, and she'd be damned if she concealed her gratitude for the sake of propriety.

Fithian looked to Missy, saw the warmth radiating off of her, and softened almost instantly. If Missy trusted Denton enough to give him that look, then she would as well.

Finally, Missy placed a restraining hand on Buddy Jr.'s shoulder. He turned around, and saw both of the women in his life looking at Denton the way parents look at children who are growing up too fast, but growing into something wonderful. When the heir to the Crundwell fortune turned back to Denton, the former knew he was once again in the latter's good graces. He just hoped other people were noticing the smiles he was getting from representatives of the three big families in town.

"I'm wondering if there isn't somewhere more discreet for us to speak," Denton lied. He hadn't been wondering that, because he still didn't know exactly what he wanted to say. But he knew to a near-certainty that there would never be a better time to say whatever it would end up being than now.

Buddy Jr. nodded in short, understated nods. "This house was designed with discretion in mind." Which struck Denton as self-evidently untrue (he recalled the palm tree out front), but perhaps he meant there were many rooms well suited to discretion within this paean to expenditure. Or perhaps the architect had *had* discretion in mind, and was just very bad at his job.

I'll find out soon enough, he thought as he followed the single-file love triangle out of the ballroom (and surely there was nothing discreet about this little aristocratic conga line) and to a place where they could speak in relative privacy.

They retired to a quiet room down length halls, some three and a half corners from the ballroom. Denton despaired of ever finding his way back without Buddy Jr.'s help, so there was reason enough to ensure this exchange remained civil.

The room was large and plush, with a high ceiling and soot-blackened fireplace against the far wall. Buddy Jr. strode over to it, plucked some logs from a copper bin just next to the fire poker, and placed them in the fireplace as though they were made of porcelain.

Denton surveyed the rest of the room. Imposing bookcases full of leather-bound volumes gave the space an air of dignity, though it was the sort of dignity that looked you up and down and sneered, as if to say *my dignity is bigger than your dignity*. "Is this your private study, then?"

Buddy Jr. nodded without turning from his work. "Yes, in a sense." Denton couldn't help but notice that this room was free from the black funereal drapings that so dominated the rest of the house.

Fithian set off at a purposeful stride, making for a very specific book amongst the countless volumes. She reached a hand out to one book that was, as far as Denton was concerned, indistinguishable from the others. It gained distinction as she plucked it off of the shelf, and four other books came with it, all in a row. They were false books, hollowed out and glued together to conceal what lay behind them. What lay behind them being three glasses and a bottle of something Denton suspected would get him *very* drunk in no time at all.

"Apologies," she offered as she carried the three glasses to a small table near the center of the room, set among worn, buttoned leather chairs, "but we're not used to having company in moments such as these."

"Oh, don't apologize, I'm quite honored to be present at all." Denton was somewhat distressed by how sincerely he meant this.

Missy joined Fithian at the table, placing small trays under each of the glasses. "To keep them from creating rings on the table," she offered without being prompted.

"If you'd like a pull of that," Buddy Jr. called to Denton as he retrieved a tinderbox from the same copper pot as the logs and set to unpacking it, "I can have a fourth glass fetched for you."

"It's very good whiskey," Missy informed Denton. "Hence, our decision to keep it hidden within the literature."

Fithian poured the first glass. "And, to be quite honest, it's sometimes fun to have secrets."

Yes, Denton reflected, *it sometimes is.* Of course, it's less fun to be the one from whom the secrets are kept. "Do you three come here often, then?"

"As often as we can," Fithian replied as she poured the second glass.

"You understand our situation, of course." Missy took the first glass and plopped gracelessly onto one of the chairs behind her. Denton was struck by the movement, and it occurred to him how rare it was to see a woman dressed as finely as she moving the way normal human beings do. It was, he imagined, considered unbecoming.

Sensing an opportunity, Denton remembered himself – specifically, the fictional version of himself with which these three were acquainted. He paced to Missy, and knelt down in front of her. "I have been meaning to ask – how is *your*...situation?" He cast a theatrical glance towards Fithian. He was almost positive she already knew, but appearing to be as discreet as the whiskey behind the books could only help his case.

"She knows," Missy confirmed quietly. "And thank you so very much for asking. I am…I am well. I am sad, you understand, but it was necessary. That child would have had no chance at a happy life, especially now, given the town's current…" here her lips cracked into a mirthless smile, "…situation." She placed a hand on Denton's shoulder. "And I do feel so much better, besides. I cannot thank you enough."

"Oh, simply terrific!" came a posh little voice from the corner of the room. "It does warm one's heart, gratitude."

"Oh *no*," Denton said out loud.

Missy cocked her head to the side. "Excuse me?"

"I mean, by that, to say oh, *no*, you have nothing for which to thank me. It is all in a day's work for a man possessed of my skillset. Unless," he added with a sideways glance to Buddy Jr., hard at work striking up a fire, "there are evildoers to chase. And now, if you will excuse me, I am afraid I must cough into the nook of my elbow." Denton did just that, using it as an excuse to peer into the corner of the room where No-Good Bulstrode stood, floofing his feathers, invisible to all save Denton.

GET OUT, he thought as loudly as he could. Yes, Fithian was right, it *was* fun to have secrets, and he felt it was also valuable to have at least *one* leg up on Miss Carsis. But, alas, here was No-Good Bulstrode, her ears in low places. And he couldn't well shoo the turkey away, at least not without looking like an absolute lunatic to the three people whose confidence he very much needed to secure.

Suddenly, he was performing for an audience. He only realized how surprisingly relaxed about the whole situation he'd been, now that he was able to contrast it with the anxiety of having Miss Carsis present by proxy.

FWOOSH. The fire caught in the fireplace with a theatricality suitable for an incipient cabal. Buddy Jr. rose and turned to the three guests he knew about, and the one he didn't. "Are you sure we can't get you a drink, Mr. Hedges?"

With a final glare at Bulstrode, Denton plastered a smile back onto his face and looked to his host. "I'm certain, but thank you so kindly."

"Of course. You had something you wanted to discuss?"

"Hm? Oh! Oh, yes, of course." Buddy Jr. was close enough to the mark. Denton wanted to discuss something – it was just a matter of figuring out what.

If only he had time to think. How best to secure their continued support? How best to utilize their support to accomplish his own ends?

Well, how were the disparate colonies being slowly united? Why, they found a common enemy. Nothing brought friends together like a common enemy.

So who could be their common enemy?

Denton opened his mouth, and the words "Governor Rumney Marsh" came out, which seemed like a good start.

XVI

A COLONIAL GOVERNOR, AS FAR AS DENTON WAS concerned, was a professional tattletale. They *technically* enforced the laws, but as was always the case with technicalities, this meant that they didn't. This task was delegated to bailiffs and sheriffs and probably some other iffs. A Governor's power lay in their own prostration before the British throne. If the Governor's governed agreed that they didn't much take to the Governor's means of governing, the Governor was fucked. That is, up until they could fire a dispatch across the Atlantic, at which point the King would send back a wax-sealed finger wagging, delivered at the business end of a cannon.

In the years prior to Colonial unrest, Governorship was something of a sinecure. Now, as the Crown's need for authority figures capable of enforcing Colonial law became more and more dire, self-importance outpaced self-awareness in many of their arbitrarily chosen appointees. Exhibit A may as well have been Governor Rumney Marsh.

Marsh, Missy informed Denton, hailed from the North of England. Judging by her tone of voice, this was among the least auspicious of the cardinal directions. He had been appointed Governor of Fidget's Mill in Seventeenfiftysomething, and this would have come as news to some of the lower sorts in town, even now. The man was ubiquitous to the moneyed classes, but nigh invisible to the not-so-moneyed. And why else would they know him? Marsh didn't really *do* anything, which in a way made him the perfect man to serve as nominal head of the town.

Now, in the wake of Buddy's passing, he seemed to be lining himself up to assume power, which was a marked step up from the last decade or so of assuming he had power.

"So," Denton asked with a sideways glance at Bulstrode, "how, exactly, he is doing that?"

Missy shrugged. "Specifically? I'm afraid I can't say – I'm kept too far removed from the conversations. But the conversations are happening, between him and my father, far more frequently than they ever had before."

"Her father remains a sympathizer of King George's," Fithian pitched in.

"And they've taken to closing the door." Missy hung her head slightly. "They didn't used to do that."

Denton nodded. None of that would hold up in, say, a court of law. But that wasn't what mattered. What mattered was that he needed to know what Governor Marsh was doing, so they could come up with a way to stop him from doing it. Not because the doing of the *it*, whatever the it was, would be bad. Rather, because the *stopping* of the doing of the it would be good.

Good for Denton, anyway. A common enemy was a start, but they needed some plan of unified action. All of them working together. That sort of thing.

They couldn't start doing that, though, until they knew what it was they were supposed to be doing.

"I'd be just chuffed to bits if you'd accept my help," Bulstrode clucked from Denton's peripheral vision. "I can stick the missing bits of this picture into place!"

Denton did his best to project a *SHUT UP* in Bulstrode's direction. He knew what lay down that path. He'd accept information from Bulstrode, and before he knew it he'd be flying on the back of a giant bird that Miss Carsis had made out of an eggplant, and oh by the way now he owed her a gallon of his children's blood or something. No. He was done with her, and didn't much care whether or not she was done with him.

"We are all of us in this room committed to the Cause, correct?" Denton phrased this very delicately. There was no real Cause in the Colonies. There were Causes, manifold Causes of endless variation. What 'The Cause' meant to one person might be similar to their neighbor's 'Cause', or it might be wildly different from their spouse's 'Cause'. But no two, it seemed, were ever perfectly unified.

And as long as nobody called attention to this fact, at the very moment when Denton was attempting to fudge a unity that didn't exist, he should be fine.

Missy nodded at once. "Yes." Fithian was close behind.

Buddy Jr. smiled and shrugged. Denton could understand his reticence; the Crundwells stood to lose the most from a radical shift in the Colonial structure. "I suppose I am."

"Well," Denton continued, internalizing an explosive sigh of relief, "then I may speak freely. Governor Marsh is an obstacle to the Cause, is he not?" Again, Denton was rolling the die here. If any of his three would-be compatriots asked him to specify *why* Marsh was an obstacle, he would be at a loss to oblige. Rumney Marsh was nothing but a tool by which he could hew together a close working relationship between himself and members of the three families. Denton cared little for or about the Governor in any sense beyond such social calculations. But he asked his question with confidence, and if being a lawyer had taught him anything, it was that confidence could be more persuasive than facts.

"He is," Missy was once again first to aver. Fithian and Buddy Jr.

seconded her motion at just about the same time. Denton made a mental note to focus on Missy as he cultivated these relationships; of the three (comparative) moppets standing before him, she seemed least inhibited by her youth.

Phew. "Then it is agreed. We must see his objects frustrated at every turn. The challenge, then, is in ascertaining his objects!"

"Or," Bulstrode put in from the corner, "forgo the objects altogether, and instead give him the old scrufftoss entire!"

"What?" Denton asked aloud. He couldn't help it.

"Huh?" Missy also asked aloud.

"Nothing," Denton mumbled.

"Yes, let's do keep a tighter rein on our outbursts, eh? They'll think you mad!" Bulstrode clicked his way further into the room. Denton cursed himself for engaging with the blasted Familiar at all.

Suddenly, Denton understood what Bulstrode had been trying to say. And, what was worse, he thought it was a good idea.

Goddamnit, he kept to himself. It didn't count as accepting Bulstrode's help if he just used an id…*stole* an idea from him, did it? It was stealing. It was the opposite of accepting help. Well, no, the opposite would be helping someone. But he wouldn't owe the damn turkey a thing, nor Miss Carsis. *Especially* nor.

Still, the idea of in any way allowing Bulstrode to have influenced his thoughts, consequently sending him down the path to achieving his goals, rankled Denton. He still had his pride to think about.

Or maybe he'd left that up a tree in the middle of the woods, that he'd scaled for no reason other than being terrified of non-existent pursuers.

Denton sighed. He'd been quiet for too long, and for some reason none of the three sitting before him had bothered to chip in with anything. So he closed his eyes and made a great show of rubbing his brow. He hadn't zoned out, you see, he had merely been thinking very hard.

"Or perhaps we needn't," he mumbled.

Fithian raised an eyebrow. "Needn't what?"

"Ascertain his objects." Denton lowered his hand and locked eyes with Buddy Jr. "Perhaps we can simply…remove him."

"No!" Buddy Jr. nearly shouted. "How can you suggest such a thing at a funeral?"

"…because that's where we're having this conversation?"

"I'll not talk to death when my sister i-"

"Who talks of death?"

"You do!"

Denton reviewed what he had said. "No?"

"Yes! When you said 'we can simply…remove him.'"

"Yeah?"

"Did you mean this as a euphemism for assassination?"

"No?"

Buddy Jr. cocked his head to one side, and cast his eyes thoughtfully to the ceiling. "…no?"

"No."

"Then why the pause?"

"I was just trying to come up with an elegant way to say 'kick him out'".

"Oh."

"Yeah."

Buddy Jr. rubbed the back of his neck. "Sorry."

Denton ran his hand through his hair, and son of a bitch he needed to stop doing that. "s'alright." He looked around for the fifth, um, person in the room. No-Good Bulstrode was nowhere to be found. This was no more reassuring than if he'd spied the turkey cluck-chuckling from inside the fireplace. The first thing to know about dealing with turkey demons, he was finding, was that one should never have done it in the first place.

They sat silently for a long moment, until Missy perked up again. "So how do we do *that*?"

Which was a very good question. And, Denton was pleased to see, one that was phrased inclusively. *We*. How do *we* do that. Buddy Jr. Crundwell, Fithian Lowestoft, Millicent Ditteridge, and Denton

Hedges.

He had finally found his 'in' with all three families.

Poor Rumney Marsh.

XVII

"WHAT CAN YOU TELL ME ABOUT RUMNEY Marsh?"

Brisby took a sharp breath through his nose, and let it out slowly. "He's why I'm here right now." Denton assumed Brisby meant *in Fidget's Mill*, and not *in the barbershop*. If Governor Marsh wanted someone to get their haircut, he'd have to write King George III and ask *him* to order the trimming.

It was two days after the funeral, and the Hedges cabal had made precious little progress. So they each vowed to start casting about for any information that might prove useful, from sources who wouldn't suspect the motivation for the questioning.

Naturally, Dr. Brisby Houlihan came to mind.

The physician closed his eyes as the barber snipped away, occasionally mumbling things like "snip snip" and "here come the snippers". Denton had debating waiting to quiz Brisby on the Governor, just in case the barber were someone to be worried about, but as a rule Denton refused to worry about somebody who introduced himself as "Fidget's snip man".

Then again, maybe that was precisely the kind of person Denton *should* be worried about, especially when their job was to wave sharp objects in the vicinity of one's eyeballs.

Then again again, it was Brisby's vision on the line, and the man didn't seem the least bit anxious. So Denton wasn't either.

"Governor Marsh," Brisby continued, "came to visit me, gosh, it feels like so very long ago. He...coerced me into serving as Customs Commissioner here, which was not only well outside my expertise, but quite inimical to my interests, among these being the enjoyment of full-bodied locomotion and respiration." Brisby underlined this fact with another deep breath. "I must interface with the man quite often, and have no choice but to do so, seeing as I am living on his property."

Denton, seated in the barber's chair next to the one in which Brisby sat, jerked upright. "Your place of temporary residence…the larger residence behind it is Governor Marsh's?!"

"Well, technically, the larger residence in *front* of it, but yes."

"Snip snip," whispered Fidget's snip man.

Brisby ignored him. "Though I interface with the man often, in the discharge of my duties, I'm afraid I know very little about him. I don't make a habit of socializing with him, you see."

"I do." Denton leaned back in his chair again, the better to stir his thoughts. After a few more seconds, punctuated by more variations on the barber's favorite theme, Denton leaned forward, because that's what you do when you have a Thought. "What do you say to Governor Marsh, when you have your sit-downs with him?"

"Oh," Brisby shrugged.

"No shoulders!" cried Fidget's snip man.

"Sorry. Um, I mainly update him on the comings and goings of the ports. Mainly comings, as there are so few nautical goings."

Denton leaned forward a bit further. "And then he sends word to England?"

"I assume so."

"Do you know, perhaps, if his reports to the Crown contain more information than the raw data you supply him?"

"Like what?"

"Anything. The temperament of the people, the flavor of the alehouse dialogues, anything of this sort."

"I honestly couldn't say."

"Could you guess?"

"Not in good conscience."

Denton frowned. This wasn't helpful.

But, in a way, maybe it was.

"Do you think he would let you see his reports, if you asked him?"

Brisby gave a scoff that would have made Chip Ditteridge proud.

"Almost certainly not. I did once inquire, as to whether or not I might read a letter he wrote to Secretary Conway. Conway – and I must confess I'm not as well-informed of English politics as I would like – but my *impression* is that Conway is generally sympathetic to the colonial cries for greater independence from the Crown. I was merely curious, you see, as to what sort of tone a man like Marsh, who I am nearly certain is a royal stooge through and through, would take when writing to a superior whose own sensibilities diverge so markedly from his own. The reasoning I gave was not this, of c-"

"Then why did he write to Conway at all?" Denton interrupted.

"Because," Brisby replied with the patience of a saint at the back of the buffet line, "Conway is Secretary of State. I'm thrilled to meet someone who knows even less of English politics than I!" Brisby chortled.

The barber sniffed moistly. "No shoulders!"

"Right, sorry."

Denton struggled to keep a smile off of his face. He was fairly certain he had everything he needed from Brisby, and it was more than he could have hoped for. Marsh wrote to the English Secretary of State, who may have sympathies with the Colonists. This left the door open for *Marsh* to have hidden sympathies of his own. Or, perhaps not. Either way, he was loathe to allow his correspondence to be read.

I can work with this, Denton thought through the sound of gears whizzing to life. The legalistic part of his mind was getting a workout in a way it hadn't for quite a while. He was dangerously close to having fun.

"Ta-da," announced the Snipmeister without enthusiasm. "You have been snipped." He handed Brisby a mirror, into which the physician frowned for several silent seconds.

"Denton," he finally said, "I wonder if you might be so good as to accompany me to the hat store."

XVIII

DENTON HAD HAD A BRIGHT IDEA. HE WAS A MAN of letters, nimble with the quill, and yet he had neglected this most conspicuous gift of his.

Until now.

While Governor Marsh was royally appointed, and so had no real accountability to the governed, these were topsy-turvy times. *Theoretically*, a groundswell of popular support against the Governor could be sufficient to bring about his removal. Or, at the very least, they could force the issue by chasing him out of town. This latter course was an escalatory act for which Denton had no great enthusiasm, but in the end, the means by which Rumney was ousted hardly mattered. What mattered was that Denton work together with a Crundwell, a Lowestoft and a Ditteridge, and so cause them to consider him, in some sense, an 'us'.

Denton's plan, one enthusiastically embraced by the cabal, was relatively simple; so simple, in fact, that it demanded more patience than effort. Which was, in a way, incredibly frustrating, but that's just the way things were falling in to place.

On one particularly snowy late January evening, Denton sat down to his desk and wrote out a letter to James Otis Jr. After a knowingly vain plea for Otis and Samuel Adams to delay the release of their Circular Letter (because, good heavens, February was fast approaching…), Denton went straight into the business at hand:

A great political windfall could be secured in Fidget's Mill, if only James Otis Jr. would write a formal letter, using his new and still-crisp Speaker of the Massachusetts Legislature letterhead (and with the support of the rest of the House, either direct or implicit), petitioning Governor Rumney Marsh of Fidget's Mill to make public his correspondence with the Crown. The justification for such a presumptuous request was that, and surely this wasn't the case, but you do know how rumors can spread, *apparently* there were rumors that Governor Marsh had been dispatching dishonest reports of the Mill to England, which skewed in an unflattering direction. Such a pity, this kind of gossip, but there was one quite easy way to put this all to bed.

And this was where Denton was counting on Brisby's reports of Marsh's inaccurate reports to be accurate. If Governor Marsh simply turned over the correspondence without issue, Denton would be left thrashing about for ways to villainize a cooperative villain. But he couldn't imagine that would happen. In his limited understanding of Marsh, Denton had pegged him as proud and vain. When faced with a request tendered by a congregation he likely thought of as little more than chattel, a request for which there was no real precedent, backed by no formal means of enforcement or punishment for non-compliance, Governor Marsh would almost certainly deny the request. Wouldn't he?

Now this was where Denton was counting on his own survey of the zeitgeist to be accurate.

If Governor Marsh cast *himself* as the villain by rebuking the Colonial legislature, thus denying what little opportunity the colonists had to feel as though they guided their own destinies, it would be quite easy to whip the Fidgetonians into an anti-Marsh frenzy. Wouldn't it?

Assume, for a moment, that it would be. There would be other practical benefits to a Fidget's Mill unified against their Colonial Governor, wouldn't there?

Denton had devised this scheme in order to fall in with the three families, but before long he realized he had stumbled on to something much larger. If he could fall in with the families, *and* pull the entire town together in defiance of British rule, securing non-importation could be a simple matter of whispering it into someone's ear at a town meeting and watching it spread! Having just witnessed the power of the people, the rich families would have little choice but to comply with their request!

And, on the off chance that they mistakenly believed they *did* have a choice, Denton would have the ears of all three families, into which he could whisper a few convincing refutations. After months of struggling, everything was falling into place with dizzying rapidity.

Perhaps he would be home with his family before the snow had melted. They had built a snowman together once – maybe they could do it again this year. It wasn't too unreasonable to hope so…or so he hoped.

Denton wrote his letter, sealed it up, and sent it out, thinking himself a model of discretion. Of the four people aware of this plan – Buddy Jr., Fithian, Missy and himself – he was by far the least trustworthy, and as he knew he could be trusted, his co-conspirators were beyond reproach; he knew this scheme would remain their little secret, until it was ready to be unleashed upon Governor Marsh.

He really ought to have known better.

There had always been some great confusion as pertained the rules. That there *were* rules, No-Good Bulstrode had no question. That he *intuited* the rules was similarly self-evident. How these rules came to be, and how they were enforced, and what punishments might be in store for transgressions…now *those* were good questions.

Or perhaps they weren't. Bulstrode had no idea.

One of those pesky rules was this: a Familiar could be invisible to someone, or he could appear to them as a regular, run-of-the-Mill …whatever form they had taken. A turkey, in Bulstrode's current case. But once they had *wholly* revealed themselves to someone, as Bulstrode had to Denton and Mr. Increase, they could never hide themselves from said person again. Which made eavesdropping difficult.

And so, each time Denton and his tripartite cabal met, Bulstrode would have to poke his little turkey head around the corner to see if Denton was facing the door or not. If so, another ingress would have to be found. Once an entrance unobserved by Hedges had presented itself, Bulstrode would render himself invisible to the three family members (an act which did take some sustained concentration) and click-toe as delicately as possible into the room. After all, Denton would still be able to hear the sound of his claws on the wood.

Then it was a matter of finding somewhere inconspicuous to conceal this regrettable body for the duration of the meet. Bulstrode often cursed another of those strange, eldritch rules: a Familiar might take any animal form it chooses, upon signing the metaphorical Black Book and joining a magically-inclined human, as was the remit of all Familiars (Oh, there was a whole different bucket of tentacles: Familiars were naturally predisposed toward servitude, and being so disposed, were often baffled by the controversy around the slavery issue amongst humans. Perhaps Mr. Increase subconsciously sensed this, which might explain why Bulstrode got the impression that the free man hated him in some existential way). But, once a form had been adopted, it could not be cast aside until the work for which the human and Familiar aligned themselves were completed. Or, in other words, once the *human's* work had been completed. Familiars were little more than spooky parasites. The relationship was symbiotic, but there was never any mistaking which was the host, even if the parasite was the only one who lived forever.

Which meant until Miss Carsis' work was done, Bulstrode was going to remain a turkey, a befeathered cannonball with a British accent. Ideal for bopping around a town in the thick of the New England woods, not-so-ideal for slinking unseen through residential spaces.

And so, Bulstrode would waddle into wherever the meeting was taking place, and begin a desperate search for a turkey-sized hiding place. There was no telling when Denton might turn around and spot him – he'd quite foolishly called attention to his eavesdropping the first time, which Miss Carsis pointed out *at some considerable length* was a stupid thing to do. Subterfuge depended upon informational imbalances in one's own favor, that was one of the things she said. One of the many, many things.

So Bulstrode had taken to hiding under chairs with floor-length skirts, or in cabinets with hinges that didn't look like they'd squeak. He once, seeing Denton turning towards him, panicked and leapt into a chamberpot.

And then there was that one time, during the meeting at which Denton and co. finally agreed to have Denton write his letter to James

Otis Jr., that Bulstrode hid in a wardrobe that was full of animal pelts that grumbled.

"Um," Bulstrode whispered, "hello? You wouldn't happen to be a lump of critterskins, would you?"

"No," the not-lump replied.

"Oh. Well, in that case, might I ask of what you *are* a lump, then? As your lumpishness seems beyond dispute."

"Myself is a-"

"Oh, sod off!" This Bulstrode shouted, and he was quite stunned to find the doors remaining resolutely un-thrown-open by Denton. The shout was amateur, but Bulstrode couldn't help it. It was frustrating, to find oneself secreted away in a cupboard with the pesky Dread Familiar. Recovering himself, Bulstrode fell back to a whisper. "Alright, out with it! What are you doing in here?"

"The same thing as Yourself, Myself supposes. Eavesdropping." The Dread Familiar also whispered – it, too, had revealed itself to Denton. And it, too, apparently had a form poorly suited to espionage.

"Well, looky-looky who's highly presumptuous."

"Does seem a fair presumption. All things considered."

"That the presumption tracks to the actual state of things doesn't justify the initial presumption."

"Hm." The Dread Familiar made a thinking noise. Not that there was such a thing as a thinking noise – Bulstrode just somehow knew that this gutteral *hgnnnnnnnn* was the noise the Dread Familiar made when it was thinking about something.

"Do be quiet," Bulstrode hissed. "I can't hear a word they're saying out there."

"Myself apologizes." *Hgnnnnnnn.*

"You're still doing it!"

"Doing what?"

"Making the noise!"

"What noise?"

"The thinking noise!"

...*hgnnnnnn*

"Listen here…what's your name?"

"Myself's name?"

"Yes, yes, your name. How am I to address you?"

Hgnn-

"Jake's sake, man! I see you on the street, booking it in a direction opposite my own, and I wish to capture your attention. What must I shout at you?"

"…Yourself will laugh at Myself."

Bulstrode thought of Denton, just on the other side of this thin wooden cabinet door, and of how Denton seemed physically and spiritually repulsed by his laugh. It was upsetting enough, to have one's natural expression of mirth, that most wonderful of emotions, be so disturbing to someone. The thought of being caught out in his hiding place, stuffed in with the Dread Familiar, all because he had been laughing…it was almost funny.

Oh dear.

Feeling a little giggle coming on, Bulstrode thought very hard about suppressing the laugh, and less hard about suppressing the words "I assure you, I will not laugh. Let's hear the name, then."

"It is not a good name."

"I'll be the judge. Out comes the name, please!"

"Yazbirth Bicklebog."

"Come again?"

"Yazbirth Bicklebog."

Bulstrode, much to his personal satisfaction, did not laugh. "Mhm. It's a family name, is it?"

"Ourselves do not choose Ourselves' names, as Yourself well knows."

"Oh, indeed. Though we do choose our shapes. And, as long as we're becoming so chumly, I'm ever so excited to learn what yours is. Unless 'shadow' is the thing, naturally."

"…" *Hgnnnnnn*

"Oh, alright, steady on. It's not as though I've asked you whom you serve, as you seem so secretive on that front. Tell you what, I'll simply take a gander at you as we debark from this wretched cupboard, when the time comes. When they st…" Bulstrode let that thought die a slow death. "Quite embarrassed to say, I've not been paying much attention to this secret meeting."

"Nor has Myself."

"Oh dear. Well, at least we have that in common."

And so it was that Denton's letter to James Otis Jr. remained a secret from the two Familiars and their consorts, without his having realized it was ever anything *but* a secret.

After the anti-Marsh cabal broke up, Bulstrode hopped from the cupboard and turned immediately to see Yazbirth's emerging form.

"Out you come!" Bulstrode called.

Hgnnnnn, replied the darkness of the cupboard.

"Unless you stumble upon a craftily concealed compartment by which you might chart an alternative escape, th-"

"Oh, alright."

Yazbirth Bicklebog quite dramatically unfolded himself from the cupboard. Bulstrode could hardly believe he'd ever fit in it to begin with.

"My word," Bulstrode hushed, "you're a big one."

"Mhm," Yazbirth agreed, looking down at his furry, ten-foot-tall frame. "Myself…this is quite embarrassing, but Myself chose this form quite some time ago."

"I could have guessed as much. 'Quite some time ago' is, I suppose, a fair enough representation of when the sort you're going round as were extant."

Yazbirth Bicklebog's heavy head hung especially heavy. "Yes, Myself made the selection of this form back when Itself would have served as effective camouflage. And then Myself's consortself died, prior to Ourselves' managing to accomplish Himself's goal. Since such time, Myself has been…" here Bicklebog took a break for a limp flopping of his mighty, moss-covered arms, "a giant sloth."

It wasn't until this moment that Bulstrode felt the need to truly suppress a laugh. Yazbirth had just made a revelation, without entirely realizing it. The reason the Dread Familiar traded in shadowcraft wasn't to maximize intimidation – that was just a happy byproduct. No, Yazbirth often appeared in silhouette because it was embarrassed. Of its appearance, of what its appearance signified about its track record as a Familiar, and of its name. For millions and millions of years, Yazbirth Bicklebog had existed in a perpetual state of embarrassment, and for the rest of eternity, Yazbirth Bicklebog would continue to exist in the same state.

"Yazbirth…er…Mr. Bickelbog…" Bulstrode pulled out his silkiest, most reassuring tones here, "there's no need to be ashamed of being a giant sloth. Your consort's death was not your fault."

Yazbirth looked at Bulstrode as though nobody had ever, in its unfathomably long existence, said that to him.

"Has nobody ever said that to you?"

"No…never."

"Not even your current consort?"

"Not even Himself."

"Who is Himself, Yazbirth Bicklebog?"

And Yazbirth Bicklebog told Bulstrode. And Bulstrode wished for longer legs, that he might kick himself. Because it really was quite obvious, in hindsight.

XIX

IF THE PLOT THICKENED ANY FURTHER, CHIP Ditteridge reflected, it would calcify.

His daughter had taken to meeting, ostensibly in private (but, she should have known, there's no real privacy in a community of this size), not only representatives from the other two families, but that slave doctor as well! A story had been circulated by which the slave doctor's abandonment of the ballroom just as the New Year (and the poison) struck was an heroic gesture, but Chip knew better. At no point in this fanciful story did Hedges and the negro stevedore dash off into the woods, only to come scrambling back in the following morning. A substantial detail like that is only omitted when it carries a measure of guilt.

At first, Chip had quietly organized a search of the woods. Did the two run off with anything, and hide it in the snow? A dozen slaves went out in search of answers, and came back empty-handed. After a great deal of haughty scoffing – just so they knew that if Chip had gone out, he'd have found something, but also he couldn't go out because he was very important and also busy – he sent half of them back to his manor (less stately than the Crundwell's, but still quite impressive), and turned the remaining six into a rudimentary spy team. They would tool around the town, observing, recording, and reporting back. It was through this slave-run surveillance squad that Chip discovered the anti-Marsh cabal, in fact if not in purpose.

What were they up to? There was no way for him to know, not that he could see. That they were meeting to discuss matters inimical to the interests of the British crown seemed a foregone conclusion. So, then, their interests were inimical to Chip's. If popular opinion turned against the throne, they would find the Ditteridge clan stood loyally beside it, and protestations of having come around to the Cause of greater self-determination for the Colonies would be too little too late. If the tide turned against the Crown, in other words, the Ditteridges would be swept back across the Atlantic.

Did Missy not realize this? Did she not remember why they were moving to the Colonies in the first place? If Chip hadn't had such extensive connections back home, they wouldn't have been given the option to leave at all. Not after what young Francis did…

Returning home was not an option. Francis would be imprisoned – at best – and Chip couldn't imagine the Ditteridge clan surviving such a humiliating blow. Long-term residence in the Colonies was the only option.

But then here came Denton Hedges, corrupter, shape-shifter, destroyer. Chip was going to be goddamned if he let this little upstart splinter his family! The Ditteridge name was too prestigious – it would not be undone by Francis' failure to govern his passions, and Denton's fancying that he could follow his wherever they led!

Come to think of it, Francis and Denton had a lot in common. Chip shuddered at the thought, though it did little to dull the howling fury with which he contemplated Denton. That was perhaps an interesting reaction that Chip did not investigate too thoroughly.

Mr. Increase was back in the storehouse on the docks, counting boxes full of British textiles. The irony was not lost on him, that he had taken a break from working with a man monomaniacally pushing a non-importation policy on the town to come and catalogue imports, but Mr. Increase had a job that paid him, which was more than most men of his pigmentation could say, and he wasn't about to stop doing it just because the scaffolding of the town was threatening collapse at any moment.

Besides, he and Denton were pretty much in the clear, after the nightmare of the party. Neither of them were suspected by the families, neither of them owed Miss Carsis any more favors, and neither of them had anything much to do. A period of quietude had descended upon the Mill, and it was a beautiful thing.

But somehow, as soon as Mr. Increase heard someone scuffling their way between the claustrophobic shelves of the storehouse, he knew the lull was already over.

The man who finally popped out of the lumber labyrinth and into Mr. Increase's workspace was a slave. Increase could spot them a mile away, though it was hard for him to articulate just how. One might imagine that identification would be through the presence of supplicatory body language, like stooped shoulders or a tucked chin. But in Increase's experience, the opposite often held true. As a general matter, slaves had strong shoulders and no compunctions about looking you dead in the eye.

No, the way Increase spotted a slave was by their being, when enjoying the relative freedom of solitude, just slightly too excited to be alive. Somebody who can take their freedom for granted is free to take just about everything else for granted, too. This was one of the few problems they *didn't* have.

It was common to see slaves milling about the town, seemingly on their own recognizance. But really, topography served as their cage. Fidget's Mill was hopelessly isolated, and too small to hide in. Where would they go? Granted, the Mill was one of the few settlements in Massachusetts with a halfway substantial slave population. A slave escaping to Boston would almost certainly find a way to disappear until the heat died down. But how would they get to Boston? Word traveled fast in the Mill, and nobody wanted to risk being ostracized just for helping a slave escape. They had principles, many of them, but they also had families to feed.

Besides, the slaves often made the same crude calculation; there were worse places than Fidget's Mill to be a slave, and if they made an escape attempt, they may well end up at one of them. This last consideration was what truly enraged Mr. Increase. Complacency dethroning dignity. He knew he had no real right to judge, that he couldn't well imagine how the horror of being enslaved would color one's decision-making processes.

But, still.

"Can I help you?" he sneered.

The slave quite plainly recognized Increase's tone, but chose to ignore it. "I'm here to help *you*." This was said in a thick accent Increase couldn't place. Here was *hee-ah*, and help somehow began with a sybllant 'h'.

Mr. Increase slowly lowered his ubiquitous clipboard. "Is that right?"

"It is. My…" he inspected the back of his hands for a moment. Much like the accent, this was a gesture with which Mr. Increase was unfamiliar. But he could guess what it meant, in a general sense. "Mr. Ditteridge has me and…others watching your friend."

"What friend?"

"The false slave doctor."

"Oh, right. Denton." Mr. Increase lowered the clipboard to his hip. "Why?"

"Because Mr. Ditteridge saw…Denton and you. Coming out of the trees."

All at once, Mr. Increase felt like he was back in those woods, fearful sweat freezing to his brow, running down his back in icicles. They had been seen. Perhaps they were not out of the woods yet at all. "What? What do you mean?"

"New Year's, he-"

"I got that. But now you're observing us, because Chip…" Mr. Increase noticed the slightest twitch of the eyelid as the slave heard the first name of his Mr. Ditteridge, "…saw us emerge from the woods? What does he know? Or suspect that he knows?"

"Nothing. Nothing that he tells us. This is why we watch."

"Do your…do the others report to him honestly?"

"Yes," the man smiled, "though not fully."

Mr. Increase breathed a sigh of relief. "What does Chip know?"

"He knows that your friend meets with his daughter, and others."

Son of a bitch, Mr. Increase thought as he ground his teeth. What was Denton up to? "Does he know where?"

"Yes."

"Where?"

"The Crundwell home."

Good heavens, the lawyer was nervy. "What *doesn't* Chip know?"

"That your friend sent a letter to Boston."

Despite the assurance that this information had not made it back to Chip, Mr. Increase's chill deepened on Denton's behalf. This man knew where the letter was being sent? Presumably, then, it was known to whom the letter was addressed. How careless Hedges had been! It was easy to lose sight of the stakes, in such an insular community as Fidget's Mill, but they were dabbling in interoceanic geopolitics. This wasn't a game. Denton was getting careless; that had potential consequences for Mr. Increase.

"What were the contents of the letter?"

"I can't say."

Mr. Increase tilted his head slightly.

"It's not known to me, I should say."

Finally warming up, Mr. Increase put his clipboard on a nearby table (a gesture many in the town knew meant "let's talk") and strode over to the man who had come bearing such useful information.

"What's your name?" he asked.

"John."

Mr. Increase rolled his eyes, and placed a gentle palm on "John"'s shoulder. "Your real name, son."

"…Adewale." This was said not with the reticence of profanity, but with the solemnity of a sacred vow, not to be undertaken lightly.

Mr. Increase smiled. "Adewale. I'm all sorts of grateful to you, but why did you tell me this, at great personal risk to yourself?"

Adewale leaned his head back slightly, as though this were the stupidest question he'd ever heard. "Because you should know."

Yes, Mr. Increase reflected, sometimes it really was that simple.

XX

MADNESS. THIS WAS NOTHING SHORT OF gibbering madness.

"He's fairly dismal," No-Good Bulstrode allowed, "and I'll not give you the goof on that score. Why, I expect he'd concede the same, wouldn't you, you mossy tosspot?"

"Oh, sure," Yazbirth Bicklebog concurred.

"But he's actually quite pathetic, once you scope bedrock. No offense meant," Bulstrode tacked on for good measure.

Yazbirth merely shrugged, and then they both turned to their audience of one.

Miss Carsis stood, arms folded, uncertain of how to respond. This was madness. Familiars were meant to hate each other on sight. Even Familiars whose consorts were allies – that was just one of the Rules. Familiars hated each other.

And yet here they were, not only falling in, but vouching for one another! Madness!

"I don't..." It was rare that Miss Carsis found herself speechless, and so those few occasions on which she did always demanded a long moment for silent reflection and consideration. "This is...ah...it's never..."

Two minutes passed in this fashion, with dozens of sentences begun and abandoned after a couple of words. Finally, after much careful thought, she landed on a way forward.

"This isn't...eh..."

Five minutes after that, she landed on a more sustainable way forward.

"This just isn't done, you two. Familiars consorting with each other. It just isn't done."

Bulstrode shook his head. "You'll not hear any disputations from me, as pertains to the preeminence of tradition amongst the virtues."

Now Miss Carsis shook her head. "Tradition is not one of the virtues."

"Well, not traditionally, no. But traditions were made to be broken, were they not?"

"No. They were made to be upheld."

"Yazbirth! To the peepers, please!" In what appeared to be one well-rehearsed movement, Yazbirth scooped Bulstrode up in his arms and raised him to eye level with Miss Carsis.

The witch was visibly disgusted by the curious intimacy of the gesture. "This just isn't done!"

"Now listen here, our Yazbirth Bicklebog has a c-"

"*Our* Yazbirth Bicklebog," Miss Carsis harrumphed.

"Yes, *our* Yazbirth Bicklebog here has a case of the extenuating circumstances." Which Bulstrode then explained, bringing Miss Carsis up to speed on the untimely death of their Yazbirth Bicklebog's consort back when giant sloth was in any way a wise choice of form. "So, you see, he's been falling in with whoever would have him for a rather unfortunate number of years, in the hopes that accomplishing some rather unfortunate number of goals for the same number of consorts might, in some way, allow him to change his form into something more…well, less unfortunate."

Miss Carsis stared for several long moments. "And?"

"And he's in the nasty habit of finding ethical disagreements with his consorts, either in the ends or the means, so he's been falling right out with folks before being able to accomplish said unfortunate number of goals for, oh, how long would you say?"

Bicklebog heaved his arms a few inches into the air. "A few hundred thousand."

"Select your metric, friend."

"Years, yes, years."

"A few hundred thousand years," Bulstrode returned to Miss Carsis, "he's been adrift on the strength of his convictions. Now he's revealed to me his current consort, who has frustrated you in all manner of ways and means. This is a revelation which would permit you to remove them from the equation, and it is a revelation I am permitted to relay to you on the condition that you allow him to consort with *us,* as our ends are al-"

"Two Familiars to one consort! Madness! It jus-"

"But it *could* be, couldn't it? Who's to stop us?"

This was a dreadful question, but one Miss Carsis had asked herself in an array of circumstances over the years. This was, after all, an epoch of rebellious sentiment, but rebelling against a terrestrial government was qualitatively different from rebelling against whatever terrifying forces kept the universe in check.

Familiarity was, basically, a verbal agreement. One sometimes scribbled in a mystical book, but that was for form's sake more than anything. Nobody exactly checked the books, did they?

But still. *Something* prevented Familiars from changing forms before they had accomplished their consort's goals. That wasn't imaginary. Whether or not that something was a some*one* or not, it didn't change the fact of the matter. But, all the same, it changed *everything.*

Did Miss Carsis have the courage to find out? All she cared about was laying a bed for Sonny and Tobin, ideally a bed in a great big mansion. But if she decided to go tempting whatever it was that kept the clocks wound and running on time, a pleasantly manageable situation could escalate almost overnight. And yet, Bulstrode was her right hand in these matters, and removing a rival witch was important to him. And so, in true parasitic fashion, it became impor-tant to *her*. After all, if her number one turkey got a bit too pally with a Familiar who could tell him an inexhaustible number of stories about leaving a consort by choice…

She jerked her jaw from side to side. "So," she addressed Bulstrode and *only* Bulstrode, "you know for whom this wooly buffoon Familiars, and won't tell me unless I agree to consort with him?"

"It's less that I'm declining to reveal the information to *you*, and more that I'm retaining the confidences of *him*." Bulstrode leaned his head into Yazbirth's chest and rubbed affectionately.

Miss Carsis heaved slightly. "Are you aware that th-"

"This isn't the way it's done? Or something to that effect, I imagine? Yes, I am quite aware. Couldn't be otherwise, the way you're going on about it."

"Insolence! You accursed-"

"Yazbirth! Kissing distance!"

Yazbirth extended his lichen-festooned arms, pushing Bulstrode to within a foot or so of Miss Carsis' face. They had absolutely prepared these ahead of time, she realized with more disappointment than anger.

"I'm terribly sorry for the tone in which this discussion has been conducted. If you've no interest in this *quid pro quo*, which I queued up in good faith on your behalf, then you may simply decline and all will be as it was. But if you wish to get the *quo*, you'll have to give the *quid*."

"It would be a simple matter of deducing who his consort is, given enough time."

"Then," Bicklebog rumbled ruefully, "Myself will take Myself's leave, and leave Yourself to Yourself's own devices."

Bulstrode shimmied in Yazbirth Bicklebog's capacious upturned palms. "And for what it's worth, dear, I wouldn't have guessed who it is. Despite it actually being quite obvious."

Miss Carsis pointed a lithe, bony finger directly at Bulstrode's beak.

"That's a rotten thing to do, teasing me with information like that."

"So sorry, but business is business."

"This is business?"

"I wouldn't have said it was personal."

Miss Carsis folded her arms again. "Taking on two Familiars is too dangerous. Perhaps in times of less unrest, it might be a risk worth taking. In the interest of broadening knowledge, like. But the mere fact that there are no witches around telling stories of what happens when one follows through on a rather obvious idea…well, my suspicion is that what happens is that the witch is no longer around." She rolled her head clockwise, grimacing as she stretched her neck. A little headache was coming on after all.

"But," she continued, "perhaps I can locate another consort for our good Yazbirth Bicklebog here. One whose goals would be accomplished alongside my own, thus coming to the same thing, in the end. Would this be acceptable?"

"Yes!" Yazbirth agreed without pause. Bulstrode was right – this was a rather pathetic creature, at bottom. Desperation did not become a demon, but neither did convictions. Despite herself, she admired the creature. It could, in theory, have chosen at any time in its long history to just see a Consortation through to the end, just to stop being a giant sloth. But the great oaf seemed to feel it was better to be a giant sloth with principles, than some other, sleeker, sexier creature on a mercenary streak.

This made Yazbirth Bicklebog perhaps the most moral creature ever to set foot in Fidget's Mill.

"Very well. Candidates suggest themselves to me already. In the meantime, go and break with your former consort. Bulstrode will catch me up."

"Of course!" Yazbirth unceremoniously dropped Bulstrode and stumbled from the room.

Once he had gone crashing back out into the night, Bulstrode turned to Miss Carsis from his usual position at ankle-height. "Certainly not Denton. Whose goals align with your true intentions to the extent we need, in order for you to not renege on your word?" The latter half of this question was offered with pre-emptive reprimand. Miss Carsis was not a fan of that tone in the least.

"I can think of a few people," Miss Carsis snapped back. And yes, she probably could. She just hadn't thought of them *yet*.

Yazbirth Bicklebog, being a giant sloth, didn't really walk anywhere. He galumphed. This galumphing was amongst the manifold things for which he was embarrassed.

Under the auspices of a quarter moon, poor Bicklebog galumphed up the hill towards Dr. Brisby Houlihan's place of temporary residence. Upon reaching Brisby's stoop, Yazbirth kept on galumphing, for he had not yet arrived at his destination. Almost, but not quite.

Nobody in Governor Rumney Marsh's family had been present at King Charles I's beheading, but his great grandfather had been present for the drawing and quartering of John Cook, the prosecutor in the case against King Charles I. That was close enough.

It was important for a true Englishman to have some blood relative who was present at the execution of King Charles I, particularly since it was also important for a true Englishman to be living in England. Rumney couldn't bear going 0 for 2, and so he happily accepted a few degrees of removal from the removal of Old Chuck's noggin as, well, acceptable. He was a true Englishman no matter where he lived, and if maintaining that title meant lying to himself, there was no harm in that, and that was the truth.

Why was this important? Because in these troubled times, talk was cheap, and very few people had money, so there was a lot of talk. Any given conversation, then, would skew in favor of the man (or, Rumney permitted, possibly woman) who could arrogate unto himself the most Authority. Not in any legal sense – dialectic authority. If some rebellious ass goes running his mouth off, there's nothing more powerful than being able to shout "what do you know about the cost of rebellion? My great grandfather was there when King Charles I's head was rolling into a basket!"

Oooh, that always shut them up. Most of the folks here who sympathized with greater distance from England had been here in the Colonies for generations. Yeah, what did *they* know? Great Granddaddy Marsh knew, and he passed the knowledge down to Rumney! Well, he knew by proxy, since John Cook knew! Close enough.

Rumney had spent so long convincing himself that his great grandfather had been present for the regicide, that he sometimes believed he *himself* had been there. And so who better than he, as the only living man who was, like, kind-of present at King Charles I's execution, to understand the vagaries of power?

Nobody. Which was why, despite occupying a Colonial sinecure with no real power, Governor Rumney Marsh took every possible precaution in securing his position. Nobody was more acutely aware of how powerless Rumney Marsh was than Rumney Marsh, which was why it was vitally important that he not *lose* what little power he had.

That was where Yazbirth Bicklebog came in. Figuratively, in the sense of 'this is the psychological profile which drew Yazbirth Bicklebog to Rumney in the first place', and literally, as in 'at this point in time, Yaz-birth Bicklebog galumphed in through the door.'

Rumney, who had been scrutinizing some old family portraits (just another night at *chez* Marsh), turned to the Familiar giant sloth and smiled. Once upon a time Yazbirth had sensed Marsh's uneasiness, and had come to him with an offer of Familiarity. And as far as he could tell, there was nothing really required of him, beyond a verbal agreement. Bicklebog had just wanted to change his shape, or whatever. To do that, he needed to help people. So he'd agreed to help Rumney, aka Himself, keep Fidget's Mill on a knife's edge, thus allowing the Governor to control which way things leaned and teetered.

That had sounded good in theory, right up until the practice entailed attempting to snuff out the bright light that was poor Missy Ditteridge. Marsh had no sunny thoughts as regarded the future of the Mill, and so, rather than allow it to slip into extinction in such a way that might be lain at his feet, he had gotten it into his head to speed its demise in such a way that would appear entirely to the doing of the Mill's backwards, incestuous denizens.

Yazbirth held fast to the shame he felt for following through on this dreadful assignment. It would help make this easier.

"Good evening, Yazbirth Bicklebog. Th-"

"Myself must tell Yourself something."

Rumney turned from a portrait of his great great grandfather, who had probably already been born when Galileo was on trial, and was therefore *present* under a sufficiently generous ontological rubric, to stare at Yazbirth Bicklebog head-on. "What?"

"Myself has found Someoneself else...self."

"...huh?"

"Myself can no longer be Yourself's Familiarself."

Rumney could say nothing in response. He stared, mouth open. A bug flew in, was overwhelmed by the halitosis (despite lacking nostrils), and zipped back out. "Who?"

"That's not import-"

"It *is* important! Who is it? How long have you been seeing them?"

"Not long. Which, erm, is to say not yet."

Aghast, Governor Marsh strode over to the far wall and gazed up at a portrait of his mother, who as far as he knew had not been present for anything of historical interest, ever. So he looked for another portrait from which he could draw some strength.

"Myself simply means," Yazbirth continued, heedless of Marsh's aimless wandering, "Yourself's replacement, by which Myself does not mean Yourself is *replaceable*, simply, erm, let Myself begin again."

Marsh spun on his heel, pointing an accusatory finger. "You're leaving me for a Colonial rebel, is that it? This is persecution! And I know all about persecution, my great great gra-"

"Yourself doesn't understa-"

"Oh, I understand perfectly well! You smell which way the wind is blowing, and you're jumping shit while th-"

"Ship."

"What?"

"Yourself said 'jumping shit', when Yourself almost certainly meant 'ship'."

The Governor thought on this for a moment, and then rushed towards Yazbirth. "Yes, do you see how I need you?" And this was, to a certain extent, true. Rumney could indeed 'smell which way the wind was blowing', and it was blowing him towards a battery of jagged rocks. If Yazbirth Bicklebog left, anything could happen to Rumney. Well, anything that fell under the purview of 'bad things'.

Yazbirth hung his head and slapped a paw on Rumney's shoulder. The gesture was meant to be reassuring, but Yazbirth's paws were heavy, and his fur was perpetually damp, so the gesture was about as reassuring as being splattered with mud by a passing carriage.

To be fair, though, Rumney could understand why Yazbirth Bicklebog was so desperate to change. The Familiar was in no way oblivious to its unsettling effect.

"Myself is truly sorry," Yazbirth Bicklebog cooed. "It's not Yourself, it's Myself."

Marsh slipped out from under Yazbirth's paw, stopping a few strides away with his back turned.

"There is a way," the giant sloth offered, "for Yourself to remain Myself's consortself."

Refusing to turn all the way around, Marsh looked coyly over his left shoulder.

"Join Ourselves! If Yourself's objectives could but align with Ourselves' own, as soon a-"

"Who is 'Ourselves' in this scenario? Who've you taken to, huh?"

"To whom has Yourself taken, Myself thinks Yourself means."

Marsh shot a furious finger Yazbirth's way. "Don't you dare correct my grammar, you, you pronoun up-fucker!" The finger retracted into a fist, and a thumb popped out, so that it might arc towards Rumney's chest. "I'm an *Englishman*, goddamn you! Perhaps you lack convictions, you long-extinct soldier of fortune, but I'll not swap sides simply because I've been offered a better deal!"

"Yourself must understand," Yazbirth persisted in enragingly neutral tones, "that Myself has existed long before the nations of today, and will exist long after Theirselves are but dust. The only compass by which Myself's actions can be coherently guided are Myself-interest."

"A-HA! So you don't even care about the current state of the Colonies!"

"Of course not. This should not be a surprise to Yourself."

"..." Rage melted from Rumney's visage, leaving behind a mask of misery. Yazbirth Bicklebog was a demon, make no mistake, but he still had feelings. And it made his feelings feel unhappy, to see Governor Marsh looking this way. "Get out," he whispered.

"Of course. Myself is sorry. Goodbye." Yazbirth gave a little bow, which from a giant sloth is still a rather big bow, and saw himself to the door. Rumney sighed, and at this point may have done well to look to that oft-ignored portrait of his mother, who Rumney's father had left for a younger woman, but who nonetheless had to suffer through a lifetime of marriage to the hateful man, on account of his firm disapproval of divorce. She had actual first-hand experience of being jilted, but Rumney wasn't thinking about that right now.

All he was thinking about was finding out who...for *whom* Yazbirth Bicklebog had left him. He was thinking about how he could get back at them, the new consort and his old Familiar alike. He was thinking about how Hell hath no fury like a consort scorned.

XXI

DENTON HEDGES RECEIVED A REPLY FROM JAMES Otis Jr. on the same day he received a long overdue letter from his family. Without thinking about it, he opened Otis' letter first. That he chose Otis over his family without thinking about it disturbed him, once he finally did stop to think about it.

Included in the envelope was a short letter to Denton, and a completed copy of the Massachusetts Circular Letter, drafted by Otis and Samuel Adams. Denton had known it was coming – they had told him about, what felt like eons ago – but seeing it here in his hands made it *real*. The Circular Letter was coming, just over a week from now, and once it was officially released the British would almost certainly strike in some very material way. The only defense the Colonies had, particularly Massachusetts, was unity of purpose and unity of action. In this case, through the economic coercion of non-importation. Removing Governor Marsh was necessary for strengthening Denton's bonds with the three families, but it was merely one further step in his quest. It wasn't the end; the end wasn't even in clear sight end.

And time was running out.

The body of the Circular Letter was much as Otis and Adams had intimated it would be. The Townshend Acts were unconstitutional, as Massachusetts lacked representation in parliament. But the solution was not parliamentary representation – that would have been absurd, given the distances involved. The solution was simply to allow the Colonies to tax themselves. Greater economic independence, sure, but no radical calls for national independence, nor even a singular national identity that would encompass all of the Colonies. It was rebellious, Denton supposed, but still relatively moderate, compared to what some people were calling for…

But England wouldn't have heard the extremes, and so wouldn't appreciate the middleground this Letter found. All they would see was a letter that stank of incipient sedition, circulated amongst the Colonies. There would be repercussions. And if Denton couldn't get the Mill to sign off on non-importation, the British lackeys Marsh and Ditteridge would make sure that the repercussions started here. Which would make them percussions, Denton observed, an apt enough word to describe the docks being bombarded by cannonfire.

Is that what would happen? Who knew – but it was plausible, and that was scary enough.

Having finally read the long-touted Circular Letter (and how privileged he felt, to be among the few to read it prior to its official publication), Denton turned to Otis' curt missive.

A petition to Gov. Marsh regarding his dispatches to England will be delivered to him tomorrow. This timeframe given in the assumption that you are receiving this letter today. Best of luck.

Denton nodded and tucked the personal letter and the Circular Letter into one of his jacket's interior pockets. He'd have to think of a safe place to keep those, but until then, the jacket would do nicely. Finally, he picked up the letter from his family and tore it open.

Upon reflection, he reflected as he stared at an envelope torn clean in two straight down the middle, *I ought to have used a letter opener.*

He pulled the two halves of the beloved letter from their shells and pushed them together on his desk. No matter that the letter was torn – it still made him smile, made his eyes ache and vision swim with the promise of tears, should he keep subjecting himself to this.

It was so easy to forget how much he missed them, when he had politics and witchcraft to distract him. Or maybe it was just *easier.*

What the letter said wasn't especially important to anyone other than Denton. Young Lawrence was showing promise on horseback; younger Annabelle was demonstrating an uncanny aptitude for mathematics, and Peggy speculated on just how far the world would open for a woman handy on the metaphorical abacus. And what of Peggy herself? Well, she was keeping busy. She'd been keeping up her *salon*-hostings, inviting local rascals with ambition in to discuss the issues of the day, and (here was the difference) what to do about them. The focus had shifted from thought to action. Denton feared for her ever so slightly; this was hardly the time for a woman to be making waves. But all the same, he trusted her sense of discretion – wasn't she so often the one keeping *him* in check?

In reading it, he heard her voice. Not in his head, but outside of it, as though she were standing just behind him, just out of sight, dictating it directly to him. What she was saying wasn't especially important to anyone other than Denton, but to Denton, it was everything.

He put the letter down and closed his eyes for a moment, because the cool air in the room was starting to dry them out. Yes, sometimes cool air could do that. When he opened them a couple of minutes later, he still heard Peggy's voice, but only inside his head.

Outside of his head, there was Fidget's Mill.

XXII

"WHAT IN THE HELL IS THIS MEANING OF THIS?!" Governor Marsh screamed as he waved a piece of paper around over his head.

Brisby tried to glimpse some of the writing on the piece of paper, but couldn't manage to read words traveling at such a high velocity. "It's, uh, a letter?"

"I know that, don't I? What's the *meaning* of it?!"

"I suppose that would be decided by the words inscribed upon it."

"This is an outrage! Can they honestly expect me to comply?"

Brisby took to muttering down to his shoes, as he felt they would be more likely to listen to him than Rumney in that moment. "I'd really need to read the letter to tender an opinion." He felt a light tap on his head, and saw a ball of crumpled paper fall between said shoes.

"Go on, read it! Read the hateful scribblings of people who know not their place!"

With an unintended groan, Brisby bent and plucked the letter from the floor of Rumney's drawing room. It was curious, the physician reflected as he unfolded the paper, that the Governor had called him in for a drink this evening. He'd never before summoned Brisby for anything other than professional consultations, and yet for the past several hours Marsh had been subjecting him to a seemingly endless parade of personal irrelevancies, beginning with what he'd had for breakfast that morning. Didn't Marsh have any friends upon whom he could heap such tedium? To whom had he unburdened himself, prior to tonight?

Perhaps it was all just prelude to this, the moment of Brisby reading the letter. Perhaps this was a professional consultation after all.

The letter was short enough, written in simple, straightforward prose. One James Otis Jr. was requesting, on behalf and with the support of the Massachusetts Colonial Legislature, a full record of Governor Rumney Marsh's correspondence with England. The justification for such a request wasn't explicitly stated, but it could be spotted boldly between the lines; Marsh was suspected of dishonestly representing the Colonies in his letters to the English Secretary of State.

"How dare they question my integrity?!" the Governor raged. "I am their Governor!"

Brisby did his best to smooth out the crumpled letter, and set about trying to do the same with Marsh's feelings. "Um," he began, "I suppose that's why. It is very much in vogue at the moment, questioning authority."

"Where?"

"What?"

"Where is it?"

"Where's what?"

"Questioning authority?"

"...I don't unders-"

"You just said it was in something. In where?"

"In vogue. It's an expression I heard somewhere."

"Where?"

"I don't remember."

"Bah!" Marsh waved a dismissive hand, and Brisby very much wanted to accept the gesture at face value and beat a hasty retreat. But, for some reason, he didn't.

"My professional opinion," which was a slightly dishonest way to preface his suggestion, given that his qualifications were medical rather than political, "is that you ought simply turn over the requested correspondence. This would be the surest way to absolve yourself of any wr-"

"Bah again!" The Governor heaved himself out of his chair and strode over to a decanter of whiskey set on a well-polished silver tray, in turn set on a mahogany table with angels carved into the legs by hands as skilled as they were unpaid. He refilled his glass, and plopped the decanter back down on the tray. "What sort of a precedent does that set, I ask you?"

"A cooperative one?" Brisby gave his own empty glass a small frown. His host failed to notice.

Marsh plopped himself back into his seat. "I've no reason to cooperate with them! I'm not popularly appointed; I am here by royal appointment! Royal as in the Crown! Crown as in the king's hat! The King as in the one from whom all blessings flow, and to whom all subjects owe fealty!"

"My professional opinion is that the crux of the matter is th-"

"The what?!"

"...the crux of the matter."

"Go on."

"I think it lies in th-"

"Where?"

It was distressing to Brisby that, despite being a both a medical man and a drunkard, it took him until now to realize just how stone-cold sloshed Rumney was. The decanter was now very nearly empty – but it was Dr. Houlihan's professional opinion that it had begun the evening very nearly full.

Brisby pursed his lips, thought for a moment, and decided to proceed in the same simple, straightforward style as the letter in question. "The whole reason people are upset is that they dispute their being subjects at all, at least in the traditional sense."

"That's not my problem! I won't allow them to bully me into accountability!"

There were a number of things Brisby would *not* say, at this point in time. Most of them dealt with Denton Hedges. There was nothing especially suspicious about the timing of this letter, as far as Brisby knew. Had there been, it would have been easier to couch its arrival into a narrative of intrigue. He could have tapped his chin and said "HMMMM" very loudly, which would undoubtedly have been quite exciting for the Governor.

To be perfectly honest with himself (and why not), the idea of tapping his chin and saying "HMMMM" very loudly would have been exciting for him as well.

But he had no theories ready to air, because they weren't theories yet. They were feelings, with a person attached. That person was Denton Hedges, and the feeling was that the man was far savvier, and far more revolutionarily minded, than he let on. He certainly hoped there was more to the man than met the eye, because there wasn't much for the eye to meet. Still, Brisby had no real love of revolution. His position was closer to indifference than resistance. He was a largely apolitical man, and he had been happy with his station in life. He had a practice he was proud of, working in a field he enjoyed, doing work that satisfied him, and relaxing every night with a family he loved. What did he care about parliamentary representation? Why should he get involved in politics? His involvement here had been foisted upon him, and all he wanted to do was his job, to completion, so that he could return to his beloveds once again.

Whenever that could come.

If Denton (or whoever) was set upon shaking up the status quo, things could *only* go poorly for Brisby. Whether he wanted it or not, he was now a part of *authority*. He was the Customs Commissioner, acting on behalf of the King, however indirectly. And so, he supposed, he did have a vested interest in the status quo. He did 'want' to oppose revolutionary tendencies.

He would have to be political. So, time to think about this letter politically!

"If you don't want to set a precedent for being…cooperative, may I suggest a form of curtailed capitulation?"

"You want me to what?"

Brisby tapped his temple once, for his own benefit. "You can grant their request, with stipulations attached. Demonstrate your willingness to be open, without compromising your position of, uh…strength." Strength was not a word Brisby would ever have applied to Governor Rumney Marsh, but he was being political, wasn't he?

"What do you mean?"

Good grief, how had this man attained any power, illusory or otherwise? He seemed to be afflicted with a serious case of the question marks. "I mean, agree to show your correspondence to a trusted representative of the legislature, or emissary approved by the same. They will review the letters, see that you have done nothing to dishonestly represent Fidget's Mill to the royal court, and report back to the legislature. By doing this, the crisis has passed, and you have done nothi-"

"I'm going to stop you right there," Marsh cut in. "What if I *haven't* been doing nothing to dishonestly represent Fidget's Mill to the royal court?"

"…which is to say that you have been doing something to dishonestly represent Fidget's Mill to the royal court?"

"More or less."

"…is it more, or le-"

"More."

Brisby buried his face in his hands. "Why?"

"…what do you mean?"

"Why did you write dishonest things about the town in your letters?"

"…"

Brisby lowered his hands. "What did you tell them?"

"…"

"Governor Marsh?"

"itoldthemthathingswerego-"

"I can't understand you."

"I told them that everything was going well!" Marsh emphasized these words with a great flinging of spittle. "I just wanted them to think I was good at my job! Is that so bad? Is that a crime?"

Brisby gave this a moment's thought. "Technically I suppose? Lying to the King? I don't know much about the law…" But, he ruminated, Denton would probably know all about that…

"I didn't *lie*. I just omitted certain things, and sometimes replaced those things with other things that I made up. Which, alright, is *technically* lying, but last time I checked…"

"…last time you checked…?"

"I don't actually have a follow-up to that."

Alright, Brisby considered. Think politically. In theory, Otis and co. should love this. They were getting favorable representation to the Crown. Pick somebody to take a peek at Marsh's correspondence, show that he was portraying them more favorably than an honest account would have drawn, and let the whole matter be put to bed.

But that was looking at the situation logically. What did it look like politically?

The letter from Otis didn't *specifically* accuse that they were being poorly misrepresented to the Crown. It was *implied*, but the only accusation that could be drawn *directly* from the language of the letter was that they were being misrepresented to the Crown, full stop. A positive misrepresentation was still a misrepresentation. And given the current pique of the town, any misrepresentation could be spun into…something. Something that would be bad news for folks like Brisby who liked things just the way they were.

"So…" Brisby returned his hands to his face, and kept them there for several seconds. When he lowered them, it was less because he had thought of something brilliant, and more because he was having a hard time breathing properly. "You can't let them see your correspondence. That's my professional opinion. Just make as populist a case as you can, for hiding behind the shield of royal authority."

"Don't show them? Why not?"

Brisby blinked hard and shook his head. "Because…" He *could* explain the whole word-parsing thought process he'd had, but once again, he suspected it'd be more productive to lay that out for his footwear than the Governor, dozens of sheets to the wind as he was. "Do you need a reason? You didn't want to show them to begin with!"

"Good point." Rumney Marsh stood up and walked out of the room. Fifteen minutes later, a servant entered the room and informed Brisby that the Governor had retired for the evening. So Brisby saw himself out, walked back across the yard to his current residence, and fell into bed. He didn't sleep, because all he could think about was civil unrest. And, should his identity as Customs Commissioner become more public knowledge, a mob knocking on his door and asking to see him with a minimum of question marks.

So much for his happy practice, and his happy patients, and his happy family, and his happy life. Unless he could do something to protect himself, that was. That something bad was on the horizon was clear enough – the letter from Otis wouldn't have been sent in a vacuum, or without motive. So what was coming? The only way to protect himself – and so his job and his family – from it was to find out what was coming, and get out of its way. Or maybe get out in front of it.

And Denton would know all about that as well, wouldn't he?

Yazbirth Bicklebog stood at the foot of Brisby Houlihan's bed, staring at the man lying flat on his back, wide awake, staring up at the ceiling. The Dread Familiar thought of appearing to the doctor, and making a case for consortation. But he didn't. Millennia of desperate wandering had helped him tune in to psychic distress, and then to distinguish different kinds. He couldn't read people's minds, but he could get the gist of them, like skimming the headlines of a newspaper over someone's shoulder. Brisby didn't want the same things as Miss Carsis, and Yazbirth was quite certain that hers was the side that would ultimately triumph. She was quite a frustrating ally – she continued to assure him that she was hard at work finding a consort for him, don't you worry about that, but so far he'd been left to feel one out on his own.

The physician was in distress, but not a sort of distress that Yazbirth could utilize. The Dread Familiar sighed and walked straight through the wall, which was a talent he had but, for some reason, could only used when he was distracted, not thinking about anything. When he had his wits about him, he always used the door.

Yazbirth galumphed out into the night, but not before casting a wistful glance back towards the Governor's mansion. Lights burned brightly in the windows, but Bicklebog knew perfectly well that that didn't mean anything. Marsh loved a well-lit mansion, whether he was awake to enjoy it or not.

That was the sort of thing that had bothered him when he was Familiaring for Marsh, but that he now missed.

XXIII

WHEN THE SERVANT, WHO FITHIAN LOWESTOFT thought was named John, escorted her into the Crundwell mansion as he had many times now, she didn't even bother to thank him, as she had those many other times. She was in a rotten mood, and she knew it, and she hated both of these facts.

Her father had been speaking to Bunny Crundwell about dates for marriage to Buddy Jr., all of which fell within the year. Her unhappy matrimony, months away!

Buddy Jr., despite his genitals, had no greater say in the matter than she did. Being the nominal head of the family meant that he had responsibilities, whether he liked it or not. And as his mother was all too happy to remind him at every opportunity, those responsibilities were nothing less than the preservation of the Way Things Are. How to do that? Why, marry a Lowestoft, of course. Because who cares if *she* wanted to keep Things the Way they Were for herself? Nobody, that's who. It was all about the Mill.

Well, the joke was on them – or she hoped it would be. Because here she was again, sneaking off into the night for the express purpose of ensuring Things cease to be the Way they Are. Shake up the town, and she and Buddy Jr. wouldn't have to get married. Buddy Jr. could run off with Millicent, and Fithian would be allowed to continue living her life, keeping Things more or less the Way they Were at that moment.

There was inspiration to be found in irritation, she assured herself. It was just a shame that irritation bore such boorish behavior. Slavery was a despicable institution, and the last thing that poor fellow who let her in needed was her giving him the cold shoulder. She was loath to think of what the *first* thing that poor fellow needed might be.

Well, maybe if the town were sufficiently shaken, as a snowglobe, the social distinctions would be leveled to such an extent that she could simply ask the man, and get it for him. But follow that train of thought too far, and one wound up in a state of anarchy. Then again, at the other end of the spectrum lay an altar, with space for her and Buddy Jr. So if she couldn't chart a middle course, it might be best to skew towards the former.

As Fithian slipped into the room near the center of the mansion, where the meetings with Denton, Buddy Jr. and Missy had been so often conducted, a shadow watched her from outside, and peered inside of her mind.

Perhaps, Yazbirth Bicklebog giggled to himself, there was something to work with in that woman.

Denton was pleased as punch. Although, given his track record with punch in Fidget's Mill, perhaps a different analogy would better serve him.

He was chuffed as Bulstrode, maybe. He was very happy, however one chose to phrase it, because the end was finally in sight. The letter was out to Governor Marsh, whom they had no doubt would refuse the request contained therein. From there, it would be a simple matter of stirring up popular discontent and wielding it like a truncheon, bludgeoning him into submission. Which, in this case, just meant asking him to resign his post, and making sure there were some blunt objects in his field of view as the request was posed.

With the Governor out of the way, there would be no direct influence the Crown could wield, at least until another Governor could be appointed and dispatched. This would give them plenty of time to finally bring the town into line with the rest of Massachusetts, from a commercial standpoint. Which he was now well positioned to do, thanks to the greater sense of unity fostered by the ouster of Marsh. Everything Denton had been working for, all of the suffering he had endured, was for this: trade agreements.

So:

Buddy Jr. was happy to guarantee, to a degree of certainty just shy of *actual* certainty, that he could deliver a Crundwell family in support of non-importation. He was willing to consent to the marriage to Fithian (with no intention of actually seeing it through, of course) on the condition that he be given full discretionary control of the Crundwell family fortunes. If he could get a verbal agreement from his mother on that, in front of witnesses, he was quite confident that non-importation was as good as done.

Fithian agreed that, with sufficient finesse, she could perhaps find a way to make marriage to Buddy Jr. conditional upon a Lowestoftian stance of non-importation, with just as much interest in seeing the marriage actually occur as Buddy Jr. had. It felt wonderful to her, to use this awful arrangement as a weapon against those who saw fit to bargain her life away for a poor imitation of financial stability.

In the part of his mind reserved for unpleasant thoughts, Denton observed the ease with which this was all happening, and wondered if there was perhaps a world in which he arrived at this same point *without* having to array popular support against Governor Marsh. Might it not have been sufficient to challenge Marsh to a duel? Wealthy toffs loved that sort of thing. But no, how would that have helped? It wasn't even *about* Marsh, that was the most distressing part. He had no idea whether Marsh was good or bad, but he certainly felt the latter for using a man's livelihood as a bargaining chip, particularly when it may never need to have been gambled in the first place…

He shut that particular trapdoor in his mind and put a very large couch upon it as he returned to his objective: the challenging pitch for non-importation would fall to Missy – her father would stand to gain exactly nothing from non-importation, and Missy had no leverage with which to bargain. They would have to come up with a way to bring him around before the Circular Letter hit. But assuming they did, Denton's work would be done. He would have accomplished the seemingly prosaic (but actually herculean) task of getting Fidget's Mill to adopt non-importation before the release of the Circular Letter, and he would be proud of this for the remainder of his life.

From there, Massachusetts would have a unified front from which to wage economic warfare on England, and Denton would read of that proxy war's progress with great interest, from the comfort of his living room in Boston. Would he be a low-stakes hero of sorts? Could he utilize this to breath life into a legal career in Massachusetts, and recapture something he'd been missing since his time in Virginia?

It was this topic he had in mind when a slave who Denton thought was named John quietly entered the room. He had a habit of doing this, which Denton wrote off as a simple lack of education, as pertained to the manners of the manor. Had he known that it was a deliberate attempt of "John's", aka Adewale's, to eavesdrop in bits and pieces, that he might keep his new friend Mr. Increase as well informed as possible of what they were discussing, Denton might have done some serious soul-searching regarding the dangers of casual racism.

"Guess," Adewale huffed. The hardest thing about pretending to not speak English was in being consistent with your malapropisms. It could be fun, coming up with amusing new ways to bungle a simple message, but the danger was in having *too* much fun and forgetting what you pretended to be confused about last time. Still, it was a welcome change of pace – there weren't many areas of Adewale's life in which he could honestly say the greatest danger was in having too much fun.

Buddy Jr. sighed. "Tuh. Gues*tuh*. Guest." The Crundwell son wasn't angry – he spoke to Adewale as a parent might to a cat who had knocked over a nice kettle of silver. The kitty doesn't know any better, so it doesn't make sense to get mad at them. But you *want* to.

"Guess," Adewale repeated. He felt the corners of his mouth creeping upwards, but managed to pull them back into a frown. That was how Chip Ditteridge always preferred his slaves – frowning. Smiles made him suspicious. Buddy Jr. was a much kinder soul, though not so kind that it occurred to him to free his slaves. So a frown would do for him just fine.

Then again, it also never occurred to Buddy Jr. that Adewale was not, in fact, his father's slave, just as it never occurred to Chip Ditteridge to wonder where one of his had gotten off to. Nor did Missy recognize him as one of her father's. Adewale was, bizarrely, slightly hurt by this collective and substantial failure to care.

"Who is the gues*tuh*?"

"Bribsy."

Denton sat forward in his chair. "Brisby? Dr. Brisby Houlihan?"

"Yes."

The four conspirators looked at each other in turn. Denton raised an eyebrow to Buddy Jr. "He doesn't often call here anymore, does he?"

"No, I've not heard from the man since New Year's."

Fithian, who had been pacing around the room, leaned on the back of Missy's chair. "Might he suspect our cabal?"

"He's an emissary of the Crown," Missy grumbled. "If he knows of us, we may run into some…problems."

"Oh," Denton started. "You guys knew that too?"

"Everyone knows. He's the only one who doesn't know that everyone knows."

Denton turned to Adewale. "Did Brisby say what he wanted?"

"Talk to you."

Buddy Jr. pointed to himself. "To me?"

"No." Adewale shook his head, and pointed directly to Denton. "To you."

Brisby knows. Denton was prepared to say as much, but he looked around the room and saw he didn't have to. If Brisby knew Denton was here, then Brisby almost certainly knew the rest of them were. And he'd have questions.

Denton snapped back to reality and faced his three compatriots. "I vote we bring him in and hear him out."

"And if we don't like what he has to say?" Missy asked as she shifted in her chair. The motion reminded Denton of a cat getting ready to pounce.

"We'll figure that out once we've heard it." Denton nodded but said nothing to Adewale, because *he* was well acquainted with proper manners in a manor.

"Please send Dr. Houlihan in," Buddy Jr. told Adewale. He added, "Thank you John."

From the moment Brisby was ushered into the room, he was a veritable typhoon of unsolicited information. Governor Marsh would be declining the request tendered in your letter because oh also yes I did see the letter and at once knew it was your doing when Governor Marsh asked for my personal opinion on the matter or well maybe I should say my professional opinion though between you and you and you and you and me my only real qualifications are medical and therefore my professional opinion in this-

On and on and on, and at the end of it all, Denton had found exactly one bit of informational driftwood to cling to, to stay afloat in the roaring torrents of irrelevance. And that was the very first thing Houlihan said: that Governor Marsh would be refusing their request to review his correspondence with England. This was wonderful news! For an old pro pamphleteer like Denton, it'd be no trouble at all disseminating news of the Governor's defiance of the Massachusetts legislature, and orchestrating a seemingly grassroots ouster. Now all that remained, really, was brainstorming ways to help Missy bring her father around on non-importation…

"What's going to happen?" Brisby moaned. "I have a family, you understand? I'm afraid for my life, I'm afraid for my practice, I'm af-" He collapsed, landing on his ass. "Ouch."

Denton crouched down next to his pitiable maybe-friend. "What do you have to be afraid of?"

"I…I'm the Customs Commissioner!"

"We know," Buddy Jr. mumbled.

"…huh?"

"Everybody knows," Fithian elaborated.

Missy at least had the decency to smile at Brisby, and not his expense. "Best way to hide your true occupation wouldn't be in the house behind Governor Marsh's, for starters."

"Having a plausible reason for being in the Mill to begin with would help too," Fithian added with the other kind of smile. "Don't you have one of those?"

"Yeah," Denton couldn't help but twist the knife a little, "don't you, Brisby?"

The doctor let his shoulders slump. "Yeah, yeah, real funny. But the point is, I'm the king's flunky here. Well," he sniffed, "one of them, anyway. And when Rumney goes..."

"You'll be fine." Denton patted him on the shoulder. "Don't worry about it. Everything is going to be fine."

Fithian leaned in to agree. Except she didn't. She sat in her chair. And continued to sit. She tried to move her head, and failed. She kept staring at the same blank spot on the wall she'd been staring at. Was nobody else in the room noticing her immobility? What had happened? She wanted to scream, to get the doctor to quit crying and *help her*, but she couldn't open her mouth.

Her vision began to collapse in on itself...only that wasn't right. The room was getting darker. But nobody else seemed to notice! Was she dying? Was this dying?

"Don't be frightened," a slow, phlegmy voice suggested. She saw a shadow in her peripheral vision, impossibly huge, yet hopelessly empty. "Myself would simply like to talk to Yourself."

And there was something...understanding about that voice. There was something in it that said *we've got a lot in common, you and I.*

So Fithian listened. Not that she had much choice. When the time finally *did* come to choose, however, she said 'yes'.

XXIV

FORGET ITS UTILITY – THERE WERE FEW THINGS more satisfying than having a secret. Fidget's Mill was a town full of secrets, populated by people who had no idea how to keep them. Which was part of why everyone in Fidget's Mill was so perpetually unsatisfied. But when one stayed kept, boy, it was very nearly magical.

Denton could only boggle at Mr. Increase, who had just laid out, more or less, all of the discussions he had been having behind closed doors with his trio of co-conspirators. "How could you…?"

"I have my ways," Mr. Increase replied. He struggled to keep a smile off of his face. It was a losing battle.

"Look," Denton mumbled as he resumed packing his bag. He'd just begun the process of preparing his exit from the Mill when Mr. Increase knocked on his door at the Klump Regency. "It wasn't a conscious decision to exclude you, you understand. It just, well, it just developed nicely as a quartet, th-"

"I don't care about that. I'm not here to beg for inclusion."

Denton was visibly relieved by this, which annoyed Mr. Increase. "Well, that's good. Because we're just about done with this whole farce, anyway. I trust you saw those pamphlets, calling for the removal of Governor Marsh?"

"You wrote them."

"Well, *I* wr…yes. I did."

Mr. Increase walked over to the desk in front of the window, and picked up a piece of paper. There were a lot of words written on it, though hard to read underneath the bold lines slashed through them.

"Hey!" Denton leapt clean across the room and snatched the page from Mr. Increase.

Increase, his hand still raised as though the paper hadn't been taken, smiled. "Your words are causing quite a stir, as I'm sure you're aware."

"I am. That's very much the intention. I expect there'll be a popular demonstration led against Governor Marsh tonight – I'm quite confident there will be, in fact." Denton grinned in what he must have thought was a predatory snarl, but was in fact the baffled cheer of a puppy who hasn't mastered object permanence yet. "Let's just say there's something in the air."

"You're going to kick something off."

"Not *me*." Denton stared at the ground for a moment, and returned to his packing. "At any rate, Marsh will be gone before the sun christens the new day. By tomorrow, Missy will have convinced her father to support non-importation, as the Crundwells and Lowestofts have already pledged to do. And, if you'll permit me to congratulate myself on my impeccable timing, the day *after* tomorrow will see the release of Otis and Adams' Circular Letter. Massachusetts will be present a unified front, from an economic perspective, negotiations will be undertaken, and before you know it, we'll be taxing ourselves." Pleased with *something*, Denton nodded emphatically and slammed his luggage, once pretend-stolen by a witch, shut. "And I'll be home with my family."

"And have you considered where anyone native to the Mill will be, at that point?"

"..." Denton's eyes raked across the edges of the ceiling, as though something of profound interest had been carved into the wood up there. "Yes? Still here, I imagine."

"That's not what I mean, and I'm quite certain that you know that." Mr. Increase walked over to the cabinet-dresser, and pulled open the left door. "This town subsists solely on its imports. We grow nothing. We produce nothing. We consume. How are we meant to support ourselves? I know this question has been raised to you before. You've had plenty of time to think of a response."

Denton thought for a moment, then waved a hand dismissively. "Imports from Boston, of course. I can personally arrange regul-"

"Oh, you've thought that through, have you?"

"As a matter of fact, I have. It's going to be hard for you here, I appreciate that. But sacrifices must be made for the Cause."

"What sacrifices have you made?"

"I missed my son's birthday, and don't you dare insinuate that I've not risked anything by doing what I've been doing."

So Denton *did* have sharp edges after all. What a welcome discovery. "I'm not here to demean your...contributions."

"Also, and I apologize if you were preparing to say something conciliatory but I've only just thought of this: I won't be spoken to about reckless endangerment of the town by a man who indiscriminately poisoned an entire party!"

"Indiscriminate?"

"You just poured it in the punch!"

"The limited attendance of the party was itself the discrimination!"

Denton waved his arms in front of his face. "I don't want to get into it all again, I just thought of that and thought it was a good point."

Mr. Increase stomped his good foot. "You can't attack me like that and not allow me to defend myself!"

"Why did you come here, Mr. Increase?"

"That's not fair! I was making a point and you interrupted me!"

"Sometimes life isn't fair, man! Say your piece!"

"My point was that importing from Boston is actually wildly impractical, given the distances and res-"

"We'll find a way to make it work. These are times of uncommon Colonial unity and extraordinary acts of generosity."

"I cannot think of a less apt summation of our current predicament."

Denton poked himself in the forehead, pressing his finger into the center as though trying to make a hole for a unicorn's horn. "What did you come here to tell me? I have much to see to in the coming days."

"I came to deliver two warnings. The first is this: Chip Ditteridge knows of us. Our involvement in the New Year's incident, I mean."

Denton's snapped his hand back down to his waist, accidentally slapping himself in the balls. "GUH. What do you mean?"

"I mean exactly what I say. He cannot *prove* it, but he suspects. And furthermore, he knows of your meeting with his daughter, along with Buddy Jr. and Fithian, and sending letters to Boston. Which makes *one* of us."

"Sorry," Denton couldn't stop himself from saying.

Mr. Increase waved the apology away. "So then, how to you expect young Missy to convince her father to adopt non-importation, when he will immediately suspect this to be one stage in a stratagem of your devising?"

"How can you know this? How can you be sure?"

"I have my-"

"Ways, fine." Denton shook his head dismissively. He scrunched his eyes shut, and screwed his fists into his temples. "For how long have you known this?"

"…oh, not very long," Mr. Increase lied. He'd known it long enough. But, well, he supposed he *was* slightly hurt at being excluded from the room where all of the most interesting discussions in the town were being held. So he'd kept his own little secret, and was just now realizing that this may have been a grave tactical error. Denton wasn't the only one not thinking of the general welfare of the town, it seemed.

"I'm afraid my impeccable sense of timing is now working against me," Denton whispered to nobody in particular. He stared at a knot in the wall for several seconds, before whipping his head to Mr. Increase as though the free man just made a surprising animal noise. "I must go speak to Missy, this instant. If she speaks to her father before the movement against Marsh begins…he could well see how this all connects! Gah!"

Denton threw open the door and sprinted out of the room. It would be several hours before he realized that Mr. Increase had told him that he had *two* warnings, but Denton had only heard *one* of them. By that point, though, he could pretty well guess what the second one would have been about.

Fithian reached through the deep blue curtains with her fingers, and pulled them apart as delicately as she might a…lover's buttocks? She'd never been particularly facile with the similes, and she was too nervous to think straight.

She had been talking with Denton, Buddy Jr. and Missy, and then a giant sloth had appeared to her and told her all kinds of things. The long and short of it was that the sloth wanted to help Fithian, and it knew that Fithian wanted certain things that her three allies might not.

And then the sloth said, go to 33 Gutter Lane, for there you will find a witch. Fithian didn't believe in witches, but she had the good sense not to explain this to an invisible sloth demon.

So here Fithian was, hoping to pop her head in quickly, say hello, Yazbirth Bicklebog sends his big stinky regards, and then head back out to watch Governor Marsh's ouster. She wouldn't miss that for the *world.* Except which door was 33? Confused, she stepped up to the third door from the left and knocked. A young woman answered immediately, which would have surprised Denton very much indeed.

Inside, Fithian was directed through the curtain, into the kitchen of the witch. At least, Fithian assumed this was the witch, though she had imagined the witch would look far less surprised.

"Miss Carsis?" she ventured.

"Yes. Yes." Despite picking up a fairly strong sense of Fithian's motive, for one fleeting moment she thought the woman might have somehow discovered Miss Carsis' role in Tobin's vanishing act. Upon sensing that to be false, she found it far more difficult to answer a second question: should she tell Fithian?

And what if she did? Fithian would tell her friends. Word would spread. Secrets rarely stayed kept in the Mill unless one kept one's own counsel. And forewarned is forearmed. No, if she told Fithian right now that her brother was safe and sound, ready to return, the girl would find herself lighter of heart, and tomorrow Miss Carsis would find the town hardened in its resolve to resist Tobin and Sonny, aware of its being manipulated.

None too happy about this conclusion, Miss Carsis deadpanned "please tell me why Yazbirth Bicklebog sent you here."

"It…she…he?"

"Take your pick. They're 'it's that skew 'he', but you can bet it'd be a different story were our society organized matriarchically."

"Right. Well, he told me that he wanted to Familiar for me…may I use Familiar as a verb?"

"Please yourself."

"Excellent, um, he wanted to Familiar for me, and he told me that I should speak to you ab-"

"So sorry to be brusque, but this is a busy night and my patience with that damned sloth is at an end." Not to mention Fithian's presence was making her unaccountably uncomfortable. The witch was helping Tobin because of his love, true, but here she was faced with another kind of love, no less powerful for being familial. Why was it acceptable to facilitate one at the expense of the other?

Well, one was chosen and one was a byproduct of fate. Miss Carsis had never cared much for fate, always preferring an active choice to a passive acceptance. But a less preferable love was still love, and lying to love felt *wrong*.

"He was very much mistaken", Miss Carsis continued, "a contract between you two is just that: between you two. I do not enter into it at all, save incidentally, due to a prior arrangement I made with that wretched hellion." Miss Carsis strode to the curtain and pulled it back. "Now if you'll excuse me, I've so very much to do."

Fithian, looking like she had just been struck by lightning on a sunny day, shook her head. "Yes, I'm sorry to have intruded." She rose slowly, and plodded her way to the door.

All the way home, Fithian mulled over why Miss Carsis was so busy tonight, when Yazbirth had given her the impression that the witch derived her power from stoicism. It was a long walk home, and all the while Fithian tried and failed to come up with explanations that didn't involve the incipient "protest" against Governor Marsh.

What was the witch planning? She picked up the pace and rushed to the Klump Regency, hoping to catch Denton and brainstorm further.

Yazbirth Bicklebog had had hundreds of thousands of consorts, perhaps even millions. And with each and every one, he developed an intense emotional connection. When they died, he was devastated, until he managed to find another, at which point he would be fine until *that* one died. It was a horrible way to exist, but it was the only way he knew.

Rarely, however, would he terminate a consortation before the likely death of his consort. He was flooded with a bewildering cocktail of emotions, but increasingly the most distinct note was one of overwhelming guilt.

And so, feeling sick at his infidelity, Yazbirth sent his new consort Fithian on a pointless errand to Miss Carsis, giving him the opportunity to slip back over to Governor Marsh's. This was such a confusing time! His brand-new consort was conspiring against his trusty old consort, with whom he had history. Where should his loyalty lie? His old consort had had him poison an unborn child and its mother, but his new consort was trying to kick his old one out of a job. Hardly moral equivalencies – the choice was clear. But that didn't mean he had to leave Marsh high and dry, did it?

He prowled the perimeter of Marsh's mansion as the sun began to set, until the anxiety could be borne no longer. Yazbirth slipped directly through the wall, and found Marsh lying despondently on a couch, staring into the dying embers of a fire.

"Myself cannot stay long," he rumbled. Marsh not only didn't seem surprised – he hardly seemed to notice at all.

"Have you seen those damned tracts someone scribbled against me?" Marsh's eyes never left the fireplace.

"Yes, though Myself cannot read, and so the content of them remains a mystery."

"They're packed with all manner of libel."

"This is unfortunate, though relevant to that which Myself wishes to discuss with Yourself."

Yazbirth waited for some kind of reaction, a turning of the head, or a rising to the elbow. But Rumney Marsh obliged with neither, opting instead to gaze at smoking logs. So the once-Familiar continued, "Myself fears that Yourself is in danger. Myself more than fears, to be candid. This is knowledge Myself possesses. Yourself is in danger of great unpleasantness. Tonight."

The Governor closed his eyes. His brow softened, as though he were listening to an unspeakably beautiful melody. Hopefully a dirge of some sort, Yazbirth reflected. That would be apt. "Thank you for warning me, Yazbirth."

"Will Yourself take steps to protect Yourself? Will Yourself retire to a safer location?"

"Will I run away, you mean? No, I will not."

"Why not?"

Finally, Rumney rose to his elbow *and* turned his head to face Yazbirth. "Because then they'd know how poor of a job I've done." The Governor smiled, nodded, and slid back into his previous recumbence. "If I stay, perhaps I can still rectify the situation. Reason with them, explain to them that, yes, I *was* dishonest in my dispatches to England, but in ways which were flattering to the town." He nodded again. "I may yet turn this around."

And that, Yazbirth was quite certain, was the last Rumney Marsh wished to say on the issue. "Well…take care of Yourself."

"Mhm. You too."

"Thank Yourself." With that, the giant sloth about-faced and made for the exit. This time, he used the door to get back out.

Once he'd gone, Marsh sniffed once, and once more replayed the fantasy of quelling a mob raised against him. It was a fantasy devoid of specifics – he had no idea how one quelled a mob. But in his daydream, they came angry and left contrite.

Before long, Marsh fell asleep. He had nightmares.

XXV

FEBRUARY IN NEW ENGLAND WAS A LOT LIKE Denton's father: cold, white, and short-tempered. One thing it was quite definitively *not* was a good time to run.

It was a measure of Denton's desperation that he ran through the snow-packed streets of Fidget's Mill, squinting against the gusting wind with icicles for teeth and one hell of a grudge. The setting sun mocked him not just by its deceptively warm tones, but by what felt to Denton like an accelerated descent. When the sun went down, the mob would begin to move against Governor Marsh. Denton had told Missy to approach her father about non-importation before then.

All Denton could do was hope she hadn't done it yet, and keep running, and more importantly keep getting up after he fell, and even more importantly keep making sure he fell in ways that avoided injuries that would prevent him from getting up again.

"Father, might I have a word?"

Chip Ditteridge looked up from his book, to see his traitorous daughter leaning against the doorframe – only leaning sounded a bit too casual. She was clinging to it as though it were still attached to a tree, and there were a fifty-foot drop beneath her feet. Her hands were turning white from the strain. That was the sort of thing Chip might well have overlooked, were he not so sharply attuned to his daughter's anxiety.

And she should have been anxious. She had been associating with the other families, and that coward who Chip was quite sure had attempted to poison him on New Years', and also succeeded in poisoning some other folks.

Smiling his unctuous best, he closed his book, but kept it rested in his lap. "Of course, Millicent. What about?"

Missy sighed and floated into the room, pulling the door shut behind her. "I've been thinking."

"What about?"

"Economics and trade agreements."

Neither said anything for quite some time. Missy had, after much consideration and input from the other three members of her anti-Marsh braintrust, decided that the strongest approach to take here would be head-on. She loved her father, but he just wasn't bright enough to pick up on subtlety. She never thought this as an insult; he would be the first to admit this, but if he wouldn't, you could convince him he should pretty easily. No, the best approach with her dear Dad was to be blunt and brief.

Chip, meanwhile, was floored by his daughter's candor. He'd been expecting some degree of finesse, or a convenient string of well-rehearsed platitudes that would just happen to lead them into whatever it was she had been discussing at those secret meetings. What he had not anticipated was, well, what she had just said, and how she had said it.

Chip scoffed haughtily, because that was what he did whenever he felt confused or threatened, in much the same way that a horned lizard will shoot blood out of its eyes.

"Economics and tr-"

"I heard what you said." Chip plucked the book out of his lap and plopped it on the table next to him. "Why don't you tell me what's your scheme, here?"

"I've been thinking."

"About economics and trade agreements?"

Missy paused for a moment, then set to pacing around the room. Chip hated to see his daughter discommoded, but given the current situation, he didn't hate it all that strenuously. "Yes," she muttered, "and I have heard rumors that the Crundwells and Lowestoft families will soon be pursuing a pl-"

"Whence these rumors?"

"Hm?" Missy slowed and turned her head towards her father.

"You didn't happen to hear these directly from Buddy Jr. and Fithian, did you?"

The pacing halted all at once, and Missy rotated the rest of her body to face her father. "What do you-"

"Don't lie to me, dear. Please. I know about the clandestine meetings at the Crundwell mansion, and a few other things that went on there besides."

Did Missy realize she was slowly positioning herself behind the back of the chair across from Chip, as though preparing to duck behind it in the event of a shoe or squash being thrown at her? When she spoke, her voice was smaller than the likelihood of a shoe or squash being thrown at her. "I don't know what yo-"

"What's the man's name? Denton Hedges?"

The name elicited a physical reaction from Missy, as though it had struck her with the force of a large cherry, or a fresh loaf of bread.

Chip continued, choosing to press at the moment of weakness. "Did you know that he was the fiend that poisoned us all on New Year's?

Killed some folks, sent some others scampering?" He leaned forward slightly, deeply regretting what he was about to say, but seeing no way around saying it. "Forced the hands of Bunny and the Lowestoft man, making the marriage of Buddy Jr. to Fithian nothing less than necessity?"

Now Missy wasn't cowering behind the chair – she was using it to remain upright. Poor girl. She hadn't known that her father knew about her and Buddy Jr., and she certainly hadn't known that about Denton.

"I already knew that about Denton," she mumbled. "Heard the rumor, anyway. I don't believe it."

Chip made to lean forward a bit more, but as he was already as forward as he could get, he just stood up. "I saw him traipsing out of the woods, like a common criminal!"

"He never left the house, father."

"He did! I saw him with mine own two eyes!"

"You are mistaken."

And it was the damndest thing; the certainty with which Missy said this made Chip wonder, for just a moment, if perhaps he *wasn't* mistaken.

"Denton Hedges is a good man," she continued, making up in conviction what she lacked in volume. "How he helped me, you ought to be thanking him as well."

Chip scratched just below his right eye. "I don't know what you mean."

"…ah?" It was then that Missy cursed her filial assumption of omniscience. She'd always been unhappily cowed by her father, even when she knew herself to be his superior in every way save diameter. When Chip had turned out to know seemingly everything about her personal life, she naturally assumed, without even thinking about it, that he knew *everything about her personal life*. Which would extend to the termination of her pregnancy. Which, it was immediately obvious, Chip did not know about.

"How did he help you? What do you mean by that?"

"It's quite a long story."

"I have time," Chip rumbled as he fell back into his seat.

As the cushion squeaked disagreeably under his weight, the door to the room swung open, and Denton Hedges barreled through. "Millicent!" he cried. He added, "Chip!" upon spotting her father once again fusing with his favorite chair. Not knowing how to cover for his dramatic intrusion, he went with "The Ditteridges, together at last!"

"What in the hell are you doing her?" Chip growled. "I mean, here!"

"I could ask you the very same question!" Denton fired back.

"I live here!"

"I know that, but it wouldn't stop me asking the question, would it?"

Chip didn't say anything to that, which Denton took as tacit concession of the point. So he continued, "I simply dashed over to see if you two were having any *interesting conversations*," this last delivered in a wide arc that ended at Missy.

"I already brought it up," she said with hopeless indifference. "He already knew about us."

"Oh, dear." Denton turned back to Chip. "For how long?"

"I saw you and that negro coming out of the woods on New Year's!"

"Well, as that most certainly never happened, I can make the happy observation that you know far less than you think."

Once again, the unflagging surety of this refutation forced Chip to investigate the fidelity of his own memories. This veered dangerously close to philosophy, which Chip simply *refused* to countenance.

"I do too," he replied. "You poisoned the party!"

"I can honestly say that I did not poison the party."

"Nevermind that – to what end have you been corrupting my daughter's beautiful porcelain head with talk of economics, and trade agreements, and other subjects intended for gentlemen?"

Denton shook his head and turned back to Missy. "I'm afraid your father is going to be a problem, and we simply don't have time to address this with any particular tact."

"What does that mean?" Missy wondered aloud.

Chip blanched. "That sounds like a threat to me!"

"You aren't threatening my father, are you?"

"I couldn't be," Denton explained reasonably, "because I was speaking to you."

This explanation did not sit especially well with Missy. "You didn't answer my question."

Denton shrugged his most lawyerly shrug.

"We'll see who threatens who!" Chip once again rose from his seat, as he could do precious little to defend himself in such a comfortable position, and wasn't about to endanger his favorite chair besides. "I'll sick my most muscular slave upon you! JOHN! JOHN!"

Adewale appeared in the open door almost immediately. "Almost immediately" being the time it took for Denton and (at long last) Missy to recognize him as the slave who had been ferrying them around the Crundwell mansion.

"Huh?" Denton barked without realizing it.

"Ah yes!" Chip cackled, misinterpreting Denton's confusion. "Take him, John, and m…" he let John's latest chore fade into nothing as a second figure appeared in the doorway.

"Ah," Denton blurted, this time at least realizing that noise was coming out of him. "I shouldn't be surprised, should I?"

"No," Mr. Increase replied, "you really shouldn't."

Adewale slipped silently into the room, Mr. Increase limping along after him. "John" strode directly up to Chip Ditteridge, and poked him in the forehead. "You can either cooperate or not, Chip. Believe it or not, I'd prefer you did. I've no interest in debasing myself by resorting to the sorts of violence you employ as a matter of course."

"You speak English?" was all Chip could manage in reply.

"No," Adewale replied, thus demonstrating a firm grasp on that dry British humor as well.

Mr. Increase leaned around Adewale, tilting his head rakishly towards Chip. "As a counterpoint to my good friend Adewale, I would be not in the least put out if you chose to be uncooperative."

Finally, Missy asked the question of the hour: "Cooperative or uncooperative with what?"

"Us," came the entirely unsatisfactory reply.

XXVI

WHEN A FOURTH MAN TRIPPED OVER NO-GOOD Bulstrode, the demon pondered his own ontology. He was invisible to the solitary clutches of frustrated men with poor social standing and a lengthy list of grievances. They were all simply milling around the town, wandering until they found another itinerant blob of humanity, with which they would unite like a cell that had divided and then thought better of it. Eventually, they would become a mob, as planned. Denton was nothing if not a gifted scribbler – which was a nice way of saying that he was really nothing *but* a gifted scribbler – and what he lacked in comprehension of individual humans, he made up for in his understanding of humanity en masse. Which, phrased in this way, made it sound as though Denton should be at his best schmoozing large groups of people. Thus the paucity of language is laid bare, Bulstrode reflected.

However, how Denton had managed to rile everyone up in synchrony with nothing more than well-timed leaflets, as opposed to, say, whispering dreadful suggestions in their ears when the moon was high, Bulstrode would never comprehend. He would also never comprehend why four…now *five* people had tripped over him. He could occasionally walk through solid objects, though when he rendered himself invisible, he retained his corporeal solidity. He'd tried focusing said density away, as he did his opacity, but no dice. That was when the third guy had tripped over him. Each time, the tripee would shoot back to a half-seated position, look directly at Bulstrode with transcendent confusion, and, seeing nothing, pick themselves up and do their best to save face amongst their quite drunken friends.

The annoying thing about this was that, as the crowds grew ever larger and ever more boisterous, nobody *ever* bumped into Yazbirth Bicklebog. They passed through him as though he weren't there at all, and Yazbirth's lack of reaction made clear that the feeling was mutual. The giant sloth just plodded along behind him, staring at nothing in particular, passing through the throng as though it were so much man-shaped fog.

Perhaps there was a silver lining to Yazbirth's being condemned to the same shape for untold millennia; he had become so accustomed to his form that he seemed to have little to no trouble controlling it. From a metaphysical standpoint, anyway. Yazbirth was the clumsiest familiar Bulstrode had ever seen, though to be fair, he supposed that came with being a giant sloth.

"Might I pose you a question, my Xenarthran friend?"

"Hm?" Yazbirth craned his mighty head down to Bulstrode. "Friend?"

"Of course!"

Could giant sloths blush? Bulstrode suspected not, nor would a Familiar need to blush, on account of having neither a circulatory system nor the blood to circulate therein. And yet, Yazbirth Bicklebog seemed to have a bit of a roseate glow to his cheeks.

"Yes, well, my *friend*, I simply must ask; how is it that you manage immateriality?"

"All Familiarselves are immaterial, yes?"

"...that's a difficult question."

Yazbirth's already-massive eyes grew even wider. "Is it? Myself thought that a Familiarself could never die. This has been Myself's burden..."

"Could n...are you thinking of the word *immortal*?"

"Which one is that?"

"The one what means 'undying'."

"Ah. So Myself was, thinking of that word. What's the first word Yourself said?"

"Immaterial." Yet another person tripped and fell over Bulstrode. "Just there! Did you spot how that tosser went tits up over me?"

A distressingly lengthy silence preceded Yazbirth's response. "Yes."

"Did you actually spot him, or do you dissimulate that I might continue my disquisition uninterrupted?"

"..."

"Dissimulate means lying."

"Oh, yes. Sorry."

Bulstrode tapped to a halt. "Up, Yazbirth!"

Yazbirth scooped up his turkey guide and held him at eye level. "I'm no consort, chappie. You needn't fib for my pleasure. You promenade this evening under your own auspices."

The sloth nodded.

"So cheer up!"

Frantic, the sloth warped his face into a rictus.

"Much better. Now, my question was – put me back down, please, thank you – my question was how you manage to navigate these crowds without anyone smashing right into you, as they so often do me."

"Huh?" As Yazbirth asked this, five people collided with him at once. They were on the road to Rumney Marsh's, and the crowd was too thick for a giant sloth to fall in easily.

Ah, Bulstrode realized, it has to do with focus. If Yazbirth isn't thinking about himself, then he becomes *less there*, and people walk through him, and vice versa. The moment he attains some degree of self-consciousness, he becomes very definitively *there*.

Perhaps there was an interesting observation to be wrung from that, but Bulstrode wasn't the one to do it. He was too busy being stepped on and tripped over.

As if Rumney Marsh needed any further evidence that the universe was a cruel and spiteful place, he wasn't awoken by the angry mob until he'd finally started having a good dream.

The shriek of the glass roused him from his slumber quite indelicately. He was wide-awake before the pear-sized rock that had come shooting through the window crunched into the dresser against the far wall.

Rumney was not a spry nor sprightly man, and yet he was out of bed and on his feet before the second rock was thrown. Fortunately, the second rascal had a bum arm, and so the projectile *thwunk*ed against the side of his house, several feet to the right of his window. It managed to knock an original portrait of himself off of the wall, though. And it sounded significantly larger than the one that had managed to slip through his window.

The third rock was sharper, which Rumney discovered when it spun through the window and slashed at his left bicep. The Governor cried out, clapping a palm over the insult to his authority. Blood dribbled out from between his fingers, so stunning him that he failed to flinch as a fourth rock whizzed past his head, tousling his hair as it flew.

Rumney seat-dropped to the ground and scooted up against the wall directly below the window. It was the only place he could think of, that would be safe from the increasingly dense fusillade of rocks being flung at his window. Shards of glass continued to rain down upon him, but lucky him, most of the pane had already been demolished. This he discovered when he threw himself on the ground below the window, and felt a tiger swipe at his entire rear flank, nails fully extended.

"Goddamnit!" he screamed, stunned by the crack in his voice. He rolled over as carefully as he could, struggling to avoid disturbing the bed of broken glass any further, and saw the reflective geometry beneath him already caked with blood.

If the rabble outside didn't get him, he'd end up bleeding to death in here.

"Wait!" he shrieked out the window. "Please! Stop, for just one moment!" And to his overwhelming surprise, the barrage of rocks slowed to a halt. The departing din left an aural cavity, which Rumney filled with thick, phlegmy panting. And, beneath that, the dull thudding of something large against the heavy wooden door to his home.

Slowly, trying to forgo the use of his hands entirely (for where could he put them, that wouldn't flay him further?), he got his feet under him and slowly pushed himself upwards, until the top of his head was just peeking over the bottom of the window frame, like a sun that had set on a gruesome battle and was terrified to discover the aftermath by its implacable light.

Metaphorically, of course. There was no sun to be found out Rumney's window. Plenty of light, thanks to all of those torches. But no sun.

Rumney had the sickening sensation that he'd already seen his last sunrise. The increasingly splintered thudding against his door downstairs made the perfect tempo for a dirge, didn't it? Not that he expected his death to be greeted by the slightest whiff of solemnity.

His death. Dear God.

"Please," he cried, struggling to summon up a fraction of the volume he'd managed when under fire. The position he was in was singularly uncomfortable, balancing on his toes, knees trembling in a deep crouch. A man significantly more fit than he would have already begun sweating, holding such a pose. Rumney's entire body was racked with tremors, his calves screaming in agony, and yet he knew he could continue to hold it. Adrenaline is powerful, and Rumney had never had much of an opportunity to build up a tolerance.

The toll was taken in his voice. It was thin and reedy, and it'd be a miracle if any of the dozens of people gathered below his window would be able to hear it.

"Please," he whimpered again, "what do you want?"

"We want you GONE!" came the immediate reply from the front of the mob. The rest of the monster's body roared in approval. Had they appointed this spokesperson to address Rumney as a collective, or had he appointed himself? Both possibilities implied their own battery of frightful corollaries.

Knees throbbing in a dull ache, Rumney summoned as much breath as he could for the reply. "What have I done?"

"You've lied to the King about us, and we caught you out!"

A roar of approval.

"I can-" Rumney slipped on the blood that was pouring out of his arm and pooling at his feet. As a reflex, he threw out a hand to catch himself. Too late, he recognized that this was a very bad idea. His palm landed flat on a piece of glass, which slipped under his falling weight and slid into the meat at the base of his thumb. He was too hoarse to scream again, so he simply emitted a gravelly groan as he crashed to the floor, peppering the right side of his body with crimson pinpricks.

Lying on the ground, bleeding and exhausted, Rumney began to cry. He couldn't hear himself for long, though, because the thudding against his front door finally stopped, a throbbing ellipsis leading to a thunderous exclamation. And now that the overture was completed, here came the symphony of splinters breaking under heavy-booted tread.

They were inside.

Rumney listened to them crashing their way up the stairs, rabbling quietly to one another (which was, somehow, more chilling than if they'd all been screaming for his head). He considered pushing himself upright, to meet them on his feet, but it hardly mattered anymore. So he remained curled into a near-fetal repose in a cradle of blood and glass, fighting back tears and waiting for his bedroom door to swing open.

It sounded as though a perpetually-breaking wave were roaring down his hallway, plucking up the furniture and carrying it along, not because it wanted to, but because it was so effortlessly mighty that it could do nothing else. Almost at once, though, the wave halted.

And then the mob found a new height to its perversity. They knocked three times on the door to Rumney's bedroom, and softly.

Rumney lifted his head, which from his position meant tracking horizontally across the room, until he saw the lately-knocked-upon door springing from a wall, blushing, bedazzled, beautiful. He savored this image for a brief moment, and then it melted. Wiping these latest tears from his eyes, Rumney sniffed. This was the final insult – they were going to make him invite them in.

They knocked again, three polite taps. He could hold out if he wanted, but this was a siege he wouldn't win. What would England think, when they got wind of this? They would have his back, most certainly. But how long would that take? Too long. Too long.

Another three knocks. No sense of escalating intensity – they were as amiable as could be, those knocks. "Come in," Rumney nearly whispered.

The door to his bedroom swung open, and a seemingly endless parade of men, all invariably of the lower sort, filed in. They were quiet, orderly, inevitable.

The man in front was most certainly the man who had done the talking out his window. But Rumney didn't recognize him. He didn't recognize *any* of these people. Which was when he finally appreciated just how poor a Governor he had been. Too little too late.

"I did lie to the Crown," Rumney burbled.

"Of course you did." The man in front sounded so *reasonable.* Was this not a fire-bellied mob? Had they not taken up torches but left their senses at home? How did they suddenly seem so…*disciplined*?

"I did lie, but I lied to make Fidget's Mill seem better than it wa-"

"We don't want to hear it." Muttered assent from the body impolitic. *Wedontwanttohearitnowedont.*

"I swear." Marsh's words were little more than shaped breath. "I swear to you. I can produce the correspondence. You needn't believe me. You can believe your own e-"

"No more lies." *Yeahyeahyeahnomorenomoreyeah.*

"Please!" Rumney mustered his strength, and fought through the pain to push himself up to something approaching a seated position. "On what would you wish me to swear? On my honor? On my parents' name? On the Crown itself? Name it, and I will swear upon it!"

"And what do oaths mean to you, eh?" *Yeahwhatdooathsmean-yeahnotmuchnonotmuch.*

Well, there was nothing to lose. Rumney stopped fighting back tears and let them flow. There was no humiliation in it to him. He'd suffered enough of that when he invited his inquisition in as if they were old friends. "What do you want from me?" he blubbered. "What can I tell you, if you won't listen to anything I say? Do you want me to leave the Mill? Fine, I'll go! I'll not even pack a bag! Give me but a coat, and I will-"

"You won't need a coat." *Nonocoatyouwontbecoldno.*

All at once, hands were on him, picking him up, dragging him out of his bedroom. He knew, before they were halfway to the stairs, that they were going to throw him down them. The mob did not disappoint. Rumney howled as he tumbled down, rolling and bouncing, connecting with the stairs only three times. On the first strike, he landed on his right shoulder, very probably dislocating it. The second hit was primarily absorbed by his left ankle, which Rumney *felt* shattering. This spun Marsh in mid-air, bringing him to a halt head-first on the ground.

He sank into a bottomless reservoir of black, surfacing periodically to catch glimpses of angry faces, sharp objects and the lifeless, lightless expanse of the snowy woods surrounding Rumney's mansion.

A hand slapped him on the face. "Wake up," the hand suggested.

Rumney failed to oblige, and so the hand redoubled its efforts. Finally, the ex-Governor regained his senses. "Wha?"

He felt more hands on him, on his bare skin. He looked down at his nakedness, a pale pink, becoming both blue by blood loss and exposure, as well as deep red – after all, the blood wasn't so much lost as misplaced. The innocent alabaster of the snow beneath his bare feet was speckled with red and, increasingly, with black.

Black? Rumney blinked himself to some degree of sensibility and took a closer look at himself, and the orgy of hands upon him. They were smothered in pine tar, which they were in turn smearing upon him.

"Please," he repeated without conviction, knowing full well that this was how the world ended for Rumney Marsh.

But the man in front said not another word, nor did any of his other attackers. They simply continued to apply the sticky, chilly pine tar, until it coated him from nearly head to toe. Wordlessly, a bucket of chicken feathers were dumped atop him. There was no ceremony to the gesture, which somehow made it all the worse. A grand pronouncement might have made the occasion feel more momentous. As it was, they simply dumped a bucket of feathers on him and prodded him in the back with a pitchfork until he started walking in his new, paltry, poultry coat.

They wanted him to walk through town, Rumney knew. But at the very least, he would not oblige them in this. He turned to the dark maw of the woods, and waded through the knee-deep snow.

Behind him, the man in front opened his mouth to call to Rumney. If he went that way, he would die. And their object was certainly not to kill him. They wanted to humiliate him, and, sure, rough him up a bit. The man in front felt they had accomplished both of these goals admirably. "Wait!" he called, but the Governor didn't stop. And while he didn't want the man to *die*, he also wasn't about to lose face with the mob by going after him. So they let Rumney walk, and it wasn't too long before he had left the quivering oasis of light provided by their torches. Once he was out of sight, the mob turned inward and wondered, gosh, now what?

"Myself never wanted this," Yazbirth Bicklebog said to Rumney. The giant sloth had gestured for Bulstrode to take a hike, and the turkey had thankfully complied. On his own, he took off after Rumney, wandering towards the woods, naked save a thin veneer of tar and feathers.

Rumney's teeth chattered. That was the only reply Yazbirth got.

"Myself is so, so sorry."

No response.

"Please say something?"

Rumney said nothing.

Yazbirth knew perfectly well that he had no body heat, the way a living creature sometimes will. But, still, he was large a made of fur, was he not? That wasn't nothing, was it? Couldn't be. So the giant sloth, thinking of nothing save the well-being of his beloved old consort, wrapped Rumney in a warm embrace. And, thinking of himself not at all, Yazbirth Bicklebog failed to attain a sense of density. His arms passed directly through Rumney Marsh, as though he had made to hug a mirage.

And before Yazbirth could think more of himself and try again,

Rumney Marsh collapsed into the snow.

Yazbirth Bicklebog spent the night thinking of nothing but himself, for long enough to burrow through the snow and dig a deep hole. Which was fine, because he knew he couldn't bear to think of what he was filling in the hole with.

XXVII

FORCE WAS HOW DUMMIES GOT THEIR WAY. Denton came up with that one himself when he was but a boy, and unfortunately he debuted it upon a bully who was just finding the rhythm to which he wanted to torment Denton that day. I'm smart, Denton contended to the bully, whose name escaped him. I'm smart and that's why you feel like you have to bully me, because you know you'll never be as smart as I am. You may be stronger, and you may be able to *force* me to eat this beetle, but you do it because you know you could never *convince* me to eat this beetle. Force is how dummies like you get their way.

After he ate the beetle and a few other grubs besides, Denton went home having learned a valuable lesson about the limits of education.

But, suddenly, he found himself on the other side of the equation. Mr. Increase had told Denton to draft a statement precisely to his liking.

"Why?" Denton inquired.

Mr. Increase smiled tolerantly. "So Chip here can si-"

Chip scoffed haughtily from his kneeling position on the floor. "That's *Mr. Ditteridge* to you!" He added, "ouch!", on account of Mr. Increase backhanding him in the chops.

Denton flinched. Force was how dummies got their way. "Don't hit him," he implored Mr. Increase as urgently as the last droplet peels itself off the lip of a water pump.

"You're going to draft a statement," Mr. Increase coolly resumed, "and Chip here will sign it."

Denton nodded. He considered reminding Mr. Increase that they were, generally speaking, friends, were they not? Because hearing himself proscribed actions in the same tone of voice – and in the same sentence – as the guy who just got slapped in the face was not great for the digestion.

"Ah, I see." Denton continued nodding, and then finally reminded himself to stop. "Um," he turned to Chip, "if the options are being *forced* to sign a non-importation agreement, and being *convinced* that you really *ought* to sign one, what are the chances that we might find our way along the latter course?"

Chip sulked at Denton, before craning his head to Mr. Increase. "May I speak?"

Increase waved a permissive hand, though spoke as one might expect a balled fist to: "Just be sure to say something nice."

Ignoring the not-so-veiled threat, Chip cleared his throat. Denton would give him this much: the man retained a remarkable amount of dignity, even on his knees. "Once the element of compulsion is introduced into the discussion, persuasion is removed. You understand? I'll be convinced of nothing." He hung his head. "But I have a daughter…" at this he tossed the silent, flinty Missy a withering glare, "…and a family, and it is in my interest to avoid returning to England. So draft your wretched document, and I will affix my signature. Not because you have swayed me through rhetoric, but because you have cowed me through violence."

"We've not been violent," Mr. Increase mumbled.

"We've not been *very* violent," Adewale corrected.

Increase conceded that point with his shoulders.

Chip turned the full fury of his gaze upon Missy now. "But you, my dear Millicent, you have been swayed, have you not? Swayed by a swain? Ha!" Because of course he was the sort to laugh at his own jokes.

"It's more complicated than that," Missy groused. She meant it.

"Oh, I'm sure it is." Chip treated them all to three haughty scoffs, each haughtier than the last. "I hope you are quite proud of yourself."

Missy averred that she was, but in a flat whisper. She probably meant that too, even if it didn't necessarily apply to this specific moment of her father's humiliation.

Said father was none too pleased to see that his humiliation was hereditary. "Pah! Away with you, bastard, give me a line upon which to sign!"

Not wishing to prolong this moment of agony any longer than he had to, Denton slipped out of the room, retiring to a quieter study well-equipped with the tools of his trade.

Yes, he chastised himself, *welcome to the other side of the equation.* Persuasion had failed, and so here he was, drafting a letter in which Chip espoused and subscribed to a full-bodied definition of non-importation, cutting off all economic ties with England, thus falling in line with the remainder of Massachusetts. Thus accomplishing Denton's goal, on the eve of the Circular Letter's release. It was all so perfect.

Except the signature he would get for this letter would be tendered under duress. Force. He was getting his way by force, and since force was how dummies got their way, this would make Denton a dummy.

Denton had never thought of himself as a dummy.

What had his father said, when Denton came home telling tales of his heroic stand against bullies, and also a detailed account of what armpits smell like?

He hadn't said 'I'm proud of you', had he?

No, almost certainly not. But he made positive noises that could be interpreted as something approaching pride, by an adolescent desperate for validation. Positive noises were rare from Chester Hedges; they were basically the same as another kid's dad throwing them a parade.

"I stood up to some bullies," Denton had said.

His father had replied, "did you win?"

"…I don't know?"

Papa Hedges thought about this for a moment. "But you didn't lose?"

"How would I know?"

"You'd know," his father said with a smile that spoke of experience.

"…then I guess I didn't."

And then his father had tousled his hair and gone to bed. This was one of the best conversations Denton had ever had with his father. What did it mean? Probably nothing – dear old dad was drunk at the time, as he almost always was. But it had convinced Denton that, in principle, what he'd done was right, even if it left room for improvement in practice.

Principle and practice. Everything came down to that.

In *principle*, he ought to tear up this sheet of paper before he had a chance to write a single word on it. He wouldn't lower himself to the bethic depths of bullies.

In *practice*, doing so could materially weaken the unity of Fidget's Mill, and so weaken the unity of Massachusetts, and so weaken the strong negotiating position the Colonies would almost inevitably have to chart out in the coming years.

How was this even a decision? He'd worked so hard, for what felt like years and years (but was really better measured in months), to reach this point. And now what he wanted was within his grasp. Did he, a man whose chief professional interests were in truth and justice – well, justice, anyway, kind of – really wish to attain his goals through dishonest or physically coercive means? What sort of a precedent was he setting for himself? How could he return home to face his family?

Would his father be proud of him, if he ever found out?

(A-ha!) Miss Carsis' voice cried in his head.

Fuck yourself, Denton retorted, no longer overly concerned with whether it was the real Miss Carsis that spoke to him or a figment of his imagination, suspecting quite strongly he would find out soon enough, after that ill-advised retort.

Practice and principle. Principle and practice.

Am I smart, or am I a dummy?

Everything was so much more complicated when you were an adult! Denton ran his fingers through his hair, and this time didn't bother to stop himself. He had earned the right to feel up his scalp, he felt.

What did everyone want out of this meeting?

Chip wanted to not have to sign anything.

Missy wanted Chip to sign on for non-importation. She seemed surprisingly sympathetic to the Cause, and the most ideologically driven person in the room, aside from perhaps Denton himself. Or maybe she was even more driven than he was – she was, after all, passively presiding over the shakedown of her father.

Mr. Increase wanted…Mr. Increase wanted the Colonies to be thrust into a crisis, not because he was an anarchist, but because he was a egalitarian, and his experience had taught him that chaos bred equality through necessity. Getting Chip to sign on for non-importation would be the first domino in a chain that led to his desired state of madness.

Only something about that felt insufficient to Denton. Increase had contented himself with distant intrigues for long enough – why take the irreversible risk of…

Distant intrigues…

Obvious! Mr. Increase was taking this risk on behalf of John, Chip's slave who had gone rogue and fed information pertaining to the anti-Marsh cabal to Mr. Increase, and who come to think of it was probably not born with the name 'John'. Increase was putting himself in harm's way in exchange for the information, which…

Two questions presented themselves, and they were almost certainly the most pivotal questions of the evening.

Question the first: Why did Mr. Increase want information about the anti-Marsh cabal so desperately, and why would he have been so satisfied with it as to endanger himself for John's sake? For someone as driven by self-preservation as Mr. Increase, it would take a considerable portion of gratitude to get him looming over a patriarch of the town as he now as.

Question the second: What was John's *specific* request, to get Mr. Increase alongside him in this position? Did the slave anticipate manumission as a result of greater distance from England? If so, Denton was afraid he was going to be sorely disappointed. But surely, he must know this. So wh…

Denton stopped thinking politically, and started thinking like a human being again. Emotions and drives and wants and needs. He thought of John, thought of the way he had looked at Chip Ditteridge. And in that cragged expression, Denton found the answer to his second question.

John wanted Chip Ditteridge dead. The whole shrinking-from-violence routine was a put-on (though Denton was fairly certain Mr. Increase's casual-indulgence-in-violence routine wasn't, or at least not entirely). This wasn't *just* in return for John providing information; Mr. Increase likely agreed to help John kill Chip in return for securing an endorsement of non-importation prior to the deed being done.

This answer suggested a whole new plethora of questions (did Mr. Increase honestly expect anyone to honor an agreement made moments before the signee's murder? How did Mr. Increase expect to pull this off with Missy in the room? Or Denton, for that matter?), as well as both increasing the importance of the first question, while simultaneously dialing back its urgency.

Whatever. Denton had one thing to deal with right now, and one thing only: getting Chip out of that room alive. Not because he had any particular affinity for Chip – just because he had no affinity at all for death.

He picked up his pen, put it to the paper, and several minutes later walked back in to the room Mr. Increase had so dramatically commandeered. Because if he could get Chip to sign a little piece of paper on his way out, because he *wanted* to, not because he *had* to, so much the better.

XXVIII

THE QUESTION OF ENDINGS IS UNIVERSAL. NOT whether or not things will end – even for Immortals such as Familiars, expiration will coincide with the slow, cool death of the universe. No, the vexing question is *how. How* will things end? How will I die, each man and woman asks themselves at least once. This is the privilege of an individual; the marshaling of one's mental faculties for self-reflection and projection.

Theoretically, large groups could easily avail themselves of these same faculties. Just as, theoretically, King George III could sail across the Atlantic and signify complete independence for the Colonies by kissing Denton Hedges on the lips. It *could* happen, in the sense that it is within the realm of possibility. But, as anyone who had ever tried to drink Ben Franklin under the table could attest, there was a cavernous gulf between 'possible' and 'probable'.

After Governor Rumney completed his death Marsh into the snowy hills surrounding his mansion, the mob that had reached a bloodthirsty pitch that the would-be mastermind Denton had failed to foresee faced the question of an ending. How would they disperse? *Would* they disperse? Their collective pique was up, and it would be strange indeed to file home in an orderly fashion and lay their heads down.

Bulstrode, who was no stranger to silent suggestions, tapped his way among the shuffling flock in search of a shepherd, whispering things like "my, you could stuff quite a few gourds into the bags under *your* eyes, you sleepy tit!" A few people were receptive to Bulstrode's psychic exhortations, but failed to be swayed by them on account of having not the slightest clue what they were supposed to mean. He wasn't *prima facie* opposed to greater confusion and chaos tonight, but nor did he consider it in his interest. They'd killed the Governor, hadn't they, so it wasn't as though they could return home and call the night a wash. But if they made things worse by exacerbating the confusion and chaos, England might choose to respond by and in force. Which was fine by Bulstrode – the rival witch was dead, which meant his consort could once again reign supreme in this little corner of the world. But a British-controlled Mill wouldn't help Miss Carsis see the two lovebirds back in anything resembling a position of power, not one little bit. So, all in all, it would be best to see the mob home.

"Buggered, aren't you? Sure look it! A pillow'd do you a treat, I expect." Still no response. No-Good Bulstrode bristled at the un-knowing indifference. Perhaps it would be helpful to be closer to their heads? "Yazbirth! Tall-such, on the double!"

Bulstrode remained quite decidedly un-picked-up. "Yazbirth?" No answer. Oh, hell! Where'd the pitiful creature gotten to now?

"Himself is dead!"

Fithian had watched a soup of heads with tattered hats and knotty hair coalesce in the streets and float off in the direction of the Marsh residence like a sinister dandelion. She'd spent the interim between then and now doing her damndest to tease out the impossible tangle of personal and political motivations that were giving rise to the madness of the evening. When Yazbirth's voice came cracking out of the silence with a tangible emotion she'd never before heard in it, she screamed, turned around, and threw a small vase at him.

It shattered on the giant sloth's snout.

"Oh! I'm so sorry," Fithian nonetheless offered. "You sc…you startled me."

"Himself is dead! Themselves killed Himself, and Myself is responsible!" Yazbirth crashed to his knees and wept languid sloth tears.

Fithian recoiled slightly. She'd no idea, when Yazbirth proposed being her Familiar, she was involving herself with such a high-maintenance monster. "Ah," she began, walking uneasily over to the kneeling demon, "there there."

"Where?"

"It's…that's a thing people say when they mean to give succor."

"Why?"

Fithian patted Yazbirth Bicklebog on his giant furry coconut of a head. "I haven't the faintest idea, I'm afraid."

"Myself is so…" Yazbirth looked down at his paws. Seeing a giant sloth perform such a human gesture – such a *theatrically* human gesture – was upsetting to Fithian in some profound and irrefutable way. "Myself feels like Myself could run. And…that running would not be enough." The Familiar looked up to its consort. "Is this a feeling with which Yourself has some acquaintance?"

Without intending to, Fithian made a deep, harsh humming sound, like a lioness after a hearty meal. Or perhaps just prior to one. "Do you feel exhausted, even as you wish to run?"

"Myself does."

Fithian nodded. "Do you feel as though the inequities of the world are too great to countenance, and do you at the same time feel as though you've enough fire within you to burn them all away, if only you had the resources to match your drive?"

"Myself does."

"That's anger, Yazbirth." Fithian wished to drink of that poisoned chalice once more, and so thought of her father negotiating her away for pecuniary gain. She had intended a sip, but took a full draught instead. "I've more than *some* acquaintance with the sensation."

"What does Oneself typically do with it?"

Fithian stopped patting Yazbirth, and rested her hand on his head. "Typically? Nothing. There's little a woman of my station *can* do."

"Yourself's resources fail to match the drive?"

"Precisely." Fithian loosened her grip – she'd unknowingly taken a fistful of Yazbirth's fur and squeezed it as though hoping to wring out its eternal moisture. "Typically. But…these are atypical times, are they not?"

"Not really," Yazbirth informed her, oblivious to the drama of the moment.

"…they are," Fithian countered.

"Take Myself's word for it. On a cosmic scale, these times are really not so atypical."

"I'm not talking about…stand up, Yazbirth. I'm not talking about a cosmic scale. I'm talking about a human scale."

"A human scale is hardly enough time for a coherent pattern to emerge, as pertains to the typicality or atypicality of times."

Fithian shook her head, and chopped her hands through the air parallel to the ground. "You're missing my point. I was simply trying to say, in an arch way, that perhaps now that you and I are making common cause, and we are both angry, we can do something about that anger together. Yes?"

Fully upright once again, Yazbirth Bicklebog scratched his chin with one hooked nail. "Ooooooh. Myself sees, and apologizes for the misunderstanding."

"No need to apologize. It's quite alright."

"Yourself is sure?"

"Yeah." Fithian cleared her throat and adjusted the armpits of her dress. They had a tendency to ride up and dig in. "Now, what shall we do about our anger?"

This was where a more dramatically savvy interlocutor would have smiled, because there was nothing more to say just then. But instead, her interlocutor suggested they file a formal complaint with the English Secretary of State, and the conversation had to continue for several more minutes.

All the while, Fithian was touching and patting and poking Yazbirth Bicklebog without thinking about it. Had she fully comprehended the significance of a corporeal Yazbirth, she might have expressed some concern. Yazbirth had been thinking about little except himself since he had tucked Marsh into his eternal slumber beneath a thick blanket of snow. And as anyone more well acquainted with anger than the generally easygoing Yazbirth would have known, anger blooms most dramatically when it has one's full attention.

XXIX

"SO," WAS NOT A PARTICULARLY COURAGEOUS way to begin this delicate ultimatum. Denton nursed an amiable disappointment in himself, but reserved the right to promote the sensation to classic disgust, depending on how the rest of this tricky situation played out.

"So," he reiterated, because repetition made it sound as though he were happy with his decision to say 'so' the first time, "here is my thinking." Denton brandished the page he had completed in the other room. "I've written this." This was not going well. "I've written this for Chip to sign, *but*."

When no *but* was immediately forthcoming, Mr. Increase cocked his head forward and pushed an eyebrow upwards. The man had the natural air of a patrician, but Denton would never say so to his face; Increase didn't seem the type to take that as a compliment. "What's the *but*, Denton?"

"*But*, I don't want him to sign it if he doesn't want to."

Mr. Increase, Adewale, Missy and Chip all said "…", but each somehow managed to say it in a very different tone of voice.

"Hear me out," Denton added hastily, as though they were all clamoring to speak over him, and as though he had something for them to hear. He was utterly rudderless here – and for a man who thrived on preparing thick legal briefs and spending nights internalizing the facts of a case beforehand, improvisation came with difficulty or, more commonly, not at all.

Get Chip out alive, that's all he could think about right now. Break it down into steps, and step 1 would inevitably be *get Chip away from the others.*

Flapping the statement like a white flag, Denton swallowed as confidently as he could and turned to Missy. "Your father is an honest man, would you say? Please speak honestly yourself."

"Honest how?" was Missy's response, which did not inspire a great deal of confidence.

"Ah…intellectually. Is he stubborn?"

Chip scoffed haughtily. "*He* is right here, you kn-augh!" He turned up to Mr. Increase. "Will you stop hitting me?"

Mr. Increase shrugged. "Eventually."

"My father is…" Missy glanced at him hesitantly. "…he favors consistency above all things."

"Which is a delicate way of calling him stubborn," Adewale translated, "which he is." Chip squinted pure hatred at his slave.

"Well…" Denton reassessed. He was really hoping for a 'yes, he is quite open-minded and only ever draws a conclusion substantiated by solid argumentation and powerful evidence'. Hope was a slippery foundation, and he should have known that. "I want to convince him."

"That's why we're here," Mr. Increase drawled.

"No. I want to *convince* him." Denton turned the statement over in his hands, scrutinizing his own writing. After a moment, calculated for maximum effect, Denton lifted his eyes to Chip. This was important – he would not address this to Mr. Increase, or Missy, or anyone else. He wanted to restore a sense of agency to Chip Ditteridge, as well as hopefully reclaiming some for himself. "Give me an hour. Lay down your preconceptions, cast aside your biases, and listen to me. That's all I ask. If, at the expiration of the hour, you do not wish to sign, I will personally tear up this statement, which I can promise you is of greater substance to me than you can possibly imagine."

Chip shook his head. "I already told you, th-"

"Everyone else will leave the room. It will be you and I."

Adewale took a step forward. "Now wait just a mo-"

Missy put a restraining hand on his arm. Denton watched a tremor wrack her father – anything even *approaching* intimacy between his daughter and a black man was nauseating to him. Denton wondered why he was bothering to tread across this treacherous landscape, endangering himself to save such a loathsome man.

He didn't have to wonder for long, though – a man didn't deserve to die simply because he was loathsome. Were that so, there would be nobody left who was qualified to wield any kind of power.

Adewale looked at Missy, who stonewalled him with an immovable glare. He then looked to Mr. Increase, who half-rolled his eyes. "Certainly can't hurt, can it?"

"An hour?" Adewale's façade of relative gentility was slipping. There was real hunger in that voice now.

Mr. Increase turned to Denton. "How would a half an hour suit you?"

Denton hadn't been counting on the full hour – he'd expected a negotiation that would terminate at twenty minutes. Thirty was an unexpected windfall. "I suppose I can condense my arguments," he groused as though this were a painful concession.

"Wonderful." Increase turned back to Adewale. "Thirty minutes for them. This is acceptable." He wasn't asking, and Denton found a curious satisfaction in knowing that Mr. Increase was still in charge.

"Yes it is," Adewale grumbled.

"We'll just step outside, then." And as Mr. Increase raised his arms to gesture Adewale and Missy out into the hall, he gave Denton a wink in passing.

Oh, son of a bitch. Now he had to unpack what *that* meant. Did Increase know what Denton was planning? Had he been *counting* on Denton to figure out what the true purpose of their visit was, and to find a way to save Chip? There was a fiendish elegance to that possibility that felt…well, very Increase. It would allow him to fulfill his obligation to Adewale in seemingly good faith, while still side-stepping the more hateful consequences of it.

Or was that wink a warning? Was Increase letting Denton know that he was aware of his plan, so that Denton *wouldn't* go through with it? Because he actually *did* want Chip dead?

Why did he have to wink, that son of a bitch?

Left alone with Chip, Denton puzzled over the best way to ease him into th-

"John means to kill me, does he not?"

Denton's eye twitched. "I believe he does, yes."

"Why?"

Was he serious? Denton couldn't tell. "Because I'm fairly certain his name isn't John. Among other grievances."

Chip plodded a sullen lap around the room. He stopped to stare wistfully out the window, because no matter the stakes, that was what one did in moments of placid contemplation. "Suppose I fled through the window?"

"I'm afraid I'd have to call for Mr. Increase once again."

"So you're not here to safeguard my survival."

"I am. I promise you that."

Chip turned his head by degrees, speaking to Denton in profile. "And how are we going to make good on that promise, may I ask?"

Denton ran his hand through his ha…ugh. "I'm in the very midst of working that out. In the meantime," Denton brandished his statement, "might I persuade you to review this document with me? I'll walk you through the reasoning behind each concession, and hopefully persuade you of th-"

Sometime around then, Denton recalled that despite a thorough reading of the classics and a robust education in assorted fields of leisure, Chip was still a dummy. In Denton's memory, he recalled it in the moment just prior to being struck on the head by a marble bust of some long-dead Ditteridge. But if he was being perfectly honest, it was probably the bust-strike that facilitated the recollection.

Chip was a dummy, and so only knew how to get what he wanted through force.

"Ouch, dang it!" Denton shouted. "I'm trying to help y-" He dodged as Chip hurled another of his relative's heads across the room. "Stop it!"

The doors swung open, and Mr. Increase, Adewale and Missy filed in. Each had a very different reaction to the crashing and screaming they'd overheard, respectively amusement, excitement and fear.

Denton tried to wave them away with one hand, as he kept his eyes locked on Chip, knees bent and ready to leap away from any more progenitor projectiles. "Go back outside! I'm reasoning with him!"

Chip scoffed haughtily.

"How's that coming along?" Mr. Increase called over the crash of some fine silver Chip was frisbeeing at Denton's neck.

"There's plenty of room for improvement!" Crash, clatter, clink.

"You must think me some sort of fool!" Chip raved as he scrambled about the room, looking for more things to throw. "Non-importation will be the death of me, as surely as would be the noose! Slower, even! I should rather the latter, in fact!"

Adewale leaned back slightly, as if to take in the wonder of the situation. "Is that so?" He set off towards Chip at a slow stroll.

"Yes, but not by your swarthy hand, fiend!"

"Then perhaps I'll make you do it to yourself."

"STOP IT!" Missy screamed at them both. Chip stopped dead in his tracks, and for a wonder, so did Adewale. "Look at yourself, dad. Just look at yourself, look at the situation, and describe it to me."

Chip stopped, and looked at himself, and looked at the situation. The last step seemed a mental leap too far, though. "You want me to do what?"

"Describe it to me."

"Describe what?"

"The situation. What are you doing, right now?"

"…I'm standing here."

"Where?"

"Beside the china cabinet."

"Why are you standing beside the china cabinet?"

"…"

"Dad? Why are you standing beside the china cabinet?"

Denton could only marvel at the situation unfolding before him. Chip was being cross-examined by his own daughter, and he was folding under the pressure. Mr. Increase and Adewale looked just as thunderstruck as Denton, if not moreso.

"Dad?"

Chip's thought process was nearly audible. It sounded a lot like two snails kissing. "I'm…I'm standing beside the china cabinet because I was looking for something heavy."

"And did you find something heavy?"

"I did."

"What did you find?"

"I found…I found a snowglobe."

"What's inside the snowglobe?"

"Snow?"

"No, dad, it…first of all, it's not real snow. Second of all, I mean what is the place represented inside the snowglobe?"

"It's…our old home."

Missy nodded condescendingly, as one might to encourage a puppy to come down the stairs for the first time. "Not old to mom, or

Francis, or Catherine, or Norm, or Tom, right? They're still there?"

Chip looked guiltily at the snowglobe, as though the rest of the Ditteridge family were *there*. "Yes, they are."

"And where is the snowglobe with a small model of our home in it now?"

"In my hand."

"The hand that's up above and behind your head there?"

"That's the one." The shame in Chip's voice was heartbreaking.

"Why is your hand up there, with the snowglobe in it? Why did you need the snowglobe in the first place?"

"...t'thr't..."

"Nobody can hear you, father."

"To throw it at Denton Hedges."

"Why did you want to throw it at Denton Hedges?"

This was what Missy had been driving at all along. The simplicity of her approach was nothing short of beautiful to Denton – it never would have occurred to him!

"I..." Chip swallowed, and finally began to lower the snowglobe. "I wanted to throw it at him because...he wouldn't let me leave..."

"How did you want to leave?"

"...through the window."

"Why did you want to leave through the window?"

Here Chip regained some semblance of his old mulishness. He thrust a calcareous finger at Adewale. "Because he wants to kill me!"

Rather than go through the trouble of disputing the claim, Adewale just bobbed his head to the side. He wouldn't admit it out loud, but he was afraid dishonesty would prompt a grilling from Missy, which he didn't feel prepared to face.

Missy, too, seemed slightly discountenanced by both Chip's assertion and Adewale's silent confirmation. But she plowed ahead with the blunt force afforded by her frustration. "So you wanted to leave through the window, and Denton said you couldn't?"

"He wouldn't let me!"

"How did he try to stop you?"

"He said…well…he told me he would call for Mr. Increase if I tried to leave through the window."

"And why didn't Denton want you to leave through the window?"

"Because…because he wanted to read me his statement, and convince me of its wisdom."

"And you didn't want to hear it."

"That's right."

"So you threw priceless family heirlooms at him."

"…yes."

"You threw priceless family heirlooms at him because you didn't want to hear him expostulate on economics."

"…well when you insist on phrasing it so reductively, it does sound quite r-"

"You threw priceless family heirlooms at him so you could leap out the window."

"…"

"This is the conduct of a gentleman?"

Chip gasped. To have his status as a gentleman challenged by his own daughter?! Unheard of! Ludicrous! But still, a difficult challenge to answer in the affirmative, given the situation.

"I…" Chip's dry, sandpaper swallow was as loud as a gunshot in the shocked silence of the room. "I suppose not."

Missy looked to Denton, and gave him one of the most heavily freighted looks he'd ever received. She had just done him the inestimable favor of throwing a bridle on the situation, taming it…and then passing it off to him. 'I set them up', that look said, 'now you knock them down'.

Denton was so stunned by the sagacity and generosity of the gesture, he struggled to find words for several seconds. And then, after a prolonged clearing of the throat, they came: "Yes, well, it's not too late for us to speak to one another, is it? As gentlemen?"

Chip sulked. If it weren't for the few pretentions to sophistication he still retained, Denton fancied Chip would be stuffing his hands into his pockets, lifting his shoulders and kicking at rocks. "No, I don't suppose it is."

"Perfect!" Missy clapped her hands, and spun freely towards Adewale. "You can go, by the way. If anybody kills my father tonight, it'll be me. That was a joke," she clarified to a room full of people who couldn't be sure.

Adewale scoffed, with enough haughtiness to temporarily impress Chip, despite his better judgment. "Have you any idea of the grudge I bear against your father?"

"Here's a bargain: protect my father against the fury of anti-English sentiment that will no doubt be coming to some sort of a head soon, and I will grant you your freedom at the end of the calendar year."

Now *everyone* in the room gasped.

"That's a leap beyond cruel," Mr. Increase grumbled through gritted teeth, "to dangle the freedom a man ought have by right of birth over his head like that."

Missy shrugged. "Slavery itself is cruel. So is murder."

Adewale shook his head, unable to articulate his rage. "You can't…there's no comparison between the two."

"Probably not. But I don't really care. The world is a cruel place."

In that moment, Denton worried that Adewale's head would just explode. "Who do you think you are, telling me about the cruelty of the world?"

"I'm Millicent Ditteridge, and I own you."

Denton struggled to comprehend what he was looking at. Missy hated what she was saying, that much was plastered plainly on her face. But she didn't hate it nearly as much as Adewale and Mr. Increase did. What the hell was she doing?

She's doing what she has to do.

"If my father is still alive and well at the end of 1768, then you are a free man, in the most important sense - legally. That's the deal. It's cruel. I know that, so don't waste your breath telling me."

Eyes locked on Adewale's, Missy seemed to grow, to expand, to thrive under the intensity of his glare. The amount of hatred in this room was nothing short of dizzying.

"Do you even know my name?" Adewale snapped.

"No," Missy replied with leaden finality.

Wordlessly, Adewale turned and left the room at a pace just slightly faster than 'in control'. Mr. Increase shook his head at Missy – now it didn't matter what that wink of his had meant. If he tried to kill Chip through alternative means, Adewale would pay the price. Missy had outmaneuvered him. "You're a monster," he snarled at her. "You decry the institution of slavery in one breath, and in the next you de-"

"Ideals are wonderful things, Mr. Increase. But they are ends that no means can reach."

Increase looked as though he wanted to say something in response, but instead he shrugged and left the room. Missy waited a minute, then cast a glance to her father and made her exit, closing the door behind her.

Denton and Chip stared at each other for five silent minutes.

"Well," Denton resumed, "now that that's out of the way, may I talk to you about the benefits of non-importation?"

Chip heard not a single word Denton said for the next twenty minutes, and then signed the statement. Denton thanked him and left the room. As he was closing the door, the hinges creaked loudly, sounding just like a grown man weeping.

XXX

SO WAS THAT FORCE OR PERSUASION THAT HAD gotten Denton the signature? Which won, principle or practice? Denton suspected that the only comprehensible answer to that question was that it didn't matter – nobody else cared. What mattered was that he had gotten the signature, and would rush news of it to the printers to have in heavy circulation by tomorrow afternoon.

It did matter to *him*, of course. But what did *that* matter? Missy was right. These were cruel times.

It wasn't until that moment that Denton realized just how heavily the decision to terminate her pregnancy must have weighed on her. She had seemed so steely and resolved when Denton first met her, but what he had missed were the agonizing nights of deliberation that had led her to that point. She sacrificed incipient motherhood to preserve one of the illusions upon which the town was constructed.

Between Missy and Mr. Increase, Denton was beginning to suspect that everyone in this town was materially stronger than he was. Which just meant he would have to be smarter.

So, in a way, it really *did* matter whether he'd secured Chip's grudging consent by force or persuasion. Because if Denton was actually a dummy, he should probably be notified now, before he started being overly impressed with his own machinations.

As he padded through the eerily silent streets (the mob must still be off calling Rumney Marsh all manner of rude words, poor fella) towards the printer, Denton tried to parse the nuances and complexity of Missy's staggeringly simple approach to overwhelming her father. All she had done was ask him questions, until he was forced to give answers that made him look and feel like an idiot. This was, on a smaller scale, basically lawyering. Perhaps a woman could apply to b-

Denton rounded and found No-Good Bulstrode.

"Ah!" the turkey demon clucked. "There you are! Bit of unfortunate news, followed by a bit of slightly less unfortunate news."

Denton brandished the signed statement in his hand. "Walk with me to the printer, Bulstrode. I've gotten Chip's assent for non-importation! As long as Buddy Jr. and Fithian can come through, my work in Fidget's Mill is finally done!"

"Well, bully for you! Shall I forgo boring you with the affairs of the Mill, in this case?"

"No, by all means. This will give us something to discuss on our journey." *So that I don't have to think about other things*, he decided not to say out loud. Though for all he knew, Bulstrode could hear his thoughts just as easily as his speech. They certainly sounded loud enough in his head.

"I'll begin with the more deplorable turn of the evening. You're aware of the raggedy band of chappies what went to give Rumney

Marsh a good scare, pursuant to a resigning of his post?"

"I do."

"Of course you do. Well, sometimes these things don't work out the way we'd all hoped."

Denton slowed his pace. "What does that mean?"

"Well, as they were fetching him from his home, they accidentally threw him down the stairs, and then accidentally tarred and feathered him. And what does the old fool do, but go waddling off into the woods?"

Denton came to a full stop. "Where did he go?"

"Into the woods, and then into the ground."

"What?! Rumney Marsh is dead?"

"Afraid so."

Lightheadedness hit Denton like a plank of wood swung by a hurricane. Rumney Marsh was dead, because of the mob that *he* had drummed up, by *his* writing. By persuasion, he had created force, and it had been ungovernable. And, by God, what if that stray thought he'd locked up in the cellar of his mind turned out to be true? What if the entire Marsh farce – now a fiasco – had been utterly unnecessary? Denton had as good as killed Marsh. The only consolation he could draw from this would have been that it was in the service of a greater good. But what if it wasn't?

The world was indeed a cruel place.

"Jesus…" Denton rubbed his forehead aggressively. "What… I…what was the less unfortunate news?"

"The rabble seems to have curtailed their bloodlust ever so slightly."

"Curtailed their…they're still going? They haven't broken up yet?"

"Heavens, no!"

"Where are they now?"

Any group founded upon ideology will inevitably turn upon itself. A unified entity without material goals will collapse into factions, each considering itself the purest expression of the initial objectives.

Usually, however, this takes quite a bit longer than a few hours.

Bulstrode led Denton to the mob that had so recently murdered Rumney Marsh. They were crowded into an awkward Y-shaped intersection, doing their best to split into two distinct groups. Their best was just shy of good enough.

The two groups babbled noisily at one another, only listening to their would-be interlocutors enough to figure out how loudly they needed to shout to drown everyone else out.

As far as Denton could suss out, the dispute came down to this: one faction held that Massachusetts should be politically independent, full stop. The other faction believed that the Colonies should all remain English protectorates, but enjoy greater economic and political self-determination underneath that umbrella. It was, at this point in time, maddeningly academic. This would be something to worry about some day, Denton hoped, but at this point was putting the cart way before the horse, and then cutting off the horse's legs and shouting at it to crawl to the cart like a slug.

Somehow, they kept getting louder. Heads were poking out of windows, forming an ersatz audience that only seemed to encourage the furious denunciations – because, the rabble seemed to reason, they couldn't well back down when other people were watching, could they?

"This is quite a bit touchier than when I left it," Bulstrode observed.

Denton folded his arms defensively. "How far do you see this going?"

"Oh, it'll play itself out eventually."

Several seconds passed, during which Denton thought very hard about that response. "You didn't really answer my question, though."

"Very observant!"

"Christ." Denton hung his head. This too was his fault. Rumney's death, the incipient civil discord, and any malefaction that might result, all sprung from the tip of his pen. Had he never written those pamphlets, would any of this be happening right now?

Alright. If nothing else, this split the ethical complexities that had been plaguing Denton into bite-sized nuggets, bitter though they may have been. Denton had caused what was now unfolding before him, and so it was up to him to put a stop to it. It was as simple as that.

So, then…how was he supposed to stop it?

"Hey!" Denton screamed into the three-pronged, two-headed, single-minded monster. The monster ignored him. "I said 'hey!'" he reiterated to identical results.

"You might try once again," Bulstrode advised, "but louder."

Denton almost followed the advice before realizing that it was offered facetiously. "That's not helpful, Bulstrode."

"Oh, I knew that. I just sometimes enjoy making my little jokes. Don't flinch like that, I promise I won't set to chuckling."

But Denton had already stopped listening. How to stop the crowd? He fancied he could do it in a pamphlet – and they might well be inclined to listen to the pamphleteer who had riled them up so effectively. But that would take time – even if he ran home and fell to his stationary immediately, the soonest he'd be able to get it into the hands of those who most needed to see it would be the day after tomorrow. What would the town look like two days from now, should the current hysteria be allowed to play itself out?

Oh, Denton felt like a fool. His entire errand in Fidget's Mill had been to secure non-importation as a means to greater unity throughout Massachusetts. But behold, here before him was unity of purpose, or the decaying remains of the same. Was this what the future held in store for the Cause? Bickering, infighting? What was the *point*? How could they hope to accomplish anything?

There was disappointment in that thought, and sadness as well. But mostly, there was frustration. It shouldn't be this difficult! They should be able to discuss their differences like adults! They…

"Where did they go?"

Denton watched the last of the stragglers disappearing around their respective corners.

Bulstrode looked up at Denton from right next to him, a move which would have broken the neck of a real turkey. "To go have a chat, I imagine."

"Sorry, I must have blacked out. How did I resolve this?"

"How do you imagine you did?"

"...I didn't."

"Precisely! And it worked out anyway! What's the lesson, then?" Bulstrode pecked Denton once on the foot.

"Hey!"

"You're no god, and thank the actual gods for that, or else we'd all be in trouble, eh? EH?!" Another peck.

"Eh! Alright! I get it."

"Do you?"

Denton hung his head, while shifting his weight to pull his foot out of harm's way. "...probably not."

"There's a good boy. Been a pleasure, I'm sure."

With that, Bulstrode took his leave. Denton stood alone in the cold, dark, wet square for another hour. He felt like he deserved it.

XXXI

THE ENDLESS NIGHT FINALLY CRACKED LIKE AN egg, spilling the frenzied yolk of morning across the patch of snow that concealed Rumney Marsh's place of eternal slumber. Word of his death spread quickly, accompanied by a host of logistical particulars and zany sound effects. Reaction ranged from indifference to concern over what it would mean for the average citizen of Fidget's Mill.

Also of pressing interest was when and how word would make its way back across the Atlantic to the King. Such news would inevitably invite reprisals of some sort – Rumney was, after all, an agent of royal authority. Having also served as the Mill's chief line of communication between the two disparate landmasses, there was hope that it would be quite a while before George III heard tell of one of his least distinguished Governors' demise. Conveniently, a recently offloaded ship belonging to loyal Englanders sank in the harbor on the eve of a planned departure back to the Motherland. It was terribly mysterious, and Denton, who had little to do once he'd sent Chip Ditteridge's statement to print and ensured that Buddy Jr. and Fithian had made good on their end of the bargain (they had), was very interested to hear about how Mr. Increase had spent the evening in question.

Nonetheless, the sinking of the ship bought them a little bit of time, and 'a little bit' was all the time they needed. Because by then England would have bigger things to worry about than the death of a small bureaucrat.

On February 11, James Otis Jr. and Samuel Adams formally disseminated the Massachusetts Circular Letter, decrying the unconstitutionality of the Townshend Acts, and calling for the right for the Colonies (specifically Massachusetts) to levy and collect taxes internally. The letter was quickly approved by the Massachusetts House of Representatives, and copies were dispatched to comparable bodies in the other Colonies.

The small moments of life in Fidget's Mill were replete with crackling tensions, threatening to ignite into open conflagration if one so much as looked at one's neighbor funny. There was much work to be done still. The Cause was still in its infancy.

All of these things were true. But also true: Denton's work in Fidget's Mill was done. He had come for the express purpose of securing non-importation prior to the release of the Circular Letter, and by God, he'd done it. There was plenty left unresolved with the Families and Mr. Increase and Miss Carsis and Brisby, but that was life, wasn't it? Denton couldn't be expected to guide them all into safe harbors, could he? He'd done his part, and now he had a family to get back to.

He'd never been great at farewells, but he was an old hand at the midnight departure. So he quietly packed up his belongings, commissioned another carriage (this one belonging to the Lowestoft overland transport empire, so they would most certainly know of his departure sooner or later) and left Fidget's Mill once and for all, eyes fixed on the horizon over which lay Boston. Denton didn't look back once. The Mill had been nothing but trouble, and he was glad to finally be done with it.

Of course, the Mill could just as easily say the same about him. So why, Denton wondered, couldn't he shake the feeling that neither of them was quite through with the other?

Part Three:

Treated with Great Indecencies

1770

A Middling Sort

I

BY THE TIME DENTON HAD ELBOWED HIS WAY through the crowd, the Customs Commissioner was already dead.

The man's name had been…what was it? Something quite dull, like Johnson, or Stevenson. Somethingson. Whatever his name was didn't matter anymore, because the man was slowing transforming into a puddle. He would be carted away in a bucket, thrown into the harbor, and forgotten. This was the way of the world now.

Also 'the way of the world now'; ethical paralysis. Since the release of the Massachusetts Circular Letter two years ago, the world seemed to have collapsed in upon itself, and begun rushing by at ever-increasing velocities. The Circular Letter had been favorably received in other Colonies, the Virginia House of Burgesses going so far as to draft their own, more strenuously worded response to it. Where Otis and Adams' Letter made no especially inflammatory noises, the Virginian Letter called for a "hearty union" amongst the Colonies, as well as making subtle pleas for a return to the attitudes of rebellion that made the Stamp Act protests possible. If Denton hadn't said "Gulp" out loud when he read this, he had certainly thought it.

The Massachusetts General Court was ordered by England to revoke the Circular Letter. The Massachusetts General Court refused, so Colonial Governor Francis Bernard dissolved the General Court.

This led to mob violence, as the citizens so lately denied of legal means to address their grievances sought other means of self-expression.

In England, Colonial Secretary Hillsborough instructed the Commander-in-Chief of North America to take whatever force he felt was necessary to Boston. By the end of 1768, British warships loomed in the harbor, as British soldiers patrolled the streets.

This was the city into which Denton Hedges sent his children every day for school. He had been fearful in Fidget's Mill, most certainly. There were no witches or demons in Boston, which did reduce one's ambient stress level quite pleasantly. Yet he had *never* been as fearful as he was now in Boston, every day. For his wife, for his children, and for himself.

And, he hated to admit, for his father. Denton had done his level best to muscle his way back into the practice of law, but few people were interested in law just then, certainly not in the way they used to be. His father had adjudicated a number of highly unpopular cases, many pertaining to English smuggling, or the impressment of Colonial sailors. His life had been threatened several times now, but Chester Hedges had brushed the threats off as so much bluster.

And yet, here before Denton lay a spreading pond of vitality.

The font of this draining brain-matter, Corpseson, might have Had It Coming. Or he might not. It was too hard to tease out the byzantine threads of causation that led to any and every new outrage these days. Merely for being Customs Commissioner, a lever by which the British exerted influence in Boston, his home was surrounded and pelted with rocks. Perhaps he'd heard of Rumney Marsh's fate, or perhaps not – either way, a rock struck his wife, and so he armed himself and fired a warning shot into the crowd.

Unfortunately for everyone, that shot was the final warning for one Christopher Seider, an eleven-year-old boy who would never see twelve. With two children in that age range, Denton was hit particularly hard by this tragedy.

The boy's death became a rallying cry for resentment towards the British. In a move Denton detested and, from a purely strategic standpoint, grimly admired, the boy's funeral procession was attended by a throng Denton wouldn't have been surprised to discover numbered in the thousands, turning the dead boy into a talisman, giving them strength against the British.

And now here lay the boy's murderer, who had clearly been given plenty of time to reflect on his sins before being sent to meet his maker. How did Denton feel about that? Was it just?

He had no idea. He'd retired himself from such considerations, for his contribution to the Cause had exacted a high price; when he returned home from Fidget's Mill, his son's voice was unrecognizable to him. It had changed, and Denton had missed it. From that moment, he vowed to abandon the Cause whenever it seemed it would interfere with his role as a father. He would not become *his* father, this he had long since decided.

Still, it was hard to feel neatly partitioned from the dead man on the dock. Things were spiraling out of control. Boston hadn't been safe for quite a while now, but Denton suspected the time was soon arriving to make an escape to less dangerous climes.

Where that would be, he couldn't begin to imagine. As he pushed his way back into the crowd, he took one last look over his shoulder, and for a fleeting moment the Whoeverson it was on the ground looked an awful lot like Dr. Brisby Houlihan.

Lawrence Hedges lugged a bucket of water in through the front door. "Where should I put this?"

"Just on the table," Denton replied automatically. This had become standard routine over the last two years. Lawrence, elated at possessing the strength required to bring water in from the pump, had one day gone and fetched a pailful of it, unsolicited. As he came waddling in with his prize, somehow managing to spill it in every direction simultaneously, it occurred to the boy that he didn't know where the water went, once fetched. He asked his father, who chuckled his response at him. Just on the table, just on the table.

Never one to internalize instruction on the first go, Lawrence had to ask the same question the next time he brought the water in. His father provided the same response.

Over two years, it became a meaningless rite between father and son. They didn't imagine that the domestic catechism imparted any luck, nor did they fancy its cessation would spirit good fortune away. It was just some-thing that provided consistency and equilibrium, which were in short supply these days.

Trailing at Lawrence's heels was young Annabelle, who was coming to look more and more like her mother with each passing day. She sighed and stared deep into the bucket, watching the ripples born of its placement on the table slowly melt into placidity.

"Dad?"

Denton looked up from a dish he was washing. He'd washed the dish before, but done a very bad job of washing the dish. He thought he'd done a good enough job, but then Peggy had grabbed the dish to eat off of it, and Denton saw it was still becrudded, and couldn't bear the thought of his wife eating off of a dish he had done a very bad job of washing. So he was washing the dish again. "Ruh?" he responded.

"Sally says it was a good thing the Customs man was killed."

This was what some people might call a 'teachable moment'. Denton remained silent, waiting to hear where his daughter landed.

"But…well, is it?"

Denton put the dish, which he had still not washed properly, down, and turned to Annabelle. "What do *you* think, sweetheart?"

"I think…" she scratched her chin like the world's cutest little philosopher.

Lawrence knotted his brow in concentration. "I think it's good, be-"

Denton held up a soft palm. He couldn't well shush his son, as he knew what he was going to say, and *why* he was going to say it. Lawrence hadn't known the Seidel boy who was killed by the Customs Commissioner, but he had a number of mutual friends with the boy, so he had seen second-hand the grief caused by his death. In thrall to his emotions, Lawrence would undoubtedly call what happened to Whoeverson 'justice'.

But Annabelle was not so gripped by grief, and so might make a greater swipe at objectivity. She was also young, and would undoubtedly be swayed by her big brother's position. "Now, Lawrence, I most certainly want to hear your position on the matter. But it's Annabelle's turn first, as it was to her the question was tendered."

Denton looked back towards his daughter, and saw Peggy leaning against the doorframe, arms folded, smiling distantly. He smiled back at her. They could go on forever if they wanted, bemoaning the challenges inherent to raising a child nowadays. Political divisions between adults that were inherited by their children; the ever-present threat of violence at the hands of heavily armed emissaries, sent by an authority an increasing number of people viewed as foreign and illegitimate; the thorny subject of slavery that was rendered far more complicated than it needed to be. The number of thickets through which a parent needed to steward their children today was nearly inconceivable. Had *their* parents had to deal with such complexities? Denton and Peggy felt not, because it is the privilege of each generation to feel this way.

"Go on," Denton nodded to Annabelle. "I want to know what *you* think."

Annabelle thought long and hard, until finally Denton saw her brow soften. Whatever mental gymnastics she had been doing, she had stuck the landing. "I think the man should have been in trouble. But they shouldn't have hurt him like that."

Peggy stepped up behind her daughter, and enfolded her in a deep hug. "I think that's a very mature position to take, Annabelle, and I'm proud of you."

Pride was right, Denton concurred. It was strange, but it was right. It wasn't as though he had conjured his family into existence by his labors. His wife was herself, independent of himself, and it was with gentle disquiet that he acknowledged his wife's outsize role in making his children who they were. He had been, after all, so often working during their formative years. So why should he be *proud* of them, as though they were some kind of accomplishment?

That was a question he couldn't answer. He could only underline the answer enthusiastically. He *was* proud of his family, more proud of them than he was of anything he had ever actually done.

Lawrence shifted unhappily, shrugging his shoulders. He could see which way the wind was blowing on the subject of the Customs Commissioner's murder, and had the good sense to keep quiet the fact that his passions blew him in the opposite direction. Denton supposed, if his son lacked his sister's innate empathy, discretion was also something of which to be proud.

Denton just hoped that the world never became the sort of place where discretion was no longer to be lauded.

II

FOR WEEKS AFTER, DENTON WONDERED WHAT HE might have done, had he not heard the bells.

There was a glittering patina of snow on the ground, but not enough to muffle the sound from the tolling church bells. Denton looked out the window, and it was indeed night, a lengthening night made wan by the moon. Church bells at night could only mean one thing: a fire.

Denton sprang out of bed. Not because there was anything he could do about a fire, but because he was, at deepest bedrock, a barrister. And where there's smoke, there's lawyer.

As he dressed as quietly as he could (which was not very quietly at all, but she appreciated the effort), Peggy rose to her elbows, watched him for a moment, and mumbled "don't forget your scarf, dear."

Denton paused, turned around, and fetched his scarf. "Thank you." He kissed his wife on the forehead, and she signaled that this was unsatisfactory.

"Be careful," she concluded.

"You know me."

"Yes," she smiled, "I do. That's why I said it."

Denton laughed softly, and did not make the same forehead mistake twice.

He wasn't the only one staggering out onto the icy avenues that night. He spotted at least six other men who had very clearly emerged from some manner of domestic quietude in response to the bells.

"What's going on?"

Denton whipped around to see Lawrence clomping out of the house, guiding the door silently shut behind him. "No," was all Denton said in response.

"What?" Lawrence looked genuinely surprised at his father's negation of his presence.

"No. Go back inside, Lawrence."

"Why?"

"Because…" *Because I said so* wasn't an acceptable explanation anymore; another casualty to 'these days'. *Because I said so* was the remit of King George III, against which Colonial hearts rebelled. Any parent deploying that old chestnut against a child as savvy as young Lawrence would be treated to a personalized paraphrase of the Journal of Occurrences. "Because it isn't safe."

"How do you know that?"

"Because…because they wouldn't be ringing the bells to let us know all was well!"

"Do you know where the problem is?"

"The…no, I don't."

"So the problem could be *anywhere*?" Lawrence grinned mischievously, and Denton wanted to throttle the scamp. This thought did nothing to diminish his pride, it was just one of those things any halfway attentive parent feels at some point. At most points, when the child is Lawrence's age.

Denton ran his hand thr…blast, he'd forgotten his hat too! "No, I see where you're going with this, Lawrence, and I am fairly confident that the danger will not be reaching this house." Fairly confident, but not *certain*.

"But not *certain*," Lawrence intuited. Rascal!

"…not certain, no."

"Well," Lawrence reasoned with ostentatious good cheer, "maybe I ought to come with you! It might be safer, anyway!"

The other people out in the street were slowly migrating towards the center of town. The lawyer in Denton despaired of their getting there first.

This was pointless. Lawrence was closer to manhood than boyhood, wasn't he? Perhaps it wouldn't hurt to bring him along. But now, he faced the greatest parental dilemma of all: how to capitulate to the child's request, without losing face as an authority figure?

He went for the pointless-stipulaton approach. "Alright," he conceded, "you can come. But you must not speak to anyone, do you understand?"

"Sure!" Lawrence couldn't have cared less about that. He acted as though he was about to see a frivolous new play. It was slightly distressing, but he *was* an adolescent boy. He was convinced of his own immortality, and about to see a house burn down. What a time to be alive, as far as Lawrence was concerned.

Denton took his son's hand, gripping more tightly than was strictly necessary, and led him out into the snow-blown evening. He looked up over the squat collection of brick buildings that made up this part of Boston, and saw only the moon's sickly stamp of approval. There were no orange bruises on the horizon, nor any smoky smells wafting his way. The bells continued to peel, but Denton was beginning to wonder if there were any fires burning at all in Boston tonight.

They were on King Street.

Denton knew instantly that he should turn tail and run home as fast he could. He had his son with him, for God's sake! He couldn't well stand here gawking!

And yet, he could. Of course he could. And he did. Because what else could he do?

In front of the Customshouse, a row of seven British soldiers stood in a clumsy semi-circle, muskets pointed into a crowd of dozens of

Denton's fellow Colonists.

"Are those muskets loaded?" Denton whispered to the stranger standing next to him.

"Yes," the man replied.

"Jesus."

The man made a low growling noise. "This is hardly the time to be taking the Lord's name in vain, friend." That was the least friendly way one man could call another man a friend, Denton reflected.

Someone shouted "FIRE!" Denton flinched, whipping around and wrapping his son in his arms.

"Jeez, dad!" Lawrence cried, demonstrating the endless reservoirs of embarrassment teenagers held for their parents.

Denton blinked, deafened by the absence of gunshots. "FIRE!" someone else screamed, which is when Denton registered that the cries were coming not from the British but from the Colonists. They were taunting the British, trying to goad them into shooting!

"Cut that out!" Denton screamed in the general direction from whence the two 'fire's.

"Shut up!" came the harmonized response.

Lawrence bristled. "Don't tell my dad to shut up!"

"Shut up!"

Denton bridled. "Don't tell my son to shut up!"

Nobody told either of them to shut up. This should have been a victory, but given the choice of being shouted down, and drowned in this silence, Denton would have chosen another round of 'shut ups' without a moment's hesitation.

After an interminable interlude of what must have been minutes, the same voices that shouted "FIRE!" sprang back to life, fixated on the inverse. "KILL THEM!" they insisted. Now they were no longer addressing the soldiers – they were addressing their fellow Colonists.

The man to whom Denton had been speaking bent down, rose with a fistful of packed snow which he packed still tighter, and hurled it towards the soldiers.

It whizzed by one of the soldiers' heads. The man flinched, and spun his gun towards the source of the snowball. The same direction as Denton was standing. The same direction as his son was standing.

Without realizing what he was doing, Denton slapped the snowball-hurling man in the back of the head. "What the hell do you think you're doing?"

The man spun around to Denton, fist raised, but hesitated when he saw Lawrence clinging to Denton's coat. He lowered his fist, but refused to undercut the onyx-edge in his voice. "I'm serving my country."

This marked the very first time Denton ever heard a man describe the Colonies as a distinct country so offhandedly, as though it were already a done deal. As he stared deep into the furnace of the man's eyes, a fusillade of snow and ice rained down upon the trembling row of armed British soldiers.

What the hell was going on? Why was this happening? Why tonight? The crowd began closing in on the soldiers, ranting and raving and pounding their fists into open palms. Through the ghostly haze of breath given body by the cold, Denton could see the fear on the soldier's faces, their knuckles turning an even starker shade of alabaster as their grip tightened on their muskets. And their fingers were threaded through the trigger guards, Denton noted with terror. This situation was tending towards disaster, and neither side looked ready to deescalate things.

A local merchant, a guy Denton recognized as one Mr. Palmes, stepped through the screaming nightmare to address the man amongst the soldiery who seemed to have the highest rank. Denton knew little about Mr. Palmes aside from his occupation, but perhaps he could help wind things back from the crumbling precipice of tragedy?

And perhaps Denton could help. He'd made a conscious effort to disentangle himself from politics and Causes since he left Fidget's Mill, and look where things had ended up. Not that he could have single-handedly averted this; this, or something like it, had been bound to happen eventually. But it was more than slightly shameful, to feel one could have perhaps done *something*, and to have, in fact, done *nothing*.

He took a step forward, to join Mr. Palmes in the noble act of rational discourse, when his son shouted "you rotten scags!" and hurled a ball of ice towards the soldiers.

It sliced through the night in a wide arc over Denton's right shoulder, and plummeted down to the ground. It never made it to the ground, though, instead cracking into the face of one of the soldiers, shattering and splitting the man's cheek. The red-coated man – more of a boy with a gun than anything (but what was a boy with a gun if not a man [and/or vice versa]?) – fell to the ground, scrambled back to his feet, and fired straight into the crowd without hesitation.

Time passed. That was all Denton could say for sure. Did one of the soldiers look towards his son, who threw what would prove to be one of the most fateful chunks of ice in recorded history, and register his identity, what he had done? Denton couldn't say for sure. Did some of his fellow Bostonians have a moment to recognize the gravity of the situation, of what they had unthinkingly taunted into being? Who could say for sure?

All Denton could say was that time passed after the shot in stillness and silence, and even then, he couldn't pinpoint how much. Perhaps two seconds, perhaps fifteen minutes.

Time passed. And there was one other thing he could say for certain; once time was done passing, all of the British soldiers opened fire at once.

Before the first Bostonians hit the ground, Denton had picked his son up bodily, and was sprinting back towards his house, as he should have done as soon as he arrived and saw the redcoats aligned for battle on King Street.

The screams chased him down the street, punctuated (sometimes terminally) by the percussive pops of musketfire. More soldiers would be coming, and once the Bostonians regained their heads, they too would be organizing for battle.

Over the past few years there had been no shortage of escalations, but this one felt materially different. This was an escalation from which there was no hope of return. As the pounding of his feet and the rasping of his breath seemed to fill the streets, drowning out the cries of pain and protest coming from just outside the State House, that esteemed seat of Colonial governance now defended by a moat of its subjects' lifeblood, Denton's vision grew unreliable, and he feared a spill on the uneven cobbles of the road. But he wouldn't fall, he knew this for a moral certainty. Because he couldn't fall. Falling was not an option.

He had to get home. He had to get home, get his family, and get out of Boston. Because some of the soldiers may have clocked his son as the ice-hurler, or maybe they hadn't. That was a convenient excuse, but that wasn't all of it.

Denton had had enough of inaction. Could he have stopped the massacre back there? No. Of course not. But maybe he could have tried. Maybe he could quiet his conscience, at least a little bit. Instead he'd sat on his thumbs while the world fell apart around him. What sort of an example was he setting for his son? What sort of a…

Here was a coin with two very different sides. What sort of an example was he setting, by fleeing the danger? Is that what he was doing? Well, maybe. A little. But Boston was the heart of the Massachusetts colony, and whatever happened here would inevitably be pumped out to the surrounding towns.

It would have been impossible to pinpoint the moment at which Fidget's Mill entered his mind, because technically it didn't; it had never left in the first place.

Massacre would be coming to Fidget's Mill. That Customs Commissioner lying dead would be Brisby Houlihan. The men falling dead at the hands of British musketeers would be Buddy Crundwell Jr., or Mr. Increase.

Massacre was coming, and Denton wasn't running away from it in Boston. He'd already seen it. No, he was running to Fidget's Mill so he could get in front of it, and be ready for it when it came. Yes.

Was he running to Fidget's Mill, or was he being drawn? By whom?

Or what?

He would take his family with him.

That didn't answer the question.

The answers could not be found here. They were elsewhere. If they were here, he'd have found them already. But he hadn't. So they couldn't be.

He would take his family with him to Fidget's Mill because it would be safer for them; he was almost positive about this. Besides, this way they would finally see him being active, in a way they hadn't seen for the past two years. They would see him passionate about the Cause. And maybe they could be as proud of him as he was of them.

They would be proud of him in Fidget's Mill. They would have a Denton worth admiring there. He would make sure of it.

He considered making a quick detour to fetch his father, but decided against it. The trip to Virginia would take him too far afield. Denton would write him a letter to make sure he was alright, and that was all; he no longer felt quite so compelled to seek the man's approval.

Why this was, Denton couldn't say. But it was so.

In the darkness of the hour, he could once again bask in the glowing pride he felt for his family. Denton explained the disastrous situation to Peggy, and explained that they had to leave. She was hardly surprised – where Denton had opted for detachment from the Cause, Peggy had kept up her surreptitious *salon*-style meetings for rebelliously minded individuals. She was well aware of how close Boston had been to boiling over, and for how long, certainly more so than Denton had. Peggy awoke Annabelle, they all packed quickly, and secured a carriage before the sun rose and made good on the chiming bells, casting the night's pandemonium in fiery hues.

"Shouldn't we get your father?" Peggy asked Denton as they boarded the carriage.

"I don't think so," Denton replied, and that was the end of the matter.

They set off for Fidget's Mill, Denton wondering idly (but not *too* idly) if he would ever see Boston again, knowing full well that the Boston he returned to would be materially different from the Boston he was leaving.

So, the question nearly asked itself: to what kind of Fidget's Mill was he now returning?

III

CORN, PAWING VAINLY AT THE CLOUDS ON hearty stalks, cresting the horizon, spreading as far as the eye could see. Fithian surveyed the fruit of her backbreaking tillage, and saw that it was good.

Or would be, anyway.

She pointed to a lazy elevation of largely bare dirt. "Would that be our maximum capacity up on that hill over there?"

"For corn, Yourself means?"

Once upon a time, Fithian would have considered a witty retort to this, only to smother it because Yazbirth Bicklebog was trying as hard as he could to be a good Familiar. Now, Fithian had trained herself to not even fashion a retort that required smothering. This was truly an age of enlightenment. "That's right."

Yazbirth made his thinking sound, which sounded like two salmon being rubbed together very quickly. Fithian always imagined this was how Yazbirth sought the spark of innovation, and so she wondered if there might be a way to get her not-so-trusty Familiar a metaphorical flint.

On the hill, shafts of corn burst from the ground, tilted forward, uprooted themselves, and slid down the hill.

"Yourself could plant more corn on the hill, but Itself would all slide down."

Well, that wasn't quite right; it just wouldn't grow to begin with. But Yazbirth's waking dreams chugged along according to their own internal logic, and among the many things Fithian had learned about having Yazbirth as a Familiar was that dream logic could supersede logical logic.

Fithian hugged her elbows as she stared at the corn swaying gently in the wind, thinking about ways to maximize the cropage up on that little hill. Terracing? That probably wouldn't work, but it might be worth trying. Particularly if the alternative was nothing – it would be preposterous *not* to try, in that case!

But it was premature to be thinking this way.

With a careless wave of the hand that the higher sorts use to dispel flatus, Fithian signaled to Yazbirth that she was done with this dream. Yazbirth, who had received no small amount of coaching as to what each of Fithian's gestures meant, terminated what future generations might have called a simulation.

With the departure of the dream, reality came crashing back in. The Lowestoft daughter frowned and squinted against the second-hand sunlight bouncing off of the omnipresent snow. Perhaps this field, frozen and buried, could become the rally of mais Yazbirth had shown her. Or perhaps the corn would simply fail to grow, as the tobacco had in 1768, or begin a natal growth spurt only the wither and die, as last year's wheat did.

Perhaps wouldn't cut it. If Fithian couldn't grow anything this year, she would give up, and leave the town to its own devices. Those devices had sufficed for two years, but the end was in sight. Since non-importation, Fidget's Mill had effectively been living in siege conditions. As a town which generated nothing itself, instead depending on imports from abroad, the atrophy had begun almost immediately. Many Fidgetonians left (so much for parochial pride), but those who remained turned to the Lowestoft family. Having made their riches via overland transport to and from larger cities in the area, the general expectation was that the Lowestofts would find a way to keep the town alive by shuttling goods in from said cities. To which the Lowestofts said, um, no? Without any product coming in from the docks, there was no source of income with which to maintain their industry. Even if they went back to absolute basics, back when the family members themselves were the ones loading and driving carriages all over creation (a task which would be substantially more difficult without Tobin, who Fithian was ashamed to realize she sometimes just plum forgot existed), it cost money to maintain their carts, to feed and shoe the horses, not to mention themselves. Besides, the flow of goods that would be necessary to keep the entire town in whatever limp parody of functionality it had worked out over its lifespan would be more than the Lowestofts could manage by themselves.

Fithian's parents had worked with Buddy Crundwell Jr. to establish a voluntary resource-collection squad, which was a pretty way of saying that they convinced a bunch of people to go get stuff for the rest of the town (and, of course, themselves by necessity) with the Mill's ever-dwindling reserve of liquid currency. Some citizens of the Mill abstained, and some left for Boston with a list of necessaries to be obtained, where they stayed after getting a taste of how wonderful it was to live in a city where the necessaries didn't need to be *obtained*. For those that left and returned, however, a status just shy of sainthood was achieved. These were the people who kept the town *alive*, by taking time out of their busy lives to go and fetch food and lumber and metal and whatever else might be needed. To be fair, it wasn't hard to take time out of one's busy life when *not* taking time out would mean not having a life at all, busy or otherwise, but nobody said there was any logic to the saintmaking game.

Before long, the admirable stance of supporting the town by means of running high-stakes errands became less and less admirable, and more and more expected. It was just something one did, if one wanted to call oneself a halfway decent citizen of the Mill. Those who continued to abstain found themselves ostracized by an increasingly tight-knit populace. Anti-British sentiment was a beautiful unifier for a brief spate, but one can only find common cause in negativity for so long. Having a positive goal, one with easily appreciable stakes and universal impact, fostered a unique "Fidgetonian" identity, an 'us' from which to jeer at 'them'. Oh, it helped that a large portion of the town had jumped ship at the first sign of trouble. Good riddance to them; it only made it that much easier to spot the *true* Fidgetonians.

As a consequence of this democratization of responsibility, the power and influence of the three families had waned over the intervening two years. Those of the lower sorts would still avert their eyes when someone like Fithian walked by, because that was what they had been taught the world expected of them. But nowadays, some of them remembered that they could look up if they wanted. Which Fithian was all in favor of, except that when she looked into their eyes, she more often than not saw the shape of rage, like a ship in the mist. The lower sorts had seen just how easy it was to keep the town running by themselves, without the families to manage the ports or transport the goods or…whatever the hell the Ditteridges did, and so fostered a retroactive antipathy towards the three families they had once assumed to be indispensible. What else would they do, upon seeing just how dispensable the families were?

Fithian never felt as though she were in any danger – certainly not the kind of danger Rumney Marsh had found himself. From time to time she did think fearful thoughts for Missy, largely due to her blowhard father. Missy, who was now making no secret of her romance with Buddy Jr. (thus freeing Fithian from the antipodal charade), had recently won general acclaim from the town for making a supply run and returning loaded down with whiskey that had come all the way from Pennsylvania. But Chip…Chip didn't lift a finger for the town. He remained sullen and withdrawn, appearing ever more gaunt and frail in the few forays into public he made. Being so reclusive, he became a natural boogeyman to the True Fidgetonians, who suspected him of drawing supplies from British spies. Could that boil over into something more violent, and could that violence sweep poor Missy up in its senseless enthusiasm? Possible, possible. All things were possible.

What mattered, then, was remaining productive. The town was unified in a way it had never been before, and that was beautiful. But it was also terrifying for anyone who might run afoul of the hive mind. Fithian, being a member of the Lowestoft family, already had one strike against her. It was imperative that she prove her worth to the town, in an effort to justify the elevated status she had enjoyed for so many years.

So she decided to grow stuff. Seemed easy enough. Turns out, not so much.

Fithian came back to reality again, this time from a waking dream of her own construction. She arced her back, drawing her shoulder blades together, and stretched her arms out and above her head.

The next time she left for Boston – which should be relatively soon, shouldn't it? Her turn was in…a week or two? At any rate, next time she left for Boston, she would fetch a crate of corn seeds. Hopefully, she could make the fantasy Yazbirth created for her come true, and turn this fallow field into a sea of swaying gold.

If not, well, she could always move to Boston. Or anywhere. She had resources and education, and she often reminded herself of this as she stared at a dead field behind a mostly-empty mansion in a practically-dead town. The logical thing to do in this situation was to leave, leave behind a town to which she had no real loyalty, that had very nearly forced her into a loveless marriage.

That was what logical logic dictated. But Fithian was a dreamer. So she dreamed, and failed to notice the watchful eyes at the edge of her property, fixed firmly upon her.

IV

THE DOCKS HAD DONE MORE THAN FALL INTO disrepair; they had been pushed. No ships had moored there in two years. And so, despite the newfound communal atmosphere of the town, nobody was surprised to find the sun rising on a dock that had a plank or two fewer than had seen the sunset. It was economic cannibalism, a silent acknowledgement of the fatalism that had gripped the town. Were there greater faith that Fidget's Mill would survive long enough to begin importing again, destroying the docks for a few hours of heat would be the height of short-sighted selfishness. But no real effort was expended in tracking down the culprits, because deep down, the people of the Mill knew that their time was short.

In the months following non-importation, many of the overseas firms which had shipped into the Mill sent domestic emissaries to claim the goods stinking up the storehouse of the docks. But after the emissaries stopped coming, a respectable pile of loot remained on the mold-gripped shelves. Some firms had either failed to claim their goods, or simply forgotten that the goods had made their way across the Atlantic already. Either way, a great many clerical errors led to a considerable surplus of resources, just sitting in the storehouse, ownerless.

Which was how Mr. Increase became one of the first people in America to learn about eminent domain.

The backlash was immediate. The people of Fidget's Mill, about as progressively minded as white folks in the eighteenth century could hope to be, were still white folks in the eighteenth century. The idea of a black man - free or otherwise - arrogating control of all the resources currently stored in town (as opposed to those shuttled in by the volunteers), occasioned a tremulous thrum of outrage. But a thrum it remained, one that expired in impotent harmonics. Because what could they do? They'd shunted Mr. Increase off to the docks, hoping to keep him out of the way. But who was laughing now? He knew how the storehouse was organized (he was, after all, the one who had done the organizing), he knew how to navigate it, and he knew how to keep a secret: don't tell anybody else. Sure, people could barge their way into the storehouse, gut the place, drag the remaining spoils out into the light of day and sort it out amongst themselves. But Mr. Increase was, for all of his melanin, a citizen of the Mill, and one who was fairly well respected. It wouldn't do, to mishandle him as one might such a base villain as a Colonial Governor.

So they thrummed their way to the storehouse every week to receive rations portioned out by Mr. Increase, and they grumbled their way home again. For a brief period late in 1768, Mr. Increase attained a kind of power once enjoyed by the three main families of the town, but once the overland supplies became a more regular feature of life in the

Mill, the goods in the storehouse became luxury goods, pleasant excesses atop the necessities. This worked just fine for Mr. Increase – he had quite a bounty from which to draw his rations for the town, but it was a bounty that was nonetheless finite. Becoming a dealer in leisure goods allowed him to stem the flow, thus prolonging the time he could spend in the groove he had carved out for himself.

One curious consequence of this new position, a consequence Mr. Increase could not have foreseen, was that he became invested in stability. He had believed, and still did believe, that equality could best be found in chaos, that great leveler of fortunes. But for now, his fortunes were on the rise, and a leveling would more likely than not pull him down, as opposed to lifting him higher. He had become, he hated to admit, a proponent of social stasis.

Which was easy for him to say. He was free. Never had he a more marked contrast than the unhappy Adewale, his partner in almost-crime two years ago. After the humiliation he suffered, Chip Ditteridge took revenge on the only person he truly could: Adewale. Under Missy's fervent protests (for she'd had every intention of setting Adewale free as promised), Chip sold Adewale off. Where, beyond 'off', no one could say for sure – Chip kept that information to himself, lest someone get it into their pretty little head to track him down. Yes, Adewale was a casualty of the curious instution, and Mr. Increase was free. And his life just went right on. Did he feel like a traitor by being comfortable? Damn right he did.

The world had changed so very much in the past two years. Too much. Mr. Increase was comfortable in his station, and he despised that comfort, which made him uncomfortable, which made his comfort more tolerable. He wouldn't have been able to bear the comfort if he were so comfortable as to be not the least bit uncomfortable. Such was the world in which he now lived.

The voice of an older woman came rolling between the shelves like a wheel of stale cheese. "Mr. Increase?"

Mr. Increase, seated at a desk, hunched over one of his scrupulously fair ration sheets for the month, became suddenly aware of the tension in his neck. He sighed and rolled his stiff, aching shoulders in a full circle as he leaned back, tilting his head toward the ceiling. Gods, how tightly wound he'd become! All of this deskwork could turn a man into an armadillo. "Yes, Vera?"

Just a few years ago, from the ersatz atrium in the storehouse, Mr. Increase wouldn't have been able to see anyone approaching until they were practically on top of him. But now the shelves were largely bare of boxes (he'd spread them all to the least accessible sections of the storehouse, according to a deliberately byzantine system of organization comprehensible only to him), and so he could see ex-hotelier Vera Miringhoff squeezing between the shelves from almost the moment she entered the storehouse. This, as always, put him in an awkward position. Did he try to have a conversation with his visitor as they struggled their way between the shelves, which were no further apart for being vacant, or did he wait until they had reached him in the eye of the spoils store?

Typically, he chose the latter course, making a point of not looking up from the work he was always and invariably hunched over until his guest had traversed the lumber jungle. But, always and invariably, Vera Miringhoff made this impossible by posing Mr. Increase's name to the immensity of the storehouse as though it were one of life's most vexing questions.

Always, invariably, Mr. Increase was there to answer her. At least, always and invariably all of the times that he was there. He supposed that he couldn't really know if she came calling when he wasn't there…even epistemology had gotten all screwy since non-importation.

Since Denton Hedges. Mr. Increase still thought of that strange little man from time to time, but it was hard to think of anybody except Vera once she was in front of you.

"Mr. Increase," she repeated again with greater confidence as she crouched to guide her heft through a familiar cavity in the aisle. It would be surprising indeed if she weren't able to make this trip blindfolded by now. "How are you?"

It was hard to have a conversation with a woman trying, for all intents and purposes, to run a jungle gym. But practice made perfect, and Mr. Increase had lately had plenty of practice. Vera's beloved Klump Regency had been very nearly the first casualty of non-importation; the hotel drew all of its business from transatlantic travelers looking for a place to sleep between the sea and the city. It wasn't as though folks were coming in from Boston to stay at the Klump Regency. So she folded, and was shocked to discover that she didn't have any hobbies. Running the hotel by herself had been a way of life as much as an occupation. Having no hotel to run meant she had no source of income, but the good people of the Mill were more than happy to band together in support of a pillar of the community. She was, after all, too old to do anything especially useful, and nobody could bear the thought of watching the poor woman waste away to an early grave, even if there was quite a bit of her to waste.

So they supported her, and Vera allowed herself to be supported, but only because she was too old to do anything especially useful. It fell to her, then, to find herself a hobby.

Did 'busybody' count as a hobby? Or was Mr. Increase the only person she pestered so often? More questions that couldn't be answered from such a limited perspective.

"I'm doing quite well. Just very busy," he added with a tilt of the head steep enough to slide down.

"Oh, don't mind me," Vera said as she came crashing into Mr. Increase's inner sanctum. How she could crash in when there was nothing on the shelves to knock over never ceased to amaze him. "Just poking around. Do you need a hand with anything?"

"No, I think I've got everything just about under control here."

Vera either failed to detect the sarcasm, or chose to ignore it. It came to the same thing. "Oh. Okay."

The worst part of seeing Vera like this was that Mr. Increase truly felt for her. What did he feel? Why, he felt a feeling the old Increase wouldn't have had the least bit of time for: pity. Was ever there a more useless emotion? Pity was good for nothing save inhibiting the one who felt it. Back when he was struggling to get by as the unseen mover of the docks, he felt pity for neither man nor woman. How could he? He was too *busy* to pity.

But now he was comfortable. And comfort allowed him – or perhaps forced him – to feel pity for those less comfortable. Which, right now, was Vera Miringhoff, standing before him and looking uncomfortable in the skin she'd worn for over sixty years.

So he pitied her. So what? What did that mean? How did that clarify what he would say to her, or do for her? Useless, pity was useless.

And yet, that was all he could feel towards her.

A few months prior, when Increase had first identified that feeling for what it was, he had tried to give Vera some busywork to do around the storehouse. But the fact of the matter was that Increase didn't have any busywork to give her. He truly did have it all under control. Vera's finding a hobby would be wholly on Vera, which was grounds for further pity.

After a lengthy silence, full of shuffling feet and cleared throats, Vera turned around and navigated herself back out of the storehouse. She mumbled some stock farewell over her shoulder, but Mr. Increase couldn't pick up much more than the general sentiment.

He shrugged, alone again in the silence, and once again hunched over the papers on his desk. His own busywork, self-generated, self-inflicted.

Oh dear. If he wasn't careful, he might start pitying himself.

V

PITY IS A MAGICAL THING. IT CAN BLUNT A MIND so often noted for its merciless bite, as it did for poor Mr. Increase. Why, if Vera wasn't careful, she might well start to pity *him*. Or, while she was at it, Miss Carsis.

Two years ago, following the death of Governor Marsh, events seemed to be building towards a shattering crescendo. And then a document appeared, an endorsement of non-importation with Chip Ditteridge's signature affixed. Its dissemination cut through the static anxiety like a fart through a funeral, and the nervy anticipation upon which Miss Carsis had intended to capitalize for her own witchy ends wafted away. The people of the Mill had begun looking to bigger and better things, issues of trans-Colonial interest. They were looking outward, and in order to shepherd them where she wanted, Miss Carsis needed them to be looking inward.

The witch was, after all of her hard work, reduced to a far more passive role in the town. This was the People's time, and when a group thought of itself as a collective entity, rather than a constellation of individuals, it became harder to manipulate. Magically, at least. Politically and materially they became *easier* to handle, which seemed counterintuitive and regularintuitive in equal measure. After all, a single bird might allow itself to be blown about by the wind, gliding whichever way the breeze happened to take it. But a flock of birds would follow whoever happened to be at the peak of the soaring V, winds be damned.

How fascinating, then, that the flock of the Mill seemed to be soaring along in defiance of the thaumaturgical winds, despite having no central figure to follow. For a time it was Buddy Jr., and then it was Mr. Increase, and now it was nobody. Who was guiding the flock? It couldn't be self-guiding, could it? Groups needed guides. That was human nature. Right? Wasn't it?

Answering this question became, in a way, Vera's new hobby.

In all the excitement of the past few years, the people of the Mill let less-than-pressing bits of information slip away through their mental cracks, the easier to focus on Big Issues. One of those crack-slipping facts was that Vera Miringhoff and Miss Carsis were, if not friends, then well-acquainted with one another. Had he remained in the Mill, Denton might well have remembered, Vera being the one who sent him to Miss Carsis in the first place. But as most people in a position to witness the connection firsthand were people staying at the Klump Regency, which is to say the itinerant population, the semi-friendship went generally unacknowledged.

So most people saw Vera wandering the streets, popping her head into any open door or window she could find, as an object of pity. Poor woman, if only she could find herself a hobby. Pity blinded them to an alternate interpretation of events, an interpretation which happened to be true: Vera was brazenly canvasing the entire town on Miss Carsis' behalf, hoping to sort out who was in charge. The ex-hotelier missed her beloved business, but only in those rare moments of downtime she could scrounge up. She was so very busy, after all.

In those aforementioned moments of downtime, so scarce in her aforementioned busy schedule, Vera would sometimes lament how little effort she needed to expend in convincing the town that she was a pitiful, dottering old fool. A vacant stare here, a clumsy bumble there, and the illusion seemed complete. She would have liked a *bit* more incredulity from her marks, even if it would have made her job more difficult.

Vera entered 33 Gutter Lane without knocking, an unheard-of privilege she had been granted to inculcate loyalty. It was the sort of bargain-basement manipulation Miss Carsis missed – make her co-conspirator feel special, and she'll work that much harder to justify the confidence. Even if Vera was meant to be an equal, Miss Carsis couldn't help jerking her around by the nose a bit. It was, as the fable went, simply her nature.

"Huh," Vera huffed as she slumped her way through the deep blue curtains.

"Hm?" Miss Carsis returned without looking up from her book.

"You look just like him." Vera opened her palms upward to mimic staring into a book.

Miss Carsis looked up and smiled, both because that was what was expected of her and because she felt genuine warmth for Vera, in that order. "Our Increase is still as literary as ever, then?"

Vera sat down in the chair across from Miss Carsis, again without invitation. A standing invitation to sit whenever she liked had been tendered long ago – more gentle manipulation. "I don't know if I'd call it *literary*, but he's still hard at work on those books."

A younger woman, one of Miss Carsis' forever-changing roster of apprentices, appeared, poured Vera cup of tea, and disappeared. No magic had been employed, far as Vera could tell; the young girl was just quick on her feet and highly discreet. Vera took a sip, nodded her approval to the universe, and continued: "Fithian was out in her field, playing with her agricultures again."

"What's she trying to this year?"

"Couldn't tell. I didn't get very close."

Miss Carsis nodded as though she'd just taken a sip of *her* tea. As far as Vera was aware, she hadn't. "That was wise of you."

Vera took another sip of her tea, and looked into her glass, which appeared to be completely full. She sometimes forgot that there was always magic afoot when Miss Carsis was involved; it was highly *un*wise of her to ever forget that.

The witch studied the ex-hotelier exactly the same way as the latter studied the cup of tea. "Anything else afoot in the Mill, of which I should be aware?"

Rejoining the waking world, Vera took a deep draught from the bottomless cup of tea. "Millicent's pregnancy proceeds apace. No complications that I can see."

"Ah." Miss Carsis didn't much care about domestic matters, but it was good to know. Buddy Jr. and Missy had been wed seven months prior, and if they were lucky, nobody would run the numbers and realize that the incoming bundle of joy had been the cause of the matrimony, rather than the product. Could this information be useful? Probably not. But not *definitely* not. So, yes, certainly good to know. "Anything else?"

"How fares our friend Yazbirth Bicklebog?" No-Good Bulstrode inquired from a spot on the table in front of Miss Carsis. This question was solely for the witch's benefit; the Familiar hadn't allowed himself to be seen by Vera. In the beginning, when Vera was first beginning her rounds of the town, Bulstrode would plod along beside her, without her having the slightest clue. This allowed Miss Carsis to verify the reports Vera brought back; how strong was her recall, with what fidelity did she recount situations, were her assessments and interpretations of events highly colored by personal bias or generally objective, and so on. Once her trustworthiness had been determined, Vera was allowed to roam alone as she'd always thought she'd been, thus freeing Bulstrode to address other matters. Which for the turkey increasingly meant turning his thoughts to the sloth. Such was the corrosive nature of pity.

She can't see Yazbirth either, Miss Carsis silently chided Bulstrode. *You know this.*

"Have you considered plunking the sight of him into that swollen coconut she calls a head?"

Go away. Go see Yazbirth yourself, if it's so important to you.

Bulstrode fluffed his feathers. "Why, I couldn't possibly, it's been far too long, and th-"

Go away, Bulstrode.

Vera sat silently and uneasily, waiting for Miss Carsis' reverie to end. Every once in a while the witch would stare at an empty space in the room, on a table or in a doorway, and make very intense contortions of the brow. Each time, Vera considered inquiring as to what the hell was going on, and each time she thought better of it. When someone's eye was twitching like that, it was best to let them be. That was, in paraphrase, the basic philosophy by which she had attained such an advanced age.

After a minute or so, Miss Carsis returned to Earth, favoring Vera with a smile of discomfiting warmth, like a woolen blanket on a summer day. "Would you like to stay for dinner?" This was how Miss Carsis signaled that their palaver was at an end. It was an unspoken agreement that Vera would always have prior dinner plans of some sort, which she once again claimed to have now. "Shame, shame, one of these days," the witch intoned for the umpteenth time.

They rose from their seats, and Miss Carsis halted mid-rise. Her eye started twitching again, so Vera nodded graciously and made her way towards the door.

"Wait!" Miss Carsis cried. It wasn't an angry cry, but a faintly plaintive one, as though the witch didn't wish to be left alone with

…something.

But that wasn't quite right. Vera watched with a feeling just shy of wonder as Miss Carsis' forehead folded in a new and exciting way. The witch was thinking, trying to make sense of some astonishing fact. And Vera could watch as sense dawned, revealing a thin, bloodless smile that bloomed into something truly beautiful.

Miss Carsis felt laughter burbling deep within her, like indigestion. She choked it down – laughter was so very *humanizing*, something she enjoyed doing in private but sought to avoid in company – but a smile plowed through her defenses. No matter. This was something to smile about.

Do you feel that? She thought at Bulstrode.

"Oh, so sorry, I was given to understand you wanted me to g-"

Shut up and feel.

So Bulstrode felt. He felt in the way one feels one's way through a darkened room…and then he felt in the way one feels the chalky slickness of a wax candle between one's fingers. Or feathers, as the case may be.

If beaks could support smiles, Bulstrode would have matched Miss Carsis' expression. "The ponce!"

Miss Carsis turned her disquieting smile on Vera. "I want you to run to the old Marsh mansion, or the docks. I'm quite certain it will be one of the two…I'm just not certain *which*. Yet. In the meantime, please wait here. I'll have dinner brought to us shortly."

Vera stammered, falling back into her seat without intending to. Had the offer to stay for dinner been more than a formality all this time? She could hardly believe it, and now she felt a fool for failing to see it. "Ah…thank you? Thanks," she clarified. Why the sudden about-face from Miss Carsis? How was she dismissing Vera one second, and asking her to await instructions the next? Await from where?

It was highly probable Vera would be distressed by the answers to any of these questions, so she settled on one that seemed far less likely to upset: "What's for dinner?"

"Stew," Miss Carsis replied while looking into empty space just above the table.

Which, all things considered, was still a pretty upsetting answer.

She could smell him. Not literally, of course, but that was the only way to describe it. His aura was a kind of odor, not wholly unpleasant but still a ways away from pleasant. At first she had pegged the recrudescence of the stench as a ghostly memory. Who *hasn't* caught a whiff of their own past from time to time? The sudden arrival of an ex-lover's sweat, gone and here and gone again a moment later? Who hasn't mistaken a stranger's laugh for that of an old friend?

Who hasn't been put in mind of an old…not a friend, and certainly not a lover…an old acquaintance?

You sense him too, right? She asked the question casually, but there was a note of anxiety in her thoughts, and she didn't like the sound of that at *all.*

"I do," Bulstrode concurred. "Question is, what's he doing back after donkey's years away?"

One of many questions. Miss Carsis hardly noticed as the help placed two bowls on the table, nor did she notice Vera making a point of *only* noticing the bowls.

"Could he be here for the physician?"

Possible, but unlikely. If he were, why now?

"Could the Ditteridge woman have sent him word of the incipient parturition?"

Once again, possible but unlikely.

"Why so?"

Basic psychology, I suppose. No matter how fondly they may think on him – and I would likely suppose that the fondness has dimmed, given what his…work did to their familial legacies – it seems unlikely they would want the man they think responsible for aborting one baby to be present for the birth of a second.

"They expect he wouldn't be able to help himself from a repeat performance? Come now, they're not th-"

Basic psychology, I said. They wouldn't ever think something so silly in big bold letters, but there's a basement space in every human mind where the silly thoughts reign as the tyrant gods of old. Miss Carsis balled her hands into trembling fists, which Vera tried very hard to not notice. She did not do a very good job.

"So why is he here?"

Miss Carsis watched as one of her helpers slopped stew into the bowls on the table. Her smile widened as she watched Vera's face drop. The stew was quite delicious, but it turned the stomach to look at it, and doubly so to listen to it. This was by design; no self-respecting witch would eat anything that looked or sounded or smelled appetizing. It just wasn't done.

She plucked up the wooden spoon which had made its way into her bowl, took up a chunky blob of the soup, and shivered. Even after all these years, it could be difficult for her to manage the first bite. Some things never changed. Through a faltering smile, she guided the nauseating morsel to her tongue, and rejoiced.

Bulstrode had asked 'why is he here', and Miss Carsis decided that there was no sense sitting in the dark and guessing. She'd find out. And Vera might not even be necessary or desirable – he'd almost certainly work out the connection between the witch and the ex-hotelier immediately.

"Actually," Miss Carsis cooed to a stark-white Vera staring at her soup as though it were a bear trap, "not to disrupt your dinner, but I may have an errand for you to run."

"Oh thank God. I mean," Vera course-corrected, "how can I help?"

"Make a brief tour of the town. Visit everyone you can think of. Tell them, simply and quickly, that Denton Hedges is back. Then move on. Don't stop to answer questions, don't editorialize, just inform them; Denton Hedges is back." She gestured to the soup in front of Vera. "You can take that along with you, if you li-"

"That's alright!" Vera nearly shouted, already back on her feet. "I have other plans for dinner. Thank you though!"

"No matter," Miss Carsis replied. "More for me."

With startling speed, the old woman flew from the room, nothing to document her departure save the gentle waving of the curtains.

Miss Carsis sat back in her chair and shoveled some more stew into her mouth. The second bites were always so much easier than the first; it was just a matter of re-training the body. Some things never changed, after all.

She felt for him, and then felt him, and then thought at him. *Welcome back, Denton.*

VI

DENTON.

"Yes?"

Peggy looked back at Denton over her shoulder. "What?"

Denton unloaded the last suitcase from the carriage. "You called my name."

"Not lately, I haven't."

"Oh." Denton's shoulders sagged as realization dawned. "Blast."

"What's blast, daddy?" Annabelle gripped the cuff of his pants as though one of their lives depended upon the answer.

"It's a word which is almost, but not quite, rude." Denton patted his beloved daughter on the head. "So never utter the word in mixed company."

"What about in *un*mixed company?" This from Lawrence, ever the scamp.

With a look, Peggy signaled that this question was hers to answer. "It's a word only to be uttered around those one loves."

Annabelle tilted her head to one side. "But it's a rude word!"

"Precisely."

"You say rude words to people you love?"

"Not *to* them," Denton the lawyer cut in, "just *around* them."

"Because you love them?"

"Yes."

"Being an adult is complicated," Lawrence explained to his sister.

Denton smiled agreeably, but his mind was elsewhere. Specifically, it was wherever Miss Carsis was. Because her mind was with him, in a very real sense. She'd thought his name at him, so she knew he was back in town. What was it to her?

This would be very interesting to know, once he'd sorted out what it was to him. Was he fleeing the Massacre in Boston? Was he here to keep things from going south in the same way in Fidget's Mill? Something else? He'd spent the frantic ride here turning this question over and over in his mind, and he'd failed to arrive at a satisfactory answer. What it boiled down to was that he had unfinished business in Fidget's Mill, and so had felt drawn back to it. What was the business? Perhaps it was the business of sorting out what the business was.

But the more pressing question was this: what might Miss Carsis suspect his business here was? Because if she fancied he was here to frustrate her goals once again…how humiliating would it be, to be turned into a toad in front of his children?

They finished unloading the carriage and sent it away, at which point Annabelle finally observed that "this building doesn't look nice."

"Now, now," Denton chided, "old Ms. Miringhoff does the best she can, but sh…oh, dear." The Klump Regency really *didn't* look very nice, did it? The windows were boarded up, and the boards on the windows were rotten. It had never been the *most* beautiful building in town, but it also used to look more like a building than ambitious driftwood.

"Blast?" Annabelle ventured.

"Very good," Peggy allowed. She turned to Denton. "So where else can we stay?"

"Hm…I have a friend, who I believe is still here. At least, I've not heard any news of his return to Boston."

"Would you have?"

"He has a practice in the city. I've popped my head in from time to time, and he remains…not there. If he's not there, he must be here."

"Naturally."

"Yes. Well," Denton clapped his hands, as this was the only way he could think to get his kids excited about something terrible, "who wants to go for a walk?"

"I do!" cried Peggy, supplying more than enough excitement for both of the kids.

"And we can even carry our luggage with us!" Clap.

"Hooray!"

Unfortunately, the Hedges didn't raise no fools. "This doesn't sound as fun as you're trying to make it sound," Lawrence contested.

"Well," Peggy rejoined, "tough."

And with that, they walked to Dr. Brisby Houlihan's house.

Upon arrival, Denton intuited fairly quickly that this was probably not Dr. Brisby Houlihan's house anymore. If it was not as ostentatiously abandoned as the Klump Regency (no boards on the windows, nor wind rattling a door set unevenly in its frame), it was nonetheless just as obvious in its vacancy. Life brings light to a home, and this home had none. It was, then, the perfect twin of the Marsh mansion just across the field.

"If the good doctor isn't *here*," Peggy wondered aloud, "then where could he be?"

"Perhaps…he left for Boston just as we were leaving for here?" Denton was neither convincing nor convinced. He scratched his head and looked to his exhausted family. Despite the temperatures that had dipped well below freezing, they were all caked in sweat. Trudging through the snow was hard work, particularly for kids who sank hip-deep in it.

Denton was running out of places to go, but he wasn't out yet. So he screwed up a smile, clapped his hands, and after a few minutes of complaining, they were back on the road.

"Hello?" Denton called into storehouse.

"(hello?)" the storehouse returned.

Denton flinched, stunned by his own echo. Once his eyes adjusted the gloom, the surprise modulated – now it was in response to the lack of, well, anything at all in the massive structure. The storehouse was nearly empty.

"Mr. Increase?"

"This place is creepy," Annabelle whimpered.

"I'm afraid that falls to me," Mr. Increase grumbled from the darkness. Denton could see glimpses of him, limping between the shelves, but the man remained as yet obscured. "Just so very hard to keep a large wooden structure well lit. For obvious reasons."

"Thank God you're still here." Denton couldn't help but let genuine relief flood into his Unshakeable Daddy routine. He'd been getting concerned – allowing the sun to set on his family, in temperatures that were already this cold, was not an option. But he also hadn't had any *other* options available, so…but stop. It didn't bear thinking about. "Everybody else is…elsewhere."

Finally, Mr. Increase limped into view, carrying his trusty clipboard. He looked a bit soggier around the edges, but those edges were somehow still as sharp as ever. Two years had hardly left their mark. "Who's everybody, then?"

"This is my wife, Peggy, and my two children, Lawrence and Annabelle."

"Mhm." Mr. Increase nodded patiently. "Nice to meet you all, but I was inquiring as to who the 'everyone' in your previous statement was. Upon whom you called before brightening my doorstep."

"Right, of course. You'll take no personal umbrage to my not having thought of you first, I hope, it's j-"

Mr. Increase held his hand up in an imperious halting gesture, and Denton felt himself growing impatient with the man as he never had before. How dare Increase address Denton this way, in front of his family? And, come to think of it, how dare Denton speak so deferentially in front of his family? How dare his family be present for this exchange? That last one didn't quite make sense, but he was in an ill humor.

"Prior to visiting you," Denton resumed in his most booming courtroom voice, "I ordered the carriage to deposit us at the Klump Regency, with the intention of renting a room."

"The Klump went under," Increase gracelessly interrupted. "Vera just wanders now, it's quite piti…it's quite unfortunate."

"Yes, I noticed that former fact. And so, I went to call upon Dr. Brisby Houlihan, only to find his house standing uninhabited in much the same way."

"Brisby's been in prison for nearly two years."

Once again, Denton's affectations cracked under the strain of new information. "On what charge?"

"Being a Customs Commissioner, I assume."

"That's not a crime!"

"Perhaps that's why they've not yet set a date for him to see a judge."

Denton put a mental pin in that, and once again gathered up the censorious tone that had fallen down around his ankles. "Yes, well, finding neither Ms. Miringhoff nor Dr. Houlihan, I thought I would pay a visit to my favorite…Mr. Increase in town, to see…well, to see what he was up to."

"I'm working."

"…okay."

"Was there anything else?"

Christ. Denton hadn't seen the man in two years, and that's what he had to say? 'I'm working'? "Yes, as a matter of fact, there was. I have shocking news from Boston for you."

Mr. Increase raised an eyebrow as only he could.

"So if you'd be so kind as to supply my family with some food and a comfortable place to rest, you and I can bring each other up to speed."

The raised eyebrow morphed effortlessly into a smile. That, too, was a shift of expression that only a man like Increase could pull off.

VII

"AT WHICH POINT, I GATHERED UP MY SON AND ran." Denton balanced atop a short stepladder, pulling ratty woolen blankets from a box. "I'm not ashamed to admit it. In fact, I defy any sage to counsel that I ought have done otherwise."

"No, no, you were quite right to do so. Good God," Increase sighed, "a massacre in Boston!"

"Indeed. This is an historical fulcrum, you mark my words. The Boston Slaughter will go down in history…as what, though, that remains to be seen."

"The Boston Slaughter." Mr. Increase tried the term out and found it pleasing. "It has a certain ring, doesn't it?"

"Certainly better than 'the Massacre on King Street', or some such." Denton swelled with pride at his nomenclature, and nearly fell off the stepladder as a result. Once the swelling was back under control, he tossed the blankets down to Mr. Increase. "Boston was in a state of chaos when I left, and I expect the chaos will spread outward before long, even to Fidget's Mill."

"And that's why you're here, then?"

"Probably." Denton followed Mr. Increase back through the maze of shelves to the central eye, where his family sat sipping hot tea. He handed a blanket to his daughter, who thanked him as she was taught. His son nodded agreeably.

"Well, if that's the case," Mr. Increase continued at something closer to a whisper than regular speaking voice, "then perhaps your first order of business might be retrieving Dr. Houlihan from his cell."

Denton appreciated Increase's discretion, in not discussing political matters in front of his children. They cut through the open central vault and moved back towards the mess of shelving. "I think you're right. If a fraction of the anti-British sentiment I saw on display should make its way here, his life would likely be…" Denton's first thought was *forfeit*, and he shivered at what was either pessimism or prescience. Instead, he went with "imperiled."

"Precisely. Beyond that, I'm afraid I can't help you. Much has changed since you left, and I'm sorry to say it's almost all thanks to you."

"You're welcome."

"I meant 'thanks' ironically, I'm afraid. Non-importation rather destroyed the town, and most folks blame you almost exclusively. You were a convenient scapegoat, having run yourself out of town as you did."

"...oh."

"So, come to think of it, you may not fare much better here than our dear Dr. Houlihan." If Denton wasn't mistaken, there was a hint of amusement in Increase's voice. He suspected the man blamed Denton too. Was he not, after all, a citizen of the Mill?

Denton thought of the soldier turning and staring directly at his son, after Lawrence had thrown the slab of ice that, for all Denton knew, was starting a revolution. "We'll have to take our chances. At least here we can potentially do some good."

"Given your track record, I don't expect your kind of good will be in high demand."

"Ah, ha."

"I mean that seriously, I'm afraid."

"How can you?"

"Your legacy in the Mill is...you must be aware, Denton. Think of how you left us, the state in which you left us."

"I made great strides for the Cause!" He thought for a moment and amended: "We all made great strides for the Cause!"

"Yes, but what Cause specifically?"

It was stunning, to Denton, that he should already be deep in the mire of political discourse. He'd hardly been back for a quarter of a day! Where had the man's sense of discretion gone? "Well, to begin with, without me, the Circular Letter would have accomplished nothing. The British would have plied the patrons of Fidget's Mill wi-"

"Did you not just finish telling me about the Boston Slaughter? If the rebellious sentiments of the Circular Letter had been dispersed through economic means, might those people still walk among us?"

Denton stopped walking. "Are you trying to place responsibility for this atrocity on my shoulders?" He glanced back towards his family, who were watching him with interest. Good heavens, they were still within earshot! He felt the tickle of self-consciousness on the back of his neck. In the stacks, he'd been having a conversation with Mr.

Increase. Now, as before, he was talking to Mr. Increase, and performing for his wife and kids. That was how it felt, at least. Every word he thought had to be smushed through the sieve of self-awareness, which took time and effort and exacted its costs in brevity and discretion.

This was, in short, *not* the conversation to be having in front of a crowd.

"Not solely," Mr. Increase replied with a shocking lack of irony. "But would you deny any portion of culpability? Isn't that the corollary of aligning yourself with a Cause?"

Play the mediator. Teach your kids a thing or two about keeping your head. "Where is this coming from? Have I done something to offend you?"

"What, other than demolishing my town and leaving? And then returning with demands of accommodation? No, I can't think of a single thing."

"I haven't demanded accommodation!"

"Not yet, but can you look me in the eye and deny that such a demand was forthcoming?"

Denton couldn't, and so instead cast an eye towards his family. Watching, listening. Good grief. He could see Peggy silently willing him to desist, to walk away, to be the bigger man. But his son had fire in his eyes. He wanted his dear old dad to show the mean old dockman who was boss. And so, despite his better judgment, this was also what Denton wanted.

"This is rich, coming from the man who indiscriminately poisoned an entire party!"

"We've had this discussion! Foreknowledge of the guestlist, and Miss Carsis' influence, made the act discriminate!"

"So Lucretia's death was part of the plan, was it?"

"Th…Wh…don't throw that at me! I don't deny responsibility for the act, nor for its consequences. Can you say the same?"

"I take limited responsibility for certain acts, but I'll not be held accountable for the Boston Blasted Slaughter!"

Stunned by his own anger, Mr. Increase raised his voice to a shout, as he hadn't in years. He had often thought of Denton with something approaching fondness, so why, now that he had the man in front of him once again, was he filled with such rage? "Then you're a coward, son, in every sense of the word!"

Denton gasped. It was the least impressive thing he could have done in response to the insult, and a quick look to his son reaffirmed that assessment. He had to do something to reclaim his honor, and quickly!

Having no clue what else to do, Denton stuck his finger right in Mr. Increase's face. "Well you, sir, are a Machiavellian scoundrel with no principles save those which facilitate self-advancement! And don't you ever call me son, dad! Er, I mean…!"

Peggy shot up from her seated position. "Now now, boys, we're all very tense," and that was true enough. She had more to say about that, but never got the chance.

Mr. Increase, thinking of how easy it was for a man like Denton to carp on about principles, thinking of ships laden with human cargo, thinking of his mother alone in the woods with child, and then with *a* child, slapped Denton Hedges' face.

Denton once again gasped, and then for a third time when he saw the look of thunderstruck shame on his son's face. He balled his hand into a fist, and stayed it from a long arc into Mr. Increase's nose only by the sound of his wife calling his name.

Instead, he pointed a trembling finger at Mr. Increase, and informed him through gritted teeth that he would demand satisfaction as a gentleman. He turned to look at his son, and saw that Lawrence quite liked that bit.

Mr. Increase agreed.

Denton accepted Mr. Increase's agreement, and bade his family leave this wretched storehouse once and for all. They gathered up their cases, as well as several of the blankets Denton had fetched from boxes ("and we'll be taking *these*" was how Denton presented it, and Mr. Increase replied "oh I wish you *would*", because malice borne of slighted bonhomie had to work twice as hard to eradicate its foundation), and made their way back out into the cold.

It wasn't until an hour or so later that both men realized they had accidentally agreed to duel one another. How had that even happened? Denton in particular was incredulous; he returned to Fidget's Mill to flee violence, and here he was, taking on an active role in it! Both regretted the decision immediately, and wished to rush back to the other and cancel the challenge immediately. It was a rash decision, and putting aside the unexpected anger stirred up by their reunion, they still cared for one another. The anger couldn't have been so stirred unless they *did* care for one another.

Or unless, of course, neither was truly seeing the other when they looked upon each other. Unless they were instead seeing someone else.

No matter. The challenge had been issued in front of Denton's family, and when they looked at him, they saw their husband, their father (Denton blinked slightly too hard at that thought; who could say why?). And how humiliating would that be, to back down from a duel issued in front of an audience? Certainly more humiliating than being shot in front of one. Such was the curious propriety of honor.

If only they had each known that the other was just as focused on neutralizing the idiotic, arbitrary conflict as they were, the idiotic, arbitrary conflict might have actually been neutralized. If only they had known that they both had never felt more powerless in their lives, and that this was their sad attempt to reclaim their agency. If only they could admit these things to each other. But neither could. And so they would duel.

VIII

DENTON PARADED HIS FAMILY THROUGH THE hush of winter. Finally, Annabelle breached the quiet. "Are you and the negroman friends or not friends?"

"We just call them 'negroes'," Denton replied in enlightened tones, "and we are. Or were."

"You seemed like friends, until you didn't."

"Well, sometimes that happens, dear."

This was, Annabelle felt, a highly unsatisfactory answer.

Lawrence took up the conversational slack. "So you're now going to settle this affair honorably, aren't you, dad?"

"Yes," Peggy replied for him, "he will. Through rational dialectic."

"Through what?"

"Conversation." Peggy cast a skeptical glance towards her husband, marching sullenly through the snow. "Daddy will talk to the man, explain the misunderstanding which surely transpired between them, and eliminate the need for any shameful acts of violence."

"But there's nothing shameful in a duel!"

"There's the duel itself."

Denton sighed and joined the conversation: "Violence ought never be the answer, Lawrence. A true gentleman always has manifold means at his disposal to resolve a conflict."

Annabelle perked up at this. "Does it?"

"Does what?"

"So when Lawrence and I are fighting, he should have manifold?"

Denton nearly stopped walked, so baffled was he by his daughter. "Annabelle, I don't unde-"

"She thinks," Peggy explained with the trace of a laugh, "that the word 'manifold' means 'to resolve a conflict'." She smiled at her daughter. "Is that right?"

Annabelle nodded enthusiastically. She was ambitious, always hungry to learn. It was beautiful to watch her absorb the chaos of her surroundings and attempt to make sense of them, even when there was no sense to be made. God, how could he have been so distant as to forget how much she loved learning new words?

Had he been looking to the wrong child's face for reassurance? Lawrence was at a bloodthirsty age, which made him uncannily well-suited to the bloodthirsty age in which he lived. Peggy disapproved of barbaric affairs of honor like a duel, as well she should. *Denton* disapproved of the duel, but he was just then unable to admit it to anyone, least of all himself. Annabelle, though…Annabelle clearly didn't *understand* the duel.

"Listen, squirrelheart," Denton cooed as he fell back to walk next to the daughter who had once been confused by hearing another man call his daughter 'dear heart', which Annabelle took to be 'deer heart', a homonymic misunderstanding which before long morphed into a joke which, over time, came full circle and was reborn as a term of genuine endearment (not to be confused with a term of endeerment, d'oh). "Sometimes, one gentleman offends another gentleman."

"Sure," Annabelle nodded.

"And sometimes, the first gentleman then refuses to apologize for having offended the second gentleman. And so the second gentleman, being offended, must have some recourse ava…recourse means, hm, 'way of getting back at someone' in this context…they must have recourse available, to see their grievances redressed." Annabelle didn't ask what 'redress' meant, and for that Denton was inestimably proud. "The affair of honor is the traditional recourse, in situations such as these."

"So what do you do?"

"They fire guns at each other!" Lawrence shouted with glee. "Ten paces, turn and fire! BLAM!"

Annabelle couldn't have been more stunned if Lawrence's pointing finger had fired a live round. "He's going to fire a gun at you?"

"Only because I'll be firing a gun at him," Denton replied limply.

"Then why don't you not fire a gun at him?"

"Because he'll be firing a gun at me."

Peggy harrumphed. "You're not misunderstanding, Annabelle. It's just a foolish practice."

"That's true," Denton conceded, "but it's also how gentleman settle their quarrels."

Annabelle's voice took on a plaintive keening quality. "But you said violence was never the answer!"

Denton puzzled over his reply, but not for long enough. "It's not. Often the threat of violence will suffice. The offending gentleman will, in many cases – in *most* cases - repent of the insult and apologize to the offended gentleman, in this case myself."

"Mr. Increase might see things differently," Peggy commented with a deliberate lack of delicacy.

Denton nodded agreeably, while simultaneously brushing her contribution away with a dismissive wave of the hand. "The threat of violence has been tendered, and now we simply wait for Mr. Increase to apologize to me."

His daughter warped her brow in frustration. "You think he will?"

"I do. A true gentleman understands the codes of honor."

"But what if he doesn't?!"

There was no way to dress up the response: "Then we duel."

"Then why *wouldn't* he apologize?"

"Because he may not be much of a gentleman at all."

"Then you wouldn't *have* to duel, would you?"

Denton grappled with this sentiment for a second. The struggle intensified as he saw, written clearly on his wife's face, that Peggy understood exactly what her daughter was saying. "Huh?"

"If gentlemen duel each other, but gentlemen also apologize to each other, then if the negroman do-"

"Negro," Lawrence corrected.

"-esn't apologize, then he isn't a gentleman. And then you wouldn't have to duel, because only gentlemen duel. Right? Isn't that right, daddy?"

There was, Denton had to admit, a strange logic to it. It was a strange logic of simplicity, one devoid of the nuances one takes on with age. Nuances, of course, being the things that allow one to face a perfectly illogical statement and think, 'this is fine'.

Fortunately, if Annabelle represented pure logic, Denton had an agent of pure mayhem at his heel: an adolescent boy. "NO," Lawrence snarled, "it *isn't* right!"

Annabelle's eyes were, by some miraculous feat of biology, perfectly dry one instant and overflowing with tears in the next.

"Lawrence Hedges!" Peggy cried. "Don't raise your voice to your sister, particularly when she's just made such a wonderful, well-reasoned point!"

Denton watched the domestic scene with indefinable dread. This was all backwards, wasn't it? By taking cues from his son, he was reaffirming the boy's worldview. He was teaching little Lawrence to hear an argument that, Denton hated to admit, had certain merits (at least from an internal consistency standpoint), and respond by shouting it down. What kind of world was he building? A world of honor? What did that look like?

Right now, it looked like his son arguing with his wife as his daughter wept.

If he could leave the world a slightly better place than he'd found it, Denton would be happy. Right now he was unhappy. And as they trudged up to their destination, happiness seemed no closer at hand. If anything, it felt further than it had in quite a while.

"Third time's lucky," Denton mumbled under his frosted breath. He reached through the fog of his exhalation and wrapped his knuckle firmly on the door he hoped would belonged to 33 Gutter Lane tonight.

IX

MISS CARSIS HAD KNOWN DENTON WAS IN TOWN, but had gotten so distracted that she failed to realize when he was on her doorstep. It was with genuine shock, then, that she saw the Hedges clan being led into her parlor.

Denton gave a cheeky little bow as he intoned, "Miss Carsis, I hope my presence does not come as an absolute shock…" This was positively dripping with irony, as Miss Carsis' telepathic welcome led Denton to believe that his appearance now *wasn't* a shock. When, in fact, it was. "But it is a pleasure to see you again, now that my business brings me back to Fidget's Mill. I would like to introduce you to my family."

"These?"

"Yes."

The witch surveyed Denton's family and nodded approvingly. "Alright. I expect you'll be wanting a place to stay."

"Well," Denton began, clearly winding up for some slick, well-rehearsed sales pitch.

Miss Carsis blinked at him and his jaw snapped shut. Just like old times. "You can stay in the property next door. I'll have two beds prepared. You and Peggy will have to share a bed, then the broodlings can either share a bed or alternate between one on the bed and the other on the floor, it makes no difference to me."

"Ah…" Denton wished to thank their sudden host, but struggled to rush gratitude past the long line of arguments as to why Miss Carsis should agree to host them.

This was working out quite well, the witch felt. She put them up not out of generosity (or not *entirely*, anyway) but because it would allow her to very easily keep Denton under her thumb. Clearly, the intermittently savvy/stupid lawyer was in one of his latter phases, if he failed to recognize her motives. Then again, she wouldn't put it past him to recognize them and conceal said recognition. She could read somebody who wasn't aware of being read. But Denton was aware now, and so his mind was largely closed to her.

His wife, on the other hand…

"Few rules of the house," Miss Carsis declared as flatly as if she had been taking on lodgers for years, "first, you have free reign in your property two doors down."

"You said it was next door!" Lawrence cried.

"Oh, did I?" She smiled at the boy in a way Denton didn't like at all. "Silly me. Free reign next door, then, but don't come knocking on my door. If I wish to speak with you, I will have you sent for. If you wish to speak with me, you can wait until I wish to speak with you. Understood? Silence is assent."

The Hedges family assented.

"Wonderful. Second rule, keep the noise to a minimum. You may hear all manner of wild and wonderful sounds coming from my abode here, but that gives you no license to do likewise. Is this clear? I am looking primarily at you little moppets, though past a certain hour of the evening that injunction applies as strenuously to the adults, if not more so."

Denton blushed. Annabelle privately wondered just what Miss Carsis meant by that, to which the witch replied, "I'll explain it to you if your parents won't. You're old enough."

"That'll be quite alright," Denton sputtered.

Miss Carsis grinned at him. "Third thing," she addressed to the rest of the family, "is I'm a witch. I mention this so your beloved husband-cum-father can't divulge this information in the sort of hushed voice that might lead you to believe it's a thing of which to be frightened. Not that I believe he would do such a thing, of course, it's simply that people can be so tetchy about the dark arts. Hardly fair, seeing as day would lose its beautiful distinction if not for the soothing contrast of twilight, wouldn't you say?" This last question posed directly to Annabelle.

The young girl smiled her open-hearted smile. "What does tetchy mean?"

The witch laughed, a sound Denton was unaccustomed to hearing from her. It was only then that he wondered, not idly, where No-Good Bulstrode was. Miss Carsis' laugh was far more pleasant than the turkey's, though. "She's a curious one, Denton. I love it! Tetchy means, oh, let's say grouchy. Or grumpy. People can be less than gracious when a witch enters their lives, that's all I mean to say by that." Miss Carsis did *not* cast a meaningful glance towards Denton during that last sentence, which Denton took to be more meaningful than the non-existent glance would have been. There were layers upon layers, when one was speaking with a witch.

"You don't seem so bad," Annabelle replied graciously. "Anyway, I bet you'd be good at manifold."

Smile locked firmly in place, Miss Carsis tilted her head slightly, letting a lock of alabaster hair flop down over her eyes. "What do you mean by that?"

"Oh, nothing." Annabelle yawned.

"You're so generous to welcome us into your home," Denton sighed, "but I'm afraid we've had a very difficult day today, and there are a few developments in Boston I should hope to discuss with you privately. When it suits you, of course." He picked up his daughter, and felt her grow heavy with sleep in his arms. Truly amazing, was his Annabelle. Would that sleep came so easily to Denton! "In the meantime, if it's not exceedingly ungracious of us, we should perhaps retire for a bit of a rest. We can speak again this evening, perhaps?"

"Perhaps," Miss Carsis replied uneasily. She was watching Annabelle as a younger girl might have watched a jack in the box primed to spring. "What did she mean, by that misuse of the word 'manifold'?"

"She loves to learn new words," Denton replied over his shoulder as he turned to follow the young woman leading them back out the door to their place of lodging. "Sometimes she uses them incorrectly."

"Aha." They both recognized that this did not actually answer her question, and Miss Carsis was well aware that this was probably deliberate. She couldn't say for certain, because a wary mind was an unreadable mind, and Denton was feeling very, very wary of her. She reached into Peggy's and found the answer, discovering just how uninteresting it was. The girl just didn't know what manifold meant.

How distressing, though, that Miss Carsis hadn't been able to pluck this information directly from Annabelle. It was as though the young girl was already wary of her, in a way such a young girl ought not have learned yet. Lawrence, that boy was an open book, but a book with lots of big pictures and very few interesting facts. But the girl…

Miss Carsis wondered if Denton had noticed her inability to read his daughter. So consumed was she with this, that she didn't even wonder what Denton would make of her calling Peggy by her name without having been introduced.

She ought to have wondered, really. Because Denton had made a point of being hyper-aware throughout the conversation, and came away with two key pieces of information: that Miss Carsis couldn't read his daughter, and could read his wife. Where Lawrence fell on the spectrum was unclear, but he suspected, correctly, that it was closer to Peggy than Annabelle.

What, specifically, was to be done with this information? That was a different question for a different day. Or perhaps a different hour – he'd be just as attentive to his host's hocus pocus as he brought her up to speed on the Boston Slaughter.

What his attentiveness netted him was this: Miss Carsis seemed unsurprised by the news.

"I expect you'll be quite happy to hear this," he growled with atypical aggression. His system was still screeching with adrenaline from the challenge he'd issued to Mr. Increase. Or had Mr. Increase issued it? It had all happened so quickly. Weren't these things supposed to take weeks to come together, with carefully appointed seconds negotiating on your behalf, and opportunities to withdraw the calumnies? It wasn't supposed to be two fellas in a stinky, empty warehouse. It w-

Oh, Miss Carsis had been talking that whole time.

"-to hear this, of *course* not." Denton had to reverse engineer the witch's response based on tone and those last six words, but he guessed she was…she wasn't quite happy to hear about the Slaughter?

"So you're not quite happy to hear about the Slaughter?" he ventured.

"Of course not, don't be a cur. You can think of me what you will, but I don't treat the cessation of human life lightly."

"You did poison an entire party."

"That may be, but I can assure you I assayed some very solemn reflections on the subject."

"Oh? Was that before or after the deed was done?"

After a moment of very solemn reflection, Miss Carsis said "whichever." She dismissed the subject with a wave. "What's done is done and there's no sense dwelling. The only thicket worth carving through is the one which leads us home."

"That sounds nice, but I'm not convinced it means much."

A bone-dry smile snapped across Miss Carsis' face. "I second your assessment. This slaughter is as a stallion galloping through a thick fog, and we shall witness its swirling wake soon enough."

Denton used silence, a skill he'd learned over the past two years, waiting for Miss Carsis to speak plainly. Even without being able to read him directly, she could intuit his intent easily enough. "You mean to retrieve Dr. Houlihan from his cell?"

"I do."

"Through legal or extralegal means?"

Only the former had occurred to Denton. He said as much.

"You might want to reconsider that."

"And how does this incipient madness impact you, I wonder? I must confess, I was slightly surprised to hear that the Mill still stood."

"Oh? Why's that?"

"Well, given your apparent determination to see it destroyed…"

Now it was Miss Carsis' turn to use silence as a blunt object.

Denton gave a smug shrug. "Am I mistaken? Well, forgive me, then."

"The pose of ironic contrition is a poor fit for you, Denton, and I'll remind you that you're a guest in my home."

"Oh. Right. Sorry." This second apology was sincere, which in a very real way made it the first apology.

Once again, Miss Carsis dismissed the subject with a wave. It was as though she were flinging a physical object across the room, but even the heaviest of topics seemed weightless in her hands. "See to the doctor, and perhaps you and I will soon enough have cause to harmonize once again. In the meantime, I'll see to my business."

"That's fair enough." Denton rose from his seat, satisfied that the conversation was at an end.

Miss Carsis raised an eyebrow at him. "You'd excuse yourself from my table?"

"I'm no longer a supplicant, Miss Carsis, but a guest. And I claim the right of a guest to retire according to my own schedule."

That barren grin again. "Very good. I'll bid you a good evening, and wish you…" Woah. She'd almost wished him well in his duel, but she wasn't supposed to know about that yet. That particular bit of information had been drawn from Peggy's mind, where it occupied quite an ample tract of real estate near the front. So loud had the fact of the duel been, that Miss Carsis had nearly forgot she'd acquired the information by eldritch means. And as far as she was concerned, Denton was unaware of her ability to read his wife, while thinking himself safe (*that* much was clear). "I'll wish your family the same," she concluded confidently.

"I'll pass that along to them," Denton lied as he donned his coat and headed for the door. One of Miss Carsis' household help came to see him out, but he nodded graciously and assured the woman that he could manage his own departure.

"I'm sure you can," the young woman replied as she followed him to the door anyway.

X

THE NEXT MORNING, DENTON WENT TO JAIL.

The Mill Gaol, as it was called, was little more than a single cell in the rear of the cobbler's shoppe. As the cobbler's shoppe was little more than a single room at the rear of one of the many unlabeled side-streets in the city, a visitor trying to find the Gaol had a more arduous task before them than a prisoner plotting a breakout.

Unless, of course, the prisoner in question was Dr. Brisby Houlihan.

He sat, as he often had lately, slumped in the chair with the door to the cell unlocked. The "cell" was distinguished from the rest of the shoppe by some bars that looked very imposing but were actually quite approachable, once you got to know them. Which also described Sheriff Barefoot. Or, rather, *mainly* described Sheriff Barefoot. Brisby had come to view the large wooden door, accoutered with angry iron spikes, as a bit of stage decoration. The real obstacle to any prospective escapee was the Sheriff himself, who had lately taken to conducting his business from a chair just outside Brisby's cell. Several months into Brisby's imprisonment, during which he underwent the nasty business of becoming stone cold sober in stone cold-turkey fashion, the surly and sullen lawman had approached the physician with a dilemma. His ill-coordinated daughter had taken a tumble during a poorly rehearsed gymnastic routine, and her ankle was attaining the size and hue of a furious thunderhead. Could he help? Brisby could, and did, and so earned the privilege of an unlocked cell and fairly liberal opportunities (he was offered access to alcohol, but refused) to enjoy freedom within the confines of the cobbler's. The proprietor, one Mr. Ecker, hadn't cared much one way or the other – it had been a miserable lottery that saddled him with the town's sole cell, and the promised five-year limit to its tenure there had lapsed long ago. He'd been forced to house drunks who got sick all over his floor, violent lunatics who spat threats along with actual spit, and all manner of unruly rabble who were bad news for his interior decoration. Brisby was a model prisoner, quiet and polite, asking only for books and water, both with uncommon frequency. So he was granted walking-around-the-shop privileges. If the doctor wanted to take a stroll every now and then, and the Sheriff was here to monitor him, what was it to Mr. Ecker?

As long as it didn't interfere with business. And now a man was stepping into the shoppe, a man who had the shoe-crazy look in his eye. Mr. Ecker could spot the look a mile out.

Another mark in Brisby's favor – he'd always known to silently return to his cell when a customer entered the store. And that was what the doctor was doing now...until he wasn't. He had frozen, watching the new arrival with a shoe-crazy look of his own.

Sheriff Barefoot saw this too, and responded with his own flavor of shoe-crazy.

Three men stood, each looking more shoe-crazy than the last. And Mr. Ecker thanked his lucky stars, for he would surely be making a sale or two today.

At which point the Sheriff's eyes darted towards a flintlock musket propped up in the corner of the room, and Mr. Ecker wondered if this otherwise wonderful prisoner might not be indirectly responsible for ruining the interior decoration after all.

"I'm here to speak to the prisoner," the newcomer declared with a degree of self-assurance that always indicated overcompensation.

"Say your piece and leave," replied the Sheriff, who wished he was armed, more for the look of it than anything.

"I'll speak to him alone."

"You'll do no such thing."

"I beg to differ, as his legal representation."

Sheriff Barefoot flinched, which in such a massive slab of a man looked nothing short of preposterous. Few people understood just how…*extralegal* Brisby's imprisonment was. It was a popular measure, made possible only by the breakdown of legal privileges for British toadies. The measure had remained because no lawyer had wanted to risk their reputation defending a stooge. But if one was now presenting himself…

And not just any one. *This* one.

"You've got a lot of nerve, coming here and lecturing me about the law. Denton Hedges, unless I'm mistaken?"

"You're not," Brisby supplied with a slow-dawning smile. "Denton! What brings you back to the Mill?"

"Tragedy in Boston," Denton replied flatly. "Tragedy which will soon be making itself felt here."

The Sheriff bristled. "What do you mean by that?"

Once again, Denton explained the Slaughter. He was getting quite good at it, turning a traumatic event into a more and more compelling bit of dramatics. It was slightly gross, but all the same, it was perversely rewarding to see the faces of grown men and women being taken on a journey by no more than Denton's words. Shame about the deaths, of course, but who didn't love spinning a good yarn?

Denton finished his story, and the shoppe fell into a sinkhole of silence. It was always satisfying, that silence.

"So," he concluded, "if you'll send me to the local courthouse, I'll-"

"We don't have a local courthouse," the Sheriff mumbled.

"What? How is that possible?"

"We handle our problems amongst ourselves, or else we send them off to Boston if they need lawyering."

Denton shook his head. "The last place this case ought to be sent is

Boston."

"You don't have a case to send." Sheriff Barefoot glanced at the musket again, only this time without realizing it.

Brisby, who felt he really ought to be contributing something here, but was at a loss of what to contribute after spending two years as a passive observer of his own life, suggested "maybe we should lock the door to my cell, just in, ha ha, case?"

"I made haste for Fidget's Mill the moment the gunfire started," Denton continued as though Brisby's hadn't spoken, "but formal word of the atrocity won't be far behind me, I shouldn't think. Perhaps as early as today, but certainly within the next day or so. I mean to see this in court and have any charges as have been erroneously levied against my client dismissed immediately."

"Your *client* is a good man, but the King's man for all that."

"Actually," Brisby began, blissfully unaware that nobody has ever thought kindly on a person who begins sentences with *actually*, "my services to the king were coerced. I have no loyalty to the crown. I'm sure I've mentioned this once or twice over the past few years."

As per usual, Sheriff Barefoot ignored the protestations.

"If we don't have him out of here in short order, Sheriff, mobs enraged by the British villainy in Boston will storm out of doors looking for retribution, and their first stop will be here."

"You sound certain, Mr. Hedges."

"Denton."

The Sheriff snorted. "Mr. Hedges will suit me just fine. You fancy yourself quite adept at managing crowds, do you? Herding large groups of people to do your bidding? Why not wheel and deal the mob towards safer outlets for their rage? Perhaps you can have them irrevocably hobble the town a second time."

Well, if the Sheriff had cast Denton as a scoundrel, he might as well lean in to it. "I should hope that wouldn't be necessary."

Mr. Ecker pointed to Denton with a crooked, trembling finger. "This is the one? The goblin of non-importation?"

Denton's voice cracked, temporarily shaken from his pose of self-assurance. "Goblin?"

Barefoot grinned. "An apt enough description, if we're to go by your actions."

"I'm not here to argue with you. If you feel you have a legal justification to be holding this man here, then I would have you furnish it now. Otherwise, he and I shall retire to a place of safety."

"Where's that?" Barefoot didn't take a step towards Denton, but it felt as though he had. "If Boston is as chaotic as you claim…"

"There are havens to be found in Fidget's Mill."

"For you?"

Now it was Denton's turn to cast a glance towards the flintlock musket against the wall. Not that he had any intention of firing it – he just wanted to be sure nobody would be in a position to fire it at him. He had dramatically underestimated the enmity which awaited him here, it seemed. "Yes, even for me."

A glob of spit smacked into Denton's cheek. He turned and saw Mr. Ecker wiping the ratty cuff of his jacket across his mouth. The man's footwear was impeccable, but the rest of him was a mess.

Denton used his own sleeve to scrape off the sputum. "You make a habit of spitting in your own store, do you?"

The cobbler took a wet, hitching breath. "Only at goblins!"

"I'm not a goblin!"

"It's time for you to go," Sheriff Barefoot observed as though 'time for Denton to go' were a station of the clockface.

"Not without Brisby."

"You're very much mistaken there, Mr. Hedges."

Denton rolled his eyes and flopped his arms towards Brisby. "Would you like to weigh in here, Brisby?"

The doctor, sitting casually in one of Mr. Ecker's nicest chairs, glanced up with a look of supreme disappointment. Denton wondered if the good doctor realized his fate was being discussed, in a not at all hypothetical way. "How would I best weigh in?"

"Tell this muscular potato man what you want!"

"Will that count for a whole lot? I am, after all, a prisoner."

"Unjustly!"

The Sheriff scoffed. "He's safest in here, Mr. Hedges. I wish to see no harm come to the man, perhaps more so than yourself. I, after all, did not abandon him for two years, but rather stood watchful sentry."

"If that's true, you should consent to his being relocated, on a provisional basis. Give him two days elsewhere, and watch how the news of the Slaughter spreads through town. If the reaction is level-headed, I will personally see him returned here, pursuant to a proper trial. But if it *isn't*..."

"No!" Barefoot surveyed his immediate vicinity for something to slam his fist on. Finding nothing, he drove it into the considerable padding of his opposite palm. "That's cowardice, though I'm hardly surprised you can't see it as such!"

"And you would keep him here? That's idiocy, and the second clause of your most recently tendered insult applies to yourself now!"

"I could toss you in that cell this instant," the Sheriff snarled, "and the will of the people would be unanimously arrayed in support of my decision! In fact," he took a step towards Denton, "why don't I keep you there with the Doctor, and we'll let the rabble you so fear sort you out?"

Denton took a step back, and glanced over Sheriff Barefoot's shoulder. "Good heavens, man, the stalling is at an end. Are you ready with that thing or no?"

"Huh?" The Sheriff's face was placid as a secluded, scum-covered pond, but he clenched and unclenched his fists. It was easy enough to see where and how the man did most of his problem solving. Finally, he solved the problem, communicating the fact by clenching his fists so tightly that they turned a whiter shade than his face. He spun on his heel to see Dr. Brisby Houlihan pointing the musket directly at his head.

"Sorry," the doctor called back to Denton, allowing the Sheriff a dose of glancing second-hand remorse. "Had to ensure the wretched thing was loaded. I don't hold with these, you know."

Without consulting his brain, Denton's mouth made an *ugh* noise.

"Really not the thing to say, when threatening someone with a firearm."

"Why is that?"

"You're essentially telling him you've no intention of ever making good on the promise of violence which is your only claim to an upper hand here!"

"I never promised violence, nor denied I would make good on the promise which I never explicitly proffered in the first place!"

Doctors, Denton reflected, rarely negotiated. Perhaps if one combatted influenza through dialectic and biological sanctions, Brisby wouldn't be struggling so mightily with the basics of leverage and compulsion.

The Sheriff, who couldn't have looked more surprised if Brisby unzipped his skin and revealed himself to be made of fruits and vegetables, turned to Mr. Ecker, who was the only safe outlet for his frustration. "Why didn't you say something?"

"Like what?" The cobbler was standing to the side, without the excuse of being hard at work on a shoe.

"Like 'look out Sheriff, the doctor is reaching for the musket!'"

Mr. Ecker flipped his arms upwards like a marionette at a Puppetry 101 class. "How was I to know what the doctor intended to do with the musket?"

"By using your fucking brain, that's how!"

"There's no cussing in the cobbler's!"

Barefoot pointed to Denton. "He cussed first, I'm sure of it!"

"But not directly at me! Also, they've gone."

"What?" The Sheriff followed his finger to a pillar of empty space formerly occupied by Denton Hedges. "Goddamn you, Ecker!"

"There's no cussing in the cobbler's, Sheriff, and if you keep up with that I'll be forced to summon a secondary authority to reprimand you!"

"The only secondary authority in this town is my boot," Barefoot called over his shoulder as he flew from the room, "and once the secondary authority has run th…" the Sheriff probably kept the insult going, but by that point he had run out of earshot. Mr. Ecker savored the silence of the cobbler's once again. He closed the door of the open cell, lest any more rascals make trouble by imprisoning themselves unjustly as the Doctor had done, and set to work slapping leather soles together, or doing whatever the hell it was a cobbler actually did. Nobody had ever told Mr. Ecker, and more importantly, nobody had ever asked.

XI

"SHOULD I GET RID OF THIS?"

Denton didn't turn around to see what 'this' was, opting to ask as he kept running.

"The loathed firearm!" Brisby gasped. "Good gracious, it's been years since I've ran anywhere! Which is actually quite sad, come to think of it."

"Keep the firearm! It's all we have! And don't think sad thoughts until we've a moment to rest!" Denton veered around a corner, trusting Brisby to keep up with him. The considerable deposit of snow on the ground minimized the pedestrian traffic, which was good, but it also minimized podiatric traction, which was bad.

"It's just," Brisby called in a rattling wheeze, "that it both slows me down, as well as attracts attention!"

The good doctor had a point. Denton could see people poking their heads out of windows. It was uncommon enough, to see men running through town with a musket. That one of them should be a prisoner, and the other an author of a great deal of the town's recent misfortune, less common still.

How to draw attention away from them?

Denton remembered a moment from his childhood, when a beloved pet had died. It was a dog…or perhaps it had been a rabbit. He couldn't recall at this great a distance, and that was itself instructive. In any case, the creature had perished, and Denton had wept. So his father left the room, returned with a red-hot brand, and thrust it towards his son's chest. Young Denton had shrieked and fallen backwards out of his seat, pursued by a father with discord behind his eyes. 'Why are you doing this, father?' the boy had wailed. To which the father had responded, 'what are you thinking about right now?' Denton, unsure of whether or not this was a trick question, had replied 'the irate brand you hold in your hand.' 'Ah,' his father grinned, 'but not the grief for your [whatever animal it was]!' No, Denton conceded, not the grief for his whatever animal it was. His father had chased a diffuse, emotional misery away with more pressing physical ones. This was what passed for a lesson in the Hedges household. Granted, old Chester Hedges had also inflicted diffuse emotional misery of another sort with that stunt, but hey, nobody was perfect.

Denton hoped what the people of Fidget's Mill felt for him was more diffuse than Sheriff Barefoot let on, because he had a more pressing concern with which to distract them.

"Whatever you do," Denton wheezed over his shoulder, "don't stop running." He took a deep breath, and in the closest he could muster to a town crier voice without sacrificing speed, he shouted "Slaughter in Boston! Slaughter in Boston!"

And then he shouted a whole lot more, while running a long, roundabout loop back towards Gutter Lane.

The Sheriff was a big, beefy slab of humanity, but the sort who looked like he might be deceptively fleet of foot. This was itself deceptive, for Sheriff Barefoot was precisely as slow as a man of his density ought to be.

He slipped and slammed his way through the streets, following the sound of Denton's voice. Why was the buffoon shouting so?

And, more to the point, why was everybody coming outside, milling around and looking confused?

"Out of the way!" he called.

"There's been a Slaughter in Boston, Sheriff!" a woman called out to him.

"I know!" he replied.

At this, a man stepped directly in front of him. "You knew? For how long have you known?"

Barefoot shouldered the man to the ground. "Not long, now get out of my blessed way before I you all in manacles!"

"Sheriff, wait!"

"We need more information, Sheriff!"

"What else, Sheriff, can you tell us?"

"Sheriff Sheriff Sheriff!"

Goddamnit all, had these people been standing behind their doors, already decked in coats and hats, simply waiting for an excuse to trundle outside and get in his blessed way? How were they all on the street, in his blessed way this quickly?

A crush of concerned Fidgetonians surrounded Sheriff Barefoot and contracted. The lawman roared in frustration as he ground his heels into the snow, skidding to a halt. He had to wave his hands out at his sides to maintain his balance, like a clown. Curse this whole day!

"Listen to me," he demanded in a voice that would brook no dispute, "the man informing you of this slaughter is none other than Denton Hedges, the man whose designs for the Mill proved so ruinous all those years ago!"

"Two years," a Fidgetonian helpfully clarified.

"Yes, whatever. Now I am in pursuit of Denton Hedges, who has lately sprung his old accomplice Brisby Houlihan from custody!" Pre-emptively begging his God for forgiveness, Barefoot smothered his professional scruples in the name of speedy conflict resolution. Unrest born of the Slaughter in Boston, he could perhaps handle. A fugitive from justice, he could certainly handle. Both at once? That would simply not do. Best to see one of the matters closed as quickly as possible. "Brisby, you shall remember, is a lackey of British allegiance!"

Gasps, jeers. "The very British who perpetuated the Slaughter?" People asked a lot of rhetorical questions like that, and Barefoot let them. He did not, for example, say something snidey like 'no, the *other* British, who invented algebra,' because that would not be productive.

Instead, he said "of course," as though the townspeople were making a very good point that he could not have himself come up with.

"Do you think Brisby has some connection to the Slaughter?"

Barefoot wondered if he could pay his penitence in installments, or if his God would demand it all at once. "I can't possibly say at this juncture, but I intend to ask him."

The crowd, without having to consult itself, parted before the Sheriff. "Then ask him, Sheriff, and after him!"

"But," one especially pedantic townsperson added, "not in that order!"

Barefoot didn't need to be told twice. He resumed his mad dash after Denton, now having nothing but footprints to guide him.

"You're leaving prints!" Brisby cried from what sounded to Denton like an ever-increasing distance behind him.

"What?"

"Footprints! In the snow!" They'd fled past the most populous parts of the Mill, now flooded and confused with Fidgetonians asking each other if they were certain the sprinting man said *slaughter* and not, perhaps, *daughter*, for maybe he was simply beside himself with joy at his distant wife's deliverance? But if Barefoot managed to navigate the confusion and follow them this far, the mad dance-diagram of the central areas would resolve into two parallel print paths, which terminated where Denton and Brisby had most recently placed their feet.

Denton finally slowed to a halt, knowing it would make resuming his frantic sprint that much more difficult, but also knowing that trying to turn around and examine their backtrail as he ran would see him kissing the telltale snow that damned them.

"Damn," he mumbled, because that was what the snow was indeed doing. The prints were bolder than Denton had imagined them, ovular pools of darkness in frozen ivory. But they couldn't well go anywhere without leaving prints, could they?

...no, they couldn't. But *somebody* could.

Denton let his hands go limp and scrunched up his forehead. As always, it was easy enough to see where a man did his problem solving. He thought for a while, just generally, and then he thought loudly, as specifically as he could, over as large an area as possible.

And then, he turned, resumed running, and hoped.

From the edge of the field, a shadow shifted. It once again bade the subject of its observation farewell, silently, from a distance. Yazbirth Bicklebog was always so busy, the shadow never wished to disturb him.

Turning towards town, the shadow coalesced into the shape of a turkey, and said "choff!" to no one at all.

Denton and Brisby arrived at the house in which Miss Carsis was putting him up, which he supposed was either 31, 32, 34 or 35 Gutter Lane, depending on the numerical conventions employed on this single-sided street. Without explaining anything, he swung the door open and gestured the physician inside.

"But our footprints!" he cried, as he turned around to see a blanket of white which could barely be bothered to part for the coy little runlet which gave Gutter Lane its name. "Where are our footprints?"

"I picked them up," Denton mumbled dismissively. "Get inside!"

After a brief struggle in which Brisby blocked his own ingress by holding the musket horizontally, like a puppy learning how to carry a big stick through a small door, the doctor scrambled into the house. Denton crossed the threshold, then turned back to the winter. "Do you want to come in?"

"Oh, so kind of you to offer," No-Good Bulstrode clucked as he brushed away the most recently laid footprints with a sooty wing, "but I perhaps ought to double back a ways, and expunge some more of your leavings, right?"

Denton felt an overwhelming urge to pat Bulstrode on his tiny little head, but thought better of it. "Thank you for your help."

"Afraid you left me with no choice, chappie. Footprints leading right to Miss Carsis' just wouldn't have done, not at all." The turkey turned and waddled back the way Denton came, though Bulstrode's voice somehow seemed to hover in the now-empty space the mouth had lately occupied. "Not to minimize my desire to lend a hand, or wing as it were, to an old acquaintance. Rummy to have you back, boy!"

To this, Denton said nothing, for it was certainly not rummy to *be* back. Not even twenty-four hours in the Mill and he'd challenged a friend to a duel and been chased by a mob. These were truly the times that were hard on men's souls. *Say, not bad!* Denton made a mental note to jot that one down. He forgot immediately.

"Can you get rid of that?" Denton heard Peggy's voice drifting down the hall, and wished he'd gone in first.

"That's what *I* said!" Brisby whined in response.

Spacious was not a word Denton would ever have applied to Miss Carsis' home on Gutter Lane, but then, he'd never been in the lodging next door. It was mainly just a long wooden hallway, perfectly suited for drifting voices, less than adequate for human bodies. At one end of the hallway was the front door; at the other end was a closet that, under duress, one might be compelled to call a room. Mattresses that were almost certainly stuffed with hay somehow creaked under the weight of his children, who sat upon them with crossed legs. Peggy stood defensively between Brisby and the kids, arms akimbo.

Much to her credit, her first question to Denton wasn't *who is this* or *what is he doing here*, but "can we dispose of the weapon?"

"I'm afraid not," Denton replied.

"Well, then we must find a spot for it, beyond the reach of the children." Again, Denton felt blessed to have a wife that understood the exigencies of patriotism.

"But mother," Lawrence whimpered, "I'm quite old enough to b-"

Denton shushed him, and Lawrence was shushed. Without another word, Brisby handed Peggy the musket, and she tromped back down the hall. Where she expected to find a hiding place for a bulky firearm was anybody's guess, but if anybody could find such a space, it was Peggy.

Turning to the physician, Denton saw him gazing longingly at his children. His initial response was to be unnerved, until he remembered:

Brisby had a family of his own, one he had not seen in years. Had he been permitted to communicate with them? He thought not; whenever Denton had popped his head in to Brisby's practice in Boston, there was never any word on the man beyond 'still out'. But how, then, had the practice stayed afloat? This was a question for another day.

Without drawing his eyes from the increasingly uncomfortable young ones, Brisby mumbled "we really ought to get rid of the firearm at the earliest convenience."

"Peggy will find a secure place to hide it." Denton padded quietly up to Brisby and placed a hand on his right shoulder. He meant it to be comforting, but the doctor started at his touch. "Sorry."

"It's fine." Brisby crossed his left arm across his body and patted Denton's hand with his own. "I suggest this because…if you have a gun, hidden or not, at some point the gun will be fired. By you, or…" He wouldn't say *at you* to the man in front of his children, but Denton could gratefully fill in the blank. The doctor could be a bit of a fool, but he wasn't an idiot.

Peggy returned to the room, sans musket. "I agree with…"

Denton failed to fill in this blank for a moment, before recalling himself. "Yes, this is Dr. Brisby Houlihan. Brisby, this is my wife Peggy."

"I've heard so much about you," they each said to each other in synchrony, and smiled likewise.

"These are my children, Lawrence and Annabelle."

"Pleased to meet you," Brisby told them with aching sincerity. The man had a reserve of affection he'd been unable to tap for years, and here it came bubbling to the surface, despite everything. Even Lawrence seemed moved by the display of orphaned love.

The doctor turned back to Denton and, with redoubled intensity, reiterated his position on the musket.

"I've hidden it," Peggy informed him, seemingly more for form's sake than anything. She wanted the musket gone as well. In the abstract, so did Denton, but he also knew a single musket shot could prove an essential bargaining chip, should things go even *more* sideways.

"I don't think you understand the nature of the universe." It was a preposterous statement offered with enough gravity to ensnare the unsmiling Hedges in its orbit. "A loaded gun wants to be fired. And it *will* be, given enough time."

Denton meditated on this. He certainly couldn't argue the point. "The hope, then, is that one of us is holding it at the moment of discharge. Holding it the right way round," he clarified.

"Hope is wonderful," Peggy opined, "but not something upon which I'd be willing to stake the lives of anyone in this room."

Brisby, grateful for the inclusion, nodded softly to her, and turned back to Denton.

With a feeling akin to remembering some pressing obligation to which one was expected to attend several hours ago, Denton realized that the decision of what to do with the musket was going to be entirely his. He sighed, crossed the groaning floorboards to the mattress upon which his children sat, and plopped himself down next to them. Annabelle leaned her head into his right flank, and Denton wondered if she could hear his heart breaking like a promise.

What kind of a childhood was he giving these kids? He had agitated for Colonial rights on the pretense of creating a better world for them, and here they all were, fugitives from a Slaughter, huddled in a cubby barely big enough for two, next door to a witch, in a town that almost unanimously wanted their father dead. And the likelihood of the Fidgetonians bearing his offspring anything less than ill will was vanishing.

This couldn't go on. The cycle of violence had to be broken.

"I'll dispose of it tomorrow," Denton announced. "Before sundown. I promise."

The miasmic tension in the room made itself known by its whooshing outrush.

Later, one of Miss Carsis' apprentices brought them dinner. Brisby and the Hedges played word games as they ate, and laughed themselves to sleep. While at the other end of the hall, tucked clumsily above the jutting lip of the doorframe, the joyless musket slumbered patiently.

XII

THE MOON DASHED DRUNKENLY ACROSS THE night, as if loath to hear the words being spread beneath its silver corpselight.

Denton's thoughtless, opportunistic announcement of the Boston Slaughter was quickly corroborated by more comprehensive (though scarcely more illuminating) accounts. As the word spread, the word changed, from 'Slaughter' to 'Massacre'. Popular response to the Massacre was immediate, triggering a reflexive (and retributive) instinct that would have made a lioness proud. But unlike a sleeping beast awoken by idiot prey, the people of the Colonies, and Fidget's Mill more specifically, had no clear outlet through which to exercise their fury. They knew what they wanted – not to placate the British, but the extirpate them – but they had no idea how to make that happen without suffering further casualties themselves.

This, in a strange way, put them on a similar footing with Denton. He knew what he wanted – to prevent the people of the Colonies from suffering further casualties – but not precisely how to make that happen without acquiescing to the British.

Between Denton and the Fidgetonians, there was perhaps a common goal to unite them. But between them there was also Dr. Brisby Houlihan, who through no fault of his own had become emblematic of Bigger Things.

Along with word of the Massacre, implausible tales of a brazen jailbreak festered and replicated, spread by none other than Sheriff Barefoot. This accomplished the dual purpose of stoking resentment against Denton and Brisby, as well as absolving himself of responsibility for his incompetence. Mr. Ecker could have contradicted the tales, but simply couldn't be bothered.

Hours later, the sun rose on a world that had irrevocably changed. Which wasn't saying much, because that was true of every day.

In Denton's case, rosy-finger dawn reached through a high, thin window, poking him with beams of dancing dust, and said "wake up, dickhead."

Dickhead snorted and lunged up to a seated position. He looked around the room, at four sleeping faces; his wife, his children, and his …friend. Yes. They'd gone out on limbs for each other, and that was what friends did, didn't they? They did. There was no point wondering anymore.

So what did that make Mr. Increase? Hadn't they quite literally gone out on limbs for, and *with* each other?

It wasn't until he reached up to run his hands down his face that he realized how sweaty his palms were. He grunted quietly and dried his hands on a blanket doing a rough impression of burlap. Taking a handful, he lifted it to dry the hand-sweat off of his face, which he had just dried on the blanket. Another glance confirmed that everyone was still asleep, which was wonderful news, as it meant no witnesses to the unfortunate comedy lately concluded.

Alright, he resolved silently, *realistic goals*. He had overwhelmed himself last time he was here by trying to chart actionable courses with unattainable ideals. He needed a fixed point towards which to run. *Today is the day for disposing of the musket, and that is all.* If, in disposing of the musket, he could devise a way to score himself a goal, then so much the better. But that was secondary. What mattered was that the sun not set on a musket in Denton Hedges' possession.

He rose from the cot and padded quietly around the room, so as not to awaken anyone. In this he was successful, up until the moment he shook his wife and whispered 'wake up', because he couldn't find the spot where she had hidden the musket.

"Oh, hello there!"

Denton jumped at the voice assaulting him as he stepped out the door, but what made him give a dull wail was the sepulchral creaking of the door hinge. He hadn't recalled it ever doing that before.

No-Good Bulstrode stood on the gutter-sliced river of white, an onyx moon against a bone powder sky. "So glad I ran in to you," the moon clucked, as though this was the last place it would have expected to see Denton.

Shivering his nerves away, Denton ran his hand throu…he paused. He hadn't done the hand-through-the-hair tic in, gosh, at least a yonk or two. Good grief. *Realistic, achievable goals. Don't panic.* It was hard to not panic, when your anxiety was sufficient to send your hand hair-ward while it was clutching the barrel of a musket. "For a specific reason?"

"A turkey can't be glad as a general, unmoved matter of course?"

"A turkey can do whatever it pleases, but you're not a turkey." Denton delivered this as though it were a particularly damning legal argument, and to his immense satisfaction, this was how Bulstrode appeared to receive it.

"Well, that's true enough. Miss Carsis would very much appreciate a brief word with you, and if you'll pop on over, I trust you'll be similarly thrilled with your having temporarily waylaid whatever schedule you've been fancying for the day."

It was close enough, Denton figured. Without another word, he stepped a few feet to his left and knocked on the door to Miss Carsis' home.

Or made to do so, at any rate. The wood retreated just as his knuckle was rushing to meet it as though it were the door's biggest fan. It opened not on one of Miss Carsis' apprentices, but on the docent herself.

"Get in here," she hissed. Which was really something to hear, given the sentence had no sibilants in it.

The door slammed shut behind Denton, which was how he worked out that he was suddenly inside Miss Carsis' home. He didn't recall moving his feet or stepping through the door, and careful retrospection only intensified the certainty that he had done neither of those things.

Dropping the musket in shock, the better to run a hand through his hair, he once again mulled on just what the witch was capable of.

"They want you dead."

Denton, once again clutching the gun as though its defensive capacity hewed closer to a security blanket than a cannon, had a splitting headache, like he'd tried to crack his skull open and hide the musket inside. That would be one way of wrapping his head around it, ha, ha. A more fruitful way, he had no doubt.

"Which they?" was all he could say in response.

Miss Carsis clapped a hand on her forehead, and muttered under her breath. Anyone else, Denton would have assumed them to be talking to themselves. With Miss Carsis, he didn't feel entirely confident making such an assumption. "They! The people of the Mill! Have you been listening to a word I've said?"

"Oh, yes, nearly all of them. I just…" It was one thing to be abetting people whose names were being snarled by a mob. To be the person who answered to that name was qualitatively different. "How dead?"

Miss Carsis shook her head, hand still glued to her forehead.

Denton's eyebrows did a little dance without consulting him. At the end, his face was warped into a prolonged, pained wink. "Right. Silly question. But brainstorming sessions are often full of these."

"This isn't a brainstorming session." She floated across the room. Not literally – at least, not as far as Denton could tell. Miss Carsis was wearing what could best be described as an off-white apron with ambitions to be either a dress or a jumpsuit, the consequence of which were feet obscured from his view. But he thought he heard bare soles thupping along the floorboards. Hoped he did. "This is me warning you. Stay indoors. I will bring you supplies. When the furor dies down, leave town. I can't even imagine why you returned, and I confess to providing you lodging with an eye to finding out. But you and the physician have become more trouble than you're worth."

"Where would we go?"

"I'll arrange for you to go anywhere you like. Back to Boston or to Prussia, makes no difference to me. In fact, further afield might be preferable, but that's your prerogative. Again, I care not. As long as it isn't here."

Denton opened his mouth to reply, something along the lines of how Miss Carsis was evincing a disturbing lack of interest in the fate of her homeland…but all that came forth was a bubble of gastric reflux. The fact was, he was no longer in a position to claim he was here on behalf of a Cause. He had come to prevent civil unrest – beyond foolish, as though he were in the least prepared to do that – but he had *become* the civil unrest. So, really, the best way to accomplish his goal would be to get himself and Brisby out of town, as soon as possible.

It was beautiful, in a strange way. He'd become the self-chasing scapegoat giving the townspeople a second chance to run him off. The hopeful martyr that lurked within all privileged white men's hearts was gladdened by the prospect: at long last, a justification for feeling so overburdened by the world! And here was Miss Carsis, ready to facilitate the move. The kids would love a change of scenery, wouldn't they? This was all almost too good to be true.

There was, after all, no reason for Denton to stay in the Mill.

Literally not a single reason.

Except, of course, for the duel with Mr. Increase.

Which was stupid, of course.

But, still.

Just below the pocket in Denton's heart that hungered for self-pity, there was a slightly larger one that demanded self-respect. That this demand was often unfulfilled did nothing to silence its stridency. There were certain indignities with which Denton could cope. Being slandered as a villain, or tool of the British, this was one of them. It was an outrageous inversion of the truth, of everything for which he had struggled and sacrificed, and yet it was a cruel fiction which nonetheless respected him as a man capable of taking an active role in events.

The title of 'coward', though…that was something else. And that something else was what Denton could look forward to, if he fled from an affair of honor. Base coward, Denton Hedges. How could he go on, tolerating such calumny? He could move far away, and never meet a familiar face for as long as he lived. But when the wind rattled the eaves at night, he would know that, somewhere in the world, there was a town where he was spoken of as a coward.

The heart trembled at the thought, even as the brain screamed that it was not a thought worth trembling over. On balance, it was a small price to pay for his loved ones, and the good of the Mill. It was, his brain reassured him, all well and good. Bearing this burden would only heighten his mantle as a self-made martyr. It was win-win!

Yes, it was utterly stupid.

And childish.

It was childish and stupid.

But.

Still.

"Let me think about it," Denton finally replied.

"Bah." Miss Carsis waved Denton away, and he was back on his feet and marching out the door before he knew it. In his memory, this was something he consciously undertook to do, something in which he had taken an active role. But in the moment, it didn't feel that way at all.

XIII

ONE THING MISS CARSIS HADN'T SAID ANYTHING about was the musket. So he wouldn't be able to get rid of it through her.

He could throw it into a snowdrift, of course, to be found sodden and useless in the thaw come Spring. Or he could bury it. There were plenty of ways he could get rid of it, safe and easy as could be, just as he promised his wife.

But none of these ways were clever, in the way giving it to a person in return for something else would be clever.

As Denton slithered back into the home in which his family and friend were taking shelter (still sleeping, and so oblivious to just how *much* shelter they were taking) and shut the door behind him, he felt nothing more strongly than the need to feel clever again.

So upon whom could he thrust the musket, and what might

convince them to accept the thrust?

Despite the mad world into which he'd awoken, he retained enough clarity to recognize that strolling out the door with a musket in hand and no destination in mind would likely get him no further than face-down in a ditch. So he returned it to its hiding place, tiptoed back down the hall, and placed a soft palm on his wife's shoulder. Gently, he shook her like his own self-confidence.

"Peggy," he informed her.

"Mwuh?" As she lifted her head from the pillow, a lengthening bead of saliva stretched between its source and its destination, desperate to coax them back together. It was a common sight for Denton, and held an inexplicable charm.

"It's of exceeding importance than you not let the kids or Brisby out of this house. You should keep yourself similarly..." Good grief, he had almost said *interred*, "...ensconsed, within these walls."

There was a moment of dull concentration, then a bolt of serrated awareness shot through Peggy. She didn't sit up, because she didn't need to. She was *awake*, and they both knew it. "We're in danger here?"

"Yes."

"Of a mortal sort?"

"I'm afraid so. But you're all safe as long as you stay here."

Another moment of intense introspection, during which Peggy made a quick survey of the way Denton was constructing these injunctions. "And you won't be following your own advice, I take it?"

"There are things I must do."

Peggy reached out and took his hand. She squeezed it tightly, but didn't waste her breath in protest. Denton felt a warm bloom of love within his chest, followed by a shudder of revulsion. Love for his wife, who was endlessly understanding of her husband's compulsions and priorities. Revulsion for himself, who was forever putting his beloved in the position of needing to exercise her unparalleled trust and patience. Denton leaned down and kissed her tersely on the forehead, and then a few inches lower, for a few seconds longer. He wondered if there were any more strands of saliva engaged in the tragic, vain task of holding their lips together as they parted. It was a sign of the easy intimacy that he felt for Peggy, that this flight of biological fancy should be contain more romance than repulsion.

She cupped his cheek in her hand and studied him like a map of the wilderness she would soon be exploring in the dark. "That's bullshit and we both know it." She said this without malice, with nothing but patience and affection in her voice. And so the blood it drew was not crimson but a starless, bible black.

They remained that way for a long time, Denton kneeling over his wife, she lying beneath him, suspended in the syrupy depths of their children's somnolent inspirations. There could be no mistaking whom, in that moment, was tending to whom.

Denton wanted to reach out and brush away the lock of silky hair that had fallen to obscure one of the eyes that had held and beheld him through ages of famine and plenty, but demurred. Not only because he was terrified of how he might see himself, cast and reflected upon that mournful pool, but because if he reached out to her, she would feel how his hands were shaking.

Because they were shaking. A *lot.*

The more things changed, the more they stayed the same. *Boy, I ought to write that one down too*, he noted joylessly.

It *was* bullshit and they both knew it. There it was, stated in a cool simplicity that precluded objection. What could Denton say to that?

Nothing. Nothing that he could think of, anyway.

Only that he loved her, and that he was sorry. Which he did, and he was.

With that said, he rose and plodded down the long hall to the front door, feeling like the biggest idiot in the universe. This was all bullshit, and he didn't need to be doing any of this. They could wait patiently here for things to die down, and then Miss Carsis would get them all out safely.

So why was he doing this? Oh, plenty of reasons. Good reasons.

Filled with shame and ambition (and how often one begat the other), he threw on his coat and stepped out into Gutter Lane, doing his damndest to think of nothing but the musket. It was easier that way.

Someone shouted "hey!" and Denton turned towards it source, which was why the shoe hit him in the forehead instead of the ear.

Sole-slapped, he struggled to think through the spreading puddle of consternation. Had someone managed to leap his full height to dropkick him in the head? If so, it was an impressive leap and a fairly unimpressive kick.

After a moment, reason reasserted itself to its prior position of being heard and disregarded by the more chimp-like passions. No, he hadn't been dropkicked. Someone had thrown a shoe.

But who?

Probably the young girl who was pointing at Denton and shouting "there he is!"

Her voice didn't carry far through the snow, but it carried far enough to summon a group of large men who looked like they had been gathered to discuss the art of hoisting large logs over their shoulders.

As a single unit, the goon squad looked to the girl, looked to her finger, and followed it all the way to Denton. He was but a few blocks from Gutter Lane, on a wider avenue flanked by crooked, two-story hovels. That the hovels had two stories indicated that this was probably one of the wealthier parts of town, in as much as there was any wealth in the Mill not locked up in the mansions, illiquid and by now useless.

The one positive thing about being faced with a horde of lumberjacks charging through the snow was that they were comically slow. What they were capable of once they caught up to you was no laughing matter, but to watch them in pursuit brought to mind a ballet troupe of sloths.

Giant sloths…

"But where?" he cried out loud. And he took off running, because even if it wasn't the answer he was looking for, 'away from the frowny musclemen' was still an admissible response.

Much to his chagrin, he was reminded that snow slowed *everybody* down. So began a chase remarkable for its inverse relationship between speed and stakes.

XIV

THE AXE HIT THE LOG WITH A MIGHTY *THWACK*, but the log refused to split, which was an outrage. The log was only about eight inches in diameter, and a foot and a half long. Eminently splittable, that size of log.

Fithian grunted and let the axe fall to the ground, strewn with the shavings of more amenable woodchunks. Her lower back and shoulders burned, but it was the burn of a hard day's work, a burn that thrived not on oxygen but weakness. It would leave strength in its wake, and the next time she had to split wood for the fire, the burn would be less. So it had been for the past few years, and so it would always be.

Frowning, she hoisted the axe up towards her face, blade-first, no longer frightened of the instrument as she had been when she had first taken it up. Axes were for men, as was physical labor. She had never been permitted to be near one, prior to the collapse of the Mill. But now management of the Lowestoft property had fallen largely to her, and so she had arrogated unto herself these forbidden tasks. And damn it all if they weren't satisfying! Coming in after a long, sweaty day of toil, flopping into bed exhausted, only to start it all over the next day…it was wonderful! Leisure was all well and good, but how could one ever appreciate it without a marked contrast?

Halting the blade inches from her eyes with her toned back and arm muscles, Fithian inspected the edge and found it wanting. Dull, of course! The alternative was that her muscles were inadequate to the task of splitting wood, which she knew damn well wasn't the case.

Dull axe clutched in one hand, she took a wide, even *leisurely* lap of the mansion, imagining the pleasant shade of gold this field might well become, in just a few short months. Yazbirth had seemed unusually optimistic about corn. As in, unusually optimistic about the prospects of corn, in relation to the optimism evinced for other crops. Not that Yazbirth was often pessimistic about corn, and was now unusually optimistic…

Fithian had fallen into the habit of clarifying things to herself, despite knowing full well what she meant. She didn't often speak to other people anymore, but in the event that she *did*, she wanted to be prepared to anticipate and head off any misunderstandings. And, of course, there were always so many misunderstandings to be had when one's primary dialectic partner was Yazbirth Bicklebog.

Speak of the Familiar: there was Yazbirth, standing at the edge of the northmost field, staring at an unremarkable spot in the grey, featureless sky.

The whetstone was in the shed at the point where the property sloped to its lowest point, and Fithian wanted to get there sooner rather than later. She often split wood with nothing but a thin shawl around her shoulders: the body heat generated by the labor was sufficient to keep her warm in the New England winter. But if she stopped moving for too long, the chill wasted no time in slipping through her pores and swapping out her bones for icicles.

Still, she stopped to stare at Yazbirth's staring at nothing. After several moments, when she felt Old Man Winter starting to get fresh, she jogged in place a bit and called to her Familiar. "What are you doing?"

Yazbirth arced his head towards his consort, slow and steady, unaware that there was a race to win. "Someoneself is looking for Myself."

"What?" Fithian hugged herself for warmth. She'd become adept enough with the axe to unconsciously turn the blade away from herself. Fool me once, etc. "Who?"

"Myself isn't certain…" Yazbirth sniffed the air, which was purely for effect. But even the densest of Familiars needed to secure a firm grasp on theatricality, if they were to triumph in the world of humans. "But Myself suspects that Himself or Herself seeks Myself simply as a conduit to locate Yourself."

The air had gone from a crisp nip to a slavering bite. She drew her paltry garments as far around her shoulders as she could manage and nodded to Yazbirth. "Go and fetch them, then. I've got to sharpen this before I'm cut down by the cold."

"But what if Himself or Herself means Yourself harm?"

"Like I said," she called back over her shoulder, "I'm off to sharpen my axe."

Yazbirth winced at the mere intimation of human viscera, knowing that the threat wasn't idle just for being off-handed. But still, orders were orders. He set off to find the source of the niggling call that had nested in the back of his mind.

WHERE WHERE HELP WHERE WHERE HELP WHERE HELP HELP WHERE HELP WHERE HELP HELP

Each pounding step through the snow Denton took, each pounding beat of his heart in his throat, brought another call of psychic distress. Initially the hopeful beacons of despair were more comprehensive calls, imploring Yazbirth or Bulstrode or Miss Carsis or *someone* to make his or her or its location known in some spooky fashion. But as lethargy weighed down Denton's limbs, the approach of his tireless pursuers felt less like some amusing goofball comedy, and more like the inexorable creep of a grand tragedy. Their pace was slow, but consistent. Denton had been faster, but he was once again leaving prints, prints that drew closer and closer together as first his natural energy, and then his trembling adrenaline, failed him.

As he fled through the Mill, he heard shouts rise in his wake. His passage was going far from unnoticed, and if he wasn't very much mistaken, the cortege in search of a funeral he had been leading was growing larger by the minute.

Or maybe even hour. How long had he been running? It felt like an eternity. And all for something that he and Peggy both knew was bullshit. If only he had another Slaughter about which he could shout!

Wheezing, he threw himself against the corner of a building that looked and felt wet. The wood buckled under his shoulders, nearly spilling him face-first into the snow. It wouldn't have been the first time in this mad dash through the Mill, but it may well have been the last. He wasn't sure he had the strength to scramble back to his feet, should the need arise. Or afall, as it were.

He turned around to see what seemed like the entire population of the Massachusetts Colony round a corner, do a zany double-take, fixate on him, and resume the chase.

A humiliating moan escaped his chest, and he found the strength to, if not keep running, then start to almost, but not quite, fall over in the direction of 'away'.

He wondered if they remembered how he had inspired them years ago, how he had worked so hard on their behalf to

To what? Destroy the town?

Goddamnit.

HELP WHERE WHERE HELP HELP HELP WHERE WHERE HELP SLOTH

"Quickly!" Yazbirth shouted from an alley. "Follow Myself!" The giant sloth turned and ran.

Denton turned to follow, and after five exhilarating seconds, Yazbirth had traveled five exhilarating feet. "Could you just tell me where to go," Denton shouted as he slid up behind the sloth, "and I'll meet you there?"

"Oh." Yazbirth hung his head, feeling this more a rebuff of his company than a referendum on his speed. "Alright." The sloth gave languid directions to the Lowestoft mansion, and Denton sprinted away before the directions had been wholly completed. He had enough to get headed in the right direction, at least.

Alright, Yazbirth thought, the time has come. Now I shall prove my mettle and stop his pursuers in their tracks!

But how? he wondered as they filed around, through and past him.

Very unfortunate, that. Fithianself would almost certainly not be pleased with this influx of unexpected visitors. He could only hope that she was getting her axe very sharp indeed.

The axe hit the log with a mighty *thwack*, and this time the log got with the program and fell to the ground in two reasonably sized chunks.

Fithian grinned, flushed with satisfaction. She'd really let the blade of the axe have it on the whetstone, and she expected it to retain its edge for quite a while, at least until the thaw, at wh-

The air mumbled and grumbled around her. She lifted her eyes to the treeline at the edge of the field, expecting to see something portentous like a flock of birds taking wing at once, cawing in ill-boding cacophony. What she saw instead was a crow alighting upon a high, crooked bough, which could well have been *A Sign*, except *Signs* didn't typically look around and then defecate when they thought nobody was watching. Omens came in all shapes and sizes, but they usually possessed a certain portion of dignity.

She shrugged off the atmospheric disturbance and tossed the two halves of the split log onto the appropriate pile, and drew an unsplit log from the other.

The dullness of the day was rent by an apocalyptic clearing of the throat, followed by what could only be described as a bag full of horseshoes being shaken very quickly.

Whatever it was, it wasn't her imagination. Fithian returned to the mansion and grabbed a heavy coat from the hook just inside the front door, then strode back outside, clutching the axe awkwardly around the center as though she didn't know exactly how to swing it.

Her grip loosened as she saw Denton Hedges sprinting towards her, trailing what must surely be the majority of Fidget's Mill. Their chase led them directly through what would eventually be, she hoped, a swirling sea of corn. If only it were that *now*, instead of a flat blanket of white. Denton might have had a place to hide.

Curiously enough, Fithian was hardly surprised that the first time she should see Denton in years would be at the business end of a bloodthirsty mob. He was a likable enough guy, but whether intentionally or not, he tended to ride his likability right up to the precipice of contempt, and then over. It was a bit like trying to go over a waterfall in a burlap sack.

So here was the mind that had been calling out for Yazbirth's. And where was the Familiar? Likely playing caboose to the hate train, which he had surely conducted into this unfortunate station.

Gritting her teeth, Fithian switched her grip on the axe to one that was, in form and function, clearly not fucking around. She could afford to advertise that she knew how to use the axe – she still had a spectral sloth up her sleeve, if it came to that.

She knew when Denton had gotten within shouting distance because she heard him shouting. His voice materialized mid-word, for he had been shouting the entire time.

"….ET BUT I DON'T KNOW HOW TO CONVI-"

Fithian stopped listening, knowing there would be nothing worth hearing. Instead she turned her attentions inward, trying to think of ways to cast the rabble forth from her property, ideally without Denton in tow. Sure, the fool had done great and irrevocable damage to the Mill. But, selfishly, Fithian was glad of it. His actions had indirectly saved her from a loveless marriage and a life of tedious leisure. More than perhaps anyone in the town, she had benefitted from the dramatic reversals of fortune wrought by the last two years.

The least she could do was ensure the unknowing agent of her triumph not be torn apart like a delicious chicken leg.

She pushed her focus back outside of herself as Denton skidded to a halt in front of her.

"I have a gun!" he cried.

She flinched. This could make things worse, rather than better. The air didn't just mumble and grumble these days, it gossiped – she was already aware of the Boston Massacre. Any echoes of it here in the Mill would bring things to a head, which would quickly find itself on the chopping block. "Where is the gun?"

"The gun is at my current place of residence!"

"…then you don't really *have* it, do you?"

Denton opened and closed his mouth a few times, struggling to formulate words to say, struggling to draw the breath necessary to say them. He turned around and saw the mob rushing towards them as a wave eager to break upon the rocks. A small moan escaped him, and he turned back to Fithian. "You don't seem worried!"

"Why would I be? They like me." She felt the knuckle of her middle finger crack against the shaft of the axe – she was gripping it more tightly than she realized.

Efforts to loosen her grip proved fruitless – it was hard to remain calm while being half-surrounded by a slow-forming crescent of furious eyebrows, some attached to bodies that could do quite a lot of damage, the rest hanging off of faces that would happily cheer on the former category.

Yes, these people liked Fithian. And so far, she'd done nothing to temper their affection. She clearly hadn't called Denton to herself; he had come unbidden. But the moment she made any halfway conciliatory noises, she would be marked by their scorn. She could just take a step back, let them ha-

Oh, who was she kidding.

She took a step forward, hefted the axe theatrically, and wondered aloud, "what's all this about, then?"

XV

THE MOB THRUST A HUNDRED FINGERS TOWARD Denton, like a giant flesh hedgehog going on the defensive.

"He harbors an accomplice to the Boston Massacre!" came one raised voice.

Denton blanched. "No I don't!" He added, "also, it's the Boston *Slaughter*."

A young woman cried "No it isn't!"

"Any man who sympathizes with the English is an accomplice to their depredations!" This from what sounded like the mouth of a babe.

"Doubly so for a man who implements the policies of the depredators!"

A great chorus of furious agreement.

"Besides," another voice cut through the soup, "even ignoring his sheltering of the villain, he himself has inflicted heartless indignities upon our town!"

"That he has!"

"Yes!"

"Of course!"

"For this alone," came a completely different voice, as easily as if it had proffered the first sentence in this contiguous group-thought, "we ought to see him hang!"

"Here here!"

"Not necessarily here, but certainly somewhere!"

"What?"

"I thought you meant you wanted to hang him here!"

"No, I'm not wed to any particular location for the hanging!"

"Oh, my mistake!"

"Quite alright!"

Denton shook his head, summoned up his most lawyerly line of reasoning, and rose to his own defense, knowing that the sentence for conviction was death. "Listen to me!"

For a shock, they did. Denton cleared his throat and thundered, "It's the Boston *Slaughter*!"

"No it *isn't*!"

"It is!"

The mob collapsed upon itself for a moment, and trembled with consultation. As one organism, it nodded and bloomed once again. "No, it isn't!" was their conclusion.

"I named it," Denton averred with indisputable conviction, "it's the Boston *Slaughter*."

Fithian racked her eyes between Denton and the mob, puzzled beyond the ability of words to convey. "What does it matter?" she whispered to him.

"A lot," he replied in a stentorian boom, "that's what it matters!" He turned back to the mob, clapping his hands together at sternum height, as he often did in the courtroom before making a big deal out of something that didn't matter at all. "Boston *Massacre* has no euphonic resonance. It's an ugly, leaden phrase. *–oss –ass*, those are the most prominent sounds. You see?"

"Well," a voice rose from the mob, "the *Massacre* was an ugly, leaden event!"

"Or perhaps not leaden, but certainly ugly!"

"Yes, of course!"

"That's right!"

Denton simply shook his head. "Have we so little regard for language? I'm speaking purely of aesthetics now, though I'll get to the deeper semantic roots in but a moment. Boston *Slaughter* has more complimentary vowel sounds. *–oss –aught*, it rolls off the tongue as a flung duck slides down a swine's behind! You see?"

"…perhaps?"

"Not entirely!"

"I think I get it!"

"I don't."

"Ah, you're right, neither do I!"

"What's more," Denton continued undeterred, "consider the difference between the two words, *Massacre* and *Slaughter*. The former brings to mind the vagaries of war, wh-"

"This *is* a war!"

"Or ought to be!"

"Maybe will be, shortly!"

Denton raised his hands for silence, and much to Fithian's shock, *the crowd fell silent for him.*

"Please, please!" he called, "I agree with you, wholeheartedly. We've attempted to secure the natural liberties due a man by the simple fact of his existence through peaceful means, rational and economic. Perhaps the time has come for force!"

Murmurs of baffled agreement. Hadn't they just been calling for this man's life? And here he was, putting to words what they felt in their hearts! How had this happened?

"But what good, I ask you, is force exercised by a divided mind?" He let the rhetorical question hang unanswered for a moment. "None! That is how much good. We must all be of one mind, if force is to serve as an actionable course of, uh, action." At that mere slip, Fithian could see Denton's spell breaking. Some of the faces nearest to the front began blinking, as though stirring from a dream whose fantasies were more convincing than waking life had ever been.

"So we must secure unanimity!" Denton called, and once again the spell was cast – for the most part. Fithian could still see some blinkered faces resisting the trance. "How? Inspire outrage!" He thrust a closed fist into an open palm. "*Massacre* is what happens during a war. But a *Slaughter*...a slaughter is what one does to *animals*! Which is how the British think of us, is it not?"

"It is!"

"Chattel, we are to them!"

"They don't think very highly of us at all!"

"Yeah!"

"In closing, then," Denton called as he clutched his hands sagaciously behind his back, "we see that *Boston Slaughter* is incontestably the superior nomenclature for the recent tragedy."

The mob once again coiled inwards to discuss.

Denton leaned in to Fithian and hissed, "send them off, now!"

She understood precisely what he meant, and couldn't help but admire the approach. Mobs gained their ferocity from cumulative myopia. Denton had managed to halt their frothing obsession with his oblivion by placing them in a deliberative mood. This would, he hoped, make them malleable, or at least more open to suggestion than they might otherwise have been.

Fithian hoped it as well.

"All right," she shouted, "that's enough for one day. I've got work to do, and you're all keeping me from it. You can discuss amongst yourselves down at the bar!"

For a wonder, the mob immediately started to splinter and drift back towards town. Some stalwart faces towards the front remained, eyes tracing the course of blood through Denton's veins, wondering when they might split them for a more static, grounded inspection. "Off you go!" Fithian ordered in her schoolmarm-iest voice. "Shoo!"

And for another wonder, they turned and began the slow march back towards town.

Clearly, though, they would be back. They would discuss linguistics and semantics, and then they would realize that they had been duped. They would be back, with trebled ferocity, not only at being duped by Denton, not only at his having stirred up agitation at the very sort of man who he had enraged them by sheltering, but at Fithian herself. For they would smear her as an accomplice, and there would be no safe haven for her. At best, she had rendered herself a social pariah in the Mill. At worst…

"Let's go inside," she whispered to Denton before the most steadfast of the mob were barely out of earshot. She turned to find no Denton, but a row of frantic, scrambling footprints leading directly to her front door.

As Yazbirth Bicklebog beat a steady galumph back towards the Lowestoft mansion, he passed an exodus of grousing Fidgetonians. Some were arguing about the difference between matching and complimentary vowel sounds, some were disputing the nuances of various words that denoted the wholesale eradication of large groups of living organisms, and a scant (but loud) few were discussing the perfidy and deception of the British and all their lackeys.

But still, none of them ever turned around. They just kept walking, down a long and unevenly tree-lined road, back to the arrhythmic heart of Fidget's Mill. So Fithianself's axe was plenty sharp after all, Yazbirth reflected happily. It was only a shame he couldn't have been there to see her at work Himself.

Oh well. That was nothing new for Yazbirth. Always missing the excitement.

XVI

YAZBIRTH BICKLEBOG CAME STOMPING UP TO the mansion, tapped its feet on the elevated threshold (for form's sake – no snow could adhere to his thick, spectral fur) and entered the Lowestoft mansion.

Immediately, Yazbirth knew that Fithian was gone. She gave the world around her a blessed density, like the mists that drift off of a warm bath, or a beloved song floating down a long hallway. Somewhere in these less metaphorical halls the Familiar knew he could find Cullender and Opal, doing whatever it was they did these days. Bemoaning their changes in fortune? Far as Yazbirth could tell, that's about all they ever got up to anymore. Which was, perhaps, fair enough – they'd labored heroically to build an overland shipping empire, only to see it collapse through no fault of their own.

But still, lethargy was infectious, and there were few more qualified to note the tragic allure of statis than a giant sloth. Wishing to remain productive, always the natural wish of a Familiar, Yazbirth spurned the presence of the parents to seek the daughter.

Footprints lead to the stables, and wheel ruts lead down the road. Fithian and Denton had left the relative safety of the mansion. Why? Why generally, but also why so soon after narrowly escaping dismemberment by the mob?

Well, perhaps that latter question answered itself. The mansion was secure, more or less, but it was also static. There it was again, that sweet call to lie down and wait for whatever might come one's way. Unlike her parents, Fithian hadn't succumbed. And for that, Yazbirth was quite proud of her. If the m…*when* the mob decided that they really ought to have cracked Denton's skull like a bad joke, the first place they would come looking for him would be the last place they'd seen him. So an immediate escape was a terrific plan.

Unfortunately, Yazbirth had not the slightest clue where they might have gone. Fortunately, there was a relatively easy way to find out. He stepped between the two thick pillars of progress the wagon wheels had ground into the snow, punctuated by hoof-beaten depressions, and began a slothful pursuit made slower by an overly attentive obliteration of the tracks Fithian and Denton had left by their passage. Yazbirth wanted nothing more than to be productive, of course, and sometimes that was best accomplished by a measure of thoughtful destruction.

"Where's dad?"

Peggy turned from Brisby, to whom she had explained what little of the situation she understood, to see Annabelle hugging herself tightly. "He's out keeping us safe," she replied with hastily fabricated confidence.

"How?"

Ah. How indeed? Peggy pinched her lips together, as though to prevent that very question from formulating itself upon her traitorous tongue. "He knows what he's doing." Wishful thinking never went out of style, did it?

Apparently Annabelle agreed, and was either satisfied by this answer, or realized it was the best she'd get. She turned and sat back down on the bed where her brother remained asleep. Lawrence's ability to sleep through momentous events was unparalleled – Denton had once nearly severed his left ring finger in an ill-fated attempt to prepare himself a meal, and the young Hedges boy slept straight through his father's grisly imprecations toward God and cutlery. He had awoken in a state of great excitement, for he had seen the blood splattered across the kitchen and assumed that they were having steak for dinner.

Sometimes Peggy worried about her son, but sometimes his …eccentricities came in handy. This was just such a time. She'd let him sleep, and wake him up when there was something to tell him other than 'go back to sleep'.

In the meantime, though, Annabelle was awake. And the look on her face made it clear that she needed to hear 'something pretty', as Denton liked to say (and had only started saying after he got back from Fidget's Mill, come to think of it). Peggy made to walk towards her daughter, when she heard a dull clicking sound behind her. It was

Brisby, apparently trying to swallow without the aid of saliva. So it wasn't just Annabelle who needed to hear something pretty.

But what could she tell them? Denton hadn't told her much of anything, and the prospect of telling a beautiful lie that might be broken by an ugly truth was objectionable in a profoundly fundamental way. But what did that leave her?

Nothing. Which was what she said, ultimately. She placed a reassuring hand on Brisby's shoulder and tried to think strength through it, and into him. And perhaps it was a beautiful lie she was telling herself, but it looked as though the spooky transference of confidence was working.

That was the trial run. Now for the main event: Peggy sat down next to Annabelle and wholly embraced her. It would take more than a single point of contact to prop her daughter up with bogus backbone – Annabelle seemed to be made of stronger stuff than the doctor, even now, and strength held its shape.

"He's not going to be happy to see you," Fithian told Denton after they'd knocked on the door.

"Why not?"

"Because he knows you're not a real doctor now."

Denton felt as though someone with small fingers had just jabbed him in the throat. It should hardly have been a surprise that the Fidgetonians had worked this out in his absence, and it wasn't one. The shock came from the fact that Denton had entirely forgotten that this was a part of the lie he'd told the town. What other falsehoods had he told and since forgotten? "And he's still upset about that, is he?"

Fithian looked at Denton with a look typically reserved for spiders that had crawled into the sugar jar. "You gave his sweetheart an abortion, Denton."

"He asked me to!"

"You deceived him."

Fair. Oh dear. It would have been lovely, had Fithian warned Denton of the antipathy awaiting him in the Crundwell mansion a little bit earlier. For example, not as the door was literally in the process of being opened by one of the Crundwell slaves.

"Erm," Denton said for the benefit of all present. "I don't believe we've met."

From deep in the house, Zeus bellowed "IS THAT HIM?" in the voice of Buddy Jr. Thunderous footsteps followed, seeming to come not from a particular point in the house behind the blank-faced slave, but from *every* point. It was as though Denton were hearing the heartbeat of the edifice, and his mere presence was sufficient for cardiovascular agitation.

Not knowing what else to say, Denton asked the slave, whose name he would never know, if Buddy Jr. was home. In response, the man stepped casually to one side, making room for Buddy Jr.'s fist to sail unimpeded into Denton's nose.

"I ought to kill you myself!" Buddy Jr. screamed from the apex of the dismal sky. Denton, still falling slowly backwards to the ground, the crunch of his broken nose bouncing around his skull like a dog being asked if it wants to go *out*, does it want to go for a *walk*, wondered if Fithian might not have seen this coming when she suggested they consult Buddy Jr. on the disposal of the musket.

The snow cushioned his head as it snapped backwards into the ground, in much the same way that a threadbare blanket cushions the fall of a man from a third-story window. His brain, perhaps seeing the cheerful liberty of the *crunch* sound, took to bouncing around his skull in much the same way.

"I ought to demand satisfaction of you, but that would validate you as a gentleman, which you most certainly are not!"

"Blllrrrrg," came Denton's moist retort.

Buddy Jr. closed the distance instantly, rearing up to kick Denton in the ribs. Fithian placed a restraining hand on his shoulder and mumbled "alright, alright." Buddy Jr. was placated in the sense that he brought his leg down slightly before kicking Denton in the ribs, thereby mitigating some portion of the force.

The force was still sufficient to break one of Denton's ribs, though.

So Fithian had probably seen this coming.

The son of a fallen patriarch knelt over Denton, poking him above his heart as if to let him know where he could expect the next blow to be struck. "You, imposter, made the most tender ministrations over my Missy under a hateful pretense! You secured my trust by deception!"

By way of response, Denton blew a geyser of blood from his nose. It splashed back down upon his own face, and he was congested by vitality.

This, he felt, would have to do as a rejoinder. He couldn't well say 'actually, the procedure was performed by a witch and her turkey demon Familiar, and was concluded by seeding a memory in your minds of my having performed it, when, in fact, I did no such thing' without being punched and/or kicked again. So he would let his blood do the talking.

"The most humiliating part of this farce," Buddy Jr. continued, "was not the discovery that you were not a doctor as you claimed to be, nor the natural inference that you *were*, in some material way, an accessory to the murder of my father and dear younger sister. No, the most galling degradation was my inability to believe any of these things as they came to light. I defended you for weeks after you fled the town, even as my father's vision crumbled to dust and ruin around me. There has scarcely been a greater fool than I."

At any moment, Denton expected to hear Missy come running out, shouting about how that was enough, and leave the poor man alone, 'the poor man' in this case being him of course, and how violence need not beget violence. But when he finally managed to lift his head to the doorway, he saw Millicent Ditteridge leaning against the frame, arms crossed, brow furrowed.

Come to think of it, he shouldn't have expected her to play mediator. Even more than Buddy Jr., she was the aggrieved party here. He respected the feat of Herculean self-control that kept her from leaping outside and kicking Denton's head like a sour bucket.

Like a what? He was getting delirious. Probably all the blood loss. He flipped over onto his chest and gurgled his way to a limp push up position, cheating by ample usage of the knees. In his peripheral vision, he could see Buddy Jr. bracing, preparing for another strike. Fithian wordlessly inserted herself between Denton and Buddy Jr., which cooled the latter off considerably.

"It was either let them vent their fury now," Fithian whispered as she kneeled to help Denton to his feet, "or let it continue to fester and boil, until it exploded under less desirable circumstances."

"Desirable," Denton coughed. "Desirable."

"Yes, well, less *controlled*, anyway." She pulled Denton the rest of the way up and handed him a handkerchief, which he immediately slapped over his nose.

"Ow," he commented. "I suspect my rib is also broken."

"Which one?" Buddy Jr. inquired with a pointer finger extended. "This one?"

"Ouch! Yes! Do't poge it!"

"Don't what?"

Denton spat blood onto the snow, a red offense against winter. "By dose…" He snuffed against the swelling that was already claiming its prize. "By dose is brogen. Alzo. Id addizion do by ribs."

Missy rolled her eyes towards Buddy Jr. "I can't understand a word he's saying now."

Buddy Jr. smiled back. "Do we need to?"

"I still can," Fithian declared impassively, "and yes, you do. Well, perhaps *need* is too strong. But there's something he'd like to discuss with you."

His volcanic rage largely spent in the latest eruption, a newly dormant Buddy Jr. shrugged and stared thoughtfully at Denton. "You can come inside, and we'll speak of whatever has brought you back to darken my doorstep. But if you spill a single drop of blood upon a carpet, I can promise you that the rest of it will spill in short order. If I have to replace one," he reasoned, "might as well make it worth my while, eh?"

"Dat's bide." Denton spat one final gore loogie onto the snow and followed Buddy Jr. and Missy into the house. Fithian followed close behind him, casting a final glance over her shoulder.

"Much appreciated," she whispered into the winds.

"Myself's pleasure," the winds replied, as the last of their wagon's tracks were swept into oblivion.

"I may need you to come and take down some of the swelling."

Yazbirth regained the vertical and cocked his head. "Swelling?"

"Poor Denton's got a bit of a nasal situation."

"Mhm," Yazbirth replied, as if this explained everything. As far as the Familiar was concerned, it rather did. Aside from the lamentable Rumney Marsh affair, Fithian had been a perfectly peaceful consort, whose only goal was to create a sustainable, agrarian life for herself and her remaining family. Who could find fault with that? Surely he could help her accomplish that without once compromising his ethics. Surely it would be more remarkable to find a way to help her accomplish that in an ethically compromising fashion. And yet, he was hardly surprised to hear she was involved with something unsavory – wasn't that the situ-ation in which he had first discovered her?

And wasn't that always the way?

Fithian caught up to the three people who had gone before her, leaving the door open for Yazbirth Bicklebog to follow.

Ever attentive to propriety, Yazbirth closed the door behind himself.

XVII

BUDDY JR. WANTED NOTHING MORE THAN TO HIT Denton again. "What on Earth would I want with the Sheriff's weapon?"

"Ind redurnd," Denton snuffled as though faced with overwhelming enthusiasm, "I berely asg thad you gall an assebly ob the down, ad inborm dem thad deir perseptions ob be are bery budge bistagen. Wh-"

All eyes in the room turned to Fithian. "Basically," she translated, "he wants you to convince everyone in the Mill to stop wanting to kill him."

It was hard to blink loudly, but Buddy Jr. seemed convinced to find a way. A slow smile crept across his face. "What on Earth makes him think anyone would listen to me?"

Denton nearly leapt from his seat. His broken rib kept the 'nearly' from becoming 'actually'. "Ow. You're a Grudwell, dat's whad!"

"Years ago, that might have counted for something. Today, it means nothing. I can't convince the town to retire its grievances against you. And even if I could," Buddy Jr. continued without the accidental grin, "I wouldn't do it in return for a lawman's musket, for which I have no need."

"Ah," Denton began, "eh." He puzzled over this for a moment. "Id's a bery good busget."

"Cripes," Missy chuckled to Buddy Jr. from mid-pace along the back of the room, "how hard did you hit him?"

Perhaps not hard enough, Denton was forced to admit. Hard enough to realize, once he was sat in the room, making his pitch to Buddy Jr., how ludicrous this whole excursion had been. So much bullshit. Peggy had been right.

But was she? Or had he simply lost his touch? He used to be relatively adept at negotiation and, yes, even manipulation. His bargaining chips were quite worthless now, and the pot he sought to draw was well beyond his means, but there was a time when neither of these things would have slowed him down. There was always a way to bring people around to one's point of view, and Denton had always fancied himself fairly facile at finding the way.

Some revision of his self-conception was clearly necessary. He stood now before people he used to consider his allies, bleeding and just about begging, neither activity getting him any closer to his goal. A goal which was, he was finally forced to admit to himself, ill-conceived and implausible.

Why had he been so myopically focused upon the musket? It was a worthless bauble, something to be slung forth at the first opportunity. And yet he had become obsessed with its transactional value, as though there remained a chance for him to shape events to his own ends. After he'd vowed to not do exactly that! What preposterous folly! What vainglorious self-absorption! What a fucking moron he'd been, good grief.

This was no longer a time for negotiation, that was what that plummeting *thud* in his heart meant. The die had been cast, the beds had been made, the paths had been laid, and now all a man could do was watch things play out according to th…

No. This fatalism was highly unbecoming, and impossible to maintain in the face of a face as smug and punchable as Buddy Jr.'s was just then. Beside, the 'stupid waste of time' that was this business with the musket had gotten him back in cahoots with Buddy Jr., Missy and Fithian. Granted, they were no longer his biggest fans, but nor were they delivering him to the clutches of his *actual* biggest fans, who wanted nothing more than to grind him into paste. That made them, in a fairly dramatic sense, accomplices to his asylum. And boy oh boy did the mob roaming the Mill have a grim view of accomplices.

"Okay," he announced. A moment of thought accompanied the second syllable. "Okay?" he repeated. It wasn't *ogay*, it was *okay*. Confused, Fithian caught his eye, and darted her own to the westernmost door through which they'd entered the room.

Yazbirth Bicklebog stood in the door, armwrestling a floating grey blob that Denton could only assume was the swelling in his nose. His face and rib still hurt, but hey, he could speak normally now.

"Okay," he declared for a third time, the conviction in his voice trebled. Which was good, because he'd need it. He'd completely forgotten about the procedure he'd…facilitated between Missy and Miss Carsis. And now that it had been recalled to him, he remembered its byproduct. "But, correct me if I'm mistaken, but you still owe me one."

Buddy Jr. did not correct Denton, but only because he probably hadn't been able to hear him over the blood roaring through the vein on his forehead. After a pause of nearly a minute, Buddy Jr. said "what?"

"Whether or not I was qualified to perform the…procedure on dear

Millicent, the fact remains that the procedure was performed." He was deliberate about the phrasing, ensuring that everything he said was *technically* true. "As a result of which you volunteered a debt of one favor."

Another age passed. "What?"

"If you are a man of honor, y-"

In an instant, Buddy Jr. shot across the room, seemingly through furniture, in order to point a quivering finger directly at Denton's nose. "I'll not have my honor disparaged by a dissembler!"

"Did I disparage your honor?"

"Yes!"

Denton couldn't help the upward cant his lips were adopting; the lawyer in him couldn't have been more pleased at the direction of the cross-examination. "How? What did I say?"

"You said…" If only the deflation of Buddy Jr.'s anger could have been accompanied by a high, flatulent whistling.

"I merely pointed out that a man of honor will, well, *honor* contracts, whether they be tendered verbally or in writing."

Missy cocked her head forward as though preparing to spit on the floor. She didn't, because that would have been supremely silly. "And would a man of honor have falsified credentials in order to investigate an ailing woman's, erm, uh, conjugal pocket?"

"Jesus," Fithian called under her breath. Buddy Jr. clearly disapproved, but limited his shame-faced praises to a scrunching of the left eye.

"Two points," Denton offered with a corresponding number of fingers. Perversely, seeing Buddy Jr. glare at the fingers as though he could not wait to snap them off only spurred Denton on. Ah, he was getting his feet back under him, wasn't he? Not for him, the annihilative seductions of fatalism! "First, I never falsified credentials."

"Bullshit!" Buddy Jr. screamed. Did Denton spy Fithian stifling a laugh back there? He thought he did. She understood what he was up to: playing the lawyer once again. And nothing could more strenuously attest to his success than the frustration of everyone in the room.

"Whence did I claim the authority to practice medicine? Specifically. Which university?" Flatulence of a lower register would have suited the silence perfectly. "No one ever inquired as to the specifics of my accreditation, and so there never arose the need for fabrication."

"You claimed to be unlicensed!"

"Precisely my point!"

"You took advantage of us in a vulnerable moment," Missy seethed.

The understatement of her anger drove its intensity home to Denton. "I am truly sorry for that. But suffice it to say, I would not have agreed to the task had I not known I could accomplish it, safely." This was, he was relatively proud to note, the first real lie he'd told in this whole conversation. "But my second point here, I never claimed I was a man of honor."

"A-HA!" Buddy Jr. cried, as though Denton hadn't anticipated what he was a-ha-ing about. "Why would anyone expect me to honor a contract with a man who has none! Honor, I mean!"

"Because *you* are a man of honor" was all Denton had to say. What he didn't say was that, as it happened, he *did* consider himself a man of honor, and a fairly bright one at that. Which was why, in the extremity of his despair which had lately passed him by with a bloated *whoosh*ing noise, he had glimpsed a potential solution to…perhaps it was not too grandiose to say, just about every problem that currently faced him, and his family, and Brisby, and even Buddy Jr.

The town of Fidget's Mill would break even by the business, which was truly unfortunate, but they would manage. Besides, all ideals to one side, it was difficult for him to feel terribly concerned about a town that had, almost unanimously, sought to chase down him in the street and murder him in some very prolonged and no doubt innovative way.

"So," Denton plowed ahead as though he'd secured an enthusiastic agreement from Buddy Jr., "if you won't assist me in quelling the town's rage, all I want you to do is serve as second in an upcoming duel, and broker peace between the belligerent parties."

Sighing, pleased to hear he could continue as though he'd agreed to honoring the contract without having to actually agree out loud (because one thing common to all men of honor is exceptional malleability when honor is impugned, and unparalleled pedantry in defense of the same), Buddy Jr. inquired as to the identities of the belligerent parties.

"It's Mr. Increase and myself."

"Fuck yourself."

"Also, what?" Even Fithian couldn't disguise her shock. "Why are you and Mr. Increase set to duel?"

Denton dismissed the question with a wave. "It's a long story, and bears no relevance to the matter under discussion."

"I'll not serve as your second!" Buddy Jr. couldn't say it fast enough, as though merely leaving the thought unchallenged for too long would make it a reality. "Heavens, I would challenge you to a duel for myself, only I'd recall to you my insult tendered upon the threshold as explanation as to why I haven't. My God! You're a fool to remain here for a duel, you're a fool to remain here for a duel with a man who remains relatively well respected by the Mill, and you're a fool if you think I'll serve as your second!"

"I don't want you to be my second. I want you to be Mr. Increase's."

Another solid minute went past, during which Buddy Jr. didn't move very much at all. And then, once again: "What?"

XVIII

INCREASINGLY, MR. INCREASE CAME TO WONDER if his willingness to duel Denton Hedges wasn't a sign that he still cared for the man. He couldn't speak to Denton's motives for issuing the challenge, but he knew full well that his motive for snatching up the opportunity was rooted in very powerful emotions, only a few of which pertained to Denton specifically. The most salient of these was a shared guilt he felt for the miserable fate of Adewale. What was that flinty, deceptively clever man up to now? Surely having his wits squandered on the very crop Increase's mother had escaped. It was awful enough to consider in a vacuum, but to know that he bore even indirect responsibility for it…it had been slowly eating at Increase over the years, and it wasn't until now, having unexpectedly reunited with the final quarter of what he felt ought to be a remorse quartet (the other three being himself, Missy and, last but certainly not least, Chip), that he found himself needing to release the pressure in one dramatic outburst.

But so what? Knowing this would change nothing. The one thing Increase clung to, the one hope that this might find a peaceful resolution, was in the fact that the above reasoning was founded upon feelings he felt towards Denton. What would have frightened him far more would be *apathy*, for that was perhaps the most depressing state of mind in which to approach one who was once a friend. To truly befriend someone is to allow them a portion of your love, and to open yourself to reciprocation. Love is a circuitous river one that drinks of the same reservoir into which it pours itself. If your friend betrays you, as Mr. Increase felt Denton had, what then is the simplest response? To erect a dam, and halt the flow? To dig out a channel, redirecting it elsewhere? No and no; the simplest response is to pour poison into the current, and let it continue flowing.

Hatred was merely God's first crack at love, and those who doubt it need just ask Abraham, or, more to the point, Isaac. But the Creator, who wanted nothing more than vengeance upon his own rather lackluster Creation, hadn't *truly* perfected the art of malice until He created indifference. One can only guess at how He felt about the innovation, but that He utilized it liberally was not in question. How else to explain why He hadn't popped his head in to see how everyone was getting on for several millennia now?

To stem the flow of love entirely, that was an act far more dramatic and deadly than merely coloring the love with umbrage. Mr. Increase was far from the Mill's most demonstrative man, but he was capable of love. He knew the feeling well – it was a dense itch in the center of his chest. Had he loved Denton? Did he still? Perhaps, but only because, with so few friends to love, Mr. Increase had so much love to spare.

And did Denton love Mr. Increase? Who could tell?

Love could both liberate and enslave, that was something Increase had learned the hard way. As a result, he was intensely parsimonious with his affection. The flip side of this was, once he opened himself to someone, he found it nearly impossible to close himself off again.

Mr. Increase returned to the empty storehouse to find it not empty. Vera Miringhoff was futzing around, counting her footsteps up and down a corridor of shelves. As politely as he could, he told her that he needed to be alone just then.

"Oh? What's the matter?" Vera inquired.

"Just..." he considered unburdening himself to this woman, for whom no especial feeling had begun to flow just yet (save *pity*, Mr. Increase recalled with a shudder), but stopped himself. It wasn't just the look of hungry solicitation in her eyes – Increase couldn't trust someone who was that eager to hear of another's misfortunes – but it was the knowledge that, if he should ever befriend Vera, and love her as one friend can love another, the probability of heartbreak was overwhelming. Unless the friendship could be sustained, a daunting prospect in such divided times, it would either curdle and spoil, turning to hatred...or it would choke upon itself, and become apathy.

Oh, hell.

"Vera, how would you like to serve as my second in a duel?"

The woman stared at him as though a flock of sparrows had just come zooming out of his mouth. "It's not nice to tease."

As Vera left the storehouse, letting the door slam shut behind her, Mr. Increase sat behind his desk and cradled his head in his hands. Jesus, here was the self-pity again! Years ago, he wouldn't – *couldn't* – have countenanced such an indulgence. But that was then, and this was now. Goddamnit, this was now.

Clump, clump. *Rssssshhhhh.* c-CLUMP. "Goddamnit."

Mr. Increase didn't remember going to sleep, but he felt comfortable assuming that he had, as he was now awakening to a ruckus in his storehouse.

Peeling off the pages that drool had affixed to his face, he raised his eyes from the familiar spot behind his desk, and was primarily shocked to see that the storehouse was empty. But this shock passed, as it always did. Even now, which is when this was (goddamnit), he sometimes forgot that this wasn't then. *Then* being the time when the storehouse had been full of goods, as opposed to *now*, when it was the opposite. Empty of bads? No, that couldn't be right. The storehouse was empty of goods and *full* of bads.

Including, potentially, the silhouette clumping and scraping its way between the shelves.

"Alright," Mr. Increase called in a tone of voice that was please to see that we've all had our fun here, while announcing that it was time to call it a night, "who's there?"

Clump. CLUMP. "Gah. Sorry! How do I get to you?"

"With a bullet in your lung, if you don't identify yourself immediately." Mr. Increase didn't have a gun, but he thought the bluff sounded too good to pass up.

"Crundwell! Bud…see, I was certain this was the path to you just a moment ago, only there's a great big shelf in my way."

If Mr. Increase *had* had a gun, this was when he would have slowly lowered it. Not having a gun, he settled for shuffling the papers on his desk a bit. "Buddy Jr.?"

"Yes."

Which explained why he couldn't work out how to thread through the labyrinth, even denuded of opacity – Buddy Jr. was of the Higher Sort, and so never deigned to besod his seaspray. The closest he'd ever been to the docks, the provenance of his wealth and status, was probably in the back of a carriage, wearing that stupid hat he used to wear. The only reason a man could be compelled to don such a monstrosity, after all, was pier pressure.

Sometimes Mr. Increase hated himself more than anyone or anything else.

"Stop," he guided Buddy Jr. gently, "look to your right. Your *right.*

Futher. See th-yeah. Now walk straight ahead. The way you're looking, not the way your feet are pointed. There. N…stop. Too far."

This continued for an age and a day, until finally Buddy Jr. was standing before Mr. Increase, looking slightly rumpled, and wondering "How are you?"

Still seated behind his desk, Increase studied Buddy Jr. like a textbook he himself had written. "Let's not do that."

Buddy Jr. looked shocked. Or at least, he looked the way he expected people looked when they were shocked. There was a hand raised to his heart, fingers splayed, and a slight angling of the head. That's not what humans do when they're shocked, just wealthy people. "What do you mean?"

"You don't care how I am. You've never once set foot in here before, so I can only assume there's a very good reason for your doing so now. If it's all the same to you, I'd like to bypass the formalities and skip directly to your purpose. I'm very busy," he added, hoping Buddy Jr. had been too engrossed in his clumsy approach to have seen Mr. Increase delaminating a bespittled page of inventory from his cheek.

The Crundwell boy's demeanor loosened immediately, as relief grabbed him by the shoulders and kneaded. "Thank goodness," he sighed. "May I sit down?"

"If you can find something upon which to sit," Mr. Increase allowed with a generous sweep of the hand.

Buddy Jr. made a quick visual survey of the room and took his point immediately. There wasn't much by way of seating, and Mr. Increase's lap was probably out of the question, for a whole host of reasons. "I suppose I'll stand."

Mr. Increase nodded at this, appreciating the wisdom of the decision.

For several moments, Buddy Jr. said nothing, simply swinging his hands front to back like a profoundly lethargic skier. He was, it occurred to Increase, struggling to think of how to begin. No doubt he had planned to position himself over a chair, perhaps unbutton his coat, lower himself down, and more than likely cross one leg over the other. Then Buddy Jr. would have said something like "ahhhh," before launching into whatever bit of business had brought him to the Atlantic edge of the town.

But not having a seat, Buddy Jr. was lost. So Mr. Increase primed the pump: "Wh-"

"It has come to my attention," Buddy Jr. began, seemingly startled by his own speech, "that you are to engage in a duel with Denton Hedges, who has lately returned to Fidget's Mill, and prompted a considerable degree of brouhaha and ado in so doing."

Increase got comfortable in his seat, or as comfortable as a creaking wooden antique would allow. Buddy Jr. had rehearsed a whole thing, and so would need to run the whole thing out.

"As you are no doubt aware, I have a history with Denton Hedges, in as much as you do, and mine is marked with no less degree of calumny than yours, save the final insult which would have catalyzed an affair of honor, an insult apparently levied against yourself but stayed in my case. And so, making an allowance for the enmity I no doubt bare against one Mr. Denton Hedges, I would be so obliged if you would...*permit* me to act as your second in the duel."

If Mr. Increase had been drinking anything, he would have sprayed it all over his desk like a breaching orca. Having no beverage at hand or in mouth, he swung himself to the edge of his seat and clamped his hands onto the edges of his desk. "You what?"

Buddy Jr. traveled backwards through his speech, moving his lips slightly as he did so. "...stayed in my case. And so," he resumed at full volume, "making an allowance f-"

Increase raised a silencing finger, and Buddy Jr. gladly heeded it. "You, a Crundwell, wish to be second to me, a negro?"

"In the duel. That's correct."

Coherent thought broke down, leaving Mr. Increase no way to assess the situation beyond flavors of pie and colors of frog. Logic cracked like the stained-glass window to a cathedral bursting inwards, as though struck by a meteor, pastoral tranquility swelling and shivering and finally shattering, a fractal cascade of light and hues and sharps and smooths on a journey to kiss the shrieking vicar of higher cognition to ribbons.

What the *fuck*. Mr. Increase had never wanted anything more than to see the people in power laid low, and now here was just such a person (however much his power had waned, Buddy Jr. remained a staple of the Mill) suggesting just such a symbolic repositioning. However particular the situation, however limited the humbling, however it was happening, it was still *happening*.

"Yes," Mr. Increase agreed, without investigating the idea much further. The image was too good to pass up. The favored son of the Crundwell clan, acting at the behest of a lowly dockhand! A rather prominent part of his mind wondered what Adewale would have made of the spectacle. Would he not have found it superlatively pleasurable? Would he not have then approached at the conclusion of the duel to offer his congratulations?

Might this not be a way to do right by him?

"Really?" There, behind Buddy Jr.'s eyes, swirled the rest of a rather tortuously reasoned pitch for himself as second. Whatever planning he'd done, meeting and overcoming resistance clearly comprised the bulk of it.

"Yes." Just imagine the scene! Increase certainly was, and doing little else. What might his mother have said, could she have seen him now? Or, as (goddamnit) this was now, *then*, which this would eventually be. Her son, who she bore alone and afeared in a clearing in the woods, now standing proudly in the field of honor, with a white man – and not just any white man, but *the inheritor to the Crundwell legacy* – acting as his second? The thought set his eyes to stinging and leaking, but still he did nothing to banish the offending fancy.

So taken was he by the image, that the Mr. Increase of the mind failed to complete the scene. He was looking behind himself, to see a humbled Buddy Jr., and failing to look ahead, to see himself pointing a gun at Denton Hedges and pulling the trigger. When he finally did turn his mind to this inevitability, long after Buddy Jr. had said a grateful farewell and gone on his way, he found himself unexpectedly at peace with the idea. He had no desire to actually kill Denton; that much hadn't changed. He still thought the duel was a hysterically stupid idea. But…now there were other factors to keep in mind. Increase still had a certain degree of affection for Denton, if he was being honest…but was it enough to counterbalance his desire to see a Crundwell serving as *his* help? Granted, it was Buddy Jr., an abolitionist, and not his father, for whom it would have been a *true* humiliation, but, well, things were so rarely *precisely* as we'd like them to be.

Not that he was doing it for the appearances. No, of course not. Public opinion had never weighed too heavily on Mr. Increase's mind. He had gotten along, for so long, on his own. What need had he for others, in his advanced age? None, or very little, anyway. The appeal of having Buddy Jr. serve as a second was far too tantalizing to pass up, but it was for purely symbolic reasons. Yes, of course.

Perhaps Increase would aim high, or otherwise try to miss Denton. Well, not miss, but merely maim. One thing was for certain though – the duel *had* to happen. Increase couldn't bear the thought of coming so close to a validation of all he'd worked for, for all those years, even if he hadn't done any of said work in years, and even if the validation came largely independently of the work he'd done…this was all beside the point! It also wasn't as though he needed validation. It would just be nice, that was all. That was a point, but not *the* point.

The duel would happen, and Buddy Jr. would serve as his second. Increase was pleased with this decision, as it left him to hope that there might be a peaceful suit after all. Buddy Jr. hated Denton, sure, but hate was preferable to indifference, was it not? Buddy Jr. negotiating a peace on Mr. Increase's behalf would be just as powerful as him standing by for the duel itself. This could all work out, Mr. Increase gave himself the courage to imagine. Perhaps this will all work out to everyone's betterment, even. Yes, he could see it now. He could see himself sighting Denton down the barrel and pulling the trigger not for passion, but for the poetry of Higher Sorts and Lower Sorts cast out of sorts.

Oops. *Not* pulling the trigger. That was what he'd meant.

XIX

DENTON TURNED ON TO GUTTER LANE AND DOVE into a pile of trash. He'd meant to dive *behind* it, but urgency had gotten the better of accuracy. His broken rib registered a forceful complaint.

Peeling a soiled onion rind off of his face, he peeked out of the pile and watched Vera Miringhoff puttering about outside Miss Carsis' door. What the hell was *she* doing here? Granted, he'd sniffed out their association way back when Vera had sent him Miss Carsis' way. And granted, Vera no longer had a hotel to run. But the ex-hotelier had the air of business about her, pacing and mumbling to herself as though she were rehearsing a monologue just before going on stage.

Eventually, she nodded to herself and knocked on the ever-moving door to 33. This door, a different one than had admitted Denton last night, was opened by one or another of Miss Carsis' apprentices, and Vera stepped inside.

Several moments passed before Denton emerged from his refuse refuge. Largely because few things inspired caution like an entire town hell-bent upon your destruction, but partially because remaining inside the pile of trash meant he wouldn't have to see how much of the pile had gotten into the fabric of his clothing, or indeed his very being.

The good news was that aesthetics bore the brunt of the befilthening. The bad news was that 'smell' fell under the umbrella of aesthetics. He was ripe, and aghast at the thought of having to return to his worried family in such a state – a child should never see his father, with a swollen, purple face, clutching his broken rib, covered in other people's garbage. This was somehow a potent part of the humiliation to Denton – it wasn't even his garbage. It was *somebody else's*. But there was nothing to be done about it. He was cold and exhausted, and perhaps his children were still asleep.

I mustn't wake them with my knock, he thought as he hobbled up to the door and extended a closed fist.

He stayed the knock, holding his fist up to the door, knuckle first, as though cursing it and any of the other furnishings that may have been fashioned from its tree of origin.

Was there a secret knock? He and Peggy hadn't worked out a knock. So how would Peggy know it was him? The door opened onto a long hallway, at the opposite end of which was the room where they resided. He could shout that it was her beloved husband Denton come a-knocking, but he had no guarantee that somebody else wouldn't hear, for whom he was no more beloved than husband. A forceful wrap would be a more discreet way of cutting the silence of their temporary lodging, but *too* forceful would wake the children (assuming they were asleep, of course), thus inviting witnesses to their father's dank indignity.

Of course, there was the *other* worst case scenario – his absence may well have bred anxiety, and that damned musket was still sitting in there, loaded, loathing its load…

How the hell should he knock on this door? He couldn't stand here all day and debate the matter; if Vera was the busybody Mr. Increase claimed, she could be stepping out of the door directly next to the one in question any minute now, off to her next bean-spilling.

What as the least threatening knock possible? Denton shrugged, bent his legs in the event that a hasty leap to the side became necessary, and knocked three times, firmly, but slowly.

Knock…

Knock…

Knock.

For several seconds afterward, nothing happened. Had they not heard? He lifted his hand to knock again, a bit firmer and a bit faster.

Knock…

Kno-

The door swung open, and four hands grabbed him by the lapels and pulled him inside. They slammed the door behind him.

No less than ten seconds later, Vera Miringhoff stepped out of Miss Carsis', looking just as purposeful as she had upon entering. So purp-oseful, in fact, that she failed to notice the scramble of fresh footprints in front of the door right next to 33 as she trundled back to the more heavily-trafficked sections of town.

They stepped to either side of Denton and hurled him down the hall a few feet, face first. As the uneven floorboards rushed up to meet him, he wondered if he could wring a bit of extra pathos from Brisby by pretending that it was the toss that had broken his rib. Wouldn't work, of course, and Denton gladly accepted the pain that came as a result of the landing, as penitence for thinking about how to make people pity him. Hadn't he just been mulling on how to avoid appearing pitiable?

Yes, he thought to himself as Peggy and Brisby flipped him onto his back, *but that was different. That was my family. Brisby's just a friend.*

Denton's friend Brisby lunged at him with half of a broken plate, pressing it into the base of his neck. "I've got this knife against your carotid artery, you s-"

"Brisby," he mumbled.

"Shh! Let me finish! Your carotid artery, I was saying, and if I w-"

Denton shook his head and turned to Peggy. "Peggy!"

Brisby's shoulders drooped an inch.

Next to him, Peggy studied Denton's face for several intense moments, before he realized why she was hesitating: she was terrified, and had almost certainly amped herself up for action by fixing Denton's face in her mind, as being the only face she wouldn't reflexively try to cave in with that well-bound book in her hand. And here was Denton, without his usual face, instead presenting one made discolored and lumpy by the attentions of an old friend of his (Denton couldn't help but reflect that Buddy Jr. landed smack in the middle of the Old Friend Spectrum, right between 'holding a shard of kitchen-ware to my throat' at one end, and 'challenging me to a duel' on the other).

Finally, realization lit up Peggy's face, though the light was far from the warm, sensual glow Denton was used to. "Oh Christ, get off him Brisby!"

Brisby's shoulders drooped another inch. He had a whole spiel about the carotid artery, and nobody wanted to hear it. "Why?"

"Because that's Denton!"

The doctor was on the verge of disagreeing, but the words caught in his throat as he turned his head back. "Good golly!"

Peggy pushed Brisby out of the way with more force than Denton had ever seen her use against another human, sprawling him backwards onto his ass. "Ouch," he reported, but Peggy paid him no notice.

She cupped Denton's face in her hands, her touch soft as memory. "What happened?"

"I think we'll just be keeping the musket," Denton replied, thinking that this would be a funny little joke to cut through the tension.

"Fuck the musket!" Peggy cried, which was how Denton knew that his funny little joke had been very little, not very funny, and not at all joke. He mulled over a far more sophomoric follow-up, but opted against it, because in his experience there was no comedic alchemy that could take tears of terror and turn them into tears of mirth.

Which was not to say that he had a lot of experience, of course.

Peggy leaned over to embrace him, but Denton put up a gently halting hand and inhaled sharply. Mortified, his wife withdrew with remarkable speed. "What's wrong?"

"I'm fairly certain my rib is broken."

Brisby perked up – he was on much firmer footing here. "How come?"

"Well," Denton wheezed as he pushed himself up to a seated position, "it made a loud cracking sound, and then it started hurting a whole hell of a lot."

"Are you certain?"

Denton and Peggy both looked at him as though he weren't a qualified medical practitioner. Which might sound too specific to be conveyed in a mere look, but anyone on the receiving end of just such a look as often as Dr. Brisby Houlihan knew otherwise. After a moment, Denton asked where the children were.

"Sleeping," Peggy replied, "assuming we didn't awaken them with our rumpus."

The feeling in Denton's chest was equal parts relief and frustration.

Relief because he might just have a chance of getting the muck washed off before his kids awoke – frustration because what kind of a kid sleeps through a wrestling match in a creaky hallway? Denton didn't know from whence their commitment to sleep, but they most certainly didn't get that from him.

Reminding herself that yes, her children might still be asleep, and just as concerned with their seeing their father this way as the father himself was, Peggy dropped her voice to a near-whisper. "Who did this to you?"

"Buddy Jr." Denton had tried to match her whisper, but the name came out as a phlegmy belch.

The Hedges were the sort of husband and wife who shared everything, *everything* with each other, because they knew that they could. It was the easiest thing in the world, when one never did anything that couldn't be shared, and had absolute confidence in the other's ability to understand those things that, all the same, might have been easier not to share.

In short, Peggy didn't need Denton to explain to her why Buddy Jr. would have upped and socked him in the face. Nor did Brisby, which made this part of the conversation as simple as you like: they just looked at each other for a moment, until Denton mumbled "I think a slap would have sufficed just as well."

Another little joke that fell flat as a flapjack. Brisby patted Denton on the knee. "Well, come on. Let's get you up…" The doctor peeled his hand off of Denton's knee, and with the utmost of trepidation, sniffed it. He asked Denton a question with his eyebrows.

Denton shrugged. "I leapt into a pile of garbage."

Peggy asked a follow-up question with her eyebrows.

"I had to hide from Vera."

As if this explained all, Brisby nodded to Peggy, and together they carried Denton outside, and gave him a bath of icicles.

Lawrence and Annabelle had been stunned, when they finally woke up, to find their father lying on the mattress, propped up by pillows and folded blankets. His shirt was off, and Brisby had his head mere inches from their father's paunch, as if trying to guess what he'd had for dinner by smelling it through his belly button. Annabelle, first to rise from her slumber, shouted "daddy!", which awoke Lawrence, who shouted "d-uh, father!", because only little girls shouted 'daddy'.

Denton explained what had happened, but not the same way he explained it to Peggy. They were, after all, just kids.

"So what are you gonna do to *him*?" Lawrence wondered in a tone of voice that said 'I've got a few suggestions'.

Denton made an abortive attempt to tousle his son's hair, but the pain in his rib stopped him. Once again he inhaled sharply, this time punctuating the insufflation with a sharp cough. "Jesus," he mum-bled. The mere act of lying down multiplied the pain he felt by several factors. Inaction was agony. *Boy, there's a title, if I ever write a memoir*, he noted without amusement.

Which focused his mind, once again, on the potential final chapter.

"I need to ask a favor of you," Denton said to Brisby, and everyone in the room thought some variation on the theme of 'uh oh', because history had demonstrated that nobody ever did a favor for Denton Hedges, and later thought 'I feel great about that decision'.

But still, it was hard for a trained doctor, which is what Brisby definitely was, to refuse the wishes of a patient. "What's the favor?"

"I'd like you to serve as my second in the…" he glanced towards his children, back to Brisby. "D-U-E-L." And Denton's children, bless their little hearts, couldn't bring themselves to let their father know that they could spell.

Peggy sighed. "You're not still doing that, are you?"

"Why wouldn't I? Er," he amended, "aside from the obvious reasons, why wouldn't I?"

"Does an inability to stand upright unassisted count as an obvious reason?"

"…yes."

"How about an inability to raise your arm out in front of you to touch your son's head with an empty hand?"

"…yes."

"I find these reasons no less compelling for being obvious."

"Well," Denton said, because that was all he could say to that. He and Peggy stared at each other for a long time, having a conversation only they could hear. At the end of it, Peggy shook her head and stood up, mumbling about fetching Denton some water.

Much to Brisby's frustration, this put the ball back in his court. Denton looked to his doctor, and his children's gazes followed his. "Well?"

Hey kid! Who won that last point?

Once he sped past the terror of his own past, Brisby replied "if your condition improves sufficiently, then I will indeed serve as your second." Not a refusal, but nor was it an agreement. He thought himself quite clever for that one.

"Well," Denton said again, but this time pursuant to a complete thought, "you're a good doctor, aren't you?"

"Of course I am!"

"If that's so, then I expect my condition will improve rapidly."

"I'm su…damn."

Denton smiled and, damn them both, so did Brisby. It was easy to smile, with the dueling ground so far away. But watching their idiot grins from the hall, Peggy didn't find it to be far enough.

XX

WHEN IT CAME TO SHERIFF BAREFOOT'S NE'ER mentioned childhood, there tended to be one of two assumptions made: that he was either the bully who snatched some beloved object from the scrawny kid and held it above his head, or he was the scrawny kid from whom the bully snatched a beloved object to hold it above his head. These assumptions were made because both seemed like plausible origins for a casual totalitarian. That the iron fist was forged in a furnace of fury was obvious enough; the question was whether the flames were first kindled at the moment of conception, or else by some traumatic experience in the formative years.

The answer, of course, was neither. Because reality is often so banal.

Sheriff Barefoot, who had been born with a name that suited him far less than the occupational honorific he would come to claim, had been the sort of kid who would stand quietly to the side as he watched the bully snatch a beloved object from the scrawny kid and hold it above his head. His stood passively, but not impassively, shaking his head at the indignity of it all, and often daydreaming of how satisfying it would be to walk up to the bully and give him the old what for. Daydreaming was, for a boy of such average proportions, as near to the real thing as he ever wanted to get.

Not long after he'd left school, biology finally took a hint; Young Barefoot grew unchecked in all directions at once. Finally, he was big enough to give the bullies of the world the old what for, but unfortunately he had left behind the world of schoolboy roughhousing. Now the bullies of the world were less about snatching beloved objects and more about stabbing beloved organs. This did little to diminish Barefoot's enthusiasm for justice – that particular function was accomplished by his joining the local Watch. He'd gone in anticipating a noble, even knightly organization of manly men, who recited colonial ordinances over their evening repast instead of (or in addition to) prayers. But he instead found a group of rowdy boys, all of them his senior in both rank and age, who flagrantly disregarded any semblance of authority, save the authority they could personally wield over others. After all these years, he had found the den into which the childhood bullies had all crawled.

Their greatest sin was caprice, their second greatest illiteracy; if the criminal element in Fidget's Mill had ever thought to demand the Watch demonstrated axiomatic consistency in their approach to establishing and exercising the law, the entire town would have been deafened by the sound of bursting blood vessels. How to combat this, then-Constable Barefoot wondered? The answer seemed obvious enough: cling more tightly to order and oversight than was strictly necessary, or even advisable. He'd never been the clinging sort; if anything, he was a bit of a contrarian. So, in a way, it made perfect sense. The popular thing to do was rebel, so the contrarian thing to do was fall in line.

Which Barefoot did, with a vengeance. It was a sorry fact of the world that might often trumped right, but Barefoot hoped that right *with* might might trump might without right.

Which it did. And in a surprisingly short period of time, Constable Barefoot became Sheriff Barefoot. Surprising to everyone except Barefoot himself, of course. He grew astonishingly popular with the people in England who cared how their laws were being observed in the Colonies. Granted, it was a small contingent, but a contingent that nonetheless could stump for Barefoot where and when it counted, and so send promotions scrawled upon regal letterhead across the Atlantic.

Apparently, when Sheriff Barefoot was off looking at something else, God had upended the world like a sore loser at the poker table. All of a sudden, falling in line was popular, and rebelling was the contrarian thing. And so he did his best to roll with the tide once again, only this time, it wasn't so easy. His daydream had come true; he was in a position to stop the bullies from picking on the scrawny kids. It was just that now he *worked* for the bullies. As he fretted over how to retain that position while turning his back on the very practices that had gotten him there, it had never occurred to him that, perhaps, that wasn't exactly the position in which he had actually landed. He grew no less obsessed with the law, but found no shortage of contortions by which he could bend the law to reflect the will of the town. The result was highly literate, and just as capricious. Which, in a way, was worse than caprice without regard for the law.

Such was the unfortunate, well-meaning, stepwise evolution by which Barefoot became the bully; he had spent so many years focusing single-mindedly upon the law as the means to enforce justice, that he never paused to consider whether or not any given law actually overlapped with justice. A watchhouse of rowdy boys had shown Barefoot the vices to be found in a non-legalistic approach to the world, but they hadn't shown him the potential virtues, and so he assumed there were none to be shown.

And so, as Sheriff Barefoot sipped on some whiskey to slake the thirst he had worked up last night, rousing crowds to violence against Denton Hedges and Brisby Houlihan, he saw no cognitive dissonance is considering them bullies, and himself a victim. They had taken his musket! Why had they done that? It was humiliating and unfair.

He rose from his desk and crossed the floor of Mr. Ecker's, because the halcyon days of the watchhouse had passed. With a deceptively delicate touch, he pushed open the door and watched the setting sun flirt with the fresh snowfall. Yes, the clouds looked juicy; there would be snow tonight. Curses! That would make the search even more difficult.

The search being for, of course, the musket.

The Sheriff was naturally upset with Denton and Brisby, but mostly in a legal capacity. They were lawbreakers, and he would see them pay for their transgressions in accordance with the law.

But taking his musket was a *personal* offense, and so took precedence in his mind. Finally, he found himself in that classic scenario of childhood, in a role he'd never expected: those bullies Denton and Brisby had snatched his beloved firearm from him, and were dangling it over his head. But it was just the three of them; there was no third party to even daydream about giving them the old what for. That fell to Barefoot, and Barefoot alone.

This was all spectacularly unprofessional. He would never have copped to these feelings, no matter how in his cups he was, no matter how familiar his interlocutor. That the personal could override the professional in this way was the ultimate humiliation, revealing one of the tragic consequences of the humanity he so often denied himself.

For this, he would never forgive them. *Could* never. And so he would marshal all of the resources at his disposal to see them captured and brought before him. If they were brought before him under the unblinking eye of public scrutiny, they would be tried and prosecuted in a court of law, as soon as laws were devised for them to have violated.

But if Barefoot should come upon them in a still, moonless alley, he would personally hand down a sentence from which there was no appeal.

Denton and Brisby were the bullies, though; of this Barefoot was certain. This all made perfect sense, because it was a conclusion reached by a series of small steps, and all conclusions reached by a series of small steps made perfect sense. They were the bullies, and he was the only person who could give them the old what for.

As crystalline flakes winked through the liquid sunset, making the Mill beautiful in a way Sheriff Barefoot knew it was not, he daydreamed about the old what for.

Vera hadn't realized just how long she'd been creeping in the alley, watching Sheriff Barefoot stare vacantly out the door of the cobbler's, until she turned her head and felt a fine dusting of snow slide down her hair.

Was he dreaming of the musket, as Miss Carsis imagined he would be? There was no way for Vera to know. Except, of course, to ask.

Wrapping the shawl Miss Carsis had lent her tight around her shoulders ("It makes you look slightly more incompetent, in an unassuming way," Miss Carsis had said in an inexplicably kind voice), Vera meditated on what a wretched blessing it was to be assumed a fool. In no sense was she the sharpest tool in the shed, but Vera could still cut well enough, which was better than most her age could say. But she had an air about her – homely, that's how people had described her, to her face, but speaking to a third party. She was the sort of person people had no problem saying what sort of person she was while she was in the room, and to her, that just about summed it all up.

Why? In her many years she had never been able to arrive at a more satisfactory answer than 'something about my mug'.

But no matter. Her old friend Miss Carsis had found another use for her dubious talent, and so off she went to see Sheriff Barefoot, a man so naïve as to believe there was nobody more cynical than him.

Vera threw on a look of dopey good-humor. "Looks like snow, eh

Sheriff?"

"It does," he replied without wholly dignifying her.

"Still after those troublemakers, then?"

"Yes ma'am." He nodded his head down the street. "We'll have search parties combing the town this evening, as we expect they'll attempt to move under cover of darkness. Right now, I'm just waiting for the sun to set." He lowered his eyes to investigate his shoes, perhaps wishfully thinking he had crushed them beneath his heel already (Denton and Brisby, not the shoes). He had not looked at Vera yet, but she was used to that sort of thing and had long since ceased to take it personally.

"And you've not found your musket, have you?"

Ah, eye contact at last! Were she a younger woman, she'd have said Barefoot was undressing her with his eyes. But given her age, and given his asceticism, he was more likely frisking her with his eyes, just in case she had the musket on her person. "No," he said at last, "I haven't. And you haven't come to bring me word on it by chance, have you?"

"I don't have word on it, no. I'm afraid not."

"Hrmph." Satisfaction flooded Barefoot's face, as if this was long-awaited validation of a bold scientific theory. He nodded and returned his attentions to the middle distance.

"But I can get you the musket."

The Sheriff whipped his head back towards Vera with whiplash speed and made a face that, were it a noise, would have been BOI-OI-OI-OING. Seemingly unaware that he was not a sprightly young man anymore, and clearly unencumbered by the fact, he leapt from the stoop and charged towards Vera, leading with his forehead. Once he was nearly nose-to-nose with her, he asked her to repeat herself as politely as one could hope for, given the situation.

"I can get you the musket," she repeated.

"That's what I *thought* you said."

"I can get you the musket on one condition."

"No," he declaimed, "absolutely not. Unless you are admitting to me that you are an accomplice to these men, th-"

"Which I'm not."

"Be that as it may, if you possess the musket, or certain knowledge of where the musket may be, but are using this knowledge to in some way blackmail me, then I must warn you-"

"Quiet." And because that was not the sort of thing a woman like Vera was supposed to say, it always worked. She held up a single finger on her right hand, which somehow conveyed *I am older than you, I am wiser than you, so listen to me* without a word. "I don't have the musket, and I'm not certain where it is. But I can find it, and I can get it."

"You would steal a musket that was stolen from me?"

"I can't imagine the thieves will press a suit."

Barefoot shook his head. Blackmail was, he was absolutely certain, not legal. Which made it wrong. "Perhaps I detain you as a suspected accomplice?"

"Perhaps," was all Vera said in response. But she said it with such unassailable confidence, Barefoot found himself shifting his weight uneasily, as though preparing to dodge a blow. There was more than a whiff of the alleged town witch in that 'perhaps'. Tales of one Miss Carsis and her powers were nothing new, and Barefoot was inclined to believe them simply because witchcraft was illegal, and they wouldn't have made a law about it if it weren't real.

Did this woman have the witch behind her? The Sheriff had done well to avoid crossing Miss Carsis (assuming she did, in fact, exist) for this long – he didn't feel inclined to switch that up, when the convulsions wracking Boston were no doubt racing their way to an already unstable Fidget's Mill.

Perhaps he would play along for a time.

"Or perhaps," he graciously allowed, "I could hear your condition."

Which he did, and then he made the BOI-OI-OI-OING face again.

As Vera waddled off into the falling curtain of night, Barefoot called for a Constable to follow her discreetly. Recalling that he had no Constables to call, he stomped back into the cobblers and plopped his fists down on Mr. Ecker's desk.

"How'd you like to be a deputy?"

Mr. Ecker looked up from his work, which as far as Barefoot could tell was spit-shining a shoelace. "What's in it for me?"

Barefoot trotted over to his own desk, fished around the second drawer from the top, and came back with a big shiny badge. Before he had time to slap it on the table, Mr. Ecker volunteered for the position.

XXI

'FOLLOW VERA, SEE WHERE SHE GOES'. THAT WAS what Sheriff Barefoot had told Mr. Ecker to do, and so that's what Mr. Ecker was doing. What Sheriff Barefoot hadn't said was 'make sure she doesn't see you following her', and Ecker was nothing if not detail-oriented. So when Vera turned around and hailed him with a friendly hello, he was only too happy to go and have a chat with her.

She stood arms akimbo as Mr. Ecker closed the distance, and said something that got lost in the hush of the snow. "What's that?" Mr. Ecker inquired.

Vera repeated herself: "Barefoot set you to following me?"

Now within chatting distance, Ecker returned her smile. "He did, though I can't rightly say why. Beyond to see where you go."

"Naturally. Well, how's this: I'll save you some time by just telling you where I'm going, and you can go back and tell the Sheriff where I went." Somewhere in the back of her mind, she felt bad for employing her mock-gormlessness on someone as genuinely clueless as Mr. Ecker. But closer to the front of her mind, she knew that such a clueless individual could sometimes be even more dangerous than a…clueful one like the Sheriff.

Mr. Ecker's face lit up like any number of illumination methods that had yet to be invented. "You wouldn't mind?"

"No, not at all! I'm off to the storehouse on the docks, to see my old friend Mr. Increase. Just to catch up, you see. So why don't you head on back to the Sheriff, and let him know? That way you can have the rest of the evening to yourself."

"Ah, I really appreciate that! Do you suppose the Sheriff will allow me to keep this badge?" He brandished the big shiny deputy's badge, dropped it, and picked it up.

A shock of shame wormed its way through Vera. The poor fool just wanted to keep his badge. The pathos of it was almost enough to make her reveal her actual destination. Almost. But actually not even close. "I couldn't say one way or the other."

This seemed close enough to 'no' to dampen Mr. Ecker's spirits. So Vera continued with a helpful suggestion: "Perhaps just tell him you lost it? Dropped it in the snow and couldn't find it again?" Barefoot would likely find the story highly plausible, she thought but did not add.

"Another swell idea!" The cobbler exclaimed. "Thank you once again!"

Vera shrugged off his gratitude and bade him farewell. They went their separate ways, and it never once occurred to Mr. Ecker that Vera was walking in the exact opposite direction of the docks.

Before Vera came in, Miss Carsis had been sitting at the table, leaning on her elbows, forehead resting in her palms. When she felt Vera approach, she leaned back and pulled herself together. By the time one of her helpers opened the door, Miss Carsis was sitting ramrod straight, looking properly mystical.

But inside, she was still leaning on her elbows, forehead resting in her palms.

Staying one step ahead of everybody was hard work, even for a witch. Her powers were far more limited than most people suspected – like hypnosis, they required a certain degree of subconscious cooperation from their subject, even if that cooperation was passive. It was the difference between hand-sculpting with clay and hand-sculpting with a tree stump.

In point of fact, it was the Familiars who possessed most of the power. The consort was merely the mechanism by which the power could be harnessed. If the Familiar was a mad gale, the consort was the windmill. It was exceeding good fortune that the Familiars seemed constitutionally incapable of recognizing this fact (except, somehow, for Yazbirth Bicklebog).

And so, what Miss Carsis' true power came down to was in being cleverer than anybody else, and seeming to do so effortlessly. In her rare moments of solitude, the effort this actually required caught up with her, and pummeled her lungs like a boxer at the speed bags. Denton Hedges had his nervous tics, but Miss Carsis would gladly have traded a hand brushing through her hair for the shortness of breath that afflicted her miserable reflections.

Years ago she had set herself a goal; to help Sonny Crundwell and Tobin Lowestoft find a way to live and love together, in full view of the world, in the town that they called home. Ever since, she had been laboring to see it accomplished. The means by which she had labored were sometimes graceful, more often disgraceful, but always dictated by pure necessity. And until Denton Hedges had arrived in town, she'd been largely successful.

But then Denton arrived.

With him came uncertainty, for which she struggled mightily to account. So she had alternately obstructed and assisted him, in as far as she could without compromising her own goals, in the hopes of seeing the dope off, back to Boston. Finally, after far too long, he had gone, allowing her to resume her struggle to be one step ahead of people who she better understood, and so could better preempt.

But then Denton came back.

Once again, he played havoc with her plans. It was as though Miss Carsis had laid a careful chain of dominos, several thousand long, and Denton had galloped through with a horse, and set fire to her hair for good measure.

She put him up right next to her, so that she might keep an eye on what he was planning, and her woman on the street Vera had helped to fill in the blanks. Not because she cared what *he* was doing; she just wanted to ensure whatever it was wouldn't conflict with what *she* was doing. She was so, so close. She had been laying the groundwork for

Sonny and Tobin's return, and the time was almost ripe.

What news from next door, then? Denton was to duel Mr. Increase, and each had determined their seconds. This was a wonderful turn of luck, for it took barely any imagination to see how this could work to her advantage. As long as the duel *happened.*

It wasn't that she wanted to see Denton and Mr. Increase shooting at each other. It was more that it was expedient for her that they should. Particularly having Buddy Jr. on as Mr. Increase's second – this could all easily break her way. Besides, she didn't *not* want to see them shoot at each other, so bring on the ten paces.

Which was why she had deployed Vera to approach Sheriff Barefoot with an ultimatum: have the musket returned to him, in return for not interfering with the duel. For if Denton and Brisby were to appear on a hill at sunrise, even across the dueling ground from Mr. Increase and Buddy Jr., the people of the town would swamp them and tear the lawyer and the doctor apart before the dockhand could pull the trigger.

As Miss Carsis offered Vera a cup of tea, and Vera accepted, the witch learned that the Sheriff was reluctantly intrigued by the offer. And while there was no clear acceptance, nor had he dismissed it out of hand. Granted, he had sent Mr. Ecker after Vera, which implied some suspicion, but the cobbler had been easy enough to deflect. Miss Carsis and Vera had a good laugh at the Ecker's expense, and they both felt bad about. But both assumed the other didn't feel bad about it, and so they humored each other, neither objecting to the mean-spirited giggle that neither enjoyed.

All that was left, then, was to sneak next door and retrieve the musket. Bulstrode had listened through the wall until Denton's breath and heartbeat implied slumber, and then crept through the closed door to have a look around. As he had never appeared to anyone lodging there save Denton, there was no risk of discovery, and so he clicked around the house, bold as brass, looking for the musket.

Being atop the high shelf of the doorframe as it was, Bulstrode nearly missed it from his lower perspective. Fortunately, whoever had last returned it there had done a rather shoddy job of it, and Bulstrode caught the dull glimmer of the barrel peeking just an inch over the right edge.

Armed with this information, Miss Carsis had devised the plan, and brought in Vera. Now, the time had come to creep next door and snag it, a task that could only be accomplished by a human.

No-Good Bulstrode once again listened for the telltale signs of sleep, and tip-clawed his way back into the next door lodging. As he returned to Miss Carsis' through the front door a minute later, he silently cursed his inability to attain incorporeality, as Yazbirth could accidentally. "Our Denton's out like last seasons' breeches, though the depth of his slumber leaves something to be desired. He could well shift his weight and be prodded to waking by his broken bones. The Doctor's attained a more reassuring pitch of dormancy, and the kids are naught if not prone to coma, so-"

The witch shook her head. "Can Vera go or can't she?"

"Oh, she really should!"

Miss Carsis turned to Vera and said "go", which Vera did. After she'd left, closing the front door behind her, Miss Carsis stopped trying to be a step ahead of everything, and allowed herself to take a step back.

Denton was asleep, Brisby was asleep, the kids were asleep. What about Peggy? She voiced this concern out loud to Bulstrode, who pondered it for a long, thoughtful moment, before replying "He's got the wife here, hasn't he?"

"Yes!"

"...I suppose she's not well recognized around town, in the way our Denton is. So it's not wholly beyond the realm of stepwise reasoning that she might go for a lovely little stroll." It was the popping of her jaw that told Miss Carsis she had been grinding her teeth. "And so it's just as likely she could return at any moment, isn't it?"

"Yes," Bulstrode granted, "I suppose it is."

With that, Bulstrode scrambled back out the door. Oh, what he wouldn't give to walk straight through the wall.

He opened the door just enough to poke his little head through, but not enough to keep from bumping Vera as she pawed lamely at the top of the doorframe. "Let's keep things to a tranquil level best suited to pillow talk and threats made in libraries," Bulstrode led by whispered example, "but I must inform you that time is rather of the essence, as the Mrs. Denton could be ret-"

Vera whipped her head down, causing the entire hallway to creak in surprise. Bulstrode flinched. "The musket's meant to be up here?!" she wondered in the loudest whisper Bulstrode had ever heard.

"Yes," he replied, "so let's grab it and make o-"

"It's not here!"

Bulstrode ruffled his feathers in consternation. "Of course it is."

"It's not! Look!"

"Eye level!"

"What?"

"Ah, right. Kindly lift me!"

Vera obliged, lifting him over her head like a participation trophy.

The jutting lip of the doorframe was bare, save the lingering odor of unspent gunpowder. The musket had been here, but was no longer.

"Oh, hell," Bulstrode observed.

XXII

BAHBAHBAHBAHBAHBAHBAH!

The pounding on the door echoed through the storehouse, met only with itself at all turns.

Again: BAHBAHBAHBAHBAHBAHBAH!

The vacuity of the building mocked Barefoot's furious thudding. So, finally, he tried turning the doorknob, and discovered that the door was unlocked. He turned to the impromptu squad of civilians behind him, led by Deputy Ecker, and wordlessly advised them to hold their tongues. They got the message.

Barefoot led them into the dark storehouse, the quaking light from their torches shafting through the bare shelves, casting the shadows of a behemoth's boneyard.

"Vera Miringhoff!" he cried into the darkness.

-ghoff! the storehouse replied.

"Mr. Increase!"

-rease!

"We've come for the musket, and nothing more!"

-ng more!

Tired of the mockery, Sheriff Barefoot turned to his men and spoke to them in a tone of voice that the empty space before him wouldn't hear. "Split up and search the place. If you find Vera or Mr. Increase, ask them where the musket is. Ask nicely," he specified, seeing the look in some of their eyes.

They broke up, and set to struggling their way through the unlit labyrinth of shelves. Sheriff Barefoot and Deputy Ecker remained at the entrance, the former folding his arms impatiently (*not*, he would have specified, because he was cold), watching his breath crystallize and dissipate before him. "You wouldn't happen to know if there are multiple entrances or exits here, would you?"

Ecker shrugged. "I don't get down here so much. Not a fan of the water."

Barefoot threw a thumb towards the door over his shoulder. "She came in this way, then?"

"I'd assume so."

After a second or two of agreeable nodding, the Sheriff pursed his lips in thought. "You didn't stick around to watch her go in?"

"No." Deputy Ecker scratched the side of his face innocently. "Should I have?"

It was very hard to get truly *angry* at someone as well-meaningly dense as Ecker. So Barefoot settled for seething at him. "Yes. Of course. How else could you be *certain* that this is where she went?"

"Because she told me she was," Ecker came back defensively.

"…she told you?"

"Yes. And I trust her. Vera is a honest woman."

"You tru…" Barefoot didn't bother finishing the thought. He

pressed his fingers into his eyes and bared his teeth at visual oblivion. "Everybody!"

-ybody!

"Come on back to the front!"

-he front!

"We're rolling out again!"

-t again!

There came a grumbling from the dancing orbs of fire throughout the storehouse, a grumbling which rose to the threat of a clamor.

"Um," one of the untrained civilians Barefoot had plucked off the street called back, "I don't think I remember how to get back!"

-t back!

"Me neither!" came another voice.

-either!

"Nor I!"

Nor I!

Barefoot drew a breath so sharp that he choked on it, and set to coughing. "Help them all out," he coughed at Deputy Ecker, and then coughed his way out of the empty maze that coughed right back at him.

"Also I lost my big shiny badge and now I can't find it so I can't give it back!" Ecker, and then the darkness, called after him.

The Sheriff heard him over his own coughing, but pretended that he hadn't.

He ran a long, circuitous route back to the cobbler's, on which he pondered his unhappiness. The wonderful thing about fresh snowfall was that it could be an occasion for youthful wonderment, as evidenced by the children he passed who were rolling snowmen and hurling snowballs…but it could just as easily be the setting for lonely melancholy, as it was now.

So absorbed was Sheriff Barefoot in his unhappiness, he nearly missed the woman running towards him, calling his name. She was wrapped in no fewer than one hundred blankets, her human form obliterated by coziness, her gender only belied by the lightness of her voice. She carried a thick ovular satchel on her back.

"Sheriff?" she called. "Sheriff!"

Barefoot turned towards her like the moon reluctantly revealing its dark side to the Earth. "Ma'am? Everything alright?"

"You're the Sheriff?" she asked him hesitantly, nodding to a clutch of playing kids behind her. "I asked those kids back there, and they sent me to you, though you know kids sometimes have a mischievous streak."

Always pleased to see a woman erring on the side of caution, Barefoot produced his big shiny badge and the big shiny smile he saved for interactions with unfamiliar citizens. Not that there were so many citizens with whom he was unfamiliar. In fact, it had been a while since he'd failed to recognize someone in such a small town. Yet he was certain he didn't know this woman… "I'm the Sheriff, alright. Sheriff Barefoot, at your service."

"Thank heavens," she said in a great whooshing exhale, "I've been looking everywhere for you."

"Well," he replied through his big shiny smile as he repocketed his big shiny badge, "you've found me. Now how can I help you?"

"You can make me two promises."

The Sheriff felt a twitch in his eye, and hoped it wasn't as noticeable as it felt. "Oh? What promises might you be seeking?"

"First," she began as she hiked the blankets further up over her head, "that you'll not harass a good Samaritan trying to do their part."

"The Samaritan being yourself, I assume?"

"That's correct."

Barefoot thought over this for a moment. He never made promises lightly, because his promises were unbreakable. But, with a ticklish sensation, he felt he knew what good deed this Samaritan might be fixing to do for him. And if he was right, a promise was a small price to pay. "Alright," he told her, "I promise you'll receive no harassment from me. And a promise from me is a *promise*, you understand?"

The man's barrel-chested honesty was unmistakable. Thus

comforted, Peggy Hedges drew her clacking burden tighter over her shoulder and smiled. "I do. The second promise is that I need your help, saving my husband's life."

Chivalry grabbed Barefoot by the spine and rattled it like a chimp at the bars of its cage. A lady needed help! "What? What's the danger? Who is your husband?"

"My husband is Denton Hedges," she replied with a casual confidence that caught Barefoot off guard. "My name is Peggy."

He stared at her for several seconds, and then past her for several more, and then at her once again. Never in his life, had he heard of a Sheriff being interrupted in his manhunt by the hunted man's wife. This took him a moment to work out, even though the conclusion wasn't in question: he couldn't harass her to tell him where Denton was. He had made a promise, and his promises were unbreakable. Damn his convictions!

"Alright," he finally replied, "alright. Why…you realize I am pursuing your husband, correct?" To kill him if I can, he stopped himself from adding. But, he cursed silently, could he still go through with it? Being confronted with the man's wife, face made tender with concern, humanized the bully Denton in a way that was profoundly inconvenient for Barefoot.

"I do," Peggy admitted in a tone of voice that implied full awareness of Barefoot's unspoken addendums. "Largely for this, correct?" She unslung her burden, dropped it into the snow, and unwrapped it. The musket. Barefoot's musket.

With a disarming lack of dignity, the Sheriff fell to his knees before the firearm he had despaired of ever seeing again. His beloved object, unexpectedly returned to him. "Aah!" he honked at the musket. Lifting his head, he honked once more at Peggy.

"My husband is a good man," she told him as though he hadn't just fallen to his knees and honked at her, "and I'm quite certain you would agree, were you to encounter him in less antagonistic circumstances. He fetched his friend Brisby from your custody not due to sympathy for the British, which I should hasten to add the doctor himself does not possess, but out of the loyalty he extends to his friends. He has done Fidget's Mill a poor turn, I would not deny that. But there was never any malice in his heart." Despite the sincerity of her plea, her rosy cheeks threatened a smile. "He can just be a bit of a fool sometimes."

Sheriff Barefoot, despite having little interest in and less use for love, couldn't help but find the conclusion to her pitch endearing. She really loved Denton, and she seemed a kind, honest person. How could a scoundrel be loved by such a woman? Barefoot's antipathy for Denton hadn't quite been tempered by her display, but it had been flagged for later review.

"And now," she continued, "he stands prepared to be executed by his own foolishness, by the hand of a friend. And if he will do nothing to save himself, then I must intervene on his behalf. But I can't do it alone." She wiped her eyes, two quivering pools of crystal blue, and Barefoot suspected the tears were shed as much for her inability to save her husband on her own, as they were for the need to save her husband to begin with. "I return the musket to you on the strength of your first promise, which you have granted. But in return, I ask you for a few minutes of your time, that I might persuade you to grant the second promise: to stop the duel."

The Sheriff rose to his feet once again, gripping the musket tightly in his hands. It would be a distant day when he loosened his grip again, he felt sure of that. Staring at the familiar blemishes along the barrel, the cherished grain of the wooden stock, he realized just how beloved this object truly was. And somewhere in the sub-basement of his mind, he noted how distressing it was that a man like Denton could be loved by a woman like Peggy, but the only thing Sheriff Barefoot could love in the same way was a weapon.

Yes, perhaps he would hear Peggy out. It certainly couldn't hurt.

He told her as much, and added, as they strolled back towards the cobbler's, "I do appreciate you returning my firearm in such generous circumstances. Vera attempted to do the same, on terms much closer to blackmail."

Peggy frowned. Despite having his eyes fixed on his musket, Barefoot knew she was frowning – he could *feel* it. "Did she?" Peggy asked pointedly.

"She did. She claimed she didn't have the musket, but knew where she could get it. I've never felt entirely comfortable with that woman," he purred to his gun, "she feigns a simplicity that doesn't become her at all."

"Such an unctuous quality in a woman," Peggy concurred, though she wasn't entirely talking about Vera. Denton had mentioned that he had seen Vera stepping into Miss Carsis' the other night. And now here she was, trying to barter the rifle away for…what? "What terms did Vera have, for granting you the rifle?"

Barefoot smiled humorlessly. "The precise opposite of yours. She wanted me to ensure that the duel proceeded as planned, without any interruptions."

A faint groan escaped Peggy, and her pace increased. Barefoot was fairly certain she was unaware of the quickening. "Then I may need more than a few minutes of your time, Sheriff. I'm afraid I need your help more urgently than I realized."

As Barefoot quickened his own pace to match Peggy's, he wondered with something just shy of awe if this woman might not convince him to save the life of a man he had, moments ago, his heart set on destroying. But hey, it wasn't as though he'd *promised* to kill Denton.

XXIII

"GONE?"

"Gone."

Miss Carsis successfully restrained herself from slamming a fist on the table, at great expense to her blood pressure. To No-Good Bulstrode she snapped, "find out where she went, and why."

Without a word, Bulstrode slipped through the door (not literally), out into the same deepening night in which Peggy had made off with the musket.

"What should I do now?" Vera asked.

That was the question, wasn't it? What a mess this had become. She supposed this was what she got for trying to stay one step ahead of a clan of dolts as dense as the Hedges. Rational actors' actions could be predicted with a certain degree of reliability, but there was no anticipating what fools might do. Far from being one step ahead of the Hedges, she had felt one step behind from the jump; at first trying to utilize him for her own ends, then trying to have him chased out of town, then offering to personally escort him out of town, and finally hoping to see him killed, as a final solution to her problem. It wasn't that he deserved to die; it was that he was just so…inconvenient.

She considered it a personal failure that facilitating a man's death was the only solution to her current problem, but for whatever shame may attend it, it *was* a solution. Potentially a very neat one.

So what should Vera do? Miss Carsis sighed and told her to stay put, and hold down the fort.

Vera nodded. "For how long?" she asked, simply out of curiosity.

"Two or three days, perhaps." The witch sat motionless on her chair for several seconds, and then leapt up and threw on a cloak in one sweeping motion. "I need to see them, bring them up to speed."

Vera kept nodding, because she had not stopped nodding. She wasn't about to ask who 'they' were.

"Ensure nothing dramatic happens in my absence," Miss Carsis advised as she rushed towards the door.

"But what if it does?"

The final glare Miss Carsis gave Vera said *ensure that it doesn't*, which wasn't helpful at all. But Vera would never say anything like that to the witch. So she kept on nodding, until Miss Carsis was out the door and stillness had reclaimed the house.

No-Good Bulstrode was too late. He had stepped through the front door to see Peggy slipping back through the door directly next to the one out of which he had stepped.

"Oh, toss," he mumbled under his non-breath. Well, he could still follow her footprints back to wherever she'd come from.

And so he did just that.

Denton awoke to Brisby squawking. As he regained his senses, he realized that the squawk had semantic content, shaping syllables that formed words that corresponded to the sentiment of consternation.

"You *WHAT?*" Brisby had squawked.

"Quiet," Peggy snapped at him with a nod towards Denton and the sleeping kids. Brisby mumbled a quiet apology.

Denton tried to voice his own syllables that formed words that corresponded to the sentiment of dismissing concern, but all he could manage was a swampy groan. Peggy and Brisby looked to him, and closed in.

"How are you feeling?" they asked in unison.

"Grmph…" Denton leaned his head towards Brisby, but spoke to Peggy. "What's he so shocked about?"

She updated her husband on her nocturnal activities; returning the musket to Sheriff Barefoot, extracting a promise to prevent the duel, his revelation that Miss Carsis had attempted to ensure the duel occurred uninterrupted. Through all of this, Denton and Brisby listened in awestruck silence.

"Why is it so important to the witch that the duel comes off?" Brisby asked for them both.

Shaking her head, Peggy replied "I don't know," in a cautious tone of voice that belied a great deal of thought already expended on the subject.

"So," Denton wondered, as wonder was all he could do just then, "the duel is still happening?"

Peggy flinched, as though the mere thought of it occurring carried a mild shock. "You and Mr. Increase will meet on whatever dueling ground you choose. You will go through the motions, only to be interrupted by the Sheriff as you do. This should be acceptable, yes? You will not have shrunk from the challenge, thus preserving your delicate sense of honor," and there an unmistakable note of mockery crept into her voice, "but neither will you be forced to complete the barbarous exercise. Acceptable?"

It was, Denton marveled, and he said so. Peggy's solution was elegant, and achieved without any real sacrifice on their part. He couldn't help but laugh. "This compounds beautifully with the arrangement I made with Buddy Jr. There'll be no duel for him to interrupt, for he will arrange a peace between Mr. Increase and myself."

"But what happens after the Sheriff intervenes?" Brisby asked.

"As I just mentioned," Denton reiterated with some annoyance, "there w-"

"But when have things ever worked out the way we plan? Let's say the Buddy Jr. thing doesn't plan out."

"Pan out. But it will."

"I don't see how you can sit there and be so confident, after all we've been through." And, Brisby didn't add, you didn't even have to spend two years in a cobbler's. He didn't feel he had to, as he watched Denton collapse under the weight of recent memory. "Let's say it doesn't pan out. Sheriff Barefoot intervenes. Then what? Will we be arrested?"

"It will certainly appear that way," Peggy granted, "but once you're safely out of the view of the public, you'll be loaded into a carriage with myself and the kids, and we will leave this damned town once and for all."

This was a prospect Denton faced with no small sense of relief. This was all so much bullshit, and nothing drove that home like being chased by an entire town with murder in their eyes, and then having one's nose and ribs broken by an old friend. The sad fact was that the chaos of the Boston *Slaughter* – he would never back down from this being the superior name – was not coming to Fidget's Mill; it had already come, and it had come in the form of Denton himself.

Returning to Boston wasn't an option – if anyone had, in fact, seen his son throw the chunk of ice that kicked the whole thing off, they would be just an unsafe there as they were here.

But they could always return to Virginia, to live with his father in his childhood home.

With that thought salient in his mind, Denton threw up on himself a little bit. Brisby blanched with envy; he didn't know adults were allowed to do that.

XXIV

RIDING A HORSE AS GREY AS THE HEAVILY besodden snow, Miss Carsis approached the picturesque cabin just as the setting sun was getting fired up about its trip to the flip side of the globe. She wondered if the sun was almost always that giddy and expansive, only dulling itself for its journey over Fidget's Mill.

Pondering the heavens as she opened the door (without knocking) and stepping across the threshold, Miss Carsis rejoiced at how near to the end she had come. The two men in this cabin had become something approaching an occupation for her, and she would be superlatively pleased to have this whole affair behind her. Even if, deep down, she would miss the distraction it brought.

She could hear shuffling from the next room over, and so called to them. "It's only me, boys." In synchrony, Sonny Crundwell and Tobin Lowestoft popped their heads out from behind the doorframe. They smiled at Miss Carsis, and she smiled back at them.

All was as it had been two years ago, the last time they had gathered here. And yet, everything was different.

Sonny and Tobin had spent the past two years bouncing around New England, dropping their erstwhile co-conspirator a line now and again, before Miss Carsis finally called them back for the endgame. And after catching them up on everything that had occurred since Denton Hedges' return (who, she had forgotten until seeing their faces warp at mention of his name, they had come to believe was responsible for the poisoning plot that had killed Lucretia), she now laid that endgame out for them, as clearly as she could: the duel between Denton and Mr. Increase was going to happen, and all involved would be disgraced in the eyes of the town. How, she asked rhetorically on the Mill's behalf, could anyone engage the traitorous cowards Denton and Brisby on the field of honor? How could they besmirch the very concept by tacitly validating the right of these two men to fall under its rubric? One of the involved parties would be, of course, Buddy Jr. The patriarch of the crumbling dynasty would be lightly ostracized by the Mill's higher sorts. But, emaciated though it was, the ruins of the Crundwell empire would still need someone to oversee them. This, finally, was when Sonny would make his triumphant return, to claim his place as rightful heir!

Sonny and Tobin looked at each other after Miss Carsis finished, and then back at the witch. It was Tobin who spoke first: "That's …that's really not at all related to what you said you'd been working on over the past two years."

"Yes. But don't you see? This is precisely the moment to bring these machinations to a head!"

"But…" Sonny finally replied, "…why?"

Miss Carsis had imagined a number of possible reactions from the two men before her, and all had been variations on the theme of fawning gratitude. It was several seconds before she could get her feet back under her. "Why? What do you mean, 'why'?"

She watched as a look passed between them, a look that said they had been discussing something and weren't eager to let her in on it. "Well," Tobin began, "I suppose we've been wondering, erm, why we should want to go back at all."

A bird outside scolded Tobin for his temerity. "Since when?" Miss Carsis exclaimed in a frighteningly unexclamatory tone of voice.

"Well, since we got to the cabin here."

"I…" Miss Carsis didn't know what she…, just that she… *something*, something not very nice at all. "I don't understand." She hoped they appreciated what they had just heard – it was a rare and exotic situation that led Miss Carsis to confess ignorance.

"Well, we'd g-"

"For god's sake, stop saying 'well'!"

Tobin jumped. "Mhm. Sorry. W…um. Of course we were wholly on board with the scheming, until very recently. But traveling around, we started to wonder why it mattered so much, that we be appreciated in the Mill. We made friends in other cities, held down jobs and supported ourselves. It wasn't nearly as hard as we expected." Miss Carsis knew that *we* was Tobin being generous and covering for Sonny. The Lowestoft riches, after all, had been built largely upon Tobin's shoulders. Sonny had inherited his wealth, and so was the one unaccustomed to doing actual work. "And then you brought us out to this cabin, and…we remembered what it's like here. It's unpleasant. It's beautiful, but unpleasant. And we don't feel as though we need much more than a place to live, and each other. Which we can do just about anywhere." They held hands and mooned at each other, and so Miss Carsis found the limits of her sentiment. It was getting downright saccharine in here.

As calmly as she could, she offered a rebuttal. "I've spent years of my life working on this. And now you're not interested anymore, because you're suddenly happy to live in some Philadelphia hovel?"

They were genuinely shocked. "We thought you'd be happier," Sonny said.

"Why would I be happy?!"

"Less work for you."

As calmly as she could, she screamed and hurled a chair across the room. "*Years of my life, Sonny!*" As Sonny and Tobin reviewed the exchange later in their own lives, they both agreed that the chair had waited for Miss Carsis to finish shouting before exploding against the far wall.

"Ours too," Tobin replied with uncharacteristic sharpness.

Miss Carsis rubbber her forehead, took a deep breath, and regained her usual unflappability. "Wheels are in motion, boys. You don't have a choice."

"There's always a choice."

"How original. What are you willing to wager, to that effect?"

Tobin joined Sonny in silence.

No one was more surprised by this eruption of fury than Miss Carsis. But she couldn't help it – here were two kindred spirits, united with her by their marginalization. And here was a betrayal, borne of their acceptance of the position into which they'd been cast. More than the time she'd wasted, the years of her life during which her every maneuver, every decision was made with them in mind to one degree or another, more than this, it was the sense of betrayal that wounded her.

She knew it was unreasonable, but she couldn't help it.

And wasn't there also an element of personal pride? She wanted to know that, after years of scheming and dreaming, she could pull off something as substantial as supplanting a power player in the town. Whether or not Sonny wanted to take the reins from his brother was of little concern to Miss Carsis – she wanted to know that, by her labors, he *could* if he wanted to.

Thus, she reached a low point in her career as a sneak. "Do this for me," she told Sonny, "be where I tell you, when I tell you, do to what I tell you…and I will give you this cabin, or any property in town, with no further claim upon your future. You can be happy here." And seeing their faces, seeing the love they had for each other, and how that love made them a bloc immovable by reason or coercion or even magic, Miss Carsis availed herself of a last resort, a desperate measure to be used only when any and every alternative had been exhausted. She said "please."

This time, her audience appreciated the stunning rarity of what they had just witnessed. So it was with great care that Sonny told her "no. I'm sorry Miss Carsis, we are truly and deeply grateful for everything you have done for us. But no."

I killed Lucretia, she wanted to tell him. *She rots in a hole because I was laboring for you, thinking only of you and Tobin. If you flee the Mill, then her death will have been for naught.*

No, no, no. The word burned the canvas of her mind from the center outwards. No. Nobody had ever said no to her before, at least not in decades. No. She'd carefully crafted a persona for herself, whose requests were impossible to deny, and so had the force of demands. No. And now here she was, debasing herself with the cant of supplication, and still they said no. No. And what could she do about it? No. Nothing. No. That was the joke of witchcraft. No. Nobody had ever said no to her, so when somebody finally *did* say no, she had no idea what to do about it. No. No! No.

She had never wanted anything as much as she wanted for Sonny and Tobin to be free to be themselves, together. And now they were abandoning that, so they could run away and…

…

They were doing exactly what they had always wanted. They just weren't doing it in the Mill. And so they just weren't doing it with Miss Carsis' help.

So *this* is what it felt like to be used, and tossed aside when one was no longer useful.

She cleared her throat, and took as deep a breath as her tightening chest out allow. "I am so happy for you two. Truly, I am." And so she appeared to Sonny and Tobin. And so she continued to appear until they once again, and for the final time, vanished over the far horizon, chasing the sun to those parts of the world where it could always be as giddy and expansive as she saw it just before night fell.

Well, she reflected with a lump in her throat, *shit.* Win some lose some, that was a philosophy with which she'd never held. But then she'd lost.

Next time, she would win. No matter what.

XXV

BRISBY COULDN'T BE PERSUADED TO LEAVE THE house alone yet, so Peggy swallowed her distaste for the duel, a feat only made possible by her knowledge that she was now a play-actor in a cut-rate farce. Acting as second to Denton's second, she tracked down Mr. Increase's second Buddy Jr., and began the negotiations for the *where* and *when* of the duel. It was the work of but a few minutes to bring the negotiations to a close: the duel would take place on an abandoned field just over a hill on the northwestern extremity of the town. The sloping hillside boasted two chief benefits: the first being that it was land that belonged to no man, the second being that the grounds could not be seen from town. Nobody had any illusions about privacy – no matter what time they all left town, some townsfolk would see them go, and the duelists would hardly have taken three paces before some nosy Fidgetonians crested the hill in hopes of seeing a man bleed to death.

Still, it seemed good form to at least make an effort. So they would duel in the field, which Peggy would later discover was called Snot Holler. Had she known that, she would undoubtedly have pushed for an alternative venue.

The initial time frame was to be two weeks from the date of the negotiation, two weeks being Brisby's guesstimation on when Denton would be able to stand up and lift a firearm. Peggy's husband was holding up admirably well against the agony of a fractured rib, as long as he could be ensconced in a tomb of pillows and blankets, and spoon-fed like a baby. The moment he moved, or was moved, or felt a gentle draft making a tour of his home, he would whimper loudly. It broke Peggy's heart, and upset the children. Denton would do his best to placate their concerns by lightening the mood through humor, which also upset the children. One joke, which went a little something like "what's the difference between bread and a rib? One you break with friends, the other is broken by a friend, in my specific case, and is excruciatingly painful," made Annabelle groan and wail at the same time. It was a noise nobody ever wanted to hear again.

So Denton devoted two weeks to convalescence, listening impotently to the world changing without him. The Boston Slaughter, which would undoubtedly (and unfortunately) be consigned to history as the Boston Massacre, had indeed triggered a wave of anti-English rage in Massachusetts, but unlike previous paroxysms, this showed no sign of tapering off into supplication once again. A fuse had been lit, and the only questions left to be answered were how long the fuse was, and how much gunpowder lay at the end. Denton reviewed his contributions to the Cause, in the form of securing non-importation all those years ago, and swelled with pride at his role. Brisby helped to keep the swelling under control, and Denton regulated the rest; if he left it unchecked, he might well be forced to investigate their contributions with a more scrupulous eye. Who knew if they would survive such scrutiny?

At the end of two weeks, Brisby shook him awake and whispered "today is the day." Denton nodded, rose to his feet, and then woke up on the floor with his stomach on fire.

Once Brisby got the pain under something approaching control, he offered his professional opinion: the discomfort of the rib was still too great, and had caused Denton to lose consciousness upon standing. Denton, in turn, brought his extensive legal education to bear in leveling a verdict on Brisby's contribution: "You're joking."

"No, I'm afraid I'm not.

"No…*I* was joking."

"…did you strike your head du-"

"Just help me up."

Hoping to catch Mr. Increase before he went out to the field, Peggy rushed from the house, through the streets made soggy with the ghost of snowfall. She came upon a modest procession trekking towards the field, at the head of which strode the man of the hour and his second. She informed them of Denton's collapse, and witnessed mixed feelings dance across Mr. Increase's face with mixed feelings of her own. The duel would have to be postponed. There was nothing for it.

When she returned home, Peggy was met by a frantic Brisby dashing down the long hall to the front door.

"He's getting delirious," Brisby panted.

Without a word in response, Peggy did her own dash down the hall, to see Denton lying on the bed, looking decidedly cogent. The only thing that spoiled the illusion was his constantly darting his eyes to an empty space in the air, near the center of the room.

Denton and Peggy never held anything back from one another, no matter how unbelievable. So, suspecting (and hoping) she knew what this was, Peggy hustled to Denton's side, crouched next to him, and whispered "which one is it?"

He grinned – there was never any reason to doubt that his wife trusted him wholly, but it still warmed his heart to see a piece of abstract knowledge instantiated. "Yazbirth Bicklebog."

"Can I see him?"

Denton nodded to the air just over her shoulder, and the air said "Myself would have made an effort to be more presentable, had Myself known Myself would be meeting Yourself today."

Slowly, Peggy turned around, and came face to knee with Yazbirth Bicklebog the giant sloth. Even more slowly, she traced her eyes up the mighty buffoon's frame of matted fur and stylish lichen. Much more quickly than either of these actions, a smile spread across her face.

Dr. Brisby Houlihan watched this with mounting horror, wishing he hadn't worked so hard to avoid the mental health lectures at school. Was madness an airborne, communicable affliction? Thinking back on his experiences in Fidget's Mill over the past few years, he concluded that yes, of course it was.

Denton and Yazbirth conversed for a time, the latter regretfully informing the former that he couldn't heal his shattered rib. A Familiar could take things away – as Bulstrode had the unborn fetus, or Yazbirth had with the swelling on Denton's nose. But a Familiar couldn't fix things – for that, a consort with powers of his or her own was required. Fithian didn't have these powers yet, and didn't seem in a great hurry to acquire them. So Yazbirth could take Denton's pain away, a service of which Denton availed himself – partially. But as the rib would remain broken, Denton wanted a trace of the pain to remain, as a reminder. A sharp stinging in the chest would let him know when he was overextending himself, but the notification would remain a sharp stinging, never again escalating to consciousness-obliterating agony.

Stunned by his patient's sudden recovery (the hallucinations seemed to pass as quickly as the pain), and so stunned by his own exceptional talents as a physician, Brisby suggested Denton take up target practicing in the two weeks between now and the rescheduled duel, "just in case". Denton refused the offer without hesitation. Even if Sheriff Barefoot were not primed to stop the duel before it started – which he still was, Peggy had been reassured both by his words and actions when she had gone to notify him of the new day of the duel – and even if Buddy Jr. were not still briefed to sue for peace with Brisby when the seconds met prior to the duel proper – which he couldn't say for *sure*, having not spoken to Buddy Jr. in quite some time, but he felt comfortable counting on given the man's fascination with honor – even if both plans failed, Denton still had no intention of shooting Mr. Increase. He had never in his life picked up a gun (well, the musket, but that didn't count), and if picking one up should now be unavoidable, he could still make the decision to keep his finger off the trigger, no matter what. Conflicts could be resolved through words, and reason, and exertions of the intellect.

Denton instead spent the two weeks holed up, taking advantage of the hospitality of a witch who apparently wanted to see him dead, spending time with his family. And crazy as it was, despite where they were, despite knowing that there was no safe place for him in the entire town outside of these walls, despite the looming threats that closed in from all quarters, Denton was happy for those two weeks in Fidget's Mill, as he never had been here, and never thought he could have been. He loved his family, and was loved by his family, and that love could never be dulled by circumstance. Dear God, why had he come back here? Why had he stayed here? He should have left with his family. If he could feel this happy *here*, he could have gone *anywhere*, and been even happier than he was now. It was trite, and it was obvious, and deep down Denton felt he had known it all along. Yet it was the simplicity of the realization that kept it from seeming true. The world was an unbearably complicated place, and Denton had at some point decided that there was no room for such straightforward, treacly sentiment. So he had made his own life unbearable complicated, not because it had to be, but because it seemed it probably ought to be.

And now here he was, with less than two weeks to revel in his no-shit epiphany, and a sinking feeling in the pit of his intestines that something was going to go very wrong at the end of it.

What a fool he had been.

At long last, the day of the duel arrived (for the second time in as many weeks). April sixth (which was only going to happen once this year no matter what). For the first time in nearly a month, Denton stepped outside, into a pre-dawn morning he could hardly credit as belonging to Fidget's Mill. He had rarely ever seen it when it wasn't absolutely covered in snow, as though God had come to regret creating the town at all and was doing his level best to bury it. And yet here was Gutter Lane, the eponymous Gutter running along the moist cobblestones, moss sprouting up from the poorly set grouting between them. It was chilly, but not freezing – a thick blanket was sufficient to keep the frost at bay.

This was, Denton noted, very similar to how the town looked when he first saw it. This thought gave him a feeling a bit like the one that accompanies a return to one's childhood stomping grounds after a long absence, to discover that everything is much smaller than one remembered it being.

Brisby and Peggy stepped out of the house behind him, the latter shutting the door. She had insisted on coming, and Denton hadn't put up too much of a fight. They left the kids inside, trusting Lawrence to act his age and take care of his sister. He was, Denton had driven home to him, nearly a man now. This was a speech he'd planned to give eventually, but he hadn't foreseen giving it with tears in his eyes. But that was alright, because strong men also cry. Lawrence the Young Man nodded solemnly, and reassured his parents that they could trust him. They were glad to hear it, but just in case, they left a spectral babysitter, giving Yazbirth permission to make himself visible to them if they started to get too rambunctious.

They'd initially approached Fithian about babysitting, but she'd been the one to volunteer Yazbirth. Despite her self-imposed aloofness from the affairs of the town, she wanted to see the duel. As did most people. Fidget's Mill was a small town, and secrets had a bad habit of becoming not-so-secrets, given enough time.

So Denton, his second and his better half weren't the only ones moving towards Snot Holler under an empty sky. The moon had set, the sun had yet to rise, and the stars had fled. There would be no celestial witnesses to whatever occurred on the hill, and Denton shivered at the thought of being abandoned by even his Creator. The sinking feeling kept sinking until it couldn't sink any more – it was a sunken feeling.

With a bolt of dread through the heart, Denton realized that, terrified of the abysmal vault above as he was, he was even more petrified by what the sun would show him when it finally dawned. Perhaps there was Someone watching him out there, cackling across the dreadful expanse of oblivion. Denton had been given two weeks of bliss with his family, and now here he was, shuffling blindly towards an uncertain conclusion, wishing for nothing more than to remain in the stygian void for eternity.

Part Four:

The Fear of Tyrant Custom

April 6, 1770

A Middling Sort

I

"THERE'S A TURKEY IN YON CELL," MR. ECKER noticed blithely. He'd been very little but blithe, ever since Barefoot had reversed the deputation.

The Sheriff looked, saw, and groaned. As if he didn't have enough to worry about, knowing he would have to face down the full fury of Fidget's Mill, a fury which he himself had stirred, and tell it to just relax for a second and then go home because there wasn't going to be any dueling today. As if he wasn't having a fowl enough day as it was, har, har, har.

Walking towards the cell, he thought about just locking the door and leaving the tar-black turkey there until there was time to deal with it. He thought about grabbing a broom and shooing the darned thing out with it. Not once did he think about where the darned thing might have come from in the first place.

If he had, he might not have waddled into the cell with it. "Alright, out you come," Barefoot mumbled with arms outstretched. And he was right about that – the turkey slipped right between the bars of the cell.

Before he could wonder aloud just what the hell was going on, he looked over his shoulder to see Miss Carsis swinging the door of the cell closed.

"Goddamnit!" he cried, rushing towards the iron door with the big heavy lock that Sheriff Barefoot had fought strenuously to obtain. It was, he had been assured, just about impossible to open without the key.

Which Miss Carsis was now twisting in the lock. Sheriff Barefoot had never been so acutely aware of the noises each individual mechanism in the latch made when engaged. *KershhclclCLUNG-tickticktinglejingleTHRUNK.*

BONG went the bars as Barefoot thrust his full weight against them. He bounced off of them, and knew that he had hurt his shoulder. The is to say, his shoulder didn't hurt yet, but he knew that it would. He was too angry to feel pain just then.

Not even dignifying his headlong charge with a sprightly step backwards, Miss Carsis shrugged at Barefoot, making the face most people make when they spill something dark on a light carpet. The damned turkeymonster resumed what Barefoot could imagine was a well-worn place at the witch's heel, and looked up at him with blank little sockets that resembled nothing more than human nostrils.

"Terribly sorry about this," the turkey told him, "though we're quite glad of your cooperation, unwitting though it may have been."

Sheriff Barefoot stared at the turkey who had just spoken to him like a hoity-toity Englishman. Slowly, he raised a finger and pointed at it. *That* set his shoulder to hurting.

Miss Carsis looked far less apologetic than Bulstrode, but that wasn't to say she looked entirely *un*apologetic. "There's something to which we must see," she said, "and once it has been seen to, I shall return." She flourished the key in her hand, and, with a wave, made it disappear. To see a powerful and feared witch (and all doubts of her being a practitioner of the dark arts had been banished when the turkey spoke, which, now that Sheriff Barefoot laid it out, didn't really make *all* that much sense as a therefore, but all the same it *did*) demeaning herself with the same flaccid sleight of hand tricks most commonly practiced the world over by dense nephews of whom little was expected, was perhaps the most incredible part of this whole thing.

But there was precious little time to mull on it; he saw at once what this was about.

"Is this about the duel?" Barefoot tried to look as authoritative as he could while gripping the bars of a prison cell from the wrong end. "I gave my word!"

"Things change," Miss Carsis replied, and there was no real way to argue with that. She swept out of the room, *swept*, which was particularly memorable, as she was wearing nothing with much by way of sweepy bits. The turkey followed, but didn't make a big deal about it.

What Miss Carsis would have known, had Barefoot the sort of mind that could be easily read, was that the word to which Barefoot felt beholden had been given to Peggy to *stop* the duel, rather than Vera to *ensure* the duel. Even if Vera had failed to deliver the musket, after all, Barefoot's newfound hatred for Denton was no secret. And so by locking Sheriff Barefoot up, Miss Carsis was preventing Barefoot from preventing the duel. Which, funnily enough, was what she was now off to do. Feeling used and exploited by Sonny and Tobin had given her a new appreciation for how it felt, and who in town had been more thoroughly mistreated in that manner than Denton Hedges? She wanted to see no harm come to him, and so her first step was locking up a man she believed wanted to see harm come to him, because of a stratagem initiated by herself.

She also might have known this if she hadn't been so eager to sweep out of the room.

As Sheriff Barefoot fought vainly against a rising heartrate, rising to drown the embarrassment of his own stupidity, and his fury at the turkey's duplicity, he heard a scribbling noise from the corner. His first thought was 'vermin', and that was true enough: Mr. Ecker was over in the corner, attempting to draw a picture of the shoe sat upon his desk.

So disoriented had he been by the whipcrack reversal of fortune, Barefoot had completely forgotten his erstwhile deputy was still in the room. What luck, then, that Miss Carsis had as well!

"Mr. Ecker!" he said at a normal speaking volume, which was when it first occurred to him that maybe there was a problem here. There was literally no way Mr. Ecker was unaware of what had just happened. "Mr. Ecker."

The cobbler swung his head blithely toward the imprisoned Sheriff, and blithely blithed, "yes?"

"You need to fetch a locksmith."

"Why?"

The Sheriff pondered several impolitic responses, before settling on the gentlest option he could. "Because I'm locked in this cell. As you may well have noticed."

Mr. Ecker swung his head back to his drawing. "Can't say I did."

"…" The only thing to do, as far as Barefoot could see, was to play along. Screaming would get him nowhere. "I find that very hard to believe."

"Oh, my eyes have been on the way out for a while now."

"There was quite a bit of shouting, in case you missed the visual cues."

"Same story with my ears. Same sad story."

If this was a part of some brilliant strategy by Mr. Ecker to enrage the Sheriff until he could simply crush the bars in his ever-tightening grip and tear them from their foundations, then it was surely as near to working as it would ever get. "I can't help but notice that you're hearing me quite well."

"They comes and goes, the old ears do."

Barefoot was clenching his jaw so tightly, it was a labor to enunciate clearly. He wanted to say "Coming right now, are they?", but said some-thing closer to "Curring 'ight 'ow, rr'ay?"

"Were for a bit, but I'm afraid I can feel 'em going as we speak." With that, Mr. Ecker plopped his hand back on the page and resumed the blithe sketched that was blithely inspired by no more than blithe anger. At least, that's what it looked like to Barefoot. But anger at what? Anger at…

Of course.

"This is about the revoked deputation?" he boggled. "I've told you, the deputation was temporary, forced by circumstance."

"You didn't mention that when you gave me the badge," Mr. Ecker sulked, indifferent to the miracle of his suddenly restored hearing.

"There wasn't time then!"

Ecker looked at the shoe as though he were dreaming of cobbling some spikes onto it, and clobbering Barefoot to death with the result. "You could have at least let me keep the badge!"

"You shouldn't have told me you'd found it! You should have just pretended it had stayed lost, if you wanted to keep it so badly!"

"Well how was I supposed to know you weren't gonna let me keep it after I found it from being very much lost, for real?"

"I told you!"

"Well, you still could have!"

"No I couldn't have!"

"Yes you could!" The pencil in Mr. Ecker's hand *snapped*, which would have been more impressive if the cobbler hadn't quietly said "whoops" right after.

The Sheriff slammed his forehead into the bars. "Ow," he said. There are very few good reasons to slam one's head into cold iron bars, but Barefoot felt it warranted by the situation. "No, I really couldn't. The authority stems from the badge, and you were granted the authority on a provisional basis, in response to a crisis that was speedily resolved. Thanks to you," he added uncon-vincingly.

"Authority stems from the badge?"

"...I'm speaking in metaphors."

"That makes no sense. Suppose a man were to brain a deputy and steal his badge. Does that make *him* a deputy?"

The Sheriff closed his eyes and binged a few little bongs on the bars with his forehead. "A metaphor, Mr. Ecker."

"I'm well aware," he sneered in a tone of voice which said he was not at all aware of what a metaphor was. He shot up from his seat and took a few tentative steps towards the cell. "But here is where I think authority comes from. I am in pris...*you* are in prison, and I am not.

Also, the lady took the key."

"That's why I told you to go to the locksmith."

"Oh. Well, the other stuff still works."

Negotiating without leverage was stupid, but Barefoot had no choice. "You are aware," he told Mr. Ecker, "that if you do not aid in my immediate release, and today's duel occurs as Miss Carsis intends, I will have no choice but to name you as an accomplice in one or the other duelists' murder?"

Mr. Ecker shrugged and returned to his seat. "That's if anybody lets ya out, Sheriff." With that, he put the drawing of the shoe away, because there had never been any point to it other than to give vent to his anger. In its own strange way, it had worked. As he turned his head to the Sheriff, he tilted it hard to one side, eyes bulging. He reached up, felt behind his ear, and pulled out the key Miss Carsis had made disappear. "Woah!" he cried, which was fair enough, because he'd just been the subject of the greatest *something in your ear* trick in history.

And yet he made no moves to release Barefoot. The rusty tang of the bar stinging his nostrils, the cold flakes of it tracing a tactless pillar down his forehead, Sheriff Barefoot went over and over that last comment as though he were vetting its alibi. Second to last, if one considered 'woah' a comment. Yes, he was assuming he would eventually get out. Why wouldn't he be? Wasn't that a perfectly reasonable assumption? They (which was a galling thought, as Barefoot had spent the majority of his life being *they*) would have no right to hold him here indefinitely. Granted, he had done the same to the physician for two years, but that was different.

Yes, it was different, he was sure of it. And soon enough, he would figure out precisely how.

The will of the people had been arrayed against Brisby, a vestige of Colonial influence. Sheriff Barefoot, despite having been appointed by Royal edict, had shifted his loyalties to the people he served. *That* was a difference, right?

Though if Denton was to be believed, Brisby had no more loyalty to the Crown than Barefoot himself. It was just that nobody had listened...

And, goddamn him, he had just tipped his hand to Mr. Ecker. Barefoot had been off to stop the duel. Had he been able to actually stop it, he felt confident retaining authority in the town would have been a simple feat of inertia. But now, he was locked in a cell, retroactively charged with seeking to prevent the bloodletting the town had, since discovering the fact of the duel, come to consider as nothing more or less than atonement for what had happened as a result of non-importation...

Without quite knowing how, the Sheriff had sidled his way back to the bench nailed into the sole wall of the cell and sat down. What if he were never released? What if the people of Fidget's Mill decided he no longer reflected their will, and chose the path of least resistance – inaction, letting him remain locked up – instead of a choice that might require a bit of debate, and potentially gainsaying the will of the witch?

The political complexities with which Barefoot had busied himself for the majority of his life melted away in a single fluttering heartbeat. His life had become simplicity itself; hoping and praying and wishing that he would not rot away in this cell.

More disturbing, more existentially shattering than the prospect of being imprisoned in his own cell for the rest of his life; there was something liberating in that simplicity.

II

THE FIRST RAYS OF THE RISING SUN CARVED through the mist like conquistadors through a wild underbrush. The effort seemed to drain them of their color and vitality, and so the light that breached the haze to fall on Snot Holler was a grey imitation of illumination.

In another world, Denton could have imagined Snot Holler being a beautiful place. It was a slow roll of verdure that did nothing so drastic as peak at the top, but instead suggested a generous crest before sloping down to a glassy pond on the far side. The hideous name of the place was impossible to square with its modest charm.

And yet, the name fit all the same. The etiolated sunshine upon the flat, windless pinnacle of the hill gave the splendor a skeletal bent, as though Snot Holler overlaid the skull of a giant, a skull in which dark thoughts still rattled. Someday, Denton felt certain, when the population of the Colonies had doubled and quadrupled, someone would purchase this glorious landscape, and a mansion would be built atop the hill. And it would be haunted from the start.

Perhaps by none other than himself.

He shivered at the thought, and Peggy saw him shiver. She gripped his arm and squeezed. The squeeze was firm, and admitted to no uncertainty; Sheriff Barefoot had looked her in the eyes and told her that his promises were unbreakable, as if it were as much an objective fact as gravity. Her husband would not be dueling today, no matter how much it looked as though he would.

And hadn't he been so confident, even just earlier this morning? Where had his brash insouciance gone? Not that Peggy missed it in and of itself, it had just been nice to see her husband feeling on top of things for a change.

"Look," Brisby whispered as they trudged up the hill.

"At w-" Denton started to ask, but then he saw them: suggestions in the mist. Pillars of shadow that rose to human height, shadows through which lay the sweet misery of extinction.

"You're a dang cunt," shouted one of the portals to oblivion.

As Denton, Peggy and Brisby drew closer, the holes in the morning filled with human features. The features belonged to three young children, of the sort Denton had seen frolicking in the snow an eternity of Christmases ago. Now they had come to Snot Holler, to see a grown man shot dead.

Expecting to be shot at but not insulted, Denton had no reasonable response to this particular volley, except to say "no I'm not."

"Yes," one of the other kids informed him, "you are."

Brisby jumped in with his professional opinion: "He's really not."

"Actually," the third kid retorted, "he is."

"And so are you," the second kid added.

Peggy gripped Denton's arm tighter. "Don't listen to them," she whispered, and that was good enough for him.

There would be more spectators. He knew it. If these little twerps knew about the duel, the whole town must know. They had just shown up to get the best seats in the house; it was only a matter of time before the people with responsibilities found excuses to defer them, and made their way out to Snot Holler.

As the sun rose, and the mist grudgingly floated off to darken some other patch of dayspring, Denton's supposition was proving correct. Fidgetonians silently migrated out to Snot Holler, mostly in groups. The duel was proving a social occasion, like a jaunt to the theater. Denton was, in fact, treated as he imagined performers were prior to the lifting of the curtain. Except for a few half-hearted insults, he was generally ignored. This was bittersweet; he had anticipated the mere act of showing his face in public would summon up a mob and stoke their resentments to a slathering pitch, so the familiar indifference with which they handled him was a welcome relief. Granted, they did this only because they anticipated his death to be attained in an altogether more entertaining fashion than they could devise, but that was the downer's perspective on the day.

Still, their apathy towards him rankled slightly. Was he not, after all, the center of attention? He recalled the reverence with which he was heeded during a courtroom disquisition. When it was his turn to talk, people had listened, and he had liked it. Just what he had liked about it eluded him; he was never the 'look at me look at me' type in informal settings. It was, he guessed, something about the fact of it being *his turn* in some officially sanctioned capacity. And now, it was *his turn* to duel. It was a situation he would have been just as happy to avoid, but if he had to be in this situation, it cheesed him off that his primacy was going unrecognized.

The cheesing became stone-cold disgruntlement when Mr. Increase and Buddy Jr. hiked their way up the hill, and were greeted with the cap-doffing adulation Denton felt ought to be his just as much as Mr.

Increase's.

It wasn't Mr. Increase's fault that he received the very attention of which Denton was deprived, and to his credit the free man seemed genuinely impatient with the display. But Denton couldn't help the tickle of resentment he felt for the man in that moment.

Lowering his gaze from the sky, Mr. Increase locked eyes with Denton, and favored him with a look of such warm recognition that the tickle dissipated without even a memory to mark its passage.

Why, they asked each other with their eyes, are we doing this? How did this happen?

Peggy was right; this was all bullshit. He had denied it, and then granted it, but now he *believed* it. Hadn't he been happy with his family, closed up in a little home? Wasn't that all he needed? Why did he need to prove himself to a town full of strangers he had never intended to see again, from a town to which he had never planned to returned (and yet knew he'd had no choice *but* to return to, if not in his waking life then most certainly in his nightmares)? What the hell was he *doing*?

He took a step in Mr. Increase's direction, and the murmur of the spectators halted in an instant. They seemed to close in from all sides, like an inquisitor's vise clamping the head of a heretic.

"You're to have no personal dealings with your fellow duelist," Brisby whispered to Denton. The latter at first wondered why the former was whispering, until he answered in at a normal speaking volume:

"I just need to say something to him." Denton's voice boomed across Snot Holler, dueling with its own echo. So there was a clue as to whence the latter half of Snot Holler's unfortunate name.

Denton's words had a physical effect on the crowd, which had tightened into an inescapable amphitheater of flesh. They seemed to bow their knees slightly, to allow the placatory sentiment to go soaring over their heads and into the deepening blue of the sky, hopefully all the way to the sun, where it would be incinerated.

The 'something' Denton wanted to say to Mr. Increase was clear enough to everyone – he didn't want to duel anymore. This knowledge only redoubled their excitement; it was rare to see a duel between unwilling participants.

"You can't," Brisby replied in another whisper. "I'm sorry. But don't worry, I can. Buddy Jr. and I shall clear this right up."

"Yes," Denton whispered back, "I know. Of course."

From his shoulder, Peggy once against squeezed Denton's arm, this time threading both hands between his bicep and chest. She was careful not to brush against his sensitive rib cage, even though she stood on his unoffended side, and her care was well placed. 'There will be no duel', her half-embrace reiterated, and because she believed it, Denton believed it.

After all, even if Buddy Jr. somehow failed to sue for a peaceful resolution in the role of Mr. Increase's second, Peggy had secured Barefoot's word that he would step in and put a stop to this farce. No, there would be no duel.

"That's alright," Denton returned in a similar whisper, having learned his lesson. "Off you go to inspect the weapons. And," he added in a whisper from even deeper down the well of silence, "when Buddy Jr. offers you an honorably bloodless conclusion to the affair, you will take it."

Brisby grinned at both the prospect of a morning uncolored with crimson, and the cheeky way Denton said this, as though Brisby had not just reassured him of this fact second ago. "Of course." With that, off he tromped to meet Buddy Jr. upon the field of honor.

Swept away by excitement, Denton turned to his wife and told her "everything will be fine", neglecting to whisper. His reassurance thundered across the Holler, cracking the sky and loosing a gale of laughter from the Fidgetonians that had surrounded the duelists. Their laughter deafened him to his own happy sentiments, and he suddenly felt exactly as he had when he once spent an hour searching for a favored pencil that turned out to be tucked behind his ear. It was a moment of discovering something so obvious that it should never have needed discovering in the first place; the people of Fidget's Mill had a bone to pick with him, and they would not go home until his bones had been picked clean. One way or another, everything would not be fine.

He just hoped Sheriff Barefoot commanded enough respect in the town to rush him off to safety.

III

EITHER DESPITE OR BECAUSE OF HIS NAME, Sheriff Barefoot never felt more comfortable than he did when he was wearing a thick-soled pair of boots. It was, perhaps, part of the reason he had been relatively comfortable throwing together a tin-pot gaol in the cobbler's. Not that he *wanted* to be splitting space with a buffoon like Mr. Ecker – just that if he had to be, it might as well be in a place where he could get his shoes fixed in short order.

It was, oddly enough, his shoes that broke him from his hopeless malaise. Sitting on the bench in his cell, elbows planted on his knees, he had let his head hang in a way his mighty neck had scarcely allowed. Eyes open, he stared at the ground as though it were an abstract painting that wouldn't be in vogue for centuries, a senseless swirl of color and shape.

And then, in an uncaused instant, coherence reclaimed the world, and Barefoot considered the boot. His boots were deep brown leather, which hugged his leg to three or four inches below the knee, where they terminated in a fuzzy cuff of sandy tan. A smooth line of something firm traced a crescent across his toes, and seemed to reach directly into the much-loved thick soles, drawing strength from the ground itself. They were Barefoot's winter boots, designed not to breathe but to stabilize. They were powerful footwear, fashioned by none other than the damnable Mr. Ecker.

"Say," Barefoot asked his feet, "what's the toe portion of these boots made of, anyway?"

Mr. Ecker, always happy to talk shop, opened his mouth to wax specific about his work. He used his open mouth to make a round "OWP" noise as Sheriff Barefoot leapt from the bench, wound up, and kicked the lock of the cell door as hard as he could.

A ferocious *CLONG* rumbled through the cobbler's, and though Sheriff Barefoot was not an inch closer to freedom, there was no mistaking his renewed intention to gain that single inch, an intention buried into each reverberation of the beclonged bars. And there were quite a few reverberations, which died in the silence that was only now reclaiming the room, after fleeing to the farthest corners. Barefoot stared at the trembling lock, and the trembling Ecker stared at Barefoot.

Finally, as though at some mute signal, Barefoot leaned back, bent his knee, and kicked the lock a second time. And then a third. And a fourth. *CLONG. CLONG. CLONG. CLONG.* Each kick seemed to draw strength from the echoes of the last, just as the Sheriff's gleeful rictus expanded in response to each kick.

The lock on the door was impossible to pick, the locksmith had been very proud of this fact, and mentioned it often prior to, during, and after installation. And, as per Barefoot's specifications, it would be the work of a dedicated team of engineers over a week or so to pry the bars of the cell from the foundations into which they had been driven. But to the Sheriff's knowledge, the door to the cell had never been tested against a big man kicking the hell out of it, over and over and over. Perhaps he wouldn't boot his way to freedom – in fact, he was nearly positive he wouldn't.

But this was better than sitting on his ass and waiting to die, and still retained the beautiful simplicity of that pathetic option. He would kick this door until, one way or another, he didn't have to kick anymore.

Miss Carsis, Vera and No-Good Bulstrode arrived at Snot Holler just as Brisby and Buddy Jr. were striding towards one another, the latter bearing a gilded wooden box in which lay the firearms with which the duel would be conducted. Vera remained unaware of Bulstrode's presence, but this did little to dissuade Miss Carsis from chatting with her Familiar all the way to the field of honor. Vera knew better than to ask to whom the witch was talking, which was the main reason Miss Carsis had let her come at all.

The crowd, through which even the most insistent struggled to shoulder their way, parted for Miss Carsis. If asked why they had made room for her, every man, woman, and child would have looked askance at the asker. They hadn't made room for anybody – they'd been standing precisely where they now stood the entire time. Of this, they were all certain.

Denton looked over and saw the trio poking their way to the front of the crowd. He frowned at them, and to his surprise, Miss Carsis smiled back. Was she mocking him? She seemed to take evident pleasure from standing here on the dueling ground. Ah, but she must have been certain the duel was going to happen. She didn't know that the ace up her sleeve, Sheriff Barefoot, was now up his! He'd see who was smiling in an hour's time, indeed he would.

With a great many "excuse *me*"s and "*excuse* me"s, Fithian Lowestoft clawed her way to the front, following the vanishing path she had watched Miss Carsis cut. Finally reaching a position next to Miss Carsis, Fithian surveyed the human coliseum with nothing short of terror.

"What the hell is this?" she exclaimed in a sharp whisper.

"A duel," Miss Carsis replied without turning her eyes from the event in question.

"That's not…the point of a duel is that it's between two men. It's not a spectator sport, for God's sake!"

The witch shrugged. Should she tell her about Tobin? Would it make a difference? 'Oh, your brother came back but then he went away again, and I don't know where to.' What good would that do? Once again, Fithian made Miss Carsis feel like her skin was trying to spin itself upside-down. She wanted nothing more than to end the conversation as soon as possible.

Fithian, however, had quite a ways to go before she was done. "And what if the bullet fails to fly true, and hits someone in the crowd?"

"Then it's very lucky we have a physician on scene," Miss Carsis replied with a dry nod towards Brisby.

"This was all your doing," Fithian said before she thought. But, her brain conceded, perhaps her mouth had a point. Miss Carsis had effortlessly stridden through a sea of people. She hadn't forced them out of the way with a magical swipe of the arm – she had gently suggested that they move, with a spooky finger-tap on the shoulder. What would have stopped her from gently suggesting that everyone in town take a lovely stroll out to Snot Holler, to watch two grown men take shots at one another? Or quietly reassuring them that there was nothing wrong with standing directly behind one of the men at whom a bullet was soon to be zooming? After all, if one of the townspeople was hit, wouldn't the man with the gun be the one taking the blame? Plenty of questions arose, and Fithian was fairly certain she knew the answer to all of them. So she asked the question she still needed answered: "Why are you doing this?"

If Miss Carsis' head had inflated like a balloon and the witch sailed around the world with it, Fithian would hardly have been more surprised than she was by what Miss Carsis actually did: she turned, tears brimming her eyes, and smiled. "Your brother and Sonny are happy together. I brought every ounce of my being to bear, but it wasn't enough. They did it for themselves. They did it without me." She sniffed, and seemed to suck her sadness back into her. All that remained was a sagacious smile. "They did it. They're out of the Mill, they're together, and they're happy. I just hope that's enough."

The hairs on the back of Fithian's neck didn't just stand up – they seemed to reach up and grab the hair that fell back across her shoulders, and tugged on it as though it were the reins of a runaway horse. "What? What do yo-"

"Shh," Miss Carsis suggested, and Fithian was surprised at just how suggestible she could be. "The seconds have nearly concluded their palaver. My time has arrived."

Fithian failed to hear that last part. She turned her eyes, swimming with tears for her dear brother Tobin, back towards the duel. As she watched Brisby and Buddy Jr. return to those whose lives had been up for negotiation, she realized just how little she truly cared for all of this.

Competing loyalties and political maneuvering, it was complexity without purpose. What mattered was so much simpler; what mattered was her family, what mattered what the love she had for her brother Tobin. What mattered was a love she had given up as lost, but which had now been dangled before her, obstructing her view of anything and everything else. What mattered was reaching that insubstantial promise of return, a promise that was not an obstruction but a path without ending. The anything and everything else – that was true obstruction.

But still, she stayed to watch the duel. What was she going to do, *not* watch the duel?

There would be no duel. It was Miss Carsis' will that there would be no duel, and this was going to be a goddamned win. It would hardly make up for the loss of Sonny and Tobin, and the loss *caused* by them, but it would be a balm to salve her until the next win, at least.

She focused on Buddy Jr. as he spoke with Mr. Increase, burrowing into the former's mind and burying suggestions that carried the force of…

…

Buddy Jr.'s mind lacked any sense of purchase. The dirt, as it were, was fallow. *How very Crundwell of him*, she noted joylessly.

She tried again, pressing harder.

Buddy Jr. slapped at the back of his neck, as though dispatching a mosquito.

Oh shit.

If she pressed any harder, the man's head was liable to pop off. Yet he reacted as though, well, as though there weren't a very powerful witch trying to claw her way into his head.

No. Unacceptable. Not another loss. Damn the pigheaded Crundwells!

She tried again. Something inside of her own head went *crick*. Stumbling slightly, she did her best to lose her balance gracefully. She recovered after a second, and could only marvel at the would-be heir to the Crundwell dynasty. He was driven.

He would have made a powerful warlock. Luckily for the planet, he'd never pursued that course; nobody capable of such obstinate bloodlust could have been anything but a very bad warlock indeed.

Another loss, then. Miss Carsis wanted nothing more than to fly home and bury her face in an uncomfortable pillow. Yet she remained; what was she going to do, *not* watch the duel?

IV

BRISBY RETURNED TO DENTON WITH A GREAT big frown and a great little box. The box was approximately twenty inches long, nine inches wide, and three inches high, fashioned from the marbled meat of a mahogany tree, textured with grooves that looked more suggested than carved from the sinuous panels. Thin, golden tendrils traced the extremities of the box, surrounding and limiting themselves in stave-like thickets.

It was the sort of box in which all sorts of things would fit. Brisby could be bringing him, for example, three apples. Or a small hat. Or a used paintbrush.

But that wasn't what was inside of the box. That wasn't what Brisby was bringing to him. The great big frown that Brisby had now shuttled to within two feet of Denton's face (the dread receptacle naturally coming along for the ride) communicated that quite clearly.

Without taking his eyes from Denton, Brisby turned the box towards the incipient duelist, pressed his fingers into the groove that spanned the lip and body of the box, and pulled it open.

Had the entire crowd here gathered fallen silent, or had their murmuring simply fallen away from his awareness? Denton neither knew nor cared. All he knew was that the world was utterly silent, until it was rent by Brisby's best attempt at consolation: "I got you first choice, at least."

"By which you mean, I *have* to choose one."

"Erm. If you like."

"I don't like, Brisby."

"I'm sorry."

Denton gulped as he leaned over to inspect the contents of the box. His peristalsis was loud enough to startle a crow at the end of the field into flight.

The two flintlock pistols didn't look like weapons for humans; they looked like trumpets for woodchucks. They had long wooden handles of an even deeper wood than the box in which they were stored, and complex silver firing mechanisms, which all looked sufficiently stark and imposing. But then, their golden barrels terminated in ludicrous, convex horns. Could a lead ball pass through the horn? Of course. A billiard ball could probably shove its way through, with sufficient coaxing. A better question: could a lead ball pass through the horn with any semblance of accuracy?

It depended, Denton supposed, on one's definition of accuracy.

The most terrifying thing about these pistols, even more than the prospect of entrusting his life to them, was the seductive pull Denton felt for them, lounging in a bed of Delphic purple velvet. He extended a finger to rock the cradle of manly romance, and was stunned to find the digit trembling. Only why should he be stunned? It would have been more shocking to find himself steady.

He lifted his eyes to the bearer of this bad news. "Why?"

"Buddy Jr. said Mr. Increase would refuse all satisfaction that was not preceded by a very loud 'bang' noise."

This couldn't be right. Denton cast a single glance in Mr. Increase's direction, and knew at once that the problem lay with Buddy Jr. That cur was whispering the same poison into Increase's ear! 'Brisby says Denton will have no satisfaction save that drawn from the barrel of a gun,' that was what Mr. Increase was being told. How else to explain the look of sour incredulity? Oh, Buddy Jr. was a man of honor. But the young Crundwell fancied that consenting to serve as Mr. Increase's second eradicated the debt he owed to Denton. Now, looking around at the gallery of eager cannibals that had surrounded him, Denton felt himself the greatest fool his family had ever produced. How could he have expected a man who not only lived in the town, but in a very real way *represented* the town to itself, to compromise himself in the eyes of his neighbors by brokering peace between the titan of the docks and the prince of the underworld? And beyond that, how could Denton have been shortsighted enough to think Buddy Jr. would put his reputation on the line for a man he fancied had utilized false pretenses to invade his beloved's…most delicate terrain, while she was herself in a delicate situation?

Buddy Jr. had shafted him, and Denton felt something only just shy of certain that Miss Carsis had taken Sheriff Barefoot out of the equation. That explained that wicked smile. So what that left was the choice of which pistol he would use for the duel.

For the first time in years, he took a deep breath. Because for the past few years, he had kept himself wound tightly enough to bounce a coin off of, plotting and planning and trying to outsmart everyone he met to accomplish some prosaic goal that was, at bottom, just so much bullshit. Not that the Cause was bullshit, and not that nothing mattered – he'd never, even in this moment of despair, sign off on such sophomoric nihilism. It was bullshit in the sense that Denton had invested his personal happiness in Causes and ideals. These were things that he ought to have pursued strictly because they were worth pursuing, and not because they might make his family proud of him, or because they might make him not want to immediately avert his eyes from any and all reflective surfaces he encountered.

If he had wanted to be happy, he should have made a life with his family. If he had wanted to do right by his fellow Colonists, he should have done so with the understanding that it might well conflict with his happiness. Instead, he had tried to accomplish a million things at once, and the labyrinth had collapsed into two paths, both of which led to the exact same place.

Did he want the pistol that was currently pointing towards the north, or the south?

He once again lifted his hand to the weapons, and was this time stunned to find that his hand *was* steady. The rockslide of self-inflicted complications had ground to a halt, and as the dust settled, he found that the mountain remained. Could life always be this simple? Almost certainly not, considering this simplicity was a symptom of a terminal affliction – honor.

But did it always have to be as complicated as he'd made it?

He asked himself this as he wrapped his hand around cool grip of the northbound firearm, savoring the caress of the velvet across his knuckles, and called it from its resting place.

V

THE HEDGES CHILDREN HAD AWOKEN TO AN empty house, and so began calling for their parents. It wasn't until they made for the front door that Yazbirth Bicklebog appeared to them, at which point they just screamed for a long time. Being generally unfamiliar with the nuances of childrearing, or children, or humans, Yazbirth, despite his unfathomable age, could think of nothing to do other than to repeatedly ask them if this was normal.

Finally, they calmed down. Lawrence calmed down so much that he fainted, and Annabelle calmed down so much that her mouth only made raspy little ribbit sounds instead of the full-throated shrieks she was trying to make.

Yazbirth consulted his Encyclopedia of Ways to Entertain Children, which had not been updated since the invention of pants. It was, essentially, a metaphorical book of margins in which Yazbirth had doodled. Much as he hated the suffering of living things, he also knew that children *loved* suffering. It was perhaps their defining characteristic. "Would Yourself like to find small animals to smash together? To see which breaks first," he helpfully explained. As the babysitter expected, this calmed the ribbiting child, and had no discernible effect upon the unconscious one.

Annabelle, for her part, realized that the monster didn't mean her harm – it just wanted to play. In fact, she felt slightly foolish for jumping to such a rash initial conclusion. Sure, it was startling to have a giant sloth materialize in one's living space and shout 'THERE IS NO

CAUSE FOR CONCERN, FOR MYSELF IS WATCHING YOURSELVES IN SECRET'. But that did not *necessarily* imply that the magical sloth monster meant them any harm. I really ought to have kept my head and asked questions, Annabelle upbraided herself.

She ignored Yazbirth's unfortunate suggestion for playtime – it would be worth circling back to address, but she had more pressing concerns. "Do you know where my parents are?"

Hgnnnnnnn. With slowness borne of either superlative confidence or superlative stupidity (or perhaps both), Yazbirth raised a hook-nailed paw to his chin. Had Denton told him what he was to say to his human children if they asked where he had gone?

"They didn't go to a duel, did they?"

Hgnnnnnnn. Would Peggy be a happy camper if Yazbirth told her sentient excretions the truth?

"If they did, you must tell me."

"What a relief," Yazbirth sighed. And it was. Clear, concrete orders – that was where a Familiar was most at home. "Yes, Theirselves did go to a duel. Yourself's Father is off to shoot at another Manself, and to be shot at by the same."

"Well," Annabelle decided, "that's unacceptable."

Yazbirth thought very hard about this concept. The whole point of Familiaring was to find *everything* acceptable. Your consort tells you what to do, and then you do it. "Hm....are you certain?"

"Certain about what? That my daddy in a duel is unacceptable?"

"Yes."

"Yes I am."

"Oh."

With that, Annabelle once again made confidently for the front door. She entertained the possibility that yet another long-extinct creature could materialize to bar her passage, but the possibility seemed remote enough to ignore.

"Uh, please do not go outside," Yazbirth rumbled.

Annabelle turned and looked at the Familiar over her shoulder, but refused to turn all the way around – her intention to go nowhere but forward was impossible to miss. "Why not?"

"Because, Myself is supposed to be watching Yourself."

"Then follow me, and watch." Annabelle opened the front door, and called in from the brisk dawn, "bring Lawrence!"

Yazbirth was almost positive that he was not a very good babysitter at all, and had no trouble accepting this fact.

As the Hedges children slipped out into the morning, Chip and Missy Ditteridge rode towards Snot Holler in an unassuming carriage driven by a single horse. Missy had tried to keep news of the duel from her father for as long as she could, but word inevitably made its way to his fat, hairy ears. Oh, how she loathed him, and loathed having to share such a small space with him. She felt certain she would never forgive her father for what he had done to Adewale. This was, to no small degree, partially because she felt a great deal of responsibility for what had happened. Chip was a status quo man; there was a very good chance he'd just plain forgotten he could sell his slaves off, and never would have remembered if Missy hadn't introduced the idea of *releasing* Adewale, which carried with it that mortifying corollary.

And now here he was, liquored up already, eager to make haste from the mansion (which he had demanded be constructed at such a remove from the Mill proper it might as well be considered its own principality), to Snot Holler, clean on the other side of Fidget's Mill. The carriage ride before them would be on the order of *hours*, perhaps, all in this suffocating silence. And what were the chances they would actually make it in time to see the wretched duel, she kept asking her father over and over? Good, he would reply. Great. The best.

Dwelling upon the injustices of the world, Missy hardly noticed the carriage clatter to a halt. It was only when Chip brushed aside the curtain, surveyed their point of arrival, and returned with a look of fury that Missy started to notice much of what was happening outside of her head.

"Why in the hell did we stop?!" Chip mooed.

Missy, who was always much happier to interact with the slaves than her father, reached out to open the door to the carriage, and let out a round gasp as it swung open of its own accord. Well, not its own accord – the accord of a pudgy man with dull red hair like the frayed end of a rope, blue eyes like a riptide and a face like a rotten pumpkin.

"Either of you Crundwells?" the man asked in what was perhaps only a generation or two removed from a thick Irish brogue.

"Who wants to know?" Chip thundered back. This, Missy realized, was a mark of just how far her father had fallen in his own estimation. Not too long ago, he would have scoffed haughtily at the *idea* of being anyone as crass as a Crundwell. Now, she could see him playing this string out in his mind, seeing if he might not get something out of pretending to be a Crundwell for a few minutes.

The man leaned his head to the side of the carriage, and relayed the question to someone they couldn't see. A brief conversation ensued, at the end of which the man returned his attention to Missy, this time with a knife in his hand. He thrust his arm forward and drove the blade into the base of Missy's throat, just above the collarbone.

Chip couldn't quite believe his beloved daughter was being stabbed to death until he heard the assailant's blade clack dully against her clavicle. This was outrageous. His daughter was being stabbed to death in front of his very eyes, and they hadn't even asked him a follow-up question!

Not knowing what else to do, because this was truly a preposterous situation, he scoffed haughtily. He scoffed the haughtiest scoff he had ever scoffed in his entire life. This did nothing to remedy the situation. Chip was officially out of ideas.

But the time for ideas had passed. Gripped by an ancient parental instinct, feeling as though he were moving in a dream from which he would surely awaken, any moment now, he clamped a hand onto the murderer's arm just above the elbow and brought his knee up sharply, in hopes of breaking the man's arm. His hopes were in vain, for he was too large to lift his leg fast enough, or the carriage was too small, or both, it hardly mattered, because soon he would be waking up. The man pulled his arm back, and as he retreated, he drove the bone-clanking blade into Missy's stomach and yanked it downwards. From the wound, she birthed her own womb.

God is punishing me, she decided. She'd never been especially religious by the standards of the time, but this seemed as good a time as any. Besides, it was perfect, wasn't it? She'd had an abortion, and now she was being aborted. That doesn't happen by accident. It would be impossible to live in a world where coincidences of that sort could occur. Who could bear to live in a universe of such caprice? Better to be divinely ordained. And being Just and Merciful, God would never let this happen were it not a punishment. So this is what I deserve, she decided. I put love for my friends before love for God, and now I am punished. This is what I deserve.

With God in her heart, she would repeat this mantra until the end.

Operating on dream logic, Chip bent over to gather up his beloved daughter's workings. He heard but did not see the door behind him open, and saw the terror he should have been feeling (but could not feel) in Missy's colorless face. Don't worry, he wanted to tell her, this is just a dream. Such grisly and inexplicable things do not happen so quickly in waking life. That would be ludicrous. That would not be the kind of world in which civilized people such as ourselves are permitted to thrive by a Just and Merciful God. This is just a dream, there is nothing to be afraid of, and soon enough, we will awaken at home in England with Doris and Francis and Catherine and Norm and Tom, and we will not fight or argue, we will love each other with the purity only possible when the children are very young and the parents are very naïve.

Chip wanted to tell Missy all of these things, but he didn't, and couldn't, because he never had the chance. Missy had been right about one thing that morning: the world was an unjust place.

VI

WAS IT WORTH DENTON'S TIME TO HOPE? HE didn't think so.

Even still, as he and Mr. Increase approached one another at the center of the field, to stand back to back and begin their journey of ten paces, he entertained a daydream in which this could all be resolved with nothing more than language. And were Mr. Increase the only factor to consider, the daydream could well have come to pass. But he wasn't. They were surrounded by townsfolk that had had their fill of language.

Each of their footsteps through the dew-bedazzled grass cracked like soggy test runs of the forthcoming gunshots. The duelists locked eyes during the approach, but said nothing until they had arrived at the arbitrary epicenter of the violence.

"This is foolishness," Denton whispered lower than the wind could reach.

Mr. Increase seemed to have deduced Buddy Jr.'s deception just as well as Denton had; there was unfeigned remorse in his eyes, and a depth of self-doubt Denton could never have imagined seeing beneath the thin planks of pride that typically walled Increase off from the world. "I know it is. I have no wish to see you dead."

"So how do we avert this tragedy, beneath the watchful eyes of the whole town?"

Leaning in even closer, his voice dropping even lower, Mr. Increase's suddenly mournful eyes sparkled with their old clever rascality. "I have a plan."

Denton felt his face was primed to light up in a much less subtle way, and so he sat on the flush of positive feelings as hard as he could. It wouldn't do, to break into a great big grin just prior to taking his ten paces. "What is it?"

Mr. Increase turned around, presenting his back. Denton did the same, leaving the two duelists facing in opposite directions. "I shall shoot you in a non-vital part of yo-"

"What?" Denton turned his head sharply to see Mr. Increase's face over his shoulder – the old fool must be grinning fit to split, trying out a joke like that at a time like this. "That's not a solution!"

Several Fidgetonians hissed at Denton, and so he put his eyes forward once again, knowing that if he didn't, the good folks of the Mill would do it for him.

"It is," Mr. Increase averred. "You're young, and will heal. I am an able marksman. I can place the bullet in your right arm, which arm you already treat delicately due to the unfortunate business with your rib. There will be no discernible variation in your lifestyle."

"Fuck *you*, no discernible variation in my lifestyle! Why don't I shoot *you* in a non-vital area?"

"Are you an able marksman? Ow," Mr. Increase added as he felt Denton poke him in the side with a backthrusted elbow.

"You know I'm not an able marksman. But so what? I don't want to ent-"

"TEN PACES," rose a cry from the rabble. The answer came from similar calls from fellow Fidgetonians, and the echoes of Snot Holler itself.

"Relax," Mr. Increase jabbed into Denton's ear.

"Fuck *you*, 'relax'! *You* relax!"

With that, they began their ten paces.

On the first pace, Denton reviewed the emotional rapids he had traversed since peeling sleep from his eyes while the moon was still high. Despair, resignation, equanimity, and now fury. All before breakfast. A man should never feel more than two emotions prior to breakfast. Surely that was in the Bible, or something. If not, Denton planned to write it down in some very important document, and have that be his gift to history.

On the second pace, Denton considered what might happen to that other gift to (and from) history, his family, should this all turn out as poorly as he now suspected it would. He had, quite foolishly, made no arrangements for their continued well-being. The kids were with Yazbirth, which was probably safe enough. What would become of Peggy? With the exception of Sheriff Barefoot, Denton didn't think anybody in town who might intend her harm knew who she was. Could she slip out of town with the kids? Maybe. But how could he have gotten himself into a situation such as this, with nothing more than a 'maybe' for his wife and children?

On the third pace, his mind wandered to what would become of the Cause after his death (*possible death*, he corrected himself with distressing lassitude). The answer, of course, was 'whatever would happen if he should survive this'. He had contributed something material to the Cause, in securing non-importation in Fidget's Mill. But his value was limited and spent, being isolated to this particular contribution. His life bore no intrinsic worth to the Cause. If anything, through his son and the boy's damned contrarian/ice-hurling streak, Denton's net impact on the Cause may well have been negative.

On the fourth pace, he upbraided himself for thinking this way; to assume even an overall negative impact on the Cause was to overestimate his own footprint in history.

On the fifth pace, Denton looked down at the vanishing prints he was leaving in the grass, which bowed beneath him but wasted no time in rising after he had passed, like royal subjects on the eve of rebellion. He immediately lost interest in this particular metaphor – too on the nose.

On the sixth pace, he wondered just what, from a physiological standpoint, Yazbirth Bicklebog had done to *his* nose to remove the swelling. The nose had remained broken, tender to the touch (or even too much direct sunlight, though perhaps that was all in Denton's head). But the swelling that had impaired his speech had been taken. How had Yazbirth worked such selective magic, and where had the swelling gone? For some reason, it seemed more preposterous for inflamed tissue to vanish entirely, than that it should have been converted to a swimming moon of jelly and stored in a mason jar somewhere.

On the seventh pace, he thought about his family again. He had found no new thoughts or observations about them in the intervening ratiocinations; he just liked to think about them. This time, his father Chester made a brief, disapproving appearance, and too little too late Denton realized that he didn't care. His father would probably be dead soon enough, if he weren't already, and he would take his generous scorn and barren pride with him. Who cared what he might think as he drew his final breaths?

On the eighth pace, Denton made the vain wish that he could have had all of these realizations a long, long time ago. If only Miss Carsis didn't seem so set on seeing him shot (or at least shot *at*, and hey, why was the witch looking so upset? It didn't seem like her, to look so sour about something she herself had facilitated. Wasn't she happy with what she hath wrought?), Denton might well have asked her about slamming him back into a younger body, returned to the previous decade with the hard-won knowledge he brought to the field of honor in the wretched 70's.

On the ninth pace, he made a whole lot of other useless wishes, because if he was going to abandon the dictates of the real world, he might as well do so recklessly, right? He wished he was better at reading people, he wished he could read books faster, he wished that he had been able to get by on fewer hours of sleep, he wished he could have learned a manual trade in his youth, he wished that he had learned how to swim, he wished he had learned how to play a musical instrument, he wished he had any ear for music at all, he wished he didn't have these goddamned nervous tics, he wished he'd not left his love for Peggy unspoken quite so often, he wished he could wipe away the pretty lies he had told his children, he wished he could let them know that the world was a terrible place and that was why the pockets of wonder and joy within it were so precious and essential, he wished he could let them know that some things are worth fighting for and some things are worth dying for, he wished he could let them know that everyone has a responsibility to do what they think is right but that everyone also ought to be doing what they think is right for the right reasons, he wished he could let them know that he had been trying to do the right things for the wrong reasons all of these years and that there was little to be proud of in this, he wished he were more coordinated, he wished he'd learned to dance, he wished he had spent more time outside, he wished he had seen more of the world, he wished he hadn't spent so much time living in his own head, he wished he hadn't spent so much time afraid of failing, he wished he had failed even more than he already had and more spectacularly at that, he wished he had learned more about birds or flowers or something so that he could walk through a field and point to something beautiful and give it a name, he wished he knew how to appreciate beauty without categorizing it, he wished he didn't have such a hard time digesting beef because the taste was great it was just hell on his insides, he wished he had had more friends, he wished he had been born in a more temperate climate, he wished he could have lived to see how the Colonies emerged from this paroxysm of revolt, he wished he had spent more time reading fiction, he wished he could fly, he wished he could breathe underwater, he wished he could travel through time, he wished he could turn into any animal he wanted even if he didn't know what it was called or even if it wasn't a real animal at all, he wished he knew what happened after you died, he wished he believed the answer was as simple as 'you go to heaven or hell', he wished he had never been born, he wished he could never die, he wished his family the best.

On the tenth pace, he turned around and lifted his pistol against the protest of his ribs, and pointed it directly at Mr. Increase, who was doing much the same, but apparently without dissenting opinions from his bones. The two men glared across Snot Holler, in a pool of teeming silence, over a divide of easily bridged misunderstandings. Denton kept his flinty glare, mirror-honed for occasions very different from this one (but easily transferable), locked on his adversary. This was, after all, the best way to keep his adversary locked on him –specifically his face. As long as Increase kept looking at his face, he wouldn't be looking at his hand, and so wouldn't notice how much that hand was shaking.

Because it *was* shaking. A lot.

Denton was no marksman, able or otherwise. With his hand shaking this much, he couldn't, in good conscience, pull the trigger. The chance of missing Increase entirely and striking an innocent bystander was too high. And there was not a single doubt in Denton's mind that this was planned, by Increase or Miss Carsis or both or whoever or everybody. He was the kind of man whose hands trembled, and the entire world knew it. But that didn't matter. What mattered was that his gun might as well be unloaded – he wasn't going to pull the trigger, no matter what, not even to fire his round into the sky and quite dramatically forfeit his shot. His final stand would be a pacifistic reaffirmation of what he had always believed, though often doubted – there were ways to resolve conflicts without recourse to violence.

Unfortunately for him, Mr. Increase did not feel the same way.

VII

SHERIFF BAREFOOT AND MR. ECKER FAILED TO hear the gunshot because the former was too busy kicking at the door to his cell. Despite the pleadings of the latter, the former continued his vain assault long beyond the point of exhaustion. His legs were on fire, and his back screamed, but the smile upon his face was inextinguishable. Here was something he could do, and goddamnit, he would do it until somebody stopped him.

With this thought in his mind, Barefoot was nevertheless staggered briefly when the front door to the cobbler's swung open, as though from a kick as ferocious as one of his own. A round pumpkin-faced ginger man hustled in through the door, followed by a posse of five other men of comparable hues and dimensions.

"Alright, that racket is driving me bonkers. What's up with that racket?" The man sniffed and snorted, hiking up a belt that looked to have been peeled directly from the living flesh of a heifer and clumsily affixed with a buckle. He was tall, though not as tall as Barefoot - perhaps just shy of six feet. Barefoot had never in his life seen this man or any of his accomplices, and yet he knew on sight that they meant to cause a rumpus.

Well, Barefoot thought, let them. It will be a challenge, but I can subdue them.

As soon as I get out of his cell.

The Sheriff straightened his shoulders, ignoring the complaints being lodged by each individual vertebra, and addressed the rumpus squad: "Town business. Can I help you, gentlemen?" It was only after asking that question that he noticed the red-black smears on the lead ginger's hands. There had been blood upon those hands, and he had done a poor job of wiping it off.

"Mr. Ecker," Barefoot hissed out of the corner of his mouth, not taking his eyes from the goon troupe who were clearly more sinister than your garden variety goon. Whose blood was that? A citizen of the Mill? "Mr. Ecker!"

The lead man grinned, parted his lips to reveal a surprisingly well-managed dental situation. His teeth were the dull yellow of cigarettes past, but they were almost all there. It was, more than the blood, the sight of the full-dress chompers that chilled Barefoot. A man with such depths of hatred in his eyes, but enough presence of mind to care for his personal hygiene, was truly a force to be reckoned with. It bespoke a man who was not crazy, but merely driven. A crazy man would stop at nothing until he found whatever he considered to be justice; such a man would eventually tire himself out. A driven man would stop at *almost* nothing, except for showers and teeth-cleanings and restroom breaks and snacks and naps ice-breaker exercises to improve morale. And a man who was willing to stop from time to time was, in the long run, the one who was *truly* unstoppable.

"Mr. Ecker!" Barefoot didn't bother trying to keep quiet this time. The damned cobbler wasn't listening to him, but was instead staring dimly at the newcomers to the room.

The man grinned at Mr. Ecker. "Your friend is trying to get your attention, buddy."

"Hruh?" The cobbler shook himself as though he were bucking off his malaise. But the malaise replied 'not so fast, literally', and settled right back down on top of him. Mr. Ecker let it, because that was easiest.

"What're you looking at?" yodeled one of the pumpkin-faced man's cohorts.

Mr. Ecker gawped like a fish out of water, and then replied, "I've never seen such red hair on a man before."

A moment of pin-drop silence popped into a torrent of laughter. It was laughter that immediately preceded an act of violence; Barefoot had heard just such a laugh too many times. He had, in his more shameful moments, uttered such a laugh in the past.

"Gentlemen," he boomed with all the dignity he could muster, "I'm afraid I'm going to have to ask you to leave."

"Wha," another of the troll patrol managed through his many-teethed mirth, "you two need a bit of privacy, do you?"

"What're you getting up to, then?" Another asked, to more thudding, hateful chuckles.

Barefoot refused to be cowed: "I mean to say I'm afraid I have to ask you to leave Fidget's Mill entirely."

"And what if we tell you to go to hell?"

"Then I'll have you arrested. I am," Barefoot said for his own benefit as much as theirs, "the Sheriff of the Mill. Who are you, might I ask?"

"Sheriff," the lead man said in a grating sing-song voice, "I am the bearer of bad news."

"And I expect you'll favor me with a cute inversion of the common turn of phrase by telling me you don't hate to be."

"Well, shit," the man laughed, "never had somebody get ahead of me on that one. Well, here's your bad news: you're locked up."

"A temporary logistical misunderstanding easily resolved. Isn't that right, *Mr. Ecker*?" Despite the emphasis in his voice, Barefoot was disheartened to see Ecker making no moves towards his release. This was, he was forced to admit, the right move. They would kill Ecker with the least pretext. He considered his own prospects to be little better.

Unless, of course, they considered him a neutralized threat by his placement in the cell? Perhaps they would leave him to rot, thinking this the cruelest option available to them. In which case…

He had to get Mr. Ecker to throw him the key, without them seeing. But how? The cobbler wasn't exactly a master of discretion. Or picking up on subtle clues. Or following clear, explicitly worded orders. The cobbler was not really good for much except cobbling, and even then…

"Mr. Ecker…" Barefoot began.

The pumpkin-faced man sensed the newfound resolve in Barefoot's voice, and cut him off without the sinister, self-conscious parody of *bonhomie* he had been affecting. "Where can I find the Crundwells?" He took a casual stroll over to Mr. Ecker, produced a knife from his pocket, and pressed the blade to Ecker's throat.

Barefoot readied himself for a lengthy hostage situation, the ransom of which was information on the Crundwells, but his minimal preparations were for naught. The man drove the point of the blade through Ecker's throat, producing a swampy gurgle from the increasingly late cobbler, which opened into an inhuman crunching and trickling as he drove the blade through Ecker's neck, snapping tendons and slicing arteries.

The Sheriff screamed nonsense syllables, throwing himself against the bars. That wasn't how that moment was supposed to play out! There were rules to these situations! Violence was to be dangled from the end of a long stick as a threat, not delivered without comment as a matter of course!

"I need to find the Crundwells," the man repeated, "I have some bad news for them."

"Why the hell did you kill him like that?" Barefoot finally managed.

The pumpkin-faced man looked genuinely puzzled by this. "I should have killed him different, should I?"

Without a word exchanged between them, the wrecking crew with whom this man traveled set to tearing books off the walls, yanking pages out, and scattering them about the place. They might be dumb, the Sheriff boggled, but within their limited skillset they were clearly well above average. Their actions were clear enough to Barefoot; they were laying kindling, stuffing it between the planks that made up the walls and floor, creating paper chains to maximize the spread of the flame. They meant to cook him alive.

"You're dead, Sheriff." The man announced disinterestedly as he approached the bars of Barefoot's cell. "The Crundwells are alive, and they're here. Now, we can either kill just the Crundwells, or we can kill everybody, seeing as that'll have gotten us the Crundwells, on account of logic. You tell me where to find the Crundwells, I'll kill you quick as you like, to show my appreciation. Otherwise, you're a slow roast."

"Who are you? Why are you doing this?" Barefoot's voice was small and pitiful. He hadn't realized he was capable of making sounds like that; more than anything, he wished he could have died without having ever realized it.

"None of your goddamned business," came the reply that would brook no further questioning. "Next words out of your mouth are where I can find the Crundwells, or they're not. Either way, you've made your choice."

The Sheriff, the man whose sole job was to uphold law and order, thought about this more carefully than he'd like to admit. Assuming these men could be trusted to keep their word (and he very much doubted that their word was as steadfast as his own), he could either give up two lives, Bunny and Buddy Jr., to save the lives of everyone else in the town. Would this make him a hero, or an accomplice to two murders? The alternative was, by his inaction, potentially allowing the entire town to be put to the sword. Even if he didn't believe these men capable of slaughtering literally everyone, he had no doubt of their sincere desire to do so, should they prove up to the task. The body count would be infinitely higher, but his personal responsibility for the death would be less. Wouldn't it? Passively allowing wholesale destruction, as opposed to actively facilitating two targeted assassinations. Th-

"You took too long," the man said as one of his cronies handed him a lit lantern. From whence the lantern, and from whence the light? Barefoot wasn't sure – he'd been too lost in his own thoughts.

"Wait!" he screamed as the man hurled the lantern into the corner with the most highly stacked kindling, just beneath the desk at which Mr. Ecker's body sat, cobbling sandals for the angels in heaven.

The men did not wait, but instead left the cobbler's. Whether by design or purely as a matter of logistical ease (Barefoot suspected the former), the room was laid thickly with kindling everywhere except the Sheriff's cell. Consequently, the fire spread quickly along the records of Ecker's existence, but took their time dealing with the issue of Sheriff Barefoot's ontology.

It would be hours before the Sheriff ceased to burn and molt and peel and scream and live and live and live. By then, his cessation was hardly noticed, as his grisly melodies had been taken up by a choir of scorched throats crying out for damnation to finally take them.

VIII

HERE'S WHAT HAPPENED: MR. INCREASE PULLED the trigger. The cock released, and the flint dipped downwards at considerable speed, like a tiny flamingo dredging for brine shrimp. Instead of shrimp, however, the flint of the gun nosed aside the frizzen, an L-shaped piece of steel which concealed the priming powder. In so doing, the collision between the flint and the frizzen generated a rain of sparks which blessed the pocket of gunpowder resting in the flashpan. Thus behold and hallelujah, the sparks ignited the powder, and the resultant little Big Bang breathed life through the touchhole in the barrel, where the same miracle was worked writ large upon the main powder charge in the combustion chamber. A lead ball .445 inches in size, smoothed into a shape that fell considerably short of spherical perfection, was propelled down the sixteen inches of the pistol's golden barrel at one thousand feet per second. As the imperfect circle had only to travel the distance of twenty paces, it did not take long at all for the bullet to reach Denton. It passed through his favorite waistcoat, creating a small, singed hole that was nearer to geometric perfection than the payload itself, though still nowhere close enough to satisfy a scrupulous mathematician. And at any rate, Denton was hardly in a position to appreciate the aesthetics. The bullet punched a far less aesthetically pleasing hole in his stomach two inches below the right nipple, where it shattered another rib, bounced down to take a small chunk out of his hipbone, and pinballed back up to finally come to rest between two of his vertebrae, near the base of his spine. Despite the good fortune of his vital organs remaining inviolate, the shock of the impact took Denton's legs out from under him, and he fell backwards as his knees buckled. Before he hit the ground, Peggy was screaming.

Here is what Denton was aware of: he had made the conscious decision to not pull the trigger, and was in the process of deliberating whether or not he might simply lower his gun to signal his intentions. Then he heard a *ponk* sound, and the world went red, and then white, and then black. The left side of his face had sprouted a field, his legs had vanished, and his wife was screaming over the *ponk* with which the Holler had not yet finished. He opened his mouth to tell her it would be alright, wherever she was, but the only reassurances he could offer her were the molten truths that coursed through his veins, now evacuating his body, perhaps disgusted by all of the lies that had paved the way to this moment.

He was aware of the world contracting, becoming smaller and smaller until it was only Peggy and Brisby kneeling over him, a jury in the round looming over their shoulders, the unhappy verdict chiseled into their features. Guilty, their eyes said, and Denton had no defense for himself. Guilty, guilty, guilty, sentenced to die by his friend's hand.

Where was Mr. Increase? He tried to put this question to his wife, but either she could not hear him over the sound of her own sobbing, or else he had failed to shape the words with any kind of articulation. Both seemed equally likely.

Brisby was saying something reassuring in a tone of voice that implied he, too, needed reassurance. Denton was prepared to offer it, but once again could not find the words. It oughtn't have been so difficult; wasn't he pouring all of his truth upon the Holler? A lie should have been the easiest thing in the world just then. The second easiest, anyway. They all knew what the easiest thing for Denton to do was just then.

Once again, his world had collapsed into a very simple binary. Keep fighting to live, or give up and die. It was not a good place to be. This was, perhaps, a necessary counterpoint to his earlier epiphany.

Sleep tried to claim him, but Denton resisted, because he knew that this was death in sleep's clothing. He was not ready to die, though he could certainly see the appeal.

Dr. Brisby Houlihan took it as a good sign that, as he labored frantically to stem the bleeding, none of the spectators who had gathered on Snot Holler ever tried to intervene. They had closed ranks, tightening the human noose, but their faces had lost the thirst with which they had arrived. As they ought to have, Brisby thought, and damn every one them. He and Peggy were kneeling in the blood that they had come to see. Were they happy? They didn't look it.

Had Denton had his wits more about him, and were his mouth not a liquid rose in perpetual bloom, he might have pondered whether or not Miss Carsis' gentle powers of persuasion had finally broken. Were the Fidgetonians wondering why they had left their homes to witness this? Were they wondering how they could have ever come out to the field of honor expecting to see anything other than the lowest impulses of their species gussied up with the empty-pocketed robes of the Higher Sorts? Maybe, maybe. As it was, they were simply watching two people trying to save the life of another.

Brisby turned Denton over roughly, examining his back for an exit wound. "The bullet's still inside," he said to himself as much as Peggy. Snot Holler considered this to be everyone's business, and carried Brisby's observation to the cheap seats.

"Can you tell where?" Peggy's voice was flatter than Brisby had ever heard it, a result of her trying as hard as possible to keep it from wavering. The time for sobbing was over. Perhaps it would come again. But for right now, Peggy knew that she needed to be in control of herself. And so she was.

Brisby shook his head solemnly. No, he couldn't. "Right now our priority needs to be stemming the bleeding." The doctor did not add 'I assume', but he could have; he had never actually treated a gunshot wound before. He'd never done much in the way of surgery, but this was hardly the time to mention the fact. "We can heat a kni…" The doctor watched in awe as Peggy wordlessly plucked Denton's unspent pistol from his hand, allowing her own hand to linger on his for a moment. Struggling tearfully to keep her terror from finding an outlet, she methodically examined the unfamiliar weapon (Peggy seemed to be the one often finding uses for the firearms her husband procured and failed to utilize himself, Brisby observed) until she found how to extract the small bounty of powder in the combustion chamber. Asking Brisby's opinion with a glance, and receiving an approving nod from the doc, she pulled Denton's stained waistcoat and shirt up over his chest, ignoring the near-perfect symmetry the bullet carved in his clothes, and poured the powder out onto the wound.

Denton gasped sharply, and began choking on his own blood, coughing and sputtering.

"I'm so sorry," Peggy whimpered, and Brisby couldn't imagine a single one of the assembled Fidgetonians could fault her for the tears. "I'm so sorry. I love you."

Words had abandoned Denton, but he reached out and took her hand, squeezing as tightly as he could. It was not much of a squeeze at all.

Checking, double checking and triple checking that the ball was out of the gun, Peggy pressed the flintlock mechanism of the pistol to the powder-coated wound on Denton's stomach. She did all of this without so much as consulting Brisby with a glance. There was no time, and Brisby could do nothing but admire her. He was nervous and reticent because he knew a little bit about medicine, and was terrified of overstepping the boundaries of his knowledge. Peggy didn't know anything about medicine, and so was driven by a single, simple imperative; saving her husband's life. Any and all knowledge was fair game, including that baffling law of physics that allowed a spark and some powder to go pop when they met.

Peggy pulled the trigger of the gun, which was canted on its side to get the flintlock as close to Denton's chest as possible. The barrel of the gun was, therefore, pointing directly into the crowd of people. They leapt backwards, many letting out startled shouts and yells, which was as lively as Peggy had seen them all day.

The powder on Denton's chest ignited, and Peggy's senses were immediately overwhelmed. With the drowning moans of her husband's agony, with the smell of his burning flesh, with the sight of his skin blackening and his face warping in agony, with an apocalyptic rumble that shook the entire hillside.

Peggy first took this to be a convulsion of her grief-stricken body, but upon further inspection, this was a sensory input available to all the assembled townspeople, and reiterated by Snot Holler even more dramatically than the sounds of her husband's throaty cries.

"What the hell was that?" Brisby wondered aloud, feeling quite foolish that he had been upstaged by a housewife whose medical training surely stopped at kissing booboos.

Words failing her as surely as they had her husband, Peggy could only point back towards the treeline that hid Fidget's Mill from view. Brisby followed her finger, and his jaw slowly dropped. He forgot Denton entirely and rose slowly to his feet. One by one, the people of Fidget's Mill turned back towards the town, following the finger of the woman whose husband they had harried and cheered to his potentially fatal encounter upon the hill. They stared in silent shock, and then vocalized horror, as the town that they had abandoned for a fleeting glimpse of bloodshed, the town in which they had all been born and raised, poisoned the horizon with a pillar of bile-black smoke.

The storehouse on the docks, where Mr. Increase had hoarded the remaining supplies for Fidget's Mill, was on fire. And then, by that baffling law of physics that allowed a spark and some powder to go pop when they met, the tower of smoke became an obelisk of flame, a tribute to oblivion.

IX

SOMETIMES IT WAS NICE TO HAVE A LIMP. IT LENT gravitas, or (god forbid) inspired sympathy. But it also slowed a man down. And now, as Mr. Increase was struggling mightily to keep pace with Miss Carsis, Vera, Buddy Jr. and No-Good Bulstrode sprinting towards the volcanic crater that was, until so recently, the storehouse, he cursed his bum leg nearly as much as he cursed his glasscutter eyes. He hadn't counted on his hand to be so steady, nor his gun to be so accurate. Who would have imagined such a whimsical little peashooter could pack such a punch? Denton had scarcely hit the ground before Mr. Increase was swamped with remorse, wanting nothing more than to rush forward and bury the hatchet with his friend, lest the friend be buried without a hatchet to cut his way through to the next life.

He'd aimed for the arm! Just to graze the arm! God, why didn't he simply throw away his shot and trust Denton would do the same?

Buddy Jr. gripped his shoulder tightly; Buddy Jr., who had lied to them both and so brought this comedy of errors to such a tragic conclusion, had pulled him back and told him that they both needed to get out of there. And so they went. And then the horizon erupted.

Now they were running, running, limping down the hill as the Holler behind them captured the reports of the misfortune that had come to plague the Mill, and dwelt upon them endlessly.

"I want to know what's happening," Miss Carsis panted to Bulstrode. Of those assembled, only Mr. Increase was aware that Miss Carsis' outburst wasn't rhetorical.

"Of course," the turkey replied as he shot forward, as the bullet that had burst from Increase's gun, though his little talons pumped at the same speed they'd been going this whole time. The sight was so disorienting, Mr. Increase nearly tumbled the rest of the way down the hill. Fortunately Buddy Jr. spotted the instability, and once again gripped his shoulder, this time to stabilize rather than stymie. Sometimes it was terrible to have a limp.

The other three broke off to go who knew where, but Mr. Increase kept on heading straight, straight for the docks, straight for the storehouse, straight for whatever was left of it.

Here it was, his dream. Chaos. The great equalizer. Hadn't he said that, in a simpler time? And wasn't he excited by the prospect, even now?

Annabelle crouched behind a large coil of rope, and stared directly into the second sun. Lawrence, who had been rudely awoken by the explosion, couldn't stay mad at the rude awakening for long; there was nothing more exciting than witnessing destruction on a large scale. And this was, for certain, a large scale.

What had begun as a small fire in the center of the storehouse had, with sufficient poking and prodding (for the timber in the docks was always and forever moist), grown into a conflagration. And completely unbeknownst to the man with the red cactus hair, Mr. Increase had a considerable store of gunpowder amongst his hoarded goods. There commenced a jumbo-sized reenactment of the process of combustion that had sped a lead pellet into Denton's belly. The powder ignited, announcing its intentions by way of a brash concussion, which made the world still and ready for a blossom of devouring flame. A meal was made of a mighty joist which spanned the ceiling and had held the elements at bay for decades, untroubled by slanting rain, battering hail and crushing snow, only to be finally laid low by fire from beneath. The support beam that was once the tallest tree in Essex County splintered and pelted the desk at which Mr. Increase had passed years of his life with its vengeance, glad to have the first vain jab at the ground before the rest of the roof came thundering down after it. The walls, teetering drunkenly without the ceiling to hold them up, finally collapsed inwards, like penitents bowing their heads before a burning messiah. The inferno darkened the sky, licking the wounds it had only begun inflicting.

Lawrence Hedges thought it was "awesome".

"It's not awesome," Annabelle corrected him. "It's very scary. The docks are on fire."

"No, they're on *water*!" Lawrence corrected her. "And the fire is *on* the water! It's awesome!"

"It's not! It's scary!

"It can be both," Yazbirth Bicklebog, ever the peacemaker, mediated. "But Ourselves really ought not linger here too long. The Menselves responsible for this may still be nearby."

"Why did they do this?" Annabelle asked, knowing neither of her companions would have the answer. "Is this because of the thing that happened in Boston? Or is this because of my daddy?"

Yazbirth thought about this, and concluded, once again, that it could be both. "Come on, Kidselves. We should find Dentonself." All three turned their backs on the flames, dancing to its own arrhythmic popping and rumbling, each filled with a terrible sense of foreboding. Even if this wasn't directly related to Denton…anybody could see that it was, in some unspeakable, inconceivable way.

At least, it certainly seemed that way to Annabelle.

The carriage was standing on a gentle rise just outside town, its doors flapping lazily in the breeze, the stench of death pouring out thickly enough to stick to the bottom of a man's boot.

Knowing full well what he would find inside, No-Good Bulstrode zipped over to the open door to peer into the rolling sepulcher. There was no sense going back without verifying, after all. And whatever lay behind the thick black curtains, Bulstrode knew he had seen worse. Much, much worse.

Even so, Bulstrode was happy to not have a stomach to turn at the macabre still life. The swarthy carriage driver outside had met a cleaner, quicker end, granted what Bulstrode continued to be the ultimate liberation: freedom from the mortal coil. Chip and Missy had been cut open and bled, and retained consciousness for long enough to crawl into each other's arms.

Which was a pity, because they'd seemed nice enough.

Bulstrode didn't really *care*, per se, nor did he have to on a technicality, because he wasn't sure Miss Carsis would either. But that didn't mean the ancient Familiar was indifferent to the suffering of living creatures. Quite the opposite – Bulstrode considered himself more intimately concerned with the well-being of all living things, because he was blessed and cursed with a glimpse of The Big Picture. Creatures of Earth, with their laughably limited lifespans, could fool themselves into thinking that there was some kind of free-floating, objective Meaning to life, often divinely ordained, which could take on such outsize importance as to sanction or even enjoin the immiseration of others. Bulstrode, on the other hand, was aware that existence was a Cosmic Goof, an Eternal Whoops devoid of any meaning not generated by living entities. So the only metric of ethical action, then, was limiting suffering, and, if possible, increasing well-being.

Not that this made ethical decisions any easier; there were complications, as when a short-term infliction of suffering might promote wholesale happiness in the long run, or vice versa. This was, in fact, almost always the case. But it was a framework through which to make decisions, and against such a skeleton ethic, Bulstrode had no compunctions about calling what had been done to Chip and Missy (by, presumably, the same person or persons who had turned the storehouse into a bonfire) an act of evil.

In acting in accordance with the complications, Bulstrode knew that he and Miss Carsis sometimes did terrible things. But he used a little talon to draw a line between doing terrible things for the greater good, and doing *evil* things for their own sake. Bulstrode considered himself the king of the former category, and the sworn enemy of the latter.

He sped back towards town, to find out who sat upon the rival throne.

Fithian had worried she would feel exposed, being thrust into a dangerous situation without Yazbirth to back her up. But to her pleasant surprise, she felt as self-assured as she had before the sloth had ever come into her life.

When Mr. Increase had pulled the trigger, and Denton had collapsed, Fithian felt herself slip into a kind of daze, which was only broken when Peggy cauterized Denton's wound with a more loving kind of gutshot. Just in case that hadn't shattered her reverie, the storehouse exploded. I'M UP, she wanted to shout at God. QUIT IT ALREADY, I'M UP.

After that, she had rushed to Denton's side, as though there were anything she could do to help. Yazbirth might have been able to take away his pain – or some of it, at least, as Denton clearly had quite a lot to be taken – but the friendly sloth couldn't do anything to actually contribute to the man's recovery.

So if the supernatural couldn't hack it, what could little old Fithian do?

She knelt down beside Brisby, and asked "would it help if we moved him back into town? Or," she amended with a quick glance back towards the black gash through the blue, "somewhere safer?"

"Yes," Brisby responded without appearing to think about the prospect at all. He was busy poking and prodding at Denton, with a look of concentration that said *I know what I am doing*, or at least *I hope I can convince you that I know what I am doing.*

Fithian nodded, said "give me a few minutes," and leapt back to her feet. She was a Lowestoft, and she had contributed to the lowly Lowestofts moving into the Mill and becoming the big-shit Lowestofts who helped run things. How had they done that? Why, overland transport, of course. This was her specialty. Granted, it was usually large crates of well-packed supplies she was moving, and not mewling gunshot victims tender to even the breeze's caress, but the principle was surely the same. She could move him to somewhere safe – the Lowestoft manor, perhaps? Father and mother would be less than thrilled, but father and mother could also go fuck themselves because they'd tried to marry her off for business.

As she ran back towards the manor, she made a mental inventory of everything her family had, and what she might use to move Denton as safely and comfortably as possible. Safety she could do; comfort might be more fleeting. But Yazbirth could take care of the pain, couldn't he? She put out the mental call for her Familiar, hoping he would hear her over the rising din of the Fidgetonians returning to town.

The closer she got to town, the more clearly she could hear their agonized cries. Whatever had started with the destruction of the storehouse was far from over. How much pain could Yazbirth take away in a single day? she wondered, not in the least bit idly.

X

"CHIP AND MISSY DITTERIDGE HAVE BEEN DONE asunder!"

Miss Carsis heard Bulstrode's voice before she saw him come zooming around the corner.

"The villains," he continued, "are a band of scruffy fellows upon whom I have never once goggled."

"How many are there?" Miss Carsis asked, much to Vera and Buddy Jr.'s confusion.

"How many what?" Buddy Jr. asked.

"Quiet," the witch told Buddy Jr., and he was.

Bulstrode fluffed his feathers six times. "Half a dozen in sum. There's one bodger who's clearly top bodger, a roly-poly ginger bloke with hair like the wind-blown scruff of a coconut."

Miss Carsis waved her hand in a gesture that was at once grateful and impatient. "But who *are* they?"

"That, I couldn't ascertain. But they're asking everyone about the Crundwells, and then doing something deliberately unpleasant like giving them a stab through the eye, or lighting their favorite house on fire."

Miss Carsis dug her heels into the ground, coming as near to screeching to a halt as a human can manage, and wheeled around to Buddy Jr. "There's a fat fellow with red hair and five friends doing terrible things in Fidget's Mill, asking about your family all the while. Any clues as to who that might be?"

"Ah…" Buddy Jr.'s velocity was converted into pure confusion, as he scanned the trees to either side of them, as though within their hangdog eaves he would find what he needed to make sense of this seemingly out-of-nowhere question. "I can't…I don't think so."

"I need you to be more certain, one way or the other."

"No. I can't imagine who that could be."

"Well, alright." She nodded and turned to Vera. "Take Buddy Jr. back to my house. Lock yourselves inside. You'll be safe."

They were now close enough to the town to hear the crackling of flames and occasional cries of terror, and to smell the smells that arose when those two sounds met. "*Will* we be safe?" Vera wondered timidly.

"Yes."

The ex-hotelier nodded, and took Buddy Jr. by the arm. "Then let's go."

Buddy Jr. allowed his arm to be taken, but refused Vera's tugging at him to move. "But why are people looking for me?"

"Not just you," Miss Carsis corrected him, "your whole family. And I have no idea, but that's precisely why we can't let them find you."

"You think they would do me harm?"

Despite the dire situation, the witch favored him with a cheeky smile. "It certainly does seem that way." Much to her surprise, this next part came easily. Perhaps it was just having done it once already. First time was always hardest. Someone had probably said that once (and, one might reasonably assume, twice). "Sonny and Tobin live happily together. They're happy, and they're away from here. They're safe. Now run," she concluded to them both.

"But where will you be?"

Miss Carsis waved them away, and despite wanting to stay for the answer, Buddy Jr. let himself be dragged off by Vera, who was surprisingly strong for her age.

Fithian hit the front door of the Lowestoft manor with enough force to snap one of its hinges. Heedless of the damage, she sprinted through the house to the kitchen, where a spare key to the stables was kept in an empty clay jar on a high shelf.

She barreled into the far wall of the kitchen, upon which was hung the damp shelf in question. The in-question shelf teetered and the jar toppled and fell, shattering on the ground, hardly able to contain its excitement in giving Fithian the key. Bending at the knees, hardly aware of their popping like the flames of the storehouse, she snapped the key up, rose to her feet, and dashed towards the back door.

Or started to. Once the impulse to *go go go* could be quieted, perspicacity knocked politely on the inside of her skull and said 'excuse me, but the planks of wood from atop which you plucked the key to the stables were awfully damp, weren't they?'

Yes, as a matter of fact, they were.

Knowing full well that time was of the essence, Fithian nonetheless turned around to investigate the damp.

What does water spilled onto dark wood look like? It could certainly look like blood, couldn't it? Something that looked like blood upon the wood mustn't *necessarily* be blood, must it?

She dabbed a quivering finger into the puddle of possible-water that was definite-blood. It stained the tip of her finger red, stank of once-vital iron.

So, then, whose blood was it? It was a small puddle, one that could have come from anyone, and could signify anything. Moreover, it looked contained; there were no errant splatters or sprays. Just a little circle of blood. Could be anyone's.

Even her parents'. Fithian rushed towards the easternmost door in the kitchen, which led to the rear staircase. "Mother?" She called up to them. "Father?" Raising a hand to push on the door, she was surprised to find the door push back. It was jammed. Her heartbeat rose, in pace and location; it throbbed from the center of her throat.

Once again, she pushed on the door, this time putting her shoulder behind it. The door budged an inch, but refused to yield further. Its give, however, came mainly from the top. Which meant that there was something heavy pressed against the base of the door.

The hand that wiped the tears from her eyes moved of its own accord. All she could think about was who – not what but *who* – was lying dead just on the other side of this door. Fithian pushed harder, this time focusing her energies on the portion of the wood that was both posing the question and concealing the answer.

As she threw her hip into the base of the door, a thin runlet of blood rushed out like a hungry tide that had no intention of returning to the sea. Fithian leapt back and gasped as the pool spread, and suddenly she was assailed by a vision of the waneless tide not slowing its expansion but accelerating, coating the kitchen floor, and then the halls, and then the dew-stained grass surrounding the manor in a thin crimson pond, into which the edifice would slowly sink, with Fithian trapped inside.

It was a preposterous vision that was no less traumatizing for its absurdity. The body on the other side of the door belonged to Fithian's mother or father, she knew this in her heart of hearts. There was nothing to keep her here, and so she turned and walked towards the rear door that would take her to the stables. She walked because if she ran now, she knew she might not be able to stop until exhaustion claimed her.

Of course, she could only chastise herself for the decision. Because if she had run straight out of the house, maybe she wouldn't have had to confront the man.

She spotted him down the hall, holding a flaming torch, looking as though he'd just seen a ghost, and the ghost had tried to explain the principles of jet propulsion to him. He was tall, with close-cropped hair that would probably have been strawberry blonde, were it given a chance to grow. There were old scars and fresh blood on his hands. Despite her better judgment, Fithian froze at the sight of him.

"You a Crundwell?" he asked in a thick accent Fithian couldn't identify.

Fithian clenched her fists so tightly, she was positive they must be bleeding. "Did you kill my parents?"

The tall man waved the torch in a lazy circle which bore no apparent relationship to what he was saying. "I was sent here to find Crundwells. Your folks wouldn't give me a straight answer. I don't like an answer isn't straight." He said this with a tetchy defensiveness, as though he expected Fithian to concede that her parents really did deserve to die for not giving an answer wasn't straight. "You a Crundwell?"

"Go to hell."

"No, *Crundwell*," the tall man corrected her with another wave of the torch. The flame of the torch stretched itself, and the curtain nearest to the man set what must have been some kind of record for bursting into flames. It went from one hundred percent fine to one hundred percent on fire in one *WHAASH*ing instant. "Oh, drat and damnation!" the man cried.

Not expecting the ruse to work, while simultaneously knowing it would, Fithian pointed to the flaming curtain and shouted "the curtain's on fire!"

"I see it! Oh, blast it!"

"You have to put that out!"

"I will, I will!" The tall man took off his jacket and began slapping at the flames. Just as the flames claimed his jacket and began slapping at its owner, Fithian turned and ran out towards the stables. There were tears in her eyes, which she let roll down her face and fall, tracing her final journey from home. She ran through barren fields which would never see corn, though she had gotten to see it, hadn't she? But what the fuck did that matter? It hadn't been real.

As she unlocked the stables and hitched a flat, two-wheeled pallet to a single brown horse with piebald spackling, smoke rose from the Crundwell home, and flaming fingers poked through the windows to wave toodle-oo. The tall man had clearly intended to burn the place to the ground – why else would he be wandering the halls with a lit torch? – but she hoped her appearance had thrown him for enough of a loop that he would forget to remove himself from the premises as it burned.

Then again, she hoped he found his way out – she couldn't imagine a more loathsome idea than her parents being cremated with their murderer.

And, come to think of it, who the hell *was* that man? Fithian didn't need anyone to tell her that there were devils at work in the Mill, and apparently they were searching for Crundwells. But why? And more than that, how could this be allowed to happen? For as long as the Lowestofts had been in Fidget's Mill, Fithian had not heard a single word of villainous gingers with a grudge against the Crundwells. And yet, the Lowestoft dynasty had been annihilated in its infancy by just such a force. It wasn't just unfair – it was *unreasonable.*

Fithian drove the horse back towards Snot Holler feeling like a fool. A fool for ever laying plans, or having dreams. A fool for wanting to see this flat patch of fallow made golden with corn. A fool for wanting to maybe one day leave the Mill, and see the rest of the Colonies. A fool for wanting to control her future. What was the point? No matter how carefully she arranged her affairs, the world was full of tall strangers with old scars on their hands.

She never turned around to watch the manor burn, because she didn't need to. She could hear it, and smell it, and feel it.

XI

YAZBIRTH HAD HEARD FITHIAN'S PSYCHIC calls, but thought they were either a dream or a memory. There was, after all, so much distress in the Mill just then, and Yazbirth's gift and curse was to be uniquely attuned to it all. Eventually, though, Fithian was plunged into some dreadful well of despair, at which point Yazbirth Bicklebog fully experienced her pain.

"Ourselves must fly, Childrenselves!" he bellowed as he scooped Annabelle and Lawrence up under his arms and went sprinting down the avenue, lined with terrified Fidgetonians begging and baraining for sanctuary; the strangers were laying waste to the town, killing innocents and burning down their houses, all relentlessly demanding an answer to the same question, phrased a thousand different ways: Where were the Crundwells? By this point, most Fidgetonians would gladly have offered them up, their only pause being not knowing where to find them. Many Bad Samaritans had directed the aggressors up to the Crundwell mansion (though one had panicked and sent his inquisitor to the Lowestoft manor, much to Fithian's misfortune, and even more so to her parents'). Most did their best to convey the reality that Buddy and Lucretia were dead, and Sonny was missing. They gave up the Crundwells freely and willingly, in the hope and understanding that to do so would be to spare their properties and their lives. In this, they were soon corrected. Fidget's Mill was the town Crundwell built, the more articulate of their aggressors claimed, and so it must be torn to the ground. The only reason to single out the Crundwells themselves was for, as it were, special attention.

Were the terrified townspeople in this as-yet unmolested outskirt in any way attentive to their surroundings, they would have noticed what appeared to be two children zooming through the streets, several feet above the ground, headfirst and apparently heedless of their destination. But what import were two hovering rugrats? The citizens of the Mill had greater concerns. Who were these men, and where had the come from, and why were they so obsessed with the Crundwells? A great many words were bandied about to describe the torments: punishment, retribution, test, evil, abomination, justice, crime, cross. But the one which was most oft repeated was *unfair*. It was unfair. What had the people of town done to bring this upon themselves? What had they done to deserve this? Nobody had ever seen any of these men before, and try as the Fidgetonians might, they couldn't find any plausible way to connect the assault with Denton Hedges or Brisby Houlihan. It was as though a hero had gone on a mighty quest to slay a dragon, and had in fact slayed the dragon, only to be bitten and killed by a poisonous horse that was non-native to the area, and had been smuggled through customs by some asshole who wasn't even involved with the original quest.

Unfair.

Yazbirth continued to rumble down the alleys, constantly having to remind itself not to try running through walls at speed while holding the stubbornly corporeal children. How did humans stand it, not being able to pass through walls? It felt as though it were taking an eternity to find the way out of the damned town, out to the fields where Fithian was in pain. And though it seemed to be taking forever, it wasn't because the Familiar was lost. Never once did Yazbirth take a wrong turn – he could follow Fithian's misery like a thread through the labyrinth. Oh, how desperately he wished Fithian's agony were diffuse enough to prompt some wrong turns. Poor Fithian, wretched pain.

Miss Carsis found the pumpkin-faced man sitting on a stoop, trying to get a small rock out of his boot. It was an inauspicious way to find a villain; she'd have rather expected to see him shoeing a horse with whoopee cushions or rechristening babies to all be named 'Smeg-ma' or something. But no, there he was, one leg crossed over the other, the crossed leg terminating in a torn sock, bobbing to the rhythm of his arms as he shook out the overturned boot.

"Pebble in your boot?" she asked him casually.

He looked up at her and, much to her frustration, smiled just as casually. "Indeed and unfortunately."

Witchcraft was largely about suggestion, and so with a wave of the hand, she suggested to the man that he hit himself in the face with his own boot as hard as he could. He did, bopping himself on an already-mangled pug nose. He cried out in surprise and anger.

"What is your name?" she asked.

"Gah, you're a witch, then? OUCH," he noticed. Bulstrode withdrew his beak from the sole of the man's exposed foot, but kept his spectral neck primed for another jab.

"What is your name? Why do you so harry my town?" She gave her hand a gentle wave, as though turning the page of a massive book. The languid fluidity of the gesture was categorically different from the pumpkin-faced man's further pumpkining of his face with his boot that it was hard to believe the two were connected. So thought the pumpkin-faced man's son, anyway, who was watching this grisly farce from the shadows.

"Tell me your name," Miss Carsis continued, "and you can stop hitting yourself."

"Hamilton Shidy!" he shouted directly at his boot, the outsole of which was beginning to fill with blood.

"And what, Hamilton Shidy, is your business in Fidget's Mill?"

"You a Crundwell, are you? A Crundwell witch?"

Miss Carsis sighed and looked to Bulstrode. The turkey returned her gaze, understood, and bit off one of Hamilton's toes.

From Hamilton's perspective, the pinky toe just detached itself. He felt it pop off, and – for some reason this was worse – *saw* it slide down his exposed sock, like a lover's fingers roaming beneath the blankets.

He roared like a bear, and the witch smiled joylessly. "I'll not ask again, but I expect an answer all the same. You have nine toes left, and then ten fingers, and then two eyes, and two ears, two arms, two legs, two testicles, a penis and finally, a tongue. Thirty-one opportunities to answer me or not." She nodded to Bulstrode.

Hamilton screamed.

"Now thirty. And I can assure you, Mr. Shidy, that should thirty more opportunities elapse, your final punishment will be not death but life. I cannot make you immortal, but I can draw out your existence for several times its natural span." None of this was, in any sense of the word, *true*. But it sounded impressive, and Miss Carsis knew that suggestion was about fostering belief. Hamilton had seen two – scratch that, Miss Carsis amended over his screams, *three* – of his toes pop off of his feet like Champaign corks with free will and no imagination. He'd watched the sole of his boot rushing towards his face, despite his own emphatic desire to not strike himself in the nose with a boot. There were people in the world who were immune to Miss Carsis' telepathic nudges, and then there were those who were so susceptible as to be as malleable as marionettes, except easier to use. Hamilton, she was pleased to see, fell into the latter category.

Miss Carsis was mulling upon this happy fact when Bulstrode shouted "Behind you!" She turned just in time to see a bunched fist closing the distance to her face. Her knees buckling without consulting her, she didn't so much duck as fall, watching as the hard-knuckled hamhock of Hamilton's son slashed through the empty space which had, until just recently, been occupied by her head.

With a jolting lack of grace, Miss Carsis' head came to occupy formerly empty space on the ground. Stars were born, lived, and burned out all around her, but were pushed aside by Hamilton's son, falling atop of her.

"That's my father you're dismembering!" he snarled and spat. She waved a hand at him, and the son raised his own hand to slap himself.

But he stopped mid-motion, and instead snatched Miss Carsis' raised arm out of the air, and pressed it to her side, pinning it there with his leg. He repeated this with the other arm. The witch struggled, but failed to free her arms. Hamilton's son was a hulking fellow who had skipped few meals in his life, which he demonstrated by driving a fist straight into Miss Carsis' nose. Charles Shidy hesitated for a moment when, upon withdrawing his fist, Miss Carsis was staring straight into his eyes, even as blood dribbled out of her mangled nostrils. She made no sound. She didn't blink. She just stared. And despite the fact that there was no magic happening, Charles was transfixed, unable to do anything but stare back.

Yelping at the pain in his foot, Hamilton rose from his seat on the stoop, staggered over to his son, said "look out, Charles!", and bopped him on the head with the boot still clutched in his hand.

Charles Shidy awoke from his hypnosis and replied by making a *gurk* noise. He swatted at the boot with the hand that had so lately slammed into Miss Carsis' face.

"She's riding me like a mule!" Hamilton shrieked as he battered his son with an open palm and a boot. Charles rolled off of Miss Carsis in an effort to flee his own father. It was a foolish boy who assumed he understood the vagaries of witchcraft. Miss Carsis had been practicing it for what seemed like her entire life, and she still didn't understand how it worked, entirely. But she knew enough to know that the hand gestures and spoken spells were a exactly like moving your hands while you spoke, or talking to yourself to try and remember something; helpful, but not necessary.

Magic happened in the mind.

Miss Carsis stood and brushed the dirt off of her, as Hamilton limped after his son, shouting apologies between cries of OUCH.

"What's wrong dad?"

"It's my toes, damnit! Also, I am being controlled by a witch!" He swiped at Charles with his boot again, apologizing with each thrust.

"Excellent work," No-Good Bulstrode congratulated her.

"A compliment I am pleased to return," Miss Carsis replied with a smile. “Run home, now, and ask Buddy Jr. just who these Shidy characters are. I’ll stay here and finish up.”

“You’ll be quite alright?”

They turned to the Shidys. Hamilton had managed to get his son in a headlock, and was trying to coach him on how to get out of it.

“I can’t!” Charles choked.

“You have to! And then you’ll have to strike me upon the head until I am unconscious.”

“Oh, I certainly…*hrrrkkk*….I certainly can’t do that either!”

“Damnation, boy, it’s a sad father whose son won’t strike him upon the head when told!”

Miss Carsis turned back to Bulstrode, but said nothing, because nothing needed to be said. The turkey-demon sped off towards Gutter Lane.

Before too long, they’d both wish they’d said something. Anything.

XII

WINCING UNDER THE LASH OF ADRENALINE, Fithian drove the horse harder than was necessary or wise. She chose to focus her attentions on the clomping hooves of the stallion, rather than the screaming and shouting and burning noises that were rolling out of the Mill behind her. Once she was clear of the town, she heard a small explosion snap across the field. But as before, she refused to turn around. There would be nothing gained by subjecting herself to that.

Cresting the final rise before Snot Holler, she could hear the frantic mumblings of Peggy and Brisby. She couldn’t make out their words, but the Holler carried their tone to Fithian well enough. And the frantic voices were good – it meant Denton still lived, imposing a sense of urgency on the proceedings.

They glanced in Fithian’s direction, to signal their acknowledgment of her approach, but did not stop talking on her account. As she drew closer, she could see that Denton was apparently conscious, but quite clearly delirious. He reclined in the sort of blood puddle Fithian had imagined swallowing her home, and was mortified to find the image recurring in her mind: Denton slowly sinking into his own vital excretions, Peggy weeping and clinging vainly to his lapels, trying and failing to keep him in the land of the living.

But alas, it was only a vision that was soon to depart. What sent it on its way was the observation that Peggy was not, from the look of things, the weeping sort of person. Maybe once upon a time, but not anymore.

"We can rest him upon the pallet," Fithian called without preamble as she dismounted the horse.

Peggy sized up the horse, the pallet, and Fithian. "How will we come with you?"

"…" Fithian sized up the horse, the pallet, and herself. "I am afraid, in my haste, I did not make allowa-"

"Doesn't matter," Peggy replied with a shake of the head. She returned her eyes to her husband's, and spoke in a reassuring whisper. "We're going to take you somewhere safe."

Denton smiled; that was the first thing anybody had said directly to him in quite a while. He had felt himself a prime mover in Fidget's Mill since his return, and now here he was, immobile on a hill as matters of great import happened all around him, not only without his input but almost certainly independent of any of his prior contributions. "Where's safe?"

"Away from here," Brisby replied. It was, Denton couldn't stop thinking, remarkable to see the man at work. He was in most cases a buffoon, but when it counted his bedside manner was brisk and confident. When Dr. Brisby Houlihan told Denton that 'away from here' was safe, then by god, Denton wasn't about to ask questions like 'yes but actually where because "away from here" is a pretty broad category'.

The doctor turned to Peggy and began discussing how best to lift Denton up onto the pallet safely. Well, it had been nice to have people speaking to him as though he were still alive, while it lasted.

He had been doing a lot of thinking since the unpleasantness with the pistols. Laying on the ground, witnessing the woman he loved most talking about him to the man who, in some strange fashion, had become a good friend, Denton felt he was privy to a glimpse of what his funeral might look like. Granted, at his funeral the mourners would not be discussing ways to keep Denton alive. At least, not unless they had been very confused by the invitations they had received. But they would be talking about *him*, all about him, though he would not be there to hear, rebut, amend, or contribute. Might he be listening from on high, smiling down upon their posthumous affections?

Maybe, but it was in trying to visualize this that Denton struck upon a less mysterious conundrum: *who would actually come to my funeral?*

Peggy and the kids would, of course. Mr. Increase? He hoped so. Would his father? Possibly, but Denton didn't much care either way. If Chester Hedges showed up, it would be out of a sense of obligation. Denton wanted to know who would, of their own volition, attend a memorial service for the lately departed Denton Hedges. Outside of his immediate family…maybe Brisby? Almost certainly not anyone else in the Mill…although it certainly would be amusing to have Mr. Increase pop in, full of apologies. He hoped Mr. Increase would come. Maybe some of his fellow Sons?

Sons of Liberty, that was.

Denton had tried living a life dictated by Big Ideas, about purpose and pride and responsibility and honor and justice and sacrifice and so on, and where had it gotten him? Laying in a field called Snot Holler with a bullet in his torso, and most of his blood on the wrong side of his skin. Tragic that it took this long to realize, but Denton finally considered the one variable he had neglected to assess: himself. He was no Patrick Henry; he was no John Dickinson. He was Denton Hedges. It wasn't that they were special, or he was incapable of greatness. Because the opposite held true as well; Patrick Henry and John Dickinson were no Denton Hedges. It was just stupid for one man to weigh his accomplishments against another's. Ambition was important, but so was self-awareness. The man or woman who could master both would be master of all they surveyed.

Denton reflected, as he did his level best not to scream as Brisby and Peggy and Fithian hoisted him onto the horse-drawn pallet, that he had mastered neither. Indeed, the former had mastered him. And so in the interest of the latter, he formulated a new guiding principle for his life:

If I survive this, he swore to himself and his God, who was becoming more and more deistic conception by the second, *I will live my life in such a way that people will want to come to my funeral.*

As another explosion from the Mill crept across the Holler, made soft by the distance like the sneeze of an angel, Denton wondered if anybody would be left to attend the funeral of Fidget's Mill. Probably not.

They dropped him onto the pallet rather unceremoniously. He shrieked. They all apologized.

Good riddance to Fidget's Mill, Denton thought as Fithian climbed onto the horse. *For real this time.* Peggy and Brisby stood next to the mounted Lowestoft. "But actually, where is safe?" Brisby asked, made once again timid by his departure from the bedside.

"We can go north, to New Hampshire," Peggy offered.

Fithian nodded agreeably. "What's in New Hampshire?"

"No idea. I've never been. But it's not here."

The three of them thought upon this for a moment, and Denton also thought upon this, but had resigned himself to not being included in the process of thinking upon things that had substantial bearing on his own well being.

"Also," Peggy added with a shiver in her voice, "I've just remembered the children."

Everyone assembled said something to the effect of 'aw, jeez'. They'd all forgotten about Lawrence and Annabelle, because in their defense, they had far more immediate obstacles occupying their attention. Still, Denton knew it would be quite a while before he could forgive himself for neglecting to factor his own children in to his escape plan, even if he wasn't very heavily involved in organizing it. He suspected Peggy would feel the same way.

Fithian looked panicked for a moment, and then smiled. "Oh, that's alright."

"What do you mean, that's alright?" Peggy snapped, and then she looked across the Holler and sighed in relief.

"Huh?" Brisby followed her gaze and, alone amongst the four of them, saw what appeared to be the Hedges children flying through the air, soaring several feet parallel to the ground, headed straight for them. "HUH?" He doubled down.

"Yazbirth!" Fithian cried. "Let him see you!"

At which point a giant sloth materialized around the children, clutching one under each soggy armpit. The kids were screaming, except they were smiling, and actually they weren't screaming at all. That, Brisby realized, was just him.

Denton and Peggy assumed that Yazbirth had come to reunite the children with their parents, and so were surprised when the sloth carefully but quickly plopped the kids on the ground and rushed to Fithian. "Yourself was distressed?!"

Fithian seemed to have forgotten her own distress, and grimaced at its being returned to her. "Yes, I was. But I'll be alright."

"Yourself is certain."

"I am."

"Ah. Alright." Yazbirth placed its claw-hook hands upon its hips and looked back towards the Mill, arms akimbo. Denton found the corners of his lips curling – it was such a human stance.

"Daddy!" Annabelle cried, doing her best to scramble up onto the pallet with him.

Brisby once again became Dr. Brisby Houlihan, taking Annabelle gently by the waist and lifting her onto the pallet. "Easy," he cooed. "Don't move too much." Annabelle, never needing to be told things twice, folded her legs under her and let Brisby perch her on the edge of the wooden pallet, where an iron bar had been riveted into the planks to hold them together.

Lawrence, taller than his sister, could step up to the side of the pallet without climbing. "You'll be alright," he told his father with the brazen confidence of youth.

"What happened?" Annabelle asked, as though Yazbirth hadn't already told her why her father had come out to Snot Holler. She needn't have covered for the sloth-demon as old as time itself – there was little Peggy or Denton could have done to punish the creature for violating their instructions, other than perhaps make it feel kind of bad for a minute. But Annabelle did not want Yazbirth to feel kind of bad for a minute, and besides, she was too young to know the limits of her parents' strength.

"I did a very stupid thing," Denton replied, "and I paid the price for it. But the good news is, I've also learned my lesson."

"You're done doing stupid things?" Lawrence helpfully prompted.

The father's smile beamed down upon the son. "That I am. Now, let's be on our way. We'll want to be as far from here as possible by nightfall."

"Where are we going?" Annabelle asked.

"North," Fithian replied.

"What's to the North?" The tall man inquired.

"New Hampshi-" Fithian spun around on the horse. Approaching them at a steady walk was the tall man who had killed her parents and burned her house down.

He pointed to Denton on the pallet, soot puffing off of him with each movement. "Now, *he's* a Crundwell, isn't he?"

XIII

HAMILTON SHIDY BOXED HIS SON'S EARS, AND yelled "damn you, boy, if you won't fight your old man when he's bewitched!" Miss Carsis was now piloting a Hamilton with two free hands, one shoe, and seven toes. She'd considered buying time until Bulstrode could return with information on Hamilton's purpose for hunting the Crundwells at the expense of the Mill, whatever light Buddy Jr. could shed upon it, but she was growing bored with the play for time. So, with a shrug of the shoulders, she had Hamilton drop his boot and try to strangle his own son to death.

"I'll just attack the witch!" Charles Shidy kept telling his father. "She's the one vexes you so! Blurgh," he added as Hamilton wrapped his hands around Charles' neck.

"It's easy to say you'll do just such a thing," the father pointed out, "but harder to do when she won't give you a minute's respite from my bludgerings!"

Miss Carsis sighed and had Hamilton redouble his assault upon his son. Alright, if she was being perfectly honest with herself, she hadn't strictly been playing for time. There was a pitch-black amusement to be found in this Oedipal struggle she was playing out. But it was a fleeting entertainment, a joke that was funny the first time, less amusing the sixth. The grin that had set up a dull ache in her cheeks melted away, replaced with slack tension in the brow. Were she not so supremely confident of her having the upper hand in the situation, she might have taken that baseline anxiety as a kind of omen. As it was, she was only aware of an unexpected variable in this tragicomic equation when she felt the ring of ice press against her right temple and heard a click. She didn't hear the Shidy goon pull the trigger, or the crack of the gunshot.

Most of the witch fell to the ground with a decidedly unimpressive *thwump*, like a sack of dirty laundry. Some of the witch, the bits where the magic happened, splattered a bit further. But all of the witch was dead, a fact which Hamilton was only too happy to verify with a blunt pocket knife once he regained control of himself.

Once he regained control of himself a *second* time, he stood up and thanked the young man, whose name he had probably been told but had certainly forgotten, who had put the witch down like the wild animal she was. They closed ranks and set off again, resuming their eternal search for the Crundwells.

Had she the presence of mind, between the realization of impending death and the death itself, Miss Carsis would have been quite shocked that her demise should be so prosaic. She had always expected she would live to some preposterous age, her power unchallenged until the very end. If not, she had imagined she would be destroyed by some rival practitioner of the dark arts, in an explosive and exciting battle of wits and witchcraft. She had certainly never imagined being shot in the head by a pimply twenty-year-old kid. That humiliation would have been compounded had she lived to discover that she bore a considerable portion of the blame for bringing the Shidy clan to Fidget's Mill in the first place.

After a great deal of calming and some light hypnosis, No-Good Bulstrode had gotten Buddy Jr. to tell him about the Shidys. It was a short and stupid story. Bulstrode listened to it, and then listened to the screaming outside, and could scarcely believe that the two were connected.

And then the death of his consort fell upon him as a mother bear upon the weakest of her cubs. He emitted a high, mournful gobble, which split Vera and Buddy Jr.'s eardrums, forever limiting their ability to hear the higher registers.

In a flash, Bulstrode was gone from Gutter Lane.

Zooming through the streets, he drank deep of the tiny tragedies humans so often allowed, even sought, to define them. He came to know each resident of the Mill by their agonies. Their deaths, small though they were, were no less tragic than the losses sustained amongst Bulstrode's group of acquaintances. But nor were they any *more* tragic. They were all just there. Facts. The world had become full of tiny tragedies, which compounded into one less-small misery, but none rang quite as sharply, nor resonated more aggressively, than the loss of Miss Carsis.

Fact.

Bulstrode had always tried, and often failed, to avoid developing bonds of affections with his consorts. Tried and failed and tried and failed. Such was the not-so-small tragedy of being a Familiar. Human misfortune came with an expiration date. Familiars had to carry their pain through the eons. The turkey-demon envied humanity its mortality, while simultaneously bemoaning the trait amongst his consorts. This was something none of them, including Miss Carsis, had ever been able to understand.

Miss Carsis' body was lying unattended in a muddy stretch of the road, her ivory-white hair matted and stained by the unworthy Earth. Bulstrode would return to bury her.

But first, he would have his revenge.

But first first, had one final task. For Miss Carsis. Not his best consort, not his worst consort. Just a consort. But the only Miss Carsis.

"No," Brisby shouted back to the tall man in his doctor voice. "None of us are Crundwells."

The tall man surveyed them all for a moment, and then shouted to Fithian, up front on the horse. "I'll leave you all go free save the Crundwell if you fess up which one he is! Or she," he added with a nod towards Peggy.

"None of us are Crundwells," Fithian replied with a shake of the head. "I don't know what your fascination with the Crundwells may be, but y-"

"Why's that one laid out so?" The tall man pointed a long, skinny finger at Denton.

"Gutshot," Denton replied with a red smile.

"Dang," the Shidy man replied with genuine remorse. "Who gutshotted you?"

Peggy flopped her hands in the air, knowing no other way to express her confusion. "Why do you care?"

"Some of my brothers, they go in for the slower deaths. I prefer them quick. No percentage in making a man hurt, I always say. Or a lady," he once again amended in the interest of equality. "Point being, you tell me which is the Crundwell, won't be no suffering. But if one of my brothers gets a hold of you, or Jesus Please Us, my da…won't be quick." With that, he shrieked in a register higher than Buddy Jr. or Vera would have been able to hear, cupped his hands over his genitals, and flopped face-first onto the ground.

In replaying the moment, wondering what the hell just happened, Denton realized that he'd seen a fleeting streak of midnight swipe across the Holler just prior to the tall man's collapse. He turned his head in the direction it had traveled, and turned just in time to see Bulstrode spit out a small boiled carrot. Er…

The turkey thrust it backwards with one claw, and padded up to Denton and company. "My Miss Carsis has been done in. I am very upset and wish to see the men responsible made profoundly unhappy, and then dead. I will explain to you who they are, and then you will agree to help me. Agreed?"

Brisby stepped forward, profoundly unsurprised by the talking turkey. He'd used up all of his surprise on the giant sloth. Besides, he was being Dr. Brisby Houlihan. "Denton is in critical condition. He can do nothing to h-"

"Denton will be fine. Miss Carsis isn't." There was something approaching emotion in Bulstrode's voice. It retained its chipper English lilt, but there was something old and angry beneath it, like children skating on a frozen lake as a leviathan patrolled the winter-sealed depths beneath them. "I am asking you to make right what you have set wrong."

The man of the hour, dizzy and exhausted on the pallet, lifted himself as high up on his elbows as he could manage. "What do you mean?"

"Oh, for fuck's sake. I mean the Shidys. Listen closely."

XIV

A FEW GENERATIONS AGO A FAMILY BY THE NAME of Crundwell sauntered up to Fidget's Mill from Virginia. They fled the source of their wealth, a once-fertile patch of land that had been farmed into extinction. A fallow field looks just like a healthy one in the winter, though, and an unscrupulous buyer might be dazzled enough by last summer's yield of tobacco to assume next summer held much the same in store.

So the Crundwells, knowing full well they had drawn their last harvest from their land and possessing precious few scruples of their own, sold the property for a considerable sum and sauntered up north.

The family to whom they sold that property went by the name of Shidy, because that was the name they had been saddled with at birth. Had they been given the choice, they probably would not have called themselves Shidy. But given the choice, they would have done a number of things differently.

One assumes. One, if one is Buddy Jr. or Bulstrode, can only assume most of what comes next. One can only assume that it wasn't long before the Shidys discovered they had been sold a barren patch of land at exorbitant prices. One can only assume that the purchase of said land ate up a large portion of the Shidy's accumulated wealth. So one can only assume that they quickly fell towards (and perhaps into) destitution.

Would they have cursed the Crundwell name every night before and after they said their prayers? Or might the cursing have become a part of their nightly communion with their god, asking for justice to be served in some capacity? How many years passed before the Shidys decided that there would be no supernatural justice meted out on their behalf, and that the righting of such a great wrong fell to them?

One would have to ask a Shidy, but good luck finding one in a talking mood.

However much time passed before the Shidys began to teach their children that there were no greater villains than the Crundwells, the hated family had of course fucked off to an obscure little hollow in the New England coastline. They had built Fidget's Mill from nothing, and unknowingly created a largely itinerant community that was, against all odds, insular enough for them to thrive without attracting undue attention. This was hardly by design; they had no idea that the Shidys had begun to hunt for them, because they had already forgotten about the Shidys entirely.

But if the Crundwells didn't remember, the Shidy clan most *definitely* did. They would never, ever forget. And history often favors those with long memories – there are few better ways to sneak up on someone than through a forgotten pocket of the past.

More assumptions and guesses, then: the folks who used the docks at Fidget's Mill to transport their goods to Boston were, generally, merchants who would never have associated with folks of such a depressed social station as the Shidys. And besides, said merchants would hardly want to advertise the fact that they had taken the cheap route and imported through Fidget's Mill, instead of straight through Boston. Being successful was all about projecting success, and nobody would ever associate thrift with being successful (even if the two were, in point of fact, often intimately related). The upshot of this, then, was that there was little risk of the Crundwell name being flaunted about in Boston within Shidy earshot. For decade after decade, this must have held true.

Until, that is, Denton Hedges came back from Fidget's Mill two years ago.

He had never been a social butterfly, nor did he often attract large groups of people to listen to his glittering anecdotes. But he almost certainly would have mentioned Fidget's Mill in casual conversation, would he not?

Bulstrode put the question to Denton, who nodded solemnly and silently. Yes, he had probably mentioned Fidget's Mill to people. Yes, probably in public places. It had just never occurred to him that that would be a problem.

He could see where this was going.

Somehow – Bulstrode could imagine a number of scenarios to account for the 'somehow', but none of them actually mattered – the name "Crundwell" filtered back to the Shidys, wherever they were in the Colonies now. And though generations had passed, and none of the original protagonists of that long-ago land deal were still alive, the name "Crundwell" had apparently been passed down like a treasured family heirloom, one they were all eager to see shattered on the ground, each shard buried at the bottom of a different cave. And so the Shidys, who may well have been scattered all across the Colonies, regrouped in New England, from whence the name "Crundwell" had called to them in Denton's voice, and began to make a far more orderly search of

Massachusetts, that tiny little Colony with so few places to hide.

Somehow again – and for this Bulstrode could imagine fewer scenarios of no greater import than the earlier ones – the Crundwells tracked down Sonny Crundwell and Tobin Lowestoft. It was perhaps a simple matter of Sonny coming to them – he and Tobin were wandering across New England between 1768 and 1770, and would likely not have thought to employ pseudonyms. Why would they have to? It wasn't as though they had been aware there was family floating around that seemed to exist solely to play out a single-sided blood feud. Sonny dropped his name while opening a tab at a bar, perhaps, and his dropped name fell upon the wrong ears. Sometimes matters of great moment occur in just such a haphazard way.

Why had they the presence of mind to not kill Sonny, but instead to follow him? How could they have known he would be returning to Fidget's Mill, recalled by Miss Caris, and so leading the Shidys to the rest of the Crundwells? Did they realize that the opportunity to at long last have revenge for this ancient offense was in the offing? Or had they simply been biding their time to attack Sonny, when the witch called him back home with the best of intentions?

There was no way Denton and Miss Carsis could have known, as they were each pursuing their own personal goals, that they were bringing the end-times to Fidget's Mill. But their actions indirectly summoned the Shidys, who neither Denton nor Miss Carsis had even realized existed, and now the entire town was paying the price.

Denton knew he shouldn't, both because it would be highly disrespectful and also because it would hurt, but he couldn't help it: he (almost literally, judging by the way his cauterized bullet hole felt) burst out laughing.

Everyone stood silently and let him get the giggles out, but no one joined in. Brisby did crack a smile, though, and hoped nobody else saw.

"Need I remind you," Bulstrode reminded Denton, "that my consort's flesh vessel lays in a shallow grave of mud and filth."

Struggling to get himself back under control, Denton placed a soft palm over his gunshot wound. "No. No, I remember. It's just..."

laughter came burbling back up the surface, but he managed to halt it. "This whole situation…" and then the laughter won.

Peggy, Annabelle, Lawrence, Fithian, Brisby, Yazbirth and Bulstrode stood upon Snot Holler, as Denton cackled and hacked and wheezed and laughed, each snort and sputter being taken up by the Holler and flung to the four corners of the world. This whole situation, the laughter repeated. The sentence never ended. But that was ok. It was clear enough what Denton meant.

XV

THERE WAS ONLY ONE REAL QUESTION, WHEN faced with all of this information. Everyone was thinking it, but none had the courage to voice it. Especially not while Denton was still laughing like that.

Once he finally stopped, Peggy cleared her throat and made things simple: "Is any of this our problem?"

Fithian, the only "real" resident of the Mill present, turned on Peggy immediately. "What the hell does that mean? People are dying down there! My *parents*!"

"People are dying everywhere." Peggy raised her hands defensively, seeing the verbal onslaught gathering steam behind Fithian's eyes. "My goal is not to be insensitive. I just don't see what we can reasonably be expected to do here. Not to mention, the entire town has only just dispersed from watching, and indeed anticipating, my husband being shot. Forgive me if I am not *entirely* devastated by this turn of fortune."

"That does come across as slightly insensitive," Brisby informed her.

Peggy waved the doctor's professional opinion away. "If it were a simple matter of going and getting help, I would be the first to make the trek. But I'll not have my family endangered to save people who would have gladly killed us bare-handed not twelve hours ago."

"But we have demons!" Lawrence cawed. "The demons can fight for us!"

"Myself does not harm," Yazbirth mumbled in a way that very definitely implied the word *anymore*.

"I'll happily chip a man's giblets," Bulstrode declared in a way that didn't need to imply anything at all, "but I need a consort to do so. I'm incorporeal without one. One of you must nut up for me. She's excluded, of course." He nodded towards Fithian. "Can't double up."

"Didn't you just chip his giblets?" Brisby asked, cocking a thumb towards the screaming Shidy without a cock.

"No," Bulstrode averred in a voice an octave or two beneath his usual.

"You can count me out too," Peggy declared with folded arms. "And the kids. I'm sure I don't need to tell you that."

Bulstrode nodded, clearly disappointed. He turned to Brisby.

"Ah…" he said.

Bulstrode nodded, not surprised. He turned to Denton.

A smile once again crept across Denton's face. "Some consort I'd be."

"Be my consort, and I can ensure your continued survival. Refuse my offer, and you will be slang out upon the mercy of an imperfect science with little understanding and still less humility."

"Hey," Brisby retorted after a long pause, "that's not fair!"

"No? Have you made the acquaintance of germs yet, doc? Microorganisms and amoebae?"

"What did you call me?"

Bulstrode clucked his disapproval and turned back to Denton. "Confident your kids will grow up right without a father?"

Denton's smile was gone, if it had ever been there at all.

The turkey hopped onto the wooden pallet, clicking his way up to the patient. "Bound to be aggro, then? That's what I'm after. It's how I feel myself. Be my furious consort, we'll off and be angry for a bit together, and then you're back with your family, right as rain."

"And Yourself can escape being stuck as a turkey forever," Yazbirth elucidated for the benefit of everyone else.

Bulstrode shrugged. "That's a consideration, I'll not bat you about there. But not the chief consideration, not by a long shot."

"So what *is* the chief consideration?"

“That, my friend, is between myself and my consort.”

Peggy approached the pallet and took Denton’s hand gently in her own. Mr. Hedges looked at Mrs. Hedges, and the two communed in silence for a time. Everyone gathered there upon the Holler, even the children, knew to keep the sacred silence unbroken. The screams and bangs coming from Fidget’s Mill were slightly less considerate, but there were extenuating circumstances.

Finally, Peggy turned to Bulstrode. “You can promise me, with certainty, that my husband will be returned to me, not just alive but in such condition as to remain so for quite some time?”

“I can,” Bulstrode agreed. “Here.” In a chilling replay of the magic he worked on Millicent Ditteridge (and perhaps, Bulstrode noted to himself, I should tell them that the poor woman is dead; it was so easy to forget these things, given how much was happening), Bulstrode held his beak over Denton’s bullet wound. There occurred, then, a most terrible slurping sound, like a dread god draining the ocean through a bendy straw. Denton felt relief wash through his fingers and toes, down from the top of his head, as pain drained along his bones and through his arteries, all to the ring of scorched flesh on his stomach, and finally out into the waiting beak of No-Good Bulstrode. Denton watched the agony leave his body in a thin stream of black particles, like lead filings drawn to a magnet.

A few of the filings fell to the planks of the pallet as Bulstrode lifting his head and asked “how do you feel now?” Denton looked and, if he wasn’t very much mistaken, saw the pain shavings boiling small holes into the wood.

“Ah…the pain has abated, I’ll admit.” He started to rise, but Bulstrode and Brisby both shouted “AH AH AH” together.

“The *pain* has abated,” Bulstrode informed him with a doctorly confidence that Brisby himself could never have matched. “Your injuries dangle inside of you like ham from the butcher’s window. Once our task is completed, I will take the bacon down and place it upon the scales, which shall at long last even out. You will join me on a stroll to the center of town,” he continued, anticipating Denton’s question, "and together we shall give the Shidys a one-off lesson on forgiveness. After that, we'll separate and never have to see one another again."

Uneasily, Denton slid to the side of the pallet and swung his legs over. Peggy and Brisby helped him down to the ground. He winced as his feet made contact, more from the expectation that it would hurt than from any actual discomfort. It didn't hurt, though – he could feel that he was still in bad shape, feel the bullet rolling around inside of him, but it was something he was aware of in the way one is still aware of a heavy night of drinking after the next morning's hangover is already under control.

Peggy rushed in at the sound of his sharp inhalation, but Denton smiled and wrapped an arm around her. "Reflex," he whispered in her ear as he moved in to kiss her cheek. Her cheek was a little bit wet. It broke his heart.

He leaned his head against her shoulder and sighed. She wrapped a gentle arm around the back of his head, running her hands through his hair so he wouldn't have to (she knew Denton's tics better than her own), and whispered "I'll take the kids to Portsmouth."

Denton smiled against her. He wouldn't have been able to suggest it himself, so he was unspeakably grateful that she had. His family couldn't be standing exposed in Snot Holler forever; they had to get out while the getting was…not literally the worst it could possibly be. Lifting his head, he looked down at Bulstrode. Or where he had expected Bulstrode to be. The turkey had wandered off to speak with Annabelle.

"I have one final condition," Denton announced, "before agreeing to become your consort. Other than stop talking to my kids."

Bulstrode flipped his head as though he had long hair that had fallen into his eyes. "Yes?"

"My family will be fleeing north to Portsmouth."

"And me," Brisby added, very much as Brisby, not at all as Dr. Houlihan. "If that's alright."

"My family and Brisby will be fl-"

"I can take them," Fithian offered. "I've got nowhere else to go."

Denton paused, and turned to Yazbirth. Feeling the bullet grinding against his spine, he turned his entire body from the feet, as opposed to torqueing from the hip. "You'll be going if Fithian goes, I imagine."

The sloth smiled. "Yourself imagines rightly."

"Alright." Denton clapped and returned his attention to the turkey. "So, everyone here except you and me will be going to Portsmouth. When we've concluded our business in Fidget's Mill, before we go our separate ways, you must take me to New Hampshire and help me find them again. I trust it should be easy enough, with Yazbirth there."

Bulstrode took a shocked step backwards. "What on earth do you mean by that, you bigoted bumfer?"

"Um…you're both telepathic? I assumed you c-"

"Well, you know what they say about assuming. Sends everything tits up, so it does. I'll see you get to the edge of Portsmouth safe and sound, but then I leave you to your own recognizance. Yazbirth can help, as he'll be there." The sarcasm of this last was unmistakable.

"You won't see me safely to my family?"

In a chilling imitation of Peggy's cadence, Bulstrode asked, "is that my problem?"

No, they decided, it was not.

Denton kissed his wife goodbye, and kissed his children goodbye, and kissed his wife once again. He kissed Fithian once on the cheek, and Brisby once on each. Yazbirth he hugged, though with reservations – it would have been a simple thing for the sloth to crush him to death in his mighty arms. And yet Yazbirth's embrace was as gentle as his wife's, if not slightly more so. On that very distressing note, Denton wished them all safe travels, and they wished him best of luck. With Fithian on the horse, Brisby riding pillion, and Peggy crouched on the pallet with the kids (Yazbirth offered to carry them, but there would have been too many questions asked regarding the apparently flying children, so the sloth settled for acting as an invisible caboose to catch anyone who might fall off of the flat pallet), Denton watched the only people he loved in the world, and the only ones he might be able to call his friends, disappear over the far side of the Holler.

Well, perhaps that wasn't quite true. Perhaps Bulstrode was a friend, in a way. And perhaps Mr. Increase still was. There was hardly anything left for him in Fidget's Mill, but perhaps there wasn't *nothing* left. That was worth returning for, was it not?

That and the assurance of continued existence, of course.

"Let's go," Denton said to Bulstrode, who it turned out was already several yards ahead of him.

"Book it!" the turkey gobbled over his shoulder. He rushed forward, knowing he was pushing Denton slightly too hard, but not caring overmuch. Bulstrode had learned much from his time with Miss Carsis, more than he had learned from most Consorts. One of the chief lessons was one that had served her well, right up until the end: there were few things more important in the art of suggestion and persuasion than fostering belief. Perform a small trick to establish credibility, and people will be inclined to believe any subsequent promises you make, no matter how outlandish or unbelievable. Perhaps 'inclined' wasn't the right word – they would fall all over themselves to, well, fall for even the most outrageous bluff.

Humans, Bulstrode reflected with neither mirth nor pleasure, loved nothing more than to be lied to.

XVI

MR. INCREASE SAT ON A SQUAT PILING AND watched his life's work smolder. The din of misfortune had migrated further into and throughout the town, carrying with it the fires that dreamt of impersonal conquest. How much of Fidget's Mill was currently, or recently, on fire? Perhaps a third of it, maybe more. And all of that had started here at the storehouse, which had been obliterated by a single spark. Give it time, Increase thought with a great deal less anger than he'd expected. Give it time and the skeleton of the building would join the meat on the ground as a thick black shawl.

More than once, sitting here on his squat piling and watching his life's work smolder, he considered the possibility of walking into the dying inferno. He had spent years and years in there – why not spent his final moments in the same place? There were still crackling pockets of flame, where the embers seethed impatiently, eager to continue their loathsome work, if only they could be provided a new source of fuel. Increase could toss himself in, be incinerated, and who knew, maybe a slab of wall would be dislodged by his dive and crush his flash-fried corpse, just for good measure.

It was an appealing image, no doubt about it. But it was something he considered no more plausible than the equally appealing image of rewinding time and saving the storehouse just as the villains responsible for the fire were setting about their work. Increase had never been the 'dive into the fire and hopefully also be crushed to death' type. Oh yes, there was a 'dive into the fire and hopefully also be crushed to death' type, and Increase had met plenty of them. He had never managed to get along with them.

No, Increase considered, perhaps he was more the 'not careful enough what he wishes for' type. This was what he had always wanted from the beginning, wasn't it? Chaos. Granted, his brand of chaos had been slightly less, erm, chaotic. But in principle it was the same – he had always believed that violent social unrest was a great equalizer, and the essential first step on the path to a better, more unified and enlightened society. To a certain extent, he still believed this. But seeing what instability looked like outside of the nautical ecosystem of the merchant ship at sea, blown up and superimposed over an entire town, Increase learned too little too late that there was a necessary corollary to breakdown: buildup. Somebody, or something, had to stick around to pick up the pieces and put them back together in that more unified and enlightened way. Chaos was unsustainable, and progress wasn't self-generating. That felt obvious now, in the giant's graveyard of the storehouse. But it was easy not to see. Increase just hoped it would be harder to forget; this was not the sort of lesson he wanted to learn twice.

Perhaps it was necessary to have violent men. But if so, it was even more necessary to have those who could wait out the bloodshed, arise from the wreckage and say 'boy, let's not do *that* again'.

Later than he'd have liked, Mr. Increase realized he was better suited to this role. He was glad to know Adewale was out there, stirring up trouble. Granted, it would be nice if the trouble were being stirred for the right people, but sometimes trouble for its own sake was valuable. But that wasn't for him. Mr. Increase would sit here, on a squat piling outside the storehouse, and wait for the fires to die, and the wreckage to settle. Once it did, he'd be able to go inside, salvage what he could, and start the process of rebuilding. And maybe this time, he could fill it with shelves that weren't so fucking confusing to navigate.

As he staggered down the street in his gore-stained coat, Denton looked an awful lot like a handful of rats that had killed a man, stripped him, climbed on each other's shoulders, and put on the man's clothing in the hopes of sneaking into a cheese shop through the front door. He had blood caked onto his still-swollen face, and the bullet brushing against his spine – while not causing any pain, thanks to Bulstrode's ministration – forced him to adopt a shambolic gate, compounded by the stress of knowing that any step could be his last, if the little ball of lead got fresh with the part of his spine that let his brain and his legs talk to one another.

This pitiful march required such unbroken focus, there was precious little conversation between Denton and the impatient turkey demon, the latter so eager to reach Hamilton Shidy that he would dart ahead several yards, turn and wait for Denton to catch up, then dart several more. This process repeated over and over, leaving Denton time to wonder why the turkey didn't just slow down and stroll with him…but more importantly, how did Bulstrode seem to know, with such confidence, where they had to go?

When they got there, Denton knew. He rounded the corner and saw her lying face down in the mud.

Bulstrode, finally slowing down, tiptoed up to her, as though loathe to wake her from a pleasant dream she must certainly be having. Was that the case? If anyone might be qualified to speak on what happens after death, it would likely have been a demon such as Bulstrode. Denton formulated a million questions in his mind, about where she might now be, what experiences she might be having, whether or not she was aware of them here. But, for once in his life, good sense and social decorum prevailed. This was a moment that called for solitude.

The moment lasted until Bulstrode brought it to a gentle close. "I would very much appreciate it," he clucked almost sub-audibly, "if you might be so kind as to flip her over. So her eyes might glimpse the sky."

Denton had been expecting Bulstrode to suggest some dreadful rite to bring her back, and so needed a moment to catch up to the actual, non-adventurous nature of the request. "Uh…sure." With great care and effort, he dropped to his knees and gently tucked his fingers beneath her shoulder.

Was this the first time he had really touched Miss Carsis? He thought it might be. There were no tremors of energy, nor visions of the power that had once inhabited this body. There was merely cold, waxy flesh, beneath mired garments.

No – she had grabbed his wrist, the first time they had ever met. Gently, yet with power.

"It's ever so disrespectful to leave her here, but at the moment it can't be helped. We'll nip off, address the Shidy business, and return to see she's accorded the respect she deserves." Bulstrode's explanations were hardly necessary; Denton knew, as he grunted over the grinding sensation in his gut and flipped Miss Carsis (he had a hard time thinking of her…*it* as *Miss Carsis' body*) in a delicate arc, that this was the right thing to do. But still, the turkey-demon continued: "She played at being Earthy, but I knew her better." Beaks lacked the articulation to smile, but Denton could *feel* a smile on Bulstrode's beak. "She was always a witch of the empyrean vault, if you see what I mean."

Denton did, but still did not say anything, for the same reason the congregant doesn't raise his voice into the silence of a cathedral simply because the priest is taking a breath.

"A sky witch, she was. Ha!" Bulstrode exclaimed. It was an artificial laugh, and thank whatever heavens Bulstrode might know about for that. "Blimey, haven't I gone maudlin? I've got a new consort now. That's you, you old scarecrow. Come, let's off and away!"

Not waiting for a response, and so not giving Denton time to ask what Bulstrode expected him to be able to do to help, Bulstrode darted forward a few yards, stopped, and paused without turning around. Bulstrode was waiting for Denton, but wasn't going to turn around again until they had rounded a corner, when an about-face wouldn't force him to look at her body once again.

So Denton followed, although he did turn around once before they rounded the corner.

XVII

THE SENSATION WAS, GENERALLY SPEAKING, familiar. Denton, being nothing if not a bundle of nervous energy, would sometimes seek to make good on his bundlehood by twisting himself into curious contortions when sitting in a chair, particularly around the house when his bearing wasn't being scrutinized. Having his legs folded at strange angles looked painful, but it was actually quite comfortable. Perhaps *too* comfortable – as he would rise to his feet to go about his day, one or the other (or maybe both) of his legs would have fallen quite asleep, and prove more difficult to bestir than even Lawrence.

This was a very fancy way of saying that at least two or three times a year, Denton would stand up from a seated position, only to fall down because his legs were still asleep.

What happened on the mud caked, fire-framed roads of Fidget's Mill was a lot like that, except Denton had a sneaking suspicion that his legs weren't just having a quick nap this time.

With a thin squeak he hit the ground face-first, and felt something in his stomach continue to fall. He rolled onto his side and examined the bloodstain on his coat, which was once again spreading, this time even more quickly than in the moments after its creation. The wound had tasted oblivion, and was now being given a second chance at life. It would not waste its precious time as a languid seep – the wound now *gushed*, oblivious to the fact that living fast meant dying young.

This was especially frustrating to Denton, because he was still relatively young, and he hadn't lived especially fast. And yet, using his arms to push himself upright, trailing his dead legs like a mermaid who had only just gotten a pair of gams, Denton knew from the look in Bulstrode's empty button of an eye that death was coming whether he was ready or not.

"Heal me!" Denton cried, realizing the absurdity of the words as they left his mouth.

"I'm afraid I can't," Bulstrode replied with what, for a turkey demon, must have been a tone of genuine remorse. "So sorry to have cocked you about with the tit for tat business." He turned and plodded up to Denton. "That bullet did you a treat, I'm afraid. Not a good treat, like a bit of chocolate or an unexpected yet desirable sexual advance. It was a bad treat, like a bit of chocolate with coconut in it, or an expected yet undesirable sexual advance."

Denton, still laying crotch-down with his shoulders pressed to vertical, looking like the nightmare creature that seals tell their cubs will come and get them if they don't behave (the boogeyseal), stared at Bulstrode for a long, red moment.

"It was a fatal shot," Bulstrode clarified. "Always was. Your tummy got the message right away; it just took time for word to reach your upper and lower bits. There was never anything to be done. I'm so sorry, I truly am."

"But I can't just stop here! You still need me! You can't do anything without a consort!"

Bulstrode slalomed his head from side to side. "I'm afraid I cocked you about there as well."

"You…"

"Brisby was right. I did snip that bad man's giblets, right under your nose. Well, close enough. I told you a naughty little fib."

"Why the hell would you do that? You mean I could have stayed with my family?" Denton began crawling towards Bulstrode, and despite knowing himself to be perfectly safe, the turkey took a step backwards. The lawyer laid low was truly a hideous sight.

"Well, I also told your wife a naughty little fib."

"What ar-"

"Halt a moment, and hear out my reasoning! I brought you with me for your benefit, not my own! I sought to repay you for the m-"

"*My* benefit?! Since when have you cared in the least bit for me?"

"Since Miss Carsis grew contrite for the way she bandied you about. She made a mess of it, but she was doing her best to put things back in as neat a row as she could for you. She didn't…well, it's a blasted shame what happened. But what's done is done. And what was done was you started dying even more quickly than usual." Bulstrode tapped at the ground with his talon, perhaps the turkey equivalent of running his hand through his hair: "This was the inevitable next step in your decline. I won't heighten your distress by causing you to glimpse yourself in this moment, but you're a far cry from the dapper gentleman I encountered at the cockfighting ring. Now, had I left you to your family, your death would have been slow, and ugly, and unpleasant. Your whole body would start going on the blink, as it is now – there's a chance you'll be conscious when your bowels go for the final time, I'm afraid to say. Worst of all, this is all the result of a duel even more foolish than your bog standard duel. That's how they would have remembered you. As it stands, I've created a little adventure for the two of us. Your farewell to your family is dignified, bipedal, and generally hopeful as you plod off to rescue the town, or perhaps avenge it. They remember the duel as nothing but a prelude to this heroic finale, in which you meet your demise concomitantly with the damnable Hamilton Shidy."

Denton still stared, stock-still, but the redness of the moment had passed. Perhaps because it was now pouring out of him, coating the ground in a selfish, vain embrace that would never find satisfaction. The color was certainly going out of the poor man's face. "But how will they ever know that that's what happened?"

"I'll pop in on them soon enough, once they're settled, and let them know what a hero their good old husband and/or father and/or friend is. Was. Sorry, as I'm sure I've mentioned."

This wasn't right. Denton had spent so long, expended so much effort, laboring under so much crippling stress, trying to make a real impact on Fidget's Mill. And here he was, bleeding out on the street, shot by his old friend over a pointless squabble, watching the town literally burn down around him because of a generations-old dispute that had literally nothing at all to do with him, except in the general sense that he had perhaps spoken a bit too freely at a bar somewhere. But how could he have known?! Goddamnit, this wasn't fair! All of the shit he went through for non-importation was now, finally, starting to pay off on an intra-Colonial scale. The Boston *Slaughter* was terrible business, but it was only the start. The world was changing, and the changes were going to be felt around the world, for generations to come. Of this, Denton was certain.

He was grateful that Bulstrode had crafted this fiction for his family, in which he died a hero. He would, perhaps, finally accomplish in death what he never had in life; securing the pride of his loved ones. Granted, he wasn't really accomplishing it. All he had done was get shot by a friend – Bulstrode was going to make the rest up.

So yes, there was gratitude, but mostly there was eye-popping rage. He wanted to see the changes he had worked so hard to bring about …or, at least, he had worked so hard to create the conditions propitious to their attainment! Or something like that! Whatever, goddamnit, he was a part of what was happening in the Colonies, and he was being denied the chance to watch his efforts bear fruit.

"No," he said quietly to himself.

Bulstrode reclaimed the backward step he had yielded. "Sorry? This is a different sorry that signifies my not hearing, or perhaps not quite comprehending what you said, though the apologetic sorry still holds."

"This isn't where I die," Denton declared. "This isn't *how* I die."

Genuinely interested, Bulstrode took another step towards Denton.

"How so?"

Denton opened and closed his bloodless lips several times before any sound came out. "It can't be. It isn't fair."

"You'll find this rich, I'm sure, but you might consider yourself lucky. It's precious few chummies who go out doing something heroic."

"But I won't! Not actually!"

"Well, that's true enough. But it'll seem that way, once I've told folks as much. So that'll be the new true."

"After all I've done. It isn't fair!"

Bulstrode took a third step towards Denton, now nearly nose-to-beak with him. "I'd be quite surprised to find you've made it this far without having heard, and I'm sorry to have to be the one to break the news so late in the day. But I'm afraid that life just isn't fair."

"I understand that life isn't fair, but this is ridiculous." So said Denton Hedges at the moment of his death.

He fell face down in the mud, just as he did when he was clouted upon the head his very first day in the Mill. And, this was a laugh, Bulstrode realized that he had needed the man after all: he was unable to turn a body over by himself. So, unhappy about it but unable to change anything, Bulstrode left Denton flopped out on the ground with his face buried in the mire of the Mill, and went to find Hamilton Shidy. Along the way, he brainstormed some better last words for Denton Hedges, but struggled to find an epitaph that more concisely summarized the middling little life of that curious little man.

Bulstrode took his time on the Shidys. This, too, was unbecoming of a Familiar. But for as long as he had no Consort, he wasn't a Familiar. He was just your run of the Mill demon.

So he took his time, because he had so very much of it.

XVIII

EVENTUALLY, THE SUN DECIDED IT HAD SEEN enough, and therefore, so had everyone else. It dipped down towards the horizon but lingered for longer than was strictly necessary. Aglow against the asphyxiate blue of twilight, Fidget's Mill was an oasis of fire in the black woods. In its own strange way, the town had never been more beautiful. The secret was to see it from a long way off; drawing too close would cause the dreadful masterpiece to liquefy into a meaningless mush of colors and brushstrokes. Also, there was still a great deal of screaming to be heard in the Mill, and few things undercut beauty like people screaming for the wrong reasons.

Oblivious, or perhaps indifferent, to the beauty behind him, Mr. Increase sat patiently on his squat piling, his back to the burning Mill, with eyes only for the storehouse. The flames inside had found much to sate their hunger, but they had paced themselves poorly; already, they were beginning to starve and die. Good riddance.

Even over the muted din of the Mill in its throes, Mr. Increase heard the familiar *click click click click* of poultry in motion. He didn't turn around to greet No-Good Bulstrode, but then, they'd never had that sort of relationship.

Bulstrode stepped up to Increase. Not in front of him where they would more easily be able to see each other, but right alongside, so they could both watch the storehouse together. And that suited Increase just fine; he could hear the turkey molting, shedding its feathery flesh. The rule of Familiarity was that a Familiar, once its consort's aims had been achieved, was once again free to adopt a new form. His latest consort was dead, but from a legalistic, pedantic viewpoint, Denton's ends had been achieved. He had left his mark on the world: a scorch on the part of the map that used to say *Fidget's Mill.*

Now it was somebody else's turn. There was a new prime mover in town, even if he didn't yet realize that's what he was. Mr. Increase would need it broken to him lightly, but there was plenty of time for that.

For now, as the sun dipped all the way below the horizon, No-Good Bulstrode molted his feathers, his form collapsing like a star, his raw function searing its intentions and irrelevancy into the universe.

And thus the demon exposed, in the shapeless moments before its rebirth, in the aimless instants before it contracted its new unknowing consort, in the febrile seconds before it at once proffered and demanded prostration, an eternal servant reigning over ephemeral masters, as it had been since the dawn of time, as it would be until the cosmic twilight, with no purpose to its existence save a desperate attempt to find a purpose, said "I expect you'll be wanting a hand with all this?"

Also by Jud Widing

Westmore and More!
The Year of Uh